LION OF SENET

BOOK ONE
OF THE SECOND SONS TRILOGY

JENNIFER FALLON

orbit

www.orbitbooks.net

ORBIT

First published in Great Britain in October 2005 by Orbit
Reprinted 2005, 2006, 2009

A CIP catalogue record for this book is available from the British Library.

ISBN 978-1-84149-351-0

Typeset in Granjon by Palimpsest Book Production Limited,
Polmont, Stirlingshire
Printed and bound in Great Britain by Clays Ltd, St Ives plc

Papers used by Orbit are natural, renewable and recyclable
products sourced from well-managed forests and certified
in accordance with the rules of the Forest Stewardship Council.

Mixed Sources
Product group from well-managed
forests and other controlled sources
www.fsc.org Cert no. SGS-COC-004081
© 1996 Forest Stewardship Council

FSC

Orbit
An imprint of
Little, Brown Book Group
100 Victoria Embankment
London EC4Y 0DY

An Hachette UK Company
www.hachette.co.uk

www.orbitbooks.net

For Amanda,
and as always, Adele Robinson

For in and out, above, about, below,
Tis nothing but a Magic Shadow-show,
Play'd in a Box whose Candle is the Sun,
Round which we Phantom figures come and go.

THE RUBÁIYÁT OF OMAR KHÁYYAM
(translation by Edward J. Fitzgerald, 1859)

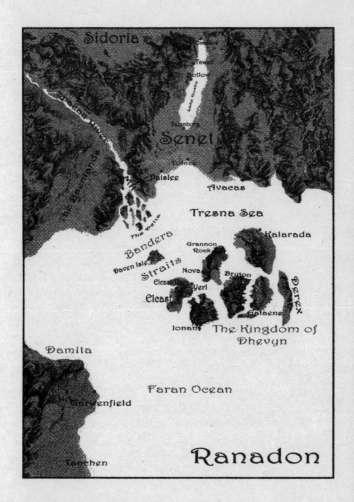

PART ONE

OMENS

I

From the top of the cliffs the world appeared bathed in blood. The dawn was ruddy, stained crimson by the red sun as it began to set in the west, chased out of the sky by the larger, brighter, yellow sun on the eastern horizon. The scarlet clouds hung heavy and thick and tasted of ash. There had been an eruption somewhere, Tia realised, as she stopped to study the view. No wonder Neris had gone missing. Eruptions always had that effect on him.

The heat was oppressive, despite the overcast sky. On this world with two suns, it never truly cooled down.

Except during the Age of Shadows.

Tia wiped the sweat from her brow and looked down towards the river. From the cliff top the delta spread out before her: a confused network of channels and sandbars constantly shifting with the moods of the fickle Spakan River. The water was muddy and sluggish; it reminded her of a series of veins and arteries, bleeding into the lighter waters of the Bandera Straits. There was little vegetation. The line of smoking volcanoes that marred the northern horizon spewed out their smothering ash often enough to ensure that everything struggled to survive here in the Baenlands. To the west, Tia could just make out the patchwork fields where their few crops fought to thrive in the ash-choked soil, and beyond them the fields of Ranadon poppies, the only thing that grew around Mil with any enthusiasm.

Behind her, a few faint wisps of thin smoke from the houses of the settlement drifted upwards, hanging motionless in the still air for a moment before being swallowed by the cumbrous clouds.

The silence was complete. Even the wind that normally howled through the delta had taken a moment to catch its breath. Tia looked along the rim of the cliff to her left. In the distance she could just make out Neris, perched perilously close to the edge.

With a sigh, she began to walk towards him, making no attempt to hide her approach. She didn't want to startle him.

It took her nearly half an hour's walk over the rough, stony ground to reach the man perched on the edge of the precipice. The solitary figure did not move as she neared. His hair hung long and untended down his back, and it looked like he'd been wearing the same shirt for a month. For a brief, irreverent moment, Tia was glad that there was no breeze. He wasn't a pleasant creature to be downwind of when he was like this. He was sitting cross-legged on the cliff top as if he was carved from the rock itself.

Neris knew she was there. He was mad, but he wasn't deaf.

'Have you ever noticed,' the madman remarked as she came up behind him, 'that the only time we get truly spectacular sunrises is when there's been trouble somewhere? There's a moral in that, I think.'

'What do you mean?' Tia asked cautiously. Although he sounded rational, she knew him too well to be fooled.

'It's like life,' he mused. 'If nothing bad ever happened, you would have perfect skies every day, and you'd be bored witless. But this . . .' he said, waving his arm to encompass the magnificent, fiery skies, 'this comes from a disaster. Somewhere out there, the Goddess has spoken.'

Tia halted in her approach. It was never a good sign when Neris began to speak of the Goddess. 'It's just a volcano, Neris.'

'The Goddess has spoken.'

'You don't believe that.'

The madman shrugged. 'It doesn't really matter whether I believe it or not. Millions of people all over the world will climb out of bed this morning and look at this sky and think the Goddess is trying to tell them something.'

He was right, Tia knew, but she didn't want him dwelling on it. That line of thought was just a step away from Neris recalling his own contribution to what people believed about the Goddess and that was an extremely dangerous thing, particularly as he was sitting on the edge of a cliff with a drop of some eight hundred feet below him.

'People choose to believe or not believe,' she shrugged. 'If they want to have faith in a stupid myth, that's their problem, not yours.'

Neris turned to look at her. Dark hollow circles ringed his eyes, his pupils were contracted, his eyes unnaturally bright. He was high on poppy-dust, she realised, which meant he might stay calm for a while, or he might fall into the depths of depression, or he might suddenly launch himself off the cliff in the mistaken belief that he could fly.

For a fleeting moment, she wished she'd thought to bring Reithan along. Reithan was much better at dealing with Neris than she was. Tia was too impatient, too angry.

'What is faith?' Neris asked.

'I don't know.'

'Which is why you'll never understand the power of the Goddess and her minions.'

'Neris . . .' she began, feeling helpless to divert the conversation from such a dangerous topic. 'You mustn't keep blaming yourself . . .'

'Then who should I blame, Tia?'

'Antonov Latanya,' she replied without hesitating. 'And that evil bitch Belagren.'

Neris smiled. 'I wish I was like you, Tia.'

'Why?'

'Because you still have hope. You still believe there's a chance you can set the world aright. Even Johan doesn't believe that anymore. We old men have lost our faith.'

'Faith is for fools,' she scoffed. 'Faith is for the idiots who believe what the High Priestess tells them. Faith is for monsters like the Lion of Senet, a man who murders in the name of the Goddess.'

'Yet you believe that somehow you can make it better. You and Reithan and the other young people here in Mil. Deep in your hearts, despite a wealth of evidence and experience to the contrary, you all truly believe that given half a chance, you could make everything better. What's that, if not blind, foolish faith?'

Tia bit back the retort that leapt to mind. He was sucking her into his argument. That was the danger with Neris. He was insane beyond redemption and hopelessly lost to his addiction, but he was still the smartest man who had ever lived, and it was foolish in the extreme to argue with him.

'Lexie's making blincakes for breakfast,' she said, deciding to change the subject rather than fight a losing battle.

'Is she making them the proper way?' he asked, with the sudden eagerness of a child.

'Of course.'

Neris was quite adamant about the recipe for the thick, chewy blincakes that he loved, and would refuse to eat them if the ingredients weren't added in exactly the right quantities and exactly the right order.

Unaccountably, his shoulders suddenly slumped, and he hunched over, hugging his thin arms around his body. 'I'm not hungry.'

'But you love Lexie's blincakes.'

'I love nothing,' Neris corrected miserably.

Tia knew her father too well to be upset by his declaration. She sighed and took a cautious step closer to him. 'Neris . . .'

'Why don't you ever call me Father?' he demanded suddenly. 'You never call me Father.'

'The last time I called you Father, you told me not to. You said you didn't deserve it.'

'Did I really say that? I wonder why?'

Tia knew why, but she had no intention of getting into that discussion either.

'If I promise to call you Father, will you come down?'

'I shouldn't be your father. Johan's a much better father than me. You should go live with him and Lexie.'

I already live with Johan and Lexie, she wanted to say. *If*

*they'd left me in your tender care I'd never have made it past
my second birthday.*

'Johan's not here,' she reminded him instead. 'He's gone
to find Hari and the others, remember? You'll just have to
keep being my father until he gets back.'

Neris didn't answer her. He stared out over the delta as
Tia tried to calculate how fast she could get to him should
he decide to jump.

A noise behind her made her turn sharply, then a wave
of relief swept through her as she saw Reithan climbing up
the rocks behind her.

Reithan was twenty-eight, dark-haired and brown-eyed,
like all the Seranovs of Grannon Rock. He was a cunning
fighter, an experienced smuggler and Tia's best friend. He
was also an old hand when it came to dealing with Neris.

The madman turned at the sound, too, and smiled thinly
as Reithan came to stand beside Tia. 'Ah! That's cheating.
You've brought reinforcements!'

'Neris, what are you doing?' Reithan demanded impatiently.

'Contemplating the nature of faith.'

'Well, how about you do it somewhere a little less
dangerous?' he suggested.

'Are you afraid I'll jump?' Neris teased.

'You won't jump,' Reithan replied with conviction. 'If
you jump, you'll die, and that would mean you'd have to
stop torturing yourself.'

Neris stared at Reithan for a long time, as if savouring
his words before digesting them. Then, without warning, he
grinned and scrambled to his feet. Loose pebbles tumbled
over the edge. Tia stifled a gasp.

'I never thought of it like that,' he announced. 'Torturing
myself. Yes, I like that.'

'Neris—' Tia began, holding her hand out to him. The
madman teetered on the edge of the precipice, grinning like
a fool.

Reithan was quicker. He lunged forward and grabbed
at Neris's tattered sleeve. Although he looked as if he would

struggle, Neris was wasted and thin from a lifelong addiction to poppy-dust, and had no hope of defeating Reithan's size or strength. The younger man pulled Neris away from the edge and shoved him past Tia, placing himself between Neris and the cliff.

'If I truly wanted to die, you couldn't stop me,' Neris warned as he regained his footing. His bright eyes were glistening with amusement. Tia could have throttled him. She hated it when he was like this.

'If you ever truly want to die, just let me know,' Reithan suggested sourly. 'I'll happily put you out of your misery, old man.'

'You know, Reithan, I believe you would,' Neris replied with a suddenly lucid glare. Then he turned to Tia as if nothing untoward had occurred. 'Blincakes, did you say? Lexie is far too good to me. We shouldn't keep her waiting, you know. Come, come. She'll get angry if we let them go cold . . . what you're doing up here at this time of the morning is beyond me. Truly, Reithan, you're a bad influence on Tia.'

Neris turned and began to pick his way down the rough goat track that led towards the village. He chattered to himself as he walked, as if Reithan and Tia were beside him, listening to every word. 'She's never going to catch a husband if you insist on leading her astray . . . perhaps I should see about introducing her at court. I was a nobleman once, I think. Or was it her mother? I can't remember . . . Johan will know . . . or Lexie. Lexie makes excellent blincakes . . .'

Tia started a little as Reithan came up behind her and placed a brotherly hand on her shoulder.

'Are you all right?'

She nodded. 'He just scares me when he's like this.'

'I know. But you can't watch him all the time.'

'He was talking about the Goddess again.'

Reithan glanced up at the sky with a frown. 'He won't be the only one talking about the Goddess this morning,' he predicted grimly.

'You don't believe there's a Goddess, do you, Reithan?'

'Of course not, but a lot of people do. And you can wager

your right eye that Belagren is plotting a way to make this look like a divine event, even as we speak.'

Tia knew he was right. 'We'd better get to Lexie before Neris does. I made up that bit about the blincakes.'

'Come on, then,' Reithan said. 'And next time you go charging off to rescue Neris, come and get me first. If he'd decided to jump, you'd never have been able to stop him.'

'I just thought—'

'I know,' he said sympathetically, then smiled. 'Come on, let's get down to the longhouse. Look at you, you're shivering.'

It wasn't the weather that made her shiver. The gooseflesh that prickled her skin came from a much less tangible source. She glanced up at the blood-red sky again, unable to shake the feeling that this morning's eruption really *was* some sort of dire omen. Somewhere on Ranadon, it was certain, someone would find a way to use this eruption to cause trouble.

Then, silently berating herself for being a superstitious fool, she shook off the ridiculous feeling of impending doom and followed Reithan and Neris down to the village.

2

It was just on dawn when Belagren heard the screams. They woke her from a deep sleep that had been filled with pleasant dreams. She was sitting on a vast golden throne, while every soul on Ranadon knelt before her, begging for her blessing . . .

Annoyed at being woken from such an agreeable fantasy, the High Priestess opened her eyes and cursed softly. The red light of the night sun filtered through the cloth walls, filling the tent with dull crimson light.

'Madalan!'

When her aide did not reply, Belagren rose from her pallet and walked to the entrance of the elaborately embroidered silk tent, throwing back the flap. The camp was in an uproar, people were running to and fro, but most were heading towards the Labyrinth.

'What in the name of the Goddess is going on?' she demanded of a young man dressed in a dark red robe running past her tent. 'Who is making that ungodly noise?'

The Shadowdancer skidded to a halt before her and bowed. He was young, perhaps twenty-three or -four, only just risen from the ranks of acolyte. Belagren knew his face, but couldn't think of his name. He was very handsome. All her Shadowdancers were. She quite deliberately recruited these young men and women for their beauty. It set them apart.

'I think it's coming from the Labyrinth, my lady.'

Any fool could tell that much, she thought impatiently.

'Perhaps they've broken through?' he suggested, seeing the look of displeasure on the High Priestess's face.

Belagren had been wondering the same thing, although the screams sounded as if they were filled with pain, rather than triumph. Lifting the hem of her red robe out of the dust, she followed him through the campground set up amid the ancient ruins, towards the entrance to the Labyrinth. She was not particularly tall and had some difficulty in keeping up with the long-legged stride of her companion. The High Priestess glanced around at the tents as she hurried along. Some of them, she noted with displeasure, had been here so long they were taking on a disturbing air of permanence.

But maybe . . . finally . . . after all this time . . .

Belagren was almost afraid to finish the thought for fear of jinxing herself.

Some long-extinct volcano had destroyed this place, raining deadly debris and ash on what must have once been a vast and beautiful city. It was impossible to tell how old the city was, or who had built it. Much of it was nothing more than strangely shaped pieces of masonry jutting out of the landscape like frozen sentinels watching over the dead. Even now, after nearly a century of excavation, they still found the occasional, mummified remains of the original inhabitants. Their bodies were tall and long limbed, their clothing strange, and their expressions were always fixed in terror, as if they had died in unspeakable agony.

The entrance to the Labyrinth stood like a gaping mouth drilled into the side of a small mountain. There was something inscribed in the rock over the arched entrance, but nobody knew what language it was written in, or what it said. Scholars from the universities in Avacas and Nova had puzzled over its meaning for years. The more superstitious souls among her followers considered it a warning of some kind.

Belagren had her own private translation. In her mind, the words over the entrance to the Labyrinth promised only one thing: *Through here lies the path to ultimate power.*

All Belagren wanted – all she needed – to etch her name in history irrevocably, was access to the information hidden behind those damn traps that Neris Veran had set deliberately to keep her out.

Fortunate for him that he's dead, she thought, thinking of several rather gruesome things she would like to do to the architect of her dilemma.

If he was dead.

Belagren had her doubts about that, but even the Lion of Senet, with all the resources he had at his disposal, had never been able to find a trace of Neris. In the absence of any evidence to the contrary, she had no choice but to accept that he was out of her reach and move on.

Perhaps Neris really *was* dead. If that was the case, then Belagren had another problem – but one she really didn't want to think about right now. Even if they finally got through the Labyrinth, even if she killed hundreds of her people breaking through the traps (and the Goddess alone knew how many were left to find), without a mind like Neris Veran's she had no hope of deciphering the information she needed. Not unless the Goddess sent her a miracle –

preferably in the form of another mind who could understand the incomprehensible mathematics of the ancients.

The notion that the suns did not orbit Ranadon, but
appeared and disappeared in their skies at the whim of the
Goddess, was a fundamental belief among the people of this
world, and had been for as long as anyone could remember.
The Sundancers had nurtured those beliefs for countless
generations, interpreting every volcanic eruption, every
flood, every drought, every stillborn child as the will of a
vengeful and capricious Goddess.

But as time passed, as inquiring minds began to turn
their thoughts to the heavens, faith had gradually been
replaced by curiosity. Someone invented a telescope and, for
the first time, people questioned the teachings of the
Sundancers. Universities flourished. People stopped
attending the temples and began to suggest that they could
rule their own destinies. The steady supply of younger sons
and daughters from noble families sent to serve the Goddess
dwindled. The Lord of the Suns, the spiritual leader of
Ranadon, became a powerless figurehead, good only for
attending balls and openings, mouthing useless platitudes to
a population who no longer cared what he said.

And then the Age of Shadows came.

The younger daughter of a proud and ancient Senetian
noble house, one of the few who still clung to the tradition
of sending their younger children to serve the Goddess,
Belagren had just finished her novitiate when the second sun
disappeared. Even now, almost three decades later, she still
remembered the fear that had gripped the people of
Ranadon. To experience true night; to wake to a world where
the second sun no longer shone during the day, to a world
gripped by cold and darkness, rattled by earthquakes,
shrouded in ash from the volcanic eruptions . . . her stomach
clenched just thinking about it.

She had been part of the expedition sent north to the
ruined city of Omaxin, as Paige Halyn, the Lord of the Suns,
searched desperately for answers. It always struck Belagren
as ironic that a man so useless and ineffectual could have

been so astute. The city *had* contained the answers they sought, but only Neris Veran had been able to understand the hints left behind by the long-dead citizens of Omaxin.

She still remembered sitting in the darkness, huddled around an inadequate fire in the midst of these haunting ruins with Madalan Tirov and Ella Geon, speculating on the power of such information, should it fall into the wrong hands. In the space of a few hours, their discussion had moved from idle speculation to a workable plan.

The following morning, Belagren announced that she had been visited by the Goddess, who had revealed to her what must be done to return Ranadon to the Age of Light.

Neris was easily taken care of, Ella saw to that. His silence and cooperation were ensured by his pathetic worship of Ella and his addiction to poppy-dust. While undoubtedly brilliant, he was a weak and easily corrupted man. The Lord of the Suns had proven a harder nut to crack. Although he didn't deny her visions, neither did he embrace them willingly. But he hadn't counted on the scope of Belagren's plans, or her connections. With the help of the Lion of Senet, for the past seventeen years she had been able to remake the world to her liking.

She had created the Shadowdancers and claimed that they were specially blessed by the Goddess, thereby bypassing the Lord of the Suns and his inconvenient morality. In theory, they were still subject to the Lord of the Suns's authority, but in reality, Paige Halyn was powerless to stop her.

That she had ordered Neris to seal the domed building, to prevent others from learning what she knew, was the only mistake she had made in her remarkable rise to power. He had sealed it with a vengeance, then thrown himself off a cliff in the southern port of Tolace, so that nobody else could learn the truth.

The High Priestess was not a fool. She knew she could overrule logic with faith for only so long. She had done it once and it had worked spectacularly, but without continuing proof, without solid evidence that the Goddess truly had her ear, she was in danger of losing everything.

And every day the problem grew more urgent. If the second sun orbited the first, then eventually it must go away again. If Belagren couldn't predict it – if another unexpected Age of Shadows happened in her lifetime – she would be exposed.

Her fate, should the unthinkable happen, did not bear thinking about.

But maybe today, she prayed as she entered the Labyrinth. *Maybe this is the last obstacle. Maybe . . .*

The entrance to the Labyrinth was part of one of the few structures that had survived the ancient disaster. It wasn't always the death trap it was now. Once it had been nothing more than a series of interconnecting tunnels leading into a large domed building that was all but obscured by the weight of the ash and debris that had buried the city thousands of years ago. The bodies had been cleared out some time ago, long before Belagren had come to Omaxin with Neris, Madalan and Ella, but she'd heard rumours that there had been thousands of skeletons found inside. Many of them were locked in embraces with their loved ones, the bones of their children clutched in their laps. The skeletons had crumbled to dust as soon as they were disturbed. In her more reflective moments, Belagren wondered what it must have been like, to flee inside the dome for safety, only to die much more slowly from starvation or asphyxiation.

Her thoughts were dragged rudely back to the present as they entered the torch-lit tunnel. The screams were louder here, echoing off the smooth curved walls. There were traces of faded murals on the walls that Belagren had never had the time or the patience to examine.

About thirty feet into the tunnel, she was forced to step over the remains of a twisted doorway. Neris's first trap. It had killed three of her people when they broke through. She could almost hear him laughing at her from beyond the grave when they'd brought out the bodies, sliced to shreds by the deadly rain of shards he had loaded in his trap. That was the day that Belagren had truly begun to fear for her future. The lingering apprehension in the pit of her belly never truly let her rest.

The screams grew louder as they approached the next obstacle, some fifty feet past the first trap. It was followed by several more gates that had proved to be nothing more than false traps. They'd wasted months, sometimes years, carefully studying and dismantling the next four gates, only to discover there was nothing sinister about them at all. She'd grown lax by the time they broke through the sixth gate. Fortunately it had only killed one man – Lester Somebody-or-other – and then only because of his arrogance. A nobleman by birth, he fancied himself equal to any problem set by a mere peasant. The peasant had proved him wrong. He was crushed under the weight of a large slab of masonry that fell from the ceiling right at the moment of his triumphant declaration of victory.

Belagren climbed carefully over the huge granite slab and glanced down. As far as she knew, they had never been able to move the slab, and Lord Lester the Long Forgotten was still underneath it.

As they neared the seventh of Neris's deadly traps, the workers moved aside to let the High Priestess through, bowing as she passed, averting their eyes for fear of being singled out. She reached a narrow bridge that had been constructed over the gaping hole in the floor, caused when four more of her people had accidentally triggered the seventh trap.

Belagren forced herself not to slow her pace as she crossed the rickety bridge in the wake of her young escort. This trap, of all Neris's diabolical devices, was the one that had come closest to killing her. Expecting the traps to follow the same pattern as the first six gates, her people were confident that after the death at the previous gate, the next four gates should be more of the previous four – false traps that looked impressive but were little more than elaborate devices to slow down the workers trying to get through the labyrinth. A few minutes before the floor section had collapsed, she had been standing on it, studying the figures etched into the barricade, as the old scholar from Nova University on Grannon Rock, Kellor Highman, and his bright young assistants had explained the problem to her. The lock on this gate was simply a series of numbers, they assured her. All they had to do was discover the sequence and press the tiles in the right order, and the door would open for them.

She had stood back to watch them work. She had watched them die instead.

Once past the collapsed floor and the uncomfortable memories it evoked, Belagren hurried on past the next four gates, each of which had proved to be harmless. She was no longer prepared to make that assumption, however. They had treated each gate as if it were deadly. Belagren privately expected every gate to cause the whole mountain to come down on top of them, which actually concerned her more than the lives lost trying to break through. She could replace a few scholars and labourers. But if the Labyrinth was destroyed; if she was denied access to the cavern at the end of it . . .

The results – for her – would be catastrophic.

The screams were beginning to fade, thankfully. Whoever was making such an awful noise was either on the brink of exhaustion, or – and this was the more likely explanation, given where they were coming from – on the brink of death.

As she rounded the curved hall, she stepped into chaos. The people who had been working on the twelfth trap, all of them red-robed Shadowdancers (she trusted nobody else down here now), were all shouting at once. The torches flickered in the darkness, making it hard to distinguish one panicked face from another. There were several bodies lying at the base of the wall where the tunnel ended, all of them burned beyond recognition. The screaming woman was lying further from the wall, writhing in agony, her face and left shoulder melted away so deeply that the red muscle underneath was clearly visible. Several others held her down, while someone attempted to pour water over the burns. It was a useless exercise. Better to give the poor woman a large dose of poppy-dust and let her die in peace, than waste time treating such wounds.

'What happened?' Belagren demanded of nobody in particular.

'Acid,' a tall, grey-haired woman answered her from behind. 'They accidentally triggered the trap. It rained acid over everyone standing near the wall.'

Belagren turned to face Madalan. 'You broke through, then?'

She didn't ask who the dead were or if anyone else had been injured. She didn't care. All she cared about was getting through this damn Labyrinth and back into the building that a dead madman was so determined to prevent her from entering.

'Not yet,' Madalan shrugged, 'but now that we've sprung the trap, it should only be a matter of time.'

Belagren nodded, but before she could answer, another young man came running through the tunnel, calling for her.

'My lady!' he panted, sketching a hasty bow as he stopped in front of her. 'You must come see! Quickly!'

'See what?'

'The sky, my lady!'

With a puzzled glance at Madalan she quickly retraced her steps through the torch-lit Labyrinth on the heels of the messenger. Blinking as she stepped out into the light, the High Priestess squinted for a moment, then followed the pointing finger of the young man. Belagren bit back an involuntary gasp.

A billowing cloud of ash, stained scarlet by the rapidly sinking first sun, blotted out the sky to the south. There had been an eruption, she realised immediately, perhaps on land, but so far south, it was more likely in the Tresna Sea.

Belagren glanced around at the startled faces of her followers and quickly raised her arms, holding them wide.

'It is a sign,' she cried. 'The Goddess has spoken to us!'

All around her, the Shadowdancers began falling to their knees, staring up at the sky. Her mind racing, the High

Priestess looked around with relief at this obvious sign of their faith, then turned her attention south once more. 'Our sacrifice has not been in vain. See for yourselves. The Goddess is with us, and the souls of those lost today will be welcomed into her loving arms. Let us pray.'

As one, the people around her, Shadowdancers and servants alike, bowed their heads in prayer. Belagren glanced over her shoulder to find everyone but Madalan caught up in his or her devotions. The older woman smiled as she emerged from the entrance to the Labyrinth. The convenience of a sign from the Goddess at such a time was not lost on her old friend.

'The Goddess is with us,' Madalan said blandly, as she stood beside the High Priestess.

'This truly is a momentous day,' Belagren agreed, then added quietly in a voice meant only for Madalan, 'We have to get back to Avacas.'

3

The ground trembled from another aftershock and low clouds of volcanic ash blocked out the sun as Dirk Provin and his brother Rees scrambled up the steep incline of the levee wall to inspect the damage wrought by the tidal wave. Dirk could taste ash on the still air, and his eyes watered as he followed Rees and the rest of the townsfolk up the slope. The shale was slippery and sharp, but he paid no attention to the small cuts that sliced his hands. The first sun had set, and the second sun sat low on the horizon waiting its turn, but the world was still shadowed by the aftermath of the distant volcano.

'Where do you think the eruption was?' somebody asked. Nearly everybody from the town had hurried to the levee to inspect the damage. They had felt the earthquake during the night and knew what it meant, but until the expected tidal wave had unleashed its fury, they had stayed well clear of the northern beaches.

'The mainland,' Master Helgin panted from behind Dirk, as the portly physician struggled in the wake of the younger, fitter men. 'It could have been as far away as the Galaquil Mountains.'

'No, it was in the seabed between here and Senet,' somebody else predicted. 'A mainland eruption wouldn't cause this much damage.'

'Now that we've returned to the Age of Light, I thought we'd seen the last of these damn eruptions,' someone else said.

'Is the Goddeth angry?'

Dirk glanced over his shoulder at the boy who had spoken, a little surprised to find young Eryk scrambling up the slope behind them. Eryk was thirteen and quite small for his age. He had unruly black hair and soft green eyes that reflected a great deal of emotion and very limited intelligence. He spoke with a distinct lisp when he got excited, and it was generally agreed that he wasn't the brightest jewel in Elcast's crown. The lad caught up to Master Helgin, then, seeing the look of disapproval on Dirk's face, offered the old physician his arm. He smiled triumphantly at Dirk, as if to say, *See! I'm here because the master needs me.*

Sometimes, Dirk thought, turning to follow his brother, *Eryk isn't nearly as slow as people think he is.*

'Well, if she is angry, Eryk,' Master Helgin puffed, leaning heavily on the boy's arm, 'it would be pleasant to think she's venting her wrath on somebody else for a change.' Stopping for a moment to catch his breath, he wiped the sweat from his forehead with a kerchief before starting off again.

Dirk glanced over his shoulder at the physician and frowned. That was a foolish thing to say, particularly as Tovin Rill, the Senetian Governor of Elcast, was only a few steps ahead of them. Dirk's eyes swung to Tovin, but the big blond mainlander seemed not to have heard the remark.

'Are there likely to be many casualties?' Lord Tovin asked when he reached the top of the levee. Dirk's older brother, Rees, stopped beside him, shaking his dark curly hair. Stocky and solid, Rees looked so much like Wallin Provin, standing on the levee silhouetted by the scarlet clouds, that Dirk had to remind himself that he was looking at his brother, not his father.

'There's no settlement around here, just farmland,' Rees explained. 'This part of the coast is too prone to storm surges.'

'We don't often get tidal waves in Senet,' Lanon Rill remarked. The governor's son had scrambled up beside his father, flashing a quick grin over his shoulder at Dirk. It had nothing to do with the tidal wave. Lanon was gloating because he'd beaten Dirk to the top of the wall.

'No, you just have the quakes that cause them and swamp us on a regular basis,' Dirk heard Helgin mutter crossly.

Dirk threw the old man an exasperated look before scrambling the last few feet to stand beside his brother.

As the townsfolk reached the top of the wall they fell silent, overwhelmed by the sight. The scene that greeted them was one of utter desolation. The tide was out now, and as far as the eye could see in the dim light a barren black beach strewn with the flotsam of the tidal wave's long journey stretched before them.

The monstrous wave had dumped its load well past the beach. The tree line that yesterday had marked the start of the fertile farmland beyond was all but flattened, the soil now poisoned by seawater. Rees pointed to the sodden fields with concern. 'The crops . . .'

Tovin Rill shook his head, stunned at the carnage. 'I'll have the damage assessed. We can apply to the mainland for relief. The Lion of Senet will not see you starve.'

No, Dirk thought, *but what will it cost us?* Like all the islands of Dhevyn, Elcast was suffering under the weight of the crippling taxes imposed by Senet. He could imagine his mother's reaction to the news.

Tovin scowled suddenly and turned to Rees. 'Of course, Duchess Morna would probably rather you starved than accept a single sack of grain from Senet.'

Rees looked uncomfortable at the reminder. 'I'm sure my mother will be grateful for Senet's help, my lord.'

The massive granite levee on which they stood had protected the rest of the island from the fury of the wave. Not for the first time, Dirk wondered who had constructed the wall. With the exception of Elcast Keep, it was the only structure on the island that hadn't been rebuilt a thousand times over. Almost a hundred feet below them, the wet black sand glistened in the dull morning, the base of the levee cluttered with debris thrown up by the ocean. He wiped his streaming eyes and squinted into the distance.

'Something's moving.'

Rees glanced at Dirk before scanning the beach carefully. 'Where?'

'Over there,' he told him, pointing towards the devastated tree line.

'It's probably just seaweed blowing in the breeze.' Tovin shrugged, looking in the direction of Dirk's pointing finger.

Dirk shook his head. 'There's not a breath of wind this morning.'

'There's something alive down there!' somebody else called. Every eye on top of the levee suddenly fixed on the tree line, waiting to catch a glimpse of the unexpected movement. Dirk studied the scene carefully, trying to sort out the tangle of debris in his mind.

'It's a ship,' Lanon announced. 'See! You can just make out the end of the bowsprit at the base of the trees. And over there! It's part of a mast.'

'If there was a ship caught in the wave, there'd be no survivors. It would have been smashed to kindling.' Tovin looked at his son apologetically. 'Poor bastards probably didn't even know what hit them.'

'There is definitely something moving down there,' a female voice called further along the wall.

Rees turned to Tovin expectantly. Although Rees was

the heir to Elcast, there would be no rescue party sent to investigate without Tovin's approval.

'It'll take hours to get around to those trees now the road's been washed out, but I suppose we'd better investigate,' the governor decided. He was silent for a moment, then turned to one of his officers who had come to view the scene along with the curious townsfolk. 'Ateway, send someone to fetch a rope and then take a couple of men down the levee wall. See what you can find. And take Master Helgin with you. If there is a survivor, no doubt he'll need medical attention.'

Helgin had finally managed to reach the top of the levee. He looked down the sheer, steep wall and took a step backwards, suddenly pale. 'I ... er ... perhaps, my lord ...'

Tovin smiled unpleasantly. 'You're quick enough to criticise Senet's efforts to aid the Kingdom of Dhevyn, Master Helgin. Surely you're willing to step forward when there's a chance to take an active part yourself?'

'I'll do it,' Dirk volunteered. Tovin Rill had that look in his eye that he got when he was riled. He'd obviously heard the physician's earlier snide remarks. 'Master Helgin is afraid of heights, my lord,' he explained.

'I'll go, too!' Eryk offered eagerly. Wherever Dirk went, Eryk was determined to follow.

'No, you won't,' Rees declared, grabbing the lad by the collar before he could jump off the wall in his enthusiasm. 'Are you sure about this, Dirk?'

He nodded to his brother, then turned to Tovin Rill for permission.

Tovin glared at Dirk for a moment and then nodded. 'Your young apprentice apparently has more balls than you do, Helgin. Does he know enough to be of any use?'

'He is his father's son, my lord,' Helgin replied stiffly. 'And yes, he knows enough to render aid.'

'If there is any aid to be rendered,' Rees remarked doubtfully, still clutching the crestfallen Eryk by the collar. 'It would be a miracle if anyone survived such a wreck.'

Tovin nodded in agreement and looked out over the

beach. 'Aye. Whoever it is, if he's still alive, he's been spared by the Goddess herself.'

Dirk was the last one down the wall, but he had little trouble negotiating the perilous descent. He and Lanon had often scaled the levee these past few months, although they took great pains to ensure that their adventures remained a secret from both the governor and the Duke of Elcast. The area around the levee wall was strictly prohibited, mostly because of the same thing they had come here to witness this morning. The shallow seabed between Elcast and Senet was riddled with underwater volcanoes and the beach was often lashed by monstrous waves, although rarely one as large as this. His father had declared the whole area off limits after three children had been killed by a smaller wave that had arrived without warning when Dirk was only a small boy.

Ateway and the two Senetian soldiers he assigned to the task headed off across the damp black sand as soon as Dirk was freed of the rope. With a quick wave to those who stood watching them from high on top of the levee, he turned and hurried after the men.

Ateway glanced at Dirk as he fell into step beside them. 'You know, that physician of yours is going to get himself arrested someday. Lord Tovin's only been here a few months and he's a very devout man. You should tell Helgin to guard his tongue.'

As if that would do any good, Dirk thought. Still, for a Senetian, Ateway was probably one of the better ones, so Dirk was disinclined to aggravate him. He settled on a change of subject instead.

'Do you miss Senet?'

'Not really. You've a good life here on this island, when all is said and done. And you manage to avoid most of the earthquakes. Sometimes Senet shakes so hard, it's impossible to stay on your feet.'

'We get the tidal waves, though,' Dirk pointed out. 'It's your earthquakes that cause them.'

Ateway frowned. 'It's the Goddess that causes the waves, lad. Don't you go thinking anything else.'

'Why?' he asked, as they trudged across the damp sand.

'What do you mean, *why*?'

'Why does she cause them? Why does your Goddess insist on visiting disaster after disaster upon us?' Dirk wasn't trying to bait him. He was genuinely puzzled by the blind faith of Senetians in all matters relating to the Goddess.

'Because the people turn from her,' Ateway informed him uncomfortably, ill equipped to argue theology. 'And if enough people turn from her, then she dooms us to another Age of Shadows until they get the message,' he added sternly.

'But her disasters affect everyone, the ones who follow her and those who don't. Why doesn't she just do something to the sinners and leave the rest of us alone?'

Ateway glared at Dirk for a moment then shook his head. 'You should ask a Shadowdancer that sort of question.'

'Haven't you ever asked them?'

'Of course not!'

'Why not?'

Ateway was saved from having to reply by the shout of one of the soldiers who had gone on ahead to inspect the tangled debris caught in the felled trees bordering the farmland. Dirk temporarily abandoned his quest for spiritual enlightenment and hurried towards the soldier who was ripping away the branches and shattered planks from the wreckage to uncover the body beneath. Dirk dropped to his knees and placed his ear to the man's chest.

'He's dead,' he announced, looking up at Ateway. 'And as cold as a fish. If someone was alive down here, it wasn't this man.'

'There'll be more of them around,' Ateway agreed with a nod. 'We should get help to bury them.'

'Let's find the survivor first,' Dirk suggested.

They worked through the morning to uncover the victims of the shipwreck. They found eighteen bodies before Ateway gave a shout to indicate that he had discovered one still breathing. The soldiers laid the dead men out in a row along the black sand as they uncovered them. They were barefoot and roughly dressed, but nothing they wore gave any hint as to the identity of their unnamed ship. They were thin, too, as if they had been at sea for some time, or perhaps they were just generally undernourished. Their injuries ranged from multiple shattered bones to one young boy no older than Dirk, who didn't have a mark on him. They were Baenlanders, he guessed. He'd heard it was a struggle to survive in the Baenlands. It was the reason so many of them took to piracy.

'Goddess, I can't believe this one's not dead!'

Dirk hurried over to where Ateway was kneeling over the body of a dark-haired man whose left leg was twisted at an unnatural angle. His arms were broken, his face was covered in blood from a savage gash over his left eye and his left shoulder appeared to be dislocated. But his chest rose and fell with surprising regularity. He was unconscious, and would no doubt awake to unbearable agony, but unless his wounds turned septic, or he was suffering from internal injuries, Dirk judged that he would probably live.

'We'll need splints,' he told the Senetians. 'And a stretcher. And something for the pain. When he wakes up, it's going to be pretty horrible.'

Ateway nodded and ordered one of the soldiers to head back to the levee wall for help. Dirk gingerly turned his attention back to his patient and examined him more closely.

He was not a particularly big man, but he was well muscled, tanned and obviously fit from a life spent on the deck of a ship. His dark hair was flecked with grey at the temples, and Dirk guessed the sailor was well into middle age. Dirk was not skilled enough to tell if he had more serious injuries. For that reason, he hesitated to move him, afraid that he might make things worse. He'd seen that happen last year, when one of the grooms had been thrown hard from a horse to the cobbled stones of the Keep's courtyard. His friends had rushed to help him up and now the poor boy couldn't feel a thing below his armpits.

Dirk was suddenly very sorry he'd volunteered to come along. This man needed Master Helgin's skills, not his own rudimentary knowledge of healing.

He sat back on his heels and stared down at the man. 'I wonder who he is?'

Ateway laughed humourlessly. 'The luckiest sod on Ranadon, that's who he is.'

Dirk didn't reply. With a dislocated shoulder, at least three broken bones that he could see, a nasty head wound, and the Goddess alone knew how many internal injuries, *lucky* was a very relative term.

Tovin Rill arranged for a wagon to meet them at the base of the levee on the other side. The unconscious sailor was hauled up the sheer side on a makeshift stretcher, encased in the splints Dirk had fashioned from the shattered decking of the wrecked ship. Many of the townsfolk had stayed to watch the sailor's rescue, while others had returned to their homes to get ready for the day.

Helgin was waiting at the top of the wall. Dirk breathed a sigh of relief as he handed the man over to the care of his master. The old physician examined the sailor's wounds, then gasped suddenly when he saw the man's face. Dirk wondered at his reaction, thinking that maybe the head wound was worse than it appeared. But he was given no chance to question Helgin about it. The physician hurriedly pulled a blanket over the man and had him bundled away before Dirk could ask him anything.

Rees had finally released Eryk and came to stand beside Dirk as he watched Tovin's men lift the stretcher into the wagon under the critical gaze and impatient direction of the old physician. Master Helgin's obvious nervousness concerned Dirk. He wondered if he had forgotten some procedure.

'Well, you can bet this will be the talk of the town for weeks to come,' Rees remarked.

'He's badly hurt and I'm not certain I helped much.'

'You did plenty,' his brother assured him. 'And you scaled the levee wall like a spider. I am actually impressed, little brother.'

Dirk smiled briefly, not really listening. Tovin Rill sat astride his stallion with Lanon at the base of the wall, watching the proceedings with interest. Eryk stayed on the top of the wall with them, standing beside Dirk, unconsciously mimicking his stance.

'You've got one problem though, Lord Dirk,' Eryk suggested sagely.

'What's that, Eryk?'

'You're gonna be in big trouble when your mother finds out.'

4

'Elcast!' Vonril shouted as he finished feeding the mules for the night, glancing up at the ash-laden clouds with a frown. They had finally begun to break up late in the afternoon, and small rays of sunlight pierced the gloom in the most unexpected places. It had been overcast and gloomy all day, and the nearby town was abuzz with talk of a giant tidal wave that had destroyed a ship and ruined the coming harvest. He moved towards the cooking fire and sat down beside his mother. 'Why in the name of the Goddess did we come to Elcast?'

'Don't swear,' Kalleen said, cuffing the young man absently. 'We're here on Elcast because I decided to come.'

'Then surely we could have found a better place to camp than here?'

'Here' was a small clearing in the Duke's Forest, about

two miles from the town of Elcast. They had come for the
annual Landfall Festival, but it was still weeks away, and so
far the takings had been lean. Elcastrans were notoriously
tightfisted, Vonril was constantly complaining. They had
been so close to Senet, too. A week, perhaps two, and they
could have been on the mainland. But their mistress had
decided that once they left Derex, they were headed in the
opposite direction.

'Here is just fine,' Kalleen announced, her face shining
with sweat. She was sitting too close to the fire for such a
warm evening. 'Besides, rumour has it that since Lord Tovin
was appointed Governor, the Landfall Festival on Elcast will
be much bigger than in previous years.'

'That was yesterday, when they actually had something
to celebrate. If you believe the townsfolk, they'll all be
starving come winter.'

'Come winter, we'll be long gone, so it makes no difference to us now, does it?'

'But why not Senet? Why not go to Senet?' Vonril
sounded like a whining child.

'Because we're Dhevynian, you moron. All foreigners
need a permit for Senet,' Lanatyne told him, throwing
another split log on the small campfire. 'And a permit for
Senet costs more than we make in a year.'

Inside the wagon, Marqel listened to the conversation
thoughtfully. Normally, Kalleen would have taken Lanatyne
to task for insulting her son, but she was distracted this
evening. Things were looking grim for the troupe. Tonight
was a chance to recoup at least some of their losses, but they
couldn't stay on Elcast indefinitely, and even arriving so
many weeks before Landfall was a gamble. They might be
asked to move on, perhaps even before the Festival. Nobody
liked their kind hanging about.

'Marqel? Aren't you ready yet?'

Marqel clambered down from the wagon, tying the
ribbons Kalleen insisted she wear into her long, fair hair. She
crossed the small distance to the fire, still fiddling with the
childish adornments. When she was finally done, she brushed

down her little girl's tunic and presented herself with a pout to the troupe leader for inspection. She wore a short tunic that fell to just below her knees, and her face was scrubbed clean as a milkmaid's. Her hair was the colour of ripened wheat and fell long and straight and heavy, without even a hint of a curl. Kalleen eyed her critically for a moment, then nodded.

'You'll do, I suppose. Just keep that smart little mouth of yours shut. At least until after he's handed over the money.'

Marqel pulled a face in reply. Kalleen had sold her as a virgin to one of the patrons who had attended their show in the town square yesterday. Kalleen had been selling her as a virgin all summer as they travelled around the islands of Dhevyn, eking out a living as acrobats, fortune-tellers and entertainers. Marqel was well rehearsed by now. She knew how to simper. She knew how to look wide-eyed and frightened. She had even mastered the art of breathlessly begging her patrons to 'be gentle with me, sir . . .'

'And don't you go doin' nothin' that'll give us away,' Vonril added.

Generally, men who could afford to buy a healthy young virgin were in positions where, if they suspected cheating, they could make life very difficult for the troupe. Vonril was nervous of his mother's scheme, and every time Marqel was sold he grew more anxious, certain their ruse would be discovered.

Marqel thought he worried unnecessarily. She saw the guilt in the eyes of the men who bought her. She knew they were paying for something they could never admit to. She had a hidden treasure trove gleaned from such men – coins, jewellery, even a tiny music box that tinkled a delightful tune whenever she secretly opened it. Those treasures were the only bright spot in an otherwise hopeless existence, with no future prospects other than the life of a whore or a performer with Kalleen and Vonril and Lanatyne in Mistress Kalleen's Travelling Troupe of Amazing Acrobats.

'Now, you remember,' Kalleen warned. 'You don't do

nothing till he's paid the money. You pass it on to Murry and then act all innocent and dumb like . . .'

'I know what I'm doing, Kalleen,' she sighed impatiently. 'This is the eighth time I've been deflowered in as many weeks.'

Marqel was safe from Kalleen's fist. She always made sure she was out of range before she gave the fat old hag any lip. It was a hard-earned lesson. Besides, tonight at least, Kalleen would do nothing that might bruise her pale flesh. She would be delivered to Hauritz the Butcher unmarked.

'You just watch that mouth of yours,' Kalleen repeated with a frown. 'Murry!'

Murry was a big, bearded man who claimed he came from Damita, even though he talked with a distinctly Senetian accent. He appeared from the other side of the blue-painted wagon he shared with Sooter, the troupe's other roustabout. Marqel and Lanatyne shared the smallest wagon, while Kalleen shared the largest with her son, Vonril. Although Kalleen's wagon was the most comfortable and in the best repair, nobody would have traded places with Vonril for a seat at the queen's table.

'It's time,' Kalleen informed him. 'See she gets there and that she comes straight back. And make sure she gives you all the money.'

Murry nodded mutely and beckoned Marqel to follow him.

Once they were clear of the camp, walking the ash-dusted road that led into town, Murry began to talk, reminding her, as he always did, of the need to be careful; of signs to watch for that a man was turning violent. The evening was mild, the second sun just sinking below the horizon. Tall evergreens coated in a powdery layer of fine white ash shaded the road, and the distant squawking of gulls filled the still air as they fought over the fish washed up on the shore in the aftermath of the eruption.

Marqel pretended to listen attentively as Murry repeated

the same advice he gave her each time they made a journey like this. She thought it bizarre. He was escorting her to a man who had purchased the use of her body because he thought she was a virgin, and Murry was lecturing her on how to ensure her own safety.

The lecture irked her. She stopped and stared up at the big Damitian. 'Murry, if you care so much about what happens to me, why not stop Kalleen selling me like a side of lamb in every town we stop at, instead of instructing me on how to avoid getting beaten up?'

Murry looked shocked. 'But you're a whore, Marqel.'

'I'm an acrobat!' she corrected. 'I'm not a whore. That's Lanatyne's job.'

'She was an acrobat once, too, you know, back before she broke her ankle.'

'I don't care. I'm not going to be a whore the rest of my life.'

'Then what are you, lass?' Murry asked, genuinely puzzled by her refusal to accept her fate. 'You've not much choice that I can see.'

'Well, whatever happens, I'm not going to piss my life away in this pathetic travelling circus.'

'You're a fool, girl,' he sighed. 'Come on, we'll be late.'

Marqel defied him for a moment or two, scuffing at the ground with her sandals as Murry walked on ahead. Once again, she would have to lie beneath some sweaty, sausage-fingered old man with bad breath, who would paw at her body clumsily, pounding his manhood into her until he collapsed from exhaustion. It would be unpleasant, but probably blessedly short. That was one thing about these men to be grateful for. Most of them were so guilt-ridden, so aroused at the thought of possessing her, that they barely lasted long enough to cause her any real discomfort.

With a heavy sigh, Marqel followed Murry down the road into town.

There really wasn't much else she could do.

Hauritz the Butcher let her in the back of his store, glancing up and down the alley furtively to make sure nobody had seen them. Marqel stepped into the kitchen with Murry close behind, and glanced around with interest. The room was dominated by a long polished table, and softly gleaming pots hung from hooks in the ceiling. There was a white lace cloth draped over the table and the stove was meticulously clean.

'Where's your wife?' Marqel asked curiously. No man kept house like this.

'My wife? Why do you want to know about my wife?' he demanded anxiously.

'We don't care about your wife,' Murry told him. 'Where's the money?'

The butcher dug into the pocket of his trousers and withdrew a small leather purse that clinked with the familiar dull sound of coins rubbing together. He handed it to Murry with a scowl. 'You disgust me! Selling your own child.'

That must have been the story Kalleen had given the butcher. Sometimes Marqel was an orphan, sometimes a sister, and sometimes a daughter. Kalleen was very good at reading people and using whatever lie would bring the highest price.

Murry took the purse and opened it. He couldn't read, but he could tell how much was in the purse, just by looking at it. He nodded, satisfied that the amount was correct, then looked down on the sweaty little butcher.

'You disgust me,' he retorted. 'You're buying her.'

This is all I need, Marqel sighed impatiently to herself. She wanted this over quickly, although glancing at the nervous butcher, she doubted he'd even be up to the job. Certainly not with Murry standing over him like that.

'Daddy?' she interrupted in her best little-girl voice. 'I'll be all right. You take the money home.' Then she added with a dramatic sigh, 'At least the others will get a decent meal tonight.'

Murry took the hint. 'I'll be back for you later.' He turned and grabbed the butcher by the front of his shirt. 'You hurt her, and you'll be sorry.'

The big Damitian released the butcher with a shove and let himself out of the kitchen. Hauritz sputtered in outrage for a moment, at least until the door closed behind Murry, then he took a deep breath and turned to look at Marqel. She smiled tentatively.

'You'll have to tell me what to do,' she said in a small, tremulous voice. 'I've never done this before.'

The butcher wiped his hands on his trousers and moved around the table towards her. Marqel dropped her eyes coyly and began to unlace her shift. With luck, and a bit of judicious teasing, it would be over almost before it began.

'How old are you?'

'Thirteen,' she lied smoothly. It didn't matter that she was almost seventeen. It was what the butcher believed that counted.

'Thirteen,' the butcher repeated, his voice husky, as if he couldn't believe what stood before him. 'So young. So innocent.'

So gullible, Marqel added with silent scorn as she let the shift fall to the floor.

The man gasped in appreciation. They always did. Her body was toned from long hours practising acrobatics, and she'd learned long ago that confronted with a naked female body, most men would agree to anything.

'Sir?' she ventured cautiously, taking a step back from him.

'What?'

'May I ask a favour?'

'Anything . . .' He moved closer, reaching for her, but not touching her yet, as if he was afraid she would disappear if he laid his hands upon her.

'This is my first time.'

'I know.'

'Would you give me something? Something to remember it by?'

The butcher looked up sharply and Marqel wondered if she'd misjudged him. 'I just gave your damn father a fortune in silver.'

Suddenly, unshed tears glistened in her sapphire eyes. 'I'm sorry, sir. I shouldn't have asked. It was wrong of me, I know. It's just that . . . well, I'll not ever have this moment again. And you seem such a . . . nice man. I wanted it to be special.'

Hauritz the Butcher stared at her for a moment, then walked across to the sideboard. He opened a carved trinket box and withdrew a gold coin. He held it up in front of her face. 'If you're a good girl, I'll let you have this when we're done.'

She nodded and wiped her tears away. Lanatyne had shown her how to cry like that. It worked every time.

'I'll be a good girl,' she promised shyly.

The butcher grinned, and pulled her to him.

Marqel closed her eyes, keeping the image of that gold coin in her mind.

5

The mysterious sailor still hadn't regained consciousness by dinnertime. Master Helgin shooed Dirk and Eryk out of his rooms and ordered Dirk to attend his parents. The governor would be in attendance at dinner this evening, and not for any reason would Dirk be excused.

They had bathed the battered man's numerous wounds, reset his dislocated shoulder and bound his broken limbs. The old man had stitched and dressed the wound on the sailor's forehead, but did not seem unduly concerned about it. All they could do now was wait.

Helgin had fussed over his patient like an old woman. The only reason that he gave for having the man brought to his rooms, rather than the infirmary down near the main gate, was his need to keep the sailor under constant observation. Dirk thought his decision very strange, particularly as Helgin was always telling him how important it was that a physician maintain a distance between himself and his patients. It was at Helgin's insistence that his mother had provided the physician with an infirmary in the first place.

'Will he be all right, Master Helgin?' Eryk asked, as Helgin tried to hurry them out.

'He's been unconscious for a long time,' Dirk added with concern.

'That's just nature's way of coping with pain,' Helgin assured them, wiping his brow with his kerchief. Although it was still warm, it didn't seem hot enough to make the old physician sweat so much.

'Are you sure you wouldn't rather I stayed . . . ?'

'Be off with you, Dirk, before your mother has *me* served up for dinner for keeping you late.'

'I don't have to go to dinner with the guv'ner,' Eryk pointed out with a helpful smile. 'I could stay and help.'

'I'm sure Seneschal Balonan can find plenty of other work for you, Eryk. The patient will be fine without you watching him draw his every breath.'

'You looked really worried this morning,' Dirk reminded him, thinking of Helgin's concern when he first examined the survivor.

'Well, I'm not worried now,' Helgin insisted, almost pushing them out the door. 'Now go, both of you. And mind your manners at dinner tonight, Dirk. Tovin Rill is an important man and you can't afford to offend him.'

That's a bit rich, coming from you, Dirk thought, recalling the physician's tactless remarks in Tovin's hearing this morning. But he said nothing. Helgin was uncharacteristically nervous about something.

'I'll come back after dinner and check on him.'

'No, you've got studying to do. I'm still waiting for that work I gave you last week.'

Dirk shrugged. 'That won't take long. They're just a few calculations. Besides, you said I didn't have to complete it until next week.'

'I changed my mind. And they're not just a few calculations, boy. Some of those problems kept the finest minds at the university on Grannon Rock occupied for years before they were solved.'

'Are you *sure* you don't want us to come back?'

'Positive. Now go!'

With no idea why Helgin was so anxious to be rid of them, Dirk reluctantly left the room, then, when he realised how late it was, hurried up the stairs to his room on the fifth floor of the ancient Keep with the ever-faithful Eryk close on his heels.

Since being appointed Dirk's servant, the tousle-haired Eryk had taken his duties so seriously that he was rarely out of the older boy's sight. Although he could be trying at times, Dirk didn't really mind. Eryk was a harmless soul without an artful bone in his body, and since being promoted, from an unwanted orphan that nobody was sure what to do with to the servant of the second son of Elcast, it was as if he had found his purpose in life. And the bullying had stopped, too. Eryk had always been an easy target for bigger, smarter lads in the castle and the town. Since Dirk's mother had taken the boy in, the bullies seemed reluctant to incur the wrath of one of Duke Wallin's sons, and through him, the duke, just to have a bit of sport with a slow-witted orphan.

With Eryk hovering around him like a clucky mother hen, Dirk changed out of his dirty clothes.

'You should brush your hair,' Eryk reminded him, carefully enunciating each word. He only lisped when he got really excited, although sometimes it was painful to listen to him trying so hard. 'And wash behind your ears, too.'

This from a boy who usually had to be dragged kicking and screaming to the bathtub. Dirk looked at the boy with a suspicious frown as he pulled on his boots.

'Eryk, who told you to say that? My mother?'

The boy shook his head. 'It was Lord Rees. While we were waiting for you on the levee wall, he said that every day I should tell you to bruth your hair, and thine your thoes—'

That would have been Rees's idea of a joke. He probably

made the poor boy repeat the list back to him a dozen times to make sure he remembered it. 'Well, next time Lord Rees starts telling you what to say to me,' Dirk cut in, before Eryk got too tongue-tied, 'you tell him I said to mind his own bithness.'

Eryk grinned at Dirk's deliberate mispronunciation. 'Are you taking the pith out of me, Lord Dirk?'

'Just a little bit. And stop calling me Lord Dirk, Eryk. I must have told you that a million times already.'

'It wouldn't be proper,' Eryk replied. 'I told you that a million times.'

Dirk stamped his feet into his boots and ruffled the boy's hair fondly. 'I'd better get going. When you're finished up here, you make sure you eat something, you hear?' Eryk frequently got so involved in what he was doing that he would forget to eat. In fact, Eryk required so much supervision that at times, Dirk wondered who was looking after whom.

Still tucking in his shirt as he ran downstairs, he barely made it to the Hall as Tovin Rill was taking his seat at the High Table for dinner.

The Hall was one of the few places in Elcast Keep that required artificial lighting. Even during the day, candles were required to light the cavernous circular hall. Like the rest of the Keep, the walls were constructed of roughly dressed granite, and it was always cool in here, even at the height of summer. The red light from the evening sun did not reach the floor through the thick arrow-slit windows that followed the deep granite stairs. The stairs wound around the interior of the building as if some giant drill had bored the Hall out of living rock. Rectangular shafts of ruby light crisscrossed the granite walls in a pattern that still fascinated Dirk, even after a lifetime of staring at it.

'Ah, here he is!' Tovin declared as Dirk tried to make his way to the High Table as inconspicuously as possible. 'Our heroic physician!'

With no chance of sneaking to his place quietly, he gave up trying. Dirk stopped in front of the High Table and bowed to the duke and the governor. His father sat in the centre, with his mother on the left and Tovin Rill on his right. Rees sat on Tovin's right next to Lanon, while his own seat sat empty and waiting beside his mother's. Every eye in the Hall was on him.

'Heroic, my lord?' Wallin asked with a smile. Dirk's father was just like Rees, stocky and solid, although his curly hair was more grey than brown these days. There was little of Wallin in Dirk. He was leaner, taller and more like his mother in both looks and temperament. 'Surely the boy merely did what he's being trained for?'

'Yes, Wallin, he did, but he shimmied down that damn levee wall like it was a garden trellis. Can't say I would have tackled it with the same aplomb.'

Dirk saw his mother pale as she turned to the governor. 'You made my son climb down the levee wall to rescue some shipwrecked sailor?'

'Didn't have to *make* him, my lady,' Tovin informed her cheerfully. 'He volunteered.'

Morna turned her steely gaze on Dirk. He suddenly felt five years old again. His father, he noticed with relief, was looking rather proud of him.

'You volunteered, Dirk?'

'I . . . well, somebody had to go, sir, and I didn't think Master Helgin was really up to it.'

'It was a noble thing you did, son,' Wallin declared, before his mother could offer her opinion. But to placate his wife, he added, 'Just don't make a habit of it.'

'No, sir.'

Dirk took his place beside Morna, deliberately avoiding her disapproving gaze.

'And how is our miraculous survivor, Dirk?' Tovin asked as the servants began serving the soup.

'He's still unconscious, my lord, but Master Helgin thinks he'll live.'

'I must check on him after dinner. I've never seen

anything so remarkable. He must be well favoured by the Goddess to have been spared.'

'It sounds rather more like he was well favoured by the timely arrival of my son,' Duchess Morna suggested tartly.

Tovin glanced at the duchess and smiled. 'Then you should feel honoured that the Goddess chose your son as her instrument, my lady.'

Dirk inwardly cringed, praying silently that his mother would not speak anything further on the subject. Morna Provin made little secret of her dislike for both Senet and their religion, and it was common knowledge that Tovin had been sent to Elcast to replace the former governor, Aris Lokin, because he was considered lax in his duties. Dirk had quite liked old Lord Aris and was sorry to see him recalled to the mainland.

'So, Wallin, what arrangements have you made for the Landfall Festival?' Tovin asked, when Morna's frosty silence became uncomfortable.

His father frowned warily before answering. 'The same as we always do, my lord. You'll be heading back to Avacas for the Landfall Feast, I suppose. I doubt our provincial fair would entertain you much.'

Tovin Rill laughed. 'Don't be absurd, man! I can't leave Elcast before the Landfall Festival! Besides, the Shadowdancers should be here any day. It would be most unseemly for me to up and leave before they get here.'

Stillness fell over the head table that even the servants noticed. Wallin glanced at Morna, then turned to face the governor.

'Brahm Halyn, Elcast's Sundancer, is usually the only representative of the Church who attends our Landfall Feast, my lord.'

Tovin's eyes narrowed. 'For your own sake, I hope you're going to tell me it's for no more sinister reason than the unseasonable weather we're having for this time of year, Wallin.'

'As I'm sure you know, my lord, our temple was destroyed during the Age of Shadows,' Wallin began. 'So we've not had a permanent representative of the other aspect of the Goddess on the island since then, but—'

'Yes, I'm aware of that, Wallin. It's one of the first things I intend to redress, now that I'm governor. Why haven't you made any attempt to rebuild the temple?'

'Elcast is not a rich island, my lord.'

'I'm sure you could have found the coin if you wanted to,' Tovin remarked with a scowl at Lady Morna.

The duke did not reply, but Dirk's mother did. 'We do not countenance the Shadowdancers, or that thinly disguised orgy they call their Landfall Festival, in Elcast, my lord. We have no need for them, their drugs or their rituals. I'll not have my sons perverted by them.' Her tone worried Dirk. It was openly hostile.

Tovin's expression was dangerous. 'I see now why the Goddess struck down your fields last night, my lady. It was a warning. One that you would do well to heed. Have you forgotten what the Age of Shadows was like?'

'I recall very well what the Age of Shadows was like.'

'Yet you encourage the very behaviour that made the Goddess turn from us. You deny her worship and hope you can continue to enjoy her bounty. Did that time of darkness teach you nothing? It is people like you that caused the Age of Shadows, Lady Morna.'

Dirk gasped, unable to believe that the governor would accuse his mother of such a dreadful thing. His father frowned, warning him to silence with a look.

'And you, Wallin? Do you hold with your wife's views?'

The silence was heavy as everyone waited for the duke's answer. 'Elcast serves the Goddess, my lord.'

The governor nodded slowly. 'In that case, we shall celebrate the Landfall Festival in the correct manner. You are a married woman and have no need to take part yourself, my lady, and Dirk and Lanon are too young in any case, but Rees will take part, as befits his rank as heir.'

Dirk glanced at his older brother. Rees looked horrified.

'Have the Landfall Festival if you must, Tovin,' Morna conceded with barely concealed disgust. 'But at least let me take my sons from here. They have no need to witness that foul ritual . . .'

'No!' Tovin declared. 'The Lion of Senet will not tolerate these atheist leanings in Dhevyn, my lady, and as his representative on Elcast, I will ensure that you do your duty to the Goddess, and you will see to it that your children do theirs.'

His mother bowed her head in defeat. Wallin looked distinctly uncomfortable. With a wave of his hand, Tovin ordered the servants to refill his wine cup and the meal progressed in awkward silence.

Dirk studied his mother out of the corner of his eye, understanding why she was so upset. The Landfall Festival was something she had been trying to discourage for years. With only one Sundancer in attendance, the Elcast Landfall Festival was usually little more than a country fair. Thanks to his mother's determination, the rituals practised by the Shadowdancers had never reached their island. Dirk had heard about them, though – rumours of human sacrifice, of wild orgies, of foul rites and strange magicks.

He glanced down the table at his brother. Rees caught his eye and shook his head, warning him to say nothing, ask nothing.

It was neither the time nor the place to talk of such things.

6

Morna Provin's icy silence was not, as Lord Tovin suspected, caused by her distress at the news that he was planning to rebuild the temple, or that there would be a proper Landfall Festival this year. In truth, Tovin's news did not surprise her. She had expected as much when she learned who Antonov was sending to replace Lord Aris.

No, it was not the Landfall Feast that concerned her.

It was Dirk.

The Duchess of Elcast had watched her second son standing before the High Table, watched him take his seat beside her. She watched him answer Tovin Rill's questions. Watched him frown when she so foolishly challenged Tovin on the issue of the Landfall Feast.

She was always watching him.

He had filled out these past few months, and was taller now than both Wallin and Rees. His eyes were grey, like hers, which was a fortunate thing, his hair dark and wavy. Everyone remarked how much his eyes were like hers. She was grateful for that. It took their attention away from his other features that were no more hers than they were Wallin Provin's. Morna was constantly looking for some sign that would betray her secret. In more than sixteen years, she had never known a moment's peace for fear of it being discovered.

And the older he gets, the more chance someone else will see it, too.

Morna angrily chided herself for the thought. It was one she could not allow herself to dwell on. *Wallin is Dirk's father in every sense of the word,* she reminded herself. In all the time they had been married, he had never even hinted that he thought Dirk was not his child. He had never once raised the subject, although he must have suspected the truth. Perhaps he denied it to himself. Morna wasn't sure, and it was certainly something she could never ask him. Wallin had accepted her back after the war, and had never referred to her infidelity again. He had never asked what she'd done and never demanded an explanation. All he wanted or expected was for Morna to be his wife and act in a manner befitting the Duchess of Elcast. She had done that much willingly. Wallin was her security. He was her sons' security. Without her patient and forgiving husband, she would be dead. But she didn't love Wallin Provin, not the way she had loved . . .

Stop it! she told herself sternly. *There is no point to this! It is ancient history!*

But was it really ancient history? Years of relative obscurity and peace had been shattered with the appointment of Tovin Rill as Governor of Elcast. *Would he see the resemblance?* Morna picked at her meal and finally waved to a servant to take her barely touched plate away, glancing surreptitiously at the Senetian Governor. Had the Lion of Senet sent Tovin Rill here for that reason? Did he know or suspect the truth? The danger to Dirk if the Senetians ever discovered who had fathered him kept Morna awake some nights trembling with fear.

Morna found herself running through the mental list of people who knew the truth. Some of them, like Master Helgin, she knew she could trust. Others she was not so sure about. Wallin might know, for all that he kept silent on the matter. Antonov Latanya, the Lion of Senet, might suspect something, but he had never met Dirk and never would, if Morna had any say in the matter. Rove Elan, the Lord Marshal of Dhevyn, might guess; he was the one who had brought her home to Elcast. Belagren, the High Priestess of the Shadowdancers and Antonov's mistress, had no idea, she was certain of that. The queen suspected nothing either, Morna was sure. Then again, Morna wondered if Rainan would care even if she did know the truth. The Queen of Dhevyn had her own problems.

'Mother!' Dirk hissed impatiently.

She turned to Dirk. 'I'm sorry, did you say something?'

'Can I be excused?' Dirk spoke barely louder than a whisper, but it was loud enough that Tovin heard him.

'Leaving so soon, Dirk?' the Senetian asked as he leaned back in his seat with his wine cup cradled comfortably in his left hand. 'It's bad for the digestion to rush off so soon after eating.'

'I mean no offence, my lord,' Dirk said with a disarming smile. 'I've some studying to catch up on. Master Helgin is a hard taskmaster.'

'Your father tells me you're an excellent student, Dirk. Even Lanon claims you are something of a mathematical prodigy.'

'I'm sure they exaggerate, my lord.'

'Perhaps. But one would think that if you excel in the area of mathematics, you would be more inclined to choose a future as an engineer, not a physician. We always have need of good engineers in Senet.' The governor turned to Wallin and chuckled. 'The Goddess and her earthquake keep them well supplied with work.'

'He says he likes helping people,' Lanon announced with a grin at Dirk.

Morna saw Rees cover his smile with his wine cup. There was no animosity and little rivalry between her sons, and although she disapproved of the friendship, Dirk had become firm friends with Lanon Rill since his arrival on Elcast several months ago. Perhaps she should be grateful for that. In years to come, her sons would need powerful friends in Avacas.

'You'd help many more people by becoming an engineer than you would taking on a life as a physician, Dirk.'

'But I would prefer to be a physician, my lord,' Dirk replied calmly.

Tovin looked as if he was losing patience with the boy. 'In Senet, a son takes the path appointed by his father.'

'But this is Dhevyn, my lord, not Senet.'

'You may *go,* Dirk,' Wallin announced abruptly, before his youngest son could add anything further. Morna looked at Dirk, trying to will him to heed the caution in Wallin's voice.

'Thank you, Father,' Dirk said, taking the hint. Rising to his feet he bowed to the governor, just low enough not to be disrespectful. 'Mother. My lord.'

Tovin watched Dirk's retreating back thoughtfully as he left the Hall. 'I see your hand in the boy's upbringing, my lady.'

'He is my son, my lord.'

'That much is patently obvious,' Tovin remarked sourly.

Morna caught Wallin's warning look and bit back the caustic reply that leapt to mind. Instead, she rose to her feet. 'If my lords don't mind, I, too, wish to be excused. I must see if Master Helgin has everything he requires to treat our miraculous survivor.'

Wallin looked mightily relieved that she was leaving. He nodded briefly and dismissed her with a wave of his hand. She left the High Table and walked the long length of the Hall, feeling the eyes of everyone on her.

Damn them, she thought defiantly. *Damn them all.*

Morna had used the excuse of the shipwreck survivor merely to escape the Hall. She didn't think she could stand another evening filled with Tovin regaling them with his droll anecdotes about the Lion of Senet's court. She breathed a sigh of relief as the massive bronze doors of the Hall boomed shut behind her.

Then it occurred to her that she really *should* see to it that Master Helgin had everything he needed. She was the Duchess of Elcast, after all. It was her duty.

The evening was mild as she stepped out into the courtyard; Ranadon's evening sun bathed the castle in its familiar ruby light. The earlier clouds were beginning to break up, but the air still tasted of ash, spewed forth by the distant volcano. It was generally agreed that the eruption must have been somewhere between Elcast and the mainland, maybe in the Bandera Straits. Morna thought it too much to hope that it had been close to Avacas, the Senetian capital.

Now that truly would be a sign from the Goddess, she thought, *if Antonov Latanya and his whole damn city were consumed by lava.*

She was a little surprised to find the infirmary closed and no sign of Helgin or his patient. The yard was all but deserted, so she turned back towards the Keep, thinking that perhaps the physician had installed the survivor in his rooms. It was not like Helgin to do that, but if he felt the man needed constant attention, he might prefer the comfort of his quarters to the bare functionality of the converted storehouse that Morna had designated the infirmary.

Tovin and Wallin were deep in conversation and did

not notice her return as she climbed the broad granite stairs that circled the interior of the Keep. Dirk was always asking who had built the Keep, but she had never been able to answer him. Like the levee wall and a number of other scattered buildings both on the mainland and around the islands of Dhevyn, the massive structures had stood for as long as anyone could remember. They were the only structures that had withstood centuries of constant earthquakes, and none of them was built close enough to a volcano to be endangered by the lava flows. Fortunately, Elcast's volcano had been long dormant, but it must have been active once, or there would have been no need for such a building.

If only we still had the knowledge to build so well, she silently lamented. On that one point she was actually in agreement with Tovin Rill. Dirk really would be wasted as a physician. His mathematical ability was astounding and he probably *could* divine the engineering secrets of the ancients if he set his mind to it. But living things fascinated Dirk. He had no interest in studying inanimate objects.

Besides, studying under Master Helgin meant Dirk could stay here on Elcast. For that reason alone she would have championed his choice of career, even if he'd wanted to be a pig herder. Dirk's curiosity and hunger for knowledge were quite legendary in Elcast, and they were the reasons her husband, somewhat reluctantly, had agreed to let Master Helgin take Dirk on as an apprentice last year. Normally, as the second son of a ruling duke, his future would be tied closely with his family estates. *In the old days*, Morna thought wistfully, *as a second son, he would have been sworn to serve in the Queen's Guard*. That custom had died out since the return of the last Age of Shadows.

Dirk was both surprised and quite delighted when his mother had championed his cause and convinced his father that he should become an apprentice physician. The downside of the arrangement was that it meant he would not be able to go to Nova on the island of Grannon Rock to study at the university there. Morna had managed to convince her son (and herself) that there were few men in Dhevyn who could teach him as much as Helgin.

She reached the third-floor landing, turned down the hall to the apartment where Helgin lived and knocked on his door. When nobody answered, she waited for a moment longer, then tried the latch, surprised to find it locked.

'Who's there?' Even through the thick door Helgin's muffled voice sounded quite anxious.

'It's me. Morna.'

The lock rattled and after a moment the door opened a fraction. 'Are you alone?'

'Yes.'

'You'd better come in, my lady.'

He stood back to let Morna enter the room and then locked the door behind her. She looked at the physician curiously. He leaned against the closed door. He was sweating profusely and seemed as nervous as a sheep in a slaughter-house.

'What's the matter, Helgin? Why the locks? You're acting like a fugitive.' She smiled at him. 'Did you say something to offend Tovin Rill? If you have, he showed no sign of concern at dinner.'

'I've not offended Lord Tovin, my lady. No more than I usually do.'

'Then why are you behaving so oddly?'

Helgin said nothing for a moment, then took a deep breath. 'You'll not think my behaviour odd, my lady, when you learn who it is that I have locked in this room.'

'The sailor?' Morna's gaze flew to the closed door that led to Helgin's bedroom. 'Who is he?'

The physician pointed to the door. 'See for yourself.'

With a frown, Morna crossed the cluttered sitting room to the bedroom door. She turned the latch and opened the door. The unconscious survivor lay on the large four-poster bed covered by a sheet. He was swathed in splints and bandages. A line of neat stitches stretched across his forehead from above his left eye up into his hairline. Morna moved into the room to get a closer look at him. She realised who it was just as Helgin stepped up beside her. Suddenly faint, she clutched at him for support, her eyes filled with tears.

'Oh, Goddess!' she breathed. 'It can't be!'

'It's him, my lady.'

'But . . .' Morna found she couldn't speak. Her mind was such a confusion of emotions that she was unable to form a single articulate thought.

'You'd better sit down,' Helgin suggested.

He tugged on her arm and led her back into the other room, closing the bedroom door before sitting her down on the settee. He left her there for a moment and moved away, returning with a large shot of dark liquid that he thrust into her hands. Morna was trembling so hard that she could barely hold the cup, but he forced her to drink it. The liquor burned down her throat, focusing her attention – on breathing, if nothing else.

'How . . . ?' was all she found herself able to ask.

Helgin shrugged. 'How he got here is not important, my lady. It's how we're going to get him out of here that matters.'

Panic filled her. 'Oh, Goddess, Helgin . . . Tovin's here. If he finds out . . . and Wallin . . .'

'Take a deep breath, my lady.'

Morna did as the physician ordered, surprised to find that it helped. 'I'll be all right. I'm just . . . shocked.'

'As am I, my lady. Unfortunately, we don't have time to adjust to the news.'

Morna nodded, feeling a little more in control. She took another sip of the burning liquid and looked at Helgin. 'Who else knows he's here?'

'Only you and I, at present.'

'But the others in the rescue party? Tovin was there when you brought him up from the beach. And Dirk . . . oh, Goddess, Helgin, *Dirk* was there . . .'

'Dirk has no idea who he is, my lady,' Helgin assured her, 'any more than the men who rescued him. Tovin saw nothing but a battered, half-drowned sailor, and once I realised who it was, I made certain he didn't get a closer look at him. For the time being, at least, he is safe.'

'We have to get him out of here.'

'I agree. However, he's badly injured and I would prefer not to move him.'

'And even if we did move him, where do we take him?' She jumped to her feet and began to pace the small sitting room. 'Damn, if only Tovin wasn't here! He was making noises about visiting the survivor at dinner.' She stopped abruptly and turned to Helgin. 'He might come here tonight!'

'And I will turn him away,' Helgin promised. 'But I can't deter him for long. You have to decide what you want to do, my lady.'

'That's simple! He has to die,' she announced decisively.

'I *beg* your pardon?'

'You have to announce that the survivor died,' she instructed, resuming her frenzied pacing. 'That you were unable to save him. Say that he had terrible internal injuries or something of that nature. That should throw Tovin off. Then we can move him somewhere safe and I'll find a way to get him back to his ... friends.'

'After all this time, do you even know how to contact his friends, my lady?'

'There are still Dhevynians loyal to his cause. The Draitons of Derex. The Seranovs of Grannon Rock ...'

'Yes, well, we won't get into what I think of the Seranov family, my lady,' Helgin muttered. Then he shook his head. 'But even if you were certain of their aid, do you know the risk you would be taking if your husband or Tovin Rill discovered you making contact with Senet's enemies?'

Morna was silent for a moment, then turned to face the physician. Her expression was bitter.

'What other course is open to me, Helgin?' she asked. 'The alternative is to inform my husband that the miraculous survivor of the Goddess's tidal wave is the most wanted man in all of Dhevyn and Senet.'

7

Eryk watched Dirk mutter impatiently to himself as he worked out the incomprehensible mathematical problems Helgin had set for him. It seemed to take his young master only as long as it took to write down the answers.

Eryk was in awe of Dirk Provin's ability to solve things like that. Actually, he was in awe of Dirk generally. Since being rescued by Duchess Morna, his life had taken such a dramatic turn for the better that sometimes his former life seemed like a bad dream. He never went hungry any more, he had a real bed to sleep in and people treated him with respect. Even the stable boys who tormented him so often when he was smaller didn't bother him these days. Not since Rees had quietly taken Derwn Hauritz and Taril Longbottom and their friends aside after that episode with the horse trough. Eryk didn't know what the older Provin brother said to the other boys, but nobody in the castle had picked on him since that day. But he still stayed clear of the town; even Dirk was not certain he would be safe alone down there. Derwn Hauritz, the butcher's son, bore long grudges.

Eryk was inclined to be forgiving towards Taril and his cronies, though. If not for a beating that left him half dead, Master Helgin would never have brought him to the attention of Duchess Morna, and she would never have taken him into the Keep and he would never have been made Dirk's servant. He would still be the smallest, stupidest boy on Elcast who spoke with a lisp and was the butt of all the pranks and torments that the apprentices in the town could devise.

Eryk knew he wasn't very bright, but being around Dirk made him realise that everyone had someone who was smarter than they were. *Except* Dirk. In Eryk's humble opinion, Dirk was the smartest person on the whole of

Ranadon. Even Master Helgin thought he was clever, and he'd lived on other islands where there were lots of smart people.

'Done!'

'That was quick,' Eryk remarked, then added a little doubtfully, 'Wathn't it?'

'Wasn't it,' Dirk corrected automatically.

'*Wasn't* it?'

'I suppose.' Dirk blew on the ink to hasten the drying process, then snatched the page off his desk. 'I don't know what Helgin was on about. If these are the worst problems he can come up with, then I think the scholars on Grannon Rock who slaved over them for so long must have been drunken morons to a man.'

Eryk grinned at the comment, following Dirk to the door. 'You're cleverer than them, Lord Dirk.'

'I seriously doubt that, Eryk.'

'You're smarter than *me*,' Eryk reminded him, then he shrugged. 'Actually, everybody in the whole world is smarter than me.'

'Don't be silly, everybody in the whole world is not smarter than you, Eryk.'

Eryk smiled at the reassurance, but knew better than to believe it. He knew that Dirk didn't consider himself particularly gifted. His young master thought the duchess was just a trifle overprotective and Master Helgin just a tad senile. When pressed, Dirk would admit, begrudgingly, that he didn't have much trouble with any of the work the old physician gave him in his dual role of tutor and apprentice master, but insisted that it didn't prove he was the genius his mother liked to think he was. Eryk knew Dirk found the whole subject of his intelligence just a little bit embarrassing, and fervently wished his parents would stop being so proud of him for it.

They hurried down the stairs to Master Helgin's rooms. Although Helgin had been anxious to be rid of them earlier, Eryk figured that with Dirk's studying complete, they would be allowed to stay and tend the unnamed sailor. Eryk ran

down the stairs behind Dirk, determined not to miss a minute
of this unusual event. Nothing like this had happened in the
Keep before. The most exciting thing that had happened to
Eryk lately was getting a new pair of boots for his birthday.

The sailor's injuries made an interesting change from
the normal, everyday ailments that Master Helgin dealt with
in the Keep, and the man was lucky that he had been thrown
ashore on Elcast, where a physician of Master Helgin's calibre
was on hand. The breaks in his leg and arms had been clean
breaks, so Helgin claimed, and the old physician had let Dirk
and Eryk watch as he stitched the cut on his forehead so
carefully it wouldn't even leave much of a scar. With a bit
of judicious manipulation his dislocated shoulder had popped
back quite smoothly, and once he awoke from his poppy-
dust-induced coma, the man would probably heal quite
rapidly.

Eryk was anxious to be there when he woke. Dirk had
said the man looked like he might come from the Baenlands.
He wanted to ask the Baenlander about his ship. He wanted
to ask about the Baenlands, too.

'Where are you off to in such a hurry, lads?' Wallin
asked, as Dirk and Eryk almost collided with the duke and
Tovin Rill on the third-floor landing.

'We were just going to see Master Helgin, sir.'

'As are we,' Tovin informed him. 'We've come to see
how our lucky sailor fares.'

'He's probably not awake yet,' Dirk told them. 'Master
Helgin gave him poppy-dust for the pain.'

'Never fear, we'll not disturb him.'

Just as anxious to check on the patient, Dirk led the way
along the hall to Master Helgin's room. He depressed the
latch. Surprised to find it locked, he fished his own key out
of his pocket and unlocked the door, stepping aside to allow
his father and the governor to enter.

Lady Morna and Master Helgin froze as they entered,
their conversation halting midsentence, their whole stance
proclaiming some terrible guilt, although about what, Eryk
could not imagine. The door to the other room was closed.

The cluttered sitting room, with its numerous piles of books, scrolls and jars, was on the eastern side of the Keep. The sun infused the room with warm red light that lent the scene a surreal atmosphere.

'Wallin! Lord Tovin! What . . . what are you doing here?'

'We came to check on Master Helgin's patient, my lady,' Tovin replied.

'You can't!' Morna declared.

'He can't be disturbed,' Helgin announced at the same time, stepping in front of the bedroom door.

Tovin stared at the duchess and then the old man suspiciously. 'What is going on here?'

Morna took a deep breath and smiled. She looked outwardly calm, but her fingers were knotting and unknotting the gold cord tied around the waist of her gown. Eryk had never seen her do that before.

'What do you mean, my lord?'

Tovin stared at the duchess for a long moment, and then looked at the physician. 'Show me your patient, old man,' he ordered.

'He cannot be disturbed,' Helgin repeated firmly.

'Helgin, stop being so stubborn,' Wallin said impatiently. 'Lord Tovin merely wants to check on the man. He won't disturb him. He won't even wake him.'

'I'm afraid I can't allow it, my lord. The patient is very ill. It's doubtful he will make it through the night.'

'Has he taken a turn for the worse?' Dirk asked in concern.

'You said he'd be fine before dinner,' Eryk reminded him helpfully.

Tovin glanced at Eryk curiously, then turned his attention back to Master Helgin. 'Well, old man? Is he dying? Or is he fine?'

Helgin didn't answer him. Wallin was sufficiently annoyed by now to push past his wife and the physician and open the door himself. He took a step inside the bedroom and stopped dead, then looked back over his shoulder at

Morna. The look he gave her was filled with such pain that
Eryk thought Duchess Morna was going to cry.

'Well?' Tovin demanded impatiently.

'I think perhaps you'd better see for yourself, my lord,'
Wallin said. He looked away, as if he suddenly couldn't bear
the torment in Morna's eyes.

The governor crossed the threadbare rug and stepped
into the bedroom. From his place near the door Eryk couldn't
see the expression on the Senetian's face when he saw the
sailor, but there was no mistaking his tone when he bellowed,
'Call the guards!'

'You can't move him!' Helgin protested. 'Please!'

Tovin pushed his way back into the sitting room to
confront Morna. 'You may consider yourself under arrest,
my lady.'

'*Mother?*' Dirk cried in bewilderment. 'Father? What's
going on?'

Tovin rounded on Dirk angrily. 'Did you know about
this, too? Are you part of the plot to conceal his presence
from me?'

'Plot? What plot? What are you talking about?'

'Go to your room, Dirk,' Morna ordered. Her voice was
flat and unemotional. 'And take Eryk with you.'

'No! I want to know what's happening. Why are you
under arrest?'

'Dirk,' his father said, 'do as your mother says. Leave
us.'

'Lord Tovin?' Dirk seemed to think that if his parents
weren't going to tell him what was going on, then perhaps
the Senetian Governor would.

'Your mother is harbouring a criminal, Dirk. I've no
doubt that we interrupted her and her accomplice preparing
to spirit him away somewhere.' Tovin turned to Morna, as
if he were mightily pleased with himself for uncovering such
a dastardly plot. 'That was the plan, wasn't it, my lady? Claim
the man had died during the night, before I got a good look
at him? What then? A message to his pirate cohorts to get
him off the island? Or perhaps you knew he was coming?'

Is that what his ship was doing near your coast, my lady? Was he coming to visit you?'

'You can't arrest my mother!' Dirk objected. The Senetian turned to stare at him in surprise.

'Stay out of this, son,' Wallin warned.

Dirk ignored him. 'My lord, you can't arrest my mother for harbouring a criminal. If anyone is guilty of that crime, it's you.'

'Dirk!' Morna cried anxiously.

'No, my lady, let him continue,' Lord Tovin said, his eyes dangerous. 'It seems you have quite an advocate. Please, Dirk, carry on.'

'*You* ordered the rescue of the sailor, my lord, and it was your men that brought him here to the Keep, when they could just have easily taken him to the garrison in town. My mother didn't even know he was in the Keep until you brought it to her attention.'

Dirk waited expectantly. Eryk had no idea who the sailor in the next room was, or what was really happening, but if Dirk was so sure Tovin Rill couldn't arrest Lady Morna for it, then Eryk believed it, too.

'And what of Master Helgin?' Tovin asked. 'Do you have an excuse for him, too?'

'Master Helgin is a physician, sir, and sworn to do no harm.'

Eryk was very proud of Dirk. He wasn't scared at all. Eryk would have given a great deal to have just a tiny bit of Dirk's courage.

'As you obviously wish this man serious harm,' his young master continued, 'he could be considered to be merely upholding his oath.'

Tovin smiled suddenly and turned to Wallin. 'Where did you educate this boy, Wallin? In the tribunals of Senet?'

'I did warn you he was a bright lad,' Wallin reminded him. 'He is also very lucky I haven't throttled him for disobeying me. Leave *now*, Dirk, and stay in your room until I send for you.'

Dirk might be prepared to face down the Senetian

Governor on a point of law, Eryk noted with interest, but he wasn't quite ready to defy his father when he used that tone of voice.

'Yes, sir,' Dirk replied meekly. He turned towards the door with Eryk close on his heels, then stopped and looked back over his shoulder. 'May I ask one question, before I go?'

'Is there any way of stopping you?' Tovin muttered.

'The sailor. Who is he?'

Tovin looked at him doubtfully, as if he thought Dirk should know the man's identity. The duke didn't look at him at all. Master Helgin was chewing nervously on his bottom lip, something he only did when he was very worried. After a long moment of heavy silence, it was Lady Morna who finally answered him.

'He is Johan Thorn,' she said softly, a wealth of unspoken emotion in her voice. She looked squarely at Tovin and added harshly, 'And he's *not* a criminal.'

'Johan Thorn? Isn't he a pirate or something?'

'He's a traitor,' Tovin agreed. 'And as soon as I get word to Prince Antonov, he will die a traitor's death.'

'Why? Because he's a pirate?'

'Because he is the true King of Dhevyn,' Lady Morna said.

8

When the vast city of Avacas came into view, Belagren breathed a sigh of relief. They had made good time from Omaxin, but every day she had spent away from the capital since the eruption was another day for people to start putting their own interpretation on events. Her urgency to return to Avacas had consumed her, and she had driven her escort hard to get back before too much damage could be done in her absence.

She halted her entourage on the rise overlooking the city as they emerged through the last of the mountain passes, thinking it looked unchanged from when she had last seen it several weeks ago. She could only hope that her first impressions were correct. It was nearly three weeks since the eruption, and a lot could have happened in that time without her.

'Shall we head for the palace, my lady?' the captain of her guard asked, interrupting her train of thought.

'No,' she replied, 'we shall return to the Hall of Shadows.'

'As my lady commands.'

The captain wheeled his horse around, ready to give the order to move on. Belagren desperately wanted to go straight to the palace, but it was important that Antonov not see her like this, travel stained, weary and unattractive as a result of the forced ride from Omaxin. It was important that he only see her at her best, particularly now that she was getting older. The Lion of Senet had a notorious wandering eye, and Belagren had never fooled herself that she could hold him exclusively to her. He'd had plenty of affairs over the years, but none of the women remained a threat for long. She had seen to that personally. The High Priestess managed the problem by ensuring that she controlled the young women who caught his eye. That way there were no scenes, no awkward explanations and most important, no bastards.

'You're not going to the palace?' Madalan asked beside her.

Belagren glanced at her friend. 'I need a bath. And besides, it might be better if Antonov comes to me.'

Madalan shook her head. 'Don't you ever worry that he'll tire of playing your games, Belagren?'

The High Priestess smiled. 'I am the Voice of the Goddess, Madalan.'

'Then for all our sakes, I hope she speaks to you again soon,' the older woman reminded her. 'Or things are going to get very awkward for all of us.'

The Hall of Shadows was a gift from the Lion of Senet. Some five miles from the centre of Avacas, it perched on an outcropping of rock that jutted into the Tresna Sea, affording it a glorious view of both the harbour and the city. Formerly the summer residence of a once-wealthy family now fallen from grace, it had been turned into Belagren's own private palace. Two new wings had been added in addition to an impressive temple on the grounds, the whole thing paid for by a grateful and devoted population who believed that the High Priestess of the Shadowdancers was their conduit to the Goddess.

When they reached the Hall she hurried inside. Madalan issued orders, arranging her bath and organising for a message to go to the palace to inform the Lion of Senet that the High Priestess had returned. Belagren hurried through her ablutions, certain Antonov would be here as soon as he heard of her arrival.

She was somewhat vexed when he did not appear until later that afternoon.

The High Priestess received him in her private rooms. The Lion of Senet strode into the outer chamber impatiently, pulling off his riding gloves. Antonov Latanya was an attractive, well-muscled man, a fact that had done much to enhance the legends that surrounded him. Belagren frowned as he helped himself to the decanter on the sideboard, pouring a large drink for himself. He did not offer to pour one for the High Priestess.

'His highness appears thirsty,' she remarked, a little annoyed at him.

'His highness is thirsty,' Antonov agreed, turning to face her. 'Where have you been?'

'In Omaxin, as well you know.'

'You should have been here,' Antonov scolded. 'There was an eruption in the Bandera Straits.'

So that's where it had happened. She was close – her guess had been the Tresna Sea.

'I know,' she informed him. 'It was a sign from the Goddess.'

'It certainly was,' he agreed, suddenly smiling, 'and I know exactly what she was trying to tell me.'

Belagren crossed the room and poured herself a glass of wine. It was her job to interpret the will of the Goddess. Antonov was starting to get a little above himself.

'You presume much, my lord, to imagine that you could know—'

'We've captured Johan Thorn.'

Belagren quickly took a sip from her wine to hide her shock. She had been so close to announcing that the eruption indicated their work in Omaxin was blessed by the Goddess and should proceed at a faster rate, which she intended to make Antonov finance. *Why didn't I know about this? Why wasn't I told the moment I arrived in Avacas?* And then another thought occurred to her. If Neris Veran lived, the one person on Ranadon who would know for certain was Johan Thorn.

'As I remind you frequently, Antonov,' she said, fighting to keep her relief hidden, 'the Goddess eventually answers all our prayers.'

'She certainly answered this one. More than that, she took an active part in his capture.'

Belagren smiled serenely as he spoke, aware that if she said anything, it would simply reveal her ignorance. Better to let him talk. He would tell her everything she needed to know.

'A tidal wave!' he continued. 'She sent a tidal wave, of all things. Johan was shipwrecked on Elcast.'

Belagren raised an elegantly arched brow. 'Elcast? Perhaps the Goddess has a sense of humour.'

Antonov smiled at her. He had the most intense, golden eyes and they were shining with faith. 'I believe she does. And I should never have questioned you, Bela. You've been telling me for years that the Goddess would hand Thorn to me when the time was right. Do you forgive me for doubting you?'

Belagren was almost as startled by that admission as she was by the news that Johan Thorn had been captured. Her growing sense of urgency, the whole reason for her trip to Omaxin, was the feeling that Antonov was slipping away from her. This fortuitous eruption had provided her with some breathing space. For the time being, at least, Antonov's faith in her infallibility was restored.

'Your questions were prompted by frustration,' she replied with a shrug. 'But you must never doubt the Goddess.' She stepped closer to him, touching his cheek with her hand. 'I know how hard it's been for you, Antonov. But the Goddess will never let you down.'

Antonov smiled and turned his face to kiss her palm. Belagren felt an unexpected shiver run down her spine. It had been so long since he had come to her bed. The young men she consoled herself with were handsome and well trained, certainly, but none of them could hold a candle to the aura of power that surrounded this man. It was intoxicating . . . and she had missed him so much.

Perhaps now, the time was right. Flushed with his renewed faith, he would come back to her bed and she could dispose of that witless but stunning young girl that she had arranged to keep Antonov occupied during her absence.

'I have to get back to the palace,' he told her, as if he didn't even notice the invitation in her eyes. 'I've a lot to take care of before we leave for Elcast.'

'You're going to Elcast?' The news distracted her from her disappointment.

'You don't think I'd trust Thorn to anyone else, do you?'

'Of course not . . .'

'We'll be leaving the day after tomorrow. I plan to stay on Elcast until after the Landfall Feast.'

You can't leave me! she screamed silently. *Not now! Not when I've only just got you back!*

'You'll stay for the Elcast Landfall Festival?' she inquired calmly, her demeanour at complete odds with her inner turmoil. 'I'm surprised to hear they even have one.'

'Of course they have a Landfall Feast. It's the law.'

'I wonder who they plan to sacrifice.'

'According to Tovin Rill, last year's sacrifice was a pig. For that sacrilege alone, I should destroy them.'

'That's Morna,' Belagren suggested. 'Given half a chance, she'd be burning effigies of you and me.'

Antonov nodded, his expression grim. 'I might sacrifice Thorn on Elcast. I think I'd like to witness Morna Provin watching as her lover burns.'

Belagren almost cried out in panic. She fought to keep her voice even. 'You can't kill Thorn yet, my dear. Not while his heresy lives on.'

'What heresy? Once he's dead that will put paid to his sedition. A few years from now, nobody will even remember his name.'

'They will if Neris Veran lives,' she warned.

Antonov stared at her. '*If he lives.*'

'He lives,' Belagren assured him. 'If Neris hadn't survived that cliff in Tolace, Johan would never have bothered stealing his child from the Hall of Shadows. I *know* he lives, Anton. I can feel it. The *Goddess* knows he lives.' Then it came to her, as she spoke. There *was* a way to redeem this potentially disastrous turn of events. 'Perhaps that's why she has given you this opportunity to capture Thorn alive, so that you may finally hunt down Neris Veran and destroy the heresy he spreads.'

She waited for a moment, wondering if Antonov's renewed faith was strong enough to override his desire to put an end to Johan Thorn.

'What do you suggest I do?' he asked after a moment's thoughtful silence.

'Don't kill Thorn until you have absolute proof that Neris Veran is dead.'

Antonov nodded slowly. 'If that is what the Goddess wishes.'

Almost faint with relief, Belagren nodded. 'It is.'

The Lion of Senet smiled and leaned forward to kiss her. She closed her eyes in anticipation, but his lips merely brushed her cheek. 'I'll see you before I leave?'

'Of course.'

He put down the empty wineglass, then turned and walked away from her, leaving Belagren feeling oddly let down. He stopped when he reached the door, turning to look at her.

'On the other hand, perhaps you'd like to join me in Elcast?'

Belagren stared at him. *You bastard! You knew all along what I wanted! You delight in tormenting me.*

'I'll have my things sent down to the *Calliope*,' she replied evenly.

'Well, don't be late. We sail at second sunrise on Titheday.'

9

Johan Thorn woke to unbelievable pain. He opened his eyes slowly, taking in the solid four-poster bed, the granite walls, the warm yellow light filling the room and the fact that every limb he owned seemed to be bound and splinted, and tried to figure out where he was. His last clear recollection was of sailing the Bandera Straits on a mission to rescue two of his people who had been apprehended in the mainland port of Paislee.

The pirates had made good time from their hidden settlement, deep in the delta of the Baenlands, and had been anchored off the coast of Senet for three days, fine-tuning their rescue plans, when the world had begun to shake. Johan vaguely remembered a sky blotted dark and ominous with clouds of volcanic ash.

Not long afterwards, the sea had begun to heave violently beneath them, the swell rising to impossible heights. Johan's last coherent memory was screaming at his crew to pull up the anchor and try to turn the ship into the waves.

Johan realised that it must have been a tidal wave caused by the eruption and the quakes that followed. *And somehow I survived it. But where is the rest of the crew? And where am I?*

Johan had trouble focusing his thoughts. He recognised the slightly bitter aftertaste of poppy-dust on his tongue and wondered who had tended his wounds. He also realised, with a touch of alarm, that if he hurt this much while doped up on poppy-dust, the pain was going to be well nigh unbearable when the drug wore off.

So where am I? he asked himself, trying to ignore the agony to better concentrate on the problem. *There is nothing due south of the Senet coast until . . .*

Johan closed his eyes. *Not Elcast. Please . . . let me be anywhere but Elcast.*

Hearing the door open, Johan turned his head towards the sound. His worst fears were realised as soon as the figure silhouetted in the doorway stepped into the room. He caught a glimpse of armed guards standing by the door outside, before the old man closed it behind him.

'Helgin . . . Master Helgin . . .' he sighed, closing his eyes. The irony of his situation suddenly struck him. *I have survived a tidal wave, only to be washed up on the shore of the one place on Ranadon I could be sure of a dangerous reception.* He suddenly realised how parched he was. 'I . . . I'd like some water.'

The physician walked to the bed and looked down on him. 'It's good to see you again, your highness.'

'Much as I've . . . missed your company, Helgin, you'll . . . understand . . . when I say the last person . . . on Ranadon . . . that I expected to see . . . when I woke was . . . you.'

Helgin smiled and held his head for him as he drank the water. 'It's good to see that you've not lost your sense of humour, your highness.'

The physician let Johan's head drop back onto the pillow, which sent a wave of white-hot pain through his left shoulder. Johan let out an involuntary cry, then turned his head to study the old man when the pain abated a little. 'I appear . . . to have lost . . . everything else. And don't call me . . . highness. I gave up . . . the right to that title . . . a long time ago.'

'There are still those who consider you the true king, sire.'

'Then they'd be wise . . . to keep their opinions to themselves.' He didn't want to listen to such patriotic nonsense. It was hard enough to speak coherently, without getting involved in a political discussion with an old diehard like Helgin. 'The . . . guards outside?'

'Tovin Rill's men. Antonov appointed him governor to Elcast a few months back.'

Johan smiled faintly. The drug was making him foolish. He should be in a blind panic on hearing that news. Instead he just smiled serenely. 'There's no chance . . . he hasn't . . .'

'Informed the Lion of Senet of your capture?' Helgin finished for him. 'No chance at all, I'm afraid. Tovin sent a pigeon to Avacas as soon as he discovered your identity. We've already received word that Antonov is on his way here for the Landfall Feast. He's bringing the whole family, I hear.'

'Well, I knew . . . had to end . . . sometime,' he sighed, closing his eyes. The pain was like a pulse, beating in time with his heart. 'Ironic, don't you think . . . that it will end . . . where it all began.'

Helgin glanced over his shoulder at the closed door and lowered his voice. 'You mustn't give up hope, your highness. You still have friends here on Elcast. Even as far away as Kalarada. If we got a message to the queen, perhaps, or maybe if we can get word to your people . . .'

'My *people*?' Johan laughed bitterly, which was a very stupid thing to do, he discovered, as his whole body convulsed with pain. 'My people are a ragtag band . . . of exiles . . . and pirates. They'd have no chance against the might of Senet. I learned that the hard way . . . the last time I tried to take on Antonov . . . and I had an army at my back in those days . . .'

'Then the queen . . .'

'No!' The exclamation sent another jolt of pain ripping

through his body. 'You are not . . . to involve Rainan in this. My sister has enough trouble . . . of her own to deal with.'

'But, sire . . .'

'Forget it, Helgin. We all know . . . I've been living on borrowed time.' He closed his eyes again and tried to concentrate. There was so much to think about, so much to consider. So many people . . .

His eyes snapped open. 'Is Morna here?'

'Yes.'

'Is she in danger?'

'Not at the moment. Tovin tried to have her arrested, until young Dir—' The old man hesitated for a moment. 'Until someone pointed out that it was he who ordered you rescued.'

'And Wallin? What . . . was his reaction?'

'Who can tell with Wallin?' the physician shrugged. 'It's no secret he has little love for you, your highness, but he won't let Morna come to any harm.'

'It would be better, I think . . . if I had died in that wave.'

'Nonsense!' the physician scoffed. 'You are alive and damn lucky to be so.'

'*Lucky?* I'm a dead man walking, Helgin.' He glanced down at his splinted legs and smiled. 'Or should that be dead man lying down . . .'

'I'll hear no more of that sort of talk,' the physician declared, suddenly all business. 'I refuse to believe you were spared just so the Lion of Senet can hang you. You must rest and get well again. I'll come back in an hour or so and give you more poppy-dust. I'd like to ease your pain now, but too much of the dust and you'll develop a taste for it that will be hard to deny.'

Helgin began to bustle about the room, refusing to meet his eye. Johan didn't have the strength to argue with him. Helgin was an optimistic fool. He'd been spared so that the Lion of Senet *could* hang him. The Goddess was Senetian, after all, wasn't she? It was just the sort of thing a Senetian would do.

'Helgin?'

'Yes, sire?'

'I'm going to die.'

'Now you listen to me . . .'

'If you have any . . . feelings left for me, you'd help me die.'

'Johan . . .'

'No, Helgin. I'll have none of your . . . bedside optimism. I am dead already. If my injuries don't kill me . . . Antonov will. Help me . . . cheat him. Give me something.'

'I'm sworn to do no harm, your highness.'

'Then help me . . . end my own life. If I live, and Antonov breaks me . . . the harm will be . . . immeasurable.'

'I can't, Johan.'

He sighed, not really expecting any other answer. 'Then . . . answer one question for me.'

'Anything, your highness.'

'When Morna . . . when she left me . . . when she returned to Elcast . . . she was with child. What . . . happened to it?'

Master Helgin took a long time to answer. 'She suffered a miscarriage, your highness.'

Johan wasn't sure what he was expecting to hear, but in a way, the news was a relief. It was bad enough that he was here on Elcast. Bad enough that old wounds were about to be reopened; old enemies about to be faced. He wasn't sure he could deal with the added burden of a child he could never claim.

'It's probably . . . for the best. I wonder if it was a boy or . . . a girl? I would have liked . . . another daughter.'

'You should rest, your highness.'

'Stop calling me that, Helgin. It annoys me . . . and Tovin would probably hang you for saying it.'

'I'm not afraid of Tovin Rill,' the old man announced defiantly. 'Or the Lion of Senet.'

'Then more fool . . . you,' Johan muttered drowsily. 'They scare the hell out of me.'

10

It was several days before Tia was satisfied that Neris was in no further danger, from himself or anything else. In that time she had kept a close watch over him, sometimes alone, sometimes with Reithan or Mellie for company. Even Lexie had dropped by for a time, to see how her father fared. She appreciated their concern, but hated the look of pity in their eyes.

Neris lived in a cave across the bay, high above the settlement, and nobody had ever been able to convince him that he should move down into the town with everyone else. 'I can see the Deathbringer closer here,' he would claim, and then put his fingers in his ears and sing loudly to himself to drown out the voices of reason that surrounded him.

His cave was surprisingly well furnished. They had gone to a great deal of trouble to see that Neris was comfortable. There was a proper bed with a down mattress covered by a hand-knitted quilt. A table was pushed against the roughly curved wall opposite the bed, and a hearth had been built under a fissure in the ceiling to take advantage of the natural chimney. *At least this isn't the rude habitation of an insane wretch,* Tia consoled herself. *He is well looked after.*

Neris was snoring contentedly, sleeping off his last dose of poppy-dust. Tia approached the hearth and poked around, looking for even a glimmer of heat from the coals, but they were long dead. She gathered up some of the kindling that was stacked neatly next to the hearth and began to build a fire, using the flint that she found on a shelf near the table to light it. Before long she had a small blaze going, so she sat on the floor of the cave and began feeding slightly larger sticks into the fire.

Once she was satisfied with the flames, Tia moved the

small black kettle over the heat and turned to examine the cave more closely. She knew this place so well, yet it frightened her a little. This was Neris's private sanctuary. In this cave the tortured workings of his drug-addled mind seemed to come alive. As she looked around, something else caught her eye and she moved closer to the wall to examine it.

Neris had sketched a diagram in charcoal on the wall of the cave since yesterday. It looked like an eye, drawn by the hand of a drunkard. On closer inspection, she realised it was a series of concentric circles. The inner circle was quite large, while the one surrounding it was elongated and distorted. Superimposed on that one was a much smaller disk. Encompassing the whole diagram was another elongated circle that Neris had written over. Tia curiously traced the word with her finger.

Scrawled across that circle was the word *death*.

Mellie came to visit for the afternoon, full of bright chatter. She kept both Tia and Neris entertained for hours with her hopelessly romantic plans for the future. Neris adored Mellie. Tia often wondered if in Mellie, her father had the daughter he wanted, rather than the one nature had burdened him with. In the end, it didn't really matter. Neris's mind was gone. Belagren and Ella Geon had destroyed the father she might have had before she was even born.

Neris was sleeping again when she left him, snoring softly on the bed as Tia pulled the knitted quilt over him. They had cooked him a meal of stewed vegetables and goat meat, and stood over the madman while he ate. Mellie was of the opinion that a bath wouldn't hurt, but Tia was more concerned about her father's eating habits than his personal hygiene.

'We can go now,' she said, in a voice barely above a whisper.

Mellie's young brow was creased with worry. Johan's daughter was always worrying about Neris. He was like her favourite uncle, in much the same way that Mellie's father, Johan, was Tia's favourite uncle.

Except Johan isn't a wasted shell of a man with nothing to live for but his next dose of poppy-dust, she reminded herself.

Tia envied Mellie her father. It didn't seem fair that one man could be so strong and another so weak. She envied Mellie's long dark curls and her dark Thorn eyes, and her happy nature, too. Tia could never recall being so optimistic, even when she was Mellie's age. *Perhaps the cynicism doesn't come on you until you're older. But was I ever so damn cheerful? Even when I was twelve?*

'Will he be all right when he wakes up?'

'He'll be fine, Mel. He'll probably sleep for a day or more.'

Tia checked the cave once more to satisfy herself that everything was as it should be, then led Mellie outside. She was surprised to find the second sun quite low on the horizon and the eastern sky beginning to redden with the coming evening sunrise. As she looked down towards the delta she saw something that made her forget all about Neris.

There was a new ship rocking gently in the muddy waters of the bay. The shallow-draughted *Makuan* was anchored below, her deck swarming with tiny figures unloading netted cargo with block and tackle and lowering it into the longboats tied up alongside. The ship was painted a dark shade of blue above the waterline, her masthead carved into an elaborate, demonic creature that Tia was certain had never seen the light of day on Ranadon.

'Porl Isingrin's back,' Tia told Mellie, slapping her back so hard she staggered. 'Now you'll be able to stop fretting about your father.'

Mellie smiled uncertainly. Tia thought she might be a little scared of Porl. He was a brusque, unforgiving man who had no tolerance for young girls with stupid questions. Tia pushed Mellie ahead of her down the treacherous path to the beach, wondering for the thousandth time why Johan had not yet returned to Mil.

After they rowed back across the bay, Tia and Mellie

walked along the sand beside the muddy water that lapped
the damp black sand, calling out to familiar faces as they
passed under the bowsprit of the ship. A number of sailors
called down to them, a few making lewd suggestions to Tia
that made Mellie blush.

Although she acted as if she was offended, Tia had been
raised here in the Baenlands and was intensely proud of the
fact that she was treated just like one of the boys, despite her
sex and her dubious ancestry. Tia didn't know if boys thought
her pretty and didn't care, although Gaven Greybrook had
told her earlier this year that she was the most beautiful girl
on Ranadon. But he'd been drunk at the time, so his opinion
didn't count for much. One of the sailors yelled something
complimentary about her legs that she didn't quite catch as
they passed the longboat. She scowled and made a crude
gesture with her finger at the sailor without looking up, and
continued on up the beach.

Grinning broadly at her friend's obvious irritation,
Mellie followed Tia to the thatched longhouse that was the
closest thing the pirates had to a community hall. There
was a steady stream of people going in and out as they
climbed the wooden steps of the stilted house. It was
crowded with villagers who, unlike the sailors on the beach,
paid them no mind as they pushed their way inside. The
press of people gave Tia a chance to calm her growing
apprehension.

There should have been two ships in the harbour. Porl
Isingrin – the man sent to discover why Johan was so long
overdue – had returned alone.

Mellie grabbed Tia's wrist impatiently and pulled her
towards the other end of the building. An impromptu market
of sorts was going on inside the longhouse as the pirates
sorted through the haul coming off the ship. There were
barrels of salted pork, bolts of cloth, cases of silverware
packed in straw and piles of other loot that Tia did not get
a chance to examine closely. The pirates' last foray had obviously been a successful one.

The women of the settlement were going through the

haul with practised efficiency. Some of the goods were earmarked for consumption by their small community; others were put aside for disposal in the markets of the smaller islands where the source of the goods was unlikely to be questioned. Some of the more valuable items were set aside for sale to their contacts in the Brotherhood, the organisation that controlled most of the criminal activity in both Dhevyn and Senet. Dealing with the Brotherhood made Tia nervous. Their assistance came at a high price and they were not to be trusted. But as fugitives, the people of Mil had little choice about who they could trade with.

Mellie dragged her forward until they reached a cluster of women involved in an animated discussion regarding the disposal of a trunk containing a number of books, all bound in dark, stiff leather, with their titles inlaid with gilt. One of the women seemed determined to claim the books for the schoolhouse, while another couple was arguing about the price such a haul would bring on Grannon Rock. Mellie shoved her way into the discussion. The women surrounding Porl fell silent and stood back to let her in.

As they made room, a solid, dark-haired man turned his eyes on them and smiled at Tia with genuine warmth. It was a fleeting smile, though, and it faded to reluctance as his eyes flickered over Mellie. The man might have been handsome enough once, Tia supposed, until the Lion of Senet had tried to burn him alive. Now the right side of his face was a mass of scar tissue. His right eye was little more than a slit in the puckered skin of his ruined face, and the skin on his arms was shiny and red, stretched taut across his forearms.

'Where have you two been? The ship's damn near unloaded.'

'I'm well, thanks, Captain,' Tia replied with a smile. 'It's good to see you, too.'

Porl shook his head and another glimmer of a smile flickered over his face, so quickly that Tia thought she might have imagined it.

'Here, make yourselves useful,' he said. 'Help Alasun

take these books down to the schoolhouse. She can sort them out there.'

Alasun was the tall woman with grey hair standing next to Porl. She seemed rather pleased that she had won her point about the books. The other couple, who had been advocating selling the books on Grannon Rock, muttered their disapproval and walked off.

Tia sighed as she saw the pile Alasun had already unpacked from the trunk. *Why couldn't she just leave them packed and take the whole damn trunk down to the schoolhouse?* It was as if Alasun wanted to handle every book first. To assure herself they were real.

'Captain Isingrin?'

'Hold your arms out, lass, and we'll load you up,' Porl said with a rather pained expression, obviously thinking the same thing Tia was.

Mellie did as she was ordered. She held out her arms to Porl and the pirate bent down to pick up a stack of books. 'Captain Isingrin?'

Porl straightened up, ready to pile them onto Mellie's outstretched arms.

'Captain, where's Papa?' Mellie asked. 'Why didn't he come back with you?'

The books clattered to the floor. Porl muttered a curse and bent down to pick them up. With a knot of apprehension growing in her stomach, Tia realised how much he'd been dreading the question.

The captain took a deep breath before speaking, his eyes fixed determinedly on the books he had dropped. 'Ask your mother, lass. Can't you see we're busy?'

'Why can't you tell me?' Mellie asked suspiciously.

'I've not the time,' he scowled. It made his face even more distorted. 'Now for once in your life, do as you're told, child.'

Mellie glared at the pirate for a moment, then ran off, pushing her way back through the longhouse to the front door.

'You'd best go after her. She's going to need a shoulder to cry on after she speaks to Lexie.'

'Is Johan? . . .' Her heart was pounding. She didn't even want to give voice to her fear.

'Dead?' Porl shook his head. 'No, it's worse than that.'

'How could it be *worse* than that?'

He glanced over his shoulder to make certain they would not be overheard, before leaning forward to whisper in her ear.

'We think the Lion of Senet has him.'

II

The whole town and every soul in the Keep turned out to catch a glimpse of the Lion of Senet's arrival on Elcast. Everybody, from the duke and his family down to the lowliest beggar, was there to watch.

His ship docked midmorning, but it took a long while to unload the horses and all the other trappings of Antonov's large retinue. The crowd lining the road waited with growing excitement. If they didn't love the Lion of Senet, there was not a man, woman or child alive who hadn't heard of him, and everybody wanted to see him in the flesh.

Marqel and Lanatyne found themselves an excellent vantage on the broad landing at the top of the steps outside the gatehouse in front of the Keep. They could see all the way down the sloping road towards the town, and right into the Keep's courtyard.

Kalleen had been crowing like a rooster since hearing the news that the Lion of Senet was coming to Elcast. There was also the welcome news that he would stay for the Landfall Festival and was bringing his sons with him. That meant there was a good chance either the prince or one of his brats would see their performance.

There were only two ways to obtain one of the much-sought-after permits to perform in Senet. The first was to purchase the permit from the Mummers' Guild, which was financially out of their reach. The second was to get the personal invitation from the Lion of Senet himself. The Lion of Senet was renowned for his generosity towards performers, and Senet's capital, Avacas, was simply the most lucrative audience in the world. An impressive performance in front of the right audience and they could make a fortune.

Marqel fervently hoped that Kalleen was right. If they got a chance to perform in Senet, the troupe would make enough money for her to retire from her career as a professional virgin. She leaned against the warm stones of the castle's outer wall, and turned her attention back to the steps of the Hall, where the Duke and Duchess of Elcast, their sons and the Senetian Governor waited for the prince to arrive. The larger of Ranadon's suns shone over Elcast, warming the morning as they milled about, chatting among themselves. Marqel glanced up at the sky for a moment. There had never been any darkness that she could remember. Night simply meant that the smaller sun was shining, casting its red light over the world.

True darkness, she often heard Murry say, was in men's souls.

When the Lion of Senet finally appeared, Marqel was not disappointed. Antonov Latanya was a big, handsome man, just as people said he was, riding a magnificent white stallion with a high-stepping gait. The prince rode towards the Keep along the steep main road from the town at the head of his entourage, waving and smiling to the crowd, his white-and-gold cloak with its rampant lions catching the sun, making him almost too bright to look upon.

Behind him, on two perfectly matched chestnut geldings, rode the prince's sons, and beside them on a much smaller white pony, a dark-haired girl with large brown eyes and a rather bemused look on her elfin face. The rest of the large retinue were functionaries, she supposed, although she could not imagine needing so many lackeys.

Marqel paid the little girl hardly any attention. The young princes, however, she studied closely. The older of the two was a young man of about twenty-four. He favoured his mother's side, she heard someone in the crowd remark. He was tall, but his hair was so dark it was almost black, making his skin appear translucent and wan by comparison. The 'Crippled Prince', she'd heard them call the heir to Senet, although from where she stood, she could see no sign of deformity.

In contrast, his brother was a younger version of Prince Antonov. A tawny-headed, strapping youth with a ready smile and golden, laughing eyes, he seemed to be enjoying himself immensely. Marqel watched him ride by wistfully.

'Is that Prince Kirshov?' she asked her companion, pointing to the young Prince. The movement must have caught his eye. The golden-haired prince turned and looked straight at Marqel. He winked at her with a grin before turning his attention back to the rest of the parade.

'Aye,' Lanatyne agreed. 'I hear the Lion of Senet pledged his service to the queen as a sign of his goodwill towards Dhevyn.'

'So who's the little girl?' Marqel asked.

They had ridden close enough for her to see the glint of a golden coronet hiding in the dark curls of the girl on the white pony.

'Princess Alenor, I think.'

'Isn't she the heir to Dhevyn?'

'Queen Rainan sent her to be fostered in Senet.'

'Fostered!' a man in front of them scoffed, glancing over his shoulder. 'That's one way of putting it.'

Marqel turned her attention to the future Queen of Dhevyn and found herself unimpressed. She cast her gaze over the rest of the entourage and spied a small blonde wearing an elaborately embroidered red robe astride a docile looking grey mare. She wasn't particularly beautiful, but there was something about her that caught Marqel's eye. Beside her was another tall redheaded woman similarly robed in red. Their sleeveless red tunics marked them as

Shadowdancers. Behind them rode a younger Shadowdancer branded with the rope tattoo on her left arm, as Marqel was. Feeling an inexplicable bond with the women, she found herself staring at them. 'Who are they?'

'That's the High Priestess Belagren riding the grey,' the man in front explained, obviously rather proud of his knowledge of who was who in the Senetian court. 'I think the one next to her is Ella Geon. Don't know about the other one.'

'I never thought I'd lay eyes on the High Priestess of the Shadowdancers,' Marqel said, with a hint of awe.

'The Lion of Senet never travels anywhere without his spiritual adviser,' the man remarked.

'Spiritual adviser?' Lanatyne chuckled knowingly. 'I would have thought a better title would be—'

'Lana!' Marqel hissed warningly. She had heard Lanatyne's opinion of the Shadowdancers before. It was widely rumoured that Belagren was Antonov Latanya's mistress. Marqel wasn't sure she believed the things Lana said about them, but even if she did, here was not the place to repeat them.

Prince Antonov and his entourage reached the entrance to the Keep as the nobles walked out to greet them. The Duke of Elcast was a solid, stocky man with grey hair and a barrel chest. The duchess was much younger than her husband, a tall, slender woman with dark hair and a distant air about her. She trailed a pace or two behind the duke and the governor. Tovin Rill, the Senetian Governor, was a big man, tall and well built, dressed in an elaborately embroidered blue silk coat that made everyone around him seem dull by comparison. Behind the adults were the sons of the duke and the governor. The older Provin boy was a stocky lad who looked just like his father. The younger one was taller, more like his mother.

The rest of the welcoming party waited as the Lion of Senet greeted the Duke of Elcast like an old friend. Wallin seemed pleased to see the prince. The duchess was much more reserved, almost to the point of being rude, but Antonov did not seem to notice. In fact, the prince's manner left

Marqel a little puzzled. From what she had heard, there was little love lost between Elcast and Senet, yet the Duke of Elcast obviously counted the Lion of Senet as a friend. Two of the Senetian guards lifted the older prince from his saddle and remained beside him as the greetings took place. The Crippled Prince appeared to be unable to stand unaided.

'And look at these boys!' the prince declared as the duke's sons stepped forward. 'What are you feeding them, Wallin? That can't be Rees! And this must be your youngest, Dirk! Look at them! They're growing like weeds.'

'Good Elcast air and food, that's what makes them grow, your highness.' Duke Wallin laughed.

'Well, we shall have to stay a goodly time with you and see if this Elcast air can work the same magick on my three charges,' he declared with a cheerfulness that, even to Marqel, sounded a little forced.

Marqel glanced back towards the princes, curious if Prince Antonov was referring to the Crippled Prince. Misha's face was pale and pain stricken. She doubted he was talking about Alenor, although she did look quite frail. It certainly wasn't Kirshov. She'd never seen anyone healthier.

'Now, if you could just arrange not to send us any more tidal waves for a while,' said the duchess, 'we should be fine.'

The Lion of Senet turned to the Duchess of Elcast. 'I'm sorry about the wave, Morna, but I'm not in a position to predict the moods of the Goddess.'

'Really? I thought your High Priestess spoke to her directly.'

Belagren dismounted and walked up the steps to stand beside Antonov. She was quite small, barely reaching Antonov's shoulder, but she radiated supreme self-confidence.

'Perhaps the Goddess had a reason for destroying your crops, my lady,' the High Priestess suggested.

'I imagine she did,' the duchess agreed. 'Spite, perhaps, or vindictiveness—'

'I'm sure we can count on Senet to aid her allies, my

dear,' Duke Wallin cut in, before the duchess could say anything more.

'Of course we will aid Elcast!' Antonov declared loudly. He sounded cheerful enough, but he was glaring at the Duchess of Elcast with extreme displeasure.

A cheer greeted the Lion of Senet's announcement. Since the tidal wave, there had been grave concerns on the island about how they would survive the coming months.

Not the least interested in whether or not Elcast would starve, Marqel turned her attention back to Prince Antonov. All she cared about was that she had finally seen the legendary Lion of Senet.

And with luck, by the end of the Landfall Festival, they would have their permit to perform in Avacas and she could put the clammy hands of panting, hairy old men like Hauritz the Butcher behind her.

Once the Lion of Senet's entourage disappeared inside the Keep, the excitement was over and the spectators quickly dispersed.

Lanatyne looked around at the thinning crowd. 'Come on.'

'Where are we going?' Marqel asked, falling in beside the older girl as she headed down the cobbled road away from the Keep.

'The docks.'

'Why?'

'Are you kidding? There's a new ship in port, full of lonely sailors with unspent wages. Why d'you *think* we're going down to the docks?'

'I can't work the docks. I'm supposed to be a virgin, remember?'

'Not if the butcher's been bragging,' Lanatyne chuckled.

'He won't brag,' Marqel told her confidently.

Hauritz wouldn't say a thing, she was certain of that. His reputation wouldn't allow it, not to mention the fact that his meticulous wife would probably take to him with one of his butcher's knives if she ever learned what her husband got up to while she was off visiting her sister in Yerl on the other side of the island.

They made their way down the steep curved road towards the town. The bay stretched out before them, almost perfectly circular, with only a narrow passage leading out to the open sea. On the right of the channel stood the looming bulk of Elcast Keep. On the left were tall, weathered cliffs that looked as if they'd been created at the beginning of time, sheared away in the massive quake that the Goddess had worked when she shaped the world.

Everyone referred to the wharf as 'the docks', but it was a grandiose name for a long, single wooden jetty protruding into the muddy waters of Elcast Bay. Most of the ships wanting to unload their cargoes anchored in the deeper waters of the bay, their wares brought ashore by longboat. The Lion of Senet's ship was a three-masted barquentine tied up at the end of the wharf. The keel was painted red, and above the waterline the wood was stained black, with a gold trim that circled the hull at the bottom of the gunwale. She was quite the most beautiful ship Marqel had ever seen.

A lot of the townsfolk had the same idea as Lanatyne, although perhaps not with the same purpose in mind, and had come down to the docks to stare at the *Calliope*. The crew was still unloading the passengers' baggage, but they took time out to joke with the children gathered to watch, and curse the slow-witted stevedores who were assisting them.

'It might not have been such a bad idea to come to Elcast, after all,' Lanatyne remarked, casting her professional eye over the numerous sailors. A ship as large as the *Calliope* carried a crew of nearly fifty men.

'You're going to be busy,' Marqel agreed, with a slight frown. Elcast was a relatively small island, and there weren't too many whores to be had in a town this size. Certainly there were not enough to satisfy a crew carried by a vessel the size of the Senetian ship. Kalleen would be rubbing her hands with glee when she worked that out.

About a heartbeat *after* she worked it out, Marqel knew, Kalleen would realise that she could double her profits by putting Marqel to work alongside Lanatyne.

'Look, there's a Sundancer!'

Lanatyne glanced in the direction of Marqel's pointing finger, took note of the yellow-robed man limping along the wharf, then turned to the younger girl. 'Shadowdancers. Sundancers. What *is* your fascination with them, Marqel?'

'What do you mean?' she asked, a little defensively.

'Goddess, every time we get within a mile of one, you get this glazed look in your eye, as if you're having some sort of religious experience.'

'I do not!'

'You do so. What is it? Do you think just because you're a Landfall bastard, they'll take you in? Do you think some Shadowdancer is going to appear one day and spirit you away to a better life?' Lanatyne laughed scornfully.

'They might,' she retorted. 'I've seen plenty of Shadowdancers with the rope tattoo.'

'And did you notice every one of them was Senetian?'

When Marqel didn't answer, Lanatyne smiled. 'Marqel, stop dreaming. You come from Dhevyn, girl. Even if you were the most pious soul that ever walked Ranadon, you'll never be a Shadowdancer. They don't take your kind.'

'Well, I'm not going to finish up like you. I don't want to be a whore.'

Lanatyne chuckled softly. 'From what I hear, Marqel, there isn't a whole lot of difference.'

12

Kirshov Latanya looked around Elcast Keep with interest as he entered the cool dimness through the massive bronze-sheathed doors. It was much larger than he'd expected, and looked as if it had been built to withstand the fury of the Goddess herself.

The main hall was circular, and was girded by a massive staircase that wound upward to the domed roof, some eight storeys above the ground. He had always imagined Elcast as being something of a backwater, and while the town was pretty much what he had envisaged, the Keep was something else again. Between his father, the High Priestess, the governor, the duke and all their assorted families, servants and aides, it was quite an assembly milling about inside the Hall after their welcome in the courtyard, but the crowd did little to dwarf the impressive solidity of the ancient granite Keep.

'Misha!'

Kirsh turned as Ella cried out in alarm, just in time to see his older brother collapse into the arms of one of the guards who had carried him in.

Kirsh frowned. Misha should never have ridden from the ship, but he didn't want to shame their father by asking for a carriage. He had ridden up the steep road from the harbour, keeping his seat by sheer force of will.

Ella and the other Shadowdancer, Olena, fussed over Misha, muttering with concern as the guard lowered him to the flagstones. His father pushed his way through to them and stared down at Misha's pallid face.

'What's wrong with him?'

'The sea voyage and the ride from town have exhausted him, that's all,' Ella informed him. 'He just needs his tonic and some rest.' She turned to the duchess. 'My lady?'

The Duchess of Elcast stepped forward. Kirsh studied her with interest. She was nearing forty, he guessed. A striking woman, with grey eyes, dark hair and an air about her of unspeakable sadness. She didn't look nearly as ominous or evil as Kirsh was expecting. In her youth she must have been quite stunning though, he thought. Certainly pretty enough to catch the eye of the King of Dhevyn.

And ruthless enough to plot my father's murder.

According to the gossip he'd heard, Morna Provin had

deserted her husband and baby son Rees to run off with Johan Thorn during the Age of Shadows. She had spent months at his side trying to destroy Senet, and then, when she realised she had no chance of winning, had abandoned Thorn to return to her husband. She had arrived back in Elcast as if nothing had happened and begged Wallin to take her back. That was the part Kirsh didn't understand. If Morna Provin had done all those terrible things, why was she here, free and unpunished? She should have been burned years ago.

'Misha must have his own room, my lady, if you would be so kind as to arrange it.' Ella didn't even look up, assuming her orders would be accepted without question.

The duchess looked down at Misha and frowned. 'Your large entourage has already put a strain on us, my lady. We don't have the room . . .'

'Make room, Morna,' Antonov ordered abruptly.

Kirsh was a little surprised when the duchess turned to his father with no sign of submission. 'Anton, you've arrived with half your damn court, knowing full well the inconvenience it would cause us. Don't complain to me now if the arrangements are not to your liking.'

'Perhaps one of your sons could give up his room?'

'I've a better idea,' she retorted. 'One of your sons can give up his room.' Without waiting for a response, she turned to her Seneschal, Balonan. 'Please see that Prince Kirshov's trunks are sent to Dirk's room.'

Kirsh looked for the younger son of Elcast in the crowd. He was leaning against the wall with his arms crossed next to Lanon Rill. A young dark-haired servant wearing a stupid grin stood beside him. Dirk was watching the disagreement between Antonov and Morna with metal-grey eyes – the same colour as Morna's. The boy was younger than he, Kirsh knew, and he looked anything but pleased that he had just acquired a roommate.

Lady Morna turned to Alenor. 'Your highness, you'll be sharing a room with Varian, our nurse, I'm afraid.'

'That's perfectly all right, my lady,' Alenor hurried to

assure her. The little princess would probably have said the same thing if Morna had told her she'd be bunking down in the stables. Six years living in Avacas had done nothing but strengthen Alenor's determination to be as ingratiating as possible. *That's probably unfair, he told himself. It's how she protects herself – by being as little trouble as possible.*

Kirsh had tried to understand how hard it must be for the Dhevynian Princess. Alenor hadn't been allowed to see her mother since the Lion of Senet had removed her from the Queen of Dhevyn's court on Kalarada when she was eight years old. He also knew that she was quietly terrified of Prince Antonov. That was something Kirsh couldn't understand either. *He* was not frightened of his father and could not comprehend why so many others feared him.

'There'd be another room available if a certain person was in a cell where he belonged,' Tovin Rill remarked pointedly, 'instead of his current luxurious accommodation.'

'He can't be moved,' Morna announced flatly.

'How convenient,' Antonov muttered, then he turned to Duke Wallin. 'Speaking of which, we have much to discuss. I assume your wife is capable of coping with your domestic arrangements while we talk?'

The duke was standing just behind Lady Morna. He placed a restraining hand on her shoulder before he answered. The duchess looked ready to explode.

'I've put the Library at your disposal, your highness. We can go there now, if you wish.'

'I wish,' Antonov agreed.

The Lion of Senet, Tovin Rill, the High Priestess Belagren and the Duke of Elcast left Lady Morna and her harassed-looking Seneschal to sort out the rest of the accommodation arrangements. A wrinkled old woman who looked about one hundred and ten years old – presumably the nurse Varian – took Alenor in hand and led her away. Morna continued to issue orders, stopping only long enough to glance over her shoulder at her youngest son.

'Dirk, could you show Prince Kirshov where he'll be sleeping?'

She didn't wait for an answer before turning back to Balonan. Someone had brought a stretcher for Misha so everybody's attention was centred on his brother.

A little reluctantly, Dirk pushed himself off the wall and crossed the Hall, Lanon and the servant boy trailing in his wake. Kirshov knew Lanon Rill. He was something of a practical joker, he recalled, and so unlike his father and older siblings in both temperament and looks that he'd heard people at court wonder aloud how he could possibly be Tovin Rill's son.

'Prince Kirshov,' Dirk said with a short bow when he stopped before him. It was impossible to tell what the young man thought about all of this. His voice betrayed no emotion at all.

'Kirsh.'

'Pardon?'

'Call me Kirsh. All my friends do.'

'But he's not your friend,' the servant boy pointed out rudely.

'Eryk!' Dirk scolded, then he turned to Kirsh and shrugged apologetically. 'He doesn't mean any offence.'

'None taken,' Kirsh assured him. 'But perhaps we can become friends?'

'Perhaps,' Dirk agreed cautiously.

His reply took Kirsh by surprise. Most people tripped over themselves to claim his friendship.

'If we're going to be sharing a room, we'd best learn to get along, or it's going to be a very long visit for both of us.' He smiled winningly, hoping to evoke some sort of reaction in the other boy.

Dirk was silent for a moment, and then nodded. 'I suppose. You already know Lanon, don't you?'

'Of course. How are you, Lanon? Being in Elcast must agree with you. You've grown about a foot since I saw you last in Avacas.'

'Good Elcast air and food is what makes me grow, your highness,' Lanon mimicked, in a fair imitation of Duke Wallin's gruff voice.

Kirsh laughed, and even Dirk smiled at Lanon's impersonation.

'Still planning a career as a jester, I see. Come, Dirk, show me where I'll be sleeping, and then you can show me Elcast. I want to see this spectacular levee wall I've heard so much about. Father will be busy for days and I intend to make the most of it.'

Dirk nodded noncommittally. Kirshov had never met anybody so hard to impress. 'Eryk, go ask Balonan about his highness's trunks. This way . . . Kirsh.'

The servant scampered off and Lanon fell in beside them as they headed for the staircase.

'Did you hear, Kirsh?' Lanon asked. 'Dirk scaled the levee wall to rescue Johan Thorn.'

'Did you really? I wonder if Thorn will thank you or curse you for it. Father's going to hang him, you know.' He glanced up the seemingly endless staircase that wound its way around the interior of the Keep.

'So Governor Rill reminds us on a daily basis,' Dirk observed.

Kirsh looked at him curiously. 'You don't approve?'

'I have no opinion on the matter at all,' the boy said.

His attitude was hardly surprising, Kirsh supposed. These Dhevynians were all very touchy on the subject of Johan Thorn.

They reached the first-floor landing and kept on climbing. 'I find that hard to believe, given your mother's—'

'My mother's what?' Dirk asked.

Kirsh stared at the younger boy for a moment. It suddenly occurred to him that Dirk might not even know what had gone on between his mother and Johan Thorn during the Age of Shadows. After all, it happened before he was born, and Duke Wallin was not the sort to dredge up the past without good reason. Perhaps they had just put it all behind them and tried to pretend it never happened.

With a rare show of tact, the young prince shrugged. 'Nothing . . . I just heard she used to be friends with Thorn, that's all.'

'So I gather,' Dirk replied.

The second-storey landing came and went, and Dirk showed no sign of stopping or engaging in any further conversation. He really was the most enigmatic person Kirsh had ever met.

'So,' Kirsh said, looking for a safe subject. 'What do you do for entertainment around here?'

'I don't get much time for entertainment,' Dirk told him as they crossed the third landing and kept on climbing. 'I'm apprenticed to Master Helgin, the physician. Perhaps Lanon can entertain you.'

The Senetian prince glanced at Lanon who grinned back. 'You're asking the wrong person about how to have fun, Kirsh. Dirk's idea of a good time is solving obscure equations that nobody but he and Master Helgin understand.'

Kirsh frowned. He was well educated, but only because his father had threatened to disinherit him if he didn't make an effort. As far as Kirshov was concerned, once he knew enough letters to read fluently and enough figuring to make sure he wasn't being cheated in the markets, he had all the formal education he needed. As for the rest of it, well, that was what scribes were for. Kirshov was going to be a soldier and had little interest in anything not military.

They crossed the fourth-floor landing without stopping. 'Are you really like that?'

'Like what?'

'Like Lanon says.'

'No.'

Lanon laughed. 'He is so! Master Helgin says he's a genius.'

'Don't be ridiculous, Lanon. I am not!'

'Ask him something, Kirsh. Give him a problem to solve. Make one up.'

Kirsh shrugged, then grinned at Dirk. 'Very well, what's three hundred and . . . fourteen thousand, four hundred and two, divided by . . . I don't know . . . four hundred and sixty-one.'

'Five hundred and twelve,' Dirk answered promptly.

Kirsh was astonished. 'Is that right?'

'Of course it's not right,' Dirk told him, a little impatiently. 'I made it up. But that's my point. You've no idea whether I'm right or not, so it doesn't prove anything.'

'You *could* be right,' Lanon suggested.

'I'm not. The correct answer is six hundred and eighty-two.'

Kirsh had a feeling he'd just been badly outwitted by the younger boy, but couldn't really say how. His thighs were beginning to feel the strain of the steep, seemingly endless stairs as they reached the fifth-floor landing. He looked upward, wondering how much further they had to go.

'This way,' Dirk said, pointing to the long corridor that led off the central staircase. The hall was torch lit, as neither sun reached into the hall to lighten the gloom.

Kirshov glanced down at the stairs they had climbed. 'You climb this every day?' There was no banister on the staircase, just a dizzying drop to the flagstones far below them on the ground floor.

'Several times a day,' Dirk informed him.

'And you scaled the levee wall, Lanon says? Somehow, I find myself not in the least bit surprised.'

Dirk suddenly smiled. 'Don't worry, Kirsh, you'll get used to them.'

'That I shall,' he agreed with a grin. 'In fact, I'll make you a wager, Dirk Provin. By the time we leave Elcast, I'll bet you I can race you up these stairs and win.'

The Elcastran boy studied him for a moment with those disconcerting metal-grey eyes. 'To the top?'

He glanced up at the stairs, suffering a moment's doubt about his boast, then nodded. 'To the top.'

'What will you wager? I've no money to gamble with.'

'A favour, then. If you win, I must do you one favour, whatever the cost to me. And you must do the same.'

'When am I ever likely to be in a position to do a favour for a prince of Senet?' Dirk asked.

Kirsh shrugged. 'Does it matter?'

'It's a stupid wager.'

'Yes, but you'll take it, won't you?'

The boy shrugged. 'If you insist.'

'Excellent! Lanon, you shall be our witness. The day before we leave Elcast, Dirk and I will race each other to the top floor. The loser will owe the winner one favour, to be granted at the winner's convenience. Is that fair?'

Both boys nodded. Kirsh smiled with satisfaction. Maybe this forced holiday on the backwater island of Elcast with his unsophisticated cousins would not be so boring, after all.

13

Tia Veran paced the longhouse like a caged cat. She listened impatiently as her elders talked . . . and talked . . . and talked, about what to do about Johan Thorn.

She had almost bitten through her tongue to stop herself from telling Novin Arrowsmith he was an idiot. She felt like slapping Lile Droganov. Couldn't they see that all this talking was getting them nowhere? Johan was probably being tortured to death, exposing their every secret, even as they argued.

The people who populated Mil were Dhevynian for the most part, although there were a few refugees from other places around the globe. A few, like Tia and her father, were Senetian, but generally the people who found their way to the Baenlands were those who had been persecuted by Antonov's occupation of the Dhevynian islands during the Age of Shadows. They had come here in that time of darkness and terror to gather their strength before the final, and ultimately futile, attempt to push the Lion of Senet out of Dhevyn. Johan had gathered them here with a promise of a brighter future. When that failed, they had done their best to carve a life for themselves in this inhospitable place. Until now, she had thought they were doing quite well.

She glanced across the hall at Lexie, who sat quietly at the head table listening to the discussion, displaying no visible sign of emotion. Small and reserved, her thick auburn hair tied back in a loose bun, Johan's wife was – by default – their leader in his absence, but she had never had to face a decision like this before. Mellie sat beside her mother, fidgeting with the fringe on her shawl. Tia caught her young friend's eye and smiled at her encouragingly. *Poor Mellie*. She had been distraught since learning that her father's ship had been destroyed in a tidal wave, even worse since she learned that Johan had survived the shipwreck and was now in Antonov's hands.

A pall of grief had hung over the settlement since then. *Thirty-three husbands and sons lost to a tidal wave, and our leader a captive,* Tia thought sadly. *Why are we doomed to suffer?* It seemed too much to think that random chance had once more struck out at her people and delivered another blow. *It's enough to make you believe there really is a Goddess*.

The real problem, though, was that they really didn't know very much at all. Porl Isingrin had delivered the news, but all he knew for certain was that Johan still lived. The old smuggler was taking on a load of illicit spirits in Nova, the main port on Grannon Rock, when he heard the news. The rumours were rife throughout Dhevyn, but were conflicting and confusing. Some claimed Johan was on Elcast; some that he was in the Senetian capital, Avacas. One rumour, which Lexie listened to with pain-filled eyes, was that Johan and his former lover, Morna Provin, had run away together and were now planning to retake the throne of Dhevyn from a secret base somewhere on Bryton. Tia scoffed at that one. Johan wouldn't do that to Lexie. Besides, he'd had plenty of time to consider retaking his throne these past years and had never shown the slightest inclination to do anything about it.

Tia had confronted Johan about that once, demanding

to know why he didn't try to take back what was rightfully his. The deposed king had smiled at her innocence and passion.

'It's not that simple, Tia,' he'd told her.

'Why not?'

'Because to reclaim my throne would cost too many lives. I've seen too much killing in my lifetime. I've come to the conclusion that it simply isn't worth it.'

'But what about the Landfall sacrifices? Doesn't that bother you? How many people die each year in those sick rituals?'

'It bothers me,' Johan had said. 'But not nearly as much as the people who would die if I tried to reclaim my throne.'

No, Johan wasn't plotting anything with Morna Provin. She'd abandoned him for a life of comfort and security as the Duchess of Elcast. She'd run straight from Johan's bed to Wallin Provin's. The coward had run away from the fight and gone back to her husband and promptly bore him another son, just to prove her loyalty. *Traitorous bitch.*

'Perhaps we should consider some sort of rescue effort?' Porl asked. The suggestion pulled Tia's attention back to the discussion.

'How?' she demanded, unable to hold her tongue any longer. 'You don't know where he is. You don't know if he's injured. You don't even know who has him!'

'Tia,' Lexie began soothingly. 'I think that perhaps we should . . .'

'What?' Tia snapped. 'Wait until he betrays us?'

Her question was met with a collective gasp of horror. 'How dare you even suggest such a thing!'

'Oh, please!' she cried. 'The Lion of Senet has him. I'm not suggesting for a minute that he would intentionally betray us, but I'm willing to bet my right arm Antonov Latanya or that creep Barin Welacin will find a way to break him.'

'What do you mean?' Mellie asked fearfully. 'You don't think they'll torture Papa, do you?'

Tia silently cursed her big mouth before turning to Mellie. 'I . . . don't know, Mel. Who knows what they'll do?'

Everyone looked at her. With the possible exception of Mellie, everyone knew she was right. They all knew from personal experience what Antonov was capable of. One look at Porl's scarred face, or old Finidice, who'd had her tongue cut out on the High Priestess's orders, was enough.

Lexie nodded slowly, as if she was finally acknowledging the truth. 'Mellie, can you go and find Pella for me? Ask her if she could bring some food up to the longhouse? It's going to be a long night, I fear, and I don't want growling stomachs distracting us.'

'But I want to help!' Mellie protested, afraid she was going to miss something important.

'Right now, that *is* helping,' Lexie assured her.

With a scowl, Mellie climbed to her feet and walked towards the doors at the other end of the hall. Tia watched her leave, then on impulse followed her to the door, just to make sure she didn't decide to eavesdrop.

'She's gone,' Tia assured them when she returned to the table.

'Then let us speak plainly,' Lexie said, glancing around the room. 'Tia has the right of it. Sooner or later, Antonov will break Johan, and he won't care how long it takes him. Then he will come after us.'

'Are we certain of that?' Calla asked. She was their blacksmith, a big, heavily muscled woman with close-cropped grey hair. 'Why would he bother? It's not as if we pose a military threat.'

'He'll come because we know the truth. He'll come because he won't feel he's destroyed Johan unless we are destroyed along with him,' Lexie told her. 'In fact, knowing Antonov, he'd more than likely keep Johan alive until *after* we were destroyed, just so he can ensure Johan knows how completely he's been defeated.'

'But how are we going to rescue him?' Calla asked. 'We've hardly got the resources to storm the palace at Avacas.'

'We don't need to storm the palace.' When curious silence met her announcement, Lexie lowered her eyes uncomfortably. 'Johan feared this might happen one day. He gave me quite explicit instructions about what to do if he were ever captured.'

'What instructions?' Novin demanded. 'I never heard about any instructions.'

Tia studied Lexie for a moment with a puzzled expression, then bit back a gasp. She remembered now. She had been there when Johan told Lexie what he wanted her to do if he was ever captured, although she was fairly certain Lexie had no idea she'd overheard the conversation. She was also quite sure that Lexie had agreed only because she thought it would never happen. Tia's eyes flew across the room to Reithan, Lexie's son, who was leaning against the wall with his arms crossed. He looked disinterested, but Tia knew he was listening to every word. And that he knew what Johan had ordered. She'd told him about it herself.

Reithan caught her look and shook his head imperceptibly.

'Look, I don't care what instructions he left,' Tia suddenly announced. 'We've been sitting here talking for hours. There's food on the way, so why don't we take a break for a while? Then we can come back here and discuss this with clearer heads.'

She'd judged the mood of the gathering well. Following a mutter of agreement, Lexie stood up, looking rather relieved that she had not had to elaborate. 'I agree. It's an excellent idea. Go now and see to your families. Let's meet back here in an hour.'

People began climbing to their feet, rubbing limbs that had gone to sleep from sitting immobile for so long, murmuring among themselves. Tia stepped back against the wall as they filed out. Reithan didn't move either. They waited until the last of the council had left before they confronted Lexie.

'You can't tell them,' Tia announced, as soon as they were alone.

Lexie looked at her in surprise. 'Tell them what?'

'You can't tell them what Johan's instructions were.

There's too much grief. Too many people have already died.
It would destroy what little hope we have left.'

'But you don't know what they are,' Lexie pointed out.
'How can you . . .'

'I know what he wanted, Lexie.'

Lexie sank down on her chair with a sigh.

'She's right, Mother,' Reithan said. They were the first
words he'd uttered all day.

'You think I *want* to tell them? Goddess! I can barely
even let myself recall what he asked of me.'

Tia walked around the table and took the seat beside
Lexie. 'He's right, though. And you know it.'

'Then I must tell the others.'

'Tell them he said to do nothing,' Reithan suggested.

'And what of his instructions?'

'We'll do it,' Tia announced, glancing at Reithan.

'Oh, Tia! I couldn't possibly ask that of you!'

'We're volunteering,' Tia reminded her. 'You haven't
asked us to do anything.'

'Your father would never agree to me allowing you to
do anything so—'

'My father doesn't even know what day it is, Lexie. He
doesn't need to be told.'

Lexie nodded. She knew Neris as well as anyone. 'But
even if I agreed, how would you get near him? How will
you find him?'

'You let Reithan and me worry about that.'

Reithan nodded in agreement. 'It's the safest way,
Mother. We'd have a much better chance of finding him on
our own. Once we've located him, then we can decide the
best way to deal with the situation.'

Lexie shook her head. 'No, Reithan. I can't sanction this.'

'Fine,' he said with a shrug. 'Let the others decide what
to do, then. I'm sure Mellie will want to be involved in the
discussion when you announce that Johan left instructions
that if he was ever captured, we should find a way to kill
him before he could betray us.'

Lexie stared at him in horror. Reithan was the son of

her marriage to Drogan Seranov, the former Duke of Grannon Rock. Her first husband had been killed in the fighting during the War of Shadows, and his brother now carried the title. Johan was the only father Reithan had ever known, and she was appalled to think he would so calmly discuss carrying out such an order. Reithan shared Tia's frustration with Johan's willingness to sit here in the Baenlands eking out a living, when there was a chance they could reclaim what was rightfully theirs.

But whatever Reithan's feelings about Johan, Lexie knew he was fond of his half-sister, and looked as if she couldn't believe what Reithan had threatened.

'Mellie mustn't know about this!'

'That's our point,' Tia said gently. 'Let Reithan and me go. Tell the others Johan said to do nothing. We'll find him, Lexie, and if it's humanly possible, we'll rescue him. But if it isn't, then we'll do what he asked of us.'

Lexie stared at them doubtfully. 'You're not an assassin, Tia. You couldn't kill Johan. Neither of you could.'

'Maybe not,' Reithan conceded. 'But we might be able to smuggle him the means to end his own life.'

'That might truly prove to be the only option,' Lexie admitted, then smiled wanly and placed her hand over Tia's. 'I think what I truly fear is the idea of you running amok through Dhevyn or Senet. You would have to be so careful. If anybody realised who you were, Johan's fate would be the least of your problems. And don't forget – there's a price on Reithan's head, too.'

'Reithan's had a price on his head since he was fifteen,' Tia pointed out. 'It's never stopped him in the past. And it's not like I've never seen the big bad world out there, Lexie. I've been to Dhevyn before.'

'You've been to Nova,' Lexie corrected. 'Grannon Rock is sympathetic to us and Alexin and Raban are our friends. You've never been to Senet. It was underestimating that danger that caused this trouble in the first place. If Linel and Hari hadn't been captured in Paislee, then Johan would never have gone looking for them and none of us would be in this mess.'

'We won't underestimate anything,' Tia promised.

'But what will I tell your father?'

'Nothing. Just give him some more poppy-dust. He won't even notice I'm gone.'

Lexie nodded sadly, aware that Tia spoke the truth. She looked up at Reithan. 'Are you sure about this?'

He nodded. 'I'm supposed to meet Videon in Kalarada in a few days. I should be able to speak to Alexin while I'm there. He'll have a better idea of what's happening.'

Videon Lukanov was their contact in the Dhevynian Brotherhood, whose activities were mostly criminal; they were convenient allies for the exiles. There was always a market for illegal poppy-dust among the rich courtiers on Kalarada. Tia had no moral qualms about trafficking in drugs. If their only chance at freedom was to destroy the traitorous nobility of Dhevyn through their own weakness, then she didn't mind a bit. Besides, poppy-dust was the only commodity of value they produced here in the Baenlands. Without the revenue it brought in, Mil would have starved long ago.

'I don't like the idea of getting involved with the Brotherhood,' Lexie said with a frown. 'I don't trust them. If they learn Johan has been captured they could turn on us, just as easily as they could aid us.'

'They'll have heard already,' Reithan pointed out. 'I'd rather they thought we had the situation under control.'

Lexie was silent for a time, considering. Finally she sighed and looked up at her son. 'When will you leave?'

'Now,' Reithan said. 'While you're still discussing it. We could be in Kalarada before you even get around to deciding what to have for lunch tomorrow.'

'I'm still not sure that Tia should become involved in this.'

'She might as well.' Reithan shrugged. 'She's only going to drive you mad if she stays here.'

Tia shot Reithan a wounded look.

'Anyway,' he added, 'I might need her. For one thing, she's Senetian, and sometimes a pretty girl can get information that others can't.' Then he grinned. 'And if we run out of money, I can always sell her as a virgin.'

Lexie smiled. Tia glared at him. She didn't think that was very funny at all.

'You must promise to take care of her, Reithan.'

'She can take care of herself.'

Lexie turned to Tia and frowned. 'Promise me you'll be careful, Tia. Promise me you'll not get involved in arguments, particularly about the Shadowdancers.'

'Lexie . . .'

'Promise me, Tia.'

'All right, I promise,' she said impatiently.

Voices reached them faintly from outside; the others were returning, well before the agreed hour was up. Lexie looked at them for a moment, then nodded decisively. 'All right, go. Both of you. And for all our sakes, be careful.'

Tia leaned forward and kissed Lexie's cheek. 'We'll save him if we can, Lexie.'

She smiled. 'I know you will. And if you get the chance . . . give him my love.'

'I will.'

The doors flew open as Mellie pushed through, carrying a large tray of bread. Pella was with her, carrying a heavy cauldron of something steaming, and there were others behind them, enticed as much by the aromas coming from Pella's cauldron as they were by the desire to continue the discussion.

Reithan and Tia waited until everyone was through the door and then slipped silently from the longhouse without being noticed.

14

The transformation the Lion of Senet effected in Elcast Keep was sweeping and immediate. Within hours, everything had changed. Dirk was still coming to terms with having to share his room with Prince Kirshov, when Lanon Rill knocked on the door. Eryk opened it for him and stood back as Lanon entered, carrying a large bundle of clothes that he dumped on Dirk's bed.

'Eryk, go fetch my other things, there's a good lad.'

'Whoa!' Dirk objected. 'What's this, Lanon?'

'I've been kicked out of my room, too,' he announced. 'To make way for the High Priestess Belagren.'

'So what are you doing *here*?'

'Well, given a choice between sharing with my father or you chaps . . . Off you go, Eryk, don't dawdle.'

The boy looked at his master for instructions before moving. Dirk threw his hands up in defeat. 'Go on, Eryk, you might as well fetch the rest of his gear.'

The lad nodded vigorously, and then hurried off, leaving Dirk staring at his new roommate.

'Not exactly the sharpest knife in the block, that boy, is he?' Kirsh remarked.

Dirk turned on the prince. 'Leave Eryk alone.'

Kirsh looked a little taken aback by Dirk's tone. 'Hey! I was merely remarking that your servant doesn't seem to be the smartest lad I've ever encountered.' Kirsh smiled at him, as if Dirk should find it amusing. 'Actually, come to think of it, that would be you.'

Dirk glared at the prince for a moment and then turned to Lanon. 'I don't suppose you thought I might want to be consulted first?'

'Why? Would it have made a difference?'

'Probably not,' Dirk agreed.

'Well, we'll just have to make the best of things,' Kirsh declared. 'I'm sure we'll be very cosy in here.'

Dirk looked around his overcrowded room and swallowed down a lump of despair. If he was planning to get cosy with anyone, a Senetian prince and the Senetian Governor's son were probably the last people on his list.

It was almost dinnertime before Eryk finished collecting Lanon's things. When the boys headed back downstairs, it was to discover Morna and the Shadowdancer, Ella Geon, involved in a rather heated discussion on the third-floor landing about the sick prince. Ella seemed protective of Misha – to the point of obsession. She refused to let Master Helgin examine him, and would not let Lila Baystoke, the town's herb woman, near the young man, claiming that all herb women were charlatans and she would probably end up poisoning the poor boy.

'But Master Helgin is an experienced physician,' Morna was trying to explain.

'In your opinion, perhaps,' the Shadowdancer retorted. 'But I have no need of anybody's aid, my lady. I am more than capable of relieving Misha's pain . . .'

The boys managed to make it past the women without interrupting the argument, but it disturbed Dirk to see his mother overruled in her own household. In fact, as he thought about it, he could never recall anyone arguing with his mother before. Not even his father.

As Dirk, Eryk, Lanon and Kirsh stepped down into the main hall, Balonan, the Seneschal, caught up with them.

'Master Dirk!'

'Balonan.'

'I was hoping to find you, lad. Your father asked me to pass on a message.' He glanced at the prince and bowed politely. 'Your highness.'

'What does he want, Balonan?' Dirk asked.

'He asked me to inform you that you will no longer be required to aid Master Helgin in caring for the captive, and as Prince Antonov has commandeered the Library, your lessons will be abandoned for the duration of the prince's visit.'

'Then what am I supposed to do?'

The old Seneschal smiled. 'I believe, Master Dirk, you have a prince and princess to entertain.'

The next day after breakfast, with nothing better to do, Dirk agreed to show Prince Kirshov the town. Dirk, Kirshov and Lanon were heading across the courtyard towards the gate when Alenor caught up with them. The little princess appeared rather annoyed that the boys had been going to leave the Keep without her.

'Where are you going?' she demanded, hurrying along behind them.

'We're just going to walk down to the village,' Kirsh told her over his shoulder. 'You can't come.'

'Why not?'

The boys stopped and turned back to stare at her. Alenor wore a sleeveless blue tunic and had her hands planted firmly on her hips, a look of determination on her face.

'There's no reason why she *can't* come, is there?'

'Whose side are you on, Dirk?' Kirsh asked.

Alenor treated Dirk to a beaming smile. 'There! Can I come, Dirk?'

'I suppose.' Dirk didn't know her well enough to judge her reaction if he refused. Besides, one day this girl would be his queen.

Kirsh shook his head. 'You'll be sorry, Dirk. If you say yes to Alenor once, you're never free of her.'

They walked unchallenged through the open gates of the Keep and out onto the road that led down into Elcast Town. The second sun warmed the morning, making it almost uncomfortably hot. Dirk wore his usual garb of loose linen trousers, sleeveless shirt and open leather sandals, although Kirsh had stuck with the Senetian fashion of fine wool trousers and high leather boots. Already there were damp patches staining the armpits of his expensive silk shirt as they made their way down the road. Lanon, having lived on Elcast for several months now, had learned the folly of Senetian fashion and wore much the same as Dirk. Alenor walked between Dirk and Kirshov, looking rather smug that she'd managed to get herself invited along. Lanon walked on Kirsh's right, and spent most of the journey questioning him about Avacas and catching up on the numerous mutual acquaintances they seemed to have. Alenor said very little, apparently content to simply be in their company.

Elcast Town was unusually busy. Even so early in the day the tavern on the corner of Candle Street was doing a roaring trade – no doubt the result of the Senetian sailors in town. The square was crowded with market stalls as the locals endeavoured to make as much as possible from this unexpected influx of visitors. Some of the townsfolk waved to Dirk as he passed down the ash-dusted main street, their smiles of welcome fading to caution as they realised who his companions were. One woman even spat at the ground contemptuously as they passed the bakery.

Kirsh glanced at Dirk curiously. 'Do I have horns, or a tail, or something?'

'Not that I noticed. Why?' Dirk sidestepped a thin woman pushing a handcart towards them loaded with vegetables. She glared at the two Senetian boys, then turned her disapproving gaze on Dirk for a moment, before muttering something that sounded suspiciously like a curse as she pushed past.

'Your villagers are staring at me like I'm the devil incarnate.'

'Welcome to Elcast,' Lanon said, his voice loaded with irony.

'What do you mean?'

'Elcast is part of Dhevyn, Kirsh, and you're a Senetian prince. In some Dhevynian minds, the two are one and the same.'

Kirsh stared at him in surprise. 'But why would these people think that about me? I've never done anything to them. I like Dhevyn. I'm going to join your Queen's Guard.'

'You're the Lion of Senet's son,' Dirk reminded him.

'Yes, but we've never done anything to hurt these people. My father came to Dhevyn's aid during the Age of Shadows. You'd think they'd be grateful!'

'You are joking, aren't you?' Dirk asked, shaking his head. Could Kirshov Latanya *not* know how much their occupation cost Dhevyn's people? 'Haven't you ever seen a debtor slave?'

'Who cares about some silly old slaves?' Alenor laughed nervously. 'Can we stop for some sweets?'

Appalled by her heartless attitude, Dirk opened his mouth to berate her for being so callous, but Alenor was staring straight at him. She gave him an imperceptible shake of her head, her eyes full of unspoken warning, as if trying to will him not to say anything further on the subject.

'Hey, there's Father!' Lanon suddenly called.

Dirk looked up to find the governor sitting astride his stallion in front of the tumbled ruins of the temple on the other side of the cobbled square. It had been destroyed during the Age of Shadows, as punishment for Elcast's sins, he'd heard people claim. Tovin Rill was holding the reins of a riderless horse as a small, red-robed figure climbed carefully over the tumbled masonry behind him, inspecting the ruins. Lanon called out a greeting to his father and headed across to speak to him, with the others following in his wake. Alenor fell in beside Dirk, a step behind Kirsh and Lanon.

'Be careful!' she hissed, without looking at him.

'About what?' he asked.

Alenor rolled her eyes, but didn't answer him.

'Taking in the sights of Elcast, your highnesses?' Tovin asked as Kirsh, Dirk and Alenor caught up with Lanon.

'Such as they are,' Kirsh agreed with a smile.

'You shouldn't be so quick to judge, Kirshov,' the High Priestess Belagren said, carefully climbing down the last few ruined steps towards them. 'The Goddess has a place for everyone and everything in the scheme of things. Even islands like Elcast.'

Dirk looked at her, the first chance he'd had to study her closely since her arrival yesterday. He'd expected to see the High Priestess at dinner last night, but the evening meal in the Keep had proved an exercise in organised chaos, with most of the Lion of Senet's entourage choosing to take their meals in their rooms. Poor Balonan had been run off his feet trying to satisfy everyone.

Belagren was older than his mother, small and slender, with long fair hair hanging unbound, as was the custom among the Shadowdancers. Her light robe was the colour of blood, and her fingers were heavy with gold rings. A twisted rope bracelet circled her upper left arm, and she wore a diamond-encrusted necklace. She wasn't particularly beautiful, but she had an air about her – something indefinable – that made Dirk vaguely uncomfortable. This was the woman who spoke directly to the Goddess. Perhaps it was that gift that made her seem so . . . unsettling.

'Hello, my lady,' Kirsh said, with the easy familiarity of one totally oblivious to the High Priestess's power. 'What are you doing down here so early?'

'Governor Rill and I are deciding whether to rebuild the old temple or construct a new one.'

'Building a new temple will be expensive,' Dirk remarked with a slight frown. Elcast could not afford it. Not after the ruined harvest.

'Yes, it will,' Belagren admitted, dusting her hands off as she came to stand before them. 'But one shouldn't think only of money when it comes to one's soul, young Dirk. Besides, Elcast has gone without the Goddess's guidance for much too long. Don't you agree?'

'My lady?'

'Don't you agree that Elcast is sorely in need of spiritual guidance?' She was watching him closely, her blue eyes sharp.

'I . . . I wouldn't really know, my lady.'

'Which is exactly my point,' Belagren remarked to Tovin. Then she turned to Dirk again. 'I understand it was your mother who opposed rebuilding the temple?'

Dirk hesitated before answering. 'Not that I'm aware, my lady.'

'Really? I wonder what else you're not aware of.'

'He doesn't seem to be aware of how damn hot it is,' Kirsh joked. 'Will we see you tonight at dinner, my lady?'

'Of course, Kirshov. I wouldn't miss dinner with the infamous Duchess of Elcast for anything.'

Infamous? Dirk stared at the High Priestess, but before

he could say anything, Alenor quite deliberately stepped on his foot.

'Honestly, Kirsh, I swear you never think of anything else but your stomach. It's too far away to think about dinner now. Come on, Dirk, you promised to show us the rest of the town.'

Tovin Rill laughed. 'Then show her you must, Dirk. What the Princess Alenor wants, the Princess Alenor gets. Isn't that right, my dear?'

Alenor smiled at the governor and, with a hasty bow to Belagren, she took Dirk by the hand, leading him almost forcibly away from the High Priestess. Kirsh and Lanon lingered a moment longer to say goodbye.

Once they were safely out of earshot, Dirk shook his hand free and glared at the princess.

'What are you doing?' he asked in a low, irritated voice.

'Saving your stupid neck,' she told him impatiently.

'How?'

Alenor stared at him. 'Don't you know, Dirk?'

'Know what?'

'About Duchess Morna and the High Priestess?'

'What about them?'

Alenor glanced at the others furtively, then turned to Dirk. 'This is the first time they've been under the same roof since the War of the Shadows,' she whispered.

'So?'

Alenor let out an exasperated sigh. 'So . . . If the High Priestess had her way, your mother would have been burned as a heretic before you were born.'

'The War of the Shadows is over and done with, your highness.'

'For you, maybe. But there are plenty of Senetians who think that while your mother lives it will never be truly over. I'm just warning you, Dirk. There's bad blood between your mother and Belagren, and the last thing she needs is you giving the High Priestess of the Shadowdancers an excuse to insist that her long overdue death sentence is finally carried out.'

15

Several days after they met Belagren and Tovin Rill in the town square, Master Helgin sent Dirk on an errand to collect some herbs and a salve he needed from the infirmary. Although Dirk was suspended from his duties as apprentice physician, Helgin trusted no one else with the key to his pharmacopoeia.

When he returned to his room, he discovered Lanon and Kirsh lounging on the bed, half-heartedly playing with Dirk's prized chess set. The set was a gift from his maternal grandfather, Prince Oscon of Damita. The chess pieces were carved from onyx and crystal, the board inlaid with mother of pearl. It was probably the most expensive thing he owned, and the fact that Lanon and the prince had appropriated it without asking made him furious.

He was also helpless to do anything about it. So he glanced about the room, hoping to find something else to vent his frustration on, when he noticed his servant was missing.

'Where's Eryk?'

'I sent him for some of those sweetmeats we found in the market the other day,' Lanon told him, without looking up from the board. 'We should speak to Balonan and arrange to have them served here in the castle,' he added to Kirsh. 'They're very good.'

'You sent Eryk into town?'

'I said that, didn't I?'

'Alone?'

'Of course alone!' Lanon said, looking up at him with a puzzled expression. 'Granted the boy's a bit slow, Dirk, but he's not a complete waste of space. And I gave him a note. All he really needs to do is remember where he's going. After that, I'm sure the—'

'You idiot!'

Dirk was gone from the room before Lanon had a chance to be offended. He ran down the stairs two at a time, consumed by an uneasy mix of anger and fear.

'Dirk! Wait!'

Dirk stopped when he reached the second-floor landing and turned to wait for Kirsh.

'Is something wrong?'

'It'd take too long to explain, Kirsh.'

'Come on, then.'

'What?'

'If we're going to rescue your hapless servant, we'll get to town faster if we ride.'

Kirsh bounded down the stairs ahead of Dirk and was out on the front steps of the hall, ordering horses saddled and brought out before Dirk caught up with him.

'This is not your concern, Kirsh,' Dirk told him.

'Of course it's my concern. You're my friend.'

Dirk wasn't sure when he'd been promoted to friend, and wasn't in the mood to argue about it. He was far more concerned about Eryk.

The stable boys brought out Dirk's grey mare and Kirsh's chestnut gelding faster than Dirk would have believed possible. Perhaps it was the tone of voice Kirsh used that got the stable boys moving so fast, or simply fear of who he was. Whatever the reason, they were cantering out of the gates and down the steep road into town within minutes.

It was late afternoon when they slowed to a trot as they reached the centre of the town. The market stalls had mostly closed for the day. The only vendors still plying their wares were selling a variety of cooked meats and fruit pies, hoping to catch the last of the day's trade before the tavern on Candle Street robbed them of their potential customers. Dirk looked around in concern. There was no sign of Eryk.

'Where would he be?' Kirsh asked.

'Goddess knows,' Dirk replied. He reined in and stood up in his stirrups, trying to guess which way the boy might have gone when the sound of laughter reached him. He dismounted and glanced in the direction of the noise. It seemed to be coming from the alley behind the tannery. Kirsh jumped from his saddle, tossed the reins over his horse's neck and followed Dirk into the lane.

A gang of boys stood at the end of the alley. There were perhaps ten or eleven of them, ranging in age from fourteen or so, as well as several apprentice fishermen older than Dirk. Their backs were turned as they chanted an old children's rhyme.

Slow boy, slow boy, tell us what you know, boy.
Slow boy, slow boy, tell us what you know, boy . . .

'Do you know . . .' one of the older boys laughed.

'What day it is?' another finished for him.

The question was greeted by howls of laughter from the others. When their unseen victim didn't reply, the chant started up again.

Slow boy, slow boy, tell us what you know, boy.
Slow boy, slow boy, tell us what you know, boy . . .

'Hey! Maybe he doesn't understand us! We should be singing thlow boy, thlow boy . . .'

'That's enough!' Dirk yelled angrily.

The chanting dwindled to nothing as the boys turned to face him. The oldest boy in the group, and no doubt the ringleader, was a heavyset lad of about nineteen, named Derwn. His father was Hauritz the Butcher, and even though he was only an apprentice, he knew he would one day inherit his father's shop and fancied himself a cut above the rest of the young men in the town. His mother spoiled him mercilessly, too.

Derwn stepped forward, hands on his hips, and glared at them.

'Piss off, Dirk,' he warned. 'And take your Senetian friend with you. This is none of your concern.'

'Eryk, come here!'

Although he couldn't see him, there was no doubt in his mind that it was Eryk trapped against the wall at the end of the lane. After a tense moment of silence, the group of boys parted and Eryk finally emerged, pushing his way through his tormentors cautiously. His tear-streaked face was pathetic with relief.

'Go mind the horses, Eryk,' Dirk ordered, before the boy brought further ridicule down on himself by saying anything. Eryk nodded and ran from the alley, leaving Dirk and Kirsh to face the village boys.

'If I catch you tormenting Eryk again—' Dirk began.

'You'll what?' Derwn scoffed. 'You don't scare me, Dirk Provin.'

'You should learn some respect for your betters,' Kirsh said, stepping up to stand beside Dirk. 'How dare you speak to a member of your ruling family in such a manner!'

Dirk bit back a cry of despair. The *last* thing he needed was a Senetian coming to his defence.

Derwn glared at Kirsh, then spat on the ground in front of him. 'I've got plenty of respect for my betters. I just don't happen to see any of them around at the moment.'

A nervous titter of laughter came from a few of the boys behind Derwn, but most of them took an unconscious step backwards. Dirk wasn't sure if they realised who Kirsh was, but the mere fact that he was Senetian was enough for a few of the more sensible ones to be wary. *Not that you could use the word* sensible *when describing a bunch of layabouts with nothing better to do than torment a slow-witted orphan for entertainment.*

'Kirsh—'

The prince ignored him, his eyes locked on Derwn.

'Go on. Do it,' Kirsh dared the young man. 'Take a swing at me.'

'Derwn, no . . .' someone said from behind.

'You think I'm stupid?' Derwn accused. 'I hit you once, and the next thing I know I'm being shipped off to Paislee on a slaver for breaking your pretty Senetian face.'

'That would be assuming you *could* hit me,' Kirsh replied with a calm smile.

'I'd break you in half, you arrogant piece of Senetian shit.'

'So do it. I'll even promise not to report you. You hear

that, Dirk? Assuming your prize Elcastran thug here can actually land one on me, he's not to be harmed for it.'

'Kirsh, you don't have to do this . . .'

'I'll even make a wager with you,' the prince offered Derwn. 'You hit me, you get to walk away, no blame, no consequences. But if you don't—'

'Yeah, like that'll happen.'

'If you don't,' Kirsh continued calmly, 'then you will promise never to harm Eryk again. No, better than that, you will assume the role of his guardian, and it will be your mission to ensure he comes to no harm in the future. Agreed?'

Derwn stared at Kirsh, weighing up the odds, perhaps, then nodded. 'Agreed.'

'So. Do it.' Kirsh stood there, waiting patiently for Derwn to attack. When the other boy hesitated, Kirsh held out his arms wide. 'Are you waiting for something?'

Angry enough at Kirsh's patronising tone to overcome caution, Derwn charged forward. The prince nimbly side-stepped the boy's lumbering attack and turned to face him.

'You missed,' he pointed out unnecessarily.

Derwn charged a second time, truly angry now, and again Kirsh simply stepped out of the way. Dirk glanced at the other boys and realised that not only was Kirsh infuriating Derwn, but he was humiliating him in front of his friends.

The third time Derwn charged, he was ready for Kirsh, but his fist connected with nothing but air as Kirsh ducked under the blow. Then the prince brought his fist up in a short sharp jab into Derwn's face, and the boy howled with pain, clutching at his bloody nose.

'I win,' Kirsh announced, dusting his hands off as if he had done nothing more strenuous than swat a fly. 'You may now consider yourself Eryk's guardian.'

Derwn glared at Kirsh for a moment, then fled the alley. Dirk shook his head as he looked at the prince, wondering how much worse he'd made things.

'Dirk.'

He turned towards the boy behind him who had called his name. It was the cobbler's son, Paron Shoebrook.

'We weren't going to hurt him . . .'

'Go home, Paron,' Dirk ordered wearily.

'Derwn said he was a thief . . . he said they'd been robbed a while back . . . some silver and a gold coin . . .'

'Eryk used to be too scared to steal food to survive, Paron. Why would you believe he'd steal anything from the butcher?'

The boy shrugged, his eyes full of guilt. 'I don't know . . .'

Dirk stared at the village boys for a long moment. Most of them avoided his eyes. 'All of you, just . . . go home.'

Eryk stayed close to Dirk for the rest of the day, pathetically grateful for his rescue. After dinner, he curled up in a ball on his pallet in the corner of Dirk's room and listened silently as the boys sat talking of the incident. Kirsh was smug and Lanon was sorry both that he'd sent Eryk into town and that he'd missed what sounded like a good fight.

But the incident unsettled Dirk. There was enough trouble with the Senetians as it was, without Kirsh getting involved in a fistfight with one of the locals. He was concerned about his father's reaction to the affair, too. Elcast was too small for news of the incident not to reach the duke's ears eventually. Dirk just hoped he wouldn't be blamed for it.

After a while the conversation drifted onto other things. By the time the evening sun flooded Dirk's room with its crimson light their discussions had moved onto Kirsh and the great deeds he was planning to perform when he joined the Queen's Guard.

By the sound of it, Kirsh was planning to single-handedly rid the Tresna Sea of pirates. It was a pity, Dirk thought, that the most notorious pirate in all of Senet and Dhevyn lay seriously injured only two storeys below them. Kirsh was going to have to settle for less famous, more ordinary deeds to satisfy his lust for adventure.

He listened to the prince, thinking that there were many things about Kirshov Latanya that puzzled him, not the least of which was his eagerness to join the Queen's Guard. Dirk couldn't understand why a prince of Senet would be so enthusiastic about taking a commission in the almost purely ceremonial force.

The days when the Queen's Guard had meant something had ended with the Age of Shadows. In those days, Master Helgin told him, it was called the King's Guard.

And their king had been Johan Thorn.

PART TWO

A
TOUCH
OF
VENGEANCE

16

Three days before the Landfall Feast, the High Priestess announced over dinner that everything was set for the Festival. At this point, Morna rose from her place at the High Table and strode off without a word.

An awkward silence followed her departure. Antonov was obviously displeased. Wallin looked distinctly uncomfortable, but the High Priestess seemed amused, rather than offended. She leaned across to whisper something to Antonov, which brought a smile to his face, and the meal carried on as if nothing had happened.

Prince Antonov learned about the fight in town, as Dirk knew he would. He was not angry, however. He emerged from the Library long enough to decree that Kirsh obviously had too much time on his hands if he had time to call out the local bullies, and ordered his son to undertake instruction each morning before breakfast with Lanon and the Elcast master-at-arms. Antonov's reasoning, he joked at the dinner table that evening, was that if he tired him out, Kirsh might not find so much mischief to get into. He seemed more amused than concerned, a situation that Dirk had no doubt would have been radically different had Kirsh lost the fight.

The closer the Festival came, the more Rees grew short-tempered and edgy, and Dirk's mother stormed about the Keep, blistering the ears off anyone who got in her way. Dirk saw little of Antonov and even less of the High Priestess. Apparently, discussions about the need for aid after the ruined harvest and the issue of rebuilding the temple took up most of their time. Johan Thorn wasn't mentioned either, which Dirk thought very odd, considering the deposed king was the reason Antonov had come to Elcast in the first place. Alenor said nothing about her captive uncle either, wise enough to keep her opinion to herself. Kirsh seemed unaffected. He continued to rule his little coterie with the same careless, cheerful arrogance that he had when he arrived.

Alenor hated rooming with their old nurse Varian, and Dirk often found her waiting outside their room early in the morning, impatient for the boys to wake. She was a deceptive little thing. She looked thin enough to break, and was quite reticent around Prince Antonov and the High Priestess. But she had a sharp mind, and seemed unafraid to say what she was thinking when alone with the boys.

It was rumoured that Kirshov would be her consort when she was old enough to marry, which didn't really surprise Dirk. Alenor adored Kirshov, even Dirk could see that. Kirsh treated Alenor no differently from the boys, which perhaps accounted for her less-than-royal manner when she was with them.

Having been raised a member of the ruling family in a predominantly male household on an island, Dirk had little social contact with girls of his own class. All the girls he knew were the daughters of servants or the merchants in town, and none of them were interesting enough to hold his attention for longer than a few minutes. He tended to lump all females in the same category as Rees's betrothed, Faralan, who was pleasant, well trained to run a household and as boring as watching grass grow.

The strangest thing about the visiting Senetians was Kirshov Latanya, and much to his astonishment, Dirk found himself warming to the young prince.

Kirsh was the most open person Dirk had ever met. He said exactly what he was thinking, as soon as he thought of it, with no care for who heard him or the political ramifications of what he said. He seemed to suffer none of the prejudice of his elders. Kirshov Latanya judged everyone according to his own private code, and did not care if they were Senetian or Dhevynian, noble or servant. He was enthusiastic to the point of being obsessed about joining the Queen's Guard, convinced it would be the most exciting life he could imagine. Dirk suspected the truth was somewhat less glittering, but one could not help being infected by Kirsh's boundless enthusiasm.

But Dirk was seriously disturbed about what was planned for the Landfall Festival. After giving the matter a great deal of thought, he finally decided that Alenor, of all the members of Antonov's entourage, would be the one to question about it. She, at least, was Dhevynian. To raise his concerns with anyone else might be judged heresy, and asking Kirshov was useless. He would either laugh at Dirk's anxiety, or worse, inadvertently report it to his father.

So Dirk kept his own counsel and waited for his chance to get Alenor alone.

Following Antonov's decree, for two hours at least, while Lanon and Kirsh practised under the watchful eye of Master Kedron, Dirk was free to talk alone with Alenor. He found the princess sitting on the white-painted railing that circled the training yard. Dirk climbed up beside her as Kirsh and Lanon worked with slow, deliberate movements under the critical gaze of Master Kedron.

'He's very good, isn't he?'

Both boys were stripped down to their breeches and had worked up a sweat in the warm morning. Although he was only a year older than Lanon, at seventeen, Kirsh was taller and better muscled and moved with the kind of natural grace that no amount of training could instil. Master Kedron, whose reputation extended far beyond Elcast, had trained Lanon well since he'd been here on the island, but even to Dirk's inexperienced eye, the better of the two was Kirshov. Lanon's movements were the result of hours of practice. Kirsh moved like a cat, his wooden practice sword whistling through the air, one action flowing seamlessly into the next.

Lanon was not bad. He just looked inadequate next to the prince.

'Kirsh trains with the Palace Guard at home,' Alenor told him. 'Prince Antonov said he might as well learn to fight the hard way.'

'Do you like living in Avacas?' he asked.

She shrugged and turned back to watch the training. 'They don't mistreat me, if that's what you're hinting at.'

'I never—'

'Don't worry, Dirk. Prince Antonov treats me like his own child.'

'He makes his *own* child train with his guard,' Dirk pointed out with a frown.

Alenor smiled, but did not reply. They watched in silence for a while, then she turned and looked at him curiously. 'Don't you wish you were out there with them?'

'Not really. I'm going to be a physician. I don't need to know how to fight.'

'Not even a little bit?'

'Well, I know the basics. Master Kedron and having a big brother saw to that, and Master Helgin makes me study tactics and history, but most of the time I'm in the infirmary.'

Alenor didn't answer him, and for a time they simply sat in companionable silence, watching the boys train. But it took Dirk longer than he imagined it would, to work up the courage to ask what he had really come here to find out.

'Alenor, what's going to happen tomorrow night?' he asked finally.

The princess looked at him. 'You really don't know?'

'I've heard the rumours about what happens in Senet. But—'

'Then you know what's going to happen,' she shrugged, turning her attention back to the boys in the yard. They were trading blows now, carefully choreographed by Master Kedron. The moves were designed to train certain muscles as much as improve their technique. The sharp *tack-tack-tack* of their wooden blades echoed across the small arena as Kirsh slowly beat Lanon back, even though he was supposed to be simply blocking his opponent's stroke. Kirsh had to feel like he was winning, Dirk thought. No matter what he did, Kirsh *always* had to feel like he was winning.

'Prince Antonov can't believe you don't have a Landfall Festival,' Alenor added.

'We have a Festival.'

'But not a proper one,' Alenor corrected. 'The High Priestess says it's like a disease that's spreading through Dhevyn. She says that a few good years with both suns shining and already people forget what it was like during the Age of Shadows. She says that if people keep turning from the Goddess, the Age of Shadows will come again.' Then the little princess glanced around and lowered her voice. 'But even at court, there are people who don't want the Landfall Festival to happen. That's why I was sent to Senet. Prince Antonov told my mother I wasn't getting a proper education.'

Dirk shook his head. 'Personally, I'm not sure what the Goddess hopes to gain by making all the unmarried men and women on Elcast gather on the common and take a drug that turns them into animals just so they can rut like pigs for the rest of the night.'

If his crudeness appalled her, she didn't let it show. 'Belagren claims it means they're blessed by the Goddess.'

'And what of the Landfall bastards that come from it?'

'According to the High Priestess, they're blessed, too, because they were conceived under her protection.'

'Do you honestly believe that?'

She shrugged uncomfortably. 'I do when I'm in Senet.'

He looked at her, puzzled by her statement.

'Around Prince Antonov and the High Priestess, I believe whatever they want me to believe, Dirk. It's how I stay alive.' It was the first time he'd heard Alenor openly admit that she was not a fosterling, but a hostage.

'And when you're not in Senet? What do you believe then?'

She studied him closely for a moment, as if debating how far she could trust him. 'My mother told Prince Antonov that the bastards that come from the Landfall Festival are a blight on Dhevyn. They had a blazing row over it. Not long after, I found out I was being sent to Senet to live.'

That the Queen of Dhevyn would voice opposition to the rites of the Senetian Goddess, surprised Dirk. He'd often heard Morna complain that Rainan was nothing more than a Senetian puppet. Perhaps she wasn't quite the ineffectual ruler his mother thought. On the other hand, if she had been any good as queen, surely she'd have driven the Senetians from Dhevyn by now.

'Why do you look so surprised? Your mother says much the same about it.'

'She calls it a self-indulgent orgy,' Dirk admitted. 'She claims Belagren encourages it because it gives her a ready supply of acolytes.'

'She has a point. About the only place a child with a rope tattoo can acquire real status or power is in the Goddess's service.'

'It's like putting a brand on cattle,' he remarked with a frown.

'Branding them, slaughtering them? What's the difference?'

'They're really going to sacrifice someone, then?' Dirk asked in a low voice.

'Someone is always sacrificed at the ritual, Dirk, ever since the end of the Age of Shadows. It happens in towns and villages all across Senet and Dhevyn, and the Lion of Senet intends to make sure that Elcast falls into line with the rest of the world or there'll be hell to pay. You don't think it was coincidence that brought us here in time for Landfall, do you?'

Dirk stared at her. 'I can't believe that my father will countenance such a thing.'

Alenor looked at him with solemn brown eyes. 'Then you don't know the power of the Lion of Senet very well at all, do you, Dirk?'

She slipped off the rail without waiting for his reply and went to join Kirsh and Lanon, who were pulling on their shirts, having finally been dismissed by Master Kedron.

17

From a purely material standpoint, Belagren somewhat regretted her impulsive decision to join Antonov on his journey to Elcast. No matter how much she might enjoy seeing Morna Provin squirm, or Johan Thorn brought down, the fact that she had been accommodated in the room belonging to the governor's teenage son was only the first in a long list of complaints she had about Elcast Keep. She blamed Morna for it, of course. The Duchess of Elcast was bound to be taking great delight in the High Priestess's discomfort.

There was no hot water piped into the rooms from underground springs as there was in Avacas. Taking a bath was a major expedition, involving an army of servants required to haul the hot water up four flights of insanely steep and dangerous stairs, which meant that it was already cool again by the time it reached her rooms. The chamber was small, poorly ventilated and, although she hadn't seen any, she was certain it must be crawling with insects.

Belagren walked to the window and looked down with a frown. The room had only a view of the castle's stables, not the ocean on the other side of the Keep. Being able to look out and see the water *might* have made the room bearable.

There was nothing to do here on this Goddess-forsaken island, either. Antonov had forbidden anyone to speak with Thorn, including her. When she challenged him, he had smiled cryptically, but refused to rescind the order, insisting that she trust him. There were some things Antonov could not be moved on, and Belagren could tell this was one of them, so she had amused herself by designing a new temple for Elcast that would take them several generations to pay for. Antonov would loan them the money, of course. With luck, the debt should be cleared by the time Morna Provin's great-grandsons were grown . . .

The feud between Belagren and her hostess went back a long way. They were enemies well before the war started. It had begun during the Age of Shadows, when Belagren had first caught the roving eye of the Lion of Senet. She was a Sundancer in those days, posted to court in Avacas because of her family connections.

Antonov was married to Princess Analee of Damita at the time, Morna's older sister. Heavily pregnant with Misha, Princess Analee was bloated and unattractive, and it had taken little effort on Belagren's part to coax Antonov into her bed. But Morna, in Avacas to visit with Analee during her sister's confinement, had been furious when she realised what was going on. She had even threatened to expose the affair, thinking her position as the Lion of Senet's sister-in-law gave her some sort of power.

Oh, how wrong you were, Morna, Belagren thought with a vengeful smile. *How foolish to think you could threaten me. And what a hypocrite you were! All the while condemning me for my affair with Antonov while you were making cow eyes at Johan Thorn . . .*

Belagren could remember thinking at the time that perhaps she should have bedded the Dhevynian king, rather than the Lion of Senet. Johan was new to his throne then, still uncertain in his power, but some indefinable political instinct told her that the future lay with Antonov, not Johan. And she had been proved right a thousand times over.

Johan Thorn was a fugitive. Antonov ruled the world.

Those fateful weeks prior to Misha's birth stuck in Belagren's memory so clearly they might as well have happened yesterday. It was just over three years after the second sun had vanished and the whole world was in chaos. The temperature had plunged, the seas were retreating and earthquakes rocked the whole of Ranadon, seemingly on a daily basis. The main city of Nova on the island of Grannon Rock had been all but destroyed. A volcano had erupted near the northern Senetian city of Ultoma, burying it under tons of ash and lava. Thousands had been killed and those that were left were cold and hungry. Heavily reliant on trade, the islands of Dhevyn and the southern nation of Damita had been affected worse than Senet. Johan Thorn, the untried King of Dhevyn, had come to Avacas with Prince Oscon of Damita to beg Antonov's aid.

Johan Thorn was a passionate young man in those days, new to his crown and desperately concerned for his people. And he had fallen instantly in love with the young princess from Damita. Morna had fallen just as hard for the dashing young king and, for a time, it seemed almost inevitable that Oscon would allow his younger daughter to marry the Dhevynian king.

Until Belagren decided otherwise. She didn't like the idea of Analee's obnoxious little sister married to the King of Dhevyn – or any king for that matter. It would give that insufferable little bitch far too much power, and that could well interfere with the plans that Belagren had for her own future.

It was Belagren who planted the idea in Antonov's mind that Duke Wallin of Elcast would make an eminently suitable husband for the young Damitian princess; although Dhevynian, Wallin and Antonov had been friends since childhood. The marriage was surprisingly easy to arrange, and with the desperation of Oscon and Johan to secure aid for their starving nations, they were willing to grant Antonov anything he asked for.

To this day, the look on Johan Thorn's face as he stood in the Sundancers' Temple in Avacas, watching his heartbroken seventeen-year-old lover marry a man more than twice her age she barely knew, brought a smile to Belagren's face.

Things had settled down for a while after that. Although the planet had continued to rage, venting its frustration at the loss of its second sun, Antonov's aid had relieved the immediate problems in Dhevyn. Belagren continued her affair with Antonov and heard later that Morna had delivered a son to Wallin Provin on Elcast. Belagren took great delight in sending a carefully worded letter of congratulations to the new Duchess of Elcast, and was just sorry she'd not been there to watch Morna read it.

Analee eventually gave birth to a second son, this one

whole and healthy, unlike her firstborn, who had suffered a stroke while still a baby, which left him deformed and sickly, but Senet was suffering from the forced darkness, too. Searching for anything that might help them, the Lord of the Suns ordered Belagren north to Omaxin with several other Sundancers to seek answers.

Belagren was furious. In her mind, there was nothing useful in the ancient ruins that might help stem the tide of disasters that plagued their world. She wanted to stay in Avacas. Since Kirshov's birth, Analee's position had become almost unassailable. Antonov was thrilled to have a healthy son, and he doted on the child . . . and the child's mother.

But in those days she wasn't powerful enough to defy a direct order from the leader of her Church, so she had begrudgingly gone north with Madalan, Ella and Paige Halyn's latest protégé, the young Sundancer Neris Veran.

When she returned to Avacas, she had the power to change the world.

Although they had discussed their plans any number of times on the way back from Omaxin, it wasn't until she arrived back in Avacas and saw Analee, pregnant with yet another son, proudly leaning on her adoring husband's arm, that Belagren decided how to proceed.

Analee had to go. And so did her sons.

Misha wasn't really a problem. The boy was weak and deformed, his left side withered and repulsive. It was all Antonov could do to look at the boy. She could do nothing about Kirshov, either. In Antonov's eyes, the child was perfect, and to harm him would have been to risk death.

But Belagren was damned if she was going to allow another son to cement Analee's place in her husband's affections . . .

A knock at the door interrupted Belagren's musings. She turned and called permission to enter. The door opened and the Sundancer Brahm Halyn limped into the room. He bowed awkwardly, uncomfortable in her presence. He was the brother of the Lord of the Suns, and in Belagren's opinion shared both his brother's weak-chinned features and his spineless character.

'You sent for me, my lady?'

'I have some questions for you, Brahm. Regarding Elcast.'

'I will answer as best I can, my lady.'

Belagren walked to the edge of the bed and sat down, not offering Brahm a seat. Not that there was a seat to offer him in this poky room. This audience should be taking place somewhere with a podium, so that she could look down on him, not here in this child's nursery...

'How long have you been here, Brahm?'

'Since the end of the Age of Shadows, my lady. Seventeen years.'

'And in all that time, it never occurred to you to press Duke Wallin for a new temple?'

Brahm looked down at his feet. 'There were other, more urgent matters...'

'More urgent than giving thanks to the Goddess?'

'There was the rebuilding...'

'Elcast seems fine to me. It's as if the Age of Shadows never happened here. Are you telling me that reconstruction was only completed recently?'

'Well, no, my lady, of course not, but—'

'So what's the problem, Brahm?'

'I ... I couldn't really say, my lady.'

'But you are a Sundancer! You are the spiritual leader on Elcast. It is your responsibility to ensure that the Goddess is given her due! What have you been doing for the last two decades?'

The Sundancer didn't answer, probably realising that he had no answer that could satisfy her. And in truth, he was not answerable to the High Priestess of the Shadowdancers in any case. He was answerable to the Lord of the Suns, his own brother, and that ineffectual fool probably hadn't even bothered to inquire about what was happening on Elcast since he sent Brahm here all those years ago.

'You seem quite comfortable here,' she remarked, deciding not to pursue the issue of the temple for the time being. She didn't need Brahm for that anyway.

'I have served Duke Wallin faithfully, my lady.'

Belagren frowned. 'I was under the impression that you were supposed to be serving the Goddess.'

Brahm met her eyes for the first time. Was that a spark of anger she saw hidden in their watery depths? *Have you finally grown a backbone after all these years, Brahm Halyn?*

'Tell me about the family.'

'My lady?'

'Tell me about the Provins of Elcast, Brahm. You claim to have served them well, so I assume you know them equally well.'

'I'm not sure what my lady wishes to know.'

'Tell me about Duchess Morna. Is she diligent in her observance of the Goddess's rites?'

'Of course!'

'Yet at last year's Landfall Feast I hear they sacrificed a pig. Did you not object to such an outrageous insult?'

'Traditionally, a pig was always sacrificed, my lady, before—' He didn't finish the sentence. He didn't need to. She knew what he wanted to say. *Before you came along.*

'And what of her sons?' she asked, knowing that the sudden change of subject would rattle him. She'd learned that trick from Antonov.

'They are fine boys, my lady,' Brahm declared. 'And diligent, too,' he added hurriedly.

'Rees seems poured from the same mould as his father,' she agreed. 'But the younger boy has much of his mother in him, I fear.'

'Dirk is a fine young man, my lady,' he rushed to assure her. 'He's training to be a physician.'

'An odd choice of profession for a duke's son, even a second son. Particularly one of royal blood.'

'I believe Duke Wallin simply wanted to make the most of the boy's potential,' Brahm said defensively. 'He's very bright, my lady. Remarkably so.'

Belagren stared at the Sundancer thoughtfully. 'What do you mean *very bright*?'

'Just that, my lady,' he shrugged, uncertain what she was

driving at. 'I've no doubt the lad could have gained entrance to Nova University on Grannon Rock when he was no more than thirteen. Even Avaças University would be glad to have him. I believe the decision to allow him to study as a physician was prompted by Duchess Morna's concerns that he was too young to attend university so far from home.'

Was that really your reason, Morna? she wondered.

'And have you seen any signs of this supposed vast intellect in the boy?'

A fond smile flickered over the Sundancer's lips. 'I gave up trying to keep up with Dirk Provin many years ago, my lady. He has a truly remarkable mind. I've not seen one like it since . . .' Brahm faltered for a moment and then shrugged. 'For a long time.'

'I see,' Belagren replied, drawing out the silence to give her time to think. Was it possible? Was the solution to her dilemma, the key to the Labyrinth here in Elcast, right under her nose? She wanted to laugh aloud at the irony. Morna Provin's son! The Goddess truly did have a sense of humour.

'I think I'd like to see this remarkable mind at work.'

'Dirk is . . . uncomfortable with being singled out, my lady. I'm not sure he would appreciate—'

'I am not in the least concerned about Dirk Provin's tender feelings, Brahm.'

The Sundancer bowed uncomfortably. 'I'll see what I can arrange, my lady.'

18

Dirk was too troubled by his discussion with Alenor to join the others after breakfast. Instead, he went looking for his father. Wallin Provin was a moderate man and a loyal Dhevynian and, in Dirk's experience, had never bothered much with religion. They had their rituals, certainly.

Brahm Halyn, the Sundancer attached to the Elcast court, was quite meticulous in his observance of the customs and devotions of the Goddess. But even after the war, they had never embraced Belagren's cult of Shadowdancers on the island. Dirk could not believe his father would stand back and allow the sacrifice of a human being – just to please the High Priestess of what, in his opinion, was a rather small and somewhat ineffectual cult. He was willing to accept the notion that they should give thanks to the Goddess. He was even willing to concede that the High Priestess had been instrumental in bringing back the second sun, but Dirk wasn't ready to accept the idea that the taking of a human life was a necessary part of worshipping *any* deity.

Balonan told Dirk he could find his father in the Library. He was hesitant about approaching his old schoolroom. He didn't want to bump into Prince Antonov. As he rounded the stairs on the first floor, he saw Antonov on the second-floor landing with Ella, the Shadowdancer who attended Misha. He waited until the prince and the red-robed Sundancer were out of sight before taking the rest of the stairs two at a time, then turning into the corridor on the third floor.

Dirk loved the Library. If left alone and undisturbed, he could lose himself in it for hours. Morna often had to send a servant to find him come dinnertime, and they always checked the Library first. It smelled of old leather and furniture wax. There was a long table down the centre of the room that glowed softly from years of careful polishing, which reflected the diamond-paned windows in its dark surface. The walls were lined with shelves that offered the promise of untapped wealth. There were books on history and science and mathematics and a thousand other subjects. But there were gaps on the shelves, too. He suspected there had been more books here once, but nobody was able to explain their disappearance.

The high ceiling was crisscrossed with huge wooden

beams, from which a large candelabrum hung. It had not been lit in years. There was no need. Day and night were defined by either the bright light of the second sun or the scarlet light of the first sun. Wallin was standing at the far end of the table looking over a stack of papers. He glanced up as the door clicked closed behind Dirk and smiled when he saw his youngest son.

'What's the matter, lad? Missing your studies? I thought you'd be glad of the break.'

'May I ask you a question, sir? About the Landfall Festival?'

Wallin's expression clouded. 'What did you want to know?'

'Princess Alenor told me . . . she says you're going to allow them to sacrifice someone as part of the ritual.'

Wallin sighed and put down the page he was reading. 'Alenor told you that, did she?'

'Yes, sir. But I'm sure she was mistaken.'

'Come here, Dirk.'

Wallin had not laughed off Alenor's claims. That worried Dirk a great deal. When he reached his father's side, Wallin put his arm around him.

'Son, there are a lot of things that happen in this world that you will find unpleasant. You've been lucky here on Elcast. Your mother and I have been able to protect you and your brother from most of them. But things . . . happen, sometimes . . . and they don't always make sense. People do things because they believe they are right, even if to others they seem horribly wrong.'

'Then she was right? You really are going to let this happen?'

'It's . . . tradition, son.'

'We've gotten along just fine without this *tradition* so far.'

'Yet our crops were destroyed. The Goddess sent us a warning, Dirk, and it's one we would be foolish to ignore.'

'That wasn't the act of the Goddess, Father. That was the result of a tidal wave, caused by an erupting volcano. It was a perfectly natural occurrence that just happened to have serious consequences for us, because we had the misfortune to be in its path.'

Wallin shook his head, frowning. 'Helgin's been filling your head with nonsense, I fear.'

'My head *would* be filled with nonsense if I believed burning a man alive had any effect on the natural order of the world.'

Before Wallin could reply, the door opened and Antonov stepped into the room. Although Dirk wasn't exactly afraid of the Lion of Senet, he was enough in awe of him that his mouth went dry on the few occasions that Antonov deigned to notice him.

'What's this about the natural order of the world?' the prince asked.

'I was just asking about the custom of murdering sacrificial victims on Landfall Night, your highness,' Dirk informed him. He heard a faint hiss of disapproval from his father beside him.

'*Murder,* Dirk? That's a bit harsh.' Antonov smiled benevolently. 'The souls of Landfall Festival are given as a gift to the Goddess, Dirk. It was the sacrifice of a child of royal blood that brought back the Age of Light. The lives we give to the Goddess now are so that we may remain in it.'

'What child?' Dirk asked. He felt his father's arm tighten warningly around his shoulder, but it was too late. He had already done the damage.

Prince Antonov's eyes grew bleak. 'It was my youngest son, Dirk.'

Dirk wished the floor would open up and swallow him, but Antonov no longer seemed to notice his presence. He turned his leonine head towards Wallin. Even his father cowered a little under his scrutiny.

'It appals me that your son should have to ask such a question. What have you been teaching him, Wallin? Or rather, what have you *neglected* to teach him?'

'His education is not being neglected,' the duke assured him.

Antonov turned his golden-eyed gaze on Dirk. 'Perhaps,' the prince agreed ominously.

'Dirk is a very bright boy, your highness. His mathematical ability, in particular, is quite astounding. I confess we have gone to such pains to foster that talent that perhaps a few other ... subjects ... have not received the attention they deserved.'

Antonov frowned. 'That's certainly clear enough. So, you're a mathematician, are you, Dirk?'

'I'm apprenticed to be a physician, your highness.'

'Indeed, but one wonders if you've been offered an alternative.'

Dirk glanced at his father with a puzzled look. 'I'm not sure I understand, your highness.'

'If your talent lies in the area of mathematics, I'm surprised that you haven't been offered a chance to pursue it in a more stimulating environment.'

'You mean at the university on Grannon Rock?'

'No, Dirk, I mean at the university in Avacas.'

'I wasn't aware they accepted students from outside Senet, sire.'

'There's a great deal you don't seem to be aware of, Dirk Provin.'

'Anton—' Wallin began.

The Lion of Senet held up his hand, warning the duke to silence. 'No! I'll hear none of your excuses, Wallin. I can easily imagine how this boy's education came to be so sadly neglected. And who is responsible for it.'

'I'm sure we can correct any—'

'Oh, you can trust me that the gaps in this boy's education will be corrected. I intend to do something about that myself.' Antonov turned on his heel, letting the door slam shut behind him.

Dirk looked at his father with concern. 'Father?'

'Don't worry about it, son.'

'But what did he mean?'

'I said, don't worry about it. Go join your friends.'

'But—'

'Go, Dirk.'

With the subject so firmly closed, Dirk had no choice but to obey his father.

As he slowly descended the stairs, he thought over what Antonov had said. He was almost afraid to learn what the Lion of Senet meant by 'doing something' about his education.

He had always had excellent tutors, the best his father could afford. Although Elcast was counted as one of the larger islands, they were on the western edge of the kingdom and far removed from the queen's court on Kalarada. Elcast was not wealthy, like Grannon Rock or Bryton, but even with the crippling taxes owed to Senet each year, they managed to get by, and the Elcast court was known to be a pleasant place to serve. Dirk had always believed that was the reason they acquired staff who could have earned much more in a wealthier court. Some people preferred the slower pace of life here, Wallin often boasted.

Dirk had never questioned their good fortune until now. He thought people like Master Kedron, whose ability was so legendary that he actually owned a diamond-bladed dagger, and Master Helgin, who had studied in the university at Grannon Rock and had reputedly served in the royal household, had come to Elcast for their health.

Now he wondered if there was another reason.

If Prince Antonov was concerned enough about the Queen of Dhevyn's court to take Alenor away from it, it wasn't hard to imagine that a mere physician might find his position uncomfortable there – particularly if he held opinions at odds with someone as powerful as the Lion of Senet. Was Helgin here on Elcast because he disagreed with the Lion of Senet? Because he taught science, rather than the approved religious version of events? Or did it go deeper than that? *Is there some connection between Master Helgin and Johan Thorn?*

Perhaps Helgin had served not in Queen Rainan's court on Kalarada, but in King Johan's.

Dirk found the whole situation rather puzzling. His father was an old friend of Antonov's, he knew, and had fought with him in the War of the Shadows. But other than the fact that there had been a war against the faithful led by a heretic, he realised now that he'd been told nothing about it at all. Nobody mentioned that the heretic had been Johan Thorn. Neither had they mentioned that he wasn't just a heretic, but the King of Dhevyn.

Looking back, Dirk recalled Helgin's reluctance to teach him recent history, claiming he had too many other things to learn. Perhaps they were some of the books that were missing? He remembered asking questions about it when he was younger that had spurred Helgin into suddenly over-loading him with other work, so that his curiosity was diverted. Recently, he'd been so wrapped up in his studies as an apprentice physician, that history barely rated a mention.

And nobody had ever talked about what Morna had done during that time. Dirk had always assumed that she had stayed home like a dutiful wife and administered the Duchy, while her husband was off fighting the heretics who wanted to prevent the return of the Age of Light.

When he thought about it, he realised that he knew nothing of his parents' history with the Lion of Senet – only that Morna was prone to making snide remarks about him and the High Priestess, and Wallin was always warning her to silence on the matter.

By the time he reached the ground floor, Dirk's natural curiosity was starting to get the better of him. There had to be someone he could trust to tell him what really happened. There was no point asking his parents or Master Helgin. It was obvious they had done their best to discourage scrutiny of the past. He didn't want to ask Alenor, afraid to expose his ignorance, and he doubted Kirsh or Lanon cared enough about history to have more than a fleeting acquaintance with it.

Then he smiled, as it occurred to him that there was one person on Elcast at present who might be able to tell him the truth. One person who knew *exactly* what had happened.

He needed to find a way to get in to see Johan Thorn.

19

At first, Johan spent his days drifting in and out of a drug-induced haze, waiting for Antonov with a degree of fatalistic calm. Slowly, as his bones began to knit together and the pain began to recede, Helgin tapered the dosage of poppy-dust. His rare moments of lucidity became more frequent, and he was able to reflect on his situation. He suffered no illusions about his fate; held no false hopes of rescue from it. He had chosen this path many years ago, fully aware that this was how it was likely to end. He did not try to fool himself into believing anything else.

I'll walk to my execution – or hobble, to be more accurate, he amended wryly, glancing down at his still-splinted leg – *with my head held high. I'll give no man any reason to question the courage of the last Thorn king.*

The pirate had expected Antonov to order him moved to less comfortable accommodation, even transfer him to the Senetian garrison in town, but apparently, Helgin had declared him too ill to be moved, so he had been spared that, at least.

But the Lion of Senet made no attempt to see him. He took up residence in Elcast Keep and carried on as if Johan did not even exist. Antonov didn't come to his room to ascertain that his prisoner really was Johan Thorn; he didn't even come to gloat.

By far the worst side effect of his increasing awareness was that it left Johan with far too much time to think about where he'd gone wrong. *Given a chance to live my life over, there's not a thing I'd do differently,* he declared defiantly to himself. That, he knew in his heart, was the biggest lie of all. Given a chance to live his life over, there was any number of things he'd do differently. *Next time I wouldn't make the mistake of asking the mainland for help when my people began to starve,* he told himself. *Next time the darkness comes, I'll let them suffer, because the short-term pain of the Age of Shadows is a minor inconvenience compared to the long-term consequences of allowing Senet a foothold in Dhevyn.*

Once started on that train of thought, Johan found himself cataloguing his past mistakes with brutal disregard for his own feelings. He'd had plenty of time over the years to work out where he'd gone wrong. He understood now why, frightened and uncertain, his own dukes had sided with Antonov. The Lion of Senet had seemed like a tower of strength compared to Johan's shaky leadership. Antonov's High Priestess had promised the second sun would return, and it did, right when she said it would. All Johan could offer to counter her visions was the word of a drug-addled madman ...

But it wasn't all the fault of Belagren and her Shadowdancers. Johan was more than willing to admit that he had contributed to his own downfall. Blinded by youth and inexperience, he had made several fatal errors of judgement and they had ended up costing him his crown.

Next time, I'd make every duke in Dhevyn swear allegiance to me personally, not my throne, so that I can't be deposed and my sister elevated in my stead.

Johan did not despise his sister. Rainan hadn't wanted the throne. She certainly hadn't conspired against him to gain it. He'd simply left her no choice. Take the throne when her brother fled or hand over Dhevyn to the Lion of Senet.

But that wasn't all he would change, given a second chance. *I'd make certain the Landfall Festival was outlawed. And I'd make it a capital offence to practise human sacrifice.*

Executing someone for the crime of executing someone struck Johan as being particularly ironic. It was probably the poppy-dust, he decided. It often left him strangely euphoric.

And next time, he thought finally with a sense of deep regret, *I won't let Morna go ...*

That was perhaps the most painful mistake of all.

Johan allowed himself to remember Morna only rarely — especially now, when she was here, so close to him yet so distant, separated by so many years and so much heartache that he almost couldn't bear to think about her. He had promised to let her go, and while he had never agreed with her decision to return to her husband and son, he had resolved to respect it.

If I'd kept her with me, if I'd insisted she stay in the Baenlands with me, would our child have survived? If I'd kept Morna by my side, I might have another daughter . . . or a son. But I wouldn't have Mellie. It was a futile train of thought. Too much had happened since then and it was unfair to both his wife and his daughter to dwell on what might have been.

Morna had not come to visit him, but that was no doubt Wallin's doing. A part of Johan desperately wanted to see her. Another part of him was terrified by the prospect. Would she still be the same woman? Had her years as Wallin's wife worn her down? Was she well? Was she still beautiful?

He heard the guards talking in low voices outside his door, and tried to make out what they were saying. It stopped him from thinking about the past for a time.

Other than Helgin, Johan had seen nobody since his capture. He once heard Master Helgin chatting to his apprentice, and he woke from a poppy-dust-induced doze one afternoon, certain he could hear Morna in the other room.

But nobody came to visit him.

He was healing well, so Master Helgin assured him. He could move his shoulder now, without too much stiffness, and the stitches had come out of his forehead, leaving a neat, slightly ridged scar across it. He smiled, wishing for a moment that Mellie were here to see it.

She'd be proud of me. I'm a real pirate now. I have a scar.

Johan sighed heavily. What was she doing now? Were Mellie and Lexie grieving him, thinking him dead, or had word already reached Mil of his capture?

Would Lexie remember what I told her to do if I was ever taken alive?

Would Reithan be able to control the hotheads, or would Tia fire them up with her rhetoric about reclaiming what was rightfully theirs?

Thinking of Tia and her gift for causing trouble made Johan frown. Although he loved her like a daughter, she had inherited her mother's cunning – and a degree of her father's intelligence. It was a dangerous combination. So dangerous that, for a moment, Johan debated the wisdom of taking Helgin up on his offer to get a message to his people in the Baenlands. He dismissed the idea immediately. Antonov would be watching for something like that, and he would watch Helgin more closely than most. Attempting to get a message out would cost more lives than he was willing to spend.

With that uncomfortable thought foremost in his mind, he drifted off to sleep again, but it wasn't restful. His dreams were a troubled montage of the past, the future and what might have been.

'Hello . . . ?'

A hand on his shoulder shook him awake gently. He opened his eyes and blinked owlishly at the boy standing beside the bed. He was about sixteen and, for a moment, he thought Morna had come to visit him. *Damn this poppy-dust. Now I'm hallucinating.*

The dark-haired boy smiled apologetically. 'I'm sorry I woke you, sir.'

Johan stared at him blankly. 'What? Who are you?'

'I didn't mean to startle you, sir.'

He glanced at the closed door with a frown. 'How did you get in here?'

'I told the guards I was here to give you another dose of poppy-dust, sir.'

'You didn't answer my question. Who are you?'

'I'm Master Helgin's apprentice.'

'Do you have a name?'

'Dirk Provin, sir.'

He closed his eyes for a moment to compose himself, then opened them and looked at the boy. 'Sir, this, sir, that . . . If nothing else, your aggravatingly good manners should have warned me you were Wallin's son. What are you doing here, boy? Did your father send you?'

He shook his head. 'I just came to see if you needed anything, sir.'

'No, you didn't,' Johan accused, shifting on the bed to

better look at the young man. 'You came to gawk at me. And for pity's sake, stop calling me "sir". My name is Johan.'

'As you wish . . . Johan.' Dirk smiled at him sheepishly. 'You are the most interesting thing that's happened on Elcast since the war, you know, and I wasn't born then, so I missed all the excitement.'

Johan stared at the boy for a moment. Was this young man Morna's way of apologising to Wallin Provin? Had she given him another son as some sort of recompense for the trouble she had caused?

'I'd use many words to describe the war, Dirk Provin, but I promise you, exciting wouldn't be one of them.'

'You fought against Senet, didn't you?'

'Senet and more than half my own dukes,' Johan corrected, not able to hide the bitterness, even after all this time. 'Take a lesson from that, young Provin. Never declare war on someone until you've taken a look over your shoulder to see who's standing with you.'

'Why did you go to war against Senet?'

'What does your father tell you?'

'He said a heretic tried to prevent the return of the Age of Light, and that he and all the dukes loyal to the Goddess sided with Prince Antonov to defeat him. Other than that, he doesn't say much at all.'

'Wallin always was a man of few words.'

'Is that what happened?'

'Pretty much.'

'Why didn't you want the Age of Light to come back? I heard it was awful during the Age of Shadows.'

Johan took a deep breath. Keeping up with the quick-fire questions from this boy was exhausting. 'It *was* awful, Dirk, but not so awful that I would condone cold-blooded murder performed as part of a religious rite of extremely dubious value to make it go away.'

'You mean sacrificing a child of royal blood to make the sun come back?'

'You've been to the Landfall Festival then?'

The boy shook his head with a frown. 'We don't have

human sacrifices here on Elcast. At least we didn't until Prince Antonov arrived.'

'Ah, my old friend Antonov. The Shadow Slayer, himself.'

'I've never heard him called that before.'

'It's a title he earned during the war – performing religious rites of extremely dubious value,' he added with a wan smile.

'But it worked,' Dirk argued. 'The second sun returned. How can you say it was of dubious value?'

Johan gave Dirk a long look, marvelling at the boy's ignorance. How did they do it? How did they hide such a blatant truth from everyone? But it was time to steer the conversation away from where it was heading. Johan knew he was going to die. He would not hurt Morna further by condemning her son to die alongside him.

'Did you say you were Helgin's apprentice?'

'For the past year,' Dirk confirmed. 'But what—'

'And Wallin agreed to it?' he asked, cutting off the stream of questions Dirk was obviously dying to ask. 'I'd have thought he'd want his sons raised in his own image.'

'What do you mean?'

'Well, if you're Wallin Provin's son, shouldn't you be out there learning the finer points of military tactics? The Lion of Senet might have need of your sword one day, boy.' Johan closed his eyes for a moment. 'Of course, there's nobody left to conquer any more. He has Damita by the balls. Your Uncle Baston would probably roll over and die like a well-trained dog if Antonov asked him to. And Dhevyn . . . well, he'll own that soon enough, once Alenor comes of age.'

'You really hate him, don't you?'

'Probably not as much as he hates me. Besides, I'm too tired to hate him any more. Now I just despair of what he's done to my people.'

'Is that why you gave up on Dhevyn?'

Johan stared balefully at the lad. 'You have no idea what you're talking about, Dirk Provin.'

'But if you were our king, why did you desert us? How

can you let Antonov occupy Dhevyn while you hide out in the Baenlands?'

'Is that what you think happened? That I just decided I'd had enough and walked away?'

'I don't know what happened, sir. Nobody will tell me.'

'I should think that as Wallin Provin's son, you'd find the truth a little hard to stomach.'

'Then maybe I should ask my mother about it?' he suggested. The boy was watching him closely, looking for his reaction. 'Perhaps she'll tell me the truth.'

Does he know anything, or is this a fishing expedition? 'If Morna was planning to tell you anything, Dirk, you'd know about it by now.'

'Was she really one of your followers? Is that why Alenor says the High Priestess wants her put to death?'

'Dirk, can I give you some advice?'

'Sir?'

'Stop asking questions. Stop poking around in things that don't concern you. I'd bet my right eye your father specifically forbade you to come here. So leave. And don't come back. And don't delve into the past, either. You'll find more than you bargained for and I promise you, it won't give you the answers you seek, just leave you with even more questions.'

'But—'

'No. I'll answer no more of your questions, Dirk. You've exhausted me and this poppy-dust has made me drowsy. Leave me alone. I need to rest.'

Johan closed his eyes, feigning sleep. The boy waited silently for a time, and then, when Johan showed no sign of taking any further part in the conversation, he left, shutting the door softly behind him.

Maybe I should have told him what he wanted to know, Johan mused once he was alone. He was alarmed to realise that Dirk Provin had no idea what happened during the Age of Shadows. With each year that went by the truth had slipped further and further away. Soon it would be nothing more than a legend, left to simmer in the hearts of emotional zealots like Tia, who believed that the cause was always worth the price; that the principle was the only thing worth defending.

Johan opened his eyes with a heavy sigh.

Belagren has won, he realised. *She has achieved what she set out to do. The next generation is growing up hearing only her version of events.*

How long before the truth is lost for ever?

He turned to stare at the closed door. *Have I been wrong all these years? Should I have fought on, no matter how many lives it cost?*

Somehow, Johan couldn't let himself believe that he could have misjudged things so badly.

What choice did I have? Withdraw to the Baenlands and save the lives that I could, or fight on, regardless of the cost?

And now ... well, another few years and there would be nobody left to fight.

Maybe he should have answered Dirk's questions. Maybe, in the heart of Wallin Provin's son, there was room for doubt. Room to consider that there was an alternative to what he had been taught.

Maybe.

But even if there was, Johan wasn't certain that he wanted to risk the boy's life by telling him the truth.

20

Later that afternoon, Kirshov Latanya wandered into the cool dimness of the stables looking for Dirk. Daylight striped the floor in alternating lines of shadow and luminescence, and the air was alive with sparkling dust motes that danced on the sunlight. Eryk had told him that Dirk was here, but he could see no sign of him. It was an odd place to seek the Elcastran boy. Dirk liked studious things, and Kirsh thought it more likely he would be curled up somewhere inside the Keep with a book.

When he first met him, Kirsh had considered Dirk Provin the most cold and dispassionate person he had ever encountered. Despite Kirsh's attempts to befriend his cousin, Dirk had stubbornly resisted his overtures of friendship, preferring to perform his duty as host, and not much more. He had taken to Alenor easily enough, which made the prince just a tiny bit envious, but then, she was Dhevynian, like Dirk.

Kirsh had never known anyone to hold his nationality against him before. As a rule, people sought his friendship because of it. Dirk was a friend of Lanon, though, who was also Senetian, which ruined the argument that it was only his country he held against him . . .

After several days of trying, Kirshov had almost given up on the idea of ever befriending Dirk, when he charged off into town to take on that gang of bullies for the sake of his half-witted servant. Kirsh had not deliberately set out to get into a fight with that self-important butcher's apprentice, but since then, Dirk had thawed considerably towards him, as if he'd proved his worth by standing up for himself – without invoking either his rank or his nationality.

A noise from the loft caused him to look up and he caught sight of a tousled dark head above him.

'Everyone's been looking for you,' he called up to the loft.

Dirk's face appeared over the edge as a few of the horses in their stalls looked up from their meal, curious about the disturbance. Kirsh could hear the rhythmic hammering of the smithy next door. The still, hot air in the stables was thick with the scent of hay and manure.

Dirk's solemn grey eyes looked down on him. 'Why?'

'We're going swimming,' Kirsh told him. 'The others went on ahead. I said I'd find you and join them later. Why are you hiding up there?'

'I'm not hiding. I just wanted to be alone. I need to think.'

Kirsh spied the ladder leading up to the loft and climbed

up the rungs until he was standing on the ladder face to face
with the younger boy.

'What's to think about?'

Dirk was silent for a moment, as if deciding whether or
not to confide in him. His brows drew together in a frown
and he pulled a stray stalk of hay from his hair before he
answered. 'Kirsh, doesn't it bother you that your father sacrificed your brother to the Goddess?'

The question took Kirsh completely by surprise. It was
not something he dwelt on. Although he knew the story well
enough, as a rule, nobody dared mention the subject in his
hearing, for fear of incurring Antonov's wrath.

He smiled, in a vain attempt to bring some levity to the
conversation. 'I guess if anything, it just makes me glad I
was born second, not third.'

Dirk scowled at him.

'All right, that was in poor taste,' he admitted. 'I don't
really think about it.' Kirsh had no wish to be reminded that
his baby brother had been sacrificed, that his mother had
killed herself, or that his father was hailed as a hero for insti-
gating such a tragic chain of events.

'But our lives are defined by it. The way people live,
what they think, what they believe . . . everything since the
Age of Shadows stems from that one action. Don't you ever
wonder what would have happened if your father hadn't
listened to Belagren?'

'You talk like a heretic,' Kirsh said with a frown.
Belagren had warned him of this during the voyage here.
Warned him that it was likely Morna Provin had poisoned
her sons against the Goddess.

'I'm not a heretic. I just can't understand why nobody
ever questions anything.'

'It's a matter of faith, Dirk. If you have faith, you don't
need to question.'

'Don't you? I mean, how do you know that the High
Priestess doesn't just make it up as she goes along? It's illogical just to accept her word as fact.'

Kirsh was genuinely shocked by the suggestion. 'You're

the one who's being illogical. If she's just making it up, then how did she know that the second sun would return as soon as the sacrifice was performed?'

Dirk thought for a moment, but couldn't answer the question. 'I don't know.'

'You need faith.' Kirsh climbed the rest of the way up the ladder and sat down beside Dirk, dangling his legs over the drop to the stable floor below. 'You should be careful, you know. Asking questions like that could get you in a lot of trouble.'

A small smile flickered over Dirk's face. 'Well, they're training me to be a physician, not a theologian.'

Kirsh laughed, relieved that Dirk seemed content not to question his beliefs any further. 'And a good thing, too. I'm going to join the Dhevyn Queen's Guard.'

'I know,' Dirk agreed, rolling his eyes. 'You've managed to mention that at least once every hour since you've been here.'

'Oh?'

'Do you really want to join them so badly? I know some of the lads here on Elcast want to, but they're Dhevynian, and they're not nearly as obsessed with it as you are.'

'I'm not obsessed!' he objected, then grinned. 'Well, maybe just a little bit. But don't you see? The Queen of Dhevyn's Guard is the only place I'll get to make my mark in this world, Dirk. Misha will inherit Senet. Without the guard, I'm just a second son who'll end up living off his older brother's charity. I want to be *somebody*!'

'You're the Lion of Senet's son,' Dirk pointed out. 'Isn't that enough?'

'But that's exactly my point!' he insisted. 'Everyone thinks of me as the Lion of Senet's son. Nobody ever thinks of Antonov as Prince Kirshov's father.'

Dirk sighed and swung his legs around until he was sitting beside Kirsh. 'Kirsh, you have more than most people even dream of. Why do you want more?'

Kirshov thought before he answered, which was not something he did often. Dirk had that effect on him. There was something about his cousin that made him stop and consider his reply. Perhaps it was Dirk's quiet confidence, or perhaps it was his determination to be a physician. Even a second son from a backward island like Elcast had found a way to make himself useful, which simply reinforced Kirsh's feeling of being superfluous.

'I'm Antonov's son,' he said eventually. 'I'm Misha's brother. And one day, if my father has his way, I'll be Alenor's consort. Even my poor dead younger brother has the distinction of being sacrificed for a glorious cause. I'm an accessory. Unless I can make a name for myself in the guard, that's all I'll ever be.'

Dirk digested his answer for a long time before he replied. 'Kirsh, I think you try too hard.'

'Well, that's better than not trying at all, isn't it?'

Dirk smiled. 'I suppose so.'

'Good. So now that's settled, let's go for a swim.'

Dirk looked at him for a moment with an odd expression, then shook his head. 'Where did the others go?'

'Down to the beach near the Outlet.'

The Outlet was a tiny cove where a small stream met the sheltered bay. The stream was a tributary of the larger Flenern River, the main source of fresh water for both Elcast Keep and the town that had grown up around its harbour. There was a sandy beach surrounding a small waterfall that fed a pool deep enough to swim in all year round. Further along the foreshore the retreating tide often left small fish stranded in the tidal pools among the rocks. It was a favourite place to swim, and they had spent much of their time splashing through the waterfall and investigating the rock pools. There wasn't much else to do here on Elcast, particularly for a young man used to the endless entertainment available in Avacas.

'You know,' Kirsh added with a conspiratorial air, 'if we took the path through the forest, we could sneak up on Lanon and Alenor from the stream and scare the sunlight out of them.'

Dirk grinned. He was so serious most times that it made him seem quite mischievous. 'We could, couldn't we?'

'Well, let's go then,' Kirsh declared, scrambling to his feet. 'How much do you want to bet I could jump from here?' he added, looking down at the drop to the stable floor below.

'I keep telling you, Kirsh, I don't have anything to gamble with,' Dirk said, climbing to his feet. 'And if I did, I wouldn't take odds on whether or not you could make the jump. I'd be wagering on how many bones you broke when you landed.'

Kirsh glanced down at the floor again and reconsidered. 'Well, maybe you're right.'

'I'm right,' Dirk assured him as he slid down the ladder.

'Don't you get sick of that?' Kirsh asked as he followed him down the safer route to the ground.

'Sick of what?'

'Always being right.'

Dirk jumped down to the floor and looked at him. 'I'm not always right.'

'Yes, you are.'

'No, I'm not.'

'You are.'

Suddenly Dirk grinned. 'All right, if you insist. I'll agree with you. However, by agreeing with you, I win the argument.'

'What?'

'Well, if I say I'm not always right, and you claim I am, then if I agree with you, that means I was wrong. And if I was wrong, then I'm not always right, so I was right the first time.'

Kirsh stared at Dirk in puzzlement. 'You're an idiot, Dirk.'

The younger boy laughed. 'It's logic, Kirsh. You should try it sometime.'

'You should stop thinking so much,' he complained. 'You're giving me a headache. Now, as your devoted servant would say, let's go scare the *thit* out of the others. *That,* I understand.'

21

Marqel and Lanatyne walked back to the camp in silence. Lanatyne said nothing, and Marquel was in no mood to talk.

In the pocket of her shift was a gold coin, as well as a scattering of silver coins, all earned in one afternoon's work. Kalleen would be well pleased.

The arrival of the Lion of Senet's ship had almost completely turned their fortunes around, but they only had one more night before the Landfall Festival, at which time their services would no longer be required. At the Landfall Feast, a man could have any woman he wanted, and for that one night at least, he wouldn't have to pay for it. They had one more night to make a reasonable profit before the troupe would have to rely on more traditional endeavours to earn a living.

But Marqel felt dirty. She wanted to wash away the stink of the men she'd been with. She wanted to wash them out of her mind, too, but she didn't think that was likely to happen anytime soon. She had stopped counting them. Lanatyne had warned of the folly of keeping a tally in your head. *Don't remember their names and don't try to remember their faces,* Lanatyne had urged. It was easier that way.

'You're awfully quiet.'

Marqel shrugged. 'What's there to say?'

Lanatyne stared at her for a moment in concern. 'You didn't get hurt, did you?'

'No.'

With sudden insight, the older girl nodded her head. 'It gets easier, Marquel. Once you get used to it.'

'I don't want to get used to it.'

'Well, what *do* you want, girl?' She laughed scornfully. 'That's right, I forgot. You're going to be somebody, aren't you?'

'Shut up.'

'Hey, maybe we can find a lord to marry you!'

Marqel was seriously regretting making that 'being somebody' comment in Lanatyne's hearing, when she heard the faint splashing of a waterfall in the distance. There was a small stream beside the road, which disappeared into the woods, and she guessed that was the source of the sound.

'You could be *Lady* Marqel,' Lanatyne teased, oblivious to her scowl. 'You could hold balls, and tea parties . . . and

. . . hey, there's a couple of princes on the island right now! Perhaps the Lion of Senet's looking for another wife?'

'Shut up, Lana!'

'No, he's too old, isn't he? You're a hopeless romantic. You'd want someone young and handsome. What about one of his sons? Kirshov is pretty cute. Or maybe we could marry you off to one of Duke Wallin's sons? Is that what you're hoping for, Marqel? That someone like Rees Provin or Kirshov Latanya will notice you in a crowd, fall madly in love with you and whisk you away to his castle?'

'Lanatyne, shut up before you lose another tooth!'

Lanatyne grinned crookedly. She was missing one of her front teeth – a souvenir from a customer in a small town on Necia last year, when he discovered his purse considerably lighter on leaving the wagon than it had been when he came in.

'Touchy little bitch, aren't you?'

Marqel debated for a moment the intense pleasure of belting Lanatyne in the mouth, against the punishment she would cop from Kalleen for damaging Lanatyne's face with only one night left to make a profit. Prudence triumphed over anger. She consciously unclenched her fist and turned her head towards the distant sound of the waterfall.

'I want a bath.'

'Washing isn't going to make it go away,' Lanatyne pointed out nastily.

'There's a stream near here. I'm going to wash before I go back to camp.'

Lanatyne's brows knitted in a frown. 'Kalleen says you're to come straight back.'

'She won't care if I stop for a bath. Besides, you've got the money.' She hadn't told Lana about the gold coin. Lana knew about the silver, of course. She'd be suspicious if Marqel hadn't tried to hold something back.

The young woman thought about it for a moment, then shrugged. 'I s'pose. Can you find your way back on your own?'

'I'll just follow the smoke from Kalleen's cooking,' she

told her. Kallen was the worst cook in Dhevyn. She could burn water.

'Well, don't be too long. You know what'll happen if Kalleen has to send someone to find you. We've got to be back in town in a couple of hours *and* we have to pack the wagon up so they can move it to the common.'

'I know,' she assured her. 'I'll see you back at the camp.'

Before Lanatyne could change her mind, Marqel slipped into the bushes beside the stream and followed it until she came to the waterfall. It wasn't a large fall, but beneath the cascade was a deep pool so clear you could see the polished stones on the bottom. Clambering down the rocks, she reached the sandy bank and tore off her shift, although she tucked it carefully under a rock with her precious gold coin and the silver hidden safely inside before she turned to the water.

Dipping a toe into the pool, she was surprised to discover it was quite warm. She waded into the water with a sigh of pleasure, stopping just before she was waist deep to tear the ridiculous ribbons from her hair and toss them on the bank. Then she sank below the surface, letting the warm water wash away the past few hours.

A screen of bushes hid the pool so completely that for a rare moment, Marqel felt like she was alone in the world. The second sun was almost set, leaving the clearing bathed in scarlet light. Marqel rolled onto her back and floated with her eyes closed and her arms outstretched. For a moment, the sweaty spectre of Hauritz the Butcher filled her mind. That unwelcome memory was followed by a blur of other faces, all strangers, all of them filled with panting desire.

'Hello.'

Marqel jerked her eyes open. She went under in an inelegant splash at the unexpected voice. Gasping, she fought her way to the surface, and turned to find Kirshov Latanya standing by the pool staring at her.

For a precious moment time froze, and the horror of the past few hours disappeared, replaced by a vision of youth and beauty beyond her wildest dreams.

'Kirsh?'

The magic of the moment was shattered as a little girl of about thirteen or fourteen with damp dark curls appeared through the bushes, followed by two other boys. The girl stared at her with a scowl.

'Who are you?'

'Who are *you*?' Marqel retorted. She was a haughty little thing, this dark-haired child. *It's the girl from the parade,* Marqel realised. *Princess Alenor.*

'This land belongs to the Duke of Elcast,' one of the boys told her. 'You're trespassing.'

Marqel treaded water in the centre of the pool, a safe distance from the edge.

'I didn't see any sign.'

'As if you could read one if you did,' the princess scoffed.

A surge of unreasonable hatred flared through Marqel. *How dare some stuck-up little bitch scorn me just because she's born a princess!*

'Alenor!' Kirshov scolded. 'Don't be such a snob. She's right. There aren't any signs around here.'

'That's because everyone knows this is the duke's land,' the other Senetian boy pointed out.

Before he could add anything further, Kirshov stepped forward and squatted down on the sand. He smiled at Marqel and her heart skipped a beat. 'But it's all right. You can swim here. You just surprised us, that's all. My name is Kirsh; this is Dirk, Lanon and Alenor.'

'I'm Marqel,' she told him, a little warily. 'And I didn't know this belonged to anyone.'

'It's called the Duke's Forest,' the girl reminded her. 'That would seem to imply that it belonged to the duke.'

Kirsh glared at the princess. 'Allie, stop that. There's no need to be rude.' He turned to Marqel again and smiled apologetically. 'Don't worry about her. She's still mad at Dirk and me for scaring her. Are you from around here?'

Marqel stared at Kirsh, her mind racing. This was too good an opportunity to ignore, yet here she was, stuck in the water without a stitch of clothing.

'No.'

'Well, don't let these other bullies frighten you,' he told her with a grin. 'Why don't you come out of the water? You'll dissolve if you stay in there much longer.'

'Your little friend there is standing on my clothes.'

Kirsh glanced over his shoulder at Alenor. She looked down at her feet and saw the shift poking out from under the rock. With a jerk she pulled it free and tossed it to Kirsh. He picked it up and held it out to her as if it were a gown made of the finest silk.

'My lady,' he offered gallantly.

Hesitating for only a moment, Marqel swam forward until her feet touched the bottom, and then she waded ashore. She made no attempt to hide her nakedness. *Let them look. I've got nothing to be ashamed of.* Besides, it wasn't the other boys or Alenor's scandalised stare that set her heart pounding. It was the look she shared with Kirsh. His strange golden eyes reflected something she couldn't name. Not lust. Not avarice. It was ... something else. Marqel didn't know for certain. All she knew was that it was there in Kirsh's eyes, and she was certain it was meant only for her.

'If you're camped in the forest, you'd best come up to the Keep tomorrow and inform the Seneschal,' the taller of the boys said, breaking the spell of her magical moment with cold practicality. 'Father doesn't mind people camping in the forest, provided he knows about it.'

Marqel slipped the shift over her head, patted the pocket to ensure that her coins were still there, then nodded at the boy who had spoken.

'We'll be moving to the common tomorrow.' Traditionally, on the day of the Festival and for the week following, anyone could camp on the common.

'And we'd best be getting back. Mother will flay us alive if we're late for dinner,' he added to the others.

'We should see Marqel safely home first,' Kirsh suggested.

The grey-eyed boy who had spoken shook his head. Marqel thought he must be one of the Duke of Elcast's sons. 'No, Kirsh, we shouldn't. Marqel will be perfectly safe here. We need to leave. Now.'

Kirsh looked as if he would argue the point, but the younger boy stared him down and reluctantly he gave in. 'Very well. Will you be all right, Marqel?'

'I'll be fine.'

'Perhaps we'll see you again? Tomorrow?'

'Tomorrow is the Landfall Festival, Kirsh,' Alenor reminded him.

'I will see you again, won't I?' Kirsh persisted as Alenor grabbed his arm and pulled him towards the road.

'I'm sure you will,' she replied with a smile. *At least you will if I have any say in the matter.*

'We really have to go . . .'

'Kirsh—' the duke's son warned.

'I know. Goodbye.'

The last she saw of him was the little princess leading him by the hand into the forest followed by the other two boys.

'Honestly, Kirsh, you have no sense at all sometimes,' the girl was telling him, sounding like a mother scolding an errant child. 'Don't you ever use your brains? Didn't you see her arm? She's a Landfall bastard . . .'

Marqel didn't hear the rest of it. They were too far away for Alenor's voice to reach her.

She didn't care anyway. She rubbed at the rope tattoo idly, and smiled. Perhaps it hadn't been such a bad day, after all.

22

Landfall Day dawned bright and hot, promising perfect weather and no chance that rain would force the Festival to be cancelled.

The common was at the back of the Keep, a vast open area of lush green grass cropped close by the goats that roamed it when it was not in use for public functions. It sloped down from the castle walls until it opened out into a broad flat area lined by the trees of the Duke's Forest on the far side. A line of wagons was camped on the other side of the park; the performers and merchants come to display their wares making their impromptu campsites. The tall wicker suns representing the twin suns of Ranadon were already set up, flanking a small stone altar. There were also long trestle tables being set up for the food that would be brought out later. Already, the mouthwatering aroma of roasting meat from the pits near the trees could be tasted on the breeze.

Dirk went riding with Kirsh, Alenor and Lanon to watch the preparations, but he could not enthuse himself about any of it. There was a solid post driven into the ground in front of each wicker structure representing the suns, and all he could think about was the unknown men who would be tied to those posts tonight, burned alive to keep the second sun shining overhead. The victims were not from Elcast, Dirk had been relieved to discover. They were two criminals named Hari and Linel, who Antonov had brought with him from Avacas.

Was the Age of Shadows so bad that it needed something as dreadful as human sacrifice to keep it at bay? Not according to Johan Thorn. Dirk still hadn't decided how he felt about the renegade king. Or even if he believed him.

'Race you to the trees!' Kirsh shouted, kicking his horse into a canter.

Kirsh rode like he did everything: magnificently. Lanon let out a whoop and chased after him. They headed for the tree line on the other side of the common, ploughing through the brightly coloured stalls being set up for the fair, and scattering anyone foolish enough to get in their way. A few angry merchants yelled at the boys as they thundered past, but the prince and the young lord ignored their curses and threats to report them to the duke. Alenor watched them, but she made no attempt to follow.

'When I am queen,' she said suddenly, 'I'm going to put an end to this.'

Dirk looked at her in surprise. 'But aren't you afraid that will bring back the Age of Shadows?'

'I don't care,' the princess said defiantly. 'I'll find a way to end it somehow.'

If Antonov had taken Alenor from her mother because he didn't like the way she was being raised, then he'd failed miserably to turn her to his cause. She wore a look of savage determination. For a fleeting moment, he saw the steel that lay hidden beneath the fragile shell. There was more of her uncle in Alenor than anybody suspected.

Dirk decided that it wasn't a good idea to mention it, though.

When they returned to the Keep, Balonan called Dirk over and informed him that Prince Antonov wished to see him in the Library. With a great deal of trepidation, Dirk made his way up the staircase. He didn't know why the Lion of Senet wanted to see him, and feared it was because the prince had learned of his visit with Johan Thorn. He knocked on the door and opened it hesitantly as the voice within called permission to enter.

'Ah, Dirk,' Antonov said pleasantly. 'Come in.'

'You wanted to see me, your highness?'

'I do. Come here, boy. Don't stand there by the door quaking in your boots. I'm not going to bite you.'

Antonov smiled at him and Dirk found himself relaxing. Perhaps nobody had discovered his secret visit after all. The guards on Johan Thorn's room had been Tovin Rill's men from the garrison in town. He'd arrived carrying several vials that contained what looked like herbal remedies, and the guards knew he was Helgin's apprentice. They hadn't thought to question his right to be there.

Dirk walked the length of the Library until he was only a few paces from the prince. Although a big, powerful man, Antonov was both charming and disarming when he chose. He was sitting at the end of the table with a large unopened book in front of him. Its cover appeared to be made of solid gold and it was encrusted with gems. Dirk tried very hard not to gape at it.

Antonov noticed the direction of his gaze and smiled even wider. 'You know what that is?'

'No, sir.'

'It is the *Book of Ranadon* – the original.'

'I've heard of it, sire. But I never thought to see it.'

The most prized possession of the Shadowdancers and, according to rumour, the true account of the High Priestess's visions of the Goddess, the *Book of Ranadon* was something of a legend. There were copies, but supposedly the original never left Avacas. The cover alone was worth more than Elcast Island.

It was probably *not* a good idea, however, to tell Antonov that Master Helgin considered the *Book of Ranadon* to be a 'load of lies, ignorance and gibberish not worth the parchment it was written on'. Or that his mother called it 'the Book of Rubbish'.

'Would you like to read it?'

'*Sir?*' Dirk asked in shock.

'You can read, can't you, Dirk? I'm assuming Helgin taught you that much.'

'Of course . . .' Something in Antonov's eyes made him fear for Helgin. 'He's an excellent physician, sire. He used to be at court on Kalarada.'

'*Used* to be, Dirk,' the prince pointed out. 'Don't you think he'd still be there if he was as good as you imagine?'

'I . . . don't really . . . well, I never really thought about it like that, your highness.'

Suddenly Antonov smiled again. 'Well, I suppose you wouldn't, would you? Come, boy. Let us see how good Master Helgin is. Read to me.'

He leaned forwards and opened the book, flicking through the gloriously illuminated pages until he came to the place he sought, and then turned the book to face Dirk.

'From here,' he ordered, pointing to a paragraph about halfway down the page.

Dirk picked up the heavy book, cleared his throat nervously and began to read.

'And so it was that after ten years of the Age of Shadows,

of droughts and famine, of bitter cold and cruel darkness, the Sundancer Belagren, pure of heart and purpose, was visited in a dream by the Goddess who revealed to her the Path of Light.

'"Go forth," the Goddess instructed Belagren in her vision. "Dance in the shadows and bring my people back to the light."

'And so Belagren became the first Shadowdancer. She gathered to her those who believed in her vision and then came to the people. She told them, "I have been shown the way to redemption!"

'No longer would Ranadon's days be filled with darkness. No longer would the ground shake with Her wrath, nor cold and hunger plague Ranadon's people. The seas would return; Her bounty would be plentiful once more.

'But there was a price to be paid before the Goddess would be satisfied that the people were ready to embrace Her truth once more. And the sacrifice was a terrible one. The Goddess demanded that a child of royal blood must be sacrificed to Her, at the ninth hour on the ninth day of Ezenor in the year ten thousand, two hundred and twenty-one. Then, and only then, would the Age of Shadows be banished.

'But some doubted the vision. The King of Dhevyn denied the truth, and others, fearing their sons would be chosen for the sacrifice, also declared the vision false. But the Shadowdancer's message was welcomed in the hearts of true believers, and it was left to Prince Antonov of Senet, Protector of Dhevyn and husband to Princess Analee of Damita, to embrace the Goddess and offer the life of his youngest son.'

Dirk hesitated for a moment. This was rather different from the version his mother had told him. He read on:

'But alas, Princess Analee did not share her husband's faith. She and her sister, the traitorous harlot Morna Provin, abandoned their children and fled to the Baenlands and the protection of the heretic Dhevynian king...' Dirk forced himself to maintain a steady tone. 'Enraged by the Heretic's attempts to prevent the return of the second sun, the Lion of Senet set out to vanquish the faithless Johan Thorn. The Dukes of Dhevyn who were still true to the faith flocked to his banner.

'The battle raged across the Kingdom of Dhevyn until the Heretic's forces were struck down by the righteous. Then, having successfully defeated the forces of darkness, on the ninth day of Ezenor in the year ten thousand, two hundred and twenty-one, high on a hill overlooking the perfidious king's defeated army, the Shadow Slayer performed the sacred rite and took the life of his own son.

'And behold, at that moment, the second sun appeared in the sky.

'The people threw themselves to the ground and prostrated themselves before the Goddess and her High Priestess, whose vision had proved true.

'From that day on, darkness was banished from Ranadon. The renegade king was deposed by the faithful, and his sister Rainan placed on the throne of Dhevyn. As a sign of her faith, the new Queen of Dhevyn asked that the Lion of Senet leave a force in Dhevyn to watch over her people, so that never more would her people bring the Goddess's wrath down on Ranadon by straying from the true faith.

'And so it was, that led by the High Priestess of the Shadowdancers and Prince Antonov's example, the people of Ranadon turned to the Goddess once more. And each day the darkness receded until, by virtue of the people's faith, it was banished completely.

'All the islands of Dhevyn and the land of Senet wept for the sacrifice of the young prince. Princess Analee, unable to live with the guilt of her faithlessness, took her own life . . .' Dirk's voice faltered and he glanced up at the prince. Antonov's eyes were closed, his face lined with pain.

'Shall I keep reading, sire?'

Antonov opened his eyes and stared at Dirk for a moment and then shook his head. 'That will do for now. You read very well.'

'Thank you, your highness.'

'But do you understand what you've read?'

'I think so, sir. The Princess Analee—'

'Your mother's older sister.'

'Mother never talks of her much.' She never mentioned that she'd abandoned Rees and fled Elcast to fight alongside an exiled king, either, but Dirk thought it unwise to bring that up.

'Do you understand now, why lives must be sacrificed on Landfall Night?'

'I could understand why one might be sacrificed, your highness. But why so many of them?'

Antonov's eyes clouded with annoyance. 'The life I sacrificed to the Goddess was a prince, Dirk. Are you suggesting that the life of one peasant is equal to that of a prince?'

Dirk shook his head. 'I suppose not, sire, but couldn't you just find one man conceived of royal blood and sacrifice him, and let the rest live? It seems such a waste.'

'A *waste*?'

'Well, sire, I know that the Landfall Festival is an old custom. But until . . . well until . . . *this* happened,' he said uncomfortably, pointing at the open book, 'until the Shadowdancers came along, nobody killed anyone. Not that I heard, anyway.'

The Lion of Senet grew dangerously still for a moment, studying Dirk with his intense golden eyes. Then he nodded, as if some terrible decision had been made.

'We will discuss this later, Dirk. In the meantime, I must speak to your father.'

Dirk knew he'd said something wrong, but couldn't work out exactly what. 'I didn't mean to offend you, your highness.'

Antonov smiled faintly. 'You did not offend me, Dirk. I appreciate your candour. You may go. I'm sure you need to change before the festivities this evening.'

Dirk bowed hastily and backed out of the room, worried about something he could not define.

His last glimpse of Antonov as he closed the door behind him was the prince opening the *Book of Ranadon,* stroking the pages with a faraway look, as though he were back once again on that hill overlooking Johan Thorn's decimated army, taking the life of his baby son.

23

The Landfall Festival got under way later that evening. Dirk walked down to the common with his parents. Prince Antonov, Tovin Rill, Kirsh, Alenor, Rees and Lanon walked with them, dressed in their best finery. With a fine gold coronet hidden among her dark curls, and a simple blue gown made of several layers of silk so fine they appeared transparent, Alenor looked quite grown up. His mother wore a green gown made of Necia silk. It was the same one she had worn to the Festival for the past three years. Dirk always thought of it as her Festival gown. It was the only time he ever saw her wearing it. He was wearing new clothes, but that had more to do with the rate at which he had grown this past year than any notion of extravagance on his mother's part. Kirsh and Prince Antonov wore expensive, hand-tooled, knee-high boots, white trousers trimmed with gold braid and short, heavily embroidered jackets that Alenor whispered were all the rage on Senet this year. Misha did not attend. He was too ill.

Once Prince Antonov had declared the Festival open, Dirk and Lanon were free to investigate the fair with Kirsh and Alenor. Duke Wallin, Tovin Rill, Duchess Morna and Prince Antonov moved among the people, smiling and talking and mixing with the population in a manner that was not possible on any other day of the year. The High Priestess was nowhere to be seen – presumably she was occupied with the upcoming ritual. Rees vanished from sight as soon as the formalities were over, looking for Faralan, youngest daughter of the Baron of Ionan and his bride-to-be as soon as she came of age. Kirsh took command of their little troop and led them in the direction of the food, determined to get the choicest cuts of the roasting bullocks. The smell was making Dirk's mouth water.

'You should see the Festival in Avacas,' Kirsh declared as the others hurried in his wake. 'We have fireworks, and acrobats and jugglers . . .'

'We have jugglers and acrobats, too,' Dirk pointed out.

'Not like the ones we have.'

Kirsh was not deliberately arrogant, Dirk decided. He just couldn't help noticing the difference between his life on the wealthy and powerful mainland and their much more modest lives on Elcast. 'What's wrong with them?'

'I didn't say they were bad. I just said ours were better.'

Lanon stopped walking and pointed to a shabby striped tent across the common where the acrobats were performing. 'Let's go see them then, and you can tell Dirk what's so grand about Senet's acrobats.'

Kirsh shrugged. 'Very well. Let's go watch for a while.'

He headed in the direction of the acrobats' tent, with the others on his heels. When they reached the entrance, he marched through the flap and pushed his way through the spectators to the stage. There was a juggler in the middle of his act tossing a number of brightly coloured clubs in the air to the tune of a vaguely familiar melody that a fat woman with several chins was belting out on a slightly off-tune flute. The juggler caught the clubs with a flourish and bowed extravagantly. The crowd applauded and a shower of copper coins flew over their heads to land on the stage.

'That was good,' Alenor said, a little defensively. Dirk wondered if she was defending the juggler or all Dhevynians in general. The fat woman noticed them with a shocked look, and leaned back to whisper something urgently through the curtain. Then she put down the flute and picked up a small drum and began to beat a complicated tattoo as a couple of stagehands began clearing the juggler's paraphernalia and the coins from the stage. The juggler turned to the fat woman in surprise. He looked rather irked by the sudden change in the programme.

'He was mediocre at best,' Kirsh scoffed. 'Last year the juggler was tossing flaming batons.'

Lanon grinned. 'Didn't the Prefect cut all his fingers off when he discovered he was a thief?'

'Well, he might have been a thief, but he was a good juggler. Until he lost his fingers, at any rate.'

The platform was cleared now and the juggler muttered unhappily as he left the stage. The girl from the pool near the Outlet walked out from behind the striped curtains at the back of the stage.

Dirk's eyes widened in surprise. She was the last person he expected to see here. He studied her closely for a moment, a thing he'd been too distracted to do yesterday when she emerged from the pool near the waterfall like some sort of water nymph.

Marqel was no older than him, he guessed. She was dressed in a long cape embroidered with intricate arcane symbols. This close to the stage, Dirk could see the edges of the cape were as frayed and shabby as the rest of the tent. Behind her walked one of the stagehands: a large, bearded, bare-chested man, whose oiled muscles glistened in the late afternoon light.

But it was Marqel who drew everyone's eye. Her hair hung down in a thick blond braid. Her face was proud, her sapphire eyes slanted slightly upward in a face that showed a hint of great beauty to come. She was not particularly tall, but as she shed the cloak, revealing a lithe, muscular body in the first bloom of womanhood, the crowd fell silent. She wore a thin, short shift that was only marginally less distracting than when he'd seen her wade dripping and shameless from the pool. Her long, finely muscled legs and arms were bare, and around her upper left arm was a red tattoo that looked like an intricate set of knots. A Landfall bastard.

He glanced at the young princess and was not surprised to see her scowling. With some strange, unfathomable female instinct, Alenor had taken an instant disliking to Marqel. Perhaps it was their adolescent chatter all the way back to the Keep yesterday as she hurried along beside three boys lost in a fantasy world of pubescent delight sparked by the sight of a stunning naked girl emerging from the water like a vision out of a storybook.

Dirk had noticed the effect their banter was having on Alenor, and had urged the others to silence, but they sat up talking long into the night, reliving the moment over and over again. Kirsh had said surprisingly little. He just sat there, staring off into space, as if lost in another world.

The tempo of the drum picked up and Marqel cart-wheeled across the stage. The muscular man stepped forward and she ran at him, stepping into his cupped hands. He thrust her upwards and she executed a faultless somersault, landing so lightly that, even as close as he was, Dirk could not hear her footfall. The crowd roared its appreciation as she stepped forward again.

This time her assistant lifted her onto his shoulders. She stood there for a moment, arms held wide, then bent down to grab the man's hands. She kicked up into a hand-stand as he stretched his arms above his head. He walked across the stage as she changed the position of her legs – first a split, then one leg bent – then she closed her legs and arched her back. Dirk watched her in awe, trying to figure out how she knew exactly what point to hold the counterbalanced handstand to maintain a position that looked impossible. The crowd was impressed. The sound of coins landing on the stage, many of them silver, acted as a strange counterpoint to the tattoo of the drum. Finally, the man lowered the girl and stepped back. She flipped across the stage, then back again, as another assistant stepped out.

The two men clasped their hands together, testing their grip, then nodded to the acrobat. She moved between them, stepping onto their locked arms. She tested her balance for a moment and nodded. The men threw her upwards and she somersaulted once, then landed on their clasped arms.

They immediately threw her up again, and again she somer-saulted, although this time she kept her body straight, rather than tucking in her knees. What came next left Dirk almost too dizzy to follow. Every time she landed, they would throw her up on the rebound, and every somersault was more complicated than the one preceding it. She turned and twisted. The crowd fell silent, wondering how long she could keep it up, wondering if she would miss the small landing platform the men's arms offered. Wondering if one of them would falter and let her fall.

Finally, she twisted so many times Dirk was unable to count them, and she landed, not on the locked arms of her assistants, but on the floor in front of them in a deep squat.

She straightened and held her arms wide, welcoming the adulation of the crowd. Dirk clapped as hard as the others, thinking that the only person he had ever met who seemed so arrogantly sure of himself was Kirshov.

Then the acrobat looked down at the front of the stage. She cast her eye over Dirk and Lanon without pausing. Alenor also received little more than her fleeting attention. But when her eyes alighted on Kirsh, she smiled. It lit her whole face. Dirk glanced at the young prince. His eyes were filled with wonder – and some other emotion that Dirk could not name. The prince and the acrobat stared at each other for a timeless moment, then she looked away, turning her attention back to her audience.

'Ladies and gentlemen! I give you Marqel the Magnificent!' the fat woman boomed.

Marqel turned and bowed again to the crowd. A shower of coins landed and the two assistants dropped to their hands and knees to gather up the loot. Kirsh dug into his belt and produced a purse, then beckoned Marqel to the front of the stage. When the fat woman with the drum nodded her permission, the girl stepped forward to accept his offering.

'You must come to Senet to perform!' Kirsh gushed. 'That was the most amazing thing I've ever seen. *You* are the most amazing thing I've ever seen.'

'It's not up to me, your highness,' Marqel replied. She

was breathless from her performance. Dirk wondered how she had learned who Kirsh was. He hadn't told her he was a prince yesterday by the pool. 'You would have to speak to Mistress Kalleen.'

She squatted down and reached for the purse, her hand lingering on Kirsh's for much longer than was necessary.

'I'll do better than that,' Kirsh promised, no more willing to release her hand than she was to let his go. 'I'll speak to my father. I'll see that you get his personal invitation.'

She smiled. 'Then I look forward to seeing you again, your highness.'

Then with a suddenness that shocked him, Marqel snatched the purse from Kirsh's hand and was gone before he could answer.

24

The fair was something of an anticlimax after that, although Kirsh did graciously admit that the Elcast acrobats were as good as anything one saw in Senet. In fact, he grew quite tiresome after a while. He ignored the other performers. He didn't want to dance to the music, or listen to the storytellers, or watch the animal acts. All he could talk about was Marqel the Magnificent.

'Marqel the Mercenary, if you ask me,' Alenor grumbled as Kirsh continued to rave about the young acrobat while they ate their dinner.

'What do you mean?'

They were sitting on the grass above the common under the castle walls, eating the juicy rare beef on bread trenchers they had finally managed to acquire through the press of hungry people. Rees had joined them and Kirsh and Lanon were giving him a blow-by-blow description of Marqel's act.

'You were there, Dirk,' Alenor reminded him. 'She was

looking for Kirsh. Didn't you see the way she smiled at him? She was probably waiting for us at the pool yesterday, too.'

'But how could she have known we'd be at the pool yesterday?' he asked, wondering if Alenor's distrust was simply jealousy in another guise. Alenor looked at Kirsh the same way Kirsh had looked at Marqel. 'And why would she bother?'

'Because foreign performers need a permit to work in Senet. The Guild won't let them in otherwise. If Kirsh arranges for his father to invite them to Avacas, then they automatically get their permit, and it won't cost them a single dorn. I'll bet you they were saving their best performance for when we arrived.'

'She was good, though.' Personally, he didn't see anything wrong with a little bit of entrepreneurial thinking.

'She's a Landfall bastard.'

'That's hardly her fault.'

Alenor smiled. 'Dirk, you always think the best of people, don't you?'

'Do I?'

'Yes. I think it makes you one of the nicest people I know.' She leaned forward and kissed his cheek and then ran off, leaving Dirk feeling rather bemused and more than a little pleased by her praise. Dirk would have followed her, but his mother chose that moment to arrive with Lady Faralan.

His brother's fiancée always visited at Landfall, and spent the next three months under the watchful eye of her future mother-in-law, learning the finer points of running a household as big as Elcast Keep.

Faralan was a pleasant enough young woman, blonde and comfortably plump, although to Dirk's mind she was a bit dim. Well, perhaps that was unfair. She was educated in things he cared nothing for. She appeared fond of Rees, and he of her, which was fortunate. She had been coming to Elcast since she was betrothed to Rees at thirteen, and Dirk considered her as much his sister as if she was already married to his brother. Consequently, he ignored her for the most part. She would one day be the Duchess of Elcast. He would be a physician, either here on Elcast, or on some other island. There had never seemed much point in getting close.

As Faralan and Duchess Morna drew nearer, Rees jumped to his feet. Faralan had been crying and his mother's expression was thunderous.

'Where is Alenor?' Lady Morna demanded.

'She went that way, my lady,' Kirsh volunteered. 'I'll fetch her if you like.'

'Thank you, Kirshov. I would like that very much.'

Kirsh, with Lanon on his heels, bolted in the same direction as Alenor had gone a few minutes before. Dirk found himself alone in the midst of a rather uncomfortable silence between his mother, his brother and the obviously distraught Faralan. Rees was studying his boots with great determination.

'You'd best be off, too, Rees,' his mother said icily. 'I wouldn't want you to keep his highness waiting.'

'Mother . . .'

'Just go, Rees. Don't make an issue of it.'

Rees looked at Faralan, reaching for her. She shook him off angrily. 'Don't touch me! I can't believe you're going to take part in this!' Dirk guessed her distress had more to do with the ritual orgy that would soon take place than the human sacrifice that preceded it. For that matter, Faralan might simply be annoyed that she was too young to take part. The Duke of Ionan made a lot of noise about being a faithful servant of the Goddess.

'Prince Antonov ordered me to, Faralan. I've no choice.'

Dirk tried to make himself as small as possible. He felt for his brother. Having been under the dangerously benign gaze of Prince Antonov, he knew exactly what Rees meant.

Suddenly, his mother seemed to notice him. But she wasn't angry, or even particularly concerned that he had overheard their disagreement. 'Dirk, would you escort Faralan back to the Keep, please?'

'Of course,' he agreed, jumping to his feet and brushing the crumbs from his trousers. Faralan spared her fiancé one last scathing glance before turning towards the castle with a sob.

Dirk had to run to keep up with her, but once he had delivered his future sister-in-law to the postern gate, which by Dirk's definition was still the Keep – albeit just barely – he bolted back the way he had come. He was much less concerned about Rees and whatever had upset Faralan than he was about spending time with Alenor. If he'd had his wits about him, he would have volunteered to fetch her before Kirsh did. The realisation gave him pause.

They're about to burn two men alive and all I can think about is spending time with Alenor. I'm as bad as they are.

When he arrived back at the place where they had eaten dinner, he discovered Rees was gone and Kirsh and Lanon yet to return with Alenor. Prince Antonov had arrived, though, and was talking to his mother. Something about the way his mother was standing, something about the set of her shoulders, made him hesitate. Dirk skidded to a halt and moved a little to the left, into the shadow of an early blooming hibiscus. It was rude to eavesdrop, he knew that, but in his experience it was also rather informative. Nobody ever said anything really interesting in the hearing of someone they still considered a child.

'You did this deliberately,' Morna was saying, in a low, angry voice. 'Why can't you just leave us alone?'

'Leave you alone to foment rebellion, Morna?'

'*Rebellion?* Don't make me laugh! What hope does a poor island like Elcast have to take on the likes of Senet? This has nothing to do with rebellion. This is your way of getting at me. Or are you doing this for Johan's benefit?'

'If it were not for your eternally patient and forgiving husband,' the prince warned softly, 'you would have been executed as a heretic years ago, Morna. As for Thorn, he'll get what's coming to him. He cannot escape my justice now.'

'Are you really brave enough to burn him, Anton? Do you really want to stir up all those old hatreds? Put Johan on public trial and you risk losing Dhevyn.'

'Don't try to glorify his deeds, Morna. Johan has long

passed the point of fighting for a cause. He's a criminal. Nothing but a miserable pirate eking out a hand-to-mouth existence in the Baenlands by theft. He'll be tried and burned as a thief, too, not a revolutionary. Nobody even remembers the reason he started on this path.'

'You remember though, don't you, Anton? He was your friend once. You betrayed him, like you betrayed Analee. How can you live with yourself after what you did?'

'I did what the Goddess asked of me.'

'You did what that evil bitch Belagren asked of you. And you still do her bidding. I hoped that when Rainan took the throne, we'd still have a ruler capable of defying you, but then I learned you'd taken poor Alenor hostage. You've made Rainan as powerless as the rest of us. So what will you do next? Marry Alenor to Kirsh? Yes, that would fit your plans very nicely, wouldn't it? He's cast in the same mould as his father.'

'If I didn't know how much the suicide of your sister pains you, Morna, I could have you condemned for voicing such sentiments.'

'Why bother, Anton, when you can hurt me so much more by making my sons take part in your sick rituals?'

'Ah, your sons. That would be the son you abandoned to follow a heretic and the son you've raised in ignorance of the Goddess's ways?'

'What do you mean by that?' Morna demanded fearfully.

Antonov didn't answer the question. He smiled coldly. 'How monstrous of me to do anything that might destroy the illusions your sons have about their mother. Actually, you've managed to impress me, Morna. How, in the name of the Goddess, did you manage to raise Dirk without him learning the truth about you?'

'You stay away from Dirk!' The fear in his mother's voice surprised Dirk.

'The boy has potential, Morna. I fear for him left under your influence.'

'My influence? As opposed to what, Anton? Your lover,

the High Priestess, whom you let dictate your every move? Or Paige Halyn, perhaps? Our esteemed spiritual leader who did nothing to prevent the rise of the Shadowdancers when he could have nipped their wicked cult in the bud during the Age of Shadows? His inaction is as much to blame as anything you or Belagren have done. The three of you are a trinity of evil, Anton.'

'And your gift for melodrama seems to have been honed by all these years in obscurity.' The prince smiled. He sounded quite reasonable. He was not angry. Not like Dirk's mother. 'Belagren wishes your children no harm, Morna. Your sons hold an honoured position in the eyes of the Goddess. They are the cousins of the child sacrificed to save Ranadon.'

'They are the nephews of the woman who killed herself rather than share the bed of the man who murdered her baby,' Morna hissed. 'Don't kid yourself that you are anything else, Anton.'

Before the prince could answer that charge, Kirsh and Lanon arrived with Alenor between them. Lanon and Alenor were rolling their eyes over something Kirsh had said. Apparently, he was still going on about the acrobat.

They stopped and stared at the prince and the duchess curiously, picking up some of the tension between the adults. Dirk thought it about time he made his presence known, before someone discovered him hiding in the bushes. He scuttled back a little way, then stood up and ran down the slope as if he had just come from the castle.

'Faralan is safely delivered, my lady,' he announced with forced cheerfulness.

'Thank you, Dirk.' She turned to the prince and bowed. 'And now, your highness, if you will excuse us, I will return to the castle with the children before the ... ritual begins.'

Antonov bowed in return, but there was a wry smile on his face that made Dirk wonder about him. His mother had accused him of some terrible things, but he seemed totally unconcerned.

'Can't I stay, Father?' Kirsh begged. 'Please?'

'When you've come of age, son,' Antonov promised. 'In the meantime, the Lady Morna has some . . . less stimulating . . . activities organised for your entertainment in the Keep. Go now. I'll see you in the morning.'

Kirsh had not seriously expected his father to let him stay, so he wasn't exactly overcome by disappointment when he was refused. But he had not forgotten his earlier promise to Marqel the Magnificent.

'Father, will you invite the acrobats to Avacas? They're very good. Really. I've never seen a better acrobat.'

'High praise indeed, from a connoisseur such as yourself.' Antonov smiled at the hope in Kirsh's eyes. 'I suppose that means you've already told them I will invite them? Well, I shall view their act for myself and if they're as good as you claim, I'll see to it they get their invitation. Now be off with you. Lady Morna should not be kept waiting.'

'Thank you, sir!' Kirsh called as he bolted up the hill.

Morna bowed wordlessly to the prince, her eyes burning with helpless anger. And then, with Dirk at her side, she turned and followed the young prince and his companions at a more dignified pace.

25

The music from the Festival carried on long into the night, making it impossible to sleep. At least for Dirk. Lanon and Kirsh were unconscious almost as soon as their heads hit the pillows. But Dirk had heard too much, learned too much, and too many things had happened in the past day to let him rest.

A timid knock at his door stopped him from tossing and turning. He slipped out of bed, careful not to disturb Eryk, Lanon or Kirsh, and padded barefoot to the door, opening it a fraction. Alenor was waiting outside, dressed in her nightgown. She placed a finger on her lips, warning him to silence, and beckoned him out. With a quick glance over his shoulder at Lanon and the sleeping prince, he slipped through the door. Alenor led him along the hall to the stairs and began to climb upwards. Dirk followed her curiously, not saying a word until they closed the door of the old observatory on the top floor behind them.

'Why are we up here?' he asked, his voice echoing in the vacant chamber. The circular observatory took up the entire top floor of the Keep, and had an onion-domed roof that was flaked and peeling with neglect. There had been a telescope here once, so Dirk had been told, before the Age of Shadows. He had never been able to discover what had happened to it.

'Don't you want to see what's going on down there?'

'I thought you didn't want anything to do with the Festival?'

'I don't,' she said, climbing onto the window seat. 'But I think *you* should see what's happening. Come on! They're about to start!'

Dirk hurried to her side and looked down over the common. In the distance he could see the wicker suns and around them a large crowd of adults gathered for the ceremony. He was too high up to make out individual figures. So high up, in fact, that it seemed pointless even being here. Then Alenor reached under her nightgown and produced a small brass tube.

He stared at the small instrument in awe.

'What's the matter? You look like you've seen a ghost.'

'That's a telescope!'

'How else are we going to see what's going on?'

'I thought all the telescopes were destroyed during the Age of Shadows.'

'They were. Belagren ordered them destroyed because she claims it was the people looking on the face of the Goddess that caused her to turn from us.'

'That makes no sense. We can look up and see the suns any time. Why would looking at them through a telescope make any difference?'

'I don't know. She says the heavens are the key to the Goddess's power.'

Dirk took the polished brass tube and examined it thoughtfully. 'Perhaps the High Priestess was afraid of what they might learn by studying the suns too closely. Where did you get this one, anyway?'

'It belongs to Prince Antonov.'

'But . . . how?'

Alenor shrugged. 'Just because a thing is banned doesn't mean it ceases to exist, Dirk. Look, there's your brother.'

Dirk placed the tube to his eye and aimed it at the scene below. It took a little getting used to, but in a moment the small figures came into focus. The people were masked now, although the masks were more decorative than an effective disguise. He could make out Rees's distinctive red coat and curly dark hair, even from this distance. The mask he wore covered only his eyes and formed the head of a bird. The beak protruded out over his nose and the feathers over the eyeholes glinted red in the ruby light of the evening sun. Rees stood a few paces from Tovin Rill and Prince Antonov, whose mask was made of gold-tipped white feathers that perfectly matched the gold embroidery on his white jacket.

The crowd had separated into two circles, men in the inner circle, women forming the outer, encircling the wicker suns and the altar, where a large bowl filled with dark liquid sat ready and waiting. The music changed tempo as it drifted up to them on the still night air – a primal beat that seemed to underscore the mood of the gathering. There were small silver cups being handed out by the Shadowdancers. One he recognised as the tall redhead, Ella Geon. The other was Olena Borne, who had also arrived with Antonov. Standing by the altar was the High Priestess, Belagren. Of the Sundancer Brahm, there was no sign.

Dirk adjusted the focus as the cups were passed along the line. He found Rees in the crowd again, watching as his brother took a sip then handed the cup on to the next man. He seemed to be swaying on his feet.

'What are they doing now?' Alenor asked.

'Handing out small cups to everyone,' he told her, without taking his eyes off the scene below.

'The Milk of the Goddess.'

Everyone was swaying now in time to the primal beat of the drums. Ella walked to the centre of the inner circle. He could see her lips move as she chanted something that he could not hear. Then a number of uniformed figures appeared, wearing the livery of Antonov's personal guard. They were holding two men, ragged and weak, between them. The soldiers hauled the prisoners across to the wicker suns and chained them to the posts. The lines of men and women swayed hypnotically, but the two men about to be sacrificed made no attempt to resist. Perhaps they were drugged. Dirk couldn't imagine he would allow himself to be dragged unresistingly to his own execution.

'Who are the men they're sacrificing?'

'I'm not sure,' Alenor shrugged beside him. 'I think they're Baenlanders. They were on the *Calliope* with us.'

'They're prisoners?'

'They always use convicted criminals. Prince Antonov says it saves the cost of an execution.'

And it explains why nobody objects too strenuously. Dirk lowered the glass and stared at her for a moment. 'If you've never been to a ritual, how do you know all this?'

'I pay attention.'

Dirk found her answer less than satisfactory, but he couldn't really think up a suitable retort, so he returned his gaze to the common.

Dirk caught sight of Belagren, who was now dressed in a long blue robe. She moved away from the altar, clutching a flaming torch in her hand.

The crowd swayed in time to the drums as she danced towards the man tied to the post in front of the largest sun. The people cried out, so loud that the faint sound reached Dirk and Alenor, high in the tower.

Belagren danced towards the second wicker sun, where the other emaciated Baenlander slumped against the post, his eyes dull. The crowd fell to their knees as the High

Priestess cried out something Dirk couldn't hear, then she touched the flaming torch to the dry kindling piled at the base of the sun. The wicker caught with a whoosh, the flames leaping upward. She then danced back to the second sun and set it alight, too. Dirk looked away hurriedly, afraid he was going to be sick. Then he forced himself to look back. For a moment, silence descended on the crowd, then a roar of approval rose up, drowning out the faint screams of the burning men.

Dirk turned his back on the scene, his stomach heaving. The shouts were so loud they could hear them in the tower. Alenor was watching him curiously. She seemed much more accepting than he was. But then, she'd been raised on the mainland. She probably saw this every year.

'Have you ever taken part?' he asked.

She shook her head. 'I'm too young.' Then she tried to snatch the telescope from him. 'That's why I wanted to see this one.'

Another shout from the crowd drew Dirk's attention. The wicker suns were well and truly ablaze now. They must have been treated with something flammable, as each sun burned a different colour. The smaller sun burned red, while the larger lit the red night with bright yellow flames. Dirk's stomach tightened as he watched in sick fascination as the flesh blackened and curled from the bones of the man chained to the closest pyre. In his mind, he could imagine the screams. As Helgin's assistant, he'd seen his share of blood and death, but nothing prepared him for the horror of watching a man burned alive. What made it worse was that the drugged and chanting crowd surrounding the dying men – the people close enough to taste the smell of charred flesh – seemed totally unmoved by what was going on before them.

Dirk moved the telescope a fraction. He could just make out the vague shapes of the other dying man as he thrashed against the chains that held him. As he watched, the man tied to the yellow sun slumped forward, dead, hopefully, or maybe overcome by the smoke. The other man seemed to remain conscious for a lot longer, screaming, burning . . .

Dear Goddess, what a way to die . . .

Then the inner circle began to dissolve. At some signal he didn't see, the men moved towards the altar to pay homage to the High Priestess. They bowed before her. She dipped her fingers in the bowl she held, smearing each man's face with the dark, sticky substance. He turned away from the sight, sickened to the core of his being. Alenor took the glass from him and trained it on the scene below.

Dirk closed his eyes, only to discover the image of the flaming men burned into his retina. 'I can't believe my father agreed to this.'

Alenor didn't answer him. She was transfixed on the sight below her, pale and shaking as she studied it through the telescope.

'What are they doing now?' he asked in a dull, lifeless voice.

'Marking themselves with the Blood of the Goddess . . . actually, I think it's only pig's blood, but it's the thought that counts.'

'That's disgusting, Alenor.'

'It's no worse than burning men alive.'

'I mean it's disgusting that you can joke about it.'

The drums throbbed like a heartbeat. Dirk turned to look down. Alenor reluctantly handed the glass back to him. The men and women, their faces streaked with blood now, began moving among each other until some instinct or signal that Dirk could not fathom seemed to take hold of them and suddenly a couple would peel away from the crowd and vanish into the trees. Other, less inhibited souls didn't even go that far. There seemed no order to their pairing, no conscious decision.

He caught sight of Rees being led away towards the trees by one of the Shadowdancers, although he couldn't tell which one. Then Dirk focused on Tovin Rill in time to see him put his arm around a young woman who looked suspiciously like Frena, the castle baker's daughter. With a frown, he watched them push through the crowd. Frena was a simple girl, just eighteen and madly in love with Mathi, the apprentice

blacksmith, if one believed castle gossip. She was not the sort
that the governor would notice. She was not even that pretty.

'Someone you know?'

He lowered the telescope and turned his back to the
window, wondering if Alenor had read his mind, or if it had
simply been the expression on his face that gave him away.

'Rees went with a Shadowdancer.'

'He's the heir to Elcast.'

Dirk wasn't sure why that was relevant. 'Tovin Rill's
gone with Frena, the baker's daughter.'

'Well, let's just pray that he doesn't get her with child,'
Alenor remarked rather callously. 'Another fatherless
Landfall bastard is the last thing Dhevyn needs.'

'The child isn't fatherless.'

'Tovin Rill won't remember who it was tomorrow and
neither will Frena.'

'But *I* know.'

'And who are you going to tell? You can hardly admit
you sneaked up here to take a peek, can you?'

He sighed heavily as he realised the truth of her words.
'Why did you want me to see this?'

'Do you think it's wrong?' she asked, instead of
answering him.

'What sort of question is that? Of course I think it's
wrong!'

Alenor nodded knowingly. 'You do now. One day you
won't. One day you'll be down there, cheering with everyone
else.'

'Never!' he declared vehemently.

The princess appeared unconvinced. 'You say that now,
but once you take part . . .' her voice trailed off for a moment.
'I've seen it happen time and again, Dirk. Antonov brings
the sons of Dhevyn's noble families to Avacas for the Landfall
Festival every year. And no matter how much they say they
won't take part, no matter how hard they protest, by the time
they leave Avacas, they're singing the praises of the Goddess
as loud as any Senetian. I thought . . . maybe you . . .'

'What?'

She shrugged. 'I don't know. I suppose I thought that if you knew what happened, before you taste the Milk of the Goddess, maybe . . .'

Dirk patted her arm comfortingly. 'Alenor, I would never take part in anything so barbaric.'

'It doesn't matter,' she sighed. 'The truth is, I'm not sure why I wanted you to see it. You won't tell on me, will you?'

'Do you really think Antonov would harm you?'

Alenor laughed, but it was a short, harsh laugh that sounded much too cynical from one so young. 'He slit his own son's throat, Dirk.'

There wasn't really an answer to that. He was silent for a long time.

'You seem to know an awful lot about what goes on in Avacas.'

'I'm a hostage, Dirk. It pays to know what's going on.'

'I'm sorry.'

'There's nothing to be sorry about. It's not your fault.'

'But at least Antonov doesn't treat you like a prisoner.' He smiled faintly. 'Neither does Kirsh.'

'That's because I'm still the heir to the throne of Dhevyn. The Lion of Senet got away with meddling in Dhevyn's royal succession once, but he doesn't want to push his luck by doing it again. Besides, he wants me to marry Kirsh one day.'

'Do *you* want to marry Kirsh?' Dirk asked.

Alenor shrugged.

'I don't think you should marry him.'

'Why not?'

'Because he's Senetian, for one thing. If you're going to be queen you should marry a Dhevynian.'

'You don't like Kirsh, do you?'

'Of course I like him. How can you not like him? That's what makes him so annoying. Is there anything he can't do well?'

'Use his head,' Alenor chuckled, with wisdom beyond her years. 'Even Prince Antonov says Kirsh thinks with his heart. He acts first and then worries about it later. *If* he worries at all.' She jumped down from the window seat and headed towards the door, her small bare feet leaving a trail of footprints across the dusty floor. 'Come on, we'd better get back before we're missed.'

'Alenor . . .'

'What?'

'I wish it was me instead of Kirsh going to join the Queen's Guard.'

His ears burning with embarrassment, Dirk looked away as soon as he had uttered the words. He felt incredibly foolish for making such an admission and could not imagine what had possessed him to blurt out such a stupid thing.

Alenor stopped and turned to look at him. He risked a glance, expecting ridicule. But she wasn't laughing at him. She stood there in the centre of the empty observatory, a small, fragile figure wearing nothing but a simple white nightgown and an invisible cloak of solemn dignity.

'Dirk, I wish you were going to be in my guard, too.' Then she smiled. 'I'd make you my Lord Marshal.'

'Kirsh will be the Lord Marshal of Dhevyn one day, Alenor. Anyone can see that.'

'Kirsh will be a hero, Dirk. He'll do great deeds, and kill pirates and defend my kingdom and they'll sing about him for generations to come. But if I ever need a tactician, I've a feeling you'd be the better choice.'

Dirk smiled. 'Even if you meant that, Alenor, what difference would it make? It's not like either of us has a choice in the matter, is it?'

26

Marqel the Magnificent was not feeling particularly magnificent this morning. She was stiff and sore from the performance last night and hadn't slept well, either. It had been quite a while since she had risked that particular act, and she really wasn't prepared for it.

It was all the fault of those brats from the castle. Originally, Kalleen had scheduled her performance for much later in the evening when the Prince of Senet might be in the audience, although Kalleen predicted that it was much more likely the sons of the noble families would view their act first. She'd instructed them about what to look for, so they would know the highborn when they saw them. They would be better dressed than most, and cleaner, she anticipated. Antonov's sons would probably be the best dressed of all. As Kalleen had delivered her lecture to them around the campfire last night, Marqel had almost bitten through her bottom lip to prevent giving away her secret.

'We watched the parade, Kalleen,' Lanatyne had reminded her. 'We know what they look like.'

Kirshov and his friends had turned up much earlier than expected, so Kalleen had cut Vonril's juggling act short and moved Marqel up. She'd had barely enough warning to get changed and she was on, with no warm-up, not even a moment to stretch, before she was hurling herself around a stage that was really too small for such a potentially dangerous act.

Still, the act had gone well, and best of all, her memories of yesterday had proved true. Kirsh had smiled at her again, the same way he had at the pool. She had even managed to keep back a few of the coins from the purse he handed her, before Kalleen got her grubby paws on it, and he had promised to speak to his father about getting them an invitation to perform in Senet. Kalleen had been so pleased about that, she barely even glanced at the purse.

Marqel turned stiffly on the narrow bunk in the wagon she shared with Lanatyne, smiling to herself. Prince Kirshov seemed thoroughly enchanted by her skill. He seemed thoroughly enchanted by her.

There had to be a way she could use that to her advantage.

The girl beside him with the superior air and suspicious

frown was, she knew, the Princess Alenor. Queen Rainan's only child, and heir to the throne of Dhevyn. What a tiny, insipid little thing she turned out to be. The other two boys were the sons of the Duke of Elcast and the Governor, Tovin Rill. One of them was supposed to be very bright, she'd heard rumoured in the town. Not that it really mattered. The only one that mattered was Kirshov, and he had been right at the front of the stage, clapping harder than anyone else, his eyes alight with excitement as he watched her perform. Somehow, that made the aches and pains worthwhile.

'Get up, you lazy slut! Kalleen wants her breakfast.'

She turned to find Lanatyne standing over her. The young woman's face was red and puffy, and she had a wonderful shiner blooming around her left eye. Marqel pushed herself up onto one elbow and stared at her curiously. 'What happened to you?'

'Some stupid pig thought my services were free last night.'

Marquel bit back a smile. Poor Lanatyne. She'd been an acrobat once, before she'd broken her ankle in a nasty fall. She still walked with a slight limp.

'Why did you bother to go at all? You knew you weren't going to get paid.'

'A Shadowdancer was sent to find unmarried women. Apparently, the numbers weren't even. You're lucky they didn't spot you.'

'I'm too young.'

'Take enough of that Milk of the Goddess shit, Marqel, and there's no such thing. You'll rut anything that moves when you're drunk on it. Still,' Lanatyne reached under her kirtle and produced a small dagger, 'I got this as a souvenir.'

Marqel gasped. The scabbard was gold and the hilt was set with a line of emeralds. When she withdrew the blade, it sparkled brilliantly, cut from a single vein of crystal. She'd heard about diamond-bladed weapons but had never thought to see one. They were extremely rare and restricted to the Senetian nobility, as a rule. It must have been worth a fortune.

'He gave you *that*?'

'Course he didn't *give* it to me, you silly bitch. I stole it. Actually, it wasn't from the one who did this,' she winced, pointing to the black eye. 'It was from some other chap. He'd been with one of them Shadowdancers, I think, and after she was done with him, she just left him there. Must have been his first time, I think. He was scratching at himself like he had the worst dose of lice you've ever seen.'

'Goddess! You didn't catch anything from him, did you?'

'I never lay with him, stupid. I just waited till he was dead to the world with a stupid grin on his face, sleeping it off in the woods like a baby with a belly full of mother's milk. Had a bright red jacket on, he did, like a bloody great signal fire. I mean, what else could I do?'

'You'd better hide it.'

Lanatyne nodded and slipped the dagger back under the pallet of the other bunk. Marqel wasn't referring to being caught by the authorities with such a valuable item, although she could imagine the blade's owner would be rather peeved by its loss. They both knew Kalleen would skin Lanatyne alive if she thought the young woman was holding out on her.

'Come on, you'd better get moving. Kalleen's in a good mood at the moment, but it won't last if you're late with her tea.'

'Why don't you get it, then?'

''Cause I'm tired. Unlike some people around here, I didn't get any sleep last night.'

'You think *I* did?' Marqel grumbled as she swung her legs to the floor. 'With all that drumming and panting and squealing and moaning going on?'

'Well, it wasn't me that was moaning. I wasn't getting paid for that.'

'You only moan if you're getting paid?' she asked.

'Let me give you a tip, Marqel. The amount of noise you make is in direct proportion to the amount they're paying you to make it.'

'They mustn't pay you much, then,' she chuckled. She spoke from experience. Lanatyne often brought her clients back to the wagon while Marqel was trying to sleep.

Lanatyne cuffed her under the ear for her cheek. 'You're a smart-mouthed little brat, you know that? It's going to get you into trouble someday.'

'It gets me into trouble now,' Marqel shrugged, stretching gingerly in the close confines of the covered wagon. 'Did you want some tea, too?'

Lanatyne sank down onto her bunk and smiled wearily. 'That'd be lovely, thanks.'

'Then get it yourself,' she replied, ducking the hairbrush that Lanatyne hurled at her as she nimbly fled the wagon.

The common looked like a battlefield when Marqel emerged into the early morning sunlight. The remnants of last night's festivities lay scattered over the field, along with more than a few sleeping bodies – too drunk, or perhaps too drugged, to make it back to their homes. The smaller sun had set and the second sun was shining brightly, casting long shadows over the burned-out framework of the wicker suns that loomed forlorn and forgotten on the damp grass. There was no trace of the men burned at the stake. Perhaps someone had taken their bones during the night. Or maybe they were there among the ashes, burned down to nothing in the heat of the ceremonial flames. Marqel barely glanced at them, turning her attention to the Keep instead.

What's it like up there? she wondered. *Are they up and about yet? Are they being served breakfast on silver platters by grovelling servants? Is Kirshov awake?*

No, he would be still abed. The nobility could sleep late if they wished. Getting up at dawn was a privilege of the lower classes.

She turned at the sound of someone crashing through the trees near the edge of the common. A young man stumbled into the light, blinking stupidly, as if he had no idea where he was. He wore a well-cut red jacket over stained leather trousers and one very expensive boot. There was no sign of the other one. She smiled, thinking this must be Lanatyne's unsuspecting victim. His face was streaked with several lines of dried blood and his shirt was torn. The young man ran his fingers through his dark curly hair, then stumbled and pitched forwards onto his face.

Marqel waited for a moment, wondering what he would do next. The young man lifted his head and tried to rise, then collapsed back onto the damp turf. He rolled onto his back with a groan, then hurriedly sat and proceeded to throw up everything he had eaten for the past week.

Serves him right, Marqel thought unsympathetically, as she turned towards the cook fire.

'Please . . . help me . . .'

She hesitated, wondering if she should ignore the pitiful plea. A part of her warned her to just keep walking. Another part of her was figuring out how much she could earn for aiding him. He looked vaguely familiar and was obviously rich, although if Lanatyne had been over him, he was unlikely to have any coin on him, or anything else of value, for that matter.

'Help you? How?'

'The Keep. Help me get back to the . . . up there . . .'

Marqel glanced in the direction of his pointing finger and smiled. 'Oh, *that* Keep, you mean?'

'I'll see you're rewarded.'

That was enough for Marqel. She walked over to where he was sitting on the grass and helped him to stand. He leaned against her heavily as he put his arm over her shoulder and they began to hobble across the common. The foot missing the boot looked swollen, and he couldn't put any weight on it. His silk shirt was shredded and there were deep scratches scoring his chest. He stank of vomit.

'You had an interesting night, didn't you?'

He grunted something in reply.

'My name's Marqel. What's yours?'

'Rees.'

'Just Rees?'

'Rees Provin . . . Can we stop for a moment?'

Marqel halted. He balanced his hand on her shoulder and took several deep breaths. Rees was sweating profusely and obviously in a great deal of pain. Whether it was from his swollen ankle or a hangover from the drug he had taken last night, she could not tell.

'Rees Provin, eh? The duke's son?'

He nodded, then winced. Apparently nodding was not a good idea in his present condition. She smiled encouragingly, already calculating her reward. It should be enough to get her out of trouble with Kalleen for not fetching her breakfast.

'I'm ready now,' he told her, bracing himself against her. They started off again towards the Keep, struggling as the ground sloped up to the base of the high stone wall. When they reached the steps cut into the hill, Rees had to hop from step to step. He was panting heavily as they made their way upwards.

They were almost to the gate when someone on the wall spotted them and cried out a warning to whoever was manning the gate. The postern gate flew open and two of the duke's guards ran down to aid them. They pushed Marqel out of the way and took Rees's weight between them, then hurried him up the steps, calling for help. Marqel followed determinedly behind. She had been promised a reward and she didn't plan to let his lordship out of her sight until she got it.

When they reached the gate, Rees was taken through and the guards tried to close it in her face. She ducked under the gateman's arm and slipped inside. Rees was already halfway across the courtyard. A tall, stern-looking woman in a long blue dress hurried down the steps of the main building with a cry of alarm, and began issuing orders to fetch water and someone called Master Helgin. Marqel began to panic. Her payment was slipping away from her, and fast.

'Hey! You promised me a reward if I helped you!'

Everyone in the courtyard stopped and stared at her. She realised how out of place she must look in her short shift, her bare legs tanned from hours under the twin suns, traveling from island to island, the rope tattoo visible for all to see. Her fair hair was loose and she had not bothered to brush it in her haste to avoid Lanatyne's missile. Amid all these oh-so-proper castle folk, she realised she must look like an escaped slave.

'She's right, Mother. I did promise,' Rees said, leaning for support against the guards who had helped him up the steps.

The duchess stared disapprovingly at Marqel for a moment, then beckoned a thin man forward. 'Balonan, see the child gets a reward. And find her something decent to wear. She shouldn't be out in public dressed like that.'

'Of course, my lady,' Balonan said, with a short bow.

That duty taken care of, the Duchess of Elcast turned back to her son as if Marqel no longer existed. Balonan crossed the yard and eyed her suspiciously.

'Come along, then,' he said, obviously displeased by the duty thrust upon him. 'I suppose you want food, too?'

'Money will do just fine, friend,' Marqel told him, anxious to be gone from this place.

'Money, eh? Mercenary little thing, aren't you?'

'Just trying to earn a living, friend.'

'My name is Seneschal Balonan, you impudent wretch, and I am not your friend.'

'Then give me my reward and I'll be gone,' she suggested.

Balonan reached into his waistcoat and pulled out a small purse. Before he could open it, Marqel snatched it from his hand.

'Don't bother to count it, this'll do. Thanks.'

She bolted for the gate and was gone from the castle before the startled Seneschal had a chance to object.

27

Belagren slept late the morning after the Landfall Festival. The second sun was high in the sky when she finally opened her eyes. She stretched languidly with a smile of intense satisfaction, then turned to study Antonov, who was still sleeping beside her. His face was peaceful, his chin shadowed by stubble that was beginning to show more signs of grey than blond these days, but he was still a strong, handsome man. She lightly trailed her fingers over his face, hoping not to wake him for a few moments longer, simply enjoying being in his bed once more.

It was where she belonged.

The Landfall Festival was the one night of the year when Belagren could be sure that Antonov would return to her. His faith was so profound that to spend the night with anyone other than the High Priestess would have bordered on sacrilege.

They were both too old now to simply fall into the bushes consumed by lust, so as soon as the formalities were over, she had led Antonov back to the Keep and the comfort of his rooms. Antonov was familiar with the Milk of the Goddess. He'd learned the hard way to take only enough to invoke its powerful aphrodisiac effects, and avoid the other, less pleasant consequences. What had followed was a night of exhausting passion that rivalled anything she had experienced before. Antonov had never been a particularly thoughtful lover, and under the influence of the Milk of the Goddess, he bordered on barbaric. She had bruises on her arms where he had held her down and the whole of the lower half of her body ached from the abuse he had inflicted on her.

Her smile widened as she thought of the first Landfall Feast when she had coaxed him back into her arms. It was not long after Analee had killed herself. The war was over by then and Johan had fled to the Baenlands. Antonov was still grieving the loss of his wife, although he was so convinced that the sacrifice of his youngest child had resulted in the return of the second sun, he never once questioned the baby's fate.

With inexplicable male logic, the man who had spent much of his married life cheating on his wife suddenly decided he should be faithful to her memory. And in some ways, Belagren had become the victim of her own propaganda. Antonov believed so deeply that she truly had spoken to the Goddess that ever since the return of the second sun he had been treating her as if she were a deity herself.

Neris was completely lost to the poppy-dust and becoming quite useless. He had discovered when the second sun would return, but he was so befuddled by the drugs Ella had pumped into him that he was incapable of remembering what day it was, let alone work out complex mathematical problems. And he was racked with guilt, thinking it was his fault that Antonov had killed his son. Hoping to distract him, Belagren had sent Neris north to Omaxin again with instructions to seal the tunnels into the building where they had learned the secrets of the ancients, then ordered him to retire to the small coastal town of Tolace with Ella, to work out the answers she needed.

What she hadn't known then, and didn't learn until much later, was that Neris had been in contact with Johan Thorn all through the war, and was in contact with him still. If she'd had any idea that Neris's guilt wasn't over the death of Antonov's son, but the whole damn War of the Shadows, she would never have let him near Omaxin again, and she certainly wouldn't have left him alone with Ella in Tolace, brooding about his part in the affair.

Looking for another, less dangerous way to control him, Ella had discovered the remarkable aphrodisiac effects of the golden mushrooms that sprouted everywhere during the Age of Shadows, effects that were enhanced a hundredfold when they were dried and powdered. Certain the only way she could get Antonov back to her bed was to make it an order direct from the Goddess, Belagren introduced the 'Milk of the Goddess' (Madalan thought up the name) to the ancient tradition of the Landfall Festival. As there was no way to drug Antonov without his knowledge, she simply served it to everyone present . . .

There were side effects, of course, as they discovered the following day. The rash that broke out had driven some people to terrible acts of self-mutilation, but it faded quickly, so quickly that many never realised what had happened to them.

After the success of the Milk of the Goddess at the Landfall Festival, Belagren had actively begun to recruit her own people outside the ranks of the Sundancers. She trained them in the use of the drug, and then sent them out to every Landfall Festival she could find, calling them Shadowdancers to differentiate them from Paige Halyn's Sundancers. Carefully selected, they were always young, beautiful, and often from the lower classes. Those young men and women, she knew, were prepared to do quite a bit to change their status in life. A surprising number even joined her because they truly believed they were doing the Goddess's work.

She smiled at Antonov's sleeping form, thinking what a great ally he had been. Belagren encouraged Antonov to invite the sons of his friends and enemies alike to Avacas, so that he could befriend them, and win them over to his cause – a thing he was able to do with the sheer force of his personality. For years now, the heirs of Dhevyn had arrived in Avacas, sullen and resentful. They had stayed for the Landfall Feast, then returned home ardent believers in both the Goddess and the beneficence of the Lion of Senet.

Slipping out of bed carefully, so as not to disturb Antonov, Belagren slipped her robe over her head. The days when she didn't care if he saw her naked in the cold light of the second sun were long past. She made a small detour to the garderobe before moving to the table to prepare a tonic to relieve the headache Antonov would be suffering when he woke. That was another unfortunate side effect of the Milk of the Goddess. It left one with a head that felt as if it had been cleaved in two.

She tapped the powder into a small amount of watered-down wine, then swirled the liquid around until it had completely dissolved. When she was satisfied that the tonic was ready, she moved back to the bed and sat down beside Antonov. Placing the cup on the table beside the bed, she leaned forward and gently kissed him awake.

'Goddess! My head feels like it's going to explode,' Antonov complained, before he even opened his eyes.

'Here, I've something that will help the pain.'

He stared at her through bleary eyes, accepted the cup and drank its contents down without hesitation, then flopped back against the pillows.

'That stuff tastes foul.'

'Of course it does,' she agreed with a smile. 'If it tasted pleasant, it wouldn't be nearly as effective.'

Antonov looked at her for a moment, then glanced down at her bruised arm. 'I hurt you.'

She shrugged. 'You could never hurt me, Anton.'

'I should be more careful.'

Leaning forward, she ran her finger lightly over his bare chest. 'Since when has the Lion of Senet ever worried about being careful?'

'You'd be surprised,' he replied, pushing her away and bringing himself up into a sitting position. 'Are you sure you're all right?'

'I'll live,' she assured him, hiding her anger at his rejection. The days when Antonov desired her were fading fast. Now it required the Milk of the Goddess and a night of religious fervour to coax him to bed. She forced herself to smile and added, 'Although, if you're feeling guilty about my pain, you could make it up to me.'

Antonov smiled knowingly. 'Let me guess? You want me to loan Wallin a fortune so he can rebuild your temple?'

'That would be a good start.'

'A start? What more can I give you?'

'I want Dirk Provin.'

Antonov stared at her for a long moment before he replied. 'Why?'

'I think it would be a nice gesture on Wallin and Morna's part to give their second son to the Goddess, don't you? It would certainly alleviate any concerns I have that they may have turned from the Goddess here on Elcast.'

Antonov's eyes narrowed suspiciously. 'Are you sure it's not just because I wouldn't let you execute Morna as a heretic after the war?'

'If I wanted to do anything so petty as seek revenge on

Morna Provin, Anton, I would ask for her first son, not her second. Besides, what difference will it make to Elcast? Rees is the Provin heir, and he's a healthy and capable young man. Wallin was letting the boy train as a physician, for the Goddess's sake! Dirk has no future here, but he's obviously a bright boy. Under my guidance, he could attend the university in Avacas and perhaps achieve his true potential. You have to agree that's not likely to happen if he stays here in Elcast under the tutelage of an old fool like Helgin.'

Antonov thought about it for a moment and then shrugged, apparently seeing no harm in the suggestion. 'I'll speak to Wallin about it.'

'Don't *speak* to him about it, Anton, demand it of him. The Goddess knows he owes you enough favours.'

'I'll not drag the boy away from his home against his will, Bela.'

'You didn't worry about that when you took Alenor from Kalarada.'

'Alenor is the heir to Dhevyn, my lady. Dirk Provin is the second son of a minor Dhevynian duke. It's hardly the same thing.'

'But you'll speak to Wallin, won't you?'

'I said I would.'

She nodded, having no choice but to accept his word. 'Yet again you prove yourself a devoted servant of the Goddess, your highness.'

Antonov smiled and leaned back against the pillows with a yawn. 'Then do you suppose you could do something about this devoted servant of the Goddess being fed? I'm ravenous.'

Belagren leaned forward and kissed him on the lips. Insatiable hunger was another of the side effects of the Milk of the Goddess. His kiss was perfunctory and disinterested.

'I'll have something sent up. Or did you want to eat in the Hall?'

'No, have it sent up.' He closed his eyes, stifling another yawn. 'I doubt there's much of anything going on downstairs at the moment.'

Belagren took the empty cup and rose to her feet. By

the time she reached the door to call for a servant, Antonov had drifted off to sleep again.

28

Rees's dramatic return, limping and bloodied, did nothing to lighten the tension that infused the Keep the morning after the Landfall Festival. His right ankle was badly sprained and he spent the rest of the day in bed, with Morna fussing over him, her mood swinging between compassion and anger without warning. The girl who had helped him back to the castle had been Marqel, the acrobat from the Festival, Dirk heard, but she was long gone by the time they arrived to see what all the fuss was about. Kirsh was quite put out when he heard that he'd missed her.

The prince's sudden and inexplicable obsession with Marqel the Magnificent was starting to wear on Dirk, so he sought out Frena, to find out how she fared. He was sorry he thought about it the moment he opened the door of the bakehouse.

Frena and her mother were alone, except for Lila Baystoke, the town's herb woman. Master Helgin tolerated her because she had a vast knowledge of herbs, and by providing her services in the town, she kept away the more trivial cases that otherwise would have demanded his attention. She was a small woman, thin and old. It was unusual to find her in the Keep so early in the morning. The rest of the bakers and apprentices had either made themselves scarce or had not returned to work yet. The air was stifling and heavy with the mouthwatering aroma of baking bread.

Frena stood in the centre of the bakehouse by the long scrubbed table, her whole body radiating misery. Her dress, no doubt her only finery, was dishevelled and stained, and even torn in several places. The light from the ovens behind her gave her uneven complexion a ruddy glow and tinted the tears on her cheeks. She looked as if she were crying tears of blood.

'Drink the damn thing!' Frena's mother was demanding impatiently.

'But it makes me sick!' Frena sobbed, clutching a small metal cup.

'It's supposed to make you sick, you foolish girl,' Lila snapped. 'Now take it and be done with it! The blood should start tomorrow and with luck, you'll be back to normal in a week or two.'

Welma was wringing her hands as she paced up and down the flagstones. 'I'll not have a Landfall bastard shaming this family!'

'I'm not having a baby!'

'You don't . . . Master Dirk!'

Dirk stepped away from the door and fully into the bake-house, fervently wishing he had thought to mind his own business.

'Mistress Welma. Lila.'

'Is there something you want, Master Dirk? The loaves will be a tad late this morning, what with everything that went on last night.' Welma was ranked low enough in the castle that she would not deliberately offend one of the duke's sons. She glanced at the herb woman for a moment and then turned her attention back to Dirk with a nervous smile.

'I . . . I thought I heard someone crying,' Dirk stammered, with no idea how to deal with such a situation. 'Is everything all right?'

'Nothing to bother a young lord, Master Dirk,' Lila assured him. 'Just silly girl troubles.'

'You run along, my lord,' Welma suggested nervously. 'I'll have the loaves brought up to the Hall as soon as they're out of the ovens, there's a good lad.'

'Is there nothing I can do to help?' he persisted. *Like telling you it was Tovin Rill who had your daughter last night?* he added silently. *Or perhaps telling you that the shit Lila is giving your daughter to stop her conceiving could just as easily*

kill her? Helgin had long suspected Lila of dealing in aborti-
facients, but until now, Dirk had never seen any proof of
it.

'It's good of you to offer, Master Dirk, but we'll be fine.
You run along now.'

Everything Dirk wanted to say was rolled up into a lump
of choked-up words that stuck in the back of his throat. He
nodded wordlessly and fled the bakehouse, praying silently
to the Goddess who had brought this terrible thing to his
home that Lila's herbal concoctions worked, that Frena
survived it and that no child would ever come of such an ill-
begotten union.

Dinner that night was tense. Rees was recovered enough to
hobble to the table and sat beside Faralan, refusing to look
at anyone. Between Rees and his father were three empty
places at the High Table when Dirk arrived. Dirk had been
relegated to another table since Prince Antonov and his
entourage arrived, to sit with Kirsh, Lanon and Alenor.

Wallin's expression was carefully guarded, torn as he
was between the prince and his wife. Dirk felt for his father.
Prince Antonov was the most powerful man in Senet, and
in Dhevyn, too. Although Antonov had demanded nothing
of Wallin other than that he follow the letter of the law, the
Landfall Festival was a vile custom, and to obey Antonov,
he had defied the express wishes of his wife. Any man on
Elcast would know what a foolish thing that was.

Morna made no attempt to hide her fury. Rees's condition on his return to the Keep had done nothing but add fuel
to an already simmering fire. Even Kirsh was uncharacteristically quiet. Alenor sat beside him, her brown eyes wide
and nervous as the tension emanating from the High Table
affected everyone in the Hall.

Just when Dirk was certain the atmosphere could get
no worse, the Shadowdancers walked down the stairs to join
them.

Since arriving on Elcast, the High Priestess and her

minions (as his mother referred to them) had kept largely to themselves. Belagren was busy making plans for a new temple, but she had not shared the details with anyone yet. This was the first meal they had attended in several days. Leading the way was the High Priestess. Behind her walked Ella Geon, Misha's nurse, and Olena Borne, the other Shadowdancer, who was shorter and more voluptuous than her companion, with long brown hair and a look of smug superiority. Behind the women walked Elcast's own Sundancer. Brahm Halyn wore the yellow robes of his sect and looked decidedly out of place next to the Shadowdancers. He was short, thin and walked with a limp, his dark hair untidy and streaked with grey. The Shadowdancers wore sleeveless gowns of soft red silk, gathered under the breast and caught by a thin band of gold braid. Only the youngest, Dirk noticed, was marked with the rope tattoo.

Prince Antonov and Tovin Rill rose to greet the Shadowdancers. After a moment's hesitation, Wallin and Rees followed suit and, after a long and painful silence, so did Faralan and Morna.

'Stand up,' Kirsh hissed to Dirk as he climbed to his feet. Alenor and Lanon were already standing. They did not need to be told, Dirk thought, looking around the Hall as everybody else began to do the same. He watched the Shadowdancers and the Sundancer walk down the long Hall, then glanced at his mother. Her expression was one of helpless rage.

When they reached the High Table, Belagren bowed respectfully to Antonov. 'Your highness.'

'My lady. Won't you join us?'

'Thank you, your highness.' She turned to Wallin. 'You honour us at your table, my lord.'

Wallin bowed in acknowledgement of the greeting, but did not offer a reply. Anything he said would get him into trouble, Dirk reasoned, either with Antonov or Morna.

Belagren hesitated before moving to take her place. 'May I request an indulgence before we eat, my lord?'

'Certainly, my lady.'

'May I speak with our newest recruit?'

'Recruit?'

'Your second son, my lord. Surely, you're aware by now that Prince Antonov has suggested he be taken into the service of the Goddess?'

Morna let out a small cry of anguish, then clamped her hand over her mouth in horror. Dirk looked about him, uncomfortably aware that every eye in the Hall was suddenly turned to him. Since when had he been recruited into the Goddess's service? His father spared him an apologetic glance and beckoned him forward. With a great deal of reluctance, Dirk did as his father bid.

Belagren turned and studied him as he approached, nodding approvingly. 'I hear great things about you, Master Provin.'

'Thank you, my lady.'

'I hear you are much advanced in your studies. Well beyond what one would expect in one so young, particularly in the area of mathematics.' She threw Morna an accusing glare. 'Although I hear other areas of your education have been sadly neglected. Would you do something for me?'

'If I can, my lady.'

'Very well.' The High Priestess thought for a moment then glanced around the Hall until her eyes alighted on the physician. 'Master Helgin. I will give Dirk a problem to solve. You will solve it also, so that we might check the veracity of his answer.'

Master Helgin warily nodded his agreement as Belagren turned back to Dirk with a smile.

'Let me see . . . how about this: a wagon is stopped on the side of the road. You make a chalk mark on both a front wheel and a rear wheel. How far will the wagon travel before both chalk marks return to their initial position at the same time?'

'I couldn't say, my lady.'

'The problem is beyond you?'

'Well, I would need to know the size of the wheels. Without that, an accurate calculation is impossible.'

He caught a glimpse of his father smiling at his response. Belagren looked rather annoyed. 'Very well, then, assume that the front wheels are three and a half feet across and the back wheels measure...' She shrugged and looked up at Prince Antonov.

'Four and a quarter feet...' the prince supplied with a grin. 'Let's not make it too easy for him.'

Dirk closed his eyes for a moment as he worked the problem out in his head. Then he opened them and looked at the High Priestess.

'Well?' she demanded impatiently.

'One hundred and eighty-seven feet.'

The High Priestess looked to Master Helgin, who was still working out the problem on a scrap of parchment. He scribbled frantically for a few moments as the Hall waited in expectant silence, then looked up.

'Is he right?'

'Not exactly, my lady.'

Belagren turned to Dirk with a disappointed frown. 'Seems you're not as clever as everyone thinks, young Dirk. Or is Master Helgin wrong?'

Dirk shrugged helplessly. 'I guess I'm not as smart as everyone thinks.'

'No, he's not wrong,' Master Helgin called out, checking his calculations again.

Dirk glared at the physician. Of all the people in the Hall he thought he could trust to keep his big mouth shut, Helgin should have been at the top of the list.

'Make up your mind, Helgin,' Antonov snapped. He, too, looked rather disappointed that Dirk had not come up with the correct answer.

'The correct answer is one hundred and eighty-six point nine two feet.'

Antonov looked at Dirk curiously. 'Is that right?'

Dirk shrugged. 'I rounded it up.'

Anton was silent for a moment, then suddenly roared with laughter. 'What do you think, my lady?'

'I'll have to test him further, but he seems bright enough,'

Belagren agreed. There was a gleam in her eye that was almost . . . predatory?

'What say you, Dirk Provin? Do you enjoy learning?'

'Very much, my lady,' he answered cautiously.

'Would you enjoy an opportunity to further your studies? To work under some of the best tutors in the world?'

'Where would I have to go to do that, my lady?'

'The Hall of Shadows.'

'*No!*' Morna cried, leaping to her feet. 'You can't take my son!'

Belagren looked up at Morna. Was there a hint of spite in her smile? A touch of vengeance, perhaps? 'My lady, the ability your son displays is extremely uncommon. It is obvious that the Goddess has chosen him.'

'He hasn't been chosen by the Goddess,' Morna cried scornfully. '*You* chose him.' She turned to the prince, unable to hide her distress. 'Is this your way of repaying our hospitality? We open our home to you, and you reward us by stealing my son?'

'With a mind so rare, one must not leave it to be damaged by those who would adversely influence it,' Antonov replied, firmly on the side of the High Priestess. 'Your son is blessed by the Goddess, my lady. I deem it prudent to remove Dirk to a more devout environment. I'll not leave him in your care so that his mind can be poisoned.'

Wallin had to physically restrain Morna, who looked set to leap across the table and claw Antonov's eyes out.

'And what happened to the last great mind you discovered?' Morna demanded. 'Look what you did to Neris Veran! You'll not destroy my son the same way you did that poor—'

'This is not the place to discuss Neris, or Dirk,' Wallin warned, holding Morna tightly. 'I beg you, your highness, may we discuss this later? When we're alone?'

Antonov glanced around the Hall, as if he'd only just noticed the people standing there, silently watching them. He nodded. 'That would be best, I think. Perhaps your wife would prefer to eat in her rooms?'

Morna shook herself free of Wallin and drew herself up proudly. 'Don't speak about me as if I'm not here, Antonov. And yes, I would prefer to eat in my rooms. I'll not share a meal with *her*,' she declared, pointing an accusing finger at Belagren, 'or with a man as duplicitous as you.'

Morna left the table and strode the length of the Hall towards the stairs with her head held high. Dirk watched her leave, wishing he could run after her. He knew there was nothing he could do to ease his mother's pain, but he wanted to hug her, to tell her that it would be all right. He wanted to tell her that Alenor had promised to put an end to all this when she was queen. And he was curious about Neris Veran. Dirk had never heard of him before, but his fate, whatever it was, obviously distressed his mother.

'How about some music, Wallin?' Antonov said, in the dreadful silence that followed the departure of the duchess. Wallin nodded and waved to the musicians in the corner. They began to play, but it was a quiet melody, more suited to a funeral than a dinner. Belagren reached forward and placed her hand on Dirk's shoulder. Her grip was like a vice.

'As there seems to be room at the High Table now, why don't you join us, Dirk?'

'Excellent idea,' Antonov agreed, before his father could object.

With a great deal of reluctance, Dirk took his mother's place between the younger Shadowdancer, Olena, and Rees. Belagren sat next to his father and Ella next to Tovin Rill. Rees would not look at him, although Faralan spared him a sympathetic smile. He looked down at the table where Kirsh, Lanon and Alenor were watching the proceedings with interest, wishing he was with them, rather than stuck up here for all to gawk at.

Dirk was served his meal and ate it mechanically, not tasting a bite. Rees pushed the food around his plate with determination and said nothing. The Shadowdancer Olena paid him no attention, either, too engrossed in whatever the prince was saying. Dirk wished the meal were over.

'Rees!' Antonov called suddenly, jerking his brother out

of his miserable silence. 'Show the Shadowdancers my Landfall gift.' He smiled and added to Tovin Rill, 'I had it made for Misha, actually, but I thought young Rees might have more use for it.'

Rees nodded, and reached down to his belt. Not finding what he was looking for, he glanced up with a curse.

'Damn!' Dirk heard him mutter.

'You've not lost it already, have you, Rees?'

'What did you give him, your highness?' Olena asked.

'A diamond-bladed dagger,' Antonov told her. 'Cost a small fortune, too, so you'd better not have lost it, young Rees.'

'No, sire,' Rees said. 'I haven't lost it. That urchin . . . the one that helped me back to the Keep. I think she stole it.'

29

Reithan's sloop, the *Wanderer,* was painted dark red. In the bright light of the second sun, it seemed an odd colour for a ship used primarily for smuggling. But at night, when the first sun bathed Ranadon in light that turned the sea the colour of blood, it was almost impossible to see the small, sleek sailing boat. As the sun began to change the colour of the sky, Tia climbed up the companion ladder balancing the bowls she carried in one hand. She clambered inelegantly over the deck towards the stern where Reithan sat, steering the small boat with his bare foot resting on the tiller.

He smiled when he saw her. 'Ah, this is the life. I forgot how nice it is to have someone else do the cooking.'

She handed him his dinner. 'Well, don't get too used to it. It's your turn tomorrow.'

'By tomorrow we should be in Kalarada,' he told her,

examining the contents of his bowl rather suspiciously. 'What is this?'

'Stew.'

'Stewed *what* exactly?'

'It's a surprise.'

Shaking his head doubtfully, he dipped his fingers into the bowl and picked up a piece of meat. He chewed on it for a moment and then grimaced. 'You found my old boots, didn't you?'

'If you don't like it, you shouldn't keep asking me to cook.' She shrugged.

'It's my duty as your friend to ensure you have all the skills required to make some poor, unsuspecting sod a good wife one day.'

Tia pulled a face at him. 'Don't waste your time. I'm not going to marry anyone. Not ever.'

'You say that now,' Reithan agreed sagely. 'But one day, some young stud with more balls than brains will sweep you off your feet. Then you'll be singing a different tune.'

'I know plenty of young studs with more balls than brains,' she told him. 'Mil is full of them. Perhaps if I ever meet someone with more brains than balls I might change my mind, but I doubt it.'

'How did you ever become such a cynic at your age, Tia?'

She shrugged. 'I don't know. Maybe it comes from hanging around with people like you.'

Reithan smiled and kept eating. Tia ate her own meal doggedly, determined not to let Reithan know she thought it tasted *exactly* like stewed old boots. It was supposed to be pork.

'How do we sneak into Kalarada?' she asked, as she chewed on a piece of meat that would probably take several days to digest.

'We're not sneaking anywhere. I don't think there's a customs official in Dhevyn that the Brotherhood doesn't own.'

The Brotherhood was a strange organisation to pin

down, Tia knew. Elusive and secretive, they had flourished since the return of the Age of Light, and spread their tentacles into Senet as well, until they effectively controlled all crime in both countries. The fugitives in Mil were forced to deal with them on a regular basis. Nobody else had the network of contacts to dispose of the goods they acquired raiding ships in the Bandera Straits. And nobody else was willing to pay what the Brotherhood could pay for their shipments of illicit poppy-dust.

'So we have to bribe someone?' she asked, knowing that all dealings with the Brotherhood came at a price.

Reithan shook his head. 'Not this time. We're expected.'

'And then what?'

'We'll meet with Videon, hand over the merchandise and collect our money. But before that, we have to go shopping.'

'For what?'

'To buy you a dress.'

'Why?'

'Because we need to speak to Alexin.'

'What has speaking to Alexin got to do with buying me a dress?' Tia had a feeling this was another part of Reithan's devious making-Tia-into-a-good-wife plan.

He sighed patiently. 'The easiest and least suspicious way of making contact with Alexin is for you to do it. I can't send you into a tavern full of Queen's Guards dressed like a damn pirate, Tia, so you're going to have to be very brave and wear a dress.'

'Why can't we just send him a message or something? Tell him to meet us somewhere?'

'We are. And you're the messenger.'

'But why me?'

'You're cheap,' he told her with a grin, then added hastily, 'and I trust you.'

'You're lucky you added that last bit,' she said.

Reithan adjusted the tiller a fraction before he answered her. 'Seriously, Tia, it's dangerous for Alexin to have any contact with us, even when he's at home on Grannon Rock.

On Kalarada, it's suicidal. I don't want to do anything that is likely to throw suspicion on him.'

'How do you know you can trust him?'

'He's my cousin.'

'You're related to half the damn noble families of Dhevyn, Reithan, and most of them would sell you to the Lion of Senet for the price of a good sniff of brandy. If you don't believe me, just ask Johan what family ties among the nobility are worth.'

'Alexin won't betray us.'

'He'd better not,' she warned.

He studied her for a moment in the changing light. 'I'm starting to wonder if it was such a good idea to let you come.'

'Why?'

'The object of this little adventure is to find out where Johan is being held prisoner, Tia. It's not to get revenge. You do understand that, don't you?'

'Yes.'

'Good. Because if you start acting like some dread avenger, I'll tie you up, throw you below, and leave you there until this is done.'

Tia tossed the rest of her meal overboard and met Reithan's eye. 'I promise I won't do anything that will endanger you or me. Or even your damn cousin.'

'Good girl.'

'Can I ask you something, though? About Alexin?'

'Sure.'

'*Why* is he helping us? His father sold out to Senet, left your father to die and then took his lands *and* his title.'

Reithan shrugged. 'I guess he feels guilty about it.'

'You *guess*? If we're trusting our lives to this man, shouldn't you be a little more certain of his motives?'

'All right, if it makes you happy, I *know* that's what he thinks. A lot of the Queen's Guard feel the same way.'

'Then why don't they do something about it?'

'I'm sure they would, given half a chance, but with the heir to Dhevyn's throne a hostage in Avacas, they're not going to do anything to incur the wrath of Senet.'

Tia was silent for a moment. 'Do you remember your father, Reithan?'

'A little,' he admitted. 'The last time I saw him I was only about nine. It was just before he and Johan left for the last battle.'

'And he never came back.'

Reithan shook his head. 'I remember when Johan came back, though. There were so few of them that escaped. It seems like the only sound I heard for days afterwards was women wailing with grief.'

'I don't remember any of it.'

'You weren't there. In fact, I don't think you were even born yet. Johan didn't bring you to Mil until much later.'

'I don't remember that, either. Not coming to Mil, or leaving the Hall of the Shadows. Not even my mother.'

Reithan smiled. 'Trust me, I don't think that's any great loss.'

'I wonder what I'd do if I ever met her?' she mused.

'Well, as she's currently a member of the Lion of Senet's household, let's pray that happy circumstance never arises.'

'Do you think Johan is with Morna Provin?'

'Do you think you could stay on the same subject for more than three sentences?'

Tia grinned at him. 'My father says that the ability to discuss multiple subjects simultaneously is a sign of great intelligence.'

'He also says that the walls talk to him,' he reminded her.

Tia decided she couldn't win that argument, so she was better off not pursuing it. 'You didn't answer my question. Do you think he's with Morna Provin?'

'If he's on Elcast, he might be.'

'Do you think he still loves her?'

'How should I know?'

'You're his friend.'

'I'm also his stepson, Tia. If he's still in love with Morna Provin, he's not likely to confide that fact to the son of the woman he's now married to.'

'Do you mind that he married your mother?'

'No. Why should I?'

'I don't know. I just thought maybe you . . . I just wondered, that's all.'

Reithan was silent for a moment before he answered. 'I don't think Lexie loves Johan the same way she did my father, any more than Johan loves her the way he once loved Morna. But they're happy together and they have Mellie.'

'I don't think Morna Provin really loved Johan.'

'How would you know?'

'Well, didn't she give Wallin Provin another son less than a year after she left Johan? That's not the action of a woman pining away for her lost lover.'

'You, of all people, should know how little love has to do with producing a child.'

Tia didn't really feel the need to be reminded of that right now. 'I still don't think she loved him. She'd never have left him if she did.'

'You know, for someone who professes to be such a hard-hearted cynic, when it comes to matters of the heart, you spend an inordinate amount of time dwelling on other people's love affairs.'

'I don't *dwell* on them. I'm just curious, that's all.'

'You need to fall in love a few times, my girl. Then you won't need to worry about what everyone else is up to.'

'Have you ever been in love?'

Reithan wiped his plate clean and handed it to her. 'At least eight times, the last time I counted. Happens to me frequently.'

'So how come you never married any of them?'

'Because if I get married, the next thing you know, I'll have children. With my luck I'd have a daughter who grows up to be just like you, and being forced to deal with two Tia Verans in the same lifetime is more than any man should be asked to bear.'

30

With the prospect of an invitation to Senet, it was a happy troupe that gathered around the cook fire on the common once the larger sun had set and the smaller red sun had taken its place. Kalleen was in a rare mood. Not only had Marqel extracted a promise from the young Prince of Senet for an invitation, but her quick thinking had earned them another purse and no doubt a great deal more gratitude.

It had been a good Festival all round, Kalleen declared, blithely ignoring the fact that she had sold Marqel not long ago, claiming they were on the verge of destitution. But with the arrival of the Senetian ship and the unusually generous crowds, things were definitely looking up. The purses Marqel had received from Prince Kirshov and then the seneschal at the castle were an unexpected bonus and now, best of all, they were on their way to Senet. The takings in Avacas would be ten times what they could earn on a small island like Elcast. Even Lanatyne, despite the black eye, agreed that things couldn't have gone much better.

Marqel was enjoying the rare circumstance of being the centre of attention and basking in it. She earned the appreciation of her audiences easily enough, but as the youngest member of the troupe, and an orphaned Landfall bastard to boot, whenever the troupe turned their collective attention towards her, it usually meant she was in trouble.

'We'll get a bigger marquee when we get to Avacas,' Kalleen announced, as she closed the lid and locked the small trunk where she kept their earnings. She tucked the trunk under her stool and moved her bulk around to a more comfortable position. 'One with a proper roof. And new costumes, too.'

'And some new equipment,' Vonril added. 'I'll be

laughed off the stage in Avacas juggling wooden balls and batons. The audiences there expect much more.'

'Then you'd better start practising,' Lanatyne laughed. 'They'll probably expect you to catch them once in a while, too.'

Vonril scowled at the young woman. 'Then you'd better hone *your* skills, whore. The men in Senet will no doubt expect you to *move* underneath them, once in a while.'

'When I'm under a real man, I *do* move,' Lanatyne retorted with a lewd wriggle.

Marqel joined in the laughter at the expression on Vonril's face.

'Now there's a thing, Vonril,' Sooter chuckled. 'Maybe when we get to Senet, you can earn enough to pay someone to pretend they like you.'

The roustabout laughed uproariously at his own joke. The others joined in, but Kalleen was starting to look annoyed. Vonril couldn't see the funny side of it at all. He jumped to his feet, his thin face crimson with embarrassment.

'You just mind your mouth, pig!' he warned. 'Bully boys like you and your friend Murry there are a penny a packet in Avacas.'

'We're not in Senet yet,' Murry pointed out.

'Not quite,' Kalleen remarked with a grin, pointing across the common. A troop of horsemen approached from the direction of the Keep. Riding in the lead was the distinctive figure of the Lion of Senet.

'I don't believe it!' Lanatyne laughed delightedly. Sooter helped Kalleen to her feet as Murry grabbed the trunk and shoved it into the nearest wagon. Lanatyne smoothed down her skirts, then turned to Marqel and made a futile attempt to tidy her hair. Marqel shook her off impatiently as they lined up to wait for the Lion of Senet to arrive.

Antonov came with a full escort. Rees Provin rode on his right, his bandaged foot sitting gingerly in the stirrup. Kalleen stepped forward and curtsied as low as her bulk would allow.

'Your highness. You do us a great honour.'

Prince Antonov cast his unsmiling gaze over their small troupe. He did not answer Kalleen. Instead, he turned to the captain of his guard.

'Search the wagons.'

The soldiers dismounted, spread through the camp and began to tear the wagons apart. Kalleen wailed in protest as they threw out bedding, clothes, pots and pans, even Vonril's juggling batons. Marqel watched them in shock, wondering what had brought about this sudden turn of events. She looked at Rees, hoping perhaps that he would remember her, but his face was grim and he would not meet her eye.

'You can't do this!' Kalleen cried, clutching at the prince's stirrup. 'What's this about? We've done nothing!'

'Sire!'

Antonov ignored Kalleen and turned to the soldier who had called him. The man was standing on the back of the wagon she shared with Lanatyne. He jumped down to the ground and walked across the small camp to the prince. In one hand was the diamond-bladed dagger Lanatyne had stolen in the woods from the unconscious Rees Provin. In the other was Marqel's secret hoard. She paled at the sight of it. Not only would she lose it now, but Kalleen would more than likely beat her senseless for holding out on her.

The prince examined the knife, then glanced at Marqel. 'Is that the girl?'

'Yes, sire,' Rees agreed tonelessly.

'Arrest her.'

Two of the soldiers grabbed Marqel and dragged her over to stand before the Lion of Senet. She squealed in protest as she struggled against them, glancing over her shoulder at Lanatyne, who looked at her stonily. She made no move to speak up on Marqel's behalf.

'There's been some sort of misunderstanding, your highness,' Kalleen said hurriedly, staring at the dagger. Marqel could see she was fuming, but she suspected it had more to do with their rapidly fading chance to get their permit for Senet, than Marqel's fate. 'If the young lord has his property back, then no harm is done. I'll see the girl is whipped for her dishonesty.'

Kalleen meant it, too. She would beat Marqel within an inch of her life for this.

Antonov looked down at Kalleen with contempt. 'You have until the morning to be gone from Elcast. And I promise you, it will be the next Age of Shadows before you set foot on either this island or the mainland again.'

The prince wheeled his mount around with Rees at his side and headed back to the castle. Protesting her innocence loudly, Marqel was lifted into the saddle in front of the captain. Kalleen, Vonril, Sooter and Murry stood watching them as they rode off, their expressions stuck somewhere between shock and outrage.

Only Lanatyne did not watch her being taken away. Instead she scuffed at the ground with her foot and didn't say a word.

Marqel stopped struggling once they got moving, mostly because she was afraid of falling from the horse. She was not an experienced horsewoman, and sitting in front of the captain's saddle, she was uncomfortable and rather precariously balanced. Besides, she needed time to think, and she couldn't do that and fight with the captain at the same time.

Think, she told herself sternly. *Think!*

The punishment for theft delivered by the Lion of Senet might yet prove the lesser of two evils. Laws varied from island to island, and she had never heard anything really bad about Elcast, so she allowed herself to hope that the penalty for theft was simply a whipping or perhaps a few days in the stocks. On Gaetane, she'd heard they chopped off your right hand for stealing.

Kalleen's discipline was liable to be a thousand times worse.

Marqel consciously calmed herself and resolved to wait and see what was in store before she made up her mind either to accept the blame or throw herself on the mercy of Prince Antonov's court.

There would be time, later, to get even with Lanatyne.

31

The meeting with the Brotherhood went as smoothly as Reithan predicted. Videon Lukanov proved to be an ordinary, middle-aged man with the air of a prosperous merchant about him. The meeting took place in a cosy tavern near the edge of town, just below the steep road that led to the Kalarada Palace. They were served an excellent meal in the small taproom, as Videon chatted about any number of inconsequential things that had nothing to do with the business at hand. Underneath Reithan's chair sat a small locked trunk – the reason they were here this evening. Videon didn't so much as glance at it.

'So, how are things in your part of the world?' Videon asked eventually, once the plates had been cleared away. He leaned back in his chair and studied the pair of them carefully.

'Much the same as always,' Reithan told him with a shrug. 'Why do you ask?'

'There's a rumour around that Johan Thorn is currently a guest of the Lion of Senet.'

'Well, they were good friends once,' Reithan replied with a smile.

'Not such good friends anymore, though, eh?'

Reithan shrugged. 'Even if they've fallen in love, Videon, it makes no difference to the business at hand.'

'No,' he conceded. 'But it might affect the long-term viability of our arrangement.'

'If anything happens that is likely to affect our arrangement, you'll be the first to know.'

Videon nodded, apparently satisfied with the assurance, then he turned his attention to Tia. 'Your little girlfriend doesn't have much to say for herself.'

That's because Reithan made me swear by everything that I hold dear not to say a word, Tia retorted silently.

'Well, I don't actually keep her around for conversation,' Reithan told him with a wink.

'Wish I could find a woman like that, myself. Pretty as a picture, silent as a mouse.'

Arrogant, patronising little shit, Tia thought. Reithan must have sensed something of her growing aggravation. He put his arm around her shoulders and squeezed her gently. It wasn't an affectionate squeeze. It was more of a *say-one-word-and-I'll-throttle-you* sort of squeeze.

'If you happen to tire of her, while you're here...' Videon suggested hopefully.

'I might. She can't cook worth a damn.'

Tia smiled at Reithan sweetly and placed her hand on his leg under the table. He managed not to show his surprise. Even more impressive was the fact that he managed not to wince when she pinched the soft flesh of his upper thigh and twisted it as hard as she could.

Reithan pulled her closer and nuzzled her neck, just below her ear. 'You cut that out this instant, young lady, or so help me, I *will* sell you as a virgin,' he hissed.

She smiled and lifted her hand from his thigh. Reithan turned his attention back to Videon with a smirk. 'On the other hand, she does have some other... attractive... qualities.'

'So I see,' Videon agreed with a chuckle. 'And I'm obviously keeping you from them. You have the merchandise?'

Reithan took his arm from around her shoulder and bent over to retrieve the chest. He placed it on the table between them and produced a small key from a chain around his neck. Once the chest was unlocked, he turned it to face Videon. 'Ten Senetian drams. As we agreed.'

'It's pure?'

'Naturally.'

'That's why I like dealing with you Baenlanders,' Videon said as he pulled the chest to him for closer inspection. 'You're so damn reliable. Have you tried it?'

'Never touch the stuff.'

'Smart, too,' Videon remarked. He closed the chest and

waved to a man standing near the door. Tia hadn't realised until then that there wasn't a man in the room who wasn't part of the Brotherhood. No wonder Reithan was so touchy.

'Pay him, Shapon.'

The man called Shapon produced two large purses from inside his shirt and tossed them on the table. Reithan picked them up and weighed them in his hands for a moment, then tucked the purses into his belt.

'Aren't you going to count it?' Videon asked.

'Do I need to?'

'And they say there's no honour among criminals.' Videon waved to another man who stepped forward and picked up the chest. Reithan handed him the key and rose to his feet. Tia took the hand he offered her and decided not to let it go. She didn't trust these people.

'Can I offer you an escort, friend? You've a lot of money on you. I'd hate for something to happen to you between here and the docks.'

'If anything happens to me, Videon, you'll have to find another supplier. I'm sure you've got more to lose than I have.'

The Brotherhood leader smiled. 'That's what I like about you, Reithan. You're a realist. Go. Take your little friend and enjoy yourself tonight. You'll be safe. I'll see you next month?'

'As always.'

The men stood back as they crossed the room. One of them even politely opened the door for them. Tia stepped outside with relief. She opened her mouth to say so, but Reithan jerked her arm and began walking briskly down the road into town.

'Not here,' he warned softly.

They walked in silence for a way, Tia cursing the long skirts she was wearing. They'd be a serious impediment if she had to run. Eventually, they turned off into a side street. Reithan stopped and waited for a while, until he was satisfied they weren't being followed, then he turned to Tia.

'What the hell was all that about?' he demanded.

'Did you see the way he looked at me? And you! Since when did I become your damn girlfriend?'

'Oh, so you would have preferred it if he thought I didn't have some claim on you?'

Tia hesitated for a moment. She hadn't thought about it like that. 'Well, no . . . but . . .'

'Goddess, Tia! You can be such a child sometimes!'

'I wasn't being childish!'

He took a deep breath, visibly calming himself. 'All right, just forget it. But don't you dare do anything like that when you meet Alexin. You're going to endanger us all unless you can at least act just a little bit . . . feminine!'

'If acting like a simpering fool is your idea of being feminine, then you can shove—'

'Keep your voice down!' he hissed.

Tia clamped her mouth shut, surprised at the anger in his voice. 'I'm sorry.'

'You should be,' he agreed unsympathetically.

'What do you want me to do?'

'Not getting us killed would be a good start.'

'I said I was sorry.'

'We need to go back the way we came. There's a tavern just near the one we met Videon in. The Queen's Guards drink there pretty regularly, so it attracts a lot of whores.'

'You want *me* to pretend I'm a whore?'

'Unfortunately, yes.'

She thought about it for a moment, then nodded. She'd seen the whores in Mil. It didn't seem that hard. 'How will I know Alexin?'

'He looks like me.'

'Suppose he doesn't like the look of me, or something?'

'If you can get close enough to him to let him know you're with me, I'm sure he'll find you irresistible.'

'Then what?'

'Take him upstairs, and for the Goddess's sake, try to look like you're going to bed him. We don't want his friends to get suspicious.'

'Where will you be?'

'Waiting for you. In room fourteen.'

'How do you know you can get room fourteen?' she asked curiously.

'We've done this before. The tavern owner is sympathetic.'

'Who did you use to lure him upstairs the last time?'

'A friend.'

'Anyone I know?'

'Tia . . .'

'I was just curious, that's all.'

Reithan shook his head and turned to examine her critically. 'Unbutton your shirt.'

'Why?'

'So you look like a whore, not a schoolmistress.'

'Oh.' She did as he asked, unbuttoning her shirt until there was a fair amount of cleavage visible. Tia glanced down with a frown. Breasts were such inconvenient things. They got in the way when you were using a bow and they bounced around quite painfully when you ran. She would have been quite happy if she'd never developed them at all.

Reithan suddenly smiled.

'*What?*' she demanded.

'Nothing. I just forget that you're all grown up, sometimes.'

'What's that supposed to mean?' she bristled.

'Let's not go there,' he suggested with a smile. 'Are you ready for this?'

She nodded, then placed her hands on her hips and thrust her bosom forward. 'I think I can manage.'

He shook his head. 'Give me your knife.'

'Why?'

'Because I don't want you stabbing the first poor sod who makes the mistake of pinching you on the bum.'

Reluctantly, she reached under her skirt and handed over the blade she had strapped to her thigh.

'Good girl. Now, let's go see if we can't seduce ourselves a Guardsman.'

32

The taproom of the Whistler's Haven was smoky and crowded as Tia let herself in. She glanced around uncertainly for a moment, then made her way towards the other end of the room. There was a crowd of uniformed Guardsmen drinking around the bar, singing a bawdy ballad about a young soldier and the widow who was the reason he never made it to the front, and several more Guardsmen by the hearth. She couldn't see Alexin among them, or anybody who looked even remotely like Reithan.

This is never going to work, she told herself. *Never.*

She was almost to the bar when an arm slid around her waist and a man pulled her to him, breathing stale beer all over her. 'You're new, sweetie.'

'I'm also very expensive,' she told him impatiently, putting her hands on his chest to keep him at a distance.

'What's so special about you, then?'

'Fifty silver dorns and you can find out.'

The man let her go with a shove. 'For that much, you'd have to be the Goddess herself!'

Tia laughed as he let her go, and continued heading towards the bar. *I think I handled that well.* Maybe this wasn't so difficult.

'Hey!'

She turned towards the man who called her. He was a Guardsman, standing with a group of other officers in their blue-and-silver jackets around a tall table littered with empty tankards. One of the men standing near the unlit hearth was enough like Reithan to be his brother except for his fair colouring. It had to be Alexin.

All too easy, she told herself. *What was Reithan so worried about?*

'You called?' she purred seductively as she headed for the

officers. The man who had hailed her was old, probably over forty. She looked around the officers and smiled at them, saving her best smile for Alexin. He seemed totally unimpressed.

'Haven't seen you around here before, darlin'.'

'That's because I haven't been here before.'

'She looks new to the game,' Alexin suggested, giving her the onceover disinterestedly. 'She probably hasn't heard about the minuscule size of your equipment yet, Wilim.'

The other officers laughed. Wilim pulled her closer. 'What about it, then, darlin'?'

Tia tried to hide her shock. It wasn't supposed to happen like this. *Didn't these morons even pay lip service to the social niceties?*

'I . . . er . . . wouldn't you like to buy me a drink first?'

'Anything for you, my lovely!' Wilim hailed the barkeeper for another tankard and then turned his attention back to Tia. He had a firm grip around her waist and was standing between her and Alexin. 'So, do you have a name, gorgeous?'

'Tia.'

'That's pretty. Almost as pretty as you.'

The barkeeper arrived with her ale and she snatched it from him, burying her face in the foaming tankard. She looked at Alexin over the rim, willing him to notice her. Wilim began to nuzzle her neck. It was all she could do not to cringe.

'Thirsty little thing, aren't you?'

She nodded and kept drinking.

'See, even whores have to get drunk before they can stand you, Wilim,' another officer laughed.

'Drunk or sober, they never forget me, though!'

'Which probably accounts for why most of them run and hide whenever you enter the room,' the man standing on the other side of her remarked, which sent all of them into gales of laughter.

Tia fought down a rising wave of panic. *I'm going to kill Reithan,* she decided. *Right after I strangle this lecher with my bare hands.* Wilim grabbed her breast and began to knead it quite painfully. It was a damn good thing Reithan had insisted she hand over her knife. *This fool would be singing soprano right now if I was armed*.

Just as Tia was doing her level best not to scream, a fight broke out near the bar. She glared at Alexin, trying to will him to look at her, but the fight had diverted his attention, along with Wilim's. She struggled free of him as he turned to cheer on the combatants. Wilim let her go and she stumbled into Alexin.

'Reithan sent me,' she whispered urgently as he caught her.

His whole demeanour changed instantly. With a nod of understanding, he helped her to her feet and pulled her close to him. Wilim glanced over his shoulder and glared at Alexin.

'Hey! I saw her first!'

Alexin bent his head down and kissed her soundly, leaving her gasping. 'Seems she's had a change of heart.'

Wilim looked ready to argue the point, but at that moment, the fighters staggered into Wilim, almost knocking him to the ground. With a roar, he forgot all about Tia and jumped to his feet, ploughing into the brawl with fists flying.

Alexin grinned at her. 'Who says there isn't a Goddess?'

'Upstairs,' she whispered. 'Room fourteen.'

Alexin nodded and with his arm still around her waist, pushed his way through the crowd to the stairs. Almost everyone was involved in the fight by now – either actively, or egging on the brawlers. He pushed her up the stairs ahead of him into the relative quiet of the hall and didn't say a word until they reached the door at the end with the number fourteen scratched into the woodwork. It was unlocked. Tia staggered through it with a feeling of vast relief.

'You didn't start that fight downstairs, did you, Tia?' Reithan asked as Alexin closed and locked the door behind him. They could hear the faint shouts and cheers from the brawl, even with the door closed.

She glared at him. *'No.'*

'I'm amazed.'. He turned to his cousin with a smile. 'Alexin.'

'Goddess, Reithan, where did you find this one?'

'She's a friend.'

'She's not a whore, that's for certain.'

'Of course I'm not!'

'Next time, find someone who knows what she's doing.'

'Desperate times call for desperate measures,' Reithan said with a grin.

'Then you must be truly desperate, cousin.' He stepped forward and embraced Reithan warmly. 'Not that it takes any great leap of intuition to guess why you're here.'

'Then you know something?'

'Not much.' The Guardsman sat down on the edge of the narrow bed and looked up at his cousin. 'I know Johan was captured on Elcast. Apparently he survived a tidal wave.'

'Is he still there?'

'As far as I know, although it's rumoured he's to be taken to Avacas soon.'

'Not here?'

Alexin shook his head. 'Rainan wasn't even officially advised that they'd caught him. I understand there is a sternly worded letter on its way to Antonov regarding the matter.'

'Oh, well, that should frighten the shit out of him. There's nothing scarier than a sternly worded letter.'

Alexin smiled ruefully. 'I wish I could tell you more, cousin. All I know is that they have him and that Antonov is already in Elcast. Even if you leave tonight, he could be gone by the time you get there.'

'They'll take him back to Avacas then,' Reithan concluded.

'More than likely.'

'Then that's where we'll go.'

Alexin shook his head.

'What do you think you can do, Reithan? You won't be able to get anywhere near him.'

'I'm not sure.' Reithan shrugged. 'Maybe an opportunity will present itself.'

'Well, if you're planning to get your little friend here to pretend she's a whore again, I suggest she gets in a bit of practice between here and the mainland.'

Tia scowled at him. 'Wilim fell for my ruse.'

'Wilim thinks anything in a skirt is on the make,' Alexin pointed out, then turned to Reithan. 'I wish I could be more help.'

'You've confirmed what we needed to know. That's help enough at this point.'

'If you leave now, you'll get to Avacas in time for Kirshov Latanya's birthday.'

'Why does that matter?' Tia asked.

'The Lion of Senet has pledged his second son to the Queen's Guard, as a token of his esteem for Dhevyn. Prince Kirshov is eighteen this year, although it's not certain he'll take up his commission yet. Senet considers a man not come of age until he's twenty.'

'I'll bet you just can't wait to have a Latanya in the guard.'

'Actually, I feel a bit sorry for the poor boy. I'm sure he has no idea what he's letting himself in for.'

'He deserves everything that's coming to him,' Tia said unsympathetically.

'And then some,' Alexin agreed. He glanced at her then and grinned broadly. 'I don't suppose you're interested in making this rendezvous believable?'

'And just exactly what do you mean by that?'

'Never mind, just a thought.' He looked at Reithan and frowned. 'He'll make a real spectacle of this, you know that, don't you? Antonov won't let Johan Thorn die before he's made it quite clear to the whole world what happens to anyone foolish enough to defy him.'

'I'm counting on it. The more the Lion of Senet wants to gloat, the longer Johan lives. And while he lives, there's still hope.'

'Then provided the Shadowdancers don't take a hand in his fate, you might have a chance at saving him.'

'What have the Shadowdancers got to do with it?' Tia asked.

'Johan is a heretic, Tia,' Alexin explained. 'He denounced the Goddess and cast doubt on the validity of the

High Priestess's visions. Belagren will want to make an example of him, even more than Antonov.'

'Then they could take him to the Hall of Shadows?' Tia asked.

'They could,' Alexin agreed. 'But I suspect Belagren and Antonov have differing opinions as to the fate of Johan Thorn.'

'That could work to our advantage,' Reithan remarked.

Alexin shook his head sadly. 'Antonov has Johan in his power for the first time since the war. It's going to take a miracle to save him.'

Reithan smiled. 'Well, that's a relief. For a moment there I was worried you were going to tell me it was impossible.'

33

News that the thief had been arrested reached the boys not long after the Lion of Senet and his party was spotted heading back to the Keep. They ran down to the courtyard to watch her being brought in. Alenor wanted to see Marqel in chains, because, for some inexplicable reason, she didn't like her. Dirk was curious, but seemed unsurprised that Marqel had turned out to be a thief. Lanon wanted another look at her, too, perhaps in the hope that she would be dressed in as little as she wore during her performance.

Kirsh couldn't explain why he wanted to see Marqel again. He just knew that he did.

They rode into the courtyard, Marqel sitting in front of Captain Ateway's saddle. He lowered her to the ground, where several other guards took her into custody. The acrobat looked around, but she didn't look frightened, just annoyed.

'Look at her,' Alenor said. 'She doesn't look the least bit sorry.'

'What do you expect?' Lanon shrugged. 'She's a Landfall bastard.'

'What will happen to her?' Kirsh asked as Marqel was roughly marched towards the gatehouse. There were no dungeons in the Elcast castle. She would be held there until tomorrow when his father and the duke would decide what to do with her. 'What do you normally do with thieves on Elcast, Dirk?'

'Depends on what they stole. I imagine for something as valuable as a diamond-bladed dagger, she'll get a lashing at the very least.'

Kirsh frowned. The idea of the lash scarring Marqel's creamy skin made him ill. He could still see her climbing out of that pool; still remember the way she looked at him. It made him ache just to think about it.

'Isn't there some way we can save her?'

They all turned to look at him. It was Dirk who asked the question the others were obviously thinking. 'Even if there was, Kirsh, why on Ranadon would you *want* to save her?'

'It just doesn't seem fair . . .'

'She stole Rees's dagger,' Alenor pointed out. 'What's fair about that?'

'But she's just . . . well, maybe she didn't know any better.'

'She knows,' Alenor assured him confidently. 'That girl may be just a Landfall bastard, but she knows *exactly* what she's doing.'

'You're being very uncharitable, Alenor.'

'I'm being honest,' the princess corrected, 'which is more than you can say for Marqel the Magnificent.'

With the aid of one of the Guards, Rees had dismounted and hopped towards the steps where they were watching the proceedings. Grooms rushed out to lead the horses back into the stables as Antonov gave Captain Ateway directions about what to do with the thief.

'So she definitely stole it, then?' Dirk asked Rees as he painfully climbed the steps towards them.

Rees stopped and looked up at them with a nod. 'She had a whole hoard of stolen coin. She's probably been stealing everything on Elcast that wasn't nailed down since she got here.'

Dirk glared at Marqel across the yard as she disappeared inside the gatehouse. 'Even the coin Derwn blamed Eryk for stealing?' Rees nodded and Dirk glanced at Kirsh, his expression distinctly unsympathetic. 'Then I hope they lash her to within an inch of her miserable life.'

'That wasn't Marqel's fault, Dirk . . .'

'What the hell is wrong with you?' Dirk demanded, turning on him angrily. 'She's a thief and liar, Kirsh. For the Goddess's sake, get your mind out of your pants long enough to realise it.'

Kirsh watched in speechless horror as Dirk turned his back on him and strode back into the castle. Lanon and Rees looked away in embarrassment, but Alenor met his eye evenly, her expression defiant. She apparently agreed with Dirk.

'I just said . . .'

'Is something the matter?' Prince Antonov asked as he walked up the steps.

Kirsh looked at his father for a moment and realised that he probably had just as low an opinion of Marqel as did Dirk. Of course, that didn't excuse the manner in which Dirk had just spoken, but Kirsh would not involve his father in that. He'd learned as a small child not to report the indiscretions of his friends to his father. A few of his boyhood companions had disappeared when Kirsh foolishly told his father that he had been offended.

'I was just wondering what's going to happen to her, sir.'

'You've no need to concern yourself with that, Kirsh. Rest assured the thief will be dealt with in a manner commensurate with her crimes.'

Antonov headed into the Keep, leaving Kirsh with Alenor, Lanon and Rees. He glanced at the others for a moment and then shrugged. 'Well, I suppose that's that, then.'

Rees nodded. 'Aye. I doubt if the Goddess herself could save her now.'

Kirsh stared at Rees with a sudden burst of inspiration. Perhaps that was the answer. Maybe, if he asked the right person, the Goddess *could* save Marqel.

Belagren opened the door herself to Kirsh's knock.

'Kirshov!' she exclaimed in surprise. 'To what do I owe this rare honour?'

'Could I speak with you, my lady?'

'Of course, come in.' She stepped back to let him enter, closing the door behind him. 'I hear there's been some excitement this evening.'

'They brought in Mar . . . the thief.'

'Foolish girl. How in the name of the Goddess did she think she was going to sell anything as rare and valuable as a diamond blade?'

'Maybe she didn't steal it.'

'Are you suggesting she was arrested for some other reason?'

'Well, no . . . it's just . . .'

Belagren smiled. 'Come on, Kirsh. I've known you too long for you to be coy with me.'

'Can't you save her, my lady?' he blurted out.

'Save her from what? Your father's justice? Even if I was inclined to, why would I?' It disturbed him to hear the High Priestess echoing Dirk's unsympathetic sentiments.

'She's a Landfall bastard, my lady. You're always telling us that the Goddess looks after the Landfall bastards. Shouldn't you do something, then, to help her? I mean, if you can't do the Goddess's will, what chance do the rest of us have?'

Belagren studied him for a moment. 'What's your interest in this girl, Kirshov?'

'I don't have any interest in her . . . I just think . . . well, she doesn't deserve the lash, that's for certain.'

'I'll wager your father thinks differently.'

'Please, my lady. Can't you do something to help her?'

'In return for what?'

'Pardon?'

'You're asking a big favour of me, Kirshov. It's not unreasonable that I might ask a favour in return.'

'I don't know, my lady ... what can I do for you that my father can't?'

The High Priestess smiled at him. 'Don't you worry about that, Kirshov. I'm sure I'll think of something.'

The Lion of Senet's justice was as quick as it was merciless. Marqel was taken straight into the castle next morning and paraded before the High Table in the main Hall. She obviously found the size of the building overwhelming. Openmouthed, she stared upwards at the huge spiralling staircase as she was pushed through the Hall by the guards.

Kirsh, Dirk, Alenor and Lanon sat on the first-floor landing, watching the proceedings. Prince Antonov sat in the centre of the long polished table with the Duke of Elcast on his right and a scribe on his left. The stolen dagger and the music box, with its carefully saved contents, lay on the table before him. There were several gold coins, a scattering of silver and a few other trinkets, brooches and earrings and the like. Rees Provin sat at the end of the table on his father's right, his injured foot propped up on a padded stool. At the back of the Hall stood a few of the castle and townsfolk come to watch.

'What is your name, child?' Prince Antonov asked.

'Marqel.'

'Do you have a last name?'

'No, your highness.'

Antonov glanced at the rope tattoo on her bare left arm and nodded. 'Where were you born?'

'Bryton, I think.'

'You don't know for certain?' Duke Wallin asked with a slight frown.

'No, my lord.'

The duke glanced at Prince Antonov reproachfully. 'This is what comes of Landfall Night,' he muttered.

Kirsh had the impression they weren't meant to overhear the comment, and his father didn't look very pleased by the duke's remark. Antonov picked up an onyx brooch and examined it for a moment, then looked straight at Marqel.

'Where did you steal this?'

'I didn't steal it. It was given to me by some seedy little tailor on Derex.'

'And the silver?'

'That was a Senetian noble visiting Kalarada.' She met Prince Antonov's eye evenly, and added. '*He* made me call him Daddy.'

The prince scowled at her, not mistaking her meaning. Nor did he pursue that particular line of inquiry. Instead, he picked up one of the gold coins and examined it curiously for a moment. 'Who did you steal this from?'

'I didn't steal it, your highness. The butcher gave it to me while his wife was away visiting her sister.' She glanced over her shoulder at the spectators and smiled. 'He wanted me to call him Daddy, too.'

Standing at the back of the Hall, the butcher's wife let out a squeal of indignation. Hauritz began protesting his innocence as he held up his hands to protect himself from his wife's fists. Kirsh glanced at Dirk and grinned. This was an unexpected bit of entertainment.

'Enough!' Antonov shouted, appalled at the interruption. 'Be quiet, or I'll have you removed!'

The butcher's wife reluctantly stopped hitting her husband, and turned to face the High Table. She was red-faced and mortified. Hauritz looked as if he wished a chasm would open beneath his feet and swallow him up.

'That's better,' Antonov said. 'As for you, young lady, I suggest you stop making these unfounded accusations against respectable citizens.'

'But I . . .' Marqel began.

'You will answer yes or no, that is all. Do you understand?'

Marqel lowered her eyes in submission. 'Yes, your highness.'

'That's better. Now, explain to me why you stole this dagger.'

Marqel did not look up, or offer a reply.

'You try my patience, child.'

'You instructed me only to answer yes or no, your highness.'

The Lion of Senet was not amused. Kirsh smiled at the look on his father's face then glanced around, wondering where the High Priestess was. If she was going to keep her promise to help Marqel, she was cutting it awfully fine.

'Very well then, did you steal this dagger?'

'No.'

'Then how did it get in your wagon?'

'I don't know.'

'Things will go much worse for you if you lie to me,' Antonov warned.

'I didn't steal the dagger,' she insisted. 'Maybe Lord Rees dropped it. He didn't know which way was up when I found him.'

'Your impudence does not help your cause, Marqel,' Duke Wallin warned.

She shrugged. 'I can't tell you what I don't know, my lord. I *would* be lying if I confessed to something I didn't do.'

A small frown flickered over the duke's face. 'She has a point, Anton. She wasn't the only one in the camp. Perhaps one of the others stole it and hid it in her wagon. They're all thieves and rogues, these travelling performers.'

Before the prince could answer the duke, the doors at the end of the Hall banged open. Belagren strode through the Hall. She was wearing her usual red robe and glittered with the weight of the jewellery she wore, much of it, Kirsh knew, gifts from his father. He knew Belagren and his father were lovers, but the affair did not disturb him as it did other people. Belagren had always been pleasant to him. She had never tried to take the place of his dead mother; never tried to order him about. In fact, Kirsh thought her presence hardly affected his life.

'Your son informs me you are trying a Landfall bastard,' the High Priestess announced as she drew level with Marqel.

'My son should learn to mind his tongue,' Antonov remarked, glancing up at Kirsh with a rather irritated look. 'She's a thief, my lady, and no concern of yours.'

'She wears the rope tattoo, your highness. She belongs to the Goddess.'

'She belongs in the stocks.'

The High Priestess turned to Marqel and studied her critically for a moment. 'The child is mine, your highness. I claim her on behalf of the Goddess.'

'What do you want with this child, my lady?' the duke asked suspiciously.

'She is born of the Landfall Festival, my lord. The Goddess has marked her and so I claim her. It is my right.'

The prince turned his gaze on Marqel for a moment and studied her thoughtfully. 'Well, child, it seems I have a choice here. What would *you* choose? My justice, or the Goddess's?'

Marqel didn't hesitate. 'I choose the Goddess, your highness.'

Antonov looked at Belagren for a long moment, his eyes almost as full of suspicion as the duke's, then he nodded slowly. 'Very well, my lady. The child is yours.'

'Thank you, your highness. I will see she stays out of trouble until we leave.'

'Make sure you do, Belagren,' Antonov warned. 'She escapes my wrath only by your intervention. One more infraction and neither you nor the Goddess will save her.'

Belagren bowed slightly in the direction of the prince and the duke, took Marqel's bare arm in a vicelike grip and marched her from the Hall.

34

'Let's go and visit the Shadowdancers,' Kirsh suggested.

He was sitting on the bottom step of the staircase. Dirk sat beside the prince chewing on a crust of bread. Lanon was leaning against the stone wall and Alenor was standing beside him, finishing off the apple she had brought from the breakfast table. It was six days now since the Landfall Festival, and things were starting to return to normal.

Alenor glared at him suspiciously. 'Why?'

'It's . . . the polite thing to do,' he declared after a moment's thought.

'Since when have you cared about being polite?' Dirk asked.

'Since Marqel the Magnificent got arrested,' Lanon said with a grin.

Alenor looked annoyed. 'We are not going to disturb the High Priestess just so you can gawk at that thief.'

'Balonan said she's rooming with the other Shadowdancers, not the High Priestess,' Dirk told them.

'So you see, Allie, there's nothing to worry about . . .' Kirsh began with a winning smile.

'Don't even think about it, Kirsh.'

'But don't you want to find out what really happened?' Lanon asked.

'I know what happened. She stole Rees's dagger.'

'She says she didn't,' Lanon reminded them.

'All thieves say they're innocent,' Dirk said.

'If you go anywhere near that thief, I'll tell your father,' Alenor announced, crossing her arms petulantly.

Normally, that threat was sufficient to curb Kirsh's more extreme schemes, but not today. 'If you say one word about this, I'll tell my father that you and Dirk sneaked out to spy on the Landfall Festival.'

Dirk wondered how Kirsh knew about that. Had he woken to find Dirk missing and followed them, or had Alenor told him of their late-night escapade?

'How are you going to get near her, anyway?' Alenor asked. 'Even if the Shadowdancers let you in, they aren't going to let you speak to Marqel.'

'That's where Dirk comes in,' Kirsh announced, slapping him on the back so hard he almost spat out his bread.

'Me? I don't want any part of this!'

'Of course you do,' Kirsh informed him. 'It'll be your job to keep Olena and Ella occupied while we speak to the acrobat.'

'What am I going to say to them?'

'Ask them about the Hall of Shadows. It's only reasonable that you'd want to know what it's like where you're going.'

'I'm not going anywhere,' Dirk announced confidently.

'I wouldn't wager anything too valuable on that,' Kirsh warned. 'Anyway, at the moment, everyone thinks you are going, and that's all that matters.'

Dirk's future was still up in the air, and the boys had an unspoken agreement not to discuss the subject. On one hand, Duchess Morna was refusing even to consider the proposal, while the High Priestess acted as if it were a foregone conclusion. The Lion of Senet and Duke Wallin had been suspiciously silent on the issue, which made Dirk extremely nervous, fearful that the decision had already been made without any attempt to consult him on the minor issue of what he wanted to do with the rest of his life. He had made several attempts to talk with his father privately about it, but it was almost as if Wallin was avoiding him.

'So, are we going to do this or not?' Lanon asked in the uncomfortable silence that followed Kirsh's remark.

'Of course we are,' Kirsh declared. 'Come on!'

Kirsh jumped to his feet and took off with Lanon on his heels. Dirk grabbed Alenor's arm before she could follow.

'This is a bad idea, Alenor. Can't you talk him out of it?'

The princess shrugged. 'Nobody talks Kirsh out of anything he really wants, Dirk.'

Dirk nodded. He had worked *that* out very soon after meeting Kirshov Latanya.

'They won't let him talk to her.'

'I certainly hope not,' Alenor agreed with a scowl. Then she turned to follow the others up the stairs, leaving Dirk standing on the bottom step staring after her.

The High Priestess had a high enough rank to warrant a room on the same floor as the Governor and the Lion of Senet, but the rest of the Shadowdancers had been relegated to the sixth floor, just below the servants' quarters. Morna might have to suffer the Shadowdancers, but she hadn't exactly rolled out the red carpet for them. Dirk caught the others on the sixth-floor landing as they eyed the door to the Shadowdancers' room. Even Kirsh appeared a little nervous.

'It's that door there,' he informed him, pointing up the hall.

'What am I going to say?'

'Just say that . . . tell them . . . oh, hell, Dirk, I don't know. You're the one with all the brains. You think of something.'

'I think this is stupid.'

'So do I,' Alenor added crossly.

Kirsh glared at them for a moment, then shrugged. 'Fine. Be like that. I'll do it.'

Squaring his shoulders, he marched purposefully up the hall, his footfall silent on the threadbare carpet that ran its length. The better carpets were on the lower floors where they were more likely to be seen. Kirsh reached the door and knocked loudly.

The door opened after a few moments. From where they were standing, Dirk could see Olena's surprise on finding the young Prince of Senet outside her door.

'My Lady Shadowdancer,' Kirsh said expansively, loud enough to ensure that his companions could hear him. 'Might we presume on your time for a moment or two?'

'What do you want, your highness?'

'My good friend Dirk, here, wishes to learn more about the Hall of Shadows. Who better than yourself to enlighten him?'

Olena looked down the hall at them suspiciously.

'Very well, then,' she nodded after a moment. 'Come, young Dirk, ask your questions. You may join your friends later.'

'Ah, we were hoping we might learn something of the Hall, as well,' Kirsh hurriedly added. 'If you don't mind, of course.'

'Actually, I do mind,' she snapped impatiently. 'Dirk may come in. You may go, Prince Kirshov. And take your friends with you.'

Dirk moved forward with a great deal of trepidation as Kirsh stepped back to let him enter. His expression was more shocked than disappointed. He wasn't used to having his plans foiled. Dirk stepped into the room with an apologetic shrug in his direction.

'Off with you!' Olena ordered and slammed the door in Kirshov's face.

Dirk glanced around the small room. There were two narrow beds with a small table between them and a dresser under the window. Dirk wondered if the High Priestess's willingness to share Prince Antonov's bed was prompted by her unwillingness to share a room with her underlings. The window was open and he could hear the faint hammering of the castle smithy far below. A movement caught his eye and he turned to find Marqel emerging from the garderobe. He almost didn't recognise her. She was scrubbed clean, her long blonde hair braided and neat, and she was dressed in a simple short-sleeved shift that covered her rope tattoo. She looked at him curiously and then turned to Olena.

'I've put the towels away. Was there anything else you wanted me to do?'

Dirk studied her curiously. She did not seem unduly bothered by her plight.

'You may come here and listen, child,' Olena told her, taking the seat beside the unlit hearth. 'This is Dirk Provin. He will be accompanying us back to the Hall of Shadows.'

Marqel curtsied to Dirk as if he were a prince – or as if she had just learned how and was trying it out for effect. 'My lord.'

Dirk thought it better to get this cleared up at the outset. He didn't like the proprietary air the Shadowdancer had assumed. 'Er . . . excuse me, my lady, but it's not certain yet that I'll be going anywhere.'

'We shall leave the details to Prince Antonov and your father to sort out,' Olena said. 'But rest assured you *will* be coming with us when we leave. Now, what did you want to know?'

The question caught him off guard. This was Kirsh's insane idea, not his, and Olena's confidence worried him.

'I . . . er . . . what's it like?'

'The Hall of Shadows is the home of the High Priestess. The palace was gifted to her by the Lion of Senet as a reward for returning us to the Age of Light.'

'I thought the Lion of Senet's sacrifice of his son was responsible for that?' Dirk asked.

'He was guided by the High Priestess,' Olena corrected.

Dirk's first impulse was to retort: *And it's common knowledge what part of his anatomy she was guiding him by*. But common sense won out over wit.

'I . . . well, nobody ever really spoke about the Hall of Shadows, my lady.'

'There's a lot that doesn't seem to warrant mentioning in this household,' Olena mumbled.

'What about me?' Marqel asked. She sounded almost cheerful, as if she was looking forward to leaving. Still, he supposed he couldn't blame her. A week ago she was a bastard and a thief. Her fortunes had turned considerably in the last few days.

'You, Marqel? I'm not certain. That will be up to the

High Priestess. Once we have ascertained where you are with your studies . . . what's *that* look for?'

Marqel had blushed an interesting shade of crimson and refused to meet Olena's eye. The Shadowdancer laughed harshly. 'Studies, did I say? You more than likely can't even read, can you, child?'

The young acrobat's silence was all the answer the Shadowdancer needed.

'I'll bet you can count, though,' she added. 'That's a skill required for any thief.'

'I'm not a thief,' Marqel retorted sullenly.

'Yes, well, even if you are, child, that life is behind you. You belong to the Goddess now.' Olena turned to Dirk and studied him critically. 'Prince Antonov says you read very well, Dirk. And I've no doubt about your mathematical prowess.'

He shrugged, not sure if the comment required a reply. Suddenly Olena stood up and crossed her arms decisively.

'You will come here every morning after breakfast, Dirk, for two hours. You will teach Marqel to read. I don't have the time.'

'But—' Dirk protested. He didn't want to spend time teaching Marqel to read. He didn't want to spend time with her at all.

'There is no point in objecting, Dirk. I will arrange it with Prince Antonov. And now, you may go. I have things to attend to.'

35

'I don't think he likes me much.'

Olena nodded thoughtfully as the door closed behind the youngest son of Elcast. 'That's hardly surprising. You stole his brother's property.'

'I didn't steal anything.'

Olena snorted at her insistence that she was innocent, but did not otherwise react. Instead she turned to Marqel and looked at her closely. 'You may not be able to read books, but you read *people* well enough, don't you? Is that a gift, I wonder, or the result of your unsavoury upbringing?'

Marqel was getting a little bit fed up with the Shadowdancer's smug superiority. 'If you all think so little of me, why did the High Priestess intervene on my behalf?'

'The Goddess willed it,' Olena replied glibly. 'Have you eaten breakfast?'

'Yes.'

'Yes, *my lady*,' Olena corrected absently. 'Your manners need work, child.'

And my bathing habits, and my accent, and my education, Marqel thought sourly. Olena had done little else but list her faults since the High Priestess rescued her from Prince Antonov's justice.

But the Shadowdancers had not been unkind. After Marquel was taken from the court, the High Priestess had questioned her closely about the troupe, about her life as a travelling acrobat and her origins. Provided she answered without demurring, Belagren seemed satisfied.

Following her interview with the High Priestess, Marqel had been placed in the custody of the youngest of the Shadowdancers. Olena had then explained, at some length, that Marqel was now destined to serve the Goddess in whatever capacity the High Priestess deemed suitable, and that she should consider herself very lucky to have been given such an opportunity. Olena also made it quite clear that if Marqel misbehaved, Prince Antonov's justice would seem mild by comparison to the punishment the Goddess would inflict on her.

Marqel chose to heed the warning. She wasn't sure what strange twist of fate had made the High Priestess intervene on her behalf. The only thing she knew for certain was that she wasn't about to do anything to jeopardise her position until she worked out exactly what was going on.

The following morning, and every morning for the next week, Dirk Provin reluctantly appeared at the door to the Shadowdancers' room to begin his instruction.

Although he was civil and usually patient with her stumbling attempts to become literate, he made no secret of the fact that he resented the duty thrust upon him.

Despite that, Marqel was enjoying her first taste of wealth and luxury. There was no shortage of food here. She didn't lie awake, tossing and turning in the dull light of night, scratching at bites from the insects sharing her bed. She was even starting to think kindly towards Lanatyne. Perhaps the older girl had done her a favour.

On the ninth day of her lessons, Olena left her and Dirk alone to go riding with Prince Antonov's hunting party. Ella was with Misha, as usual, and she had not seen the High Priestess since Belagren had claimed her from the Lion of Senet. It was the first time in her short acquaintance with Dirk that they had not been under the constant scrutiny of the Shadowdancers. Marqel thought it might mean he would take his duty less seriously.

'We'll start with this word here,' Dirk informed her, taking his seat at the small table as Olena closed the door behind her.

Marqel looked down at the incomprehensible squiggles and shrugged. 'I don't know.'

'Remember what we did yesterday?' he asked. There was an edge of impatience in his voice. 'We went through all the letters in the alphabet. Sound the word out. What's this first letter?'

'I can't remember.'

'You're not trying. Think!'

'It's not my fault I can't remember!' she snapped. 'Not everybody's as brilliant as you!'

'Or as stupid as you,' he retorted.

Stung by his scorn but determined not to show it, she leaned back in her chair and studied him curiously for a moment. 'You don't like me, do you?'

'*What?*'

'You don't like me.'

'That's hardly the point.'

'Does the prince like me?'

Dirk rolled his eyes. 'If you mean Kirshov, then yes, I suppose he likes you.'

'If a prince can like me, then why can't you?'

'I don't have to like you, Marqel. Once you leave Elcast, I'll never see you again.'

'You're coming with us. I heard Ella and Olena talking about it. It's all arranged.'

'I'll believe it when I hear it from my father, not from you.'

'Suit yourself,' she said with a shrug. This was not going well. Her plan was not to alienate him. Suddenly, she smiled with all the ingenuous innocence she could muster. 'It's a long journey to Avacas. It might be easier on both of us if we were friends.'

Dirk stared at her with those disconcerting, metal-grey eyes. 'Why do you want to be my friend?'

'Well, it's you or the Shadowdancers,' she said with a grin.

Despite himself, Dirk smiled. 'Do you really want to be a Shadowdancer, Marqel?'

'Apparently I've been called by the Goddess,' she informed him. Then she added with a shrug, 'It's better than a life on the road with Kalleen and the others, I suppose, and now that they're banned from Senet, it's going to be hard for them to make a decent living. At least this way I know where my next meal is coming from. And nobody seems to care about this,' she added, pushing up her sleeve to reveal the rope tattoo, 'when you're a Shadowdancer.'

Dirk studied the tattoo with a frown. 'It's barbaric, branding people like cattle.'

'Olena says that Landfall bastards make the best Shadowdancers. She says it makes you tougher.'

'How?' he asked.

This was better. It was the first time he had ever shown any inclination to talk to her on matters not directly related to their lessons. 'She says that when you have the rope tattoo, you learn what rejection and suffering are all about. Then, when you are finally welcomed into the arms of the Goddess, you understand that you truly have come home.'

Dirk nodded thoughtfully. 'So the more you suffer before you become a Shadowdancer, the more you appreciate them. That's a pretty effective tactic, actually. Cruel, but effective.'

'Why is it cruel?'

'I'm surprised you of all people have to ask that.'

'I didn't have such a bad time of it,' she objected. Her life as an acrobat was beginning to take on a much rosier aura in hindsight. 'And I was a damn good acrobat.'

'And a thief,' he reminded her.

'I didn't steal your brother's dagger.'

'Of course you didn't . . . and I'm going to be Lord Marshal of Dhevyn, one day,' he scoffed.

Marqel chose to ignore his sarcastic tone. 'Kirshov will be Lord Marshal of Dhevyn eventually, won't he?'

'Probably.'

'And he'll marry that insipid little princess, too?'

'Don't speak like that about Alenor.'

Marqel grinned. 'Touched a sore spot, have I?'

Dirk blushed crimson and turned back to the book. 'We should be getting on with the lesson.'

'Poor Dirk,' she chuckled, with a sudden burst of insight. 'Pining away for the little princess, are we?'

'Mind your own damn business!'

'Doomed to a life amid dusty old books and dusty old men,' she smirked, 'while your best friend gets to marry your princess and rule Dhevyn at her side. For somebody as smart as you, you sure drew the short straw, didn't you?'

He slammed the book shut angrily and jumped to his

feet. 'You don't know anything about Alenor or me. You're nothing but an ignorant Landfall bastard. You can't even read.'

'I don't need to read,' she retorted. 'I'm going to be a Shadowdancer. I'll have you to do my reading for me.'

'Then you're a fool,' he told her coldly. 'Because I promise you this, Marqel the *Magnificent,* even in the unlikely event that you one day get to be the *High Priestess,* you would never be able to rely on me for anything.'

'If I ever get to be High Priestess, Dirk Provin, I'll have princes lining up to pay homage to me. You'll be lucky if I let you sweep my floors.'

Dirk laughed, but it was full of ridicule. 'You can dream all you want, Marqel, but no prince is going to pay homage to a thief and a whore.' He looked at her, and his eyes narrowed perceptively. 'This is about Kirsh, isn't it?'

'I never said . . .'

'Kirshov doesn't care about you, Marqel. He barely even knows you're alive.'

He's lying, she told herself, resisting the temptation to put her hands over her ears to block out his scorn-filled words. *I know he's lying.*

'I don't care about Kirshov,' she lied.

'Then why do you ask after him every day?'

'Because he's a prince,' she pointed out, crossing her arms defensively. 'And that makes him better than you!'

'It makes him a whole *lot* better than you, too,' he reminded her. Tears stung her eyes as he stomped to the door and jerked it open. 'The lesson is finished. You can find someone else to teach you how to read.'

Marqel jumped a little as the door slammed shut, feeling suddenly very small and alone. Wiping away her tears, she turned her back on the door.

He was *wrong.* She was living in a castle now, wasn't she? And eating like a queen? Hadn't the High Priestess herself intervened, claiming her for the Goddess? And wasn't she going to be a Shadowdancer?

Marqel went to the window and leaned her head against

the cool glass. After a while, she opened her eyes and looked down. The room looked out over the courtyard and the main entrance to the Keep. The wide, paved yard was bordered on three sides by the castle itself and the outbuildings that made up the stables, kitchens, storehouses and other industries housed in the Keep. She watched the castle folk go hither and thither, and felt isolated and alone. Other than a full belly and clean bed, absolutely nothing had changed.

I'll never be one of them, she thought with dismay. *I might be living in a castle now, but I'm still nothing. Still a nobody.* The realisation hurt more than she thought possible. And Dirk Provin. Well, that arrogant, jumped-up second son of a minor duke had no right to say what he did. She wasn't a thief or a whore.

I am Marqel the Magnificent, she reminded herself. Better yet . . . *Marqel the Shadowdancer.*

You're wrong, Dirk Provin, and I'll make you eat those words. One day, you will call me 'my lady'. One day, you will bow before me. One day . . .

36

Dirk was still fuming as he ran down the stairs. He'd had enough of Marqel *and* the Shadowdancers, and the Landfall Festival, even Prince Antonov. He wanted to be free of his responsibility to teach the young thief, and he wanted to be certain that he would not be packed off to the Hall of Shadows for the crime of being able to solve mathematical equations in his head. The only person who could guarantee that was his father, so it was to his father's rooms he headed, determined to get this sorted out, once and for all.

He knocked on the door and opened it without waiting for an answer, not certain his father would be there. More than likely, he was in the Library with Prince Antonov, but he had no wish to speak to the prince. He wanted to plead his case out of the hearing of the Lion of Senet.

'Dirk!'

His mother looked up from the chair by the window, hurriedly wiping her eyes. She had obviously been crying. His father was standing in front of her, his expression bleak.

'I'm sorry, Mother,' he said uneasily, wondering what he had burst in on. 'I can come back later . . .'

'No, son,' Wallin said heavily. 'You might as well come in. We were just talking about you.'

'I haven't done anything wrong, have I?' he asked, a little nervously. Had his father learned about his visit with Johan Thorn? It was too soon for him to know about his argument with Marqel.

Morna smiled wanly and opened her arms to him. 'Of course you haven't, darling. Come here.'

Dirk crossed the room warily, trying to remember the last time his mother had called him 'darling.'

'What's wrong?'

His parents exchanged a telling look before his father answered. 'The High Priestess wants you to enter service in the Hall of Shadows.'

'I know, but you won't let her take me, will you?' Dirk looked at each of them in turn with a growing sense of dread.

'In that, we've had a small victory,' Wallin told him with a forced smile. 'Although I'm afraid your mother doesn't agree with me.'

'What small victory?'

'You're going to live with Antonov,' Morna informed him tonelessly.

Dirk stared at his parents in shock.

'You'll continue your studies in Avacas until you go to the Hall of Shadows when you come of age,' his father explained. 'I'm sorry, son. It was the best we could do under the circumstances.'

Dirk's shock at the news was lessened somewhat by a fleeting, if rather selfish thought. Studying in Prince Antonov's court meant being with Alenor. But now was not the time to tell his parents that. And in truth, it seemed poor compensation for being made to spend his life in the service of a Goddess he wasn't even certain he believed in.

When he didn't answer, Wallin smiled with false cheerfulness. 'It won't be that bad, Dirk. There are some excellent tutors in Avacas, and you'll have Kirshov there for company. You and he seem to have become good friends. You'll barely spare us a thought once you get a taste of mainland court life, I suspect.'

'But why do I have to go at all?'

'The High Priestess seems to think you've been chosen by the Goddess,' Wallin said.

'For what?'

'I couldn't say, son, I'm not a Shadowdancer. But you can't deny your own ability. And I know how much you enjoy learning.'

'I learn just fine here on Elcast, Father.'

'We have a responsibility to see that you are educated *correctly*,' Morna added with undisguised bitterness.

'And Prince Antonov doesn't like the way I've been educated,' Dirk concluded. 'I still don't see why I have to leave. Can't I study the things I need to learn with Master Helgin? And then worry about whether or not I want to be a Shadowdancer when I'm old enough to decide for myself?' Dirk was quite sure he was old enough to make his mind up now, but legally, until he came of age at eighteen, he had no real say in his own future. A fact the High Priestess was no doubt counting on.

'Antonov feels that if you remain here, your thinking might be . . . influenced . . . in the wrong direction.'

From what Dirk had seen and heard over the past few weeks, that was not an unreasonable assumption. His aunt had killed herself rather than live with Antonov, and his mother had run off with a pirate. It was a wonder any of them was still free.

'Can't you do anything?'

'If we deny Antonov in this, we commit treason.'

'How can it be treason?' he demanded impatiently.

'Treason implies defying the crown. Antonov isn't the King of Dhevyn. He's just invaded us and—'

'Keep your voice down!' Wallin hissed. 'Don't you know what could happen to you – to us – if Antonov hears you speaking like that?'

'Mother called him a murderer and it didn't seem to bother him. Why should he care what I think?' Dirk winced under his mother's gaze. He hadn't meant to blurt that out.

'Exactly how much did you overhear, Dirk?' she asked softly.

'Enough.'

'Then perhaps you understand why we can't fight this. Rainan may be Queen of Dhevyn, but she rules only as long as Antonov allows it. Between him and the High Priestess, they have Dhevyn by the throat.'

'What about the real King of Dhevyn?'

'Johan Thorn?' Wallin asked in surprise. 'What's he got to do with this?'

'Dirk apparently overheard a discussion I had with Antonov,' Morna explained. 'Johan's name came up.'

Wallin turned to Morna in despair. 'Damn it, Morna, you should know better than to talk to Anton of him! Can't you mind your tongue? For your sons' sake, if not for mine.'

'Johan chose his own path, Wallin. I've wished on more than one occasion these past years that I had stayed with him.'

The duke shook his head as if there was nothing he could do or say that would make the situation any better.

'Why *did* you go with him, Mother?' Dirk asked, not sure what sort of reaction he'd get. He still hadn't come to terms with his mother's rather colourful past. It seemed so unlike her. It was almost as if the stories were about someone else.

His mother took a long time to answer. 'Because I loved him,' Morna confessed, finally. 'And believed in him.'

'Morna . . . I don't think it's necessary to—'

Morna looked up at her husband apologetically. 'Dirk will learn the truth, sooner or later. I'd rather he heard it from us than hear the Lion of Senet's twisted version of events.'

Wallin was obviously not happy about having to elaborate. He took a deep breath before he turned to Dirk. 'It all happened a long time ago, son. During the Age of Shadows.'

'When Johan Thorn was the King of Dhevyn?'

Wallin nodded. 'When Belagren announced that she had been shown the way to restore us to the Age of Light in a vision, there was a great deal of excitement. When she announced how it had to be achieved, it split the kingdom. Johan Thorn led the faction who opposed Belagren's plans.'

'Didn't he want to see the end of the Age of Shadows?'

'As far as Johan was concerned, the Age of Shadows wasn't so bad that it required the sacrifice of an innocent child to restore the light,' Morna said bleakly.

Johan had said almost exactly the same thing, Dirk recalled.

'You have to understand what it was like, Dirk,' his father explained, ignoring his wife's interruption. 'There was no sun during the day, only the red sun at night. The rest of the time we were plunged into darkness. The tidal waves and volcanic eruptions we suffer now are nothing compared to what happened when the darkness came. What crops weren't destroyed by ash, or lava, or seawater, withered and died due to lack of light. There was widespread famine. Constant earthquakes. Our cattle were dying. As the temperature dropped the seas retreated. If not for Senet, the Islands of Dhevyn would have perished. At least the mainland was able to produce enough food to keep us from complete starvation.'

'Then I'm surprised it was Prince Antonov who championed the High Priestess,' Dirk said thoughtfully. 'You'd think he'd want to maintain things as they were if the Age of Shadows handed him such power over Dhevyn.'

'It handed him power, but Senet was suffering, too,' Wallin agreed. 'Initially, the mainland was able to weather the darkness better than the islands, but it was only a matter of time before it began to suffer as we did.'

'Stop trying to make it sound as if Antonov's invasion of Dhevyn was a natural consequence of the Age of Shadows,' Morna complained. 'Tell him what really happened. Tell him about Neris.'

'Morna, Antonov didn't invade—'

'Who's Neris?' Dirk asked, before his father and mother could be diverted into an argument about whether or not the occupation of Dhevyn by Senet constituted an invasion. 'I've heard him mentioned before.'

'Neris Veran was a young man with a talent in mathematics similar to yours,' Wallin answered. 'He was a Sundancer, taken into service when he was quite young, only nine or ten years old, I think. The heretics believe that it is he, not Belagren, who discovered the secret of returning us to the Age of Light.'

'He never advocated killing a child,' Morna interjected.

'He and Johan became friends,' Wallin continued as if Morna hadn't spoken. 'He shared his heresy with Johan, and it turned the king from merely a voice of dissent into an outright opponent. The next thing we knew, we were at war.'

'And you fought with Antonov?' he asked curiously.

'I took the side of the Goddess, son,' Wallin agreed.

'You took the coward's way out,' Morna corrected. 'Antonov bought off you and every other duke who sided with him with promises of safety and light, even though what he proposed was repugnant to any civilised person.'

'As you can probably tell, your mother was violently opposed to me joining him. I followed the Lion of Senet to war and left her here on Elcast. While I was gone, she left the island with Johan and they plotted to assassinate Antonov.'

Dirk stared at his mother in shock, but she would not meet his eye.

'Why assassinate Antonov?' Dirk asked suddenly, turning to his father. 'Wouldn't it have been more effective to remove the High Priestess?'

Wallin smiled faintly, as if amused by the fact that Dirk's first reaction had been a tactical assessment rather than moral condemnation. 'Belagren was the one advocating the sacrifice of a child of royal blood, but it was Antonov who planned to carry out the ritual. Remember that your mother is a Princess of Damita. She is of royal blood, just as you and your brother are.'

'I reasoned, with very good cause, that my son was a prime candidate for the sacrifice,' Morna snapped.

'Your mother was convinced I would not raise a finger in protest if Belagren tried to take Rees,' Wallin added, as if the mere thought offended him.

'*Would* you have objected?' he asked his father.

'Don't be absurd, Dirk, of course I would have objected.'

'Yet you fought on Antonov's side. Isn't that a bit hypocritical? I mean, if you believed in his cause enough to fight for him, shouldn't you have enough faith to make the ultimate sacrifice?'

Morna laughed sourly. 'See, Wallin? Even Dirk can see through your excuses. Answer him, my dear. Tell him how you stood by and let Antonov kill Analee's son while promising your wife that you wouldn't let him harm yours.'

Wallin frowned. Dirk realised that this was a disagreement older than he. But his father made no attempt to answer her charge.

'The plot to assassinate Antonov was uncovered,' he continued. 'Antonov defeated Johan's army and placed the king's sister, Rainan, on the throne. Neris killed himself by throwing himself off a cliff near Tolace. Thorn escaped after the battle and has been hiding out in the Baenlands, ravaging the Bandera Straits and the Tresna Sea as a pirate ever since.'

'Have you seen him since he was captured?'

Morna shook her head sadly. 'He and I did not part friends.'

'Why not?'

'Because I chose to return here. After what happened to Analee, after the war, after everything else . . . he couldn't understand my decision to return to Elcast.'

'The *Book of Ranadon* spares it one paragraph,' Dirk said thoughtfully. 'Something about Prince Antonov standing on a hill overlooking Johan's defeated army. It doesn't mention the rest of it.' He didn't think it prudent to repeat the line about her being a traitorous harlot.

'You've read the *Book of Ranadon*?' Morna gasped in surprise.

'Prince Antonov has it. He asked me to read some of it to him. I suppose the High Priestess brought the book with her.'

'She would!' Morna replied. 'The *Book of Ranadon* is a work in progress, Dirk. Don't believe a word of it. Belagren makes it up as she goes along.'

'Morna!' Wallin objected.

'Don't look at me like that. Even you must admit that it glosses over the facts.'

Wallin nodded reluctantly. 'I'll grant that the *Book of Ranadon* sometimes errs on the side of brevity . . . but—'

'*Brevity?* One paragraph to cover a full-blown civil war?' She turned to Dirk, as if disgusted that Wallin would even consider the *Book of Ranadon* worthy of notice. 'Even today, the struggle for the truth still goes on. The day Antonov sacrificed his son was not the end of the conflict, as the Book would have us believe.'

Dirk looked at his mother, suddenly understanding her bitterness. She had watched her king defeated, her nephew murdered and her sister commit suicide. And Wallin had been one of Antonov's generals. It was a wonder his parents even spoke to each other, let alone live together in relative harmony.

'How did you escape Antonov's wrath, Mother?' Dirk knew now what Alenor had meant when she spoke of bad blood between Morna and the High Priestess.

'My loyalty to the Goddess was never in doubt,' his father answered for her. 'Antonov and I were friends and I was one of his generals. Your mother was spared because I interceded on her behalf.'

Dirk also began to understand why it pained Morna so much to shelter the Lion of Senet in her home.

'Do you condone what Antonov did, Father?'

Wallin shrugged. 'He was my friend, Dirk.'

Dirk could hardly believe what he was hearing. '*Friend?* He killed his wife *and* his baby son. And now you want to send me to live with him!'

'Try to understand, son,' Wallin said, almost pleading for his approval. 'Antonov is not an evil man. The Lion of Senet did what he honestly believed he had to do to save Ranadon, and regardless of what your mother thinks about the morality of it, it worked. The Age of Light returned. He wept as he took his son's life.'

'You still make excuses for him, don't you?' Morna accused in disgust.

'Morna . . .' Wallin sighed.

'What of Analee?'

'Analee died by her own hand, my dear. I know you blame Antonov, but he never meant for her to die. He still grieves for her.'

'*Grieves* for her?' Morna jumped to her feet and turned to stare out the window. On this side of the castle, you could hear the surf far below as it crashed against the cliffs. 'He defiles her memory with every breath he takes!'

Wallin shook his head sadly, but did not answer his wife. He looked at Morna's unrelenting back for a moment, obviously at a loss. He could not comfort her or relieve her pain. There were too many unforgivable deeds between them. Dirk wondered for a moment how they had managed to make a life together. Maybe they had declared a truce for the sake of their children. Perhaps his mother had spent the last sixteen years trying to make up for what had happened.

Dirk felt deep sorrow for his mother, but he knew it must have been no easier on Wallin. His father was a moderate man caught between extremes. With Antonov on one side and his wife on the other, it must have been impossible.

'Why didn't you tell me this before?' Dirk asked his father.

'Because we hoped Rainan would be strong enough to defy the Lion of Senet,' Morna replied without turning to look at him.

'Until Antonov arrived,' Wallin added, 'there was some hope you would never have to leave Elcast.'

'That's why you didn't object to me becoming Helgin's apprentice, isn't it?' he asked. 'So I wouldn't have to leave Elcast to study?'

Wallin nodded.

'There's no chance of that now, is there?'

His father shook his head sadly. 'I'm afraid not, son.'

'Will I be allowed to come home at all? Even for a visit?'

'That will be up to Prince Antonov.'

'Then I'm a hostage, too.'

'No,' his father assured him. 'You're still my son and a grandson of the Prince of Damita. No harm will come to you. Your rank alone will see to that.'

'No *physical* harm,' his mother amended bitterly as she stared out over the turbulent water. Then she turned and looked pointedly at her husband. 'But what of his soul, Wallin? Have you thought about that?'

37

In the days that followed the Landfall Festival, Morna Provin watched with a feeling of helpless rage as Antonov Latanya quite deliberately set out to seduce her son.

The Lion of Senet showed no inclination to return to Senet anytime soon. He was too devious to tear Dirk away from everything he knew and loved without giving him a chance to grow accustomed to the idea. He was not interested in making an enemy of the boy. Antonov wanted Dirk to like him. He wanted Dirk to feel comfortable in his company. But most of all, he knew how much it upset Morna to see Dirk warming to him, and the weapons he had in his arsenal were considerable, not the least of which were his own sons, Misha and Kirshov.

Antonov suggested in passing that Misha was feeling rather lonely, and if it wasn't too much trouble, would Dirk consider visiting him each day for a game of chess, perhaps? Her son had readily agreed. Although frequently bedridden, the Crippled Prince was a bright young man, and as nobody in the Keep had been willing to play chess with Dirk since he was seven years old, he jumped at the chance to pit his mind against a new opponent. Within days, the boys were firm friends. Misha even began to show signs of improvement, and was able to join them at dinner some evenings. Antonov warmly congratulated Dirk for his efforts, placing Misha's improved health firmly at Dirk's door.

Antonov's second son was the spitting image of his father. But he had inherited much of his mother's warmth and openness. There was so much of Analee in Kirshov that sometimes Morna couldn't bear to look at the boy. And that was the danger of him. One couldn't help but fall victim to his charms. There was a hard streak in him, though. Morna saw glimpses of it when he was annoyed or impatient. And he could be cruel, particularly to Alenor, but she suspected it stemmed more from thoughtlessness than any deliberate wish to hurt her feelings. Analee had been like that. With a careless word, a thoughtless, flippant comment, her older sister had been able to reduce Morna to tears.

Dirk wasn't blind to what Antonov was trying to do. He was a very smart young man, and knew enough of the truth to be wary of the prince, but it never occurred to him to be wary of his sons. There was nothing Morna could do about it. Neither Misha nor Kirshov was aware that they were conspirators in Antonov's game. The Lion of Senet was too subtle to involve them openly. He simply opened the door to friendship between the boys and let nature take its course.

The worst of it was watching Dirk and Alenor. He was quite besotted with the young princess, a fact that concerned Morna greatly. But just as she was powerless to stop the growing friendship between Dirk and the Latanya princes, she was equally powerless to do anything about Alenor. She couldn't say anything. She couldn't even hint to Dirk that his affection was misplaced. Dirk was supposed to be Wallin Provin's son. She could not tell Dirk that Alenor was his first cousin, not the distant fourth cousin twice removed – or whatever it was – that the official records claimed.

Her vague concerns that somebody might notice the resemblance between Dirk and his real father had solidified into a solid lump of fear that never left her. She was certain Antonov knew the truth – except, if he did know that Dirk was Johan's son, why was he trying so hard to befriend the boy?

She could not understand what Antonov was playing at. He acted as if he were here on Elcast for a holiday. He'd done nothing about Johan. He hadn't been to see him, hadn't ordered him moved, hadn't tried to change the guard. He hadn't even inquired about his recovery. His inaction was slowly driving her insane. The agony of waiting for something to happen was a particularly exquisite form of torture.

Morna studied her reflection in the mirror of her dressing table, noting fine lines around her eyes that hadn't been there a few months ago; the grey that sprinkled her dark hair. Living with the uncertainty was destroying her. There were dark circles under her eyes, too. She'd barely slept a wink since Johan was captured. Morna dropped her head into her hands, trying to hold back the tears that threatened to undo her.

I can't go on living like this.

'Is something wrong, my dear?'

She looked up with a start. Wallin had finished dressing. He was standing behind her, a look of concern on his weathered face. He was so much older and wiser than she was. It was only in the past few years that she had truly come to appreciate that.

'It would be a far shorter list if I chronicled what was right,' she replied, looking at him in the mirror.

'Things have been a bit . . . awkward . . . lately,' he agreed.

Morna smiled thinly. 'You have a marvellous gift for understatement, Wallin.'

'Just as you have a gift for worrying too much.'

She turned on her stool to face him. 'What am I supposed to do? Just sit here and watch Antonov try to steal my son?'

'Have you ever noticed that you always refer to Dirk as your son?'

'What do you mean?'

'I mean Rees has always been *our* son. With Dirk you're always saying *my* son. It's a foolish slip of the tongue, Morna. You might give people the wrong idea.'

She studied him closely. After a long moment of strained silence, she looked away, unable to face him.

'You know,' she said tonelessly.

'I've always known, Morna.'

She was silent for a long time. Wallin looked at her, his expression giving her no hint of how he felt. Was he angry? Was he hurt?

'How did you find out?' she asked finally.

'You came to my bed the very first night you returned to Elcast. Do you remember that? I didn't ask you. I was prepared to wait. In fact, I expected it to be months before you would be ready to become my wife again. And then little more than six months later you gave birth to an eight-pound baby boy.'

'You never said . . . never even hinted . . .'

'Nor would I have said anything, had things remained as they were.'

Morna lowered her eyes, guilt making it impossible to meet his gaze. 'I never meant to deceive you, Wallin.'

He smiled regretfully. 'Then why try to make me believe Dirk was mine?'

'I had to protect him,' she explained, as if it would somehow justify her deceit. 'If anyone had guessed the truth . . .'

'You can't protect him for much longer, my dear.'

'What are you saying?' she demanded. 'You're not going to . . . ? Oh, Wallin, please! You can't do that! Dirk doesn't even suspect. It would destroy him! He loves you. You can't . . .'

'I won't expose him, Morna. Or you,' he assured her. 'What I meant is that he has reached an age where your protection is more akin to shackles than armour. Dirk must learn to look out for himself.'

'That's your advice?' she snapped. 'Let Dirk learn to *look out for himself*?'

'What's your suggestion, Morna? Keep him hidden away here on Elcast for the rest of his life, safe under your watchful eye?'

'Well, it's certainly a better idea than sending him to Avacas with the Lion of Senet!'

'You should have a little more faith in the Goddess, Morna.'

'The Goddess? *Antonov's* Goddess? The Goddess who demands human sacrifices each year to appease her appetite? Don't give me that nonsense about the Goddess, Wallin. Dirk doesn't have a destiny and he hasn't been touched by divine purpose. He's a normal child who happens to be intelligent. There is nothing more to it.'

'He's almost sixteen, Morna. He's not a child any more. And his mind is way beyond being just "intelligent". We've both known that since he was a toddler. It's one of the reasons you fear for him. I remember the first time Dirk came to you with one of his impossible questions. He must have been only three or four at the time. I forget what it was that he asked. But I do remember you turned white as a sheet when you realised that he was questioning something no four-year-old should comprehend.'

Morna shook her head, as if by denying him she could somehow alter reality. 'Dirk is too dangerous for Antonov, don't you see? Antonov would destroy him if he learned the truth.'

Wallin placed a comforting hand on her shoulder. 'I repeat what I said earlier, Morna. You worry too much. Dirk is my son. Legally and in any other way you care to mention. Antonov cannot prove otherwise. For Dirk to be a threat to Antonov he would have to know who fathered him *and* want the throne for himself. And he doesn't know. He doesn't even suspect the truth. It's hardly likely to become a problem, is it?'

'But if Dirk knew . . . if someone told him . . .'

'Dirk has never even worried that he won't become the Duke of Elcast. What makes you think that, even if he knew the truth, he'd want to be king?'

'But—'

'No. I'll not have you tearing yourself apart over this, Morna. You are to stop dwelling on vague possibilities. If anything, *your* nervousness will betray Dirk.'

'You're right,' she admitted. Then she looked up at him fearfully as another thought leapt to mind. 'But what if Johan learns the truth? Suppose he realises that Dirk is . . . he knew I was with child when I left . . .'

'There is nothing to be concerned about, Morna. He asked and Helgin told him you miscarried.'

She stared at him. 'You told Helgin to say that?'

'I merely pointed out to him that everything would be a lot easier if Johan believed his child had not survived.'

'Helgin never said . . .'

'I instructed him not to.'

'Do you often do that? Instruct people behind my back?'

'Is it any worse than some of the things you have done?' he asked.

Morna looked away, unable to deny his accusation. Wallin took her hand gently and pulled her to her feet. She could not meet his eyes. As he embraced her, she felt guilty for feeling so safe in his arms. That he had known the truth all these years and never betrayed her made her feel unworthy of his affection.

'I'm so sorry, Wallin,' she said, her voice muffled by his broad shoulder. 'I never meant to hurt you.'

'I know,' he told her gently. 'But I know you never loved me. I knew it from the first time we met.'

Tears welled up in her eyes as she remembered that awful day. She leaned back in his arms. 'I was so angry with my father.'

'Angry? Or disappointed?'

'What do you mean?'

'You were seventeen years old, Morna, and already in love with Johan Thorn. I was twice your age and a complete stranger.'

'When he told me he'd arranged a marriage, I was so sure it was Johan . . .' she acknowledged with an inelegant sniff, surprised that even after all this time, the shock and despair of that day was so easy to recall.

'Not an unreasonable expectation, under the circumstances,' he agreed. 'Your sister was married to the Lion of Senet. I can understand why you thought that if Oscon could arrange for Analee to marry a king, he could do the same for you.'

'Yet you married me anyway? Knowing I didn't love you?'

'I hoped you would learn to love me, Morna. An idle hope, as it turned out.'

'But I do love you, Wallin . . .'

He shook his head sadly. 'You are grateful to me, Morna. And in your own way, you probably have some affection for me. But you've never loved me. Not the way you loved him.'

She closed her eyes and let him hold her, resting her head on his shoulder. 'And yet you still protect me. You took me back after I abandoned you. You pleaded with Antonov to spare my life. You accepted Johan's son as your own and never once gave me, or Dirk, reason to suspect that you knew he wasn't your son.' Morna lifted her head and smiled at him. Out of the corner of her eye she noticed the door was open. Odd, she had thought it closed. 'I truly don't deserve—'

Morna stopped abruptly, suddenly unable to speak. Wallin glanced at her curiously and then looked over his shoulder.

Dirk was standing at the door, his eyes wide. He stared at them silently for a moment and then fled.

'Dirk!' Wallin called after him, urgently.

'Oh Goddess!' Morna sobbed as her worst fears suddenly became real. 'How long was he standing there?'

'Long enough,' Wallin suggested grimly.

38

Dirk forgot the reason he had gone to see his mother this morning as he ran down the stairs and through the Hall without stopping. He ran through the courtyard and out the gate without acknowledging the greeting of the guards.

His mother's words were echoing in his head. *You accepted Johan's son as your own and never once gave me, or Dirk, reason to suspect that you knew he wasn't your son.*

He ran down towards the town and then, on impulse, veered off into the forest that flanked the road. He crashed through the undergrowth, ignoring the sharp branches that slashed at his face as he ran.

You accepted Johan's son as your own ...

He ran as if he could somehow outdistance the truth.

When he finally stopped, exhausted and bloodied, he discovered he was close to the pool near the Outlet where they'd first met Marqel. He stumbled through the bushes to the small pool and fell to his knees on the edge of the water, gasping for breath.

You accepted Johan's son as your own ...

His mother's words burned through his brain. It was as if they were written in fire, branded on the inside of his skull.

You accepted Johan's son as your own ...

Johan's son. Not Wallin's son. *Johan's* son. The bastard get of a deposed heretic king. The illegitimate result of an illicit affair between a woman who had abandoned her husband and child, and a man who would rather suffer the Age of Shadows than allow anyone to do anything that might bring back the light.

The *Book of Ranadon* had referred to his mother as a traitorous harlot, he remembered. *The* Book of Ranadon *is right!*

Dirk glanced down at his reflection in the pool. The face

staring back at him was a stranger. *You must take after your mother,* he'd heard people say, time and again. No wonder no one ever said he looked like Wallin or Rees.

Dirk plunged his face into the warm water of the pool, but it did nothing to cool his fevered mind. He came up gasping, shook his head, leaving a spray of droplets in his wake, and sat back on his heels.

So I'm a bastard, he told himself harshly. *I don't even have the dubious distinction of being branded a Landfall bastard. At least they're conceived openly, not the result of some tawdry affair.*

He'd been so sure the *Book of Ranadon* was just a pack of lies. So certain that Antonov was wrong about his mother. Even after Morna had admitted to him that she had fled with Johan during the war, he'd convinced himself that she was simply fighting for something noble. She was afraid for Rees and Johan had offered her hope.

He realised now that there was nothing noble in her actions. She was simply an unfaithful wife who had run off with her lover and then come home again, carrying his bastard.

What had Johan said? *Don't dig into the past. You'll find more than you bargained for . . .*

The sense of betrayal he felt was overwhelming. It was as if his mother's words were a terrible, invisible axe that had cleaved him from everything he thought he knew. He felt cut adrift and lost. His mother had lied to him. His father had lied to him – only he wasn't really his father. They had even lied to each other. Who else knew the truth? Helgin must have known. That cut almost as deep as the knowledge that his parents had lied to him. He had trusted Helgin.

What about Rees? Did Rees remember Morna abandoning him?

What a fool I am, he berated himself silently. *She said she left Elcast because she feared for Rees. Yet she left him behind on Elcast while she cavorted with her lover.* That should have warned him that her motives weren't anywhere near as noble as she tried to paint them. *I should have seen the truth then.*

He recalled his mother's agonised look as she admitted

her past. *Dirk will learn the truth, sooner or later,* Morna had said. *I'd rather he heard it from us than hear the Lion of Senet's twisted version of events.*

He understood now why Morna was so fearful of him learning the truth from Prince Antonov.

As he thought of the Lion of Senet, Dirk found himself reassessing his opinion of the Senetian ruler. Was anything he had done worse than his mother's acts? He'd simply followed the edicts of his religion, and while they might be questionable, his honour was above reproach. Morna tried so hard to make Dirk think Antonov was evil, yet it was his mercy that allowed her to live.

She's a hypocrite and a liar, he decided.

He found himself wanting to lash out at Morna in any way he could. He wanted her to feel even a fraction of his pain. He had never before felt so abandoned, so alone.

He glanced down at his reflection once more. The face he stared at had always belonged to Dirk Provin. Now it belonged to someone different. Someone he didn't know.

I wonder if Johan has any idea that I'm his son?

Dirk decided he probably didn't. For Morna to perpetrate her lies, she couldn't risk telling Johan he had a child.

What of Antonov? Does he know, or even suspect the truth?

And if he did learn the truth, what would he do about it? Would he permit a possible usurper to the throne of Dhevyn to survive?

That thought gave Dirk pause.

If I wanted to, I could claim the throne of Dhevyn, he realised with a start.

But why would I want it? It belongs to Alenor, not me.

As his thoughts turned to Alenor, Dirk's heart constricted. He sat by the pool for a long time, trying to make some sense out of what he knew. Eventually, he glanced up at the second sun and realised that he had missed his morning lesson with Marqel. He would be missed in the Keep. Was Wallin looking for him? Was his mother desperate to explain away her confession with another wagonload of lies?

He took a deep breath and splashed his face with water. *I have to go back. I have to pretend that nothing is amiss. How will I stand it?*

Dirk climbed slowly to his feet and consciously tried to calm his racing heart.

'I have to go back,' he told his reflection, then added spitefully, 'but I damn well don't have to stay.'

Lunch was being served when he arrived back at the Keep. He marched into the Hall and straight up to the High Table. Tovin Rill, Prince Antonov and Wallin Provin were deep in a discussion about the ruined Elcast harvest. His mother sat on Wallin's left, her eyes wide with fear, as she watched him approach the table. Rees and Faralan sat beside Morna, lost in a rather heated conversation of their own. Kirshov, Alenor and Lanon were nowhere in sight.

Dirk was calm as he stopped in front of the table. His heart no longer felt as if it would explode out of his chest. His breathing was even and measured.

'Your highness?'

'Dirk!' Wallin cried in surprise, drawing speculative glances from both Tovin and Antonov. 'We've been looking for you everywhere. Goddess! What happened to your face?' Then, as if Wallin suddenly remembered the Senetians, he added hastily, 'You missed your lesson with the acrobat. Olena was quite concerned.'

'I'm sorry, sir, I had something to take care of.'

'You look like you've been in a fight,' Tovin chuckled, as he took in Dirk's scratched face and tattered shirt. 'You weren't discussing the correct rules of pokeball with Lanon again, were you?'

'No, my lord. I was in the woods. I was attacked by nothing more sinister than a thorn tree.'

'Well, if you're here looking for Kirsh and Alenor,' Antonov said, 'they said something about a picnic.'

'No, your highness, I wasn't looking for them. I came to ask you something.'

Out of the corner of his eye he saw Morna bite back a gasp of dismay. He did not look at her.

'Ask away, Dirk. I'll answer if I can.'

'My father says you want me to return to Senet with you.'

'That's true, Dirk, but we don't have to go before...'

'I'd like to accept your offer, your highness.'

'Dirk! *No!*' Morna cried, jumping to her feet. Wallin's expression was bleak, but he made no move to object. *Why should he? He's not my father*.

Antonov glanced down the table at the duchess. He did not attempt to hide his triumph. He turned back to Dirk. 'You will be most welcome in Avacas, Dirk. But I'm tempted to ask what brought about this sudden change of heart. I heard you weren't disposed towards the idea.'

'I've had time to think about it, your highness, and on reflection, I feel I can learn a lot more in Avacas than on a small island like Elcast.'

'You demonstrate rare sense for one so young.'

'Thank you, your highness.'

Antonov looked at Morna and his smile widened. 'Well, my lady, it seems there is nothing to prevent us finally removing the burden of our presence from your household.'

'Anton, please... you can't...'

'I believe I can, my lady. Your husband has already agreed and now that I find your son so keen to accept my hospitality, I see no reason for us to impose upon your good graces any longer. If you would be so kind as to send Balonan to me after lunch, I will start making the necessary arrangements. I imagine we could be gone on tomorrow's tide.'

'Dirk...' Morna's eyes glistened with unshed tears. She was almost begging him for understanding.

Dirk found he didn't care. 'Yes, Mother?'

She wanted to ask him why. He could see that. But she wouldn't. She couldn't risk him blurting out the reason in front of Antonov, and she didn't trust him enough to realise that he had more sense than that. Dirk was quite offended. He might be hurt, but he wasn't stupid.

'Your decision appears to be causing your mother some distress, Dirk,' Antonov pointed out. He realised that the prince didn't seem concerned about it, either.

'She'll get over it.'

'Dirk . . .' Wallin said warningly.

'May I be excused, your highness? I need to pack.'

'Of course,' Antonov agreed with a smile.

Dirk bowed to the prince and turned on his heel. He could feel Morna's eyes on him as he walked through the Hall, but he didn't look back. The last thing he heard as he began climbing the staircase was Antonov talking to Tovin Rill.

'And now that business is taken care of,' the Lion of Senet was saying, 'I believe it's time I did something about Johan Thorn.'

39

Johan was jerked awake by a commotion in the outer room. He was still rubbing the sleep from his eyes when the door flew open. It banged against the wall. The pirate rolled onto his side and stared at the familiar figure standing in the doorway. He was surprised it had taken him so long to come.

'Your highness, I must object!' Helgin was complaining from the other room. 'He is still not recovered enough to—'

The Lion of Senet slammed the door behind him, cutting off Helgin's protests and glanced about Johan's room before he spoke. 'Helgin's a whining old woman. He always was. You look fine to me.'

'Your expert medical opinion means so much to me.'

Antonov crossed the room and picked up the book at the foot of Johan's bed. He examined the title on the spine, and tossed it back onto the bed, before he looked at him.

'Enjoying your convalescence?'

'I was until you showed up,' Johan replied, pushing himself up in the bed, wincing a little as his shoulder objected. His broken arms had taken longer to heal, but his shoulder was giving him more trouble than his freshly mended bones. 'I'm truly honoured that you finally found time to pay me a visit, your highness.'

'I had other, more important things to take care of.'

'More important than finally getting rid of me?'

Antonov smiled. 'You haven't changed, Johan. It irks you to think that there's anything more important in this world than you, doesn't it?'

'Total self-absorption is your weakness, not mine, Anton. To be honest, I've quite enjoyed the break – no pun intended. The food here is good, I've had time to catch up on some reading—'

'I'm glad you've enjoyed it so much,' Antonov cut in. 'You'll be in a dungeon when you reach Avacas.'

'You actually *have* dungeons? Now why doesn't that surprise me?'

'You're in a remarkably good humour for a man about to die.'

'Am I? Ah . . . well that's probably the poppy-dust,' he said. 'I'm beginning to understand what Neris found so enticing about it.'

'Have you fallen so low that you're now taking drugs to ease your conscience?'

'My conscience doesn't need easing, and no, Anton, I hate to disappoint you, but I'm not caught in the grip of the poppy-dust. You'll have to find another way to torment me, I'm afraid.' He stared at the prince for a moment, trying to discern his intentions. 'Although one can't help but wonder why you didn't come up here and run a sword through me the day you arrived on Elcast.'

'You've no idea how tempted I was,' Antonov admitted.

'So what stopped you?'

The prince smiled coldly. 'Actually, it was Morna.'

Johan's expression darkened. 'What have you done, Anton?'

'Nothing, Johan. Absolutely *nothing*. I didn't have to.'

'What are you talking about?'

'Don't you see the beauty of it? The longer I was here on Elcast, the longer I was in her home, the longer I left you lying here unmolested, the longer I went without even mentioning your name, the crazier it drove her.' He smiled ingenuously. 'I've discovered subtlety can be so much more effective than brute force.'

'You always were a sadistic bastard.'

'And you were always a fool.'

'I must have been,' he agreed ruefully. 'I asked Senet for aid.' When Antonov didn't rise to the taunt he studied him curiously. 'Do you really intend to kill me, Anton?'

'What did you think I was planning? To escort you back to Kalarada and reinstate you?'

'You don't have the right to reinstate me, Antonov Latanya. Any more than you had the right to remove me in the first place.'

'The Goddess gave me the right.'

'The Goddess gave you the *excuse*,' Johan countered.

'You still mock my faith? You believed in her once. Until Neris poisoned your mind against her.'

'Neris opened my eyes to the truth, Anton.'

'Truth? What truth? You are the proof that she *exists*, Johan! I asked the Goddess to deliver you to me and behold, she sent forth a tidal wave.'

'And who did you kill to get her attention this time, Anton? Another one of your sons?' When Antonov didn't answer him, he scowled with mock concern. 'I hope you don't ask her for such favours too often. I mean, what happens when you run out of relatives to sacrifice?'

Antonov refused to answer. Instead, he walked to the window and turned his back on Johan.

'Helgin begrudgingly admits that you are recovered enough to travel.'

'You've been waiting all this time for me to recover? I didn't think you cared.'

'I don't,' Antonov said, turning to look at him. 'You have

information I require and I don't intend to let you die until I have it.'

'What could I possibly know that is of any interest to you, Anton? Except perhaps that your whole damn religion is a farce ... But then, you never wanted to hear that, did you? Not even when I had the proof.'

'The proof is dead. Neris killed himself.'

'Then you admit that I *had* proof?'

'The only thing I'll admit is that you listened to the ravings of a drug-addicted lunatic, and were prepared to destroy thousands of years of belief based on what he told you. I have all the proof I need. I did as the Goddess asked and she returned us to the light.'

'You murdered your son because *Belagren* told you to, Anton, not the Goddess. And how do you think she knew when the appointed time was right? How do you think Belagren knew the *exact* time the sun would return? Because of some holy vision she had? Or because Neris was able to calculate—'

'Enough!' Antonov cried. 'I will not listen to your blasphemy!'

'More's the pity,' Johan said wearily. 'Your son might be alive today if you had.'

'If you had heeded the Goddess's word, Johan, you might still have a kingdom.'

'If you hadn't heeded Belagren's words, you might still have a wife.'

'You're treading on very dangerous ground, Johan.'

'What are you going to do, Anton? *Kill* me?'

For a long time the Lion of Senet didn't reply. When he did, his eyes burned with the same fanatical light that had shone in them so many years ago. Johan was filled with despair at the sight. Antonov was still as unreasonable, still as completely immersed in the lies of his faith, as he ever was. 'The High Priestess has charged me with a sacred mission.'

'Sacred mission? You astound me, Anton. I never cease to be amazed at your gullibility. Who does she want you to murder this time?'

'I must find Neris Veran.'

Johan smiled sceptically. 'And why do you think Belagren wants Neris so badly?'

Antonov actually looked surprised that Johan had to ask such a thing. 'To pay for what he's done. He must face the Goddess and denounce his heresy.'

'It wouldn't be because Belagren still doesn't know when the next Age of Shadows is due, I suppose? No, of course not. That would mean your whole damn religion is a sham. Anyway, Neris is dead. You know that.'

'Perhaps. What about your people hiding out in the Baenlands?'

'They're a handful of refugees. They're no danger to you.'

'They consider you the true King of Dhevyn. If I kill you before I clean them out, they'll worship you as a martyr for years to come and I'll never be rid of Neris's poisonous heresy.'

'Perhaps they think of me as the true King of Dhevyn because I am the true King of Dhevyn,' he suggested. Johan lay back on the pillow and closed his eyes with a faint smile. 'Anyway, whatever your reasons, do you seriously think I would tell you anything of value?'

'You'll tell me,' Antonov replied confidently. 'If I have to break every bone in your miserable body, you'll tell me what I want to know.'

Johan laughed sceptically. 'You don't know me as well as you think.'

'Oh, don't worry, Johan. I know you won't give in easily. Why do you think I wanted you recovered before I moved you to Senet? I can't have you dying on me until I'm ready for it.'

'That would be tragic,' he agreed wryly.

'My people are very, very good at what they do,' Antonov warned. 'One way or another, you will tell me everything I want to know. You will live to see me clean out that viper's nest in the Baenlands. You will live to see your dreams destroyed. I will break you, then humiliate you, then I'll kill you and dance on your corpse.'

It was no idle threat he was making, Johan realised. *Oh, Helgin, you sentimental old fool, why didn't you let me die? It would have been so much easier on everybody.*

'Antonov, doesn't it concern you a little that you're proud of how efficiently you can maim and torture people? Why do you need to hone such skills, I wonder? Surely the great Lion of Senet holds power because his people love him, not because they're afraid of him?'

'And it was the great love of the people of Dhevyn for *their* king that saw them flock to my banner, not yours, when we went to war, I suppose? Perhaps you should consider that, before you start condemning my tactics.'

'Would that be the tactic where you respond to a request for aid by invading us?'

'Your people were starving and rioting, Johan. Your whole kingdom was falling apart around you. You asked for my help and I gave it unstintingly.'

'You call invading Dhevyn an act of charity?'

'It was the Goddess who brought your people hope. My troops brought order out of chaos.'

'It's been a long, long time since the Age of Shadows ended, Antonov. You've more troops stationed in Dhevyn than you have in Senet.'

'I would withdraw them tomorrow if the queen asked me.'

'Rainan?' he laughed sceptically. 'You've taken her daughter hostage. She's afraid to ask you what day it is, let alone demand you withdraw.'

'And whose fault is that? Dhevyn had a king once. He abandoned his throne.'

Johan took a deep breath before replying, surprised at how heated the argument was becoming. He had thought himself past all this.

'This is pointless, Anton. Neither of us has anything to gain by trying to apportion blame for things done so many years ago.'

'You're right, I have nothing to gain. I already have it all.'

'Is that what drives you?'

'Perhaps. What drives you, Johan? The never-ending desire to *lose*? First you lost Dhevyn, and now you're going to lose your pitiful little substitute kingdom in the Baenlands, and then you're going to lose your life.'

Johan was suddenly weary of Antonov's company. 'Why did you come here, Anton?'

'To tell you that we're leaving for Senet in the morning. You'll be moved down to the ship this evening.'

'And chained in the hold with the rats, I suppose?'

Antonov glanced around the comfortable room that had been his prison since arriving on Elcast. 'Your days of luxury and peace are at an end, Thorn.'

'They ended a long time ago, Antonov, the day I let you step foot in Dhevyn.'

40

Leaving Elcast proved rather more complicated than Dirk anticipated. He really hadn't thought much about the consequences of his decision. It was prompted almost entirely by the desire to lash out at his mother in any way he could, and Antonov's sudden decision to leave on the next tide left him no time to reconsider. He stood in the centre of his room and looked about in despair. Confronted with a lifetime of memories to be packed, he had no idea where to begin.

'Dirk?'

'Faralan?' he exclaimed, glancing over his shoulder. 'What are you doing here? Did you come to help me pack?'

'No.'

'Then if you don't mind, I've got a lot to do before I leave tomorrow.' He studied the shelves near the window with a frown. *I might be able to squeeze the books in. But the chess set will have to stay. And the crystals*. Dirk's fascination with geology had been a passing fad when he was eleven or twelve, and for a while he had driven everyone mad with his insistence on carting a sample of every interesting rock he found into the castle for identification and study. He'd been too engrossed in his studies as a physician lately to keep up the hobby, but over the years he'd amassed quite a collection.

'I . . .' Faralan began hesitantly. She was very nervous about something, which struck Dirk as odd. 'I came . . .'

'Yes?' he prompted impatiently, turning back to face her. Faralan stared pointedly at Eryk. She obviously wasn't going to leave until she'd said whatever it was she had come to say, or say it while Eryk was in the room. 'Eryk, run downstairs and ask Balonan where my trunk is.'

Eryk looked at Faralan oddly as he sidled past her, but didn't offer any comment, even though Dirk was quite sure the boy knew he was being sent away so he couldn't over-hear the conversation. Once he was gone, Faralan glanced down the hall to ensure she was not seen, then stepped into the room and closed the door. She turned to face Dirk with her hands on her hips.

'I came to ask you what in the name of the Goddess you think you're doing,' she blurted out.

Dirk was astonished. 'I'm going to Avacas.'

'Why?'

'Do I need a reason?'

'Yes.'

'I want to further my education.'

She lowered her voice, as if she feared they would be overheard. 'Have you any idea what your foolishness is doing to your mother?'

'That's her problem, not mine,' Dirk replied, turning back to the dilemma of what to pack from the shelves by the window. 'It's also none of your business.'

Faralan grabbed his shoulder and turned him around forcefully. 'What's the matter with everyone around here? Listen to you! What's got into you, Dirk? A month ago you and Rees were denouncing the Shadowdancers and anything to do with them as evil incarnate. Now you're running off to live with Antonov, and Rees . . .'

Dirk shook free of her irritably. 'That's an arrangement my parents made with Antonov, not me, so don't go acting as if this is my fault. If Mother doesn't like the idea, maybe she shouldn't have agreed to it in the first place.'

'She had no choice, you know that.'

'Then why are you mad at *me,* Faralan? One way or another, I was destined to leave Elcast. I can't help it if Mother doesn't like the fact that I'm now looking forward to it. Would she be happier if they dragged me down to the boat kicking and screaming?'

Faralan shook her head with a frown. 'I don't understand you, Dirk.'

'You never have, Faralan, don't start trying now.'

Her eyes filled with unshed tears. Dirk muttered a curse and bit back his temper with an effort. 'What's really the matter, Faralan? You don't care if I go to Senet or not.'

'It's Rees,' she told him with a sniff. 'Ever since the Landfall Feast, he's been . . .'

'He's been what? He seems fine to me.'

'Different.'

'How?'

'I don't know,' she shrugged. 'It's just now he says things . . . it's like he's changed his mind about everything. He's talking about making sure the Landfall Festival is held every year – and he said that next year we'll have our own people to sacrifice. He asked your father to do something about the ruined temple, too, and now Tovin Rill is talking about levying a tax to fix it. And your mother's been acting really strange ever since they caught that pirate. Now you're running off to live in Avacas.' She wiped away a stray tear and sank down onto the edge of the bed. 'I used to *like* coming here each year.'

'Rees said *what* about the Landfall sacrifice?' It had sounded so unlike his brother. Dirk understood why Faralan was so upset.

She shook her head in dismay.

He sat down beside her, unsure what to say. He normally barely spoke to his brother's fiancée. He certainly didn't feel qualified to give her advice about Rees.

'Maybe he's just . . .' Dirk found himself unable to complete the sentence. He had no idea what had possessed his brother to say such things.

'Maybe I'm just what?'

'Rees!' Faralan jumped to her feet with a guilty start. She hurriedly wiped away her tears as Rees walked in.

'Haven't you heard of knocking?' Dirk asked in annoyance.

'Why? What were you doing with my fiancée that required a warning that I was about to enter the room?'

Dirk stared at Rees in surprise. Such a comment was so out of character for his brother that for a moment Dirk was rendered speechless.

'Faralan, Mother is looking for you. She needs your help getting Prince Antonov's servants moved out.'

'I should go to her, then,' she said. She turned to Dirk and smiled tentatively. 'Goodbye, Dirk. I hope you find what you're looking for in Senet.'

'I . . . I'll . . .' Dirk wasn't sure what to say. Rees was staring at him suspiciously. 'I'll make sure I'm back for the wedding.'

'Mother is waiting, Faralan.'

Faralan fled the room, and the door slammed behind her. Dirk glared at his brother as he stood up. He had never heard him use that tone with her before.

'What's your problem?'

'I don't have a problem. Do you need assistance packing?'

'No. Why are you so anxious to be rid of me all of a sudden?'

'I'm not. If anything, I envy you. You're going to have the opportunity to serve the Goddess directly.'

Dirk stared at Rees, open-mouthed. 'You think that's why I'm going? And you *envy* me? What's happened to you, Rees?'

'Nothing.'

'You used to hate the Shadowdancers. At least until you took part in the Landfall Festival. Was it so much fun that now you've had a complete change of heart?'

'I never said I hated the Shadowdancers. I just never understood them before.'

'And smearing your face in pig's blood, then screwing your brains out with a Shadowdancer made you see the light, I suppose?'

Rees's fist came out of nowhere. At first, Dirk thought his face had exploded. He staggered backwards, white-hot pain shooting across the bridge of his nose. He blinked back tears of pain and shock, clutching a hand to his bloodied face, but made no attempt to hit back. He was taller than Rees, but his brother was heavier and more experienced. He was too stunned to react, in any case. Rees had never raised a hand to him before. As far as Dirk knew, Rees had never raised his hand in anger to anyone before.

'If you ever say such a thing again, I'll beat you sense-less.'

'Faralan is right,' he accused, trying in vain to staunch the flow of blood from his swollen nose. 'You've lost your mind.'

'Is that what upset Faralan? Is that what you were telling her?'

He couldn't say anything to Rees without telling him that he had sneaked up to the tower to watch the Festival with Alenor. He couldn't let on that he knew exactly what went on. He'd get them both into trouble. Besides, with Rees in such an unpredictable mood, Dirk decided diplomacy was more prudent than provocation.

'I didn't tell her anything.'

'Then see that you don't. You've got less than a day left here on Elcast, Dirk. Try not to ruin it for everyone.'

Before Dirk could defend himself against that charge, the door banged open again and Kirsh barrelled in with Lanon on his heels. The boys were laughing about something, but their amusement withered almost as soon as they stepped into the tension-filled room.

'Hey, if we're leaving tomorrow, you and I still have a race up those stairs to . . . Goddess, Dirk! What happened to you?'

Rees stared at the prince and the governor's son for a moment, then turned to Dirk. 'Just remember what I said, brother.'

Kirsh and Lanon stepped aside as Rees strode from the room. As soon as the door closed behind him, the boys turned to Dirk, bursting with curiosity.

'Are you all right? Why did Rees hit you?' Lanon demanded.

Dirk sat on the edge of the bed and tipped his head back. He could taste the iron tang of his own blood in the back of his throat. His face was on fire.

'Who said Rees hit me?'

'He had blood on his knuckles,' Lanon pointed out. 'What did you say to him?'

'It doesn't matter, Lanon. Just find me a towel, will you?'

Lanon hurried off to fetch a towel, leaving Kirsh to stare at him with a concerned expression.

'Here, let me look at it.'

'Ow! Don't touch me! Just leave me alone, Kirsh.'

'Does it hurt?'

Dirk tilted his head forward and glared at the prince. 'What do *you* think?'

Lanon arrived with the towel, which Dirk snatched from him. The boys winced sympathetically as he carefully dabbed at his tender, swollen face.

'You need something cold on that,' Kirsh advised. 'Otherwise it's going to black both your eyes, too.'

'You're not helping, Kirshov.'

The door burst open again, and Alenor walked in. 'Guess what? I just heard Prince Antonov say that we're leaving to . . . Goddess, Dirk! What happened?'

Dirk rolled his eyes in despair. His once quiet room was proving to be busier than the Elcast Town Square on market day.

'Rees punched him in the nose,' Lanon volunteered cheerfully.

'*Why?*'

'We're still waiting to find out.'

Dirk lowered the blood-soaked towel and glared at them. 'There's nothing to tell.'

'We'll get it out of you eventually,' Kirsh warned with a grin.

'I think I'd like to hear the reason, too.'

Dirk felt like screaming as Wallin Provin stepped through the door. Was the whole damn castle planning to gather in his room?

'If you would excuse me, your highnesses, I'd like a word with my son.'

Dirk could have sworn Wallin placed an unnecessary emphasis on the words 'my son'. Although they were dying to know what had really happened, Kirsh, Lanon and Alenor acquiesced to the duke's request with a bow and a promise to Dirk that they would return later. He dabbed at his nose again, relieved to discover the bleeding had slowed.

'You should put something cold on that,' Wallin advised.

'So everybody keeps telling me.'

'Why did Rees hit you?' he asked. Then his expression clouded. 'You didn't . . .'

'*No.*'

Wallin nodded, then took a deep breath and sat on the bed beside him. For a long time he said nothing. When the silence became unbearable, he visibly braced himself before speaking.

'I'm not sure how much you overheard, Dirk,' he began, uncertainly, 'but you may have misconstrued . . .'

'"You accepted Johan's son as your own and never once gave me, or Dirk, reason to suspect that you knew he wasn't your son,"' Dirk quoted harshly. 'Just exactly which part did I misconstrue?'

The duke sighed heavily. 'You weren't meant to hear any of that, Dirk.'

'Obviously.'

Wallin shook his head and studied him for a moment. He was not a talkative man, or one given to long explanations. What others thought of as aloofness was simply Wallin's nature, and he was uncomfortable having to explain anything now. Dirk was astounded by how much it hurt to learn that this man wasn't his father.

'I never thought of you as anything other than my son, Dirk.'

'Never?'

'I'll admit to a moment of apprehension when I learned it was Johan Thorn who was washed up in that tidal wave.'

'Why did you lie to me?'

He shrugged. 'To be honest, it just never crossed my mind to say anything. You are my son, Dirk, in every way that matters.'

'Aren't I a constant reminder of her infidelity?'

'It's funny you should ask that. I wondered if I should feel that way. But I don't. In fact, it's only since you've got taller that you've even begun to resemble Johan.'

'Oh, great! Now I look like him, too! What's next? Do I have the Thorn birthmark as well?'

Wallin smiled at Dirk's poor attempt at humour. 'There is no Thorn birthmark, Dirk. At least not that I'm aware of. And you're not so much like him that it will put you in danger. But yes, the older you get, the more like him you become. For that reason, if no other, you must do your best to remain in the Lion of Senet's good graces. You may one day be in need of powerful friends.'

The bleeding had finally stopped. Dirk put down the towel and touched the swollen flesh gingerly. He was sure his nose was broken. At the very least, it must be five times its normal size.

'How long have you known?'

'Since before you were born.'

'Mother lied to you too, then?'

'She was trying to protect you, son.'

Dirk snorted sceptically. 'Is that why you're here? To make me understand? Or to beg me not to leave?'

Wallin shook his head. 'No. All the gnashing and wailing in the world on your mother's part is not going to alter the fact that the Lion of Senet wants you in Avacas. Perhaps, in light of that, it's not a bad thing that you know.'

'Does he know?'

'Antonov? I think not.'

'But you don't know for certain?'

'Not for certain, no.'

'What about Johan Thorn?'

'He thinks your mother suffered a miscarriage, and if you have any sense at all, you will let him continue to think that. I know this news hurts you, Dirk, but that pain is nothing compared to what you would suffer if it became public knowledge.'

'Do you really think a bit of public humiliation could hurt any worse than what I'm feeling now?'

'Dirk, this has nothing to do with your tender feelings. Don't you understand that your life is at stake? There are a great many people in Dhevyn who would try to use you, should the truth be known, and a great many people in Senet who think the only good Thorn is a dead one. I've no doubt you'll come to terms with the knowledge in your own time, son. Whether or not you ever forgive your mother will be up to you. Right now, I'm more concerned that you understand *why* she lied to protect you. And that you have the wits to do the same for yourself.'

'I'm not stupid, Father.'

Wallin smiled. 'No, Dirk, you certainly are not. But you're hurting. I understand that. And you're angry with your mother. Trust me, nobody on Ranadon understands how that feels better than I do. I just want to make sure that you don't let your desire to hit back at her outweigh your common sense.'

Dirk stared at Wallin with a puzzled look. 'Why did you take her back? After what she did . . .'

'She was the mother of my son, Dirk.'

'She betrayed you.'

'She did what she thought was right. It's not quite as

sinister as you think. Your mother knew Thorn long before she met me. And believe it or not, while Antonov is my friend, and I don't hold with your mother's views, I have my concerns about the practices of the Shadowdancers. It's why I didn't object when she wanted to stop the Landfall Festival from being held on Elcast.'

'Well, those happy days are over,' Dirk informed him sourly. 'I hear Rees has become quite enchanted with the idea.'

Wallin didn't seem surprised. 'It's not an uncommon reaction to the rite.'

Dirk stared at him. 'Are you going to let them? Are you really going to let them sacrifice somebody next year to appease the Goddess?'

'One day, when you're older, you'll take part in the Landfall Festival yourself. You'll see things differently then.'

Dirk thought that highly unlikely.

'Have you ever taken part in it?'

'I have to be going. There's a lot to be done with Antonov leaving. Shall we see you at dinner?' It was clear he did not intend to answer Dirk's question. The duke rose to his feet, glancing around the room.

'Maybe.'

'I know it's difficult, but if you can bring yourself to do it, see your mother before you leave. She's worried about you.'

'I'll try.'

Wallin appeared suddenly uncomfortable, as if there was something else he wanted to say, but couldn't bring himself to voice the words. 'Well . . . I'll see you at dinner then.'

'Yes, sir.'

He walked to the door, but stopped with his hand on the latch. 'Dirk . . . I couldn't be prouder of you if you were my own flesh and blood, you know that, don't you?'

Dirk nodded silently.

'You have a gift, lad. A gift from the Goddess. Whatever you do once you leave here, don't waste it.'

'I'll try not to, sir.'

Wallin nodded. 'Good . . . well, see you at dinner then.'

Dirk sat motionlessly for a long time after Wallin left, thinking about what he had said. His eyes misted with tears, which he brushed away angrily, bumping his swollen nose. He let out a howl of pain, but it was as much from his mental anguish as it was from the relatively minor agony of his bruised and battered face.

41

Kirsh was already dressed and ready to leave. He shook Dirk rudely awake just before the second sun rose. Dirk blinked owlishly at the prince in the red light of the early morning, wincing at the pain the movement caused in his swollen, battered face.

'What?' he demanded grumpily.

'We're leaving this morning,' Kirsh reminded him cheerfully.

'So let me enjoy my last few moments of peace,' Dirk begged, pulling the covers up over his head.

'You and I have a score to settle,' Kirsh said as he ripped the sheets back.

Dirk rolled over and glared at him. 'Score? What score?'

Eryk was standing beside Kirsh and seemed firmly on the prince's side. 'You have to race Prince Kirsh up the staircase before we leave, remember?'

Dirk closed his gummy eyes with a groan.

Kirsh shook him by the shoulder impatiently. 'You're not going to wheedle out of this, Dirk Provin. Come on, out of bed! Lanon's already on his way up to the top to act as referee.'

Dirk asked. 'Why Lanon?'

'He was the only one willing to climb to the top of the damn staircase.'

Dirk stared at Kirsh with despair. His face was aching,

his eyes were gummed up and his nose was congested. He was in no mood and no condition to race anyone up eight flights of steep stairs – especially not Kirshov Latanya, who was competitive to the point of obsession. It was not as if he could just let Kirsh win, he realised. If the Senetian prince thought he had given the race anything less than his best effort, he was just as likely to demand they run it again.

'Kirsh, I really don't feel like . . .'

'A pact is a pact.'

'But I can't even breathe properly! You'll win just on that alone!'

'You can breathe, Dirk. Besides, if anything, your injuries just level the playing field. You're used to those damn stairs. You've been running up and down them all your life.'

Dirk sat up slowly and swung his legs around so that he was sitting on the edge of the bed. 'There's no way I can talk you out of this, I suppose?'

'Not a chance,' Kirsh assured him.

Dirk sighed heavily. 'Very well. Do you want to get ready, then?'

'I am ready.'

Dirk glanced at Kirsh's clothes and would have frowned, except that it hurt too much.

'You're wearing that?'

Kirsh was dressed in fine woollen trousers, an expensive and exquisitely embroidered linen shirt and knee-high boots. 'Sure. What's wrong with it?'

'Nothing.' Dirk shrugged. 'Let me get dressed and wash my face. I'll meet you downstairs.'

Kirsh nodded and ruffled Eryk's head with a grin. 'Don't let him go back to sleep, Eryk. If he's not there in ten minutes, I'm coming for him. We have to leave just after the second sunrise to catch the tide, so we have to get this over and done with, or Father won't let us finish it.'

That sounded just fine to Dirk, but he knew that Kirsh wasn't going to be put off by anything as mundane as angering the Lion of Senet.

'I'll be there,' Dirk promised.

'I'll be waiting.'

Once Kirsh left the room, Dirk pushed Eryk aside and stumbled to the washbowl to splash cold water on his face.

'You're gonna beat him, Lord Dirk,' Eryk declared confidently as he handed him a towel.

He glanced down at the boy and smiled. 'You think so, Eryk?'

Eryk nodded. 'You fixed Derwn up real good.'

'That was actually Kirsh, not me.'

Eryk shrugged. 'You're still gonna beat him. I know it. Here.' The boy tapped his chest, roughly where he thought his heart might be.

Dirk frowned, not sure he wanted to be the repository for Eryk's noble dreams.

'Will you be disappointed in me if I lose?'

'You won't lose,' Eryk assured him confidently.

Dirk smiled. 'Well, I hope I'm as good as you think I am, Eryk. Are you all packed?'

The boy nodded, a little uncertainly.

'You know, you don't have to come with me. You can stay here on Elcast with your friends if you prefer.'

'But you're my only real friend, Lord Dirk.'

Sadly, the boy probably spoke the truth. Dirk glanced around the room, with its bare shelves and empty cupboards, experiencing a moment of doubt. *What am I doing?* he asked himself. Then he remembered why he was leaving Elcast and straightened his shoulders with determination.

I'm not a Provin. I don't belong here.

Then he splashed his face again, mostly to stop himself from facing the uncomfortable fact that he probably didn't belong with Antonov Latanya either.

Eryk headed up to the top floor after they left Dirk's room, preferring to be there for the finish, rather than watch it from below. When Dirk arrived at the bottom of the stairs, he discovered to his dismay that most of the people in the Keep had got wind of the challenge between Dirk Provin and Kirshov Latanya, and had turned out to watch. Dirk pushed his way through the crowd, smiling uncomfortably at the wellwishers, who slapped him on the back and offered words of encouragement.

'Quite an audience,' a voice remarked behind him.

Dirk spun around to find Prince Antonov standing behind him.

'Your highness?'

'Kirsh told me about your challenge.' He glanced around at the gathered servants and smiled. 'It would seem the pride of Elcast is firmly in your hands this morning.'

'It's only a race, your highness.'

'It's never *only* a race, Dirk.'

Kirsh came to stand beside his father, bouncing on the balls of his feet with anticipation. He was itching to get started.

'Aren't you going to get dressed first?' he asked, taking in Dirk's loose trousers, bare chest and bare feet.

'I'm dressed enough for this,' Dirk replied.

Kirsh looked at him oddly, then shrugged. 'Are you ready, then?'

He nodded. 'Let's get it over with.'

The crowd moved back to give them room. Antonov took it upon himself to act as the starter, and made sure that both boys were positioned below the first step. Dirk took his place on the inside. It might only be by a fraction, but the distance was shorter, the steps a little narrower on that side. Of course, the disadvantage was that if he stumbled, he might plummet to his death, but it was a risk he was prepared to take. Antonov smiled at them, as he pulled a kerchief from his jacket.

'A race to the top of the stairs!' the prince announced loudly, for the benefit of the spectators. 'The loser will owe the winner a favour, which may be collected at any time in the future, at the winner's convenience. Is that right?'

Both boys nodded. Dirk didn't look at Antonov. His eyes were fixed firmly on the winding staircase. He opened his mouth and took several deep breaths as Antonov spoke. His nose was still swollen and his breathing was already affected. He needed all the wind he could get. He glanced at Kirsh, whose eyes were alight with excitement. The prince cut a dashing figure in his well-cut clothes and his expensive boots, but they would tell on him the further they climbed the stairs.

'So, just to make it interesting, I have decided to throw in a purse of one hundred gold dorns for the winner!'

The crowd gasped at the news. A hundred gold dorns was more than any of them earned in a lifetime. Even Dirk was stunned by the offer. He had never even seen that much money at once.

'Are you ready?'

Dirk nodded and took a final deep breath. Kirsh said something that brought a laugh from the gathered spectators, but Dirk was too focused on the task ahead to hear. He watched Antonov out of the corner of his eye, saw the kerchief rise and then fall, and then, without any conscious act, he was running up the stairs.

Kirsh streaked ahead, as Dirk knew he would. The Senetian prince was both taller and stronger than Dirk, and he didn't know the meaning of restraint. Kirsh would give the race every ounce of strength and energy he had. Dirk's only hope lay in the fact that he was lighter, he wasn't carrying the added weight of leather boots, and he'd climbed these stairs every day of his life since he'd learned how to walk.

The crowd cheered them on as they reached the first landing. Kirsh was well ahead of him, reaching the second landing while Dirk was only a few steps above the first. Out of the corner of his eye he caught sight of Morna and Wallin on the landing, but he paid them no mind, too focused on the task at hand to even notice if they were cheering for him. He tried to pace himself, to leave himself something for the latter stages of the race, when he was counting on Kirsh tiring, but the temptation was strong to try to catch his opponent. He forced himself not to look at Kirsh, to concentrate on putting one foot above the other.

The cheers above him told him that Kirsh had reached

the third landing while he was barely past the second. His face was aching and he could feel his lungs straining for air. He passed the third landing as the crowd cheered Kirsh ahead of him on the fourth. Dirk felt a surge of annoyance. *Why are they cheering Kirshov? You'd think they would want to see me win.* But everyone loved a winner, Dirk knew, and Kirsh had endeared himself to the folk of Elcast Keep in the short time he had been on the island.

The fourth and fifth landings passed in a blur, and Dirk's lungs began to burn. His breathing rasped and his swollen nose felt like it was on fire. He risked a glance ahead and was relieved to find Kirsh had yet to reach the sixth-floor landing. He was gaining on the prince – slowly – but gaining nonetheless. His concern now was that he'd left his final push too late. Kirsh was pounding upwards and didn't seem to be flagging much at all.

Dirk's legs were heavy as he ran doggedly upwards. By the time they reached the seventh-floor landing, he was only a few steps behind Kirsh.

Now was when it really counted, he knew. Kirsh's thighs would be burning, but he just might have the strength to see it through. With a determined effort, Dirk gave it everything he had. He was breathing through his mouth now, his nose unable to supply the wind he needed to sustain his effort. Fifteen steps from the top he drew level with Kirsh, who glanced at him in surprise. They ran neck and neck for a few steps, then Dirk surged ahead, his lungs crying out in protest, his bare feet chaffed raw by the granite, his thighs on fire.

Kirsh drew level with him three steps from the top. Dirk risked a glance out of the corner of his eye and saw the look of glee on Kirshov's face. Lanon stood on the top step, cheering them on. The roars of the crowd were muted and lost in the distance.

Three steps to go and Dirk knew Kirsh was going to beat him.

Two steps left and he glanced up. Eryk was next to Lanon, jumping up and down as he cheered his master on.

His face shone with the inalienable belief that Dirk would triumph.

The thought of letting Eryk down was suddenly intolerable. With one last desperate surge he took the last step a heartbeat ahead of Kirsh and collapsed on the cold stone of the landing, as wild cheers erupted all around him. Dirk rolled onto his back and lay there taking deep, rasping breaths with his eyes closed. He was too exhausted to relish his victory, too drained to think what it meant.

'Con . . . grat . . . ulations.'

Dirk opened his eyes and stared at Kirsh. He was bent double, his hands resting on his knees as he gasped for air. Dirk didn't answer him. He didn't have the breath in him left to speak.

Kirsh managed a wan smile. 'You're tougher . . . than you . . . look . . . Dirk Provin.'

'Faster, too,' Lanon remarked with a laugh.

He felt a small hand on his shoulder and turned his head. Eryk was kneeling beside him, a look of supreme smugness on his face.

'I told you you'd win,' he said happily.

'I . . . owe you . . . a favour . . .' Kirsh added. He didn't seem to mind that he'd lost. 'Name . . . it . . .'

'Some . . . other . . . time . . .' Dirk managed to gasp. At that moment, Dirk couldn't think of anything he needed or wanted of Kirshov Latanya.

'When . . . you're ready.'

Dirk nodded and closed his eyes, better to concentrate on breathing.

It was only later that it occurred to him that he had won a small fortune. He was leaving Elcast a rich man.

PART THREE

THE
HERESY
OF LOGIC

42

It was not that far from Elcast to Senet, but for the same reason there was a massive levee wall on Elcast's northern coast to protect it from tidal waves, the Lion of Senet's ship was forced to take a much more circuitous route to reach the mainland. The Tresna Sea between Elcast and the mainland was riddled with underwater volcanoes. Floating slabs of pumice dotted the seascape, and the constantly changing seabed made it difficult to navigate safely through the shallow, turbulent waters.

The journey from Elcast to Avacas was a trying time for Dirk. Although he would never admit it to anyone aboard the *Calliope,* he was desperately homesick, missing Elcast as if a limb had been severed. He was angry with himself, too. Within a day of boarding the ship, he began seriously to regret the impulse that had driven him to announce that he wanted to go to Avacas.

He was sharing a cabin with Kirsh, Misha and Eryk, which was extremely awkward for all of them. Misha didn't travel well, and his temporary recovery while on Elcast was soon a distant memory as the sea voyage took its toll. Ella Geon was often in their cabin tending the young man, and while she seemed happy enough for Eryk to run errands for her, she had little patience with either Kirsh or Dirk getting underfoot.

Part of Dirk missed his apprenticeship with Master Helgin, and he couldn't help but wonder what was wrong with the elder Latanya prince. Misha's withered left side did not seem to be in any way related to the tortured cold sweats he suffered. At times, he was lucid and seemingly free of pain. Occasionally, he was delirious and incomprehensible. Although Dirk had never witnessed one, Misha had told him that he sometimes suffered fits that left him foaming at the mouth. When he questioned Kirsh about the nature of Misha's illness, the younger prince shrugged. He had no idea what was wrong with his brother. It was bad enough that Misha was crippled. To Kirsh, physical disability was the cruellest thing a man could suffer. Other problems hardly seemed worth worrying about.

On their fourth day out, Dirk escaped the cabin as Ella bustled in, just as the second sun was overtaking the first. Misha had been awake most of the night, tossing restlessly on the narrow bunk, and this had kept the other boys awake, too. Once in the companionway outside the cabin, Kirsh vanished in the direction of the galley, looking for breakfast. Yawning, Dirk headed up to the main deck, preferring fresh air. Illness had a unique smell about it, he decided, and in the close confines of the cabin it was more noticeable than usual.

The air was cool and refreshing on deck, and for a moment Dirk did nothing but close his eyes and let the wind wash over him. Then he made his way aft, past the horses corralled on the deck, stopping for a moment to pat the few that poked their curious muzzles through the barricade to greet him. He leaned on the starboard side railing, watching the sea heave and sigh beneath the ship. The morning was clear, the wind steady, but there was no sign of Elcast in the distance. More than anything, that featureless horizon drove home his isolation.

'We welcome the second face of the Goddess!'

Curiously, Dirk turned at the sound of Belagren's chanting, as it carried on the crisp breeze that drove the ship forwards. The High Priestess was kneeling on the poop deck near the wheel, greeting the rising sun of morning, along with Olena Borne and Marqel. The helmsman stood listening to their devotions, with his feet braced wide apart as he steered the ship towards Senet. Dirk watched them for a moment, wondering if they really believed that their devotions would make the slightest bit of difference.

'Juicy bit o' meat, that one, eh?'

Dirk turned to the sailor who had come up beside him. 'Pardon?'

'Her,' the sailor explained, pointing to the Shadowdancers. 'The young 'un. Had 'er in Elcast town while we was there. Cost me a fortune, mind you, but she was worth every penny.'

'Who? Marqel?'

'Is that 'er name? Never bothered to ask. Didn't know she was gonna be a Shadowdancer, though.'

I wonder if you wanted her to call you Daddy, too, he thought.

'Damn, if I'd known she was gonna be one o' them, I'd've waited a year or two. Then I could've had 'er for nothin' at the Landfall Feast.'

'I suppose,' Dirk replied with a noncommittal shrug. He spied Kirsh heading along the deck towards them, munching on an apple.

'Well, p'haps not,' the sailor mused as Kirsh reached them. 'Them Shadowdancers usually don't put out for poor sailors like me. 'Ere, you're highborn, lad. Maybe you'll get lucky.' He winked at Dirk, then added, 'If you do get lucky, make her do that thing with her mouth . . .'

'Who are you talking about, Rezo?' Kirsh asked curiously.

'Marqel the Magnificent,' Dirk told him. 'My new friend Rezo here was just telling me how much he paid for her in Elcast.'

Kirsh's eyes narrowed dangerously. He turned to the sailor, grabbing the front of the man's shirt. 'If I hear one word, Rezo, one whisper about Marqel among the crew, I swear I will have you keelhauled.'

The sailor shrank back in fear. If Kirsh's tone wasn't enough to frighten him, then his rank certainly was. Kirshov was the Lion of Senet's son. His threat was not an idle one.

'It weren't just me, yer 'ighness! Lots o' the crew 'ad her!'

'I don't care, Rezo. It's you I'll see keelhauled for it.' Kirsh let him go with a shove and the sailor scurried away towards the chart house.

Dirk looked at Kirsh in astonishment. 'You're going to

keelhaul him? For what, Kirsh? Reminding you that she's a whore?'

The prince turned on him angrily. 'Unless you want that nose of yours broken again, Dirk, I suggest you stop now. It's disrespectful to say such things about a Shadowdancer.'

'She's not a Shadowdancer yet, Kirsh. Besides, Alenor calls them all whores. You don't threaten to have her keel-hauled for it.'

'Alenor is a princess,' Kirsh pointed out. 'Rezo isn't, and neither are you. I could just as easily have you punished in the same manner.'

'You must be joking!'

Kirsh glared at him for a moment. Then with a slightly embarrassed shrug, he looked away. 'I guess I am over-reacting just a tad.'

'Just a *tad*? You're insane!' When his accusation drew curious looks from some of the nearby sailors, he lowered his voice. 'What does it matter what the crew says about Marqel? You know what she is, Kirsh. Telling people not to say it out loud isn't going to change it.'

'It just doesn't seem fair,' he said, feeding the remains of his apple core to the closest horse. 'She's been given a second chance, Dirk. I'm not going to let half-wits like Rezo ruin it for her.'

Up on the poop deck, Marqel and the others had finished their prayers. Marqel said something to the High Priestess, who nodded distractedly. She turned and slid down the companion ladder with ease. The acrobat had gained her sea legs quickly for a girl raised on dry land. She saw the boys and headed towards them.

'Good morning, your highness,' she greeted Kirsh with a beaming smile. Then, with rather less enthusiasm, she added, 'Lord Dirk.'

'Good morning, Marqel,' Kirsh replied, with a smile no less dazzling than hers had been. 'All finished with your prayers?'

'For the time being.'

'Excellent!' he declared. 'In that case, you can resume your studies.'

'My studies?'

'Dirk was teaching you to read, wasn't he? Since there's nothing much else to do on board, I thought we might continue them.'

'What?' Dirk asked in alarm. With everything that had gone on in the past few days, Dirk had totally forgotten about Marqel's lessons. He was certainly in no mood to resume them.

Marqel lowered her eyes with a shy smile. 'You don't have to do that for me, your highness.'

'Nonsense! I'm glad to help. What do you say, Dirk? Shall we have Marqel quoting poetry by the time we reach Avacas?'

If she had been selling herself in the taverns near the docks on Elcast, Dirk was fairly sure Marqel could quote poetry now, but not the sort Kirshov had in mind.

'If you're so keen to teach her how to read, Kirsh, you do it.'

'Don't be silly, Dirk. I'm just going to be there for moral support. You'll have to do the actual teaching.'

'I'd have to ask the High Priestess,' Marqel told them. 'But I'm sure she won't mind.'

'Off you go then,' Kirsh ordered. 'We'll wait for you.'

Looking as pleased as if she had just been rewarded with a peerage, Marqel hurried off to seek Belagren's permission to resume her lessons. Dirk scowled at Kirshov.

'What are you doing?'

'Helping Marqel learn to read,' he said with an innocent shrug.

'Are you sure that's all you're doing?'

'I've no idea *what* you're implying,' Kirsh responded stiffly.

Dirk didn't get a chance to answer. Marqel hurried back to them and stopped before Kirsh breathlessly. 'My lady said yes.'

'Excellent! In that case we shall retire to the bow, away from the stink of these horses, and proceed to educate you!'

Marqel pushed past Dirk with a triumphant little smile and fell in beside Kirsh as he headed for the bow. He stared after them with a frown, only following reluctantly when Kirsh glanced over his shoulder and ordered him to follow.

43

Antonov insisted they join him and the High Priestess each evening in his cabin for dinner. He seemed to enjoy the company of his young guests as much as that of his sons. Dirk was surprised at how much trouble Antonov went to, to ensure that he was at ease in such unfamiliar surroundings. He questioned each of them about their day and seemed genuinely interested in their answers, although what Belagren thought about it was anybody's guess. Her expression remained neutral, her comments noncommittal. But the Lion of Senet treated Alenor like a favoured niece and Dirk like a welcome nephew. In his company it was very easy to forget how dangerous he could be.

'Belagren tells me you've resumed your lessons with our young thief, Dirk,' Antonov remarked as they were served their dessert by one of Antonov's legion of silent, unsmiling servants. They ate almost as well on the *Calliope* as they had back in Elcast. Dirk was only just beginning to appreciate the benefits of enormous wealth.

'We made great progress, too,' Kirsh declared, smearing his cake with cream. Dirk wondered how they managed to keep it fresh, or was there actually a cow on board? The main course had been beef, roasted to perfection. Still, he supposed the weather had been fair and they had not been at sea long enough for the supplies they had taken on in Elcast to turn rancid yet.

'You, Kirsh?' Antonov asked in surprise. 'I was under the impression you thought reading was akin to having a tooth pulled. In fact, I can't ever recall seeing you pick up a book voluntarily.'

'Ah, well that's Dirk's influence, sir,' he replied through a mouthful of cake.

'Then I must congratulate you, Dirk,' Antonov said with a wry smile. 'You appear to be having a remarkably good influence on my son. Perhaps next you might be able to persuade him not to talk with his mouth full.'

Dirk shrugged self-consciously. Kirsh's sudden interest in teaching had nothing to do with anything he had said or done. It was entirely attributable to Kirsh's obsession with the acrobat.

'And what of you, Alenor? How did you spend your day, my dear?'

'In my cabin, your highness,' she told him with a scowl at Kirsh. 'I was supposed to go up on deck, but you said I shouldn't roam the ship unescorted. Kirsh was supposed to come for me, but he never showed up.'

'No doubt he was distracted by his sudden interest in education,' Belagren commented. It made Dirk wonder if she knew more than she was letting on. Perhaps the High Priestess suspected something of Kirsh's fascination with Marqel.

'I see an opportunity here,' Antonov announced. 'You've all been away from your studies for much too long, and as we are now blessed with Dirk's remarkably well-educated company, I see no reason why they shouldn't resume. Tomorrow, Kirshov, you *will* remember to escort Alenor on deck and you and she can *both* study while Dirk continues his lessons with the thief. I've no doubt young Dirk here is more than qualified to supervise your lessons, too.'

Nobody around the table objected. Kirsh didn't really care what he had to do, as long as he got to spend time with Marqel, and Alenor felt much the same way about Kirshov. Only Dirk was displeased with the arrangement; however there was nothing to be gained by complaining about it.

'And now for something less taxing,' the prince continued when his edict drew no howls of protest. 'By the time we get back to Avacas it will be almost your birthday, Kirshov.'

'Goddess, I almost forgot!' Kirsh exclaimed. 'How soon after that will I be able to go to Kalarada, do you think?'

'When you come of age, Kirsh. That's another two years away.'

'Yes, but in Dhevyn, one comes of age when he's eighteen, not twenty, like in Senet. And as I'm going to join the *Dhevynian* Queen's Guard . . .'

'You are still a Prince of Senet,' Belagren reminded him.

'I know, but . . .'

'I'll think about it,' his father promised, 'but don't get your hopes up. There are more things to be taken into consideration than your single-minded enthusiasm for joining Dhevyn's army.'

'It was your idea, sir.'

'I'm aware of that,' he replied with a smile. 'I just wasn't expecting you to embrace the notion quite so enthusiastically. That must be Alenor's doing, I think. I should never have stolen her away from Kalarada.' He raised his wineglass in her direction and added, 'She is such a delightful example of Dhevyn's grace and beauty that she has beguiled you completely, I fear.'

Alenor blushed at the compliment. Like Dirk, she found it hard not to fall victim to Antonov's charm, even when he was quite openly reminding her that she was a hostage.

'Speaking of birthdays,' Antonov said after toasting the princess, 'when is your birthday, Dirk? Now that you are a member of the family, as it were, we must ensure that we celebrate it properly.'

'I'll be sixteen next month, your highness, and really, there's no need to go to any trouble.'

'So soon?' he inquired curiously. 'I thought your birthday much later in the year . . . no matter. Is there anything you want as a gift? A horse, perhaps? You'll need your own mount in Avacas. As soon as we get back, we shall attend the auctions in Arkona and find you something worthy of a prince.'

'Really, your highness, there's no need—'

'Nonsense, Dirk! I enjoy spoiling my friends. Besides, I have to find Alenor another mount soon, so we shall make a day of it. She has almost outgrown that wretched pony she's so devoted to.'

'But I like Snowdrop, your highness. She's well mannered, and quiet and—'

'Quiet?' Belagren laughed. 'She's docile to the point of insensibility, Alenor.'

Antonov smiled. 'I'm afraid I must agree with the High Priestess, my dear. I swear, if it wasn't for the fact that the beast was standing upright, I'd feel the need to check the poor creature for a pulse.'

'But I don't want to lose Snowdrop, sire. Can't I keep her?'

'Of course you can, Alenor. My intention is to find you a more spirited mount, not break your heart. We shall put Snowdrop out to pasture and she will grow fat and happy in her dotage. You may visit her as often as you wish.'

Dirk watched Antonov out of the corner of his eye as he ate the last of his dessert, quite amazed at the man's generosity. Nothing seemed to be too much trouble for him. No wonder Alenor bore her situation so well.

The servants cleared away the remains of their meal as Antonov leaned back in his seat, replete and content. He glanced at the three of them and then waved his hand with a smile.

'Go on then, you're excused.'

'Thank you, sir,' Kirsh said, jumping to his feet.

'You seem in quite a hurry, Kirshov,' Belagren remarked.

'Captain Clegg promised to show us how he navigates using the suns.'

'I'm sure Dirk will find it fascinating,' Antonov said. 'But I'm surprised to find you so anxious to learn about it.'

Kirsh shrugged. 'Misha's not been sleeping well.'

Antonov nodded understandingly as they headed for the door. 'Then enjoy yourselves, boys. I will look forward to hearing all about solar navigation tomorrow evening at dinner.'

'Good night, Father. My lady.'

'Good night, Kirsh.'

Kirsh had already stepped into the companionway when Antonov called Dirk back. 'I almost forgot, Dirk, I have a favour to ask of you.'

'Sire?'

'The guards report that our prisoner has developed a nasty cough.'

Dirk was instantly on his guard. 'That's unfortunate, your highness.'

'More than unfortunate, Dirk. I mean, the man survived a tidal wave. It would be rather incongruous to lose him to something as trivial as a cough at this late stage.'

'I'm not sure I follow you, your highness.'

'He needs a physician, Dirk,' Belagren explained, 'and with Misha so ill, I can't spare Ella.'

'Would you be so kind as to check on him tomorrow?'

Dirk had to fight down a wave of panic. He tried to determine if there was something more behind Antonov's innocent request, but he couldn't read the man well enough to tell. Belagren was watching him with hawklike eyes.

'Your highness, my lady . . . I was only an apprentice physician. I'm not sure I would be of any use.'

'Don't be so hard on yourself, Dirk,' Belagren told him.

'But—'

'You scaled that damn levee wall to save the man,' Antonov reminded him. 'I would think his continuing good health would be of vital interest to you.'

'It is, sire, which is why I think he'd be better with a Shadowdancer in attendance, rather than me.'

Antonov smiled. 'You do yourself an injustice, Dirk Provin. Helgin sang your praises most highly. Visit Thorn tomorrow and do what you can to ease his suffering. If he needs any herbal concoctions, I'm sure Ella will have everything you require.'

'As you wish, your highness.'

Antonov nodded with satisfaction, and returned his attention to the High Priestess. Dirk closed the door to the cabin thoughtfully, wondering if there was anything more sinister in the Lion of Senet's request other than simple concern that his prisoner might die before he could get around to hanging him.

44

While Johan wasn't exactly chained in the hold with the rats, Antonov had done his utmost to ensure that he would not enjoy the voyage. He was shackled hand and foot in a cubbyhole not much bigger than a cupboard on the lower deck, just above the waterline. There was no bunk, just a smelly straw mattress. He had a bucket to relieve himself in but no light and no water other than the small jug delivered to him once a day with his barely adequate meal.

His shoulder ached abominably. His stomach growled with hunger and his newly healed broken leg felt like it was made of lead. The shackles had chafed his wrists and ankles raw, and he had developed a racking cough that left him weak and exhausted after each fit shook his body.

They were minor discomforts, really. Johan knew Antonov would not let him die yet, although he certainly wouldn't care if he suffered. Antonov was a master when it came to playing mind games, he reminded himself, and this was just another game. He had quite deliberately left Johan in Helgin's tender care while they were in Elcast. And for no better reason than how much more effective it would be when he tore him from such comfort and warmth and plunged him into this damp, dark pit, with no relief from the pain and no hope for anything better at the end of it.

Don't let it get to you, Johan told himself firmly.

Look what he had done to poor Morna. Weeks under her roof, knowing Johan was a prisoner there, and Antonov did nothing more sinister than attend the Landfall Festival. It must have torn Morna apart.

He wished he'd had a chance to see her while he was on Elcast. There was little chance that would have happened, though. Wallin Provin might go down in history as the most tolerant and forgiving man on Ranadon, but he drew the line at allowing his errant wife to resume her acquaintance with her former lover. Helgin had told him that Wallin had forbidden Morna to see him. With Antonov in the house, she wasn't prepared to defy her husband and risk losing his protection.

On the fifth day of the voyage, Antonov sent the Provin boy to check on him. Johan knew it was the fifth day. He had debated scratching a tally on the wall, but decided against it. Antonov would gloat to see such a transparent sign of his battle to retain his sanity. So he consciously kept track of the days in his head. He tried to recite poetry. He made up bizarre mathematical calculations in his head that he had no hope of solving. Anything to keep his mind occupied.

If I can keep my wits about me he won't defeat me.

He was a little surprised when Dirk entered the cabin bearing a small lantern. He didn't think it likely that Antonov would allow him any visitors. Contact with the outside world made it that much easier for Johan to hang on; that much easier for him to retain his sanity – but more important, his purpose.

The Lion of Senet wanted to break him, and he knew well that isolation was the most soul-destroying weapon a man could suffer. Isolation and sleep deprivation. The former would drive a man mad. The latter could kill him. Antonov had told him that once, many years ago. He claimed that if you starved a man, it would take him several weeks to die, but if you deprived him of sleep, he'd be dead in ten days. Johan had never been able to get a straight answer from Antonov when he inquired how the prince could be so certain of that fact. He had a bad feeling Antonov knew what sleep deprivation would do to a man, because he'd actually done it to some poor sod. Then again, maybe he hadn't. Maybe the game was to make Johan think he had.

'I came to see if you're sick,' Dirk announced, as he stepped into the tiny cabin and placed the lantern on the deck. He was taking shallow breaths through his mouth, as if it would somehow lessen the overpowering stench.

'Ah, that's right, you're the apprentice physician, aren't you?' He squinted at the boy in the flickering light. The sudden brightness hurt his eyes. 'Does your mother know you're here?'

Dirk glanced nervously over his shoulder at the guards posted outside the open door. 'What do you mean by that?'

He was very touchy, this boy of Wallin's. 'I mean, this is the Lion of Senet's ship, boy. Last I heard you were Helgin's apprentice. What are you doing here?'

'Checking to see if you're sick,' Dirk replied unhelpfully.

Johan laughed, which precipitated a painful coughing fit that tore through his chest, leaving him weak and shaking. When it was over, he lay back on the stinking mattress wearily. 'Antonov's tortures become increasingly more subtle.'

'Sir?' the boy asked, uncomprehendingly.

He turned his head and smiled at Dirk. 'Now he's sent me a jester. And a bad one at that.'

'I wasn't trying to be funny, sir.' Dirk squatted down beside him, placing a cool hand on his forehead. 'You have a fever.'

'I know.'

'Where does it hurt?'

'Where *doesn't* it hurt?'

Dirk glared at him.

'It hurts here,' Johan conceded, not wishing to antagonise the boy further. 'Right across the top of my chest. And I told you to call me Johan.'

'It hurts when you cough?'

'Yes.'

'Are you bringing up any phlegm?'

He nodded, a little surprised to find Dirk taking his responsibility so seriously. The boy looked down at his chafed wrists with a frown.

'Those wrists will get infected if they're not taken care of soon. And you're dehydrated,' Dirk diagnosed, sitting back on his heels. He glanced around the dim cabin with concern. 'You need to be moved from here. There's no ventilation. No sanitation.'

'I think that's the whole point, Dirk.'

Dirk's brows drew together in concern, reminding Johan sharply of Morna. She used to pull that face when she was worried about something.

'Prince Antonov doesn't want you to die, sir.'

'Oh, yes he does,' Johan assured him. 'Make no mistake about that. He just doesn't want nature to rob him of the pleasure of killing me himself.'

'Then I'll arrange to have you moved, otherwise he *will* be robbed of the pleasure,' the boy retorted.

Johan studied him sceptically. 'Do you really think the Lion of Senet will act on *your* advice?'

'Why not? He was the one who sent me here.'

Johan frowned. *Now why would Antonov send this boy to me? He's got his own physician to attend me if he is so concerned about my health.*

'What were his instructions exactly?' he asked.

Dirk smiled faintly. 'To see if you're sick.'

Johan smiled back. This boy was pretty quick for a Provin, who in Johan's experience were a dour lot. There wasn't a lot of Wallin in him.

'Actually, he said that it would be a pity if you died from a cough, having survived a tidal wave.'

'He's got a point,' Johan conceded. 'Although, in truth, I half expected him to leave me here to rot.'

'So did I,' the boy admitted. 'He surprises me.'

'How?'

Dirk shrugged. 'I don't know. He just doesn't act the way I thought he would.'

'That's the danger of him, Dirk.'

The boy studied him thoughtfully. 'You used to know him pretty well, didn't you?'

'I thought I did. I learned the hard way that I didn't know him at all.'

Dirk didn't answer for a moment. Johan had the feeling he wanted to say something, ask him something, perhaps.

'I'll come back later,' the boy announced abruptly, climbing to his feet. Whatever Dirk had been going to say, he'd thought better of it. 'I have to speak to Prince Antonov about having you moved. And I'll need some herbs from Ella, too.'

'Ella Geon? Is that malicious breeding cow still around?'

'She looks after Misha. Do you know her?'

'All too well.' He closed his eyes. 'Goddess, I feel like I've stepped into a nightmare, and all my old enemies are waiting there to torment me.'

The boy hesitated again. Something was really bothering him. Johan waited for him to say something further, but once again, it seemed as if he'd changed his mind.

'I'll be back,' Dirk said, finally. 'Is there anything you want?'

'You could load me into a lifeboat and let me take my chances on the open sea,' Johan suggested hopefully. When the boy didn't answer him, he smiled. 'Or not.'

'I meant anything to ease your pain.'

'Oh? Well, in that case, would you mind running a fork through Antonov's left eye at dinner this evening? I'm quite certain that would relieve my suffering.'

'You're acting like this is a game.'

'It is a game, Dirk. One Antonov and I have been playing for a very long time.' He suffered through another coughing fit, then closed his eyes wearily when it finally abated. 'If you truly want to ease my suffering, Dirk, don't try to save me. Let me die.'

'I couldn't do that, sir!'

Johan opened his eyes and stared at the boy curiously. 'Why not? I mean nothing to you.'

'That's not the point, sir. I . . . I just don't think I could take another human life.'

Johan's eyes narrowed. 'Are you certain of that?'

Dirk thought for a moment before answering, then he shrugged. 'I don't really know. Until now, nobody's ever asked it of me.'

'Every man has the ability to kill, Dirk. How easily he gives in to that ability is the true measure of how civilised he is.'

'You've killed men, haven't you?'

'Yes,' he admitted. 'But I'm not claiming to be civilised. You, however, obviously think that you are. I hope you're not too hard on yourself when you find out one day that you're just like the rest of us.'

The boy stared at him, obviously unsettled.

Johan closed his eyes with a weary sigh. 'Off you go, young Provin. You do what you must. In the meantime, I shall lie here in the darkness and after I've recited all three hundred verses of Glonkinal's epic poem "Journey to the Centre of a Volcano", I shall endeavour to calculate the square root of five thousand four hundred and eighty-two. I've been at it for three days now. I'm confident that today I will discover the solution.' He opened one eye and stared at the boy. 'It keeps the mind focused, you see.'

Picking up the lantern cautiously, Dirk stepped out of the tiny cabin.

'Dirk!' Johan called after him.

'What?'

'I wasn't kidding about the games. To Antonov and Belagren, everything is a game. Before you get too enamoured of your new friends, you might want to ask yourself what *your* role is, because, Dirk Provin, you're a piece being moved about the board at their whim, just as surely as I am, you can rely on it.'

Dirk stared at him for a long moment. 'How accurate are you trying to be?'

'Pardon?'

'The square root of five thousand four hundred and eighty-two is an irrational number. It has infinitely long decimal places – you'll never calculate it exactly. So how accurate are you trying to be?'

'Are you serious?'

'Completely.'

Johan shrugged. 'I don't know. I suppose I'll be satisfied if I can calculate it to the tenth decimal place.'

Dirk hesitated for a moment. 'It's six.'

'What?'

'The tenth decimal place. It's six.'

With that startling announcement, the boy vanished from sight and the guards closed the cabin door, plunging Johan back into darkness.

45

Antonov was talking to the helmsman when Belagren emerged from the gloomy depths of the ship. She squinted in the sudden harsh light and headed forward to speak to the prince. The sea was choppy this morning, the wind quite strong. Scattered clouds shadowed the surface of the water and made a mottled pattern of dark and light. Belagren found herself clutching at the railing to maintain her balance as she walked.

As she climbed the companion ladder, the Lion of Senet stepped forward to assist her up the last few steps. He smiled, but it was a pleasant, good-morning sort of smile. There was nothing intimate about it. He'd not been to her cabin either, since they left Elcast. His need for her, the lust inspired by the Landfall Festival, had passed even more quickly this year. Soon he wouldn't want her at all. Belagren was more concerned about the effect such an event would have on her power than on her libido. She could have a man any time she wanted. Ruling the world took a little more planning and organisation.

'Did you sleep well, my lady?' he inquired as he led her to the side of the ship.

'Well enough,' she responded, quite distressed by the banality of the conversation. *A few weeks ago he wanted me so badly I had bruises to prove it. Now he talks to me like he's greeting a foreign ambassador at court.* 'And you?'

'I always sleep well at sea.'

They reached the port side and stopped for a moment to watch the sea heave and sigh in its own inexplicable design. Antonov clutched at the railing, rubbing the carefully polished wood almost unconsciously. Belagren watched him caressing his ship, thinking she'd feel much more secure if Antonov looked at her even half as fondly as he looked at his damn boat.

'I wanted to speak with you, Anton,' she said, when he made no further attempt at conversation. He seemed far more interested in the distant horizon.

'Hmm?'

'About the Provin boy.'

'An interesting and intelligent young man. I confess I find myself quite taken with him.'

I know you are, Belagren thought. *Which is why I need to talk to you.*

'I just wanted to make sure that you have informed him that he'll be coming to the Hall of Shadows with me when we disembark in Avacas.'

Antonov turned to her. 'I told his parents he could stay with me until he comes of age.'

'You told Morna that to stop her making a scene, Anton. Nobody seriously expects you to foster the boy.'

'I gave Wallin my word that I would treat him as my own son.'

'You gave *me* your word that I could have him.'

'And you can have him. When he comes of age.'

'But you said as soon as we arrived in Avacas,' the High Priestess reminded him. *I don't have years for you to play your mind games with Morna Provin.*

'I know what I said, Belagren. I've changed my mind.'
He was calm and sounded quite reasonable. Belagren had
never heard him raise his voice, never seen him angry. It was
almost as if he enjoyed the fact that the more agitated his
opponent was, the more serene he became.

'What do you want with him, Anton? You have no need
of him. Other than his entertainment value, perhaps.'

'What I do or do not have a need for is mine to decide,
my lady.'

'The Goddess will not be pleased if you renege on your
promise.'

The power of her threat was somewhat diminished
when Antonov caught sight of Dirk coming towards them.
He turned away from the High Priestess and smiled warmly.
'So, young Dirk, how fares our prisoner?'

'He has an infection of the lungs, your highness,' Dirk
told him, as the brisk wind whipped the dark hair across his
face. He glanced at Belagren and gave her a short bow, just
low enough not to be disrespectful. 'My lady.'

'Is he going to die from it?' she asked.

He brushed the hair away, only to have it half blind him
again, the moment he lowered his hand. 'Not yet.'

'Is his condition liable to worsen?' Antonov inquired.

'If you leave him in that hole much longer, it will.'

The Lion of Senet seemed amused. 'Do I detect a note
of reproach in your tone, Dirk?'

'He needs to be moved out of that ship's locker you've
jammed him into,' Dirk informed him. 'He needs fresh air.
And more water.'

'You were right, Anton,' the High Priestess remarked
as she watched Dirk. The boy was hard to read. He was very
guarded for one so young. 'He doesn't approve of your treatment of Johan Thorn.'

'It's got nothing to do with Johan Thorn, my lady.
Nobody should be kept like that. The prince treats his horses
better.'

'That's because my horses are of more use to me.'
Ignoring the High Priestess, Antonov placed his arm around

Dirk's shoulder in a fatherly fashion and smiled, moving him across the deck a few paces. 'So, what do you prescribe for the patient, Physician Provin?'

'Move him to a proper cabin,' Dirk suggested, obviously uncomfortable with Antonov's familiarity. 'Feed him properly. Give him sufficient water. With that and a poultice, his body should be able to fight off the infection on its own.'

'Or you could just leave him there and let him die,' Belagren suggested behind them. 'It would save the cost of a trial and an execution.'

Dirk broke free of Antonov's paternal embrace and turned to look at her. 'If you were planning to let him die, my lady, why do you need my help?'

Antonov's eyes clouded briefly. 'If you wish to continue in my good graces, you would be wise to watch that tongue of yours, young man.'

'I'm sorry, your highness, I didn't mean to offend the High Priestess.'

'You're forgiven,' Antonov assured him. Then he frowned, his face a portrait of concern and understanding. 'I know how difficult this must be for you, Dirk, and while I'm reluctant to place such a heavy responsibility on your shoulders, I would be most appreciative if you could see to Thorn's welfare for me until we reach Avacas.'

'Sire, I really think that a Shadowdancer would be . . .'

Antonov held up his hand to halt Dirk's protests. 'Even if she were the last physician on Ranadon, I still wouldn't put Ella Geon and Johan Thorn alone together in a confined space for more than about thirty seconds. They have something of a . . .' he glanced at Belagren for a moment before he continued, 'feud, I suppose you might call it . . . going on.'

'What sort of feud?'

'Perhaps you should ask Thorn about it.'

'I'd not mention it to Ella, though,' the High Priestess added.

'Will you move him, sir?' Dirk persisted.

Antonov sighed heavily. 'Yes, Dirk. For you, I will move him. Just make certain that Thorn is aware that his improved circumstances are entirely attributable to your intervention. I'd hate for him to think I was getting sentimental in my old age.'

'Somehow, I don't think that's likely, your highness.'

Antonov smiled. 'You're a lot like your father, Dirk.'

'Sir?'

'You're a lot like your father,' Antonov repeated. 'You have that same dry sense of humour that he had when he was younger.'

'I never really noticed, sir,' Dirk answered cautiously.

'Well, sometimes we don't notice these things ourselves, even when they're obvious to everyone else. Do you like the *Calliope*?'

'Pardon?' The abrupt change of subject caught him completely unawares. Belagren knew the prince did it deliberately, just to unsettle people.

'My ship, Dirk. Do you like her?'

'She's magnificent.'

'She's the fastest barquentine ever built,' Antonov informed him. 'The most expensive, too, I suspect. She has over nine thousand square feet of sail. Fully rigged, she can do twelve knots.'

'You must be very proud of her.'

Belagren wasn't surprised by the pride in Antonov's voice. From the day they first laid her keel, she'd seen the prince stroke the woodwork, as if he could somehow convey his affection to the ship through her railings. Belagren suspected Antonov Latanya loved his ship almost as much as he loved his sons. Perhaps more. She had often wondered what Antonov would do if given a choice between his crippled son and his ship.

'We'll be taking her into the Baenlands later this year,' Antonov added. 'You should come with us.'

'I didn't think you could get a ship this size through the delta, your highness.'

'Thorn somehow used to manage it on a regular basis,' Antonov pointed out.

'Surely the pirates don't have any ships as big as the *Calliope*?'

'Perhaps not. You'll have to ask Thorn how he did it for me.'

'You want *me* to ask him, your highness?'

Antonov frowned at him. 'Dirk, there are only two things that can happen to Johan Thorn. The first is that I torture the information I want from him, then try him and burn him as a heretic. The second is for him to volunteer the information, after which I will still try him and then burn him as a heretic. Now, as you seem so concerned that my treatment is going to kill your patient, I must, for the time being at least, halt my efforts to soften him up for the Prefect awaiting him in Avacas.'

Belagren didn't like the way this conversation was going. *When did Thorn become* Dirk's *patient?*

'Your highness, I only said that he needs water and fresh air. I wasn't—'

Antonov ignored the interruption. 'And as it's your interference that will make the job harder for my Prefect to break him, I think it only fair that you make yourself useful in the meantime. Besides, if you are able to extract the information I want from Thorn – if you could get him to open up to you – then perhaps Prefect Welacin won't have to use those methods of interrogation for which he is so rightly famous.'

What's he up to? Belagren wondered. *Is he playing with the boy? Or is it Johan he's tormenting? Does it amuse him to watch Johan being tended by Morna's son?*

And who is the game about, anyway? Dirk? Morna? Johan Thorn?

'Why should I care, one way or another, what you do to Johan Thorn?' Dirk replied. He was keeping his voice deliberately emotionless, Belagren thought.

Antonov hesitated for a fraction of a second. 'I'm not sure, Dirk. I suppose I just assumed your mother had passed on some of her own . . . feelings, regarding the man.'

'She never spoke of him, sire. Neither did my father.'

Antonov studied him closely for a moment.

'Did you know he was once your mother's lover?' Belagren asked.

Dirk met her gaze evenly. 'All the more reason, my lady, for me not to care what happens to him.'

The prince looked rather smug suddenly. 'Then why do you want me to make him more comfortable?'

'I don't,' Dirk said evenly. 'You asked if he'd die if you left him there for the rest of the voyage. I said he would. You'll move him because you want him to live, your highness. Not because it pleases me.'

The Lion of Senet gave Dirk a long, considered look, and then waved his arm dismissively. 'Make whatever arrangements you need to ensure Thorn survives the voyage.'

It was a small victory, but a significant one. Dirk bowed to the prince and the High Priestess, then turned away. As he walked towards the ladder, she turned on Antonov.

'Anton, I must insist . . .'

'Not now, Bela.'

'But don't you see? He *must* be sent to us.'

Antonov was playing some game with the boy that she didn't understand. She did understand, though, that in order to get her hands on Dirk Provin, she was going to have to find a reason for Antonov to want to send him away.

'He's definitely his father's son.'

'What?'

'Dirk Provin. He's his father's son, don't you think?'

'I couldn't say,' she replied with a sigh. 'I never really knew Wallin that well.'

46

Kirsh sat himself down on the deck beside Dirk, as he was prompting the young thief through the painful process of sounding out each word of the child's primer he had found for her in the Library on Elcast. She had mastered the alphabet, finally, and was working her way painstakingly through the simple text. Marqel stumbled, and then stopped reading completely, blushing under the prince's scrutiny.

'Don't stop on my account,' Kirsh told her brightly. 'You're doing very well.'

'I'm trying,' she assured him, with a coy smile.

'Very trying,' Dirk mumbled.

'Come on, Dirk! Have some patience with the poor girl! Learning anything new takes time. It's like training horses. You have to be patient and kind to get any results.'

Dirk glanced at Marqel, wondering how she would react to being compared with a horse, but the thief only had eyes for Kirshov. The wind of their passage had mussed her thick blonde hair and her eyes were glowing as she stared at the prince.

'Well, since you're such an authority, you can teach her,' he said, tossing the small leatherbound volume at Kirsh and climbing to his feet. 'I have to go and check on my patient, anyway.'

'How is he?'

'He'll live.'

Kirsh glanced at Marqel, then grinned up at Dirk. 'Off you go, then. I'll look after Marqel.'

'Where's Alenor?'

'In her cabin. She said something about a headache. Perhaps once you've tended the prisoner you should check in on her.'

'Perhaps I will.'

Once Kirsh turned his attention to Marqel, Dirk might as well have been invisible. With an exasperated curse, he made his way below to check on Johan.

The pirate's condition had improved markedly since he'd been moved to the mate's cabin, although the dislocated crewmen were understandably put out by the arrangement. When he arrived outside the door in the narrow passage, the guard on duty nodded a greeting and unlocked it for him. Dirk stepped inside and heard the lock turn behind him as the door closed.

Johan heard the lock, noticed Dirk's questioning look and smiled. His colour was vastly improved and his fever was gone, but he still moved stiffly – a result, no doubt, of the injuries he sustained in the tidal wave. 'Antonov is probably afraid I'm going to leap off my sickbed, overwhelm you and that thug outside, then single-handedly steal his precious ship from under him.'

Dirk was getting used to Johan now. He always had some trite comment to make about his dire situation.

'Are you feeling well enough to leap off your sickbed, then?'

'If I say yes, do I get thrown back into that hole below?'

Dirk shook his head. 'We'll be in Avacas tomorrow. I don't think he'd bother.'

'Nothing is ever too much bother for the Lion of Senet, Dirk. Not when it comes to the discomfort of his enemies.' Johan swung his legs over the bunk and sat up, but remained hunched over to avoid banging his head on the upper bunk. 'Avacas. Tomorrow, you say?'

'According to Captain Clegg.'

'My, how time flies when you're hoping for a miracle.'

'Is that what you're truly hoping for?' Dirk asked curiously.

The pirate shrugged. 'If there were going to be any miracles in my lifetime, Dirk, they would have been more convenient happening fifteen or twenty years ago. It's a bit late now.'

'Won't your friends try to rescue you, then?'

Johan studied him closely for a moment before he answered. 'So this is Antonov's ploy, is it? Send you here to tend and befriend me, then pump me for information?'

In truth, Dirk had not asked the question out of anything other than idle curiosity, but neither was he a practised liar. He found himself unable to meet Johan's accusing stare.

'You're a typical Provin,' Johan snorted in contempt, interpreting Dirk's silence as an admission of guilt. 'Always at the beck and call of Senet. I don't know why the hell Wallin didn't just secede from Dhevyn after the war and declare himself subject to Avacas.'

'My father is a loyal Dhevynian,' Dirk snapped defensively. It felt strange, and rather uncomfortable, making that declaration to Johan Thorn. But Wallin *was* his father – legally, if nothing else – and Dirk planned to do everything humanly possible to avoid anybody ever learning that the truth was any different.

'Your father followed the ruler of another nation into battle against his king, Dirk. Before Antonov came along, we used to call that treason.'

'My mother followed you, though,' Dirk retorted. 'Yet she's the one everybody calls a traitor.'

Johan's eyes narrowed. 'You know about that, do you?'

Dirk shrugged. 'Some of it.' *Please don't say any more. I really don't want to hear the details about your sordid little affair with my mother.*

'Your mother understood what was at stake, Dirk.'

'Then why didn't she stay with you?'

Johan shrugged, wincing at the movement. 'She had a son on Elcast whom she never forgave herself for abandoning. A woman's love for her children is a powerful thing.'

'More powerful than her belief in you?'

'Apparently.'

Dirk stared at him for a moment, then looked away. He didn't want to get caught up in this, didn't want to hear about it. The more he knew, the harder it would be to look Antonov in the eye, and Dirk was well aware of the danger should the Lion of Senet suspect his secret.

'I've brought you some more tonic,' he said, fishing the bottle out of his pocket.

'Ella made it up for you?' he asked with a raised brow.

'Yes.'

'Then perhaps you should try it first.'

'Do you think it's poisoned?'

'If it came from Ella Geon's hand, that's a distinct possibility.'

He handed the vial to Johan. 'Antonov said you and Ella had a feud.'

'Did he now? That's one way of putting it, I suppose.'

Johan took the glass vial, then unstoppered it, screwing his nose up at the smell.

'What did she do?'

'Who?'

'Ella Geon. What did she do to make you hate her so much?'

Johan took a swig of the tonic and then coughed painfully as it spilled down his throat. When the spasms had abated, he wiped his streaming eyes and looked at Dirk.

'Do you really want to know?'

'Drink it all. And I'm curious, that's all.'

Johan appeared to debate the wisdom of telling him anything for some time before he answered.

'I had a friend once,' he said, finally. 'Ella also pretended to be his friend . . . no, it was worse than that, she pretended to love him. And then, when she'd made him totally dependent on her, when she had him so deep in the grip of poppy-dust that he couldn't even remember his own name, she bedded him for the sole purpose of getting a child from him. Then she handed him back to his enemies.'

Dirk was silent for a long moment. 'What happened to your friend?'

'He killed himself.'

'And the child?'

Johan smiled. 'Ah! Now that's why Ella hates me. When I found out about the child I decided nobody deserved to be brought up by that heartless bitch. We raided the Hall of Shadows and took it from her. It was one of the few spectacular successes we've had since we were declared outlaws. I don't think Antonov really considered us a threat until we defiled the Hall of his precious High Priestess.'

'What did you do with it? The child? You didn't . . .'

The pirate laughed sourly. 'No, Dirk, I didn't kill the child. Where I come from, we don't kill babies. I took her back to the Baenlands and raised Tia as my own daughter.' Johan smiled briefly, as if remembering the child fondly.

If you knew who I really was, would you smile with such

pride and affection when you remembered me? he wondered silently.

'Does she know about her mother?'

'Of course she knows. Why?'

'No reason,' Dirk shrugged. 'I suppose I was just wondering what it must be like to grow up knowing your mother had done something so terrible.'

Johan smiled knowingly. 'You'd be the best one to ask about that, lad. Your mother is more notorious than Ella Geon ever was.'

'Perhaps, but I didn't grow up knowing about it. Until you came along, I never even heard it whispered.'

'That's your father's doing. Wallin always was good at turning a blind eye to unpalatable truths.' He took another swig of the tonic, but this time managed to swallow it without coughing. 'I'm sorry my appearance on your peaceful little island shattered the fairy-tale world you lived in, Dirk.'

Dirk snatched the vial from his hand. 'Prince Antonov said to make sure I didn't leave anything sharp lying around.'

'That's because he knows how inconvenient my death would be. He's taken great pains to ensure that I live to reach Avacas.'

'He wants to put you on trial.'

Johan laughed sceptically. 'Do you really believe that?'

'What should I believe, then?'

'You can believe this much, Dirk Provin: given the means, I would end my life right now. Every moment I live and remain in Antonov's custody makes it that much more dangerous for the people who depend on me. If I thought you had a modicum of compassion, I'd ask you to help me.'

'To help you die? We had this discussion already. I told you I couldn't.'

'Actually, you told me you *wouldn't*. It remains to be seen whether or not you could.'

'You're insane. And I don't really believe that you want to die.'

'How could you possibly know what I feel?'

Dirk hesitated for a moment. 'I suppose I can't. But isn't dying just giving up?'

'Not when I think of the lives it will save. Do you know what will happen if Antonov finds out what I know? Do you have any concept of the suffering he'll inflict on the people I love?'

'I have to go,' Dirk replied uncomfortably. This was getting out of hand. *First I find out he's my father; now he wants me to help him commit suicide.*

'Do you always do what Antonov orders?'

Dirk ignored the sarcastic comment. 'I'll be back later to give you another dose. After that, I don't imagine I'll see you again. We'll be in Avacas by then and you'll be handed over to the Prefect.'

'Well, *there's* something to look forward to.'

Dirk turned and knocked for the guard to let him out.

'Tell me something before you go, Dirk.'

'What?' Dirk asked, looking over his shoulder.

'Why are you here? What's so special about Wallin Provin's second son that would make the Lion of Senet take him under his wing?'

'I don't know.'

'Don't lie to me. Of course you know.' Johan lay back down on the bunk and gingerly folded his arms behind his head. 'What is it, Dirk Provin? Are you such a grand physician that he couldn't bear to part with you?'

'I don't know . . .'

'Or have you traded your position as an apprentice physician to become an apprentice tyrant?'

Dirk was beginning to lose patience. 'I don't know, I said!'

'Don't snap at me, boy.'

'I'm sorry.' He shrugged, not sure why he felt the need to answer Thorn's question. Perhaps he wanted the man to know he hadn't been invited to Avacas because he was planning to follow in Antonov's footsteps. Maybe Johan would be a little less disgusted with him if he understood Dirk had left Elcast to further his education. 'I suppose . . . well, it might be because I'm good at mathematics.'

'How good?'

He looked away uncomfortably.

Johan eyed him suspiciously. 'Extraordinarily good. That's my guess. What was it you answered that first day you came to visit me? The square root of some huge number I picked at random?'

'What of it?'

The pirate closed his eyes for a moment. 'Goddess, it never ends.'

'What never ends?'

He heard the key turning in the lock on the other side of the door. A moment later the guard opened it, glancing around the cabin suspiciously before motioning Dirk out.

'The cycle, Dirk,' Johan told him wearily, as Dirk stepped into the companionway.

Then as much to himself as to Dirk, he added, 'Just when you think the danger is past, some freakish little bastard like you pops up and it starts all over again.'

47

Reithan and Tia tied up the *Wanderer* at the Paislee docks and paid the Brotherhood to watch over her before making their way overland to Avacas. Tia often wondered where their loyalties truly lay – certain neither the Dhevynian Brotherhood nor their counterparts in Senet gave much consideration to what went on at court if it didn't affect their criminal activities. It made dealing with them a very risky business. Mil's only strength in trading with the Brotherhood was its position as the most prolific and reliable source of poppy-dust. Were it not for that, Tia was quite certain the Brotherhood would have betrayed them years ago.

The man from the Brotherhood who arranged the transaction gave Reithan a small metallic marker imprinted with the fox emblem of their society. He stressed several times that Reithan should be careful not to lose it, and assured them that without the marker, they would have no chance of reclaiming their boat. Reithan tucked the marker into his pocket, and with a final, wistful glance at his sailboat, left it in the dubious care of the Brotherhood.

Although it would have been quicker to sail straight to the capital, Paislee was the centre of Brotherhood activity in Senet, and they were much less likely to attract either attention or trouble in the smaller port. There was quite a bit of commerce between Paislee and Mil. The Senetian nobility were just as anxious for a steady supply of illicit poppy-dust as the Dhevynians, and that gave them some small measure of protection. But Reithan warned Tia to be on her guard. *Safe* was a relative word in Senet. Linel and Hari had been arrested here.

They hitched a lift to Avacas with a cobbler who was heading for the city to visit his ailing mother. He was glad of the company and the added security their presence offered. A lone wagon was a ripe target. Three people stood a much better chance against attack than one not-very-courageous bootmaker.

The cobbler's name was Fortlen, and other than his tendency to talk incessantly – from the moment he woke until he fell asleep by the campfire each evening – he was a tolerable travelling companion. After three days in the cobbler's company, Reithan joked to Tia that the reason Fortlen was so willing to let them accompany him was his fear of having nobody to talk to, rather than his fear of attack. It also explained why nobody in Paislee had wanted to travel all the way to Avacas with the garrulous old man.

They parted company with Fortlen on the edge of Avacas twelve days after they left Paislee. Tia looked around her in awe as she stood beside Reithan on the side of the road. She had never seen anything like the Senetian capital. The day was overcast and warm, the heat intensified by the press of bodies in the streets. The slight rise of the land gave them a good view of the sprawling city that stretched away

towards the coast. Tia had never imagined so many buildings could be so close together in one place.

She had tried hard not to gape when they had walked
the streets of Kalarada, the capital of Dhevyn, but she had
no hope of hiding her wonder in Avacas. Tia had never seen
so many people in one place before, either. The entire population of Mil would have fitted in one crowded block of the
Senetian city.

Reithan had been here before, though, and it was to the
home of a friend that he led Tia. He pushed and shoved his
way through the crowds with the ease of a man born and
bred in a city.

'Is it market day?' she asked, side-stepping a grimy
beggar who clutched at her leg as she passed.

'No, Avacas is always like this.'

She looked around, shaking her head in bewilderment.
'But there are so many people!'

He smiled at her. 'More people live in Avacas than live
in the whole of Dhevyn.'

The news was something of a shock to Tia. It had not
occurred to her until that moment that Dhevyn might have
remained under the yoke of Senet because it truly wasn't
strong enough to take on the mainland kingdom. Perhaps
Queen Rainan paid fealty to the Lion of Senet out of necessity after all – and not cowardice, as Tia believed.

'How far is it to your friend's place?'

'He lives closer to the palace. He's a corporal in Antonov's
guard.'

Tia stopped dead and stared at him. Reithan realised
that she was no longer following, and turned to find out
what had happened to her.

'What's the matter?' he asked, walking back to where
she stood unmoving in the centre of the street. The busy
populace flowed around her as if she were a rock in a rapid
stream.

'You have friends in Antonov's own guard?'

He took her arm and jerked her forward. 'I have a lot
of friends, Tia.'

'But—'

'But, nothing. I'd trust Ivon with my life. In fact, I have trusted him with it. On a number of occasions.'

'Does Johan know you have friends in Antonov's guard?' she asked suspiciously.

'Of course he knows. Johan encouraged me to make contacts in Senet. He thought we might need them one day. Look, do you suppose we could discuss this somewhere a little less public?' He glanced around at the people moving past them. Some of them were staring curiously at the couple standing in the middle of the road, blocking traffic.

Tia let him pull her along the street. When Reithan said he had friends in Avacas, she had no idea he was planning to lead them into the heart of Antonov's personal guard. The mere thought of speaking to a member of the feared Senetian Guard was enough to make her nervous, even if he was on their side.

'Reithan!' she called, looking for any reason to delay the meeting.

'What now?'

'Can we check the wharves first?'

'Why?'

'To see if Antonov's ship has docked yet. If he's not here, there doesn't seem much point in hanging about Avacas, does there?'

Reithan thought it over for a moment, and then nodded. 'Actually, that's not a bad idea. If he's not returned from Elcast yet, I'd like to know when he's expected. Anyway, Ivon might not be home at this time of day.'

'Let's check the wharves then.'

Reithan led her in a different direction, again pushing and shoving through narrow, crowded streets that swarmed with people. The buildings were a haphazard mixture of styles: some were built of wood, others of granite or sandstone. Some were a mixture of both, with solid ground floors and flimsy upper storeys, which looked as if they might fall over in the first decent quake. Occasionally, they passed by the ruin of a tumbled house. According to Reithan, the most recent quake of any force had been nearly fourteen years ago, although tremors were so common the population took little or no notice of them. The thought of earthquakes didn't bother Tia. She had lived in the shadow of the Baenlands's active volcanoes all her life. But the crowding in the city concerned her. Mil was laid out much more carefully than Avacas. They knew the paths of the lava flows and had built around them. In Mil, houses were constructed around a central foundation pillar that moved with the ground when it shook, and the caves were always a safe haven if the eruption looked particularly severe. Here, the buildings were built to suit the people, not the terrain, and there were far too many people.

She said as much to Reithan, who looked around him for a moment and then shrugged. 'Avacas has been here for thousands of years, Tia. It might get shaken up a bit every now and then, but it's never been completely destroyed.'

He led her down a narrow lane between a chandler's shop and a tavern. When they emerged at the other end, they found themselves on the docks. The *Calliope* was tied up at the main wharf a little further around the harbour.

Tia smiled for a moment when she saw it. Despite what she thought about the man who had commissioned her, the *Calliope* was a magnificent ship. They walked along the dock to where a small crowd had gathered to watch. The Lion of Senet was ashore already, Tia guessed. There were no Shadowdancers in sight, either, which meant Tia wasn't likely to catch a glimpse of Ella Geon. Nor was there a guard of honour waiting, only a mounted groom holding a single horse. The crowd would be much larger if the prince was preparing to disembark. These were just idle onlookers.

'Look!' Reithan said, in a low, urgent voice. The man who had drawn Reithan's attention stood on the deck surrounded by guards, waiting to descend the gangway. He was chained and gaunt, bearded and pale, and he leaned on a roughly fashioned crutch. But it was unmistakably Johan Thorn.

'Look at him! He's been hurt!'

'I'm more surprised to find him standing,' Reithan answered.

'Can we get to him, do you think?' Her heart began to beat faster. It didn't seem possible that he could just be standing there, almost in arm's reach, but they couldn't do anything. She noted the placement of the guards with a practised eye, hoping for an opportunity.

Reithan looked at her askance. 'Look around, Tia. There are a dozen guards with him on the ship, and they're probably waiting for an escort from the palace. Between us, we have a sword and two table daggers. I could probably take three or four of them. Were *you* planning to take care of the rest?'

'But he's so close!' she hissed in frustration. It was all she could do not to call out to Johan, to give him hope; to offer some reassurance that they would try to help him.

'He might as well be on the other side of the second sun, right now. The important thing is that we've seen him. He's alive and he's in one piece. We can make our plans once we've spoken to Ivon.'

'I feel so helpless!'

'That's probably because right now we *are* helpless.'

Tia nodded glumly in agreement. She knew Reithan was right, but that didn't make it any easier to stomach. She watched Johan, his eyes downcast, standing on the deck surrounded by alert guards, and tried to think of a way to help him. There was none, of course, but that just made her even more determined.

'Who's that?' she asked Reithan, pointing to a young man who approached the guards around Johan. Merely by the quality of his clothes, she could tell he was noble born. *He carries himself with the assurance of one born to rule, too,* Tia thought sourly. She knew that unconscious stance well. Growing up around Johan, she'd seen it every day of her life. The young lord said something to the guards and they parted with a slight bow, deferring to his command. 'Is that one of Antonov's sons?'

Reithan squinted a little and stared at the boy, before turning to her with a shrug. 'I don't know who he is.'

Tia studied him carefully. He was a lanky, dark-haired young man. He said something to Johan, which caused the pirate to smile, then turned and walked away. He descended the gangway, where the groom was waiting, sitting astride a grey mare, holding the reins of the other riderless horse. The young lord took the reins from the groom and swung into the saddle. Then he turned and headed away from the ship without looking back. As he rode past Tia, she noticed that his eyes were the colour of dull steel.

And as cold as steel, too, she decided, disliking him on sight.

'He's probably one of Antonov's pets,' Reithan remarked as the young lord rode by.

'What do you mean?'

'Antonov is fond of taking the sons of Dhevynian nobles into his home and treating them like royalty. By the time he sends them back to their own islands, they're so devoted to him, it wouldn't matter what Rainan did, she could never count on their loyalty.'

'Which island is he from, do you think?'

'I don't know.'

'Do you think he's from Elcast?'

'He looks too young to be Wallin Provin's heir. Maybe he's the younger Rill boy. He's been living on Elcast ever since his father was appointed governor there.' Reithan shrugged, turning his attention back to the ship. 'Or it might be the second son. The one Morna had after she went back to Wallin.'

'The traitor's whelp. That figures. Anyway, what does it matter?'

'It might,' Reithan said thoughtfully. 'The guards didn't stop him talking to Johan.'

Tia stared at him and shook her head. 'You think he'd help *us*? Wallin *Provin's* son?'

'I suppose not. But he's Morna's son, too.'

'The boy has been brought to Avacas by Antonov Latanya, Reithan. If what you say is true, by the end of the week he'll be swearing his sword to Senet.' She watched with a frown as the young lord and his groom disappeared from view, swallowed by the crowd along the wharves. 'If he hasn't already.'

'Aye, it's unlikely there'll be aid from that quarter,' Reithan agreed. 'Come on, let's go investigate that tavern we passed earlier. I could do with an ale.'

'But what about Johan? Shouldn't we follow him or something?'

'He's not going anywhere but the palace.'

'But how will we know for certain?'

'Ivon will know.'

With a final, hopeful glance at Johan, she reluctantly nodded. Despite her efforts to will the pirate to look in her direction, he didn't look up. With a sigh, she followed Reithan back along the wharf towards a large tavern called the Watchkeeper's Dog.

Just as they reached the tavern doors, a closed-in carriage trundled down the wharf, surrounded by a full squad of soldiers wearing the gold-and-white rampant lion crest of Senet. The carriage pulled up at the foot of the *Calliope*'s gangway and Johan was hauled down to the wharf and bundled into the carriage with little ceremony.

'One thing bothers me a little, Tia.'

'What's that?'

'Antonov has been hunting Johan for years. You'd think now that he finally has him, he'd make a bit more of a fuss.'

'You mean, where are the jeering crowds? The triumphal procession through the streets of Avacas with the dread pirate locked in a cage for all the world to gawk at?'

'Something like that.'

Tia shrugged. 'I don't know.'

'Neither do I, and until we figure out what game Antonov's playing, I think we should be cautious.'

'As opposed to what?' Tia asked, as she stepped past Reithan into the gloom of the tavern's taproom.

48

The street down which Reithan led Tia was narrow and cluttered, the houses built so close together there was barely room to squeeze down the lanes between each building. When they finally found the house on Chandlers Street, they discovered a small cottage filled with cats. The place stank, and there wasn't a surface in the house that wasn't coated in cat hair.

Far from being a fearsome member of Antonov's dreaded guard, Ivon Modonov proved to be a rotund little man with a balding head, a warm smile and a passion for his feline companions that Tia thought a little unnatural. His uniform was stretched tight over a well-fed belly, and he was armed with nothing more dangerous than a table dagger.

Ivon welcomed them cheerfully, calling Reithan his cousin and asking them loudly about their journey from Versage, in northern Senet, no doubt for the benefit of his neighbours. Tia followed Reithan into the cluttered little house, through a dim hall into the kitchen at the back, which was cluttered with bowls of food and saucers of souring milk left out for the cats. Ivon shooed a big black tom off one chair so that Tia could sit down, and a litter of ginger kittens off another to make room for Reithan.

'Can't say I'm surprised to see you,' Ivon announced as he set about making tea for them. 'Not considering who arrived today.'

'You know about Johan Thorn, then?' Reithan asked.

'The whole palace is abuzz with the news.'

'Where are they holding him?' Tia demanded. 'Can we get to him?'

Ivon turned and studied her curiously for a moment and then turned to Reithan. 'Who is she?'

'This is Tia. She's a friend.'

'Hmm . . .' Ivon replied with a frown. 'Do you trust her?'

'Yes,' Reithan assured him, with a faint smile. 'I trust her.'

'Does she understand how dangerous it would be for me if anyone thought—'

'You don't have to talk about me like I'm not here,' Tia cut in impatiently.

Ivon glowered at her. 'And you don't have to act so uppity, missy.'

'Tia . . .' Reithan warned, before she could respond. She opened her mouth to object, then clamped her lips shut tight. Tia knew the look on Reithan's face well enough to heed his warning. Once he was satisfied that she would say nothing further, he turned back to Ivon. 'Will you tell us what you know?'

The fat little man carried the teapot to the table and laid out three chipped cups. He told another grey tabby to scat, before taking the chair on the other side of the scrubbed wooden table. 'We got word Antonov was coming home about three weeks ago. He sent a pigeon from Elcast.'

'They made good time then,' Reithan remarked.

'Aye. And brought Thorn with them. He's to be held in the palace, not the garrison, I understand. His guards have been handpicked, I know that much. There's not a one with a modicum of sympathy for Dhevyn among them.'

'So getting to him through the guards is out of the question?'

Ivon nodded. 'Completely.'

'What about you?' Tia asked. 'Can't you get in to see him?'

'I work in the quartermaster's store, missy,' Ivon told her as he poured the tea. 'It means I hear a lot, I see a lot, but I don't have access to anything important. I certainly don't have an excuse to visit with the likes of Johan Thorn.'

'Who else will be allowed to see him?'

'Not many at all, I'd say. They'll not let anybody near him.'

'I'm surprised Antonov didn't parade him through the streets in chains when he arrived.'

Ivon shrugged. 'Not so surprising, really. He probably wants to wait until Queen Rainan gets here.'

'She's coming here to Avacas?' Tia gasped.

Ivon nodded. 'It's Prince Kirshov's birthday soon. There's a huge celebration planned.'

'So she was probably invited long before Johan was captured,' Reithan concluded. 'Still, the timing couldn't be better for Antonov. If he's planning to make an example of Johan Thorn, what better time than when the Queen of Dhevyn is here to watch? Is there any way to get a message to Johan?'

Ivon shook his head. 'I doubt it. But let me see tomorrow. I might be able to figure something out by then.'

Reithan thanked him and they kept drinking their tea.

When Ivon returned to the house the following evening, the news was even less encouraging. The whole of the third floor of the west wing was sealed off and off limits to all but a select few. The list of people permitted to enter the prohibited area was depressingly short. Prince Antonov, the High Priestess, the Shadowdancer Ella Geon, Prefect Barin Welacin and his staff, and, for no apparent reason, Dirk Provin.

'Why Dirk Provin?' Tia asked suspiciously when Ivon informed them of the list. She remembered those iron-coloured eyes, wondering what Antonov's Elcastran pet had done to deserve such a dubious honour.

The fat little clerk shrugged. 'I was lucky to learn of the list, missy. I didn't ask for reasons.'

'Will you stop calling me missy? My name is Tia.'

Ivon turned to Reithan as if she hadn't spoken. 'There's none on that list liable to help you, I'm guessing.'

'Perhaps,' Reithan agreed thoughtfully. 'Although, like Tia, I'm curious as to why Dirk Provin would be allowed to visit Johan Thorn.'

'He's probably here to learn the finer points of torturing a man to death,' Tia suggested sourly.

'Maybe. Is there any way we can get close enough to find out?'

'In the palace, you mean?' Ivon asked.

Reithan nodded.

'I suppose you could try for work there. If you wait outside the South Gate in the morning you might get a position.'

'How does that help?'

'Everyone looking for work in the palace lines up there each morning at the dawn of the second sun and waits to be called,' Ivon explained. 'The palace housekeeper reads out a list of trades and positions she needs to fill and if you think you're qualified, you step forward. Some people wait for months, though,' he added. 'And some days there's nothing at all. Still, with the prince's birthday coming up, they'll probably need extra staff. Do you have any experience?'

'Doing what?'

'Cleaning?' Ivon suggested, looking at her as if she was just a little dim.

'Sure. I clean the palace in Mil all the time.'

Reithan smiled. 'She'll be fine, Ivon. Just don't ask her to pretend she's a whore. I can tell you from experience that she's not very convincing at that.'

Ivon studied her for a moment with a frown. 'Do you own a dress?'

'Of course I own a dress!' No need to tell him she'd only worn it once.

'Then tomorrow morning you must wear it. You'll never get picked wearing that.'

'We appreciate this, Ivon,' Reithan said, before Tia could ask what was wrong about the way she was dressed. Her vest was clean, and her trousers weren't even patched. She'd seen a lot worse in the streets of Avacas on their way here.

The rotund little man shrugged. 'You've a cause to fight for, Reithan, and so have I.'

'What's your cause?' Tia asked.

'Senet.'

'But you're helping us. How does that help Senet?'

'Half the wealth of this nation is wasted keeping troops posted throughout Dhevyn,' Ivon explained in a lecturing tone. 'Children starve in Avacas so that the Lion of Senet can hold onto Dhevyn. Many believe he is empire building at the cost of his own kingdom. Some of us have chosen to do what we can to aid Dhevyn in its fight for independence, so that Senet might also be free.'

Tia found herself somewhat chastened by his answer. She had never given much thought to what the Lion of Senet's schemes might cost his own people. In Tia's mind the world was divided into two sorts of people: those who were loyal to the true King of Dhevyn and those who weren't.

Later that evening, Reithan found Tia in the small yard at the back of the house, playing with a litter of tabby kittens. She had found a length of string to amuse them and the kittens were determined to kill the strange, skinny beast that wiggled along the step in front of them, tantalisingly out of reach.

Reithan sat down beside her, smiling at the antics of the kittens for a moment, before he spoke. 'So, are you ready for this?'

'For what?' she asked, pulling the string along the step. 'A lifetime of servitude?'

'Hardly a lifetime's worth,' Reithan chuckled. 'We just need to get one of us near him.'

Tia was silent for a moment, then she glanced at Reithan. 'You planned this all along, didn't you? That's why you wanted me to come.'

'I wouldn't say I actually planned it,' he told her. 'But the thought did cross my mind that you might come in handy. You're Senetian, for one thing, and with that red-blonde hair, you look it, too. You've a much better chance of getting a position in the palace than I.'

'And once I do? What then?'

'We'll wait until we find out where you've been assigned before we decide what to do next. The chances are that you'll wind up in the kitchens or the laundry and never even see the inside of the palace proper, so let's not get too excited.'

She nodded in agreement, snatching the string from the grasp of a kitten as it waggled its bottom, preparing to pounce. The kitten leapt after the string, claws and teeth bared. Tia pulled her hand clear just in time.

'There was one thing I wanted to warn you about,' Reithan added cautiously.

'What's that? Are you going to tell me not to get into any political discussions about the legality of the Senetian occupation of Dhevyn? I'm not that stupid, Reithan.'

'I was going to warn you to be careful if you should happen to meet Ella Geon.'

'Why?' Tia asked with a shrug. 'She doesn't know who I am.'

'No, she doesn't. But you know who *she* is, and I don't want you forgetting yourself.'

'There's nothing to forget, Reithan.'

'She's your mother, Tia.'

'Ella Geon is the woman who gave birth to me,' Tia corrected coldly. 'She is *not* my mother. Did you think I was hoping she'd notice me across a crowded room and run to embrace her long-lost daughter?'

'You sound very bitter. It worries me.'

'I'm not bitter.'

'No?' he asked, with a raised brow.

'All right, maybe I am a little bitter,' she conceded. 'But that doesn't mean I'm going to forget what's at stake. I'm not going to endanger you, Johan Thorn, my father and everybody in the Baenlands, just to satisfy my own selfish desire to strangle the cold-blooded bitch.'

'You'll get your chance one day, Tia. Just not here. Not now.'

'I know.'

He smiled at her and turned his attention to the kittens, one of which had decided that his boot was fair game. Tia watched the little tabby attacking Reithan, thinking that their own struggle against Senet stood about as much chance of succeeding as the kitten's hopeful attack on Reithan's boot.

She steadfastly refused to think about Ella Geon.

49

It was during his second week in Avacas that Dirk met Barin Welacin, the man responsible for interrogating Johan Thorn.

Since arriving in Senet, Dirk had gone out of his way to appear unconcerned about the fate of the former Dhevynian king – for the pirate's protection as much as his own. His feelings about Johan Thorn were ambivalent, but he had no desire to make things easier for the Lion of Senet, so he feigned indifference to the prisoner's welfare, while hoping against hope that something would happen that might spare the exiled king from his fate.

As the days passed with no attempt to rescue Johan, Dirk wondered why his people in the Baenlands had done nothing to free him. Although Dirk knew there was no ransom on Ranadon large enough to secure Johan's release, and no force strong enough to steal him from under Antonov's watchful eye, it still seemed a bit craven of his followers to simply leave him to die.

Fortunately, it wasn't that hard to stay out of the way of the people involved in Johan's incarceration. The third floor of the west wing had been turned into one big prison, and was off limits to all but a select few. Alenor speculated it was because her mother was due any day, and Queen Rainan of Dhevyn would not be amused to find her brother rotting in a leaky dungeon somewhere beneath the palace.

The sheer size and complexity of the Senetian palace

almost overwhelmed Dirk. His home at Elcast Keep had always exuded a feeling of ageless solidity. By contrast, the palace in Avacas seemed a study in tasteless and conspicuous wealth. There were more servants in one wing of the palace than served the whole of Elcast Keep, and the entire staff outnumbered the population of Elcast Town. There were servants to clean his boots, servants to take care of his clothes, servants to make his bed and servants to tend his bath. There was even a servant who insisted it was his job to dress Dirk each morning, a task he hurriedly assured the young man he could more than adequately do himself.

He wasn't just given a room in the palace, he was given a whole suite on the same floor as the royal family. The suite included a bedroom three times the size of his old room on Elcast, a sitting room, a book-lined study and bathroom sporting a tub large enough to swim in. Even more impressive was the fact that the thermal springs below Avacas had been tapped for the benefit of the palace occupants, and at the turn of a gold-plated stopcock, the bath could be filled with steaming, faintly sulphur-tainted water.

The day before his sixteenth birthday, Dirk was called to Antonov's study to discuss the proposed trip to Arkona the following day. True to his word, Antonov had arranged for them to visit the vast Senetian horse markets so that Alenor could find a new pony and Dirk a suitable mount for his birthday. As Arkona was some eighteen miles from Avacas, they had decided to make a day of it. Antonov had planned a picnic, and they were taking so many servants with them to attend their every need that the whole thing was taking on the complexity of a major expedition.

Barin Welacin was sitting in the straight-backed chair opposite Antonov's gilded desk when Dirk entered the room in answer to the Lion of Senet's summons. The Prefect was a small man, with a deceptively pleasant face and short stubby fingers that seemed out of proportion to his palms. He had dark curly hair and warm brown eyes, and looked no more dangerous than Alenor.

'Ah, Dirk!' Antonov declared expansively, as Dirk

stopped in front of the desk and bowed respectfully to the prince. 'Thank you for sparing the time to see me.'

As if I had a choice. 'I was told you wanted to see me, your highness.'

'I did, yes,' Antonov agreed. 'Have you met Prefect Welacin, yet? He's going to begin Johan Thorn's interrogation tomorrow while we're in Arkona.'

'My Lord Provin,' Barin Welacin replied, rising to his feet and bowing with remarkable deference.

'Prefect Welacin.'

'We were just discussing the issue of Thorn, in fact,' Antonov told him.

'I can come back later if you're busy, your highness.'

'Not at all! In fact, you might be able to assist us.'

'*Me,* sire?'

'His highness informs me that you spent a great deal of time in Thorn's company on the voyage from Elcast,' Barin said, taking his seat again. 'Perhaps you can offer some insight regarding the best way to deal with the man.'

'I thought *you* were the interrogation expert, Prefect Welacin,' Dirk replied, a little annoyed that he was being drawn into this. 'I can't see how my opinion would be of much use.'

'It might,' Barin replied with a shrug. 'Do you think physical torture would work on him?'

'I think you'd be wasting your time,' Dirk answered honestly, after only a moment's hesitation. He couldn't afford to give the impression that he cared about Johan's fate. 'The man survived a tidal wave, Prefect Welacin. He has a tolerance for pain that defies belief.'

'Then what do you suggest, Dirk?' Antonov asked. He was leaning back in his chair, studying Dirk intently. Sunlight streamed into the office from the diamond-paned windows, catching the gilt on Antonov's chair and making him appear bathed in his own light. Dirk suspected the desk and chair were placed quite deliberately to make the most of that effect. 'What would you do if you were trying to extract information out of a man like Johan Thorn?'

Dirk was tempted to reply that he would never be stupid enough to let an enemy remain at large for so long that it became an issue. But he didn't.

'I don't know, sire.'

'Perhaps he would respond to another sort of pressure?' Barin suggested. 'If we could capture one of his cohorts and threaten his life? That might work. I heard reports that Reithan Seranov was seen in Paislee recently.'

'Who's he?' Dirk asked, before he could stop himself. He really should learn to stop asking questions.

'A drug runner and a murderer,' Antonov informed him coldly. 'I would torture Reithan Seranov just for the hell of it, if I ever got my hands on him. Rumour has it that he's Johan's right-hand man.'

'Then you'd be wasting your time.' Dirk shrugged. 'He'd be just as ready to die for his cause as Johan is. And Johan would probably let him die for the same reason. You'd have more luck with a complete stranger than you would with one of his followers.'

Antonov nodded, wearing a disappointed frown. 'You're right, I fear. But then, we never thought this was going to be easy. Are you all set for the trip to Arkona tomorrow?'

'Er . . . Yes, sire.' As usual, the abrupt change of subject caught him off guard.

'Excellent. I would ask a favour of you, though, Dirk. Stay close to Alenor tomorrow. She's feeling a little guilty about buying a new mount. I think she fears Snowdrop will feel betrayed if she finds another horse to love. You know how it is with young girls and horses.'

Actually, Dirk didn't know, but if agreeing to console Alenor was all it was going to take to escape this room and the discussion about the best way to torture Johan Thorn, then Dirk was more than willing to accommodate the prince's request.

'I'll keep an eye on her, your highness.'

'Thank you, Dirk, I knew I could rely on you.'

'May I go now?'

'Of course.'

Dirk bowed politely and let himself out, leaving Antonov and Barin alone to make their plans.

The following evening, on their return from Arkona, Dirk was looking around the crowded anteroom for Kirsh or Alenor when the Baroness of Quaran, a coastal holding east of Avacas, cornered him near the tall windows overlooking the palace gardens, and began to question him about his mother.

Her inquiries had seemed innocent enough at first. She began by wishing him a happy birthday, but her conversation rapidly progressed to questions about whether or not Morna had resumed her affair with Johan Thorn while he was a prisoner on Elcast. And what did his father think about it? Antonov came to his rescue, interrupting the interrogation with a question of his own about this year's grape harvest. As Quaran was renowned for its wine, and the baroness was anxious to promote her produce to the prince, she abandoned Dirk for a more profitable discussion with the Lion of Senet.

Antonov smiled sympathetically at Dirk as he steered the baroness away, as if he understood how uncomfortable Dirk was, and how much his intervention was appreciated.

Although the excuse for this evening's gathering was his sixteenth birthday, dinner in the Lion of Senet's palace was always an occasion, always formal, and required Dirk to dress in finery he would never dream of wearing in Elcast. The guest list was different every evening, and every person in attendance was a person of note. To Dirk, all this lot seemed to want was to either curry favour with Antonov or gawk at Morna Provin's youngest son. Dirk was aware that he was the subject of intense speculation, but rarely was the subject discussed openly, and certainly not in his presence.

They were seated for dinner at the long table amid a forest of fine crystal and silverware, when someone asked if this morning's executions had been successful.

'Moderately,' Antonov replied, taking a sip of his wine. The servants were laying out the main course: a sumptuous arrangement of delicately roasted meats and crisp vegetables accompanied by a delicate red wine sauce. The food served in the palace was always like this – rich, aromatic and served in quantities that defied logic. He'd never seen anyone finish a meal since he'd been in Avacas, with the possible exception of Kirshov, who apparently had a bottomless pit in lieu of a stomach.

'What did you hope to achieve by them, your highness?' a man a few places to Dirk's left inquired. 'I heard the dozen men put to death this morning were rounded up at random.'

'We were testing Thorn's resolve,' Antonov shrugged, as if he were discussing the weather. 'If one believes the legends he likes to spread about himself, one would think he was a noble champion of injustice.'

'And did he prove to be so?' the Baroness of Quaran asked.

'Quite the opposite, my lady,' Antonov told her. 'And it's not as if Welacin didn't give him a chance. Before he slit the throat of each man, he promised Johan he would spare the man's life, if Johan would tell him what he wanted to know.'

'And Thorn said nothing?' The baroness's face was flushed, her eyes bright.

'Not a word. Johan Thorn maintained a stony silence throughout the whole ordeal.'

'Then your ploy was unsuccessful,' the man who had asked the question in the first place surmised. Dirk had been introduced to him earlier. He was an earl from somewhere in northern Senet.

'Not at all. If nothing else, we proved that Johan Thorn is a heartless monster. When one has shattered such a powerful myth, one cannot say that it was a completely wasted effort.'

Dirk nearly choked on his meal. *Twelve innocent men had died and Antonov is pleased because he thinks he's proved that Johan Thorn is a monster?* He glanced across the table at Alenor, but she refused to meet his eye. She was trying to be as quiet and inconspicuous as possible. Kirsh was tucking into his meal, seemingly oblivious to the conversation going on around him.

The northern earl raised his glass to Antonov. 'I admire your subtlety, your highness.'

'I can't claim any credit, I'm afraid,' Antonov said modestly. 'This masterful strategy was devised by our birthday boy, not me.'

Dirk froze as every eye at the table turned to him. He turned to stare in horror at the Lion of Senet, who smiled at him proudly.

'I'd never have thought up anything so fiendishly effective, myself,' Antonov continued. 'But it's a brilliant ploy. We just keep executing innocent men, giving Johan the power to put an end to the carnage anytime he wants. If he saves the lives of the innocent, he betrays his followers in the Baenlands. If he doesn't, then our champion of injustice is responsible for the needless death of innocent people. And it has the added benefit that I can't be accused of treating the Queen of Dhevyn's errant brother like a common criminal.' He looked across the table and smiled at Alenor. 'I've no wish to do anything that would cause dissent between your mother and Senet, my dear.' Alenor blushed, but didn't answer him. She looked as if she wanted to disappear. Antonov turned back to the rest of the diners and smiled. 'It's quite simply the most ingenious stratagem I have ever seen.'

'And young Dirk here thought of it?' the baroness asked. She was looking at Dirk with a hungry, predatory eye, almost as if she found the idea arousing.

'I never suggested anything of the kind, my lady,' Dirk protested, finally finding his voice.

'Don't be so modest, Dirk. I believe your exact words were that we'd have more luck with complete strangers than we would with his followers. Isn't that right?'

'Well, yes, I did say that, but—'

'He gets his modesty from his father, I think,' Antonov laughed. 'You remember how Wallin would never want to claim credit for anything during the war? A touching trait, I always thought.'

The guests all laughed politely at Antonov's words. Dirk sat motionlessly at the table, the conversation going on around him like a blur. *It's not my fault,* he told himself. *I didn't mean to . . .*

But the damage was done, and it took less than a day for word to spread through Avacas that the whole sickening episode had been Dirk Provin's idea.

50

'Didn't I warn you?' Tia demanded angrily, as soon as she found Reithan out in the yard of Ivon's cottage. The door banged shut behind her as she stepped out into the small courtyard bathed in red light from the first sun hanging high in the sky.

'Warn me about what?' he asked, looking up from the chair he was mending. He was bored, trapped here in Ivon's house all day, and had taken to mending the furniture to keep himself occupied.

'Dirk Provin.'

'What's he done?'

'He's got them rounding up innocent bystanders and executing them in front of Johan to make him talk.'

Reithan stood up and frowned as he brushed the wood shavings from his trousers. 'And it was Provin's idea?'

'Sella told me. She's one of the laundry maids.'

It had taken Tia two weeks of getting up at dawn and patiently waiting at the palace before she was finally called up from the crowd gathered outside the South Gate.

'Sella's brother was serving in the dining room tonight when Antonov was crowing about how clever Dirk was to think of it. I told you he was trouble, didn't I?'

'Yes, you did tell me.'

'Well?'

'Well *what*?'

'What are you going to do about it?'

'Stay off the streets so I don't get rounded up and executed for Dirk Provin's entertainment,' he replied in all seriousness.

'Reithan!'

'Well, what exactly did you want me to do, Tia?'

'I don't know,' she grumbled, sitting down on the step and wrapping her arms around her knees miserably. 'There must be something we can do.'

'There's nothing we can do. Besides, you always said you thought the only good Senetian was a dead one. Maybe that's Provin's plan? Maybe he's just found a way to rid the world of a few excess Senetians.'

'Hah! How likely is that? Dirk Provin thought this up because he's a sadistic little bastard. You can tell it just by looking at him.'

Reithan did not disagree with her assessment. He came to sit beside her on the step. 'What about Johan? Do you have news of him?'

She shrugged. 'He didn't talk, if that's what you're asking. Didn't say a word, according to Sella. It must have been killing him to do nothing while those men died.'

Reithan nodded in agreement. 'Even Johan will eventually fold under that sort of pressure. We really need to do something soon. Have you had any luck getting near him?'

'No, but I think I've worked out how to do it.'

'How?'

'I need to get Emalia's job.'

'Who's Emalia?'

'The maid who changes the sheets in the royal suites. She has access to every one of them, although I hear they haven't allowed Johan any sheets on his bed for fear he'll try to make a noose of them. Sella and Emalia talk about him all the time. When they're not talking about their love lives,' she added with a groan.

Sella was a tall girl with a very large bosom and a great deal of interest in the goings-on upstairs. Emalia was her best friend, a tiny, voluptuous young blonde whose passion was men – in particular, big, dark-haired, handsome ones. Although Tia thought the girls she worked with vapid and stupid, she had spent days feigning intense interest in their activities, folding sheets and cooing with admiration as Emalia gossiped endlessly or chronicled her conquests.

'Access to the royal suites would be a good start. But how are you going to get Emalia's job?'

'You're going to get it for me.'

'How?'

Tia looked at Reithan and grinned. 'This time, you get to be the whore.'

Reithan looked at her oddly.

'After we finish work, Emalia and Sella usually head down into the town to drink at the Lone Soldier.'

'I've heard of it. It's a pretty rough place, by all accounts.'

'According to Emalia, the tavern's main attraction is that it's frequented by plenty of big, dark-haired, handsome men. And seeing as how my arsenal of weapons consists almost entirely of one big, dark-haired, handsome man, I might as well use him.'

'Your *arsenal*?' Reithan repeated with a frown.

'I owe you for making me pretend I was a whore on Kalarada.'

'One does what one must for the cause, Tia. So what's your plan?'

'Emalia and Sella usually drink in the tavern until late at night, then stagger back to the room they share above the tea merchant's shop in Grainway Street. If they're lucky, one or other of the girls gets to spend the night elsewhere.'

'Preferably with a big, dark-haired, handsome man, I'm guessing,' he remarked dryly.

'Exactly! So, if we can arrange for you to meet Emalia, and if you can arrange to spend the night with her *and* keep her from work the following morning, then Sella will try to find a way to cover for her friend's absence. All I have to do is offer to help, and with luck, by tomorrow morning I'll be changing the sheets in the royal suites in Emalia's place.'

'What makes you think I can convince this Emalia of yours to spend the night with me? More to the point, what makes you think I'm going to go along with this absurd plan?'

'One does what one must for the cause, Reithan,' she reminded him with a grin.

The following morning, when Emalia didn't arrive for work, Sella hurriedly briefed Tia on her friend's duties, while trying to avoid the attention of the laundry mistress. Tia listened earnestly, nodded frequently and tried not to laugh aloud as Sella described the handsome chap that Emalia had found herself last night. Tia found it interesting that Sella wasn't concerned for her friend, just envious. Tia promised to cover for Emalia, and hurried upstairs, wondering if Reithan had enjoyed himself as much as Emalia apparently had.

The halls of the palace were wider than the main long house in Mil. The thick carpets that stretched endlessly along the polished floors were patterned in an intricate floral design, bordered in red. The doors to each of the royal suites were carved and gilded with the rampant lion of Senet, and sunlight streamed into the halls from stained-glass skylights placed every ten feet or so along the ceiling.

Tia did her best not to gape as she pushed the laundry cart along the hall, keeping her head lowered. Sella had given her quite explicit instructions on what she must do, the foremost of which was not draw attention to herself. Emalia would be back soon, Sella assured her. The important thing was to ensure that the routine upstairs didn't vary – that way nobody would notice she was missing.

The first room Tia entered belonged to Prince Kirshov. Tia had seen him from a distance once or twice since she'd been working in the palace. He was a strapping young man, with his father's blond good looks. But to Tia, he embodied the Latanya character, with an arrogant disregard of all those beneath him, a trait she considered all Senetians (and the nobility in particular) guilty of. The room was empty when she knocked on the door, so she let herself in and glanced around at the jaw-dropping wealth strewn carelessly around the room. Every piece of furniture was gilded. The doors to the prince's dressing room stood open, revealing more clothes than Tia thought might exist in all of Mil.

All this wasted on a spoiled Senetian brat.

She changed the sheets on the prince's bed quickly, bundling up the used sheets and tucking them into the bottom of the laundry cart. Before she closed the door behind her, she glanced around the room once more. That statue on the mantel would feed everyone in Mil for a year.

'Don't just stand there daydreaming, girl!'

Tia started at the unexpected voice and turned to face a grumpy maid carrying a bucket of sudsy water and a scrubbing brush, waiting to enter Prince Kirshov's room.

'You might have all the time in the world to squander, missy,' the woman snapped, 'but some of us 'ave work to do. Get along with you!'

Tia muttered an apology and pushed the cart clear of the door.

The next suite along the hall, so Sella had informed her, belonged to Prince Misha. The rooms across the way were Dirk Provin's. Tia thought for a moment, then pushed the cart across the hall.

A small boy of about twelve or thirteen answered her knock.

'I've come to change Lord Provin's sheets,' she explained.

The lad nodded and stood back to let her enter. Tia glanced around the room, hoping to learn something of the suite's occupant. The sitting room was scattered with books, and the door to a small study on the left was open, where even more books lay on the polished desk.

'The bed's in there,' the boy told her helpfully, pointing to the bedroom.

Tia looked down at the lad and frowned. 'Are you Lord Provin's slave?' *Trust a Provin to use a child in such a manner.*

He nodded vigourously. 'I'm his volley.'

'His what? Oh, you mean valet?'

'My name's Eryk. What's your name?'

'Tia.'

'You're very pretty.'

The compliment took Tia completely by surprise. 'What?'

Eryk blushed and looked at the floor. 'I'm thorry . . . I didn't mean to . . . I . . . Lord Dirk told me I have to think before I . . .' The boy seemed to be on the verge of tears.

'It's all right, Eryk. You didn't upset me.' She put down the sheets and reached out to place a hand on his shoulder, but he flinched from her touch.

'I'm gonna be in trouble, aren't I?'

'Of course you're not in trouble! I won't tell on you.'

Eryk brightened immediately. 'You won't?'

'I won't.'

'I don't want Lord Dirk to be mad at me.'

She studied the child carefully. 'Does he get mad at you often?'

'Only when I'm bad.'

Tia's heart swelled with pity. *What had that beast Dirk Provin done to this poor child?*

'What does he do to you when you're bad?' she asked gently, bracing herself for some terrible tale of hideous torment.

'Well . . . once . . . back home . . . the time I accidentally spilled ink all over Lady Faralan's best dress . . . he made me . . .' The child avoided her eye, as if the tale were too painful to relate.

'It's all right, Eryk. You can tell me.'

The boy squared his shoulders, as if gathering his strength before divulging the gory details. 'He made me help her with her needlework for a whole month!'

'He *what*?' she asked in disbelief.

'He made me hold the yarn for her, and wind her bobbins, and fetch and carry, and sit with the women, like I was a *girl*! It was horrible, miss! I *never* want to do that again!'

Tia stared at the boy in confusion. 'He made you help

the women for a month? *That* was the worst punishment he's ever given you?'

'The worst, miss! I asked him to just give me a beating and be done with it, but he said beatings was ... bar ... barb ...'

'Barbaric?' she suggested.

'I think that's the word. Anyway ... after he said that it was bar ... that word ... he told me I'd learn more by helping than by getting off lightly with a few tears. I'd much rather he gives me a beating, but he never does. He can be *really* mean like that sometimes, miss.'

Tia stared at the boy for a moment, then picked up the sheets.

'He sounds quite dreadful,' she agreed, a little doubtfully.

'Oh no, miss, you got me all wrong! Lord Dirk isn't dreadful. He's the smartest, kindest, bravest person in the whole world.'

51

Still trying to reconcile her vision of a man who had ordered a dozen strangers executed with young Eryk's assertion that Dirk Provin was the 'smartest, kindest, bravest person in the whole wide world', Tia knocked on the door of Prince Misha's suite.

She waited for a moment, until a voice called permission to enter. Picking up a pile of fresh sheets from the cart, she pushed open the door and stepped into a room no less opulent than the previous suites. The difference was that in this room, aromatic candles lay scattered on the gilded tables, and the occupant of the room sat wrapped in a rug before the fire, studying a chess game with great concentration.

Prince Misha's withered leg was covered by a rug, but everyone knew of the Crippled Prince. He had the pale, almost translucent skin and the fragile demeanour of a poppy-dust addict. It was a symptom she knew well, and she bit back a snort of disgust.

The whole world at his withered feet and he could do no better than to lose himself to the cowardly escape of poppy-dust.

Still, it answered one question. She understood now why Ella Geon was responsible for caring for the ailing prince. The Shadowdancer was an expert when it came to poppy-dust and its effects on the human body. Neris Veran could attest to that.

'You're here to change the sheets?' the prince inquired, glancing at the linen she carried. His eyes had the fevered brightness of an addict. 'Where's Emalia?'

'She's sick, your highness,' Tia mumbled.

'Nothing serious, I hope.'

'No, your highness, I don't think so.'

'What's your name?'

She hesitated, unsure why the prince was taking such an interest in her. 'Tia.'

Prince Misha smiled and beckoned her closer. 'I've not seen you in the palace before, Tia.'

'I'm new.'

'Then welcome to Avacas,' he said with a smile. 'Do you know anything about chess?'

'Pardon?'

'Chess. Have you ever played?'

'A little. With my father.'

Misha sighed heavily. 'I was hoping you could offer me some advice. He's going to beat me again, I fear.'

'Who's going to beat you?' she asked curiously, while a little voice in her head cried: *Change the damn sheets and get out of here, you idiot!*

'Dirk Provin. He's a fiend, I tell you!'

Dirk Provin. The mere name evoked a rush of confused emotions in her. She put down the sheets and crossed to the table, studying the board for a long moment.

'Your entire king side is useless,' she told him.

Prince Misha glanced up at her curiously. 'What?'

'Your entire king side is useless,' she repeated. 'You've got no hope of getting out of that mess.'

'Explain.'

'Well, look at it,' she told him, a little impatiently. 'Your opponent has plenty of space and is all set to move in on your queen. Look at his knight! It's in a brilliant position, because you've no way to displace it! His spatial advantage alone will lead to a win.'

'Then what do you suggest I do?'

'Be on the lookout for a good square to put a knight in, because if you can find one, your knight will become very powerful and you might have some hope of turning things around.' Then she grinned. 'Or you could accidentally knock the board over.'

Misha smiled at her. 'A tempting suggestion, but I fear Dirk would remember where each piece was placed when he last saw the board. He's like that, you know.'

'Then you'll just have to beat him the hard way,' she suggested, with more savagery than the comment warranted.

'Hmmm,' Misha agreed absently, turning back to the board, and pulling the rug a little closer, as if he was cold. 'I've never taken him yet, but I'm sure I will eventually.' He looked up suddenly and stared at her with a curious expression. 'Where did you learn so much about chess?'

'I told you. My father taught me.' She fervently wished she hadn't said a word. *So much for being inconspicuous.*

'Your father must be very good. Perhaps you could arrange for me to play him? He might be able to teach me a thing or two.'

'He's dead,' Tia blurted out hurriedly.

Misha was instantly contrite. 'I'm sorry.'

'I have to change the sheets,' she mumbled, backing away.

The prince nodded and turned his attention to the board. His hands were shaking, Tia noticed, and his skin was pallid, faintly sheened with sweat. For a moment she hesitated.

She'd seen her father like this. The Lion of Senet's eldest son was displaying all the symptoms of an addict overdue for his next fix. If he didn't get it soon, he would start to fit, she knew. She'd seen Neris do it often enough.

'Are you all right?' she asked.

He nodded, pulling the rug even closer. 'I'm due for my tonic soon, that's all. It's nothing to concern yourself with. Ella will be here shortly.'

'Ella Geon. The Shadowdancer?'

Misha glanced up at her. In the short time she had been in the room, his trembling had progressed from barely perceptible to visible shaking. 'You know her?'

Tia fought down a wave of panic. She had convinced herself that she didn't care if she saw Ella Geon in the palace. She had even convinced Reithan. But the prospect of meeting the woman who had given birth to her suddenly filled her with dread.

'No ... I've just heard about her, that's all. Look ... I really should get on these sheets. Are you sure you're all right?'

'I'll be fine, but thank you for your concern.'

Tia picked up the clean sheets, watching the prince uneasily. He was studying the chessboard again, and paid her no more attention as she crossed the sitting room to the bedchamber. She glanced over her shoulder at him before she entered the bedroom, not sure if it was wise to leave him unattended. His addiction seemed serious, although how they could let someone like Misha Latanya fall victim to the poppy-dust was beyond her.

Shouldn't someone have tried to help him before now?

But then again, maybe he didn't want help. Neris certainly didn't. He preferred the dazed half-world of poppy-dust to having to face up to reality. At least Neris had a good reason to seek an escape, though. As far as Tia could tell, Misha had nothing but wealth, power and privilege to run from.

She was tugging the sheets from Prince Misha's bed when she heard the prince cry out as the chessboard fell to the floor in the other room. For a brief moment she hesitated. What did she care if some spoiled Senetian prince was choking on his own tongue because of a self-inflicted drug addiction?

The sound of shattering glass prompted her to action. With her luck, she would be blamed for breaking whatever he had knocked over. She abandoned the bedmaking and ran back into the sitting room.

Misha was on the floor, his limbs stiff and rigid. He had stopped breathing and his lips were turning blue. As she reached him, his body began twitching uncontrollably. His eyes were rolled back in his head and he was choking, as foam dribbled down his chin. With practised ease, Tia fell to her knees and rolled him onto his side, then looked around for something to jam in his mouth to prevent him from biting through his own tongue as his jaw clenched tight. The nearest thing proved to be the king from the chess set that was now scattered all over the floor.

That's one game Dirk Provin won't win.

Tia forced the chess piece between Misha's teeth and felt him clamp down on the carved schist. His body began to jerk violently. He was sweating so much it was hard to hold him. He was bleeding, too. The glass she had heard shattering from the other room was scattered on the floor beneath him, and every thrashing movement caused another piece to slice into him. She moved around on her knees and cradled his bloody, foaming head in her lap, whispering soothing nonsense words. They made no difference, she knew, but they made her feel as if she was doing something useful. Not that there was a lot she could do. The only thing that would halt this fit was time.

The door suddenly flew open, but her relief at thinking help was at hand evaporated instantly when she looked up to find Kirshov Latanya and Dirk Provin standing at the door. The prince's eyes were blazing dangerously, as he took in his unconscious brother covered in blood, twitching on the floor in the arms of a complete stranger.

'What in the name of the Goddess is going on here?'

'Get help!' she cried, before Prince Kirshov could jump to conclusions and accuse her of anything.

'You get away from him!' Kirshov demanded, taking a step further into the room. Oddly, it was Dirk Provin who stopped him.

'No, Kirsh! She's right. Find Ella. Quickly!'

The prince glared at her for a moment, then ran into the hall, yelling for help. Dirk Provin hurried to Misha and knelt down beside him. He glanced at the prince with concern, then turned his steel-coloured eyes on Tia.

'Get that thing out of his mouth,' Dirk ordered.

'I've seen this plenty of times before,' she snapped. 'I know what I'm doing.'

'Then you should know better than to put anything in his mouth when he's having a seizure.'

While they argued, Misha's tortured limbs began to relax. Dirk reached down and pulled the chess piece from the prince's mouth and tossed it on the floor with a look that spoke volumes.

Arrogant prick, Tia thought. *What would you know about treating seizures?*

'What happened?' Ella Geon demanded, rushing into the room with Kirshov on her heels.

'He had a seizure,' Dirk explained, looking up at the Shadowdancer. 'He's coming out of it now, and other than a few cuts, he doesn't seem to have suffered any lasting harm. No thanks to our friend here,' he added looking pointedly at Tia.

'Get everybody out of here,' Ella ordered.

Misha's limbs had relaxed completely now, and he was beginning to regain consciousness. Tia made sure he was on his side, saliva dribbling down his chin, before slowly climbing to her feet. She avoided looking at Ella. Her boots crunched on the broken glass and her heart was hammering, but she wasn't sure if it was anger or fear that made it pound so desperately.

'You!' Ella called suddenly, as Tia tried to back away

from the prince as inconspicuously as possible. 'Who are you?'

'I came to change the sheets, my lady.'

'Where's Emalia?'

'She's sick.'

'Then get about your duties, girl! And you are not to say a word of this to anyone, understand? If I hear you've been spreading gossip downstairs, I'll personally see to it that you are flayed alive.'

'Yes, my lady.' Tia didn't doubt the threat. Ella Geon had quite a reputation around the palace, and it wasn't a pleasant one.

'Well? Don't just stand there! Change the sheets! His highness will need to rest!'

'Yes, my lady.'

Tia fled into the bedroom, angry tears blurring her vision.

Not even a thank-you, she muttered silently to herself as she finished jerking the old sheets from the large four-poster. *Not so much as a hint of gratitude. Well, the next time Prince Poppy-dust out there has a fit and I'm around, he can damn well choke on his own spit! And what the hell would Dirk Provin know about anything? How dare he imply that I was endangering the prince? Who does he think he is, any-way . . . ?*

'What's your name?'

Tia spun around to find Dirk standing at the door to the bedroom. She could hear Ella in the other room reas-suring Kirshov, in between fussing over Misha. Close up, he was younger than Tia had first thought. About the same age as she was, in fact. But that just made it worse. The discon-certing thing was that except for those steel-grey eyes, he reminded her sharply of Johan Thorn.

'Why do you want to know?'

'I was just . . . I was going to say thank you for trying to help Misha. You did the best you could.'

Patronising pig. 'I didn't do anything special.'

'You didn't panic. Most people would have.'

'I'm not most people,' she retorted, then gasped as she realised she had spoken the thought aloud.

Dirk Provin smiled at her. 'Apparently not. Did you want a hand making that bed? Ella's getting impatient.'

The offer left her speechless for a moment. Then she shook her head, certain that he had an ulterior motive. 'I don't need any help from you, Lord Provin.'

He looked at her curiously, as if he couldn't understand the reason for her animosity, then he shrugged and walked back into the other room.

52

Ivon made Tia some hot tea when she returned to the house that evening, still shaken from her encounter with Prince Misha. They sat around the table in Ivon's tiny, cat-filled kitchen, while Reithan and the tubby little soldier listened to her tale with growing concern. Reithan didn't say much, but he shook his head a lot and Ivon tut-tutted frequently, which Tia found intensely annoying.

'That was foolish in the extreme, Tia,' Ivon said when she finally finished her story. 'You should not have brought yourself to the attention of Prince Misha, or the Shadowdancer.'

'What was I supposed to do? Just let him lie there twitching and foaming at the mouth?'

'You should have run like hell,' Reithan advised.

'That's easy for you to say,' she retorted. 'You weren't there.'

'There's one thing about your tale that bothers me, missy,' Ivon said, shooing a cat off the table that was trying to drink out of his teacup.

'What's that?'

'You say Prince Misha is a poppy-dust addict? I've never

heard anything about it. I mean it's well known that's he's crippled and poorly, but there was never any suggestion that he was an addict.'

'Poorly? That's probably the story they spread to cover it up,' she shrugged.

'But are you sure? You're awfully young to be such an expert on such matters, missy.'

'I'm *sure*,' she replied. 'And stop calling me missy.'

'But it seems so out of character.'

Tia laughed sourly. 'You think a member of the nobility addicted to poppy-dust is out of character?'

Ivon sipped his tea as his brows drew together in concern. 'Oh, I know it's a problem, both here and in Dhevyn. But that's just my point. Prince Antonov despises anyone who has anything to do with poppy-dust. The Senetian Guard spends most of its time hunting down criminals who traffic in it. He stripped the Earl of Dochovnat of his lands and his title when he discovered him using it. And the Duke of Galean's son was executed when he was caught dealing with the Baenland pirates.'

'It's one thing to condemn others,' Reithan pointed out. 'But it's a different story when it's your own flesh and blood. In fact, if it's true, then the last thing Antonov could admit was that his son is an addict.'

'It accounts for Ella Geon being in the palace, too,' Tia reminded them. 'If there's anyone on Ranadon who knows how to deal with a poppy-dust addict, it's her.'

'She has experience in that sort of thing?' Ivon inquired curiously.

Reithan and Tia exchanged a knowing glance.

'Oh yes, you can count on that,' Reithan told him.

Ivon shook his head with a puzzled frown. 'It all seems very odd to me.'

'Well, I'm just glad I got out of there in one piece. Ella Geon threatened to flay me alive if I said anything to anyone. And I don't think she was joking.'

'You said you spoke to Dirk Provin afterwards,' Reithan said. 'What did he say?'

'Nothing of substance. I spoke to his servant, too.'

'Now what did *he* have to say?'

Tia pulled a face. 'He says Dirk Provin is the smartest, kindest, bravest person in the whole world.'

'That's quite a recommendation.'

'I'm not sure I believe it, though. I think the poor child is too grateful for the roof over his head to risk telling me what he really thought. After what Dirk Provin ordered done to make Johan talk, you can understand why his servant is afraid of saying anything uncomplimentary about him.'

'You *really* don't like Provin, do you?' Reithan remarked.

'He's a patronising snob, as well as a sadist and a traitor to his own people.'

'You're not interested in giving him the benefit of the doubt?'

'Give me one reason why I should!'

Reithan didn't answer her. He stood up and walked to his vest, which was hanging on a nail on the back of the kitchen door, and pulled a letter from his pocket, which he tossed on the table.

'What's this?'

'A letter.'

'I can see that. Who's it from?'

'Lexie. It arrived today via one of our contacts in the Brotherhood.'

Tia opened the letter curiously, turning her chair slightly to catch the evening sun streaming in through the dirty kitchen window. The letter was deliberately vague, to protect them if it fell into the wrong hands, but for those who knew her, it was easy enough to understand.

My son, the letter began, *I trust you are enjoying your journey. We are all well at home.*

I have unexpectedly heard from a distant cousin we have not heard from in many years. She is concerned for her youngest son. He is currently staying with a prominent family in the same city as you. You can imagine my surprise when we received a letter from her via your cousin in Kalarada, but it appears genuine. She fears that her son may be in danger and begs our help. In light of this, I believe it may be worth making contact with him. He might be in a position to aid you in your own endeavours. I will leave the decision up to you.

Your sister sends her love. Please tell your travelling companion that her father has been doing well.

All my love,
Mother.

Tia read the letter twice, then looked at Reithan. 'Does this say what I think it says?'

'It makes no sense to me,' Ivon complained.

Reithan took the letter from her and studied it for a moment. 'If I'm reading it correctly, Morna Provin sent a letter to Mil via Alexin, asking for help, because she thinks Dirk is in some sort of danger.'

'If it's true, she's got some damn nerve,' Tia said. 'Fancy thinking she could just run off and live like a good Senetian lackey on Elcast for all these years, then demand our help the minute something happens to one of her precious babies.'

'You can be sure *Wallin* Provin knows nothing about any letter,' Ivon remarked. 'Such a thing would be considered treason.'

'That's never bothered Morna Provin in the past,' Tia pointed out.

'Do you think you could arrange to talk with him?' Reithan asked Tia.

'Who? Dirk Provin? Not a chance! For one thing, I don't believe he'd help us. For another, if I did say anything to him, he'd probably have me arrested. And besides, I was only filling in for Emalia. She'll be back at work tomorrow and I won't even get a chance to get near him.'

'Emalia won't be back for a while.'

'What did you do, Reithan?' she demanded suspiciously.

'I introduced her to a friend of mine. He's second mate on a ship that was leaving for Damita on this morning's tide. Emalia was quite enchanted by him. I imagine she's somewhere southeast of Avacas at the moment, merrily sailing the Tresna Sea.'

Tia glared at him. 'I asked you to keep her occupied, Reithan, not arrange to have her kidnapped.'

Reithan smiled. 'You have way too much faith in my stamina, girl.'

'You wanted her out of the way and she is,' Ivon pointed out. 'One day changing beds in the royal suites wasn't going to help much.'

Tia shook her head. 'I'm still not going to walk up to Dirk Provin and ask for his help.'

'No, that would be foolish in the extreme. But we do need to find a way to sound him out. I'm rather curious to know whose side he's really on.'

'Reithan, he arranged to have twelve innocent men murdered! I think it's pretty damn obvious whose side he's on!'

'You may be right. But I'd still like to know for certain. If he has any sense of loyalty to his own people, he could be just the break we're looking for. He has access to the whole palace, and more important, to Johan.'

'He's the best friend of Prince Kirshov and the Lion of Senet's pet,' she reminded him. 'I promise you, Dirk Provin is nothing but trouble.'

'And if he is, I'll happily stand by and watch while you slit his throat,' Reithan assured her. 'But not until we know for certain.'

'He's very clever,' Ivon suddenly said.

'He certainly knows when he's on a good thing,' Tia agreed.

'No, I mean *really* clever. I heard Prince Kirshov talking about it to Sergey at training a few days ago.'

'Who's Sergey?' Tia asked.

'The captain of the guard.'

'What did he say?' Reithan asked.

'I didn't hear all of it, but I think he was complaining about having to study with the Provin boy. I mean, it's common knowledge that Kirshov hates spending time with his tutors. It's also common knowledge that Prince Antonov only lets him train with the guard if his tutors remain satisfied with his academic progress. Kirshov was telling Sergey that it was bad enough studying with Princess Alenor, but since Dirk arrived, it's been a thousand times worse. He called him the next Neris Veran.'

Tia stilled warily before she glanced at Reithan.

'Surely he was exaggerating,' Reithan suggested in a carefully neutral voice.

'Maybe,' Ivon shrugged. 'But I've heard other people talk about him, too. And if you believe palace gossip, the High Priestess has been badgering Prince Antonov about sending him to the Hall of Shadows, although why she would want Morna Provin's son, of all people, anywhere near her sacred Hall is beyond me.'

Later that evening, when Ivon was snoring contentedly next to the fire with his favourite tomcat on his lap, Tia and Reithan slipped out into the yard. The sun was high overhead and the world was saturated in its scarlet light. Reithan closed the door gently and turned to face Tia, making no attempt to hide the concern he had so carefully concealed from Ivon.

'It's not true, is it?' Tia demanded in a voice barely above a whisper.

'About Dirk Provin? Goddess, I hope not!'

'My father is a freak of nature, Reithan. He says that himself. It isn't possible that Dirk Provin could have the same ability!'

'We're in trouble if he does,' Reithan warned. 'The only thing that stops Belagren from becoming omnipotent is the fact that she can't access the knowledge that Neris left behind.'

'But if Dirk Provin is clever enough . . . if he could find a way through the Labyrinth . . .' She let the sentence hang, afraid to voice her fears.

Reithan nodded grimly. 'Then Belagren would learn when the next Age of Shadows is due.'

'And if she learns that, she'll share it with Antonov...'

'I know,' Reithan said heavily. 'If that happens, Dhevyn truly will lose all chance of ever being free.'

Tia nodded in agreement, as she thought over the problem. She'd seen no sign of Dirk's allegedly superior intelligence when she'd met him. That didn't mean it wasn't there. But if it was true, the danger he posed was extreme.

Her father had spent months devising ways to hide and forget what he'd discovered. The Labyrinth constructed by Neris Veran in the ruins at Omaxin had confounded the High Priestess and her minions since before Tia was born. In fact, she owed her existence to it. It was the Shadowdancers' attempts to coerce Neris into revealing the secrets of the Labyrinth that had prompted Ella Geon to seduce her father and produce a child that they believed they could use to control him. Johan had ruined their plans when he had rescued Neris and then later stolen her as a baby from the Hall of Shadows, but they had never stopped searching for a way to get through it, and every year that passed made the problem more critical.

Belagren's dilemma now, Tia knew, was that she didn't know when one of the suns would disappear again. The only person alive who knew *that* was Neris Veran, a mad, drug-addicted, broken man, who blamed himself for the rise of the Shadowdancers and all the suffering and death that came with them.

Neris would tell nobody what he knew, not even Johan. He had constructed the maze believing that it would be a lifetime or more before someone else came along who could find a way through it.

Tia and Reithan both understood why Neris had done what he had. They also believed that if *they* could announce when the Age of Shadows was due to return, they could expose Belagren and her cult for the charlatans they were, break Antonov Latanya's power and finally free Dhevyn from Senet.

And now Dirk Provin – that arrogant, sadistic little bastard from Elcast – was going to ruin everything.

Tia didn't doubt for a minute that Dirk would throw his lot in with Antonov and Belagren. And if he was as smart as Ivon claimed, then he might be able to find a way through the Labyrinth, discover the knowledge that Neris had gone to such pains to conceal and hand the High Priestess unlimited power.

'He has to die,' she hissed.

'But he might be on our side,' Reithan pointed out.

'Why should he be?'

'And who's going to kill him? You?'

'Gladly,' she promised savagely. 'And what's more, I'm going to enjoy every minute of it.'

53

Following Antonov's announcement over the dinner table that it was Dirk who ordered the murder of a dozen innocent men to persuade Johan Thorn to talk, everyone looked at him differently. As the palace swung into the preparations for Kirshov's coming birthday celebrations, he found people giving him a wide berth. They refused to look him in the eye. Conversations would suddenly halt when he entered a room. The tutors who were responsible for his lessons with Alenor and Kirsh each day treated him with such deference it was embarrassing.

Kirsh just shrugged when he heard about the executions, certain that his father had a good reason for whatever he did. Alenor barely even blinked at the news. She'd lived in Avacas long enough not to question what went on in Antonov's court. They believed him when he protested that he'd had nothing to do with the slaughter. But when he mentioned the rumours and the sly looks to Alenor and Kirshov, they told him he was imagining things.

But he wasn't imagining it, he knew, and nothing drove

home his isolation more than the reaction of the serving girl in Misha's chambers after he'd had that seizure. Antonov had managed to make him out to be the essence of pure evil. Dirk didn't know who the girl was, but she had looked at him as if he was a fiend. She had been openly hostile when he'd tried to thank her, too. And if that was the reaction of some nameless serving wench, what must Johan Thorn think of him?

He'd done his best to avoid contact with Johan in the weeks since his arrival in Avacas, although Antonov had urged Dirk to visit him on a number of occasions. Despite his status as a prisoner, with the Queen of Dhevyn due any day, Antonov was taking some pains to appear as if he was treating Johan Thorn as a prisoner of rank, rather than the common heretic he believed him to be. Dirk had resisted until now. He so desperately didn't want to get involved, but at the back of his mind was a small voice that reminded him that, like it or not, he *was* involved, and that even if he hadn't been Johan Thorn's bastard, he would have railed against Antonov's treatment of him.

He finally decided to visit Johan the day after Misha's seizure. The serving girl's hostility had convinced him that he should do something, even if it was just to assure Johan that he'd had nothing to do with those men's executions.

Johan's room was on the third floor beneath the royal suites in the west wing, which had been cordoned off from the rest of the palace. Dirk descended the stairs behind a guard sent to escort him to Johan's room when he had asked to see him.

The room faced the western side of the city, and the setting sun flooded it with light. The ceiling was high and decorated with a candelabrum that could be lowered by a chain, which made Dirk wonder if this part of the palace had been built during the Age of Shadows. Nobody built rooms that required artificial lighting any more.

The exiled king was leaning on the windowsill, staring at the magnificent view of the city stretched out before him. The second sun sat low on the western mountains. The first sun was just beginning to appear over the opposite hills, bathing the eastern horizon in a ruddy light. An earlier rainstorm made everything glisten with moisture, and scattered clouds moved across the sky, throwing a patchwork quilt of shadows over the city.

Johan did not turn as he heard Dirk approach. 'I wondered if you'd have the gall to face me again.'

Dirk walked through the room that was stripped of anything Johan might use as a weapon. The shelves were empty, the cupboards bare. He walked across a surprisingly rich carpet to the window. 'Sir?'

'Nice view, don't you think?'

'It's magnificent.'

'This used to be my room, you know. I used to stay here as an honoured guest once. But we were young then, and it was considered politic to ensure that the future ruling princes of Dhevyn and Senet were at least nodding acquaintances.'

'Perhaps that's why . . .'

'Why what? Why he hasn't killed me yet?' Johan turned to look at him accusingly. 'There's nothing mysterious in that, Dirk Provin. Antonov thinks I know something he wants to know.'

'You mean how to navigate the delta into the Baenlands?'

Johan laughed, genuinely amused. 'Think about it, Dirk. How hard do you think it would be for Antonov if he really cared about that?'

'Then what does he want from you?'

'He didn't tell you?'

'No. Why would he tell me?'

'Well, I just thought that seeing as how you were being so helpful in designing new and ever more imaginative ways of making people suffer, you were doing it because you knew what he was after. Was I wrong? Could you be doing this just because you can?'

'I had nothing to do with those men dying.'

'That's not what I heard. In fact, Antonov was positively glowing in his praise for your diabolical plan.'

'He's twisting the facts,' Dirk objected. 'He took something I said and made it into something else entirely.'

'Antonov has a gift for doing that sort of thing.'

'So what is it that he wants to know?'

Johan hesitated for a moment before he answered. 'He thinks I know where Neris Veran is.'

'And do you?'

'Neris killed himself during the Age of Shadows,' Johan told him with practised ease.

'Then why . . .'

'Because Antonov doesn't believe he's dead.'

'Didn't he jump off a cliff, or something?'

'A fall off a cliff won't kill you, boy. It's all those nasty rocks at the base that usually do the trick. Neris jumped off a cliff, certainly. Antonov thinks I had a ship waiting for him.'

'And that you hid him in Mil? But he was mad, wasn't he?'

'What he did for Belagren drove him mad, Dirk.'

'I don't understand,' Dirk told him, more than a little frustrated with Johan and his cryptic answers. 'I don't understand what's going on between you and Antonov. I don't understand what some long-dead madman has to do with it, and I certainly don't understand why everyone keeps trying to involve me in it.'

Johan looked at him for a moment, then turned to stare out of the window. He pointed to the sun that was slowly climbing through the heavens, as the other sun sank down behind the western hills. 'Tell me what you see, boy.'

'The sky, the suns.'

'And tell me how those suns come to be in our sky?'

Dirk hesitated. He could imagine what reaction he would get from Johan if he quoted the *Book of Ranadon*. But he had no other explanation.

'Don't know the answer? That surprises me, Dirk. I thought you'd be able to recite the whole glorious epic about Belagren's vision and Antonov's majestic sacrifice of his baby son.'

'I know the story.'

'And do you believe it?'

'I suppose. I'm not sure.'

'Not sure? All this time under Antonov's roof and you're not sure? Well, let me enlighten you, my young friend. Those suns are in our skies because that's what they have always done. They travel our skies at their own pace, and every now and then the second sun leaves for a time. We call this time the Age of Shadows. It's a cycle that's been going on since the beginning of time. This "Age of Light" nonsense is simply the biggest confidence trick in history. The Sundancers fooled generations of people into believing that it was the will of the Goddess, until Belagren . . . when she raised blind faith and ignorance to an art form.'

'But it was the Shadowdancers who . . .' He was going to say it was the Shadowdancers who brought back the light, but decided that was probably unwise. 'I thought it was the High Priestess of the Shadowdancers who had a vision.'

'Belagren and Neris were both Sundancers, Dirk. Insignificant in the scheme of things, and neither of them destined for greatness. Then, during the Age of Shadows, in a futile, last-ditch effort to make it appear he was doing something useful, the Lord of the Suns sent Neris to Omaxin to study the ruins there, and Belagren went along as the expedition's . . . cook, I think it was.'

'Is that where she had her vision?'

'That's where Neris learned the truth and confided it to Belagren. The rest, as they say, is history. She and Ella Geon and Madalan Tirov conspired to turn Neris into a drug addict to keep him quiet, and Belagren started having remarkably accurate visions. I believe they cooked up the whole idea of the Shadowdancers over a campfire and a large bottle of brandy.'

'But surely the Lord of the Suns must have been suspicious?'

'Who? Paige Halyn? You've not met him yet, I take it. He's half the reason Belagren has so much power. The Lord of the Suns is a weakling. He lets Belagren ride roughshod over his whole religion, redefining it to suit herself.'

'So what are you implying? That there is no Goddess?'

'I don't know if there's a Goddess or not, Dirk, but I do know that the Age of Shadows had nothing to do with her displeasure. I think what makes Belagren and Antonov so heinous is they *know* the truth. At least Belagren does. Antonov's faith is genuine, I fear, to the point where he is completely blinded by it.'

Dirk was silent for a long time. The revelation did not surprise him as much as it should. On some level, Dirk's logical mind had rejected the accepted version of events some time ago, but in lieu of another explanation, he had no choice but to accept it. But if what Johan claimed was true . . .

'That's heresy,' he said finally.

'I went to war over it,' Johan reminded him. 'Did you know that during the last Age of Light, the scholars at the university on Grannon Rock were on the brink of discovering the truth themselves? The heresy of logic, Belagren called it. When the sun vanished, earthquakes rocked the whole of Ranadon and Nova was all but destroyed. Belagren claimed it was proof that their theories were heresy, and then she destroyed every telescope in Dhevyn and Senet. She killed anyone who spoke out against her vision, and she got away with it – because it was dark, and the people were cold and hungry and looking for a scapegoat.'

'So the sacrifice of Antonov's baby son was performed at a very specific time, because Belagren knew when to perform the ritual to gain the best effect,' Dirk surmised. 'But I still don't understand why a dead man is so important. If what you claim is true, then the damage is done.'

'Neris told Belagren when the sun would return, Dirk. He never told her when it was due to leave again. Belagren would kill a thousand innocent men to discover that.'

'Does Antonov know the truth?'

'Of course he knows. I told him myself.'

'He claims his sacrifice was an act of faith.'

'I know he does. To this day I cannot believe a man would so blindly follow his mistress to the point of murdering his own child, without at least checking the facts.' Johan looked at Dirk and smiled bitterly. 'I believe Belagren's creed is that if you have a king by his balls, then the hearts and minds of his subjects are bound to follow.'

'I think he genuinely believes that he did what the Goddess asked of him.'

'Stop defending him, Dirk.'

'I wasn't trying to. I think what he did was monstrous. I think that the way he condones the slaughter on Landfall Night is equally monstrous. But I also think he honestly believes that he brought back the Age of Light. He's a true believer.'

Johan shook his head. 'He knows, Dirk. Otherwise, why is he so interested in you?'

The only other possible answer to that question was one Dirk didn't even want to think about. Johan mistook his silence for agreement.

'I notice you've not questioned my revelation. You don't even look surprised.'

Dirk shrugged. 'That doesn't mean I believe you. Why are you telling me this?'

'I thought you should know why they're using you.'

'Nobody's using me for anything,' he objected.

'They're using you, Dirk, and the tragedy is that you don't even realise it. They want you because Neris left the job only half completed. He was able to predict the return of the sun, down to the very hour it was due to arrive, but Belagren doesn't have a clue about when it's due to leave again. She needs you to solve the other half of the puzzle.'

'That's absurd!'

'If you don't believe me, go downstairs and tell Antonov what I've told you. By rights, he should arrest you and have you put to death for heresy. But he won't. He wouldn't dare kill you. The Shadowdancers need you too badly.'

Dirk was silent for a moment, a little daunted by the revelation Johan had laid before him. Then another thought occurred to him.

'If what you say is true, then the knowledge of when the sun was due to leave again . . . whoever held that information would have immense power,' he mused.

'You are a smart lad.' Johan turned his back on the sunset and the sunrise that accompanied it. He studied Dirk closely in the rapidly reddening light. 'I wonder: suppose you *are* as clever as Neris? Suppose you discovered what everyone is dying to know? What would you do?'

'I'm not sure I understand you, sir.'

'If you knew when the next Age of Shadows was due? Who would you share it with, if you owned that power, Dirk? Who would you tell?'

Dirk thought for a moment and then answered Johan honestly. 'I would tell my queen.'

'Rainan? You'd be wasting your breath.'

'But surely, if she knew the truth . . .'

'She knows. I hate to keep disillusioning you, Dirk, but a surprising number of people know the truth, including your father. It just suits them to ignore it.'

'You make no allowance for faith,' Dirk accused. He couldn't bear the thought that Wallin Provin might be a willing participant in such an appalling conspiracy of silence. Or that Alenor's mother would willingly subjugate Dhevyn to Senet for reasons she knew to be a sham.

'There is no such thing as faith,' Johan declared. 'There are only the power seekers and those who follow them. Which one are you, I wonder?'

'I'm neither,' Dirk told him emphatically. 'And I'm not interested in your games or your theories. I came here to tell you that I'm sorry about what Antonov ordered, but that I had nothing to do with it. The rest of it is not my concern.'

He turned his back on Johan and walked towards the door, sorry now that he had come. It seemed that everything he did just dragged him deeper and deeper into the quagmire of intrigue that surrounded Johan Thorn.

'Why?' Johan called after him.

Dirk turned to look at the exiled king. 'Why what?'

'Why do you care what I think about you? You're the son of the man who stole the woman I loved. You're the favoured pet of my worst enemy. Why do you care about my opinion?'

Because I'm your son, Dirk wanted to say.

But the words wouldn't come, so he said nothing, just turned on his heel and slammed the door behind him.

PART FOUR

THE
BUTCHER
OF ELCAST

54

Belagren's mood was ugly when Ella and Madalan bowed before her in the small audience chamber in the Hall of Shadows, which was normally reserved for more formal meetings with visiting dignitaries. The High Priestess always used formalities when she was angry, Marqel had quickly learned, and the angrier she got, the more formal the occasion.

Each of the acolytes took turns serving the High Priestess. It was considered part of their training. Today it was Marqel's turn to stand at the High Priestess's left hand, ready to do her bidding. The earlier rain had cleared, and sunlight flooded the room through the large arched windows that lined the western wall, making the Shadowdancers squint as they tried to focus on the High Priestess. She usually met with them in her office, but today she was trying to make a point, Marqel thought. The High Priestess was extremely displeased, and she intended to be certain that her underlings knew it.

Marqel had not been sure what to expect when she arrived in Avacas. After they had docked, Marqel, the High Priestess and the other Shadowdancers who had travelled on the *Calliope* had made their way to the Hall of Shadows, on the outskirts of Avacas. Ella Geon had returned to Antonov's palace with Misha.

Her first view of the Hall of Shadows took her breath away. Some five miles outside the city, the palace sat high on a narrow promontory that jutted into the ocean and made the building appear as if it had sprouted out of the sea of its own volition. It was built of a smooth white stone that Marqel could not name, which blushed pink in the light of the evening sun, its eight evenly spaced and elegant spires tipped with the red-and-gold pennons of the Shadowdancers, and one solitary yellow flag, acknowledging the Church of the Suns. That Belagren and her cult of Shadowdancers were merely a subordinate branch of the Sundancers didn't seem to matter much to either side.

They were welcomed into the palace by Issian Lore, the housekeeper. If Issian was curious about Marqel's inclusion in their party, she gave no sign. She merely assigned a servant to show her around, and then ignored her.

The room to which the servant led Marqel proved to be a long dormitory in the north wing that housed another fourteen young women, all of whom were training as Shadowdancers. The other girls, for the most, ignored her, except for a tall blonde named Caspona, who spent a great deal of time complaining to her friends that the High Priestess must have lowered her standards considerably if they were now allowing Dhevynians to join the Shadowdancers.

The following morning Marqel was escorted to the Library with the others. She was tired from a restless night spent in an unfamiliar bed surrounded by the various snores and grunts of her roommates, and was still yawning as she finished her breakfast in the vast dining hall. Afterwards she followed the other girls through the bewildering network of corridors that led to the Library.

The Library was massive. Everywhere she looked there were shelves and shelves of books; more than she could count, more than she could guess at. She stared at them, open-mouthed, until one of the girls poked her from behind.

'Goddess, you look like somebody's just murdered your favourite aunt! They're only books!'

Only books. The size of the place terrified her and, for a dreadful moment, Marqel wondered if she would be expected to learn everything here.

'Ah, you must be the new girl, Marqel.'

Marqel blinked and turned to the man who had spoken. He was a Shadowdancer, younger than she expected, his cheerful face and unruly fair hair unable to hide a pair of bright, birdlike eyes.

'How do you know who I am?'

'You walked in groaning. The High Priestess said you'd only just learned to read.' That was news she didn't want broadcast, but the Shadowdancer looked away before she could voice her displeasure. He turned and led the way into the Library through the islands of long, polished tables that filled the centre of the room, then stopped and glanced over his shoulder. 'I am Fraken. I'll be responsible for you for the time being.'

'She's probably overwhelmed by her surroundings, being so young and all,' Caspona suggested tartly from behind them. 'And she is foreign.'

The scholar smiled. 'I'm glad to find you so understanding of Marqel's feelings, Caspona. Perhaps she should study with your group this morning.'

This was obviously not the outcome the blonde acolyte was hoping for. Sunlight streamed through the high windows as Caspona shot Marqel a look that could have been bottled and sold as liquid venom.

'What is the boy doing?' Belagren demanded of Ella, dragging Marqel's attention back to the meeting. 'I charged you with bringing him to me as soon as possible.'

'If *you* couldn't get Antonov to release him, my lady, what makes you think I would have any more luck?'

The small, low-backed throne on which Belagren sat was on a podium built up high enough to ensure nobody ever looked the High Priestess in the eye. *She chose this room because she can look down on everyone,* Marqel noted with a touch of admiration. She had learned much from the High Priestess in the weeks since she arrived.

'Prince Antonov is quite taken with the boy,' Madalan added. 'I believe it amuses him to make a friend of Morna Provin's son.'

Morna Provin's son? Dirk Provin? Marqel thought she must be hearing things. *Why would the High Priestess care about him?*

'Surely, if you asked Prince Antonov again, my lady...' Ella suggested, her voice fading to nothing as she visibly withered under the High Priestess's gaze.

'And what should I give as a reason for my interest in the boy, Ella?'

Marqel listened to the discussion with no real idea what the Shadowdancers and the High Priestess were talking about, but her curiosity was piqued.

'Perhaps we worry unnecessarily,' Madalan suggested. 'Perhaps Antonov will be able to extract the truth from Thorn about Neris? If we could find him alive...'

'I'd have a mindless madman incapable of telling me anything,' Belagren snapped. 'What is so damn difficult about that maze, anyway? For the Goddess's sake, all we need to do is work out a few calculations, surely.'

'It's not that simple, Belagren, as well you know,' Madalan reminded her. 'Neris has rigged that tunnel into the ruins with some truly fiendish devices. You've seen the results yourself. The only way past the gates without somebody dying is to solve those puzzles – puzzles *he* devised, puzzles beyond the understanding of normal minds.'

Marqel studied the High Priestess out of the corner of her eye as the Shadowdancer spoke. She had never had a reason to doubt that the High Priestess was responsible for the return of the Age of Light. This was all quite extraordinary. Ella noticed the direction of her gaze, and looked at her sharply.

'It seems our new acolyte isn't as fully briefed as I thought,' she remarked.

'You'd do well to worry about finding a solution to this dilemma, rather than worry about my acolytes,' the High Priestess retorted. 'This whole nightmare wouldn't be happening at all, if you'd done what I told you. If *you* had been able to control Neris as well as you claimed you could, I wouldn't need Dirk Provin.'

'Neris took his own life,' Ella reminded her stiffly.

'And why was that, I wonder?' Belagren asked with the smug assurance of one who well knew the answer.

'Explain to me again why Neris threw himself off a cliff, Ella. Was it because he had betrayed us to Johan? Was it because he thought he started a war? Or was it that he couldn't bear the thought of another night with you in his bed?'

Ella began to tug at her long red hair, a habit Marqel had noticed that she usually fell into whenever she was feeling unsure of herself. 'The man was a drug addict, my lady, as well you know. If anyone had suspected he was suicidal . . .'

'*You* might have noticed he was suicidal, Ella,' Belagren said with venomous sweetness, 'if you weren't so busy trying to find ever more inventive ways of ruining his mind so that he was of no use to us at all. A bit more restraint and a little less experimentation on your part and none of us would be in this mess.'

'All I can suggest, my lady . . .'

Belagren glared at the Shadowdancer. 'I'm not interested in your suggestions, Ella. I want Dirk Provin. And I want you to get him for me, because if the Age of Shadows returns and I'm not forewarned, I promise you, the first head I take in retribution for Ranadon turning from the Goddess will be yours.'

'Ella appears to be wavering in her resolve,' Madalan remarked once the redheaded Shadowdancer had left the Hall of Shadows to return to the Lion of Senet's palace.

Belagren nodded thoughtfully before answering. Marqel filled the High Priestess's cup with wine and placed the golden decanter carefully on the tray.

'She seems unusually nervous, but that could be because she's scared of me. She always has been.'

'It more than likely was,' Madalan agreed.

The High Priestess picked up a chicken leg and delicately tore a small piece from it with her teeth. No grease dribbled down her chin as she ate; nothing stained the front of her red silk robe. Marqel, who had grown up around the

manners of men like Sooter and Murry, found her fastidious
eating habits quite fascinating.

'Is Dirk Provin really so important?' Madalan inquired.

'He might be. If he's as clever as they claim.'

'Are you certain Antonov has no inkling of the boy's
significance?'

'We'd do well to pray that he doesn't,' Belagren warned
ominously. 'Why in the name of the Goddess didn't I *insist*
on bringing him straight to the Hall of Shadows when I
arrived in Avacas? We've lost months tiptoeing around
Antonov, trying to be discreet.'

'Don't you think Johan will find it a bit suspicious that
we want Morna's son? He'll smell a conspiracy and you can
be certain that once he does, he'll not rest until he's unearthed
it.'

'Our problem is not what Johan Thorn will make of it.'
Belagren shrugged. 'He is powerless now. I'm more worried
about Antonov. He believes that I am the Voice of the
Goddess. I can hardly admit that I need the boy to tell me
something I've spent a lifetime convincing him I already
know.' Then she turned to Marqel and studied her curiously.
'Don't you have classes you should be attending, child?'

'I was ordered to serve you, my lady.'

'Yes, well, you'll serve the Goddess much more effectively if you know what she needs of you. What class are you
missing by being here today?'

'Herb lore, my lady.'

'Then go and learn about her gifts, my dear. That will
be all.'

'My lady,' she said with a small bow. The discussion was
just getting interesting, too. She was quite certain Belagren
didn't care whether she missed the lesson on herb lore – even
if Caspona had heard a rumour that today they were
supposed to learn the secrets of the Milk of the Goddess. The
High Priestess dabbed at her chin with a napkin and waited
until Marqel closed the door of the anteroom behind her
before she continued. Marqel leaned against the closed door
with a frown, more than a little miffed that she had been

dismissed. There was something going on, something that involved the insufferable Dirk Provin, and she was itching to learn what it was.

'Damn Neris Veran!'

Marqel heard the curse quite clearly, and turned to examine the door. At some stage, probably during an earlier quake, the frame had twisted slightly. There was a thin, wedge-shaped gap between the door and the frame, just above eye level. Without any thought for the consequences if she were discovered eavesdropping on the High Priestess, she stood on her toes and peered through the gap to observe the rest of what was bound to be an interesting conversation.

'Did he really hate us so much that he'd want to kill us?'

'He wanted to hide the records of Ranadon's movement around the suns,' Belagren said, delicately laying aside the chicken bone and wiping the grease from her fingers with the napkin. 'Killing a few Shadowdancers in the process was just an added bonus.'

'Have you given any thought to Antonov's likely reaction if he ever discovers there was no need for a sacrifice?'

'Of course there was a need,' Belagren said, picking a grape from the platter on the table. She bit into it daintily. 'You need momentous acts to mark momentous occasions, Madalan.'

'And if he suspects the truth?'

'Antonov won't – can't – allow himself to confront the possibility that he was duped,' Belagren said. 'For his own sanity he must continue to believe that it was the sacrifice of his son that made the sun return.'

Madalan nodded in agreement. 'For him to accept the truth would make him a murderer. But I'm still not certain where Dirk Provin fits in to all this.'

'By some extraordinary coincidence, the Provin boy has a similar mathematical gift to Neris. He just might be smart enough to get us through the Labyrinth and tell us what Neris didn't want us to learn.' The High Priestess took another delicate bite. 'I need to know when the next Age of Shadows is due. I must know the time down to the hour, the very minute! Otherwise everything we've worked for will be wasted.'

'Rudi calculates it will be years yet,' Madalan reminded her.

Belagren shrugged, before discreetly spitting out the seeds into a small silver bowl. 'What would that fool know?'

'At least you have Antonov right where you want him.'

'If Anton was right where I wanted him, Madalan, he wouldn't be defying me over the Provin boy,' Belagren complained.

'And the Lord of the Suns? What if he decides to interfere?'

'Paige Halyn is a drowning man taking his last few gasps as he tries to save what is left of his tired old religion. The Shadowdancers are the future, Madalan.'

'And what of the future? Suppose it *does* take years? What if Antonov dies and Misha becomes the Lion of Senet? What if the sun disappears and the next Lion of Senet doesn't believe it was you who made it happen?'

'Misha will never be the Lion of Senet, Madalan. It will be Kirshov.'

'But he's due to leave Senet. He's going to join the Queen's Guard in Dhevyn.'

'Misha is a sickly young man,' Belagren pointed out. 'Nobody will think it odd that he dies young. It will be Kirshov who rules Senet.'

'Isn't he supposed to be marrying Alenor? How can he be Prince Consort of Dhevyn and the Lion of Senet at the same time?'

Although out of the line of her vision, Marqel heard Madalan pouring another glass of wine from the decanter.

'Once Kirshov is married to Alenor,' the High Priestess explained, 'Misha will die, and Rainan will have no choice but to accept him in the dual role of consort and prince.'

'How do you know Misha will die once Kirshov marries?'

'The same way I know what's wrong with him, Madalan. Goddess! You don't think I left anything as important as the succession of Senet to chance, do you?'

Madalan stared at the High Priestess. 'You poisoned him?'

'Now that's such a nasty word, Madalan. Let's just say that Misha's pain can only be relieved by regular doses of poppy-dust. Unfortunately for young Misha, it's highly addictive. If he misses a dose of his "tonic", he suffers withdrawal, and the poor boy immediately thinks he's dying.' Belagren smiled coldly. 'So, of course, because taking our tonic makes him feel much better, everyone believes that it's helping him.'

Madalan sounded quite horrified. 'Belagren, have you any idea what Antonov would do if he realised you'd turned his son into an addict?'

'This is Misha we're talking about, Madalan. The Crippled Prince. Anton can barely bring himself to look at the young man. And he has no experience with the symptoms of poppy-dust addiction.'

'And the physicians who tend Misha? Surely they suspect something?'

'There hasn't been a physician near Misha Latanya in twenty years that I don't own, Madalan. It would be a different story if it were Kirshov who was addicted. Anton dotes on his second son.'

'And what of Kirshov? How are you going to ensure that he's on our side once he rules Senet?'

Belagren leaned back in her seat and took a sip from her golden cup. She glanced over her shoulder at the anteroom door, and for a moment, Marqel got the impression that the High Priestess knew she was listening.

'I believe that's where our new acolyte comes in.'

'Marqel? She's just a Dhevynian Landfall bastard.'

'I'm not interested in her origins, Madalan, just in what she'll become. Did you know that she's here because Kirshov personally intervened on her behalf when she was arrested? Apparently he's quite besotted by the girl.'

'But you don't know anything about her.'

'I *do* know that she's a whore, a thief and a liar. That's always a good start in this business.'

'She's very young to trust with that sort of responsibility,' Madalan warned.

'Then your task, Madalan, will be to make sure that she *can* be trusted. Between now and when the second sun leaves our sky, I must have Kirshov Latanya so bound to us that he will turn his back on everything he believes to be decent and right if I crook my little finger in his direction.'

Marqel sagged against the door, her heart pounding. *There is no Goddess,* she realised, her tenuous faith easily giving way to the truth of what she'd overheard. *No visions, no nothing. It's all a trick.* It's just another show, albeit on a far grander scale than anything Marqel was accustomed to.

Just another circus . . . just another seedy bunch of travelling performers with better costumes and more expensive props, Marqel thought.

Only, the takings in this travelling circus weren't merely a scattering of copper coins. For this performance, the players might well earn themselves a kingdom.

55

The celebration for Prince Kirshov's birthday was the most elaborate anyone could remember. It was like Landfall Night, every night, without the orgy. Or so Alenor claimed. Avacas was ablaze with light and music, the streets were full of entertainers. Every noble family in Senet and Dhevyn had sent a representative to the mainland to take part in the festivities. The city was filled with visitors — both highborn and peasant. They were here to curry favour, or take Kirshov's measure, depending on which side of the political fence they sat.

Dirk was a little overwhelmed by it all. Although he had been at court on Senet for months now, the sheer excess left him gasping. Antonov was sparing no expense. There were banquets every day and balls every night, as the noble families of Senet tried to outdo themselves – and each other – proving their loyalty to the Lion of Senet.

Tonight was to be the most impressive function of them all. Dirk had suffered through the celebrations of the past week mostly because Alenor had looked at him with the desperate, get-me-out-of-here look that she often used on him. His nights had been long and tiring, filled with endless dances with Alenor and a succession of eligible young women whose fathers he couldn't risk offending.

The ball tonight was being held in the palace and, as Dirk stood before the mirror checking his reflection for the hundredth time, he wondered if he could get an opportunity to dance with Alenor properly. He was a little fed up with having her step out onto the floor with him, clutching his arm and rolling her eyes as she scolded him for taking so long to come to her rescue. For once, he'd like to ask her to dance and have her smile and graciously take his arm, pleased to be in his company – not just relieved because of the escape he had been so well trained to offer her.

'You look gorgeous!' Eryk declared.

Laughter accompanied Eryk's declaration. Dirk spun around guiltily as Kirsh burst into his room and caught him posing in front of the mirror. Kirshov had filled out in the last few months. He was taller than Antonov now, although he was leaner, more athletic. A golden coronet held down his fair hair, and his white jacket was embroidered with golden lions. He looked every inch his father's son.

'Are you quite finished admiring yourself?' Kirsh chuckled.

'I suppose,' Dirk admitted, feeling a little sheepish.

'Come on, then! We'd better stop by Misha's room before we go downstairs. I promised him we'd call in so he could admire us in all our finery.'

'Isn't he coming to the ball?'

Kirsh shrugged. 'He's been pretty poorly since that last seizure.'

Dirk had grown to know Misha quite well over the last couple of months, and often spent time reading to him or playing chess when his illness forced him to stay in bed. Kirsh loved his brother, but as far as Dirk knew, Antonov's second son had never been ill in his life. He didn't really understand what Misha was going through.

Dirk privately wondered if Misha was simply using his illness to avoid a potentially uncomfortable evening, which he was not averse to doing on occasion. It would be hard for him to sit there and watch his younger, healthier brother feted by the nobility when he was too weak even to sit on a horse.

They had come from everywhere for the ball tonight: from as far away as Sidoria in the bleak northern wastes; the exotic islands of Galina in the far south; even from Damita, where Dirk's mother had once been a princess.

'Come on,' Kirsh demanded impatiently. 'Or do you want to stand there admiring yourself all evening?'

Dirk allowed himself one final glance in the mirror, still not certain he recognised the reflection that stared back at him. Prince Antonov had provided the finery he wore in the same way that everything else he had wanted or desired had been provided since he left Elcast. Antonov was many things that Dirk did not approve of, but miserly wasn't one of them.

'What about Alenor?' Dirk asked with a wink at Eryk as he closed the door behind them. The wide halls were filled with scurrying servants, attending the scores of guests who were staying in the palace.

'Haven't seen her all day. Not since Rainan arrived.'

'Your father let her see the queen?' Dirk asked in surprise.

'Of course he did. He's not a monster, Dirk.'

Dirk didn't comment, not wanting to offend Kirsh by getting into a discussion that would spoil the evening. He was learning very quickly to keep his opinions to himself.

The last time he'd made a passing comment twelve innocent men had died.

'She'll be at the ball, won't she?'

'She'll be there. And that reminds me. If you see that snivelling little cretin from Vivan go anywhere near her, run a fork or something through him, would you?'

'Duke Rhobsin, you mean?' Dirk asked. 'If you're so concerned about Alenor's honour, why don't you run him through yourself?'

'Don't be stupid. I'm wearing white. I'd get blood all over my clothes.'

'Oh, well, in that case . . .'

Kirshov laughed as they reached Misha's rooms. 'I knew I could count on you.'

'Anything else I can do for you, while I'm at it, your highness? Anyone else you'd like me to murder? Apparently I'm quite good at it, if you believe the gossip around the palace.'

Kirsh frowned. 'Nobody thinks anything of the kind, Dirk. Stop worrying about it!'

Dirk opened his mouth to argue the point, then shrugged, realising the futility of it all, and knocked on the door to Misha's room. There was no way Kirsh would understand.

Misha was propped up on a mountain of pillows, and he smiled at them as Ella let them into the bedroom. She bowed politely and left them alone, giving Dirk a long, considered look that made him quite uncomfortable as she left the room. Kirsh threw himself onto the side of the bed, making Misha wince in pain. Dirk remained standing at the foot.

'You two look like a couple of dandies,' Misha said.

'We're going to dazzle everyone,' Kirsh agreed. 'Are you sure you don't want to come?'

'No. I'll be better off here, I think. But you must come by tomorrow and tell me all about it. Everything.'

'I will,' Dirk promised.

Kirsh also nodded his agreement enthusiastically, but

Dirk suspected that by tomorrow morning Kirsh would not be feeling nearly so eager. Hungover, certainly, but in no mood to relive the night with his bedridden brother. Misha smiled at Dirk knowingly. He knew Kirshov too well to expect him to keep such a promise.

'Well, you'd best be off then,' Misha advised them. 'And try to stay out of trouble with the ladies. Remember, they all have fathers and brothers and some of them have armies.'

Kirsh groaned. 'Have you *seen* some of those girls? The Duke of Cheyne's daughter looks like the wrong end of a horse!'

'She laughs like one too,' Dirk added, thinking of the young woman's braying giggles.

'And what about the one from Colmath? What's her name? Piranha?' Kirsh said. 'She eats like she's scared to swallow a decent meal! And all she can talk about is crabs.'

'Crabs?' Misha asked with a raised brow.

'Her name's Pirlana, and Colmath's major industry is shellfish,' Dirk explained. 'She's rather proud of the fact that Colmath has recovered almost completely from the Age of Shadows. Apparently, her island is now producing more oysters than it did during the last Age of Light.'

'You sound like you've spent some time with the lady.'

'I have,' Dirk said with a grimace. 'Kirshov dumped her on me last night at the Ambassador of Gateane's Ball. I had to dance with her three times before I could get rid of her. I am now an expert on the Colmath fishing industry.'

Misha smiled at the expression on Dirk's face. 'Well, never fear, Dirk. Tonight nobody will even notice you. Young Kirshov here will outshine everyone.'

'You think they're going to notice me?' Kirsh scoffed. 'With Rainan here?'

'The queen knows it's your birthday, Kirsh. I'm sure she'll put aside her differences with Father for this one night at least. Even the fact that she came to Senet is a good sign.'

'I suppose.' Kirsh shrugged. He never dwelt on politics for long. 'We'd better get going. Father will have us burned at the next Landfall Feast if we get there after the queen. We'll tell you all about it tomorrow.'

Misha smiled wanly and wished them luck before they left his room and headed down to the ballroom on the first floor.

The Grand Ballroom of Avacas Palace was the largest room Dirk had ever seen. It was easily four times the size of the Great Hall in Elcast, and was festooned with gold-and-white bunting that covered the elegant, hand-painted wallpaper for the party. A full orchestra was ensconced in the corner of the room near the open balcony doors, and the balmy evening, with its red-tinted light, filled the hall with a rosy glow. It was already half full of splendidly dressed men and magnificently jewelled women, who moved about sipping wine from gold-rimmed Sidorian crystal goblets handed out by waiters wearing the gold-and-white livery of Senet. The discordant sound of the musicians tuning their instruments did little to dent the hum of conversation that filled the hall.

The ballroom quickly filled with people as the Queen of Dhevyn's scheduled appearance drew nearer. There was no sign of Alenor, so Dirk and Kirsh amused themselves by poking fun at the machinations of the noblemen and women present who were using this occasion to find suitable spouses for their offspring. They also devoted a considerable amount of effort to avoiding Lady Pirlana and her good friend Lady Harinova, the Duke of Cheyne's daughter.

'It's like a meat market,' Dirk observed.

Kirsh nodded. 'They all think you're destined for the Hall of Shadows. Be glad you've been spared it.'

'So have you. Aren't you going to marry Alenor?'

The prince shrugged. 'I suppose.'

'Don't you love her?'

'I guess I do . . . sort of. Oh, hell, you know what I mean . . .'

Dirk shook his head disapprovingly. 'Alenor loves you,

Kirsh. Don't you think you owe it to her to return her feelings?'

Kirshov studied him curiously for a moment. 'Have you ever noticed how you're always leaping to her defence? If I even look at her crosswise, you jump down my throat. If you ask me, you're the one who's in love with her.'

'Don't be stupid!'

'I was only joking. And never fear for Alenor. When I have to marry her, I'll see she's taken care of. The last thing I want is you calling me out for upsetting her.'

'Just you remember that, too,' Dirk replied with mock severity. 'I could take you any time I wanted.'

'I'm trembling with terror,' Kirsh declared. 'Goddess spare me from the dreaded Butcher of Elcast!'

Dirk looked at him in shock. '*What* did you call me?'

'The Butcher of Elcast. I heard somebody call you that the other day. And don't look at me like that! It was just gossip. Nobody listens to that sort of nonsense!'

'You apparently listened to it.'

Their discussion was interrupted by a fanfare from the orchestra. Kirsh grabbed Dirk's sleeve and they hurried to take their places in the long lines that were rapidly forming a narrow corridor leading to the gilded throne at the other end of the hall. The fanfare ceased abruptly as they fell into line, and the orchestra struck up another tune, one that Dirk thought vaguely familiar, although he couldn't place it. He didn't really care, either. He was still reeling from the news that because of that incident with Johan Thorn, he had apparently acquired the title of the Butcher of Elcast.

The doors at the end of the hall opened and a score of the Queen's Guard marched into the ballroom. Without any prompting, the crowd moved back a step to give the guards room. Garbed in silver breastplates, polished helms and royal blue cloaks, they were an awe-inspiring sight as they stepped through the hall in perfect unison until they were evenly spaced on either side of the corridor of people. Dirk glanced at Kirsh and smiled at his friend's unabashed delight at the appearance of the Dhevynian Guard. Kirsh's future lay bright and glittering before him. He could hardly wait to join them.

And I'm the Butcher of Elcast...

56

Once the guard was in place, the orchestra struck up a fanfare again, and Lord Ezry, the Seneschal of Avacas Palace, stepped forward.

'Her majesty, Rainan Thorn D'Orlon, Duchess of Kalarada, Countess of Derex, Queen of all the Islands of Dhevyn.'

Dirk leaned forward a little as the queen appeared. Antonov escorted her into the ballroom, her arm resting lightly on his. She was dark-haired and small, like Alenor, but there the resemblance ended. She wore a jewelled crown in the shape of a sun and a silken gown that seemed to have been spun from gold.

'And his highness, Prince Antonov Latanya! Lion of Senet, Czar of Avacas, High Prince of all the Provinces of Senet, the Shadow Slayer, Protector of Dhevyn.'

Walking beside Antonov, the Queen of Dhevyn seemed tiny. Dirk wondered who had given him the title of *Protector of Dhevyn*. Perhaps Antonov had awarded it to himself. Dirk was damn certain Johan Thorn had not bestowed the honour on him. Then he glanced at Kirsh with a puzzled frown.

'How come you're not out there with your father?' Dirk asked softly.

'Misha's not here.'

Dirk nodded in understanding. Antonov did not want to draw attention to the illness and absence of his heir by having only his youngest son announced. This way, nobody would be certain whether he attended or not. By tomorrow,

Dirk had no doubt there would even be those who would swear they had seen the elder prince at the ball.

Alenor walked behind Antonov and the queen. She was wearing a gown almost as exquisite as her mother's. Her hair was piled elaborately on her head and caught in a golden coronet. Dirk hardly recognised her.

'Her Royal Highness, Duchess of Vyrie, Baroness of Tawell . . .' Dirk was surprised to hear that title announced. Tawell was a Senetian barony north of Bollow on the shores of Lake Ruska. Antonov was definitely doing his best to tie Alenor to Senet. 'Princess Alenor of Dhevyn!'

'Look at Alenor,' Kirsh whispered out of the corner of his mouth. 'I wonder what they threatened her with to get her dressed up like that?'

'She looks beautiful!' Dirk whispered back.

Kirsh smiled, but did not reply. The queen moved down the line, stopping occasionally to acknowledge a familiar face. Antonov remained silent, only speaking if Rainan asked him a direct question. He could afford to act as her inferior, Dirk thought. Everyone knew where the real power lay.

As they approached Dirk and Kirsh, he felt his mouth go dry. Hopefully, the queen would only be interested in Kirsh. This was his party, after all.

Kirsh bowed low as the queen drew level with them.

'Prince Kirshov.'

'Your majesty.'

'My congratulations on reaching your majority.'

'Thank you, your majesty.'

'We look forward to you assuming your duties with our guard.' Rainan smiled, then glanced over her shoulder at Antonov. 'We shall enjoy returning Prince Antonov's favour, by welcoming *his* child into *our* home.'

Dirk bit back a gasp as a flicker of annoyance lit Antonov's eyes. There was nothing subtle about her remark, and it would be spread through the hall within minutes. Kirsh, however, did not seem to notice.

'I look forward to serving in your guard with all my heart, your majesty,' he replied with complete sincerity.

Rainan looked a little surprised when she realised Kirsh meant exactly what he said. She nodded her approval, then turned to Dirk, who bowed awkwardly, caught out by her sudden notice.

'And you must be Dirk Provin, Wallin's youngest boy.'

'Your majesty!'

'My daughter speaks very highly of you, as does Prince Antonov. How is your mother?'

'I . . . um . . . she was well, your majesty, when last she wrote me.'

'When you correspond with her next, please pass on our regards. We were friends once.'

Dirk nodded mutely, not sure what to say next. As if she understood his dilemma, the queen smiled and moved away. Then she stopped and looked back at Alenor.

'My dear, you must bring Dirk to visit with us while we are here. We'd like to hear how things fare in his part of the world.'

'Yes, Mother.' Alenor glanced at Dirk with an imperceptible shrug, as if she could not understand the queen's sudden interest in him, any more than he could.

Rainan and Antonov walked on until they reached the thrones at the end of the hall. Rainan took her seat next to Antonov, who raised his arm to give the signal for the party to begin in earnest, when Lord Ezry's voice boomed out once more.

'The High Priestess of the Sun Goddess! Mother of the Light! The Lady Belagren and His Holiness, Keeper of the *Book of Ranadon*! Lord of the Shadows and the Light! The Lord of the Suns, Paige Halyn!'

Dirk barely had time to notice the look of anger that flashed across the queen's face as Belagren and her entourage stepped into the room.

There were twenty or more people in the High Priestess's wake. Dirk paid them little mind, more interested in finally seeing the Lord of the Suns. He was an elusive figure, who rarely ventured out of his palace in Bollow on the shores of Lake Ruska. He was also a disappointing figure.

He did not radiate holiness or immense power. In fact, he appeared quite ordinary. A little taller than average, his long brown hair parted down the middle framed a face that was creased and wrinkled with age, the lines crossing each other on his forehead like a checkered tablecloth. His impressive beard reached halfway down his chest. Only his expensive yellow gown and jewelled fingers made him stand out from the crowd of Sundancers and Shadowdancers surrounding him. He wasn't exactly fat, but clearly bore the evidence of a life of good food and wine.

Belagren entered the hall a step ahead of Paige Halyn, smiling at the people lined up and waiting, as if they had been assembled just for her. Rainan had schooled her features into something resembling indifference, but Dirk could tell she was furious. It was a dreadful breach of protocol to arrive after the queen. Even worse to have themselves announced as if they were royalty.

Alenor stood beside the queen, her expression blank. Years of living in Senet had taught her to control her emotions almost as well as her mother. Antonov nodded at the sight of the Lord of the Suns, but even he looked a little annoyed at Belagren's nerve. As host, the blame for the High Priestess and her party so blatantly flaunting protocol was undeniably his.

Behind Belagren and Paige Halyn were a score of Sundancers and Shadowdancers. They all wore sleeveless yellow or red tunics tied with a gold cord. Many of the young men and women in red were branded with the rope tattoo, and wore it as if it were a badge of honour. He glanced over them briefly, not really interested in their ranks, when his eyes lit on a familiar figure.

He had to look closely, not sure if it was really who he thought she was. A few short months had wrought a remarkable change. Of the wild young acrobat that had been dragged into Elcast Keep for the crime of stealing Rees's dagger, there was barely a trace. She walked tall and proud, her wheat-coloured hair brushed to a shine and flowing down her back unbound, as was the custom among the Shadowdancers. She still moved with the same natural grace that had made her such an accomplished acrobat, but she had filled out and had lost the awkwardness of early adolescence. Marqel had matured into a stunning young woman. As she looked around her with interest, her eyes met Dirk's and she spared him the briefest of nods in acknowledgement.

Then her eyes met Kirshov's, and Dirk could almost feel the world shift beneath his feet.

Dirk did not believe in prescience. But in that moment, he knew with sick certainty that the appearance of Marqel the Magnificent could only mean trouble.

'Your majesty,' Belagren said with a deep curtsey as she reached the throne. 'Please forgive our rudeness. We did not realise you had already arrived.'

It was a bald-faced lie, and every soul in the ballroom knew it, but there was little Rainan could do in the face of the apology.

'It pleases us to overlook your slight on this occasion,' Rainan replied stiffly. 'It would not do to spoil such a pleasant evening.'

'As always, your majesty is the soul of forbearance,' Paige Halyn replied with a bow. 'Good evening, Prince Antonov, Princess Alenor.'

The Lion of Senet bowed. Alenor frowned, as she stood at her mother's left on the podium, looking down over the cluster of Sundancers and Shadowdancers. Simply by the look on her face, Dirk could tell that she had also spied Marqel among them. Or perhaps she had been watching Kirsh, whose eyes were glued to Marqel.

'Your presence honours us, my lord,' Alenor said. Her voice was dangerously flat. Dirk knew that tone well. She was furious, but whether over the slight to her mother or the fact that Marqel had reemerged, he could not tell.

'You'll be in residence in Avacas for a while then, my lord?' Antonov inquired.

'Until the Solstice Festival, your highness.'

'Then we shall have to make certain you enjoy your stay here.'

Rainan glanced up at Antonov. 'Your highness, perhaps we could discuss your social calendar at a more appropriate time. This is your son's birthday, and I'm sure your guests would rather be dancing.'

Dirk decided he liked the queen. She might be under Antonov's thumb, but she obviously didn't like it. He glanced at Kirsh, wondering what he thought about the exchange. Kirsh probably hadn't heard a word of it. His eyes were locked with Marqel's. He looked up in time to see the prince jerk his head slightly in the direction of the open balcony doors. Marqel smiled and nodded imperceptibly, then turned her attention back to the podium.

'What are you *doing*!' Dirk hissed as Antonov gave the signal for the music to start up again. The lines dissolved around them as people moved back to the food laden tables, or went in search of more wine.

'Just saying hello to an old friend,' Kirsh said, shaking off Dirk's arm. 'You remember Marqel, don't you?'

'Of course I remember her. Do *you*?'

Kirsh shrugged. 'Don't be silly. That's all in the past. She's a Shadowdancer now, not a thief.'

'Kirsh, please. Stay away from her.'

'Don't be such a bore, Dirk. It would be rude of me not to say hello. We practically lived in each other's pockets on the journey back from Elcast. Don't you remember?'

Dirk remembered very well. 'All the more reason to give her a wide berth.'

Kirsh looked a little put out at the reminder, but as the lines dissolved around them, Antonov beckoned his son forward to speak with the queen. Dirk watched him leave, wondering if there was anything he could do to head off the disaster he was certain was brewing.

Lost in his brooding, Dirk started as Alenor came up beside him and touched his arm. 'I'm sorry, Alenor, did you say something?'

'I said, did you see her?'

'Marqel? Yes, I saw her.'

'She's a Shadowdancer now. I didn't think she was old enough.'

Dirk shrugged. 'Well, I suppose she's the same age as me, but with the Shadowdancers . . . well, you know what I mean . . .'

Alenor smiled wanly. 'Yes, I know what you mean.'

'I'll see what I can do,' he offered. 'Perhaps if I—'

'There's nothing you can do, Dirk. Kirsh knows where his duty lies.'

Dirk looked at her helplessly, wishing there were some way of easing the ache in her eyes. Alenor adored Kirsh. He'd known that since the first day he met her. It infuriated him to see how little that affection meant to the prince. Kirshov accepted Alenor's love as if it was his due.

'Alenor, would you like to dance?'

She smiled at him, lifting her chin proudly. 'I would be honoured, my lord.'

Dirk smiled as he offered her his arm and led her to the dance floor. If nothing else good came out of this night, at least this one wish had been granted.

57

The rest of the night dragged for Dirk. As the sole representative of Elcast, he was required to nod and smile and discuss boring things with a long succession of dukes and princes and minor barons. He was introduced to his uncle, Prince Baston from Damita, a slender, dark-haired man with a jaded smile.

Dirk didn't like his uncle very much. He seemed more interested in restoring Damita to its previous position of influence than socialising with his nephew from Elcast. Dirk inquired after Prince Oscon, the grandfather he had never met, and was treated to a withering glare. That his grand-father had helped Johan raise an army against Senet was not forgotten. Baston was doing his best to curry favour with his father's former enemies.

'And Johan Thorn?' Dirk asked, wondering what sort of reaction he could evoke in his pompous uncle. 'Have you had a chance to visit with him since you've been in Avacas?'

Baston's face turned an interesting shade of red. 'How dare you!' he hissed, looking over his shoulder to see if anyone had overheard the question.

'I'm sorry, did I say something to offend you?' Dirk asked innocently.

Baston sputtered something unintelligible and stormed off. Dirk hid his smile behind his wineglass and turned to see what else was happening at the ball.

Alenor had been swept away by a succession of men, old and young, who sought out her company, probably to pump her for information about what the queen was really doing here in Senet. Duke Rhobsin hung around like a bad smell until Alenor relented and let him lead her onto the dance floor. Dirk had no idea what she said to him as they danced, but when it was over he stalked off fuming, and didn't go near her for the rest of the evening. *At least now I won't have to kill him,* he thought.

Dirk barely saw Kirsh, who was doing his duty by being noble to some of the more important daughters of the kingdom, while constantly looking over his shoulder for Marqel.

Dirk knew he was fretting uselessly, but he couldn't help it. Kirsh should know better. Kirsh *did* know better, he reminded himself. But he didn't seem to care. It was as if Marqel's mere presence could make him forget who and what he was.

'That was a mean bit of sport you had with your uncle, Dirk Provin.'

He started at the unexpected voice behind him and spun around to find a guardsman sipping a goblet of wine with a rather amused expression. 'Sir?'

'Ah, now, young Dirk, let's not stand on ceremony. I'm Alexin Seranov. My father is the Duke of Grannon Rock. I think if you follow the histories back far enough, we are cousins of sorts.'

'I know . . . I mean, I didn't know who you were, but I've heard of your father.'

'And I've no doubt he's probably heard of you, by now. You've made quite a name for yourself in your short stay here in Avacas.'

Dirk glared at the guardsman. 'I'm sorry, Captain, I have to go. Please give my regards to your father.' He turned on his heel, fuming. *The queen only arrived in Avacas this morning and already her guardsmen have heard of me.* The idea appalled him. *The Butcher of Elcast.* What made it worse was that the Queen's Guard were Dhevynians, his own people.

'Dirk, wait!' Alexin placed a restraining hand on his forearm. 'My intention wasn't to offend you.'

'Then what *was* your intention, Captain?'

Alexin glanced around, to see who was within earshot before he answered. 'I'm a loyal Dhevynian, Dirk, as are all the Queen's Guard. There are those that still believe, despite your reputation, that you are, too.'

'I'm not sure I understand you.'

'Let's just say that should you decide to remember where you come from, there are people who could help you. And people who could use *your* help.'

'What sort of help?' Dirk asked suspiciously.

Alexin didn't answer him. Instead, he glanced over Dirk's shoulder and smiled insincerely. 'My lord.'

Dirk turned to find Paige Halyn approaching them. Dirk found himself glad of the interruption. 'My lord.'

'So this is Dirk Provin,' declared the Lord of the Suns.

Dirk wasn't sure if he was required to answer that. The old man studied him suspiciously. 'You've made yourself some powerful friends in a very short space of time, haven't you?'

'Sir?' Dirk didn't know if he was being complimented or censured.

'I also hear you have quite a remarkable mind, young man.'

'I couldn't really say, sir.' He shrugged self-consciously. For a fleeting moment, Dirk wondered what was worse – being known as a butcher or as a genius.

'You're too modest, lad. Prince Antonov seems quite in awe of your ability.'

Dirk could not imagine Antonov being in awe of anyone. 'I think he exaggerates, my lord.'

'Perhaps he does, but to be in such high favour with the Lion of Senet is no mean feat. Your future looks very bright.'

'Some people have all the luck,' Alexin remarked.

Dirk glared at him for a moment before turning to the Lord of the Suns. 'I try my best, sir.'

'When do you come of age? I know the High Priestess has designs on you, but you might wish to consider serving the Goddess in a slightly different capacity. The Sundancers could do with some fresh blood.'

There was something in the way Lord Paige said 'fresh blood' that made Dirk vaguely uneasy. 'Not until the year after next, my lord.'

'Pity.' With a slight nod, Lord Paige moved off, leaving Dirk staring after him in confusion.

'You've a lot of soul searching to do, I think, young cousin.'

'Pardon?'

'You're earmarked for greatness, it seems. I wonder if you know what you're getting yourself into?'

Without waiting for an answer, Alexin walked away, leaving Dirk feeling rather disturbed by his warning.

Dirk drained the last of his wine and looked around, wondering where he could find another. He wasn't given to drinking to excess, but this night was proving more trying than he'd anticipated. Would it do any good, he wondered, to drown himself in wine? Would it change anything, or would he simply not care if he were drunk enough? He turned to search out a waiter and found himself face to face with Prince Antonov.

'I see you've met the Lord of the Suns, Dirk.'

'Yes, your highness.'

'He was very impressed with your progress.'

'Yes, sire, he told me that.'

Antonov nodded. 'In fact, once Johan Thorn is disposed of, I plan to take a much closer interest in your development. I'm sure you'll benefit from my patronage. With Kirsh and Alenor gone, you'll be pretty lonely here in Avacas, otherwise.'

'Alenor is leaving?' he asked in surprise.

'She is returning to Kalarada with the queen. Once she and Kirsh are formally betrothed, I can see no harm in it. And she needs experience at court. It will be a good arrangement all round, don't you think?'

Dirk knew the prince wasn't asking his opinion. He nodded slowly. 'I think she'll be very happy to return home, sire.'

Antonov studied him closely for a moment. 'Dirk, I am aware how you feel about me. It concerns me a little that after all this time under my roof, you still feel that way. I've treated you like a son. You have an opportunity to make the most of your position. I will be very disappointed in you if you choose to let emotion rule that rather remarkable head of yours.'

'I'm not sure I understand what you mean, your highness.'

'Oh, you understand me well enough, Dirk Provin. So let us clear the air between us once and for all. Let me warn you, just this once, and we will never speak of it again. If you ever get tempted to follow the path your mother favours, I will crush you like an insect under my boot heel, and not lose a moment's sleep over the fact that I have destroyed you.'

Dirk stared at the prince, unsure how to respond to such a threat. Antonov's tone had not changed as he delivered his dire warning. He was smiling, as if they were discussing nothing more important than the price of fish in the marketplace. A shiver ran down Dirk's spine as he realised how close he was to making an enemy of this man.

'I will do my duty, your highness.'

Antonov's smile widened. 'I never doubted you would, Dirk. Now, do me a favour and go and find that son of mine. We have an announcement to make, and as he is the subject of the announcement, it would look much better if he were actually present for it. Check the balcony first. I think I saw him heading that way. Off you go, and make sure he's back here before the fanfare starts.'

The prince turned away, his attention already on another guest. Dirk watched him smiling and joking, wondering how such evil could exist in such a splendidly benign figure as Antonov Latanya.

Feeling more than a little unsettled by his discussion with Antonov, Dirk escaped the ballroom, making his way through the crowd to the balcony. There was no sign of Kirsh. He hurried down the steps to the lawn, which was lit with evenly spaced torches, their flickering flames bowing and shaking in the cooling breeze coming off the Tresna Sea. They weren't needed for light, but had been placed for effect. Antonov liked fire. Dirk broke into a run, crossed the lawn and plunged into the woodland beyond.

Here in Avacas, it was as if the Age of Shadows had never been. The forests had recovered almost completely from the devastation caused by the long, dark days. He'd heard somebody at dinner the other evening claim that the sea had returned so completely that it was only a handspan from its usual level. Was Johan right about it all being a sham? Or could the death of a child really be responsible? Was it really necessary to keep murdering people on Landfall Night to ensure that Ranadon remained in the light? And what did Alexin Seranov want? What did he mean when he said there were people who needed his help?

Eventually he stopped trying to outrun his own thoughts and threw himself down to the soft ground, smelling the damp leaves and rotting vegetation. Dirk rolled onto his back and stared up at the sky. The scattered clouds appeared as if they'd been dipped in blood. *And now they're calling me the Butcher of Elcast*.

'I want to go home,' he said aloud to the night.

The silence that answered him only served to magnify his loneliness.

58

Marqel had been delighted, but not really surprised, to learn that she was to attend the ball to be held in honour of Prince Kirshov's birthday. Since overhearing the High Priestess's plans for her, she was almost giddy with the prospect of the glittering future now open to her. *They want to bind Kirshov to them,* she thought, *and they need me to do it*. For the first time in her life, Marqel found herself grateful to Kalleen and Lanatyne.

They had ridden through the streets of Avacas to the palace, through crowds that lined the roads watching the steady stream of important personages arriving for the ball. Some of the spectators wanted to see the lords and ladies in their finery, others merely wanted to gape at the Shadowdancers, to dream, perhaps, of a life they could only witness from the outside. Marqel rode in a carriage with Caspona, between Madalan and Olena, taking no notice of the crowd or the town. She had seen cities like Avacas aplenty, and they held no particular appeal for her. Outside the Hall of Shadows and the Lion of Senet's palace, Avacas was just another red-tiled seaport full of sleazy old men and cheapskate, jealous old women.

The palace, however, was an entirely different matter. Although quite overwhelmed by its opulence, Marqel single-mindedly sought out Kirsh in the crowd the moment she entered the ballroom. As luck would have it, the first familiar face she saw was not the prince, but Dirk Provin.

There was something different about him, she decided. He was taller, maybe, and just from the way he was standing, he seemed even more certain of himself than he had been on Elcast. Perhaps a couple of months in a mainland court had knocked the rough edges off the stiff-necked provincial boy.

Then her eyes met Kirshov's, and all thoughts of Dirk Provin vanished. The prince smiled at her as he had the first time they met.

He's mine, she knew instinctively.

Kirsh jerked his head slightly in the direction of the balcony and she nodded to let him know she understood. She would wait there all night if she had to.

'Which one is Kirshov?' Caspona whispered as the queen, the High Priestess and the Lord of the Suns went through the motions of being polite to each other.

'The one in white near the throne,' Marqel replied through the corner of her mouth. The other Shadowdancer was also scanning the crowd, but Caspona was under orders to make the acquaintance of the Duke of Tonkeen. Marqel glanced at her suspiciously. *Why did she want to know about Kirshov?*

'He's all right, I suppose,' the other girl conceded. 'Who's the dark-haired one standing next to him? He's cuter.'

Marqel glanced at Caspona with a frown. 'Dirk Provin? *Cute?* Are you blind as well as witless, Caspona?'

'*That's* Dirk Provin? He's nothing like I imagined . . .'

'What do you mean?'

'They call him the Butcher of Elcast. I thought he'd be much older.'

'If you ladies have finished gossiping,' Madalan remarked behind them in a voice that left little doubt about what she thought of their whispered conversation, 'I believe you have work to do?'

The music had started up again. The Lord of the Suns was talking to Prince Antonov and the High Priestess. Kirshov had moved to join them. Marqel watched as Alenor approached Dirk and said something to him, and then he smiled and led her onto the dance floor. He wore the same stupid look he always did when confronted with the princess. *Idiot*.

But as Madalan had pointed out, they had work to do. The two acolytes curtsied hastily and followed their companions into the crowd. Marqel itched to speak to Kirshov, but knew it was pointless until he was finished talking with his father. She accepted a glass of wine from a passing waiter and pretended to sip it as she moved through the crowd, surreptitiously making her way towards the balcony. She had no need to search out her 'assignment'. In fact, she'd been specifically instructed to do nothing but observe this evening. She was considered too young and inexperienced to trust yet.

Marqel intended to prove otherwise. She would deliver Kirshov to the High Priestess and to that end she had taken the precaution of stealing a small vial of the Milk of the Goddess from her herb-lore class. It nestled between her breasts like the promise of a new tomorrow. Although nothing had been said to her officially yet, Marqel knew what was expected of her and was determined to prove herself.

And she wasn't going to wait until the next Landfall Festival to do it.

'You look so different in that outfit. I almost didn't recognise you.'

Marqel spun around at the sound of Kirsh's voice and smiled at him. The music from the ballroom floated across the balcony. She was standing half hidden by a tall potted palm, but there was really no need for secrecy. The balcony was all but deserted so early in the evening. It would be much later before the crowd spilled out into the scarlet night.

'Red suits me, don't you think?' she asked, glancing down at the sleeveless Shadowdancer's robe.

'I think you'd look good in any colour.'

She blushed prettily, another trick Lanatyne had taught her. 'Happy birthday, your highness.'

He shrugged. 'Actually, my birthday was ages ago. But

you know how it is. These things are organised with a lot more important things in mind than whether or not it's actually my birthday.'

'Like the Queen of Dhevyn being here?'

'I suppose. I try not to pay too much attention to that sort of thing. Now Dirk . . . he's a different story altogether. He can't seem to help himself. Although since this "Butcher of Elcast" thing started going around, I imagine he'll think twice before he gets involved again.'

'I can't believe they're calling him that. I always thought he was a bit of a wimp.'

'Dirk can be an old woman sometimes,' Kirsh agreed with a grin.

'I thought he was your friend?'

'He is my friend. But he's still an old woman sometimes.'

Marqel smiled coyly at him. 'You didn't come out here to talk about Dirk Provin, did you?'

Kirsh glanced over his shoulder towards the ballroom. 'There's a really nice little spring down in the woods. Did you want to see it?'

'If you like.'

Kirsh held out his hand. When she placed her hand in his, she felt as if lightning were streaking up her arm. With a conspiratorial wink, Kirsh pulled her out from behind the palm and they headed down the steps from the balcony, across the torch-lit lawn and into the woods.

He didn't let go of her hand.

They followed a faint trail through the trees. The ground was soft, carpeted with a layer of dead leaves that muffled their footfalls. The woods were alive with the sound of insects, their busy feeding time crammed into the short ruddy night provided by the smaller sun. Although the woods appeared natural, Marqel suspected every tree, every shrub, in this carefully contrived wilderness had been planted for the Lion of Senet's enjoyment.

Trustingly, Marqel let Kirsh lead her through the trees, her heart so light it felt as if her feet barely touched the ground. They came upon the small clearing a little while later. The spring bubbled up from underground, tumbling over a small outcropping of rocks. A shallow pool lay at the base of the rocks, which spilled over into a narrow stream that disappeared into the trees.

'Thirsty?'

Marqel nodded, not trusting herself to speak. Kirsh led her to the spring and she squatted down beside him. He cupped his hands under the water and then brought them to her lips. She drank the tepid water from his hands, her eyes never leaving his face. Kirsh was smiling at her, his golden eyes full of delight. She spilled as much as she drank and laughed as the water trickled down the front of her robe. Kirsh laughed at her, so she splashed him. He scooped up a handful of water and threw it at her. Marqel squealed and splashed him back playfully, drenching the front of his jacket. It degenerated into a water fight after that, both of them trying to soak the other, laughing so hard they could barely stand.

It was Kirsh who called a truce, holding up his hands in surrender as he staggered back out of range. 'I yield!' he laughed, looking down at his soaking jacket.

'Do you really?' she demanded.

'Truly!' Kirsh panted, as he undid the buttons and peeled his jacket off. He shook it out and water drops flew from it in a tiny shower. 'Look at you! You're wet through.'

Marqel glanced down at her robe, then with a shrug she reached down and lifted the gown over her head. The small vial tumbled to the leaf-strewn ground. She kicked a few leaves over it to conceal it, then unselfconsciously wrung out the sodden garment. She glanced up at Kirsh. He was staring at her, open-mouthed.

'What's the matter? It's not as if you haven't seen me naked before.'

'I know, but . . .'

Marqel tossed the shift aside and took a step towards him. Kirsh seemed frozen to the spot.

'You yielded to me. That means I can demand a reward.'

'What do you want?' Kirsh managed to say. His voice

was suddenly husky, his pupils wide. For a dreadful, fleeting moment, Marqel saw a sickeningly familiar look in his eyes. The same lust-filled need that filled the eyes of the men Kalleen had sold her to. She blinked the illusion away.

'A kiss.'

Kirsh hesitated for a moment, then glanced around the clearing as if making sure they were truly alone. *He wants this to be special,* Marqel told herself. He wasn't looking around to make sure he wasn't caught.

She took a step closer to him. He reached out and took her hands, tentatively closing the distance between them. Marqel closed her eyes and waited.

When he kissed her it was everything she ever dreamed a kiss could be. His lips tasted of the sweet spring water. It was perfect.

She opened her eyes and smiled at him.

Kirsh didn't smile back. For a long moment, time hung suspended between them. Marqel fought back a sudden stab of fear, as he seemed to debate something within himself. Then he pulled her closer.

This time when he kissed her, it wasn't nearly so virtuous or pure. She wrapped her arms around his neck as he trailed his tongue over hers. Then his mouth covered hers with a force that left her breathless. They stumbled backwards and the rough bark of a tree scoured her back. She didn't care. She ran her fingers through his thick fair hair and lifted her leg around his back, using her strong acrobat-trained muscles to pull him even closer . . .

And then that bratty little princess, led by Dirk Provin, turned up and ruined everything.

'Really, Kirshov,' Alenor announced loudly as she made her presence known. 'Have your sport if you must, but at least choose something a little more . . . wholesome. You don't know where she's been.'

Kirsh and Marqel broke apart as if Alenor's voice were a bucket of iced water thrown on them. The prince flushed guiltily, glanced at Marqel, then turned to Alenor. The guilt in Kirshov's eyes as he looked away cut her to the core. The accusation in Dirk's eyes was like pouring acid onto the open wound.

'Alenor, it's not what you think—'

'Oh, for the Goddess's sake, Kirsh! Don't treat me like a fool!' Alenor turned on her heel in disgust and stalked off, back towards the palace.

With a helpless shrug, Kirshov looked at Dirk for support. 'Can't you talk to her, Dirk? Can't you explain?'

'Exactly what did you want me to explain, Kirsh?'

Kirshov muttered a savage curse, snatched his jacket off the ground and hurried after Alenor, leaving Dirk alone with Marqel. The acrobat studied him, waiting for him to say something.

'You'd better get dressed,' he muttered finally.

Marqel nodded wordlessly and picked her robe up from the ground. She shook out the damp garment, then slipped it over her head, her eyes never leaving his.

'Dirk . . .'

'We should be getting back to the party.' He turned his back to her, as if he were uncomfortable under her scrutiny. It pleased her that she could have that effect on him. If *anyone* should be feeling embarrassed, it was he. She kicked the leaves over until she found the vial of the Milk of the Goddess. *What a waste. There would be no chance now to use it.*

'I'm not a slut.'

'I never said you were,' Dirk said without looking back at her.

'But you think I am.' She came up behind him and grabbed his shoulder, pulling him around to face her. 'Kirsh loves me.'

'Kirsh is *amused* by you,' Dirk told her harshly.

'You don't understand. You're too young.'

'I'm the same age as you, Marqel, and I understand just fine. Kirsh is a prince and he's destined to marry Alenor. You're a thief and a Landfall bastard. Don't kid yourself that you could ever mean anything more to him than a bit of sport.'

'You're a cold little bastard, aren't you?' she accused. 'No wonder they call you the Butcher of Elcast.'

'No wonder you're doing so well among the Shadowdancers,' he retorted. 'They're all whores, too.'

She slapped his face and the crack rang out loudly through the clearing. 'I swear by the Goddess, Dirk Provin, one day you'll be sorry you ever met me!'

She strode off angrily, leaving Dirk alone in the clearing, rubbing his stinging face.

'I'm sorry already!' he called after her.

Marqel's eyes were blurred with furious tears as she fled the clearing. Kirsh hadn't even said goodbye. He just ran off after Her Royal High-and-Bloody-Mightiness and left her alone with Dirk Provin. *That* was Dirk's fault, too. Kirsh had asked him to go after Alenor, but he refused. He had just stood there, with his cold grey eyes and his reproachful silence, and stared at her as if she had done something evil.

He has to pay, she decided. He had turned a moment of glorious passion into something tawdry. He had sullied her dream with his self-righteous looks and his silent condemnation. For a brief moment – before that odious little Elcastran and his whiny, stuck-up little princess arrived and ruined it all – Marqel thought she had been transported to paradise.

59

Kirsh was on the balcony, much to Dirk's relief, although there was no sign of Alenor. A cluster of young women, including the dreaded Lady Pirlana and her good friend Lady Harinova, had surrounded the prince, jostling for his attention. Dirk was still furious with Kirshov, and smarting from his encounter with Marqel.

Perhaps there really is a Goddess, he thought sourly, *and this was her idea of a joke. Why else would Alenor have come looking for me?*

And why else would they have taken the path back through the woods that would lead them to the very place Kirsh was fooling around with that damn thief?

The palace sat like an island of music and merriment in the ruddy light from the evening sun. He climbed the steps to the balcony slowly, forcibly schooling his features into a pleasant expression. No matter what he thought of Kirsh in that moment, he couldn't do or say anything about it while so many strangers surrounded him.

When he caught sight of Dirk, Kirsh's relief was evident. 'Dirk, my good friend! I was just telling Lady Harinova how much you admired her dress earlier. Don't you think she looks ravishing?'

Considering that a few hours ago, Kirsh had described the hapless young woman as looking like the back end of a horse, he was doing a fine job of flattering her now. Dirk knew what he was up to. The next thing Kirsh would do is suggest that he dance with her, which would get him out of the way and save Kirsh from having to explain anything.

'Ravishing,' he agreed, before Kirsh could add anything further. 'But I fear I must deprive you of the prince's company, ladies. Your father wants you . . . us, your highness.' He added the qualification hurriedly, before the girls decided he had come to take Kirsh's place.

'A prince's duty is never ending,' Kirsh lamented with a dramatic sigh. 'Come, Lord Dirk. Let us find out what the Lion of Senet wants with us now.' He pushed his way through the disappointed young women and headed back towards the ballroom. Dirk fell into step beside him.

'Your timing is impeccable.'

'You think so?'

Kirsh glanced at him guiltily. 'Well, most of the time, anyway.'

Dirk didn't answer him. He couldn't think of anything to say to Kirshov that didn't begin with: *'What the hell did you think you were doing?'*

Kirsh could sense his anger. He stopped and grabbed Dirk's arm, forcing him to turn and face him. 'It didn't mean anything, Dirk. It was just a bit of fun.'

'She thinks you're in love with her, Kirsh,' he told him.

'Who? Marqel? Don't be silly. Whatever gave her that idea?'

'Hmmm ... let me think ... gee, could it have been you dragging her into the woods and tearing her clothes off?'

'Keep your voice down!' Kirsh hissed, looking around nervously. He nodded and smiled to someone who waved to him before turning back to Dirk. 'You make it sound so ... sordid.'

'It *is* sordid, Kirsh. And what's worse, Alenor saw you. Personally, I don't care how many girls you drag into the woods, but I'm damned if I'm going to stand by and watch you hurt Alenor like that.'

'All right. I'm sorry.'

'You need to apologise to Alenor, not to me.'

'Are you sure it's Alenor you're worried about?' Kirsh asked curiously.

'Who else would I be worried about?'

'I don't know. Maybe you're jealous.'

'Jealous? Of who? You and Marqel? Don't be absurd! You're the one who's been obsessed with her ever since we first met her.'

'You were just as taken with her as I was when she climbed out of that pool.'

'Even if I was, Kirsh,' Dirk snorted scathingly, 'I'm not stupid enough to do anything about it in the grounds of Avacas Palace while half of Senet and Dhevyn is here to watch!'

Kirsh nodded in defeat. 'All right. Point taken. I'll apologise to Alenor. Right now, in fact.'

'It'll have to wait. Your father sent me to find you.'

Kirsh rolled his eyes. 'What have I done now?'

'He said something about an announcement.'

'Oh, that.'

'That *what*?' Dirk asked. 'What's he going to announce?'

They began moving towards the doors. The orchestra was playing a lively jig and the ballroom rang to the sound of stamping feet and laughter. 'Nothing that will surprise anybody, that's for certain.'

'Well, you'd better get changed first.'

'What?'

'Your jacket, Kirsh, it's soaking wet and covered in leaves.'

'Good thought,' he agreed, glancing down at his clothes. 'Will you cover for me?' he added, slipping off the damp jacket.

Kirsh was talking about more than a temporary absence, Dirk knew. He sighed heavily. 'What do you want me to do?'

'Find Marqel. Talk to her. Explain things to her.'

'Why don't you do your own dirty work?'

Kirsh stopped just before they reached the doors and looked at his friend. 'You're the only person in the whole world that I can ask this of, Dirk. Damn, but I'm going to miss you when I leave.'

'Right now, Kirsh, I don't think I'm going to miss you at all.'

'You're mad at me, aren't you?'

'You're pretty sharp, Kirsh.'

'Will you talk to her? I'll talk to Alenor. And I promise I won't say anything to upset her, truly, I do. It'll be good practice for me for when I go to Kalarada, anyway.'

'I wouldn't worry too much about joining the Queen's Guard, Kirsh. Knowing you, you'll be the Lord Marshal of Dhevyn about two weeks after you get there. Then you can say anything you want.'

'I fear it will take me longer than that, Dirk.' He grinned broadly. 'It could take as many as three or four weeks.'

Despite himself, Dirk smiled and shook his head. Kirsh was incorrigible at times. 'You're an idiot.'

'I know,' he sighed. 'But who's going to be around to remind me of it?'

'Don't worry. You'll still have Alenor to keep your feet on the ground.'

'Alenor,' he sighed. 'Dear, sweet Alenor. I'm not good enough for her, you know. She deserves someone much better than me.'

'Alenor doesn't seem to think so.'

'Which is a good thing, too,' Kirsh announced. He slapped Dirk on the back so hard he staggered. 'Come on. Let us square our shoulders and laugh in the face of adversity while I go bravely towards my doom.'

'Kirshov, what are you babbling about?'

'Didn't you know?' he asked as the fanfare brought everyone in the ballroom to a standstill. 'Father is going to announce our betrothal. That's why Queen Rainan is here. As soon as she turns eighteen, Alenor and I are getting married.'

The announcement of the betrothal of Prince Kirshov of Senet to Princess Alenor of Dhevyn was met with a cheer and a round of polite applause. Both the Lion of Senet and the Queen of Dhevyn wore professional smiles as they congratulated their offspring after the announcement. If Alenor was still angry with Kirsh, she was too well trained to let it show in public.

As Kirsh had reminded him, the betrothal was hardly a surprise – merely confirmation of what everybody expected would eventually happen. Dirk applauded along with everyone else, wishing he could do something for Alenor. Kirsh wasn't a bad person, he knew, just thoughtless. He didn't stop to think about the repercussions of anything that he did, which was a dangerous trait in a prince. Perhaps that's why Antonov was so keen to send him to join the Queen's Guard. He would learn a degree of discipline in Dhevyn's army that he would never gain here in Senet. Kirsh was too well known, people were too afraid of offending his father, for him to ever be held accountable for his actions. A few years in Dhevyn as a guardsman would do him good.

Dirk glanced across the ballroom and caught sight of Marqel, her face flushed, her eyes bright. *Now why did I agree to talk to her again?* She was standing with several other Shadowdancers by the windows, watching the proceedings with great interest. He wondered how she'd explained away the state of her robe. Marqel's eyes were locked on Kirshov. Dirk pushed through the crowd towards her. Better to get this over and done with as soon as possible.

But just this once. After this, Kirsh can clean up his own messes.

Marqel saw him coming, but rather than turn away, she jerked her head towards the balcony. Surprised, and rather relieved that she was willing to talk to him, Dirk nodded in understanding and turned towards the open doors. He hadn't been looking forward to confronting the other Shadowdancers, and at least now he was spared having to invent an excuse to get her away from them. He glanced over his shoulder to see if she was following him, but couldn't see her.

With everyone still toasting the betrothal, the balcony was deserted when Dirk stepped outside.

'I thought you could do with a drink.'

Dirk turned to find Marqel standing behind him holding two goblets of wine. She held out one of them, which he accepted warily. Marqel was ready to claw his eyes out an hour ago; now she was fetching him drinks.

'We need to talk,' he said.

She nodded. 'I know. But not here. This is probably not a conversation either of us wants overheard.'

Dirk couldn't argue with her on that point. Together they walked down the steps and along the gravel path that bordered the torch-lit lawn.

'I'm sorry for slapping you,' she said as they walked.

'I probably deserved it.'

'Kirsh sent you to talk to me, didn't he?' Her tone was pleasant, her demeanour almost friendly.

He nodded, quite relieved that this was going to be far less onerous than he anticipated. 'You have to understand how it is for him, Marqel. He's a Prince of Senet. And now that he's betrothed to Alenor—'

'It's all right, Dirk, I understand.'

'You do?'

'Of course I do. I may not be able to read as well as you, Dirk Provin, but I'm not an idiot.' She smiled warmly. 'In fact, I propose a toast. To understanding.'

There was something wrong with the way she was behaving. The Marqel he knew was never this pleasant, never this cooperative. He gulped down the wine to hide the doubtful expression on his face.

'Bah . . . aaaggh . . . what was in that?' he sputtered as the sour wine burned down his throat. Marqel was watching him closely, her eyes as bright and hard as sapphires.

'The Milk of the Goddess,' she told him.

He tried to spit it out. Marqel was positively gloating at him, as the drug immediately began to take effect. His tongue was numb and his pulse began to pound like a drumbeat on the inside of his head. The whole world seemed to spin beneath him then he suddenly felt heat sear through him, as if a fire had been lit in his veins.

Goddess! he thought with that small part of his mind still capable of rational thought. *If this is what a mouthful diluted in wine does to you, what must those at the Landfall Feast feel after drinking it neat?*

The blood in his veins was burning. Marqel's face was flushed, her eyes glittering as she watched the drug consume him.

He tried to call out for help. He managed something incomprehensible, but there was nobody close enough to heed his cries. Marqel had seen to that. She had led him far enough away from the palace that nobody would hear them. His absence wouldn't even be noticed in that crush of people either.

What had Alenor said about the Milk of the Goddess . . . ?

He couldn't remember . . . but he was disgusted to realise that the mere sight of Marqel was arousing him. The vision of her emerging naked from the pool near Elcast Keep suddenly filled his mind, blocking out all other thought. And he wanted her so badly that for a moment desire overwhelmed all reason.

'*Why?*' he managed to gasp, as he struggled to remain in control of his thoughts, trying to push away the images that kaleidoscoped through his brain.

'I just wanted to prove that even the noble Dirk Provin isn't above man's baser instincts,' she smirked.

Dirk threw down the goblet, vaguely heard it shatter on the gravel. He clutched at his head, fearing it would explode.

'Not so superior and self-righteous now, are we?'

'Antidote!' he struggled to get out. The ability to think coherently was rapidly slipping from his grasp. 'Must be something I can take.'

'There is no antidote, Dirk,' she taunted. 'You're just going to have to suffer, I'm afraid.' She moved closer to him, trailing her fingers lightly across his cheek. 'I hear it takes about five hours for the effects to wear off, unless you can relieve the pressure. But then, to do that, you'd have to find some woman willing to let you use her for an hour or two, wouldn't you?' She dropped her hand and moved behind him. She stood on her toes and breathed into his ear. 'Perhaps Alenor will offer to help? Have you seen her naked, too? Or is it just me that fills your dreams, Dirk Provin?'

Dirk jerked away from her hot breath and turned to face her. 'Don't . . . touch . . . me . . .'

Marqel smiled languidly. 'I could fetch her if you like. Or maybe not. I think you'd rather she didn't see you like this. Of course, you then have to survive the rash. Have you heard about that? The burning . . . the itching . . .'

'You . . . *malicious* . . . *bitch*!' he stammered, afraid he might explode from the severity of the burning in his loins and the pounding in his head.

'Did you want to kiss me, Dirk? Like Kirsh was kissing me?'

'Shut up!'

'Go on, Dirk . . . you know you want to. I see the way you look at me . . .'

Dirk pulled Marqel to him and kissed her. She did not object, but then neither did she respond. When he lifted his mouth from hers, she studied him calculatingly for a moment, then shook free of him.

She was laughing at him. 'You know, I heard somebody say once that when the Goddess made men, she forgot to give them enough blood. That's why they can't think and fuck at the same time.'

He could fight it no longer. He reached for her again, tried to kiss her, but this time she actively resisted him, pushing him away with a contemptuous shove.

'Get your hands off me!' she hissed. 'I belong to Kirshov!'

Dirk wanted her so badly he was aching with it. He reached for her once more and, for a moment, he thought she might slap his face again. Her body was taut and tempting under the damp red shift. He wanted to possess her with an urgency that swamped any other thought.

But she didn't want him. With a malicious smile, she turned and began to walk away.

Dirk thought he would explode. The need for release was overwhelming. He grabbed her, expecting her to struggle. She resisted for a moment, then, with an inexplicable change of heart, relented. She turned back with a calculating smile then kissed him, open-mouthed and hungrily.

Dirk's last rational thought slipped away as she breathed in his ear, 'Make certain you enjoy this, Dirk Provin, because, trust me, you're going to pay for it.'

60

Every servant in the palace was needed on duty during Prince Kirshov's birthday celebration and Tia was no exception. Emalia had still not been heard from, so Tia had remained as the temporary upstairs laundry maid, and with the palace full to overflowing, she barely had time to catch her breath before someone else was demanding her services.

She had caught a glimpse of Queen Rainan earlier in the day, and had been able to identify a dozen or more lords and ladies, both friend and foe, as she scurried about the fourth floor, called this way and that to hand out towels and gather up the guests' dirty laundry. She hated the work – not because she had any particular dislike for being a laundry maid, but because the Senetian nobles looked through her as if she didn't exist. She had accidentally walked in on one man climbing unselfconsciously out of his bath this morning. He had made no attempt to cover himself, and had ignored her stammered apologies as if she weren't even in the room. *Conceited pig.* It was almost with relief that she knocked on the door to Prince Misha's room. At least she could rely on the Crippled Prince to acknowledge her existence.

'Tia!' Misha exclaimed as she let herself in. 'What are you doing here so late?'

'Changing towels mostly, your highness,' she explained. 'There's a lot of people here at the moment.'

He smiled. His eyes were bright and he looked unnaturally alert, almost well.

He's just taken poppy-dust, she realised. *That's why he's so animated. In an hour he'll be crying like a baby. An hour after that he'll be unconscious.* Tia knew the cycle well.

'Is the party going well?'

'Sounds like it,' she told him. 'They were all clapping

and cheering a while ago. You could hear them on the landing.'

'So, it's official,' Misha said. 'Kirshov and Alenor are betrothed.'

Tia shrugged and walked across the room to glance out of the window. Far below on the vast lawns of Avacas Palace the torches burned like fireflies dancing on the red-tinted night. Beyond the woods in the distance, she could see the red slate rooftops of the city that crowded around its walls, although, this far from the wall, the city's stench was blessedly absent. Avacas was crowded and dirty and Tia had never been comfortable here on the mainland.

Misha was feeling well enough to get out of bed, although he had only moved to a chair by the unlit fireplace. There was a rug wrapped around his legs to keep out the chills he was so prone to.

'The Lion of Senet's son married to the Queen of Dhevyn's daughter,' she said thoughtfully.

'It's not like it's a surprise or anything.' Misha fidgeted with the fringe of the rug, as if he was unable to remain still. Another telling sign that he was well into the grip of the drug. 'But I pity Alenor a little. Kirshov really doesn't appreciate what he's getting. Or what he'll become.'

'You don't think he'll make a good Prince Consort?'

Misha smiled. 'I think Kirsh has a lot of growing up to do before he'll make a good anything. It's not healthy to have everything come so easily in life.'

'Do you envy him?' Tia asked curiously, forgetting momentarily to whom she was speaking.

'Constantly,' Misha laughed. 'Don't *you* envy him?'

'I've no wish to be in his position,' she replied. 'I think I'll be far happier . . . as a maid . . . than he will be as a prince.'

'Ah, but then Kirsh doesn't usually think at all, so he probably won't notice.'

Tia smiled. Misha was an intelligent young man and, in truth, despite his addiction, she found herself quite liking him. *Well, perhaps liking him was an exaggeration.* It would be more accurate to say that she despised him marginally less than she despised most Senetians.

'He'll make a fine guard, though,' Misha added. 'And it's the best thing for him. He needs a bit of discipline.'

Tia leaned on the windowsill as she watched the grounds below. She could just make out two figures strolling along a gravelled path. The man looked suspiciously like Dirk Provin and the woman who walked with him wore the red robes of a Shadowdancer. *Now where is he going with a Shadowdancer at this hour of the night? Why isn't he staying at the party?*

'You think the Dhevynians will accept him?' she asked, turning her attention back to the prince. Personally, Tia half expected some guardsman to find an excuse to run the prince through the first chance he got. She would have.

'He'll win them over in time. And he needs to. There's too much distrust between Senet and Dhevyn.'

Tia looked at the prince curiously. 'It's understandable though, isn't it? I mean, you . . . we . . . invaded them.'

'Invaded?' he chuckled. 'You sound like a Baenlander. We didn't invade Dhevyn, Tia. Johan Thorn asked for our help.'

On the verge of arguing the point, Tia clamped her mouth shut, silently cursing her stupidity. She was supposed to be a simple laundry maid. Simple laundry maids didn't argue politics with princes, even doped-to-the-eyeballs, amiable ones.

'Well, I wouldn't know about such things,' she shrugged.

'You have an opinion, though, I can tell that much.'

'I should change the towels,' she said. She glanced out the window again and discovered the couple below now locked in a passionate embrace. *And Alexin said he might be worth sounding out,* she thought in disgust. *Look at him. Rolling around on the grass like an animal with that whore. He's not worth sounding out. He's a Senetian sympathiser, a turncoat and a traitor to his own people. I don't care who his damn mother is.*

'Who are you really, Tia?'

'Pardon?' she asked in surprise, turning her back to the window.

'You play chess like a master. You discuss politics. Emalia can't even read.'

'I'm just a servant, your highness.'

'I've a feeling there's a great deal more to you than that. Have you ever thought of becoming a Shadowdancer?'

Tia almost choked. '*Me?* A Shadowdancer? I don't think so.'

'Why not? The church is always in need of intelligent young men and women. You could do much better for yourself as a Shadowdancer than lugging sheets and towels around, cleaning up after people here in the palace. I tell you what! I'll speak to Ella. She'd be very interested in you.'

More than you could ever know, a little voice in her head chimed in.

'Truly, there's no need, your highness,' she assured him. 'I'm quite happy as I am.'

'Ah well, let me know if you change your mind.'

'I will, your highness,' she promised as she stepped into the bathroom. She replaced the towels hurriedly and fled the room after that — before Misha decided to take it into his head to make her wait for Ella Geon to return.

Tia ran down the back stairs after she left Misha's rooms. She had promised to meet Reithan near the stables when she could get away. With the party going on, nearly everyone waiting outside the South Gate this morning had been employed, including Reithan, who was taken on as a groom for the evening. Tia thought him foolish in the extreme to risk coming to the palace. Although he was not well known in Avacas, there were enough people in Senet who knew who he was, and there was no telling when the Brotherhood might suddenly decide to turn on them. He had shaved off his beard and trimmed his hair, but his tanned face was white around his chin and he didn't look that much different to her. Reithan was counting on the fact that nobody would expect to find him in the stables of Avacas Palace, and therefore would not realise who he was, even if they thought his face familiar.

Tia found Sella and told her she was going out for a breath of air and something to eat, then hurried out of the laundry and through the kitchens. Outside in the yard several long trestle tables had been set up to feed the army of servants who were attending to the guests. In addition to the legion of temporary staff that the palace had hired, every guest had brought a servant or two, sometimes a whole retinue. There were open barrels of ale set about, all of them surrounded by servants come to sample the largesse of the Lion of Senet. There was a party atmosphere in the yard. The ball would go on until well into the early hours of the morning, and many of the servants, particularly the coach drivers, had settled themselves in for a good long wait.

Tia couldn't see Reithan near the food, but Dirk Provin's servant spied her in the crush and hurried to her side, glad of a familiar face.

'Hello, Tia.'

'Hello, Eryk,' she said distractedly. She had no time now to be pleasant to the boy.

'How come you're here so late?'

Tia wasn't really listening – she was too busy scanning the crowd for Reithan.

'Did you want some ale? I can fetch some for you if you like.'

She smiled down at him and nodded, thinking it would keep him occupied. 'Thanks, Eryk. That would be nice.'

The boy scuttled off in the direction of the barrels. Without sparing Eryk another thought, Tia headed across to the vast stables where Antonov kept his horses. The saddling yard was almost as crowded as the one outside the kitchen. She pushed past a clutch of men laughing about something and headed for the ruckus coming from the direction of the lunging yard.

Somebody had organised a cockfight. The perimeter of

the lunging yard was five deep in men, both servant and noble, cheering and wagering on the outcome. Tia spotted Reithan hanging over the rail, strategically placed near Alexin, where it would not seem odd if a guardsman and a palace groom exchanged pleasantries. She caught his eye and he pushed off the rail, then threaded his way through the crowd to meet her.

'Any luck?' he asked, taking her by the arm and leading her to the shelter of the stable wall where the crowd was a little thinner.

'Reithan, there is no way I can speak to him,' she hissed, looking around to ensure she wasn't overheard. 'I'm not even supposed to leave the fourth floor.'

'What about when he goes back to his rooms tonight? Can't you find an excuse then?' When Tia refused to meet his eyes, he lifted her chin with his finger, forcing her to look at him. 'This is important, Tia. Alexin said he looked like a man who could use a friend.'

'Well, don't worry,' she told him scornfully. 'He's found one. The last I saw of Dirk Provin, he was getting very friendly with a Shadowdancer.'

'You know where he is now, then?'

'I know where he was a little while ago,' she conceded reluctantly.

'Then let's go find him . . .'

'Reithan, don't be insane! It's bad enough you being here in the stables! What if someone saw you?'

Before he could answer, a group of guardsmen walked by. They stopped talking until the Dhevynians had passed. Tia glanced over them idly, then hurriedly turned her face away as she recognised Wilim, the officer who had tried to buy her services in the tavern in Kalarada. Her eyes met his for a moment. He had the look of a man who thought he might have recognised her face, but couldn't place it.

'Tia, this may be our only chance—'

'Here! Don't I know you?' Wilim had turned to look at her again. She tried desperately to avoid meeting his eye. 'Hey! I'm speaking to you!'

'Me?' she asked, trying to sound innocent.

'Yeah, you!' He grabbed her arm to study her more closely. 'I know you, don't I?'

'I've never seen you before in my life. Let go of me!' Shaking free of him, she turned her attention back to Reithan as if the conversation with the guardsman was concluded. She smiled at him brightly and spoke as if she were simply picking up the conversation where she left off, before being so rudely interrupted. 'So, anyway, I was telling my friend—'

'Hey, don't you turn your back on me! I was talking to you!'

'Leave her alone, Wilim,' Alexin said, coming up behind him. Tia breathed a sigh of relief. He must have seen the trouble brewing and decided to intervene before it got out of hand. Reithan was looking at his boots, hunching down in his coat, to avoid recognition.

'You remember her, don't you, Alex?' Wilim asked over his shoulder. 'It was in the Whistler's Haven, remember. It's that whore you stole from me.'

'Don't be absurd, Wilim,' Alexin laughed. 'What would a Kalarada whore be doing here? Now apologise to the young lady for calling her a whore and come watch the fight.'

'It's her, I tell you,' Wilim insisted. 'What's your name, girl?'

'Mellie,' Tia told him, giving him the first name that leapt to mind.

'No, it's not Mellie. It's Tifani, or Tiana, or something like that . . . Tia! That's your name, isn't it? Tia!'

'Wilim,' Alexin said in a sterner tone. 'Leave the poor girl alone. She's told you her name. Now leave her be before you get us all arrested for harassing the Lion of Senet's servants.'

'But that's just my point!' Wilim declared. 'She's working here in the palace. So what was she doing in the Whistler's Haven on Kalarada? Spying?'

'I've never even been to Kalarada,' Tia informed him

JENNIFER FALLON

stiffly. 'And if you don't leave me alone, I *will* have you arrested. Just like your friend says.'

'Is there a problem, gentlemen?'

Their discussion had drawn the attention of a small, curly headed little man wearing a dark topcoat. Behind him walked two of the biggest men Tia had ever seen.

'Everything is fine, Prefect Welacin,' Alexin assured him. Tia gulped back a lump of fear when she heard his name. Barin Welacin had a fearsome reputation in Senet and had been placed in charge of palace security for the evening. As Misha had pointed out, there was a great deal of mistrust between Senet and Dhevyn. With so many servants of both nations waiting around, and so much free alcohol to fuel the fires of resentment, the Prefect and his band of hired thugs were under strict orders to put down even the slightest hint of trouble before it got out of hand.

Wilim turned on Barin Welacin. 'We were just reacquainting ourselves with one of your damn Senetian spies here, Prefect Welacin, but don't worry, we can keep a secret, can't we, boys?'

There were five guardsmen, including Wilim and Alexin. Barin Welacin made a barely noticeable hand signal, and suddenly there were another three huge Senetians lined up behind Barin.

'I believe the Queen's Guards are being catered for in the ballroom,' Barin reminded them pleasantly. 'Perhaps you gentlemen might like to return there now to avoid any misunderstandings?'

Tia held her breath. Except for Wilim, she suspected none of the guardsmen wanted to get into a fight with Barin and his henchmen. It would embarrass the queen, if nothing else, and they were fanatically loyal to the Dhevynian crown. But it was for exactly that reason that this was likely to turn ugly.

Before Wilim could make the situation any worse, Alexin stepped forward with a conciliatory smile. 'We came down to watch the cockfight and now we're leaving, Prefect Welacin.'

Tia let out her breath with relief. Barin smiled pleasantly and ordered his men to stand aside, to allow the guardsmen a clear path. Reithan was trying to fade inconspicuously into the background. He'd had numerous run-ins over the years with Barin Welacin, and although he'd managed to elude capture, Barin knew him by sight. The last thing they needed was for Barin to suddenly take an interest in them.

'Tia! Tia! There you are!'

Tia muttered a curse as Eryk pushed through the crush of people towards her, carefully holding a foaming tankard before him. He was smiling broadly, obviously pleased that he'd found her. Wilim turned and stared at her as the boy proudly held out the tankard to her.

'I was right! That is your name!'

After that, what happened was almost too quick for Tia to follow. Wilim lunged at her, but Reithan pulled her free of his reach before he could catch her. Barin's henchmen reacted as if someone had pulled a sword on them, and the guardsmen responded the same way. Through the middle of it all, Eryk stood there dumbfounded, as the space around him dissolved into a melee. Reithan tugged on Tia's arm to pull her clear of the fight, but found his way blocked by more of Barin's thugs, hurrying to join the fray. He glanced at her for a moment, his expression resigned, then he let her go and swung his fist at the man blocking his way. Someone grabbed Tia from behind, but she didn't wait to find out if he was friend or foe. She reached behind her and grabbed a handful of the man's organs and twisted as hard as she could. Her assailant screamed and dropped to the ground clutching his groin. With a smug little grin, Tia dusted off her hands and looked around for Reithan, but she couldn't see him.

The fight raged on around her. The five guardsmen were being beaten down by the sheer weight of numbers. Barin's thugs seemed to be multiplying at a ridiculous rate. Every time one of them went down to a guardsman's fist, another two took his place. Tia grunted and fell to her knees as a couple of the combatants bumped into her from behind. As she struggled upright, a flying guardsman, who landed unconscious beside her, knocked her over a second time. Giving up on the idea of standing for the time being, Tia crawled on her hands and knees through the forest of legs until she was clear of the fight, cursing her skirts and the fact that she was unarmed. Someone grabbed her ankle, then let it go. She glanced over her shoulder to find Eryk kicking at the hand of the man who tried to apprehend her. The angry Senetian forgot about Tia and turned his attention to the servant boy, allowing her time to escape. Spitting grit from her mouth Tia staggered to her feet, only to find herself face to face with Barin Welacin.

'Take this one as well,' the Prefect ordered calmly.

They took her from behind before she could run. She struggled uselessly against the men who held her as they tied her arms behind her back. The fight was almost over as the Senetians' superior numbers swamped the guardsmen. She looked around wildly. But for Wilim, who was the last guardsman standing, and the huge crowd that had gathered to watch, there was nobody who could help her. Another Senetian held Eryk by the collar of his shirt. The boy had a bloody nose and was covered in mud. Poor child. It wasn't his fault. Still, he was Dirk Provin's servant. She thought it unlikely that he would suffer more than a night in the dungeons. There was no sign of Reithan, either. She allowed herself a moment of hope. Perhaps he'd been able to get away.

'Take them to the cells,' Barin ordered. 'I'll join you there once I've spoken to Prince Antonov. He's going to be rather pleased with this little haul, I imagine.'

As Barin moved off at a leisurely pace in the direction of the palace, she saw Reithan behind him, slumped semi-conscious in the arms of two of the Prefect's men.

61

Dirk collapsed into bed fully clothed as soon as he reached his room. He slept heavily through most of the day, although he remembered vaguely someone banging on his door, demanding entrance. It sounded like one of the Shadowdancers, and the last thing he wanted was anything more to do with Marqel and her ilk. His door remained locked, and he pulled a pillow over his head to shut out the insistent knocking and went back to sleep.

He woke again later, with no idea whether he'd been asleep for minutes or hours. The knocking had stopped, but he was itching all over. He clambered out of bed and tore off his clothes, thinking sourly that this was what he got for rolling around on the grass like an animal. His body was livid with a rash and his skin was on fire. It seemed to be more than just an allergic reaction to the grass. It might be an aftereffect of the Milk of the Goddess. Hadn't Marqel said something about a rash? He reached for the bell cord to summon Eryk, hoping a cool bath would ease his agony, but his hand stopped before he pulled it as another thought occurred to him. Perhaps this wasn't an allergic reaction at all. There was no telling how many men Marqel had lain with. This could quite easily be the first symptom of some unspeakable disease she had passed on to him. Dirk had seen enough as Helgin's apprentice to be well acquainted with the symptoms of several ailments common among the sailors and whores of Elcast Town.

Embarrassment as much as fear kept him from calling for help. He bathed his burning skin with a damp cloth but it did nothing to relieve the itching. He fumbled around in the small backpack that he had brought with him from Elcast until he found a small jar of lotion – one of Master Helgin's favourite cures for itching, made from the stems and leaves of the jewelweed plant that grew along shady banks of the many small streams on Elcast. He applied the lotion liberally and then fell back onto the bed naked, falling into an uneasy slumber plagued with vague and disturbing nightmares. He slept the rest of the day, and woke just as the second sun was setting. The rash was gone so completely that he wondered if it was nothing more than a fevered dream.

Dirk sat up gingerly. He was ravenously hungry, but pleased to discover that his head had not been cleaved in two. It certainly felt like it had been this morning.

And he couldn't put last night out of his head.

Alenor had told him the Milk of the Goddess made you forget. Rees had not remembered a thing the morning he stumbled out of the Duke's Forest. But Dirk remembered all too well, and he cringed from the recollection. It was something of a shock to realise that he was capable of such things.

Even worse to realise that he had enjoyed it.

After a long soak in his bath and an hour or more of uselessly trying to put it out of his head, he gave up and decided to think about it consciously. Perhaps, by sorting through the disturbing images flashing through his brain, he could acknowledge them and then file them away in the back of his mind, out of sight forever.

Dirk was not an innocent. He and Kirshov had sneaked out of the palace to visit Avacas's numerous brothels on more than one occasion. Dirk was quite sure Antonov knew about it, but the prince chose to turn a blind eye to his son's extra-curricular activities.

Dirk thought they'd kept it from Alenor, too – until she took Dirk aside one evening and asked him to ensure that they stayed away from The Widow's Peak, because it was rumoured that the girls there were unclean. Dirk had been shocked, and then rather amused by Alenor's wise acceptance of the situation. Kirshov would marry Alenor thinking he was the one in charge. Dirk wondered if Alenor would ever let him discover the truth.

But last night had been different from his previous encounters. For one thing, he had the Milk of the Goddess roaring through his veins. The raging lust that it had awoken in him made him shudder as he recalled it. Dirk had always prided himself on being highborn, and the inherent nobility that came with his birthright. The Milk of the Goddess had torn away his thin veneer of civilisation.

He wondered what Johan Thorn would have to say about that.

Yet Marqel wasn't drugged. She was, however, exceptionally well trained. Marqel had been taught to dole out pleasure like fine wine, a drop at a time, with excruciating attention to detail. Her skills weren't learned sneaking around the back of a haystack or fumbling with an inexperienced youth. She'd been giving her body to a succession of paying customers in seaport taverns for Goddess knew how long, and had learned her craft well. But for his abiding distrust of the former thief, Dirk could well believe that Marqel might own him body and soul after a night in her arms. With a sour smile, Dirk realised that Marqel was still the thief he thought her to be. The difference was that now she was trying to steal men's souls.

By the time he was dressed the only thing Dirk was certain of was that he could never, *ever* let Kirsh know what had happened. Their friendship was solid, but Dirk was sure it would not survive the prince learning that he had slept with Marqel the Magnificent.

Dirk was still trying to work out what to do about it when a knock sounded on his door. His first thought was to order Eryk to open it; then he realised that he'd locked everyone out, including his servant. He stumbled out into the sitting room and unlocked the door himself. Prince Antonov strode in without waiting for permission to enter. He studied Dirk for a moment, then nodded his approval.

'You did well last night.'

'Sir?' he asked in confusion.

Antonov laughed softly. 'I hear you defused a potentially awkward situation.'

'I don't understand.'

'I'm referring to that thief we brought back from Elcast with us. I hear you intervened in the nick of time. It would have been most awkward, with the queen here, if Alenor had decided to report Kirsh's indiscretion to her mother.'

'He told you about that?'

'Alenor did.'

That surprised Dirk, but then maybe Alenor had been hoping Antonov would punish Kirsh. It was a sign of how much Antonov had gained her trust, that she would share such a thing with him, rather than with her mother.

'What did Kirsh say about it?'

'Not much. He drank enough last night to kill a horse. Fortunately, my son has the constitution of an ox, and he didn't drink enough to kill an ox. I doubt he'll be so foolish the next time.'

And I should never have gone within a hundred yards of Marqel.

'Is he all right?'

'He has a hangover that has him thinking he's dying, but he'll get over it. I just wanted to check that you survived the night unscathed.'

'I'm fine, thank you, sir.'

'Then I'll see you at dinner, perhaps? Don't feel compelled to attend. We'll be a fairly small gathering tonight, I imagine. If you're not feeling up to it, send down to the kitchens and have someone bring a tray to your room. Nobody will be offended.' Antonov turned to leave. 'Oh, and Dirk, don't make any plans for this evening. I'm having a small get-together on the terrace after dinner. I'd be pleased if you joined us.'

That meant, be there, or else, Dirk knew. 'I'd be honoured, your highness.'

'Then I will see you later.'

After eating dinner in his room, Dirk went in search of Eryk. There was no sign of the boy, and Dirk was beginning to worry about him. The palace had been full of strangers last night, and with Eryk's gift for wandering into trouble, the boy's continuing absence seriously concerned him.

When he knocked on Kirshov's door, a servant opened it and stood back to let Dirk enter. Kirsh was lying on the bed, looking pale and completely washed out. He smiled thinly when he saw Dirk, though, and struggled to sit up. The servant rushed to his side, but Kirsh pushed her away impatiently and ordered her from the room.

'I was looking for Eryk. You haven't seen him, have you?'

Kirsh shook his head, then winced, obviously regretting the impulse.

'Not today,' Kirsh replied as the maid closed the door behind her.

'He'll be around somewhere, I suppose. How's your head? Your father said you drank enough to kill a horse.'

'I wish I'd drunk enough to kill me,' he groaned. 'It's got to be less painful.'

Dirk smiled. 'You'll live.'

'So they tell me. But what about you? What happened to you last night?'

'Nothing much.' The ability to lie so smoothly was a talent he had only recently discovered, forced on him by necessity in this place. It bothered him a little that he could become so proficient at it so quickly.

'Pity. I was hoping at least one of us had a good time.'

'Ah well, look on the bright side. Maybe Alenor won't be mad at you by now.'

'Alenor! Goddess, don't even mention her name to me. Do you know what that heartless little cow said to me?'

'I can imagine it wasn't very sympathetic,' Dirk said.

'She is going to grow up into a harridan. I can see it now – my whole future stretching before me like a prison sentence. Her incessant nagging is going to drive me to suicide!'

'Don't you think you're exaggerating just a little bit, Kirsh?'

'*No!* Don't you see? She's not just going to be my wife some day, Dirk, she'll be my queen! What chance do I have?'

'None at all, I'd say.'

They both started at the unexpected answer. Dirk turned to find the High Priestess standing by the open door with Marqel. Kirsh's eyes lit up at the sight of the young Shadowdancer.

'We came to see how you were faring, your highness,' Belagren explained as she and her acolyte stepped into the room. 'I'd say you were well on the road to recovery if you can complain so vociferously.'

Dirk stared at Marqel, and she met his gaze evenly, daring him to say something. Her face was bruised and she seemed to have the beginnings of a black eye.

'I was hoping you had brought me a cure, my lady.'

'I'm afraid the only cure for what ails you is time, Kirshov,' Belagren informed him. 'However, Marqel here is quite accomplished in the art of massage, and I thought she might be able to ease your discomfort a little.'

'That would be very helpful,' the prince replied wanly. He seemed to have taken a sudden, and entirely fake, turn for the worse.

'Actually, it's probably not a good idea at the moment,' Dirk said, trying to think of something – anything – to foil Belagren's plans. The last thing he wanted or needed at present was Marqel and Kirsh comparing notes about last night's party. 'The prince is expecting his betrothed at any moment.'

'No, I'm not!' Kirsh objected, glaring at Dirk. 'I'm not even speaking to Alenor after what she said to me!'

Belagren smiled triumphantly. 'Then I suggest you leave Marqel to her ministrations, Dirk. They will be much more effective if administered in quiet surroundings.'

I'll just bet they are. Dirk had no intention of leaving Marqel to her 'ministrations'. Having so recently been on the receiving end of them himself, he knew well the likely effect on Kirshov. He glanced at Marqel, who was smiling smugly. As well as sporting a swollen face, there was a nasty bruise on her upper arm near the tattoo. Someone had hit her since he saw her this morning. He was certain he'd not been responsible. Had she been punished for something? He pushed the thought away, wondering if he had any chance of stopping the High Priestess having her way in this.

'Marqel? What happened to your face?' Kirsh asked curiously as he noticed her bruises.

Marqel hesitated for a moment and glanced at the High Priestess, who nodded imperceptibly, as if granting her permission. Dirk had a sudden and dreadful feeling that she had been waiting for him to ask that very thing. He was playing right into her hands.

'Didn't Dirk tell you?' Marqel asked.

'Tell me what?'

'That last night after your betrothal was announced, he took me outside into the gardens and raped me,' she informed Kirsh calmly.

62

Marqel had woken in a green world to the sound of groaning. The light confused her until she realised that she was lying on the ground in the shelter of a huge willow, and that the green tinge was simply daylight filtered through its over-hanging branches. The groaning took a little longer to place. She had rubbed her eyes and sat up, discovering its source as her eyes adjusted to the bright light. Dirk Provin sat on the ground a few feet away from her, his head hanging down between his knees. He had pulled his boots and trousers on, but his shirt lay on the ground beside him. His chest was scored with deep scratches.

Marqel reached for her shift and pulled it over her head. She was in a lot of trouble. She hadn't meant for this to happen. She just wanted to dose him with the Milk of the

Goddess and watch him suffer. It had given her an intoxicating feeling of power. This pompous, overly smart, insufferably arrogant young lord who thought her a thief deserved to be taken down a peg a two. She'd planned to do nothing more than tease him. Lead him on until he was desperate for release, then abandon him and go in search of Kirshov.

She hadn't truly been prepared for the change in Dirk with the drug that burned through his veins. Although she had been instructed in its use, taken in sufficient quantity, it should have left him unconscious within an hour. She must have gotten the dosage wrong. Instead of passing out, he had apparently consumed only enough for the drug to act as a powerful aphrodisiac, and things soon progressed beyond the point where Marqel had any control over the situation.

'Goddess!' Dirk had muttered, glancing up as he heard her moving.

'You look like shit,' she told him.

'You're no picture of glowing good health, yourself,' he pointed out wanly, then he clutched at his head. 'Bloody hell! I think my brain is going to explode!'

I hope it does, she thought angrily.

'Have you any idea what time it is?'

'Time you got back to the palace, I imagine.' There was still something she could salvage from this disaster. She might be in trouble, but there was still this chance to even the score with Dirk Provin. All those lessons, all those long-suffering sighs . . . that look when he had caught her and Kirsh in the forest . . . the bards were right: revenge did taste better than fine wine. 'Then you can go and explain to that insipid little princess where you've been all night.'

Dirk looked at her with narrowed eyes. As she suspected, he was still burning with unrequited love for Alenor.

Serves you right. I hope she never speaks to you again.

'I'll have less explaining to do than you, I think,' he retorted.

'What are you talking about?'

Dirk suddenly laughed. It obviously pained him, but

whatever had amused him seemed worth the agony. Marqel looked away, certain he was able to read the guilt in her eyes.

'What did they offer you, Marqel, to turn yourself into a whore?'

Marqel turned on him angrily. 'I'm not a whore. I was chosen by the Goddess.'

'You don't really believe that, do you?'

'You wouldn't understand. You're nothing but an over-educated, idealistic fool, Dirk Provin. You'll learn that very soon. I might be a whore in your eyes, but I know what my destiny is.'

Dirk stared at her for a long moment, then shook his head. 'I don't understand you.'

'Then maybe you're not as smart as everyone thinks you are.'

They had walked back to the palace together, although Dirk unconsciously kept his distance from her, as if trying to give the impression he was simply heading in the same direction. Marqel wondered what was going on behind those steel-grey, albeit rather bloodshot, eyes. She had never trusted Dirk, and her victory over him seemed a hollow one in the cold light of day.

Of course, her real problem was more immediate. She had better come up with a damn good excuse if she expected to survive the wrath of the High Priestess.

When they reached the palace, Dirk headed towards his rooms without so much as a glance in her direction. Marqel took a deep breath and walked up the grand staircase slowly, ignoring the servants who hurried past her carrying steaming cups of foul-smelling herbal teas. There were a lot of hang-overs in the palace this morning, and just as many dubious cures.

Caspona met her on the fourth-floor landing. 'Well, well, well. If it isn't Marqel the Magnificent.'

Marqel was beginning to despise that name. Not long after she had arrived at the Hall of Shadows, she got into an argument with Caspona, who accused her of being a worthless thief. Marqel had retorted by announcing she was not a thief but an acrobat, and had foolishly bragged that she had been known as Marqel the Magnificent. It was something she was afraid she would never be able to live down.

'Belagren wants to see you,' Caspona smirked. 'You're in a lot of trouble.'

The Shadowdancer flounced down the stairs before Marqel could say anything else. She watched her go with a frown. Did Caspona know something, or was she making it up, just to frighten her? Turning her attention back to the broad hallway, Marqel noticed a page hurrying by, wearing the livery of Senet.

'Hey, you! Boy!'

The child turned and bowed to her hastily when he saw that she was a Shadowdancer. 'My lady?'

'Where is the High Priestess?'

'In her rooms, I believe, my lady. That way. The door with the two suns carved into it.'

'Thank you, boy. You can go now.'

As she dawdled along the hall, her mind began to race, inventing and discarding excuses. Her whole future hinged on the next few minutes. Maybe, if she was careful, there was still a chance Marqel could talk her way out of this.

By the time she knocked on the High Priestess's door, she had her story worked out.

'You disobeyed me.'

Belagren's eyes were cold. She sat in her long red robes in the morning room of her lavish guest quarters with two of the older Shadowdancers flanking her. It reminded Marqel of the day she had been dragged in front of Prince Antonov for trial. That time, she hadn't been on her knees, though.

'How so, my lady?'

'Where did you get that dose of the Milk of the Goddess from?'

Marqel hesitated for a moment. She hadn't expected Belagren to know about that. She made a few mental adjustments to her story before she replied.

'From the herb-lore class, my lady,' she admitted. 'We've been learning about it recently.'

Belagren glanced over her shoulder at the younger of her two aides. 'Selena, I want you to go back to the Hall of Shadows. By the time I return, I want a full report on the precautions taken during the acolytes' training to guard the supplies of our most precious gift from the Goddess. It's too valuable to be wasted in such a fashion.' Selena bowed and left the room. Belagren turned her attention back to Marqel. 'So, with the benefit of a few days' training, you took it upon yourself to steal a dose of the Milk of the Goddess, and then what? Try it out on the first man you could seduce into taking it?'

Actually, she'd been hoping to use it on Kirsh, thinking that between her own charms and the Milk of the Goddess, she would be irresistible. But she wasn't about to admit that to anybody, least of all Belagren.

'No, my lady,' she murmured, her head lowered submissively. 'I thought I was doing the Goddess's bidding.'

Madalan snorted sceptically at her declaration. 'You stole something that didn't belong to you. And you have the nerve to claim you were doing the Goddess's work?'

'I had a reason, my lady.'

Madalan frowned at her. The old woman stood on Belagren's right and looked even more annoyed than the High Priestess. 'And since when does the reasoning of an acolyte count for anything?'

Belagren raised her hand to forestall Madalan. 'No, let her speak. I'm interested in hearing her excuse. I doubt it will change my mind about her, but I'm curious, none the less. Speak, child. Tell us your reason.'

Taking a deep breath, Marqel hoped her story sounded as clever out loud as it had when she silently rehearsed it on the way here.

'I used it on Dirk Provin. He may pretend to be sworn

to the Goddess, but he has no faith in our cause. His mother is well known for her—'

'I know what the Duchess of Elcast is renowned for, child,' Belagren cut in.

Marqel nodded, hoping she sounded dispassionate. Belagren was fond of hearing the acolytes speak in a dispassionate tone. 'I know how anxious you are to get him to the Hall of Shadows, my lady.'

'You presume a great deal, Marqel.'

She lowered her eyes, wondering if she'd revealed too much. 'There's also the fact that he's Prince Kirshov's best friend. If the prince ever learns of what happened last night . . .'

'Then his friendship with Kirshov might be in danger,' Belagren finished, drawing her brows together.

'I just thought . . . well, I reasoned that if Dirk was accused of . . .' Marqel could feel herself wilting under the relentless gaze of the High Priestess. 'I thought I could provide you with a reason to demand that the Lion of Senet release Dirk to your custody, my lady.'

Belagren studied Marqel thoughtfully for a moment, then turned to Madalan. 'Leave us. I wish to have a word with this Shadowdancer alone.'

Looking rather put out by her dismissal, the elder Shadowdancer bowed and left the room. Once the door closed behind her, Belagren rose from her seat and approached Marqel.

'Get up.'

Marqel climbed to her feet but kept her head lowered, not certain she wanted to read what was in the High Priestess's eyes.

'That's a very plausible story you came up with, child. Is it the truth, or did you make it up on the way here?'

Gambling on the fact that the High Priestess had dismissed Madalan for a reason, Marqel looked up and met her eye with the faintest hint of a smile. 'A bit of both, my lady.'

'You think quickly. I like that. You are also very lucky. You could have ruined everything.'

Certain she was not required to answer, Marqel remained silent.

Belagren paced the room slowly, considering schemes and plans that Marqel could only guess at. 'What else do you know about Dirk Provin?'

'He's very clever,' she replied, not sure what the High Priestess wanted to hear. 'But he's fiercely protective of Alenor. And he was *really* angry before we left Elcast, although I don't know why.'

'Yes, I noticed that,' Belagren replied thoughtfully. 'Olena said you had a gift for reading people.'

'Dirk Provin isn't exactly a challenge, my lady. He's quite transparent, actually.'

The High Priestess turned to look at her with a thin smile. 'Listen to you! A few months ago you were a snivelling, thieving gutter brat, and now you dare speak about the highborn in such a fashion.'

'Just because one is highborn, it doesn't make them any better than me.'

Belagren crossed the room and grabbed Marqel's left arm, squeezing the rope tattoo in a painful grip. 'This is what makes them better than you, child. You're a Landfall bastard.'

Marqel met her eyes evenly. 'I'm a Shadowdancer, my lady. That makes me as good as anybody.'

Belagren suddenly smiled and let her arm go. Marqel had to forcibly restrain herself from rubbing it to ease the sting.

'You will make a fine Shadowdancer, I think, Marqel. Despite your larcenous tendencies, I believe you understand us. That is rare in one so young.' She walked back to her seat and took it once more, looking over her with a calculating eye. 'I think I will keep you near, Marqel. You could learn much from me.'

'You do me a great honour, my lady.'

The High Priestess smiled coldly. 'That remains to be seen, Marqel. However, you've given me food for thought. How close do you suppose Kirshov, Alenor and Dirk Provin really are?'

'They're the best of friends, my lady.'

'That's not a situation I would like to see continue. It might prove awkward in the future. You, however, still have much to learn.'

The High Priestess rose from her seat again and came to stand before Marqel. Without warning, Belagren struck her in the face. Marqel staggered backwards, tears blurring her vision. She gingerly touched her bloodied mouth, then looked up at Belagren in shock.

'Your *first* lesson, Marqel,' the High Priestess explained in a conversational tone, as she raised her arm to hit her again, 'is that if you are going to claim you were ravaged, you need to look the part.'

63

Prince Antonov was a daunting figure, the more so when he was angry. Marqel watched him pace the empty, cavernous ballroom like the restless lion that was the symbol of his house. She stood silent and unmoving in the centre of the hall as the prince confronted the High Priestess, not even daring to glance at Dirk, who stood unsteadily beside her.

All hell had broken loose with her announcement. When the guards had finally managed to pull Kirshov off Dirk, the boy was a bloodied mess. His nose was broken and both eyes were blackened. He stood before the prince in a torn shirt splattered with blood. Kirshov was in his room, under guard.

Marqel bit the inside of her bottom lip to stop herself from smiling triumphantly. Dirk Provin deserved everything he got. More than likely, Kirshov would never speak to him again. Marqel realised she had turned a potential catastrophe into a victory. She seemed to be developing quite a talent in that area.

But the Lion of Senet looked ready to murder someone.

'How far do you think you can push me, Belagren?' he demanded of the High Priestess.

Belagren glanced over her shoulder at Marqel and Dirk. 'Your highness, perhaps we could discuss this in private?'

'Oh, don't worry about those two,' Antonov said harshly. 'Your little Shadowdancer there knows exactly what's going on, and it's about time Dirk learned the folly of his ignorance. Besides, I want there to be no misunderstanding about this.'

'Anton, you are overreacting. Kirshov was simply upset when he learned—'

'Spare me your excuses, Belagren. I know what happened. I suppose it was just coincidence that the Shadowdancer you chose to accompany you to my son's room just happened to be the one who would tell Kirshov something guaranteed to set him off?'

'That's absurd!'

'Then what was *she*,' Antonov demanded, pointing at Marqel, 'doing in my son's room?'

'Marqel is very good with massage. I thought only to relieve his pain.'

'Massage?' Antonov scoffed. 'Strange. I would have thought after the trauma of being raped, as she claims, she'd have been too distraught to do anything.'

'Anton, you are being unreasonable!'

'This is my house, Belagren! I'll be as unreasonable as I damn well please!'

The High Priestess sighed heavily. 'Anton, listen to me. I did not intend your son or anyone else harm. I was genuinely concerned for the boy. You should be less concerned with Kirshov's hangover and more concerned about what happened to my Shadowdancer!'

'Nothing happened to your Shadowdancer, Belagren, that you didn't orchestrate. You don't seriously expect me to swallow this rape story, do you? Dirk says she used the Milk of the Goddess on him. It sounds more like your Shadowdancer was looking for a bit of sport.'

Before the High Priestess could answer, the prince

turned on Dirk. Marqel watched him out of the corner of her eye, wondering what he was thinking. Was he scared of Antonov? He did not appear afraid. And, somewhat to Marqel's annoyance, Antonov seemed prepared to think the best of him.

'As for you, Dirk, I always thought you clever. But what in the name of the Goddess possessed you to tell Kirshov what you did last night?'

'I didn't tell him, your highness, Marqel did. And she lied. She claimed I raped her. That's what Kirsh got so angry about.'

'And I demand that he account for his actions!' Belagren insisted. 'He must be released to my custody immediately.'

'I have other plans for Dirk Provin, my lady, and they don't involve packing him off to the Hall of Shadows just yet.'

'He raped one of my Shadowdancers! If it were anybody else, you'd hang him yourself! It's only because you appear incapable of serving justice in this matter that I must insist you hand him over to me, so that I may ensure that he pays for what he has done.'

Marqel glanced over her shoulder hearing a commotion at the doors. They flew open and the Queen of Dhevyn swept into the room with the Princess Alenor at her side. Marqel studied the princess curiously. She looked much too small and fragile to be serious competition. Marqel could not imagine what Dirk saw in her. From what she overhead Kirsh saying earlier, she was certain the prince had little affection for her.

'Your majesty,' Antonov said with a frown.

'I heard there was trouble in Kirsh's room,' Rainan replied, glancing curiously at their small gathering. 'I was told someone attacked him.'

'You were misinformed, your majesty,' Antonov assured her. 'There is nothing to concern yourself with.'

The queen reached them and caught sight of Dirk's battered face. 'What happened to you, Dirk?'

'Rainan—'

'I was speaking to Dirk, Anton.'

The prince fell silent, but he gave Dirk a warning look. The young man smiled crookedly at the queen through his split and swollen lips. 'It was nothing, really, your majesty. Kirsh and I had a disagreement about something and he got a bit carried away. I'm fine and so is Kirshov.'

'What were you arguing about?' Alenor asked, glancing at Marqel.

'I'd rather not say, Alenor. It was . . . personal.'

'They were arguing about me,' Marqel volunteered. The High Priestess might be looking for an excuse to get her hands on Dirk, but for Marqel, the most important thing was to destroy the friendship between Kirshov, Alenor and Dirk, and she intended to do it properly. 'Dirk Provin raped me last night. When Prince Kirshov learned of it, he attacked Dirk.'

Dirk stared at her aghast. 'That's a lie!'

'You didn't . . . entertain yourself . . . with Marqel last night?' the queen asked.

'I didn't force myself on her, your majesty.'

Marqel wasn't looking at Dirk, she was watching the little princess. Alenor's eyes were suddenly brimming with unshed tears.

So much for that beautiful friendship, she thought with satisfaction. She was coming to enjoy this game. The High Priestess had done nothing to intervene, so she was fairly sure she was on safe ground with Belagren, and in the end, she was the only one Marqel was interested in pleasing – other than herself.

'In this I'm more inclined to believe Dirk,' Prince Antonov said with a scowl in her direction.

'Are you suggesting my Shadowdancer is lying?' Belagren asked.

'I'm suggesting Dirk is not capable of such a thing, my lady.'

'Even under the influence of the Milk of the Goddess?'

'Well, as you are the one who doles out that vile substance, Belagren,' the queen pointed out, 'you can hardly complain when it has the desired effect.'

The High Priestess glared at the queen for a moment, then turned to Dirk. 'I will not be satisfied until Prince Antonov releases you to my custody. When we reach the Hall of Shadows you will answer to the Goddess for what you have done.'

That got a reaction from him. 'You know she's lying, my lady.'

He's got balls, Marqel thought begrudgingly. *He doesn't appear to be afraid of Belagren at all.*

'Your first lesson, when you reach the Hall of Shadows, will be respect, Dirk Provin.'

The queen turned to look at the High Priestess directly for the first time. 'This charge seems quite fortuitous, my lady. How convenient for you that Dirk should do something so heinous that it requires him to answer to the Goddess for it.'

'I'm not sure I understand what you're implying, your majesty.'

Rainan smiled sceptically. 'I know how anxiously you have been awaiting Dirk's arrival, my lady. I've heard the rumours. Presumably this . . . incident . . . has something to do with the power games you and Antonov are so fond of playing. But be warned, High Priestess. Kirshov Latanya is betrothed to my daughter. You and Anton can play your games, but I will not tolerate any interference in my daughter's future.'

'You dare a lot to threaten me, your majesty,' Belagren warned.

'I should have dared it a long time ago,' the queen replied. 'I've let you two dictate to me far too often. I've no wish to leave my daughter the legacy I inherited from my brother.'

'Then watch yourself, your majesty, it would be most unfortunate if she were to inherit before she was ready.'

Marqel's eyes widened at the open hostility between the queen and the High Priestess. Dirk and Alenor looked just as shocked. But the queen smiled, apparently unconcerned.

'You'd have me killed, Belagren? Go ahead and try. You

might find that even if you succeed, your power will be far from certain. Antonov is beginning to tire of your schemes, I suspect. And of you.' She glanced at the prince then, who was looking quite flabbergasted. Marqel suspected they were witnessing a confrontation that had been brewing for years. 'It's taken me a long time to gain the courage I should have had to follow my brother's lead and defy you both when I took the throne. But you made a fatal mistake when you took my daughter hostage. She's been raised under Antonov's roof and had the benefit of watching you both closely for years. Alenor knows you better than you can possibly imagine. You won't find her so easily manipulated.'

The silence that descended when the queen finished speaking was thick with tension. Alenor stood beside her mother with a look of quiet determination in her eyes. Marqel saw the look of shock on Belagren's face and began to wonder if she was not the only one to have underestimated the queen. She glanced at Dirk then, but his swollen features made his expression impossible to read.

'We will be leaving Avacas tomorrow and returning to our court on Kalarada,' the queen announced into the silence, assuming a regal air once more. 'As for you, young man,' she added, turning to Dirk, 'the only advice I can offer you is that you be careful. Belagren and Antonov both have great plans for you. Rather ironic, don't you think, that he is Morna Provin's son? I believe the Goddess has a sense of humour, after all.'

The queen turned her back on them and walked the length of the echoing ballroom without waiting for a response. Alenor hesitated for a moment, giving Dirk a look that was full of bitter disappointment, before she followed her mother.

As soon as the door closed behind the queen and the princess, Antonov turned on Belagren.

'I want you gone. Take your Shadowdancer and go back to your Hall.'

'And the boy?'

'I will think about it.'

The High Priestess looked at him for a moment, perhaps calculating how far she could push him. In the end she bowed her head. 'As your highness wishes.'

'Dirk, I want to see you in my study. Now.'

'Yes, sir.'

Antonov nodded brusquely and left them alone. Belagren watched him leave with a thoughtful expression before she followed.

Once Belagren was out of earshot, Marqel turned to Dirk with a smile she could no longer hide. 'That was quite a scene, wasn't it?'

Dirk glared at her through his bruised and puffy eyes. 'Don't even speak to me, you lying little bitch.'

'Temper, temper, my lord.'

'Do you *know* what you've done, Marqel?'

'Oh, yes,' Marqel assured him. 'I know exactly what I've done. The question is, Dirk Provin, do you?'

PART FIVE

A
CHOICE
OF EVILS

64

Johan Thorn was escorted through the palace to Antonov's private study on the ground floor, with a guard so large he was actually flattered. They marched him through the palace in chains, their hands resting nervously on their swords, as if they expected an invasion force to leap out from behind the drapes at any moment. His escort stopped in front of the impressively gilded doors of Antonov's private audience chamber. The captain of the guard knocked and opened the door without waiting for an answer. Johan didn't see much of the room, as he was surrounded by a wall of soldiers. They took him straight through to the terrace beyond.

The Lion of Senet was waiting for him. The second sun had set, and the terrace, which looked down over the manicured gardens, was bathed in red light. Waiting with Antonov were Barin Welacin, Ella Geon, his sister Rainan, who refused to meet his eye, a number of Welacin's thugs and Dirk Provin. Dirk looked as if he'd recently been beaten, his shirt torn and splattered with blood. On a small table near Rainan, a scroll and inkwell were laid out, as if waiting for a scribe. Three prisoners, a man, a woman and a boy, were on their knees in front of Barin, their heads covered by black hoods. Johan glanced around suspiciously as the guard fell back. The High Priestess was conspicuous by her absence. That made him hope a little. It was unlike Antonov to undertake a gathering like this without his paramour present. Had they had a falling out, or was that too much to wish for?

'Ah, if it isn't the long lost King of Dhevyn,' Antonov announced. 'Welcome, your majesty!'

'What's going on, Anton?'

'We're having a reunion, Johan. I decided we should all get together, like one big happy family, and have a little chat.'

'You know I won't tell you anything.'

'Yes, well I thought of that,' Antonov conceded. 'And then the Goddess smiled on me and delivered these three into my care.'

He waved his arm at Barin, who pulled the hoods from the heads of the three prisoners. Johan's heart skipped a beat when he saw them. Reithan was bruised and battered, but that was hardly surprising. They wouldn't have been able to take him without a fight. Tia looked unharmed, but her eyes were desperate. The boy he didn't know, but he looked terrified.

What the hell are Reithan and Tia doing here? He closed his eyes for a moment, to calm his racing heart. *Following my orders*, he reminded himself. *Oh, Lexie, my love. What in the name of the Goddess possessed you to send Reithan and Tia to Avacas as my executioners?*

He pushed away the wave of despair and looked at Antonov with the blandest expression he could manage.

'We've been down this road before, Antonov. You didn't get anything out of me the last time you killed innocent men in front of me, so what makes you think I care what happens to these three?'

'Well, for one thing, none of them is innocent,' the Lion of Senet said. 'And please, don't insult me by pretending you don't know who they are.'

Dirk took a step forward. 'Eryk has nothing to do with this, your highness.'

'Then he shouldn't have tried to help them escape,' Antonov replied, without looking at Dirk.

The boy whimpered, his eyes begging Dirk for help, but there seemed nothing the Provin boy could do to aid him.

'But who are these two?' Dirk persisted. 'I've never seen them before, your highness, and I can promise you Eryk is not connected with them.'

Johan thought the young man looked like he'd rather be anywhere but on this terrace, witnessing Antonov in all his malicious glory. Interestingly, though, two of the guards had moved around the railing until they flanked the Provin boy. They weren't being obvious about it, but if Dirk tried to intervene, they were close enough to stop him. *Does Antonov not trust his young protégé?*

'This one is Reithan Seranov,' Barin told him. 'He's wanted for drug running, murder and a dozen more crimes against both the Goddess and the state. The girl is Tia Veran.'

Ella Geon gasped at the announcement. Johan looked at the Shadowdancer for a moment, wondering what she was feeling. Had she grieved for her stolen child all these years, or simply been annoyed that her plans had been foiled?

Antonov turned to her and smiled. 'Did I forget to mention that I've found your long-lost daughter for you, my lady?'

'But . . . how . . . ?' Ella stammered. Johan had never seen her so lost for words. He couldn't imagine what she was feeling. If she was feeling anything. He'd always had his doubts about Ella Geon and her ability to comprehend normal human emotions.

'It's the Goddess's work,' Antonov said with utter conviction. 'You see, Johan, you've never believed in the Goddess, yet every day she answers my prayers. The fact is, I don't need you to tell me where Neris is any longer. I'm sure if I ask her nicely, young Tia here will tell me everything I want to know.'

'My father is dead!' Tia spat angrily. '*She* killed him with her lies and her damn drugs.' Tia glared at Ella. There wasn't a single scrap of affection in her demeanour, no longing for her mother – just pure, unadulterated loathing.

'You didn't raise her with any manners, did you, Johan? Hardly fair to the poor girl. You should have thought about her future. What if she wants to take her place in society some day?'

'Stop playing games, Anton,' Johan said wearily. 'You've brought us all here for a reason, so get to the point. I tire of the sound of your voice.'

'You've more to hear yet, before I'm done, Johan Thorn,' the prince assured him. 'And we'll start with your sister here.'

Rainan was flanked by two of her own guardsmen. One

of them, Johan noted, was Alexin Seranov, Reithan's cousin and their main contact on Kalarada. He also looked as if he'd been in a fight.

'What more can you take from Dhevyn that you have not already?' Rainan asked bitterly. For the first time she met Johan's eye. He was shocked at how much she had aged since he'd seen her last. The strain of ruling Dhevyn, while her daughter was held captive in Antonov's court, had taken its toll on his sister.

'Her crown,' Antonov replied. 'I've grown weary of you Thorns and your continued defiance. And don't bother looking so offended, Rainan. You've paid lip service to Senet for years, but you've always harboured resentment towards me, and your little declaration earlier this evening has merely confirmed what I always suspected. I do not intend to stand for it any longer. I have decided that you will abdicate the throne in favour of your daughter. She and Kirshov will be married immediately and my son will act as regent until Alenor comes of age.'

'I'll do no such thing!' Rainan declared hotly. 'Alenor is only fourteen! I will never allow it!'

'You will, your majesty, one way or another. You will sign the abdication voluntarily and live,' he said, pointing at the table where the document was waiting, 'or I will have you killed, and Alenor will inherit the throne anyway, without the benefit of your guidance. Think about it.'

'You wouldn't dare kill me! In front of all these witnesses?'

'What witnesses? Nobody who is not firmly in my camp will leave this terrace alive, Rainan, you can be certain of that.'

Johan glanced across at Dirk. The young man hadn't moved. His expression was carved in stone. *Will you leave this balcony alive, Dirk Provin?* he asked silently. *I'm damn sure I won't.*

'Sign it, Rainan,' he said, turning to look at his sister. 'Give him what he wants.'

'How can you say that, Johan!' she demanded. 'How can you let him do this to Dhevyn?'

'I've not been able to stop Antonov doing what he wanted with Dhevyn since the Age of Shadows.'

'You see, Rainan, the years have finally taught your brother to accept reality. It's a pity he didn't come to this realisation sooner.'

Johan laughed bitterly. 'The only thing I've come to realise, Anton, is that you are a deluded fool. You think you control your own destiny, but you're nothing more than Belagren's puppet. You always have been.'

'I serve the Goddess.'

'There is no Goddess,' Johan said wearily, as he had so many times before. 'You believe in a fantasy. Belagren never had a vision. She ordered you to kill your son because Neris Veran told her when the Age of Shadows would end. Why do you think she wants Neris back so badly?'

'Neris Veran is a heretic. The most diabolical heretic that has ever lived. *I* want him back, Johan, because I will not allow him to spread his evil, pernicious heresy any longer. He suborned you, he suborned half of Dhevyn with his lies, and I will see him destroyed for it.'

'I suppose that's easier than admitting you murdered your own child for nothing.'

Antonov was losing patience with them. He turned on Rainan again. Alexin and the other guardsman had closed in on their queen, their hands resting on the hilts of their swords. Antonov's men were also poised to strike.

'Will you sign?' Antonov demanded.

Rainan hesitated for a long moment. Then she shook her head. 'I can't turn my back on Dhevyn just to save my own life.'

'You must, Rainan!' Johan urged. 'Don't make the same mistake I did. Don't let your pride stand in the way of your life.' Antonov seemed content to let Johan argue his case for him and made no move to stop him talking. 'Alenor needs you. Dhevyn needs you.'

'So that's it?' she asked, her eyes filled with tears. 'I should just stand aside and let Antonov have Dhevyn?'

'Stand aside and give your daughter the benefit of your

counsel,' he said. 'The alternative is to leave her alone and grieving – a child trying to rule Dhevyn with Kirshov Latanya by her side and the Lion of Senet looking over her shoulder.'

Rainan lowered her eyes and was silent for a long time. Then she braced herself and looked squarely at Antonov. 'Do I have your word that my daughter will be unharmed?'

'You do.'

'And I will be permitted to remain on Kalarada with her?'

'Until you try to undermine my authority,' he agreed.

Rainan spared Johan a rueful glance before nodding reluctantly. 'Then I will do as you ask.'

'The documents are ready and waiting, your majesty.'

Rainan stepped up to the table and picked up the quill. She glanced over her shoulder at Johan for a moment. He nodded silently. Then, with a look of bitter shame, she turned her back on him and signed away her kingdom.

When she was done, she threw the quill down and turned to face Antonov. He treated her to a beaming smile. 'There! That wasn't so hard, was it? I'm sure you'll come to see the wisdom of your decision. Now, that just leaves us with one other small matter to take care of.' He turned to smile warmly at Tia. 'Where is your father, my dear?'

Johan was astounded. With the stroke of a pen Antonov had once again stolen Dhevyn from her rightful monarch, and yet it seemed to mean nothing to him. Already his attention was on other things.

'I told you already,' Tia snarled. 'He's dead.'

'Yes, I heard you the first time, Tia, but I don't happen to believe you.'

'I don't care what you believe. It doesn't alter the truth.'

'Feisty little thing, aren't you? You must get that from your mother. Your father was a rather spineless man, as I recall.' Antonov suddenly turned to Dirk. 'What do you suggest, Dirk? Do you think our young friend here would succumb to the same sort of pressure we tried on Johan?'

Dirk stared at the Lion of Senet but didn't answer him.

'No suggestions? You were much more forthcoming about how we should deal with Johan Thorn. Still, I'm sure you'll have something to say eventually. Now, back to you, my dear. What will make you tell me the truth, I wonder?'

'I've told you the truth.'

'Yes. It's quite irritating the way you keep insisting on that. Would you break under torture?'

'There'd be no point,' Dirk said, finally finding his voice.

Antonov spun around to face him. 'Ah! The Butcher of Elcast finally speaks! Why do you say there would be no point?'

'People will say anything under torture,' Dirk told him. His voice was flat and emotionless. 'And besides, if you truly believed physical torment worked, you'd have stretched Johan Thorn over a rack while we were still on Elcast.'

Is Dirk faking this nonchalance, Johan wondered, *or is he truly becoming Antonov's accomplice?* He expected as much from Wallin Provin's issue, but it would kill Morna to see her son like this.

Antonov smiled. 'You really are too damn clever for your own good, aren't you? So what do you suggest then, Dirk? If you're so certain a red hot poker won't achieve the desired results, what do you recommend?'

'You might consider the possibility that she's telling you the truth.'

'Considered and discarded,' the Lion of Senet announced. 'Neris lives. Why else would Johan have gone to the trouble of taking his child from the Hall of Shadows, if not for fear of the power such a child would give the High Priestess over him?'

'Maybe you're the one they're trying to fool.'

'What do you mean?'

Dirk glanced at the prisoners for a moment, then turned his gaze on Johan. He couldn't read what was going on behind those steel-coloured eyes.

Dirk turned his attention back to Antonov. 'Perhaps that was their plan all along. To make you think he lives.'

'They continue to insist that he's dead.'

'Do they? Think about it, your highness. Suppose Neris Veran really did die in that fall from the cliff. What better way to confound you than to allow the rumour that he survived to spread? You've spent how many years, how much money, trying to find him? Johan Thorn has made you complicit in his scheme. Your every effort to find Neris feeds the rumour that he lives. And what better way to make you think he lived than to rescue his child for him? For that matter, you've no proof other than her name that this is even the right girl. She could be anybody.'

Johan stared at the boy in amazement. He'd known since the trip to Avacas on the *Calliope* that Dirk Provin had an exceptional mind, but it never occurred to him how exceptional it was until that moment. Dirk wasn't smart like Neris. Neris was a mathematical freak, but he had little or no talent dealing with anything that couldn't be added, subtracted, multiplied or divided. Dirk's intelligence was more than the freakish ability to work out ridiculous calculations in his head. The boy had a level of political acumen that was truly frightening. *He can't be more than sixteen years old and he's playing on Antonov's fears more effectively than I've ever seen anyone manage it before.* And doing it in a way that might actually spare Tia's life. Johan wasn't fool enough to think that either he or Reithan would see this night out. But if Tia could somehow manage to survive it . . .

'That's so damn clever, I almost wish I *had* thought of it,' he remarked, trusting that his denial would further strengthen Dirk's argument.

'Why?' Antonov demanded with a frown. 'What would you hope to achieve by such a ruse?'

'Because it keeps you occupied,' Dirk answered before Johan could. 'If you want proof, your highness, it's all around you. If Neris Veran really did know when the next Age of Shadows was due, don't you think the first person he'd tell would be Johan Thorn? And if Thorn knew something that important, he wouldn't be here now, your highness, he'd have been shouting it from every rooftop in Senet and Dhevyn for the past fifteen odd years.'

'You expect me to believe that Johan Thorn would be willing to die, rather than reveal his lie?'

'You sacrificed your son because you believed in your cause, your highness,' Dirk reminded him. 'Why is it so hard to believe that Johan Thorn is prepared to die for his?'

Antonov seemed dumbfounded by Dirk's logic. Johan glanced at Reithan and Tia, who were staring at Dirk in confusion.

'Do you believe in the Goddess, Dirk?' Antonov asked him suddenly.

'I believe Johan Thorn doesn't have the information you want, your highness, because it doesn't exist.'

Antonov turned to face Johan. His expression was thoughtful. 'Dirk argues a compelling case, don't you think?'

'I think it's nonsense,' Johan scoffed. 'He's been around you too long. He's imagining plots that couldn't possibly exist.'

'Are you so cunning, Johan, that you would think up such a plan?'

'If I were that smart, Anton, I'd have figured out a way to rid Dhevyn of you,' Johan retorted pleasantly.

He watched Antonov pace the terrace, trying to hide the terror he felt. He didn't know if what Dirk had said had made any impact on Antonov, and suspected that it hadn't. The Lion of Senet had his own plans, and all the clever manipulation of the facts weren't likely to alter them.

'So, Dirk, should I kill them? If what you claim is true, will killing them aid or hinder their cause?'

'Eryk is innocent, your highness. It's unlikely he's even heard of Neris Veran, so killing him would be pointless.'

'Or he could be a clever plant, sent to Avacas by your mother, to coordinate her treasonous activities with Johan's allies. It was Lady Morna, after all, who suggested you bring the boy to Senet as your servant.'

Dirk looked genuinely amused. '*Eryk?* Your highness, even you can't believe that.'

Antonov shrugged. 'It's hard to know what to believe when dealing with such accomplished liars. For now, let's assume I believe your servant is nothing more than an innocent bystander, but what of the others?'

'Killing the girl would be foolish,' he replied without hesitation. 'If she is Neris Veran's daughter and he's already dead, her death won't achieve anything. But if he's alive, you'll just drive him further underground. You've already said Neris was spineless, so he doesn't sound the type to come roaring into Avacas to avenge his daughter's death. And as I said before, for all you know, she could be some bit of fluff Seranov picked up in his travels.'

'And what of Thorn? And Seranov?'

'Kill them and you'll turn them into martyrs.'

'I think I'm prepared to risk that.'

'There's no need. Have Alenor do it. Then their blood will be on Dhevyn's hands, not Senet's.'

The soon-to-be-deposed Queen of Dhevyn gasped at the suggestion. Reithan had obviously heard all he could stand and tried to lunge at the young man, but was clubbed down with brutal efficiency by the guard standing on Barin's left.

Johan stared at the boy, wondering if he had misjudged him. *Maybe he's not trying to help us at all*, he realised with despair. *The little bastard is actually advising Antonov, and doing it well. Oh, Morna, you would die if you realised your son had come to this. Did you know? Is that why you let him leave Elcast? Because you knew he was beyond redemption? Was he like this as a child, or is this malicious gift something that only Antonov saw in him?*

'Alenor couldn't bear to have her pony put down, Dirk,' Antonov was saying. 'What makes you think I could make her order the execution of her uncle?'

'She'll do anything Kirsh asks her to do. He's going to be the Regent of Dhevyn. Tell *him* to make Alenor do it.'

Antonov turned to study him for a moment, as if debating something in his own mind, then he walked across the terrace and placed his arm around Dirk's shoulder.

'You know, I shall enjoy keeping this boy close to me. Don't you think he makes a promising student? He's so much more suited to rule than either of my boys. Misha is too sickly and Kirsh is . . . well, let's just say that Kirsh has too much of his mother in him ever to be truly ruthless. But this boy! He's everything a man could want in a son. Don't you think so, Johan?'

Johan glared at Dirk for a moment, then shook his head sadly. 'I think if he was my son, I'd die of shame that I'd spawned such a monster.'

Antonov smiled happily. 'I'm sorry you feel that way, Johan, because you see, that's the tragedy of it. He *is* your son.'

65

'You don't look surprised, Dirk,' Antonov gloated, his arm still draped around his shoulder. 'Your father, on the other hand, looks like he wishes *I had* killed him.'

I should have known, Dirk told himself angrily. *I should have realised that Antonov knew the truth. I should have anticipated this. I should have known that he would find a way to use this against Johan. The sick, evil bastard is positively enjoying it, too.*

He tried to catch Johan's eye, but the pirate refused to look at him.

'You're lying, Anton,' Johan accused, although his statement lacked conviction.

'You know I'm not,' Antonov replied cheerily. 'The lad was born less than six months after Morna Provin returned to Elcast. He's your son, Johan.'

Dirk stared at his father, trying to hide his despair. His life, Eryk's life, *all* their lives, depended on getting through this nightmare in one piece.

I was trying to buy you time! he wanted to cry out. *Nothing anybody said to her could ever make Alenor order your execution!*

But the words wouldn't come, couldn't come. He almost had Antonov convinced. One wrong word, one sympathetic look, and everything would be ruined. He looked away, unable to bear the accusation in Johan's eyes, but when he did, he found himself looking at the serving girl who had helped Misha when he'd had that seizure. The look Tia Veran gave him was one of undiluted hatred.

'Aren't you proud of your boy, Johan?' Antonov asked, twisting the knife with glee. 'I mean, look at him! He's got Morna's eyes, don't you think? A strapping young man, good looking . . . and smart? You wouldn't believe how smart he is. As clever as Neris, they claim. Now isn't that proof that there *is* a Goddess? She delivered to us another Neris Veran, spawned from the unholy alliance between you and that treacherous bitch, Morna Provin.'

'Even if he is my son, what's the point in telling me about him now?'

'Why now? Because he's *mine*, Johan.'

Dirk glanced at Antonov and, feeling like hot lead had been poured into his stomach, he realised what the Lion of Senet had in mind. He truly *had* just been playing games until now. It was clear now why Antonov had been so anxious to throw them together. Did he expect them to have developed some sort of friendship? Johan Thorn might have been able to resist watching innocent strangers die, but did he have the strength to stand back and watch Antonov torture and kill his son? The son that he'd only just begun to know? *Or his daughter?* Dirk recalled his conversation on the *Calliope* with Johan when he'd told him of the child he had stolen from the Hall of Shadows. *I raised her as my own child*, he'd said. Would Johan be able to hold his tongue if Barin Welacin used his talent for causing pain on Tia Veran?

In a sudden moment of clarity, Dirk understood why Johan had asked him to help him die. *He isn't a coward. He was trying to cheat Antonov of his entertainment.*

'Antonov, what are you trying to prove?'

'That I'm right,' Antonov snapped. 'And so help me, before this night is over, I'll *know* if Neris Veran lives. You *will* have denounced your heresy, Thorn, *and* admitted that there truly is a Goddess. Prefect Welacin!'

Barin had been waiting for his cue. He grabbed Tia by the arm and dragged her across the terrace until she was only a few feet from Johan. Reithan Seranov, still groggy from his last attempt at defiance, was beaten down again, just for good measure, as Barin motioned two of the guards forward. They grabbed Tia's arms, holding her immobile. Barin reached down and took hold of Tia's left hand. He then produced a pair of pliers from the pocket in his coat like those the farriers used to trim horseshoe nails.

'How much damage are we going to have to do to this pretty young thing before you see reason, Johan?'

Tia struggled against the guards as Barin positioned the pliers over the top knuckle on the little finger of her left hand.

'Don't tell them anything, Johan!' she cried out defiantly.

'That's the spirit, dear,' Antonov said. 'Be brave.'

'For the Goddess's sake, Anton!' Rainan begged. 'You can't do this!'

'That's entirely up to your brother, Rainan.'

When Johan didn't answer immediately, Antonov nodded to Barin. The Prefect squeezed the pliers closed on Tia's finger. Her scream tore through Dirk like a white-hot sword, but it wasn't enough to cover the sound of breaking bones. Dirk was afraid he was going to be sick. Eryk was crying uncontrollably, held in the grip of one of Barin's guards.

Then he glanced across at Ella Geon. She was a physician *and* Tia's mother, if Dirk understood things correctly. Yet she watched the proceedings with a stony expression that did not change. She did not move while her daughter knelt on the terrace, sobbing with agony, blood pouring from the stump of her amputated finger.

'Perhaps another finger, Barin,' Antonov suggested.

Johan Thorn stared at the Lion of Senet in horror. *Don't give in*, Dirk found himself silently hoping. *Don't let Antonov break you*. He felt desperately sorry for Tia Veran, but somehow he understood that the only thing that made her suffering meaningful was that Johan's secrets remained safe.

Tia screamed again, as Barin crushed the bones in her fourth finger.

'Enough!' Dirk cried before he could stop himself.

Antonov turned to stare at him, clearly surprised and disappointed that Dirk didn't have the stomach for this sort of thing. '*Enough*, did you say? Surely you're not sickened by the sight of a bit of blood, Dirk? And you ... such a dedicated physician?'

Everyone was staring at him. Dirk realised with dismay that his protest had achieved nothing but to delay Tia's torment for a moment or two, and to expose his own vulnerability.

'It seems he's not quite so firmly in your camp as you thought, Antonov,' Johan remarked. His face was pale and sheened with sweat.

'You want proof, Johan?' Antonov reached into his belt and drew out his dagger. It was a diamond-bladed weapon – rare, valuable and wickedly sharp. 'Let's see who Dirk belongs to, shall we?' For the first time, Dirk saw anger glinting in the prince's eyes. 'Take it!'

With a great deal of trepidation, Dirk did as Antonov demanded. The blade was heavy in his hand.

'Kill her.'

'What?'

'No!' Rainan cried. Her guardsmen stepped forward to restrain her. Their job was to protect their queen, and at that moment, she was in more danger trying to intervene than by being a spectator. The Shadowdancer Ella Geon's expression still did not change. Neither did Barin Welacin's.

'Kill her, Dirk,' Antonov repeated. 'Kill the girl.'

'Now?'

'Of course, now! What, isn't the audience large enough for you?'

Dirk stared at Antonov in horror.

'What's the matter, Dirk? Have you suddenly discovered you don't have the strength of your convictions?' He laughed sourly. 'It's so much easier to *order* people to do things, isn't it? Come now, lad! You're more than happy to make Kirshov or Alenor order an execution, and they're your friends. But suddenly you find yourself unable to perform the same deed in person? You disappoint me, son.'

I can't do this. Dirk looked around the terrace and realised there was nobody who would help him, nobody who could offer him a way out of this. His mind was suddenly blank, his thoughts drowned out by the horror of what Antonov wanted him to do.

The Lion of Senet watched him for a moment, then turned to one of the guards and asked for his sword. The man complied immediately, unsheathing his blade and handing it to Antonov with a short bow. Antonov accepted the blade and took a step back from Dirk. He raised the sword, aiming it at Eryk's left eye.

'Let me put it another way, Dirk. Kill Tia Veran now, and prove you are my friend, or refuse and prove you are your father's son.'

When Dirk still hesitated, Antonov began to grow impatient. 'Can I make it any clearer, boy? Kill her, or I will kill them both. Either way, she is going to die. It's up to you whether young Eryk dies with her or not.'

The boy could not understand what was happening. Still kneeling on the flagstones beside Reithan Seranov, the Lion of Senet's blade hovering inches from his face, he turned his gaze on Dirk, eyes wide with fear. 'Lord Dirk . . . ?'

Dirk thought his heart might shatter into a million pieces. There was so much trust in Eryk's dull, fear-filled eyes.

'Do it, son,' Johan said quietly.

Dirk stared at Johan in shock. He couldn't believe what he'd heard. 'You can't be serious!'

Johan shrugged philosophically. 'We're all going to die tonight, Dirk. Our deaths might be inevitable, but there's no reason for you or your servant to share our fate.'

'I'm sorry, but I can't do this,' Dirk finally admitted. He turned to Antonov and held out the dagger to him. 'I was training to be a physician, your highness. I'm sworn to do no harm.'

'Too bad,' Antonov replied unsympathetically. 'Anyway, you've taken no oath. Physicians don't take their oath until their fourth year of training. You never even completed your first year, if I'm not mistaken.'

Dirk was running out of excuses. Running out of time. *Maybe if I place the knife right and she can fake it . . .* he wondered, knowing as he thought of it that it was a hopeless plan. Eryk was crying, silent tears running down his face. Dirk took a step forward.

I won't do this!

'We don't have all night, Dirk,' Antonov prompted impatiently.

Dirk covered the remaining distance between himself and Tia in a daze. Her feet were shackled. She would not be able to escape. Tia was hunched over, sobbing uncontrollably, holding her bleeding hand against her chest, as the blood pooled on the flagstones of the terrace.

'Rainan, you might like to warn your guardsmen not to try anything heroic,' Antonov said behind him. For a moment, all eyes turned to the queen and her guardsmen.

'I'm sorry,' Dirk whispered to Johan, while everyone was momentarily distracted. Then he added, 'Father.'

It was the best he could do. The only way he could tell Johan what he'd been trying to do. The only chance he had for forgiveness.

'Do it now, Dirk,' he whispered urgently. 'There'll never be a better chance. If it's any consolation, it's what Tia and Reithan came here to do.'

At the mention of her name, Tia looked up. 'Johan, *no!*'

'I *won't*—' Dirk cried in a desperate whisper. 'I'm not a murderer.'

'Then you're playing in the wrong game, son. Now *do* it, and for the Goddess's sake, do it cleanly. You're a physician. You know where to place the blade to make it quick.'

Dirk glanced down at the dagger. It felt like a lead weight in his hand.

'I *can't*—'

'If you don't, then you'll die too,' Johan hissed urgently, 'and the only cause that will serve is Antonov's. You can't help me, Dirk, but you *can* save the others.'

'Anton, this is cold-blooded murder!' Rainan protested. Dirk glanced over his shoulder. Antonov's back was turned as he faced the queen.

'Avenge me, Dirk,' Johan commanded softly. 'And promise me you'll save Tia and Reithan if you can.'

'I promise,' he replied, so softly only Johan heard him.

The exiled king smiled. 'Give my love to your mother.'

Dirk stared at Johan for a long moment. Then, with a two-handed grip and a wordless cry of despair, he plunged the dagger, not into Tia's exposed back, but into Johan's throat as hard as he could, driving the blade up into his brain, killing him instantly. Warm blood spilled over his hands as the life vanished from Johan's eyes. He heard a woman scream, but he wasn't sure if it was Rainan or Tia.

Dirk jerked the blade free as a terrible silence descended over the terrace and Johan Thorn crumpled to the ground at his feet.

66

'*No!*' Antonov's cry sent a shiver through Tia, as she looked down at Johan's lifeless body through a veil of agonised tears. For a moment, the pain in her hand seemed insignificant compared to her grief. Then another feeling washed over her, making her almost faint with it: relief. It was followed by a wave of intense guilt as she recognised the emotion for what it was.

The Lion of Senet covered the distance between himself

and Dirk Provin in three steps. He backhanded the young man viciously, making him stagger backwards. Dirk Provin looked stunned, but whether from the savage blow, or the fact that he had just killed his own father, Tia couldn't tell. She didn't really care, either. All she really understood was that Johan was dead.

'You've killed him, you fool!' Antonov cried.

Dirk looked up at Antonov unapologetically. 'You said you wanted him dead.'

'I told you to kill the *girl*!'

'He lunged at me. I didn't have a choice.' Dirk's voice was flat. *You heartless little bastard*, Tia thought, even as it occurred to her that Johan had done nothing of the kind. *Why is he lying?*

'*Do you know what you've done?*' Antonov screamed. He was in a rage, his face contorted with fury.

Dirk didn't answer for a moment. He gingerly fingered his lip where Antonov had hit him, then straightened up to stare at the prince. 'At the very least, I've convinced your little friend there that we're not kidding around.'

Everyone stared at him in shock.

'*What?*' Antonov demanded.

'She's a nobody, your highness. She's not Neris Veran's daughter. She's not anybody's daughter. I'm sure she'll eventually admit to it, but it'll take a few more fingers and frankly, I don't see the point. She'll tell us the truth now, I promise you.'

Tia's hand was throbbing unbearably. She tried to make sense of what was happening. It was like being in an earthquake. The ground was shifting underfoot, too fast for her to comprehend what was going on. Dirk Provin stepped forward and grabbed her by the arm, jerking her to her feet.

'You'll tell us who you really are now, won't you?' he said harshly. She staggered and cried out with the pain, but he held her up. Then in a voice so low she thought she might have imagined it, he added: 'For the Goddess's sake, tell them something! And make it believable!'

Through a red haze of pain, grief and guilt, Tia began

to comprehend. She glanced across at Reithan before she answered. He seemed to understand what was going on better than she did. He was on his hands and knees on the terrace, blood dripping from a cut over his right eye, but he looked up and nodded imperceptibly.

'My name is . . . Catalin . . . Arrowsmith,' she stammered, hanging her head. She was trying to avoid looking Antonov in the eye, certain he would know she was lying. She unwittingly gave the impression she was hanging her head in shame.

'I knew she wasn't my child,' Ella announced stiffly. She appeared to feel vindicated, as if Tia's admission proved that it wasn't lack of maternal feeling that had kept her immobile while Barin Welacin tortured her.

Dirk still held her. He shook her roughly and she cried out. 'Come on. Tell us the rest of it!'

'We've seen her before in the taverns on Kalarada,' Alexin Seranov added, stepping forward. 'We thought she was one of Barin's spies, actually.'

Barin Welacin nodded in agreement. 'Aye, there was some trouble about it down near the stables. That's how we caught these three.'

'I . . . I come from Kalarada,' she continued, glancing at Alexin, hoping she'd read his intentions correctly. She could understand what Alexin was trying to do – throw doubt on her identity. But she couldn't begin to imagine what Dirk Provin was playing at.

'See how cooperative she is,' Dirk said. 'Now that she knows we mean business. So what can you tell us about the Baenlands, girl?'

'I . . . I met Reithan in a tavern in Kalarada and he asked me if I wanted to see Avacas. When we got here, he told me to get a job in the palace so I could find out what was happening to Johan Thorn. All I had to do was tell people my name was Tia Veran. I've never even been to Mil.'

Antonov turned on Reithan furiously. 'What did you hope to gain by this deception?'

'They're trying to make you think Neris Veran lives,

your highness,' Dirk answered before the drug runner could say a word. 'They probably hoped that you'd become so distracted by your search for Neris that you'd lose interest in Johan Thorn.'

Antonov stared at Dirk suspiciously. 'And how is it that you worked this out, Dirk, when nobody else did?'

Dirk Provin met the Lion of Senet's gaze without wavering. 'It's what I would have done, your highness.'

Antonov looked around him, at Johan's body, at Queen Rainan who was pale with shock, being held upright by one of her guardsmen. He looked at Ella, standing there with her icy composure, and at Barin Welacin, who seemed annoyed that he had been robbed of his chance at further sport with his pliers. He took in Reithan, kneeling on the terrace with a guard standing over him, a sword at his throat. He glanced down at young Eryk, who was curled up in a ball, tears streaming down his face. Last, he turned to Dirk, who held Tia in a vicelike grip. Dirk appeared calm but he was trembling. Tia could feel it in the hands that held her.

'Dirk.'

'Your highness?'

'Clean this mess up.'

Without another word, Antonov turned on his heel and walked away.

The silence lasted a few moments longer. Everyone on the terrace seemed frozen in shock, by Antonov's sudden departure as much as anything else that had happened in the past few minutes. It was Barin Welacin who recovered first. He glanced around the gathering, then turned to Dirk. The Prefect had apparently read the situation and come to the conclusion that the power here now lay with the Provin boy.

'What are your orders, Lord Provin?'

Dirk seemed a little taken aback by the question. 'What?'

'Your orders, Lord Provin?'

'Ah . . . yes . . . I . . . get rid of the body,' Dirk ordered, taking a deep breath. 'I want my servant released, too. And have someone clean the blood off those tiles.'

'Is that all you care about?' Rainan asked, her voice choked with emotion. 'The blood on Antonov's precious tiles? What about the blood on your hands, you—'

'Your majesty, I believe you were planning to leave tomorrow. Might I suggest that you do it *now*, tonight, in fact. It would be better for everyone, I think.'

Dirk was speaking to Rainan, but he was looking at Alexin, not the queen, as he spoke. Some sort of unspoken communication happened between the guardsman and Dirk Provin that Tia did not understand.

'Her majesty will be leaving on the next tide,' Alexin assured Dirk. When Rainan made to object, Alexin cut her off. 'If you would be so kind as to make a ship available?'

'The *Calliope* is at your disposal, Captain.'

Even Barin raised an eyebrow over that command. 'And the prisoners, my lord?'

Tia felt as if she was trapped in a nightmare; the sort of surreal landscape where nothing was as it seemed and everything changed so rapidly that it was little more than a blur.

'I'll take them to my rooms for now,' Dirk announced. Tia swallowed back an instinctive wave of panic. *Isn't anybody going to object to this?*

'*Your* rooms, my lord?'

'I'd like to question both of them some more before I recommend to Prince Antonov what should be done with them.'

'With all due respect, my lord,' Barin ventured with a frown, 'I believe I'm more . . . experienced than you, in these matters.'

'Your experience didn't help us much this evening,' Dirk pointed out coldly. 'I got more out of the girl than you did.'

'Yes, my lord, you did,' Barin conceded. 'But I hadn't killed anyone yet.'

Dirk faced the Prefect with an icy stare. 'You have your orders, *Prefect* Welacin.'

Barin seemed to debate the matter for a few moments

longer, before bowing in acquiescence. 'As my lord commands.'

Even the Prefect is afraid of him, Tia thought. She shuddered as Dirk pushed her ahead of him towards the palace, resolved that if nothing else, before the night was out, she at least would do something about Dirk Provin.

67

When they reached Dirk's rooms on the fourth floor Dirk thrust Tia inside roughly and let her go. Reithan followed a few moments later. Her hand was still pounding in agony, although the bleeding had stopped. Almost tripping on the chains around her ankles, she spun around to face Dirk Provin, determined to go down fighting, but he ignored them completely. With an abrupt command, he dismissed the guards then pushed past them into the bathroom. The next thing she heard was the sound of the dreaded Butcher of Elcast heaving his guts up like a girl.

She glanced at Reithan, then waited a few moments after the sound of Dirk's vomiting ceased. Finally, curiosity got the better of her. Holding her throbbing hand against her chest, Tia hobbled across the room with a metallic clatter to the bathroom and cautiously poked her head inside the door. Red light flooded the room from the skylight in the ceiling. Dirk had sunk down on to the floor beside the washstand. His knees were drawn up, his head resting on his arms.

'Are you all right?' she asked.

He looked up at her. His eyes were tormented and Tia was astounded to find his face streaked with tears. Dirk leaned his head back against the tiled wall and closed his eyes. 'I'm just wonderful,' he said bitterly. 'Rape, torture, patricide ... all in a day's work for the Butcher of Elcast.'

Tia had no answer for that. She was still reeling over

the fact that Dirk was so obviously upset. He'd seemed carved from ice out on the terrace.

'You'd better let me look at that hand,' he added tonelessly. 'It'll turn septic otherwise.'

'What would you care?'

With his eyes still closed, his head tilted back against the tiles, he was so exposed, his throat so bare and open to attack . . .

One slash with a knife, one thrust with a blade and you're dead, Dirk Provin. Just as you killed Johan, you cold-blooded bastard.

She looked around for a weapon. On the washstand beside the water jug lay his shaving paraphernalia, including his razor. It was no more than three steps away. But she was wearing chains. And Dirk was sitting on the floor between her and the washstand. She took one small step forward. The chains rattled loudly. Dirk looked up, then wiped his eyes impatiently. She froze midstep. He studied her for a moment before climbing to his feet, then glanced at the washstand, as if he knew what she was planning.

'For the Goddess's sake, I'm not going to hurt you!'

'What are you going to do then?' she asked belligerently.

'I meant it about dressing that hand.'

'I don't need any help from you, Dirk Provin. In fact, I'd say you've done quite enough for one evening.'

He stared at her, then pushed past her and walked back into the other room. 'Are you all right, Eryk?'

The servant nodded silently. Dirk studied the boy for a moment, to reassure himself, perhaps, that the boy was unharmed.

'He was your *father*,' she accused, following him with her eyes, determined not to turn her back on him. 'He was the true King of Dhevyn. Not only are you a callous, cold-blooded cur, but a traitor as well.'

'Shut up, Tia,' Reithan warned.

Dirk paid no attention to either of them. He ruffled Eryk's tousled head with a comforting hand, then turned to Reithan. 'What about you? Are you all right?'

He nodded. 'I'll live. See to Tia.'

She glared at Reithan for a moment and then turned on Dirk. 'You murdered Johan.'

'I did what he asked of me.'

'And you couldn't wait to do it, could you? You didn't even flinch!'

'Goddess! I should have let Barin have you. Don't you ever let up?'

'Why should I?'

'Because he's trying to help us,' Reithan said. He wiped away the blood that was obscuring his vision and sat down on the arm of the expensively upholstered settee.

'You call murdering his own father *helping*?' she asked incredulously. 'If that's his idea of helping, I'd rather he didn't do us any more favours.'

'Johan was a heartbeat away from revealing the truth about your father,' Dirk tried to explain.

'Johan would never betray—'

'Yes, he would, Tia,' Reithan cut in impatiently. 'He wasn't going to stand there and watch Barin Welacin tear you apart a finger at a time. He might have been able to ignore Antonov executing a score of innocent strangers. He probably wouldn't have broken if it were Eryk or me that was being threatened. But he couldn't take watching you being tortured.'

'But how could Dirk Provin possibly know that?'

'Because he told me about you,' Dirk said. He walked to the window and glanced down at the gardens. Without taking his eyes from the view, he added, 'He loved you, Tia. I knew that, just by the way he smiled when he spoke of you.'

'Dirk is right, Tia. Once Antonov realised what you meant to him, Johan knew he had no defence against the Lion of Senet.'

Tia stared at him in surprise. The last thing she was expecting was Reithan to side with Johan's killer. 'Why are you defending him?'

'Because he's on our side,' Reithan said, looking at Dirk evenly.

Dirk didn't deny Reithan's claim. But he didn't agree, either.

'I don't believe it!'

'And I don't care,' Dirk retorted. He turned his back on them and walked across the sitting room to the bedroom door. He stopped with his hand on the latch and looked back at her. 'My life was just fine until your precious Johan Thorn came along. I was happy. I knew who I was. I had a home and I knew what I wanted to do with my life. I found out Johan was my father just before I left Elcast, and I've spent every waking moment since that day terrified that the Lion of Senet would learn the truth and try to use it against the people I loved.

'The truth is, Tia, I don't care that you hate me. I don't care that you think I'm a monster. Right now, all I care about is that I was able to do the only thing Johan ever asked of me and, even if only temporarily, I beat Antonov at his own game. In the process, I saved your life, in case you didn't notice.'

Although she was reluctant to admit it, Tia knew there was more than a grain of truth in his words. He *had* saved her and Reithan. And he had spared them the necessity of carrying out Johan's orders. But she still wasn't ready to trust him.

'That's all this is to you, isn't it? A game. You'll forgive me for not tripping over myself with gratitude.'

He shook his head, but didn't answer her, then opened the door to the bedroom. Tia could hear him moving about in the other room. Clutching her throbbing hand to her chest, she glanced over her shoulder at Reithan.

'It might be worth trying to make a break for it!' she hissed.

'You won't get far in chains,' Eryk pointed out, before Reithan could answer.

With a guilty jump that made her hand throb in protest, Tia turned back to find Dirk emerging from the bedroom. He was carrying a small knapsack and a vial of purple liquid. He'd changed out of his bloodied shirt, too, but hadn't bothered to tuck in the clean one.

'What's that?' she asked suspiciously.

'It's poison,' he told her. 'I thought I might tip it into the palace cisterns. I've only killed one person today. I'm a bit below my quota.'

It took her a moment to realise he was teasing her. 'You're sick!' she accused.

'It's antiseptic, that's all. Did you want me to dress those fingers, or were you planning to wait until gangrene sets in and you lose your whole hand?'

'Let him look at it, Tia,' Reithan ordered.

Tia suffered him leading her to the settee near the fire-place. Dirk dragged a small side table over and placed it in front of her, then took her hands and pulled the locking pins out of the metal cuffs. He didn't remove the shackles around her ankles, though. Nor had he yet freed Reithan. Once her wrists were free, he tossed the chains aside and ordered her to rest her wounded hand on the table. Then he sent Eryk to the bathroom for a towel and a bowl of clean water.

'Why are you doing this?' she asked as he knelt in front of the table to examine her hand.

'Does it matter?' He took the bowl and towel from Eryk and placed them on the table. 'Eryk, are you sure you're all right?'

'Yeth, Lord Dirk, I promith,' Eryk said in a small voice.

'I need you to do something very important for me. I want you to find Princess Alenor for me and get her to come to my room. Do you think you can do that?' His voice was gentle, almost soothing, as if he were talking to a frightened animal.

'What will I tell her, my lord?'

'Tell her I need to see her. Urgently.'

Eryk nodded, then looked at Tia with concern. 'Will you make Tia better?'

'I'll try. Now off you go and fetch Alenor for me.'

Eryk nodded and smiled wanly at Tia before he left the room. Dirk turned back to his patient, lifted Tia's hand with surprising gentleness and lowered it into the water. The bowl immediately turned red, as the drying blood soaked away from her ruined fingers. She gasped at the pain, but refused to let him know how much it was hurting her.

'Do you think we'll change our minds about you just because you're helping us?'

'That would imply I actually cared about your opinion of me,' he replied.

'I'm not a fool,' she informed him through gritted teeth. 'I know what you are, and I saw who Barin Welacin turned to for his orders after the Lion of Senet left.'

Dirk sat back on his heels and looked at Reithan. 'Is she always this irritating?'

'Yes,' Reithan replied with a thin smile.

'Reithan!'

'Don't worry about Tia,' Reithan told Dirk, ignoring her protest. 'She'll come around when she's had time to think about it. But what *are* you going to do next?'

'I'll try to find a way to get you out of the palace. After that, you're on your own, I'm afraid.'

Reithan nodded in understanding.

Tia turned to Reithan in surprise. 'You're not going to trust this murderer, are you?'

'Right now, you don't have much choice but to trust me,' Dirk pointed out. 'Of course, if you'd rather I gave you back to the Prefect . . .' He let the sentence hang. When she didn't answer him, Dirk patted her hand dry and studied it closely for a moment. Tia couldn't look at it. She fixed her eyes firmly on the richly patterned wallpaper and tried to quell her increasing nausea.

'How much pain can you take?' he asked.

'What?'

'I can splint your fourth finger, although I don't know if you'll ever have the full use of it again, but the little finger is a mess. I need to trim away the bone fragments and then stitch it closed. I don't have any poppy-dust to kill the pain.'

She stared at him, aghast. 'Are you *serious*?'

'Do I sound like I'm joking?'

Tia glanced at her hand and gagged. Tears filled her eyes as she looked down at it. The fourth finger was purple and swollen to twice its normal size around the top joint. Her little finger was a bloody mess and missing completely above the first knuckle. He was right, she realised. If it wasn't cleaned and stitched, she'd end up losing her whole hand.

'Do you actually *know* what you're doing?' she asked doubtfully.

'Yes.'

She thought about it for a moment and then nodded reluctantly. 'I can stand it.'

68

Marqel wished she knew what to expect as she neared the broad hall that culminated in two massive, impressively decorated doors. This part of the Hall of Shadows was usually out of bounds, but the summons from the High Priestess had left her no choice but to attend her mistress in this most hallowed sanctuary.

She approached the doors cautiously, still amazed that she had survived the day, following the episode with the Milk of the Goddess. That slip had almost cost her the chance to stay in the Hall of Shadows.

Of course, Marqel thought, *I should have realised that anything to do with that grey-eyed, too-damn-smart-for-his-own-good bastard from Elcast was apt to go astray.*

Had it not been for her quick thinking, everything might have been ruined. A small, irritating voice in her head rudely reminded her that if she hadn't tried to get even with Dirk Provin by spiking his wine with a stolen dose of the drug in the first place, none of this would have happened, but she ignored it.

It was very late, but two guards stood at the entrance, their red tabards pressed and gleaming in the evening light that flooded the hall from the glass panels in the ceiling. The gilded mural on the doors behind them depicted the two suns of Ranadon, the High Priestess reaching up to them, her arms outstretched, interceding on behalf of the grateful population that lay prostrate at her feet.

The guards stood back to let her pass as she pushed open the heavy door and let herself into the High Priestess's chamber. Marqel had never been in this part of the Hall before. This was Belagren's private sanctuary and off limits to everyone but her closest advisers. The opulence of the rooms made her gape. Everything from the small side tables to the large inlaid murals on the walls was touched with gilt. The vase in the corner of the room appeared to be solid gold. The wealth that had been squandered in the entrance hall alone would feed a village for five years.

And if I'm careful, one day all this will be mine.

'Marqel!'

'My lady?'

Marqel followed the sound of Belagren's voice, turning towards the door of the bedroom. It was gilded with the same careless opulence as the rest of the apartment. Forcing down her apprehension at Belagren's tone, she opened the door.

The bedchamber was almost large enough to accommodate the Queen's Assembly, its walls panelled with hand-painted silk. The massive bed took pride of place in the centre of the room, its diaphanous curtains blowing gently in the slight breeze that came from the open doors leading to the marble balustraded balcony.

Marqel's slippers were silent on the tiles as she crossed the room. The High Priestess was still fuming over the Lion of Senet's intransigence concerning Dirk Provin, she guessed, hoping it was enough to distract her from her own misdemeanours. Marqel was new to the politics and power games of Senet and the Shadowdancers, but she had already discerned that there had been a shift in the balance of power recently; another event that seemed unaccountably related to Dirk Provin. For an insignificant second son of a provincial Dhevynian duke, he'd made quite an impact since his arrival in Avacas.

'If that's a smirk I see on your face, girl . . .' Belagren began as she caught sight of her.

'No, my lady, I wasn't smirking.'

'You wouldn't want to be,' Belagren assured her ominously. 'Not in the mood I'm in tonight. I've had just about enough of people who think they can trifle with me. Help me with these shoes.'

The High Priestess settled into her tapestry-upholstered armchair. She lifted her feet onto the matching padded foot-stool and allowed Marqel to unlace her boots. She watched Marqel the whole time, with her bright, birdlike eyes. Marqel could not begin to guess what the High Priestess was thinking. She had been watching her like that ever since they had left the palace earlier this evening and ridden back to the Hall of Shadows in Belagren's elaborate coach. Marqel wished she could tell if the constant surveillance was a good sign – or bad.

'You did quite well today,' the High Priestess said as she wiggled her toes appreciatively.

'Thank you, my lady,' she said, greatly relieved. She placed the boots on the floor beside the stool. 'Can I get you anything else?'

'Some wine, I think.'

She bowed and hurried out into the anteroom, where a selection of finely cut crystal decanters was arranged on the sideboard. Selecting one at random, she poured the dark liquid into a crystal goblet edged with gold and hurried back to her mistress. Belagren took the wine from her and smiled.

'That's better,' she sighed. 'Sit down, Marqel. I'd like to talk to you.'

With some trepidation, she perched on the edge of the chair opposite the High Priestess, like a bird ready to take flight at the slightest hint of danger.

'I'm curious about you, Marqel.'

'My lady?'

'Why are you here?'

'You sent for me, my lady.'

'That's not what I meant. When I offered you the choice on Elcast you jumped at the chance to become a Shadowdancer. Why?'

Marqel considered her answer carefully before she spoke. 'Because I want what you have, my lady.'

Belagren glanced around the room. 'You mean this? This is just the trappings of wealth, child. It means nothing.'

'But people respect the Shadowdancers, my lady. I want people to respect me, too.'

'Is it just respect you want, Marqel?' she asked curiously.

'I'm not sure I understand what you mean, my lady.'

Belagren took a good swallow of the wine, studying her closely over the gilded rim. 'You've been with us how long now? A few months? In that time, when other acolytes are still trying to find their way, you have managed to make a friend of Kirshov Latanya and an enemy of Dirk Provin. You stole the—'

'But, my lady—' she objected. Belagren held up her hand, commanding her to silence.

'You stole from us, Marqel. Whatever romantic slant you might like to put on it, you took that vial of the Milk of the Goddess and gave it to the Provin boy without permission. In fact, you've broken any number of our rules, and yet you've managed to turn everything to your advantage. The question I would like answered is this: are you incredibly stupid or incredibly lucky?'

Marqel didn't answer. She wasn't sure that she could.

'So I will repeat my question, Marqel. Are you sure it's just respect you want?'

There was no answer Marqel could think of that would satisfy the High Priestess, and fortunately, she was saved from having to think of one. At that moment, Ella Geon burst into the outer chamber, calling for Belagren. She threw open the bedroom doors, her face flushed.

'He's dead!' she announced furiously.

'I beg your pardon?'

'He's dead!'

'Yes, I heard that part, Ella. Who exactly are you referring to?'

Ella appeared not to have heard her. She began pacing like an angry cat. Marqel bit back a smile as she thought that if Ella had a tail, it would be lashing back and forth like a whip.

'One minute he was there, as large as life, and the next minute he's bleeding all over the terrace!'

'Who is dead, my dear?' Belagren asked calmly.

'Johan Thorn, of course! Who do you think?'

The High Priestess froze for a moment in shock, then swung her feet to the floor. 'How did it happen?'

'Oh, that's the bit you're never going to believe!' Ella declared, throwing her hands up.

'Perhaps, if you ever get around to telling me what happened, I could decide that for myself,' she suggested tartly.

Ella stopped pacing and turned to face the High Priestess. 'Your precious Dirk Provin killed him.'

Marqel thought she must have misheard the Shadowdancer. So did Belagren, by the shocked look on her face. 'The *Provin* boy killed Johan Thorn?'

'Right after Antonov got Rainan to agree to abdicate in favour of Alenor, with Kirshov to act as regent until she comes of age.'

'He did *what*? Without me present?' Belagren seemed more shocked at that news than the news that Dirk Provin had killed Johan Thorn. 'What happened? Was the boy provoked?'

'He was as calm as you like,' Ella told her with a shake of her head. 'Ran a blade into Johan's brain with surgical precision, actually. He's dangerous, that one. Oh! And here's the real treat. Did you know that Dirk Provin was not Provin's son, but Thorn's bastard?'

The High Priestess was silent for a long time before she spoke. 'Are you certain?'

'Antonov is. He was positively gloating over the revelation.'

'He's never said anything. He never even hinted at the possibility.'

'That's because the Lion of Senet is playing his own game, my lady. I've been warning you of that for years.'

'But he is so devout . . .'

'You mistake devotion for obedience,' Ella warned. 'Antonov worships the Goddess, Belagren, and he believes you are her instrument, but he also thinks he has a divine mandate to right the wrongs of this world. A misconception you yourself have gone to great pains to foster in him. He's still fighting for the Goddess, but he's fighting by his rules these days, not yours.'

'Where is he now?' Belagren demanded, rising to her feet. She seemed to have forgotten that Marqel was in the room.

'Antonov?'

'No. The Provin boy. Where is he?'

'Last seen, he was issuing orders in Antonov's name like he was the Lion of Senet's favourite son. You've almost no chance of getting hold of him now. Antonov said as much, just before the boy killed Thorn.'

'Did Antonov do *nothing*?' Belagren asked.

'He was too stunned, I think. We all were.'

'But *why*? What does Dirk Provin have to gain by killing Thorn?'

'It's like Ella said,' Marqel said. 'He did it because now there's no chance Prince Antonov will let you have him.' It was only when Belagren and Ella turned to stare at her that she realised that she'd spoken out loud. She swallowed her apprehension and added gamely: 'If you still want him, you're going to have to make his killing of Johan Thorn a religious matter.'

Ella looked surprised at her assessment of the situation, but nodded in agreement. 'She's right, I fear. The only way you're going to get your hands on Dirk Provin now is if you declare the murder of Johan Thorn a crime against the Goddess.'

'That's a simple matter.' Belagren shrugged. 'Johan was a heretic and Dirk Provin has robbed the Goddess of her chance to redeem him.'

'Now you have to convince Antonov of that,' Ella reminded her.

Belagren shook her head slowly and turned to stare thoughtfully at Marqel. 'No, I don't think I do. I think in this case, it's not Antonov I need to act as the sword arm of the Goddess. It must be Kirshov.'

'My lady?'

'We're going back to the palace, Ella. You are to make certain that nothing of import happens without me. I must speak to Antonov. How dare he make such a decision without consulting me first!' Then she turned to Marqel. 'As for you, my dear . . . well, I have a special job for you.'

'What do you want me to do?'

Belagren smiled coldly. 'I want you to earn the respect you so hunger for, Marqel. Let's see if you're good enough to seduce a prince.'

69

Tia didn't pass out from the pain, although Dirk fervently wished that she had. But then, she hadn't screamed, either. He was quite impressed by that. He had cleaned and stitched Tia's wounded hand as she gritted her teeth, tears streaming silently down her face.

Dirk was grateful for the distraction of her mutilated fingers. It gave him something else to think about other than what had happened in the past hour. The inner turmoil that Dirk thought might eventually tear him apart could find no outlet. On the surface, he appeared just as cold and calculating as Tia thought him to be. As he dressed Tia's mangled hand, it was easier to live with what he'd done; it served as a vivid reminder of *why* he'd done it. It would have been easier, though, if she didn't so obviously despise him.

Dirk was just finishing tying off the bandage when there was a pounding on the door. He knelt back on his heels and examined his handiwork for a moment. The bandage was as good as any he'd seen Master Helgin do. With a nod of satisfaction he climbed to his feet and crossed to the door.

Dirk opened it to find Alenor and Eryk standing outside.

'Dirk?' Her expression was grim, her eyes red-rimmed and swollen.

He stared at her silently for a moment, guessing that she must have heard what happened. He stood back to let them enter.

'I'm in two minds about you, Dirk,' she announced as she turned to face him. 'And you've got about three heart-beats to convince me why I shouldn't have the Queen's Guard kill you where you stand.'

'Go ahead and kill me,' Dirk suggested wearily as he closed the door. 'It'll top off the perfect day.'

Alenor glared at him, then glanced over her shoulder at Tia and Reithan.

'Who are they?'

'This is Tia Veran,' Dirk said. 'And Reithan Seranov.'

The princess turned to Reithan. 'You're Alexin's cousin?'

'Yes, your highness.'

The news did not seem to surprise Alenor. She turned her attention to Tia then and looked at her curiously. 'Veran? Neris's daughter?'

'The one and only.'

'Mother said there was some girl—'

'Oh, she's some girl,' Dirk muttered with feeling.

Alenor faced Dirk determinedly. Her bearing was regal, unfriendly.

'What happened tonight, Dirk? First there was that business with Kirsh and Marqel and the High Priestess and now Mother says you killed my uncle.' Dirk thought it curious that Alenor referred to Johan as her uncle. Until now she seemed to have gone out of her way to play down her relationship to the deposed king.

'You should be proud of your cousin, your highness. He played Antonov like he was a damn fiddle,' Reithan said.

'What do you mean?'

'I'm still alive and Tia's still got most of her fingers because Dirk intervened.'

'But he managed to dispose of Johan Thorn in the process,' Tia added. 'You should have seen how easily he did *that*.'

'It's true, then?' Alenor gasped, turning to Dirk. 'You really did kill Johan?'

Dirk didn't answer her. There didn't seem much point. She knew the truth before she came here. The queen had obviously told her everything that had happened.

'*Why*, Dirk?' the princess insisted when he would not meet her eye.

'Maybe he thought that with Johan out of the way, he might have a chance at the throne of Dhevyn?' Tia suggested.

'Tia, will you *please* let it go!' Reithan snapped impatiently, almost as weary of the young woman's rage as Dirk was. 'You're not helping anyone with this.'

Alenor turned to Dirk and studied him closely. 'Do you want the throne of Dhevyn, Dirk? If you truly are Johan's son, you've as much claim to it as I have.'

'I don't want anybody's throne,' he said.

'Are you sure?'

'Think about it, Alenor. Even if I did want your throne, who would follow me? I'm the Butcher of Elcast. The fiend who killed Johan Thorn, remember?'

'That's something *I'll* never forget,' Tia assured him savagely.

Dirk turned on Tia angrily. 'Don't you dare stand there all full of righteous indignation because I killed your precious king. I *saved* his life! Twice! And all the while he kept asking me to end it. You *came* here to kill him! And now, because I saved you the trouble of doing it yourself, you think you can condemn me with a clear conscience.'

Tia looked away guiltily. She caught Reithan's eye and abruptly sat down.

'Not another word, Tia,' Reithan warned.

'You could have killed Antonov,' Alenor suggested. 'Or Barin, or—'

'Which would have resulted in everyone dying,' Dirk

pointed out, collapsing into the chair by the unlit fireplace. 'Including your mother.'

'How can you be so certain?' Alenor asked.

'If I'd assassinated the Lion of Senet, do you think Prefect Welacin would have allowed anyone to leave that terrace alive?' Dirk leaned his head back and closed his eyes. He was tired, desperately so. And sick. Sick of Tia and her self-righteous condemnation, sick of Alenor and her accusing, wounded looks . . . and sick over what he had done. For a moment, out there on the balcony in the ruddy evening light with Johan begging him to rob Antonov of his sport, it had seemed the right thing to do. In that brief moment it had seemed the *only* thing to do. But now . . .

'Alenor, you have to leave Avacas.'

'What's going to happen to you?'

He gave a short, bitter laugh. 'With luck, Antonov will kill me.'

Alenor frowned. 'Either that, or he'll hand you over to the High Priestess to answer for your other crimes.'

'What other crimes?' Reithan asked curiously.

'I've had a busy day,' Dirk said. 'Right now, I'm over-whelmed with not caring about it, one way or the other.'

He looked up at Alenor, who appeared to be torn between sympathy for his plight and horror at what he'd done.

'Take your mother and get out of Avacas while you still can, Alenor. Antonov's reeling at the moment, but it won't last long. He's blinded by his faith, but he's not stupid. I don't know if he bought my story about Tia being a nobody, but even if he did believe it, it won't take him long to realise that Reithan probably knows enough to satisfy him. After that, there's no hope for anyone.'

'How can you just sit there and be so damn analytical?' the princess demanded.

'Rainan agreed to abdicate, Alenor,' he reminded her wearily. 'If she doesn't get away while she still can, the Lion of Senet will crown you Queen of Dhevyn tomorrow, then marry you to Kirsh and, with his son as regent, Antonov might as well be sitting on the throne of Dhevyn himself.'

'You're not suggesting Kirshov had anything to do with this?' Alenor asked incredulously.

'No, Alenor,' Dirk assured her. 'Your precious sweetheart is still unsullied by the taint of blood on his hands.' He couldn't believe that even now, Alenor still harboured such a crush on Kirshov that it blinded her to what was going on. Antonov had announced his plans for Dhevyn openly, yet she still clung to the illusion that her love for Kirsh would overcome everything. 'Your fiancé has a gift for remaining blithely unaware of what's going on around him,' he added. 'I wonder how much longer he'll be able to keep doing that?'

'Just because you're angry at Kirsh because of what you did to Marqel, that doesn't mean you can drag him into this. He wasn't the one who . . .' Her voice trailed off, as if she didn't have the courage to complete the sentence.

Dirk jumped to his feet and glared at her, daring her to finish what she was going to say. 'I didn't *do* anything to Marqel, Alenor, that she didn't arrange! Goddess! Why won't anyone believe that?'

'Antonov believed you,' she reminded him. 'Is that why you killed Johan for him?'

'Who's Marqel?'

'You really don't want to know, Reithan,' Dirk assured him before turning back to Alenor. 'Go, Allie. Leave. Tonight. I'll arrange to get the orders drawn up for Captain Clegg, so you can sail as soon as the tide turns.'

'What happens to us?' Reithan asked.

'You could come with us,' Alenor suggested. 'Dirk is right about that much. He has to get you and Tia out of the palace, out of Avacas.'

'I don't want to go to Kalarada,' Tia objected. 'Reithan and I need to get back to Mil.'

'You worry about getting yourself out of Avacas, Alenor,' Dirk told her. 'I'll see that these two get away safely.'

Alenor smiled briefly. 'I can't believe Antonov is letting us take the *Calliope*.'

'He doesn't actually know about it.'

'I should go, then,' she said. 'I have to say goodbye to Kirsh.'

'Leave him a note, Alenor. You have to get out of the palace before Antonov decides to object. He doesn't need your mother alive any more. He doesn't need anyone except Neris Veran.' Dirk turned to Tia and added, 'I hope he is alive, Tia. It'd be a damn shame to have so many people die for nothing.'

'Why don't you come with us, Dirk? Mother would—'

'The queen thinks I'm a murderer, Allie,' he reminded her. 'Anyway, I can't leave Avacas yet.'

Alenor stared at him with undisguised pain. 'How silly of me. Of course you can't leave Avacas. Why would you want to give up everything you have here? Mother says Antonov is grooming you to rule.'

Her accusation cut him to the core. But he wasn't going to argue about it. Alenor and the queen had to leave the palace tonight. If getting her away safely meant letting her think that of him, then so be it. He had neither the time nor the inclination to argue about it.

'Goodbye, Allie.'

The princess stared at him for a moment longer, then fled the room. Dirk watched her leave, thinking he'd lost more than a father tonight, he'd just lost one of his best friends.

70

Kirshov Latanya woke to a palace in uproar. Glancing out of the window, Kirsh noticed that the first sun was just past its zenith, the second sunrise still hours away. *So why the commotion?* He could hear the racket in the hall and was in no mood for the disturbance. His head still pounded like a drum band had taken up residence inside his skull, and the tonic Ella Geon had ordered him to drink after his fight with Dirk left a bitter taste in his mouth. Kirsh staggered to the washstand and stared at his reflection in the mirror. Dirk had only managed to land one hit on him, but it was a good one. His left eye was swollen and bruised. He dabbed at it gingerly, consoling himself with the thought that Dirk had looked a lot worse by the time the guards had pulled him off his Elcastran cousin.

He wished fervently that he knew exactly what had happened last night. Nobody had told him what was going on. After Marqel made her startling revelation, he'd been confined to his room on his father's orders, presumably so Antonov could deal with Dirk in private. The High Priestess would demand retribution, Kirsh was certain of that. *And Dirk deserved it*. But what had possessed him to do such a dreadful thing? *Was it jealousy? Spite?* He'd never thought his cousin capable of such a heinous act, yet he could think of no reason why Marqel would lie about it.

Poor Marqel. He wished there were something he could do for her to ease her pain. He wanted to hold her, to comfort her. If he was honest with himself, he wanted her in a way he never wanted Alenor. He had wanted her ever since that day on Elcast when she emerged from the pool near the Outlet.

A knock on his door turned his thoughts from Marqel. He called permission to enter, thinking it was Ella come to dose him again with one of her foul-smelling concoctions designed purely (he was certain) to discourage anyone from admitting they were ill in case they were forced to partake of her cures.

'Prince Kirshov?'

Kirsh straightened at the sound of the voice and rushed into the sitting room. Marqel stood in the doorway, looking around for him.

'Marqel?'

She lowered her eyes shyly. 'Your highness.'

'What are you doing here? I thought you left for the Hall of Shadows with Belagren hours ago?'

'I came back,' she said unnecessarily. She closed the door behind her and leaned against it. She seemed to be fighting back tears.

'Are you all right? What's wrong?'

'I . . . I'm sorry, I shouldn't be here . . .' She turned to open the door to leave. Kirsh crossed the room in six strides and pushed the door shut before she could escape.

'What's the matter, Marqel?'

'Nothing,' she sobbed.

He opened his arms to her and she sagged against him, weeping like a brokenhearted child. He held her as she cried, wishing he could do something more to comfort her. *Damn you, Dirk Provin. This is all your fault.*

'Come on now,' he told her soothingly. 'It's not that bad, is it?'

'Oh, Kirsh,' she sobbed into his chest. 'I'm so sorry.'

'You've nothing to be sorry about, silly,' he assured her, stroking her thick blonde hair. 'If anyone should be apologising, it's Dirk.'

She sniffed inelegantly and looked up at him. 'It's all my fault. I shouldn't have provoked him.'

'It's *not* your fault! I don't care what you said to him, nothing can justify what he did.' He hugged her close for a moment, then held her at arm's length, staring at her with concern. 'Did he hurt you?'

Marqel was one of those rare creatures who looked beautiful when she cried. When Alenor sobbed, her nose ran, her skin turned blotchy and her eyes reddened and swelled. Marqel's crystal tears spilled down her cheeks like a precious waterfall. 'He could have killed me.'

Kirsh shook his head. 'Dirk's not a killer, Marqel . . .'

'Tell that to Johan Thorn.'

'What?'

'Oh, Kirsh, haven't you heard? After he left you, Dirk stabbed Johan Thorn in the throat, right in front of your father and Queen Rainan.'

Kirsh stared at her in shock. 'That's impossible! You must be mistaken. Why would Dirk kill Thorn?'

'I'm not sure,' Marqel admitted with a shrug. 'Maybe it was because he found out he was Johan Thorn's bastard?'

'He's *what*?'

Marqel sniffed again, as if it pained her to tell him what had happened. 'Ella Geon saw it all. I was there when she told Belagren. That's why I came back to the palace. I thought you might do something foolish and I wanted to tell you not to. I wanted to tell you it was my fault and that you shouldn't try going after Dirk.'

Kirsh stared at her. 'What makes you think I'd go after Dirk?'

She smiled at him through her tears. 'I know what you're like, your highness. You have such a powerful sense of honour. With your father so shocked by what Dirk did that he's unable to make a decision, and Dirk ordering Barin Welacin around like *he's* the Prince of Senet, not you, I just knew that you'd feel you have to take command. But you mustn't! You have to let your father deal with this.' She took a step closer and reached up to touch his cheek. 'You mustn't pay any attention to what your father said about you and Misha. I'm sure he loves you both.'

'What did he say?' Kirsh demanded, concerned by her sympathetic tone. 'What are you talking about?'

'If you haven't heard, Kirsh, I don't want to be the one to cause you pain.'

'Tell me what he said!'

She hung her head. 'He said he would enjoy keeping Dirk close to him. He said Dirk is much more suited to rule than either you or Misha.'

Kirsh let her go and walked towards the window, Marqel's words slicing through him like a knife edged in pain. 'What else did he say?'

'He said that Misha is too sickly and you're too much like your mother.'

'And? . . .'

'Kirsh, I really don't want to repeat—'

'What else!' he shouted angrily.

Marqel flinched at his tone. 'He . . . he told Johan Thorn that Dirk was everything a man could want in a son.'

Kirsh felt like someone had hit him in the gut with an iron bar. He was staggered to learn his father thought so little of him; furious to learn that Antonov thought so much of Dirk. It made sense now, his father's fascination with Morna Provin's son. He understood now why Dirk had been invited to Avacas. And why his father had relented and agreed to let him go to Kalarada to join the Queen's Guard.

He doesn't need me any more. He's got Dirk.

'I'm so sorry, Kirsh,' Marqel whispered. 'I didn't want to be the one who told you.'

And now Dirk's ordering everyone around like he's a Prince of Senet, is he? 'I'll kill the little bastard myself,' Kirsh snarled, wishing now that he'd throttled Dirk when he had the chance.

'You can't!' she begged.

'Why not?'

Marqel looked suddenly frightened as she searched for reasons to prevent him destroying Dirk Provin. 'It . . . it would just . . . alienate your father even more.'

'Then what should I do, Marqel? Let him get away with it? Let him get away with raping you? Killing Thorn?' *Stealing my father's love?* He didn't say it aloud, but it was what hurt most of all.

'Maybe the High Priestess can help?' she suggested.

'How?'

'Dirk Provin raped me, Kirsh. That's a crime against the Goddess. If Belagren was able to get her hands on Dirk, she'd be able to see him brought to justice.'

Kirsh nodded in agreement. 'Then I'll go and see Father now and demand that Dirk be handed over to her.'

'He won't agree. Belagren already asked Prince Antonov, and he refused.'

'He refused?' Kirsh asked in astonishment.

Marqel nodded. 'I was there. He's ignoring all the laws of Senet and the Goddess to keep Dirk by his side.'

'I see.' Kirsh turned away from her, afraid she would see the pain in his eyes.

'I'm sorry, Kirsh. I know how much you love your father.'

'Where is Dirk now?'

'I don't know.'

'And my father?'

'I only just got here from the Hall of Shadows. I don't know where anyone is.' She walked up behind him and placed a comforting hand on his shoulder. 'I wish there was something I could do to make it better, Kirsh.'

He placed his hand over hers for a moment, then turned to face her. 'You're here. That's enough. Won't you get into trouble, though? I didn't think acolytes were allowed to leave the Hall unescorted.'

'I don't care. You're more important to me than the Hall of Shadows.'

'You shouldn't have risked everything for me.'

'I'd risk *anything* for you, Kirsh.'

He hesitated for a moment, then pulled her to him. There was so much promise behind her kiss, so much temptation. He held her tightly for a moment longer, then reluctantly peeled her arms from around his neck. 'You'll have to stay here. Once I've found Dirk, I'll come back for you and then we'll go back to the Hall of Shadows together. If I can hand over Dirk Provin and explain to Belagren how you helped me, I'm sure I can convince her not to punish you too severely.'

'What will you do when you find him?' she asked with concern. 'Please be careful! He's already killed one man tonight.'

'Don't worry, I can handle Dirk Provin.'

'Can you? He's very clever.'

'We'll see how clever he looks with a sword in his belly,' Kirsh snapped, a little resentful that Marqel would assume Dirk could outwit him.

'You mustn't kill him!' she cried in alarm.

'Why not?'

'You . . . you have to . . . disgrace him!' she declared hurriedly. 'You have to prove to your father that he's not worthy of the Lion of Senet's affection. If you kill Dirk, Antonov will just resent you even more for taking his prized pet away. That's why you have to hand him over to the High Priestess.'

'You're right. I never thought of that.'

She touched his face gently and looked up at him with

an adoring smile. He turned his face and kissed the palm of her hand. 'I'm betrothed to Alenor, Marqel.'

'I know,' she sighed. 'Is that why you told Dirk to tell me that you thought of me as just a bit of sport?'

'I never said . . .'

Her eyes suddenly filled with accusing tears. She turned away from him. 'Maybe that's why he thought he could have his way with me. If you didn't care . . .'

'Oh Goddess, Marqel, that wasn't what I meant! If I'd known what he was going to do . . .' Kirsh was suddenly racked with guilt. *It's my fault*, he realised. *I was the one who sent Dirk to Marqel*.

She bravely wiped away her tears. 'You weren't to know what Dirk was capable of, Kirsh. Nobody could have guessed it. He's fooled everyone, including your father.'

Kirsh had never felt so helpless. Or guilty. 'I wish I could make it up to you, Marqel.'

'There is one way,' she assured him. 'Find Dirk and hand him over to the High Priestess for punishment.'

'I give you my word he'll pay for what he did to you,' he promised.

'Deliver Dirk Provin to Belagren and you'll break the hold he has on your father,' she told him. 'The High Priestess will grant you anything you want, for such an act of bravery and faith.'

Kirsh nodded slowly. This was his chance, finally, to earn a measure of respect in his own right.

'Make him pay for what he did to me, Kirsh.'

'I'll make him pay, Marqel. I promise you, I *will* make him pay.'

71

The small family chapel where Antonov often went to pray was located in the grounds of Avacas Palace, some distance from the main building. Dirk crossed the terrace steadfastly refusing to look down to see if the blood had been washed away. The second sun was just beginning to turn the sky yellow on the eastern horizon and the heat was just starting to make its presence felt. It would be another fine, clear day, just as yesterday had been.

How could so much change in the space of one red-tinted night?

After a detour through Antonov's study to write the orders for the *Calliope* to sail, Dirk had sent a servant upstairs with the sealed parchment, under strict instructions to deliver the orders to Queen Rainan in person. Having done all he could to help Alenor, he followed the gravelled path towards the chapel, guessing that was where Antonov would be. When all else failed, the Lion of Senet always fell back on his faith. It sustained him. He might be manipulative, ruthless and cruel, but everything Antonov did, he did for the glory of his Goddess. It was one of the things that made him so dangerous.

There were two guards on duty outside the temple, which was crafted of grey schist flecked with gold. Twin lines of four elegantly fluted pillars supported a latticework of stone at the entrance, leading into a small, circular chamber with an onion-domed roof. Inside, the room was bare but for a narrow marble altar bearing two suns, one slightly larger than the other, made of beaten gold.

Antonov was on his knees, his head bowed in prayer, when Dirk entered the temple. The guards made no attempt to deny him entry. He wondered if they would be quite so accommodating when he tried to leave.

He hesitated for a moment, doubting he had the courage to do this.

'You are your father's son, Dirk Provin,' the prince said, without looking up.

'So it would seem.' His voice was surprisingly steady.

Antonov climbed carefully to his feet, his knees stiff from a long night spent in prayer. 'You know, you had me worried there for a time. For a moment I feared you killed Thorn because you were trying to challenge me. But I've spoken with the Goddess and I see now, what I should have seen then. You weren't helping Thorn. You were helping me. And you of all people have reason to see Thorn dead.'

Dirk was stunned. *He believed me? He actually thinks I did this to help him?*

'I'm sorry for not trusting my instincts about you, Dirk. You have your father's single-mindedness, I suspect,' Antonov suggested. 'Johan may have been a misguided heretic, but he certainly had the courage of his convictions.'

Dirk was in no mood to be compared with Johan Thorn. 'And where did that get him? He spent years in hiding while you ate up his kingdom, island by island.'

'Don't repeat that patriotic Dhevynian drivel in the Goddess's temple,' Antonov ordered. 'And I hope you don't believe it, Dirk Provin.'

I don't know what I believe, Dirk felt like saying.

'Or should we call you Thorn now that your secret is out?'

'It's just a name.' He shrugged. Actually, he'd given the matter no thought at all. Dirk was still coming to terms with the events of the past night. He'd had no time to consider the long-term consequences. All he knew, all he *wanted*, was for this nightmare to be over.

Antonov was watching him closely. 'It's a name that carries a lot of weight. Are you strong enough to take on the title of the Eagle of Dhevyn? I wonder how easily you will bear the load?'

'A great deal easier than you imagine, your highness,' he declared with a degree of bravado that he didn't feel.

Antonov sensed his hesitation. 'Or maybe you're thinking of challenging me? Is that it? You're an ambitious young man. Do you think you might kill me next? If you did, you'd have to fight a war against the might of Senet with Misha ruling Senet and Kirshov ruling Dhevyn.'

Dirk smiled at the very suggestion. 'One son too sick to rule, the other too much like his mother?' He shook his head. 'I hope, for your sake, those words don't come back to haunt you, your highness.'

Oddly enough Antonov looked pleased, rather than disturbed by his answer. 'I suspect history will remember you for your political acumen, not your academic achievements, Dirk.'

He forced a nonchalant shrug. 'You're assuming I want history to remember me.'

'Your actions last night leave it little choice.'

'Perhaps,' he conceded.

'You have taken a step towards the light, Dirk. You have killed the heretic and the Goddess will reward you for what you've done.'

'And if I don't want a reward?'

'Then you prove yourself even more worthy of the Goddess's blessing.'

Dirk was amazed. It seemed that no matter what he did, Antonov was going to find a way to make it fit his view of the world. He began to understand, for the first time, how this man could have sacrificed his own son. Antonov had a gift for rationalising that defied belief.

'I could just walk away.'

'I'll not give you permission to leave Avacas.'

'I think if I was planning to leave, your highness, I probably wouldn't ask for it.'

'Don't even joke about it, Dirk.' Antonov took a step towards him. 'Stay with me. Let me guide you and all the power that should have been your father's will be yours. I'll make you the Eagle of Dhevyn. Together we'll stamp out the heresy that tore Dhevyn apart and restore her to what she once was. I'll even let you marry Alenor, if that's what you want. I know how much you—'

'That's not what I want, your highness.'

Antonov looked a little surprised, and then his expression grew suspicious. 'Don't even think of leaving Avacas, Dirk.'

'Do you think you could stop me?'

'Not if you were truly determined,' he agreed. 'But if you did anything so foolish, I would have no choice but to hunt you down. And believe me, I would devote the might of Senet to your destruction.' Antonov took another step forward, his arms outstretched, his smile benign. It was all Dirk could do to stand his ground. 'I am still your friend, son. Don't make me teach you how much harder I would be to deal with as your enemy.'

Dirk nodded in understanding. 'Do you want to add the throne of Dhevyn to your empire so badly that you would embrace the son of a man you despised, just to secure it? Why do you need me? You effectively own Dhevyn now. You occupy us. Your grandchildren will rule us. You've removed Rainan and have Alenor so afraid of you she can scarce breathe when you're in the room. Kirsh will be Regent of Dhevyn. What's the problem? Don't you trust your own son to do your bidding? Or has he too much of his mother in him for your liking?'

'At times you've too much of *your* mother in *you* for my liking, I'll grant you that much.'

When Dirk didn't answer him, Antonov smiled, and when he spoke his tone was eminently reasonable. 'Come now, you're still in shock over what happened on the terrace. It's never easy, killing your first man. Don't worry, it'll get easier.'

Dirk shook his head. 'How many does it take, your highness? Five? Ten? A hundred? How many men did you have to kill before it no longer bothered you?'

'It's time for you to step down from the high moral ground, Dirk. I am merely a reflection of what you will become, and if that frightens you, it's your problem, not mine. Your actions this night have proved that you and I are carved of the same wood. When you've had a chance to think about it, you'll see that I'm right.' He smiled, reaching out his hand once more. 'Why don't you kneel with me now? Pray to the Goddess for guidance.'

'Somehow, I don't think she has the answers I need, sir.'

Dirk turned and walked towards the entrance, his body tense with anticipation. He half expected Antonov to summon the guards outside.

'Your future is here, Dirk.'

He glanced over his shoulder at Antonov. 'You'd have me betray my own people.'

'I'd have you help them,' Antonov corrected. 'Johan tore the world apart with his heresy. But you and I can make it better. We can restore the Goddess. We can help your people see the truth. That will never happen while Rainan is on the throne.'

'Well, she won't be on the throne much longer,' Dirk reminded him. 'You've taken care of that.'

'I fear Alenor will be no easier to control than her mother, even with Kirsh at her side. He is far too easily distracted. You, on the other hand, are Johan Thorn's son. His rightful heir. And with my help, you will grow into the king your father should have been.'

Dirk was appalled by the breadth of Antonov's delusion. *Does he really think I'm going to claim a throne I don't want for the glory of his damned Goddess? Can faith be so blind?*

'You'll see that I'm right when you've had a chance to think it over,' he assured him, when Dirk did not reply. 'With my help, my guidance, we'll set the world to rights.'

Dirk turned and walked back out into the bright sunlight past the guards without answering. The gravel crunched underfoot. *I have to get out of here*, he thought, sickened by the future Antonov had planned for him. *I have to get out of Avacas; out of Senet.*

He reached the terrace and climbed the steps. This time he forced himself to look down. Barin had followed his orders. The blood had been washed from the flagstones, but there was still a faint stain on the tiles. The second sun burned hot and yellow as it chased away its red companion and a fleeting thought intruded – it was past high tide. Alenor and the queen should be safely out of Avacas by now.

Dirk squatted down and thoughtfully traced his hand over the stain. The heat of the morning had dried it already, leaving a crust of tiny brown flakes that came away on his fingers.

Is this what I am? he asked himself. *Is Antonov Latanya what I will become?*

Dirk found it disturbing that he could not answer his own question.

PART SIX

THE
DEATHBRINGER

72

The second sun was well above the eastern horizon by the time Dirk Provin returned from wherever he'd disappeared to after that awful scene on the terrace. Tia still couldn't believe what she had witnessed, still couldn't come to terms with the fact that Johan Thorn was dead.

Hugging her throbbing hand to her chest, she paced the room impatiently as young Eryk, Dirk's loyal, unquestioning servant, slept fitfully, curled up on the edge of the couch. She envied the boy his resilience. He'd been there, seen everything, yet he remained certain that his master knew what was best. If that meant murdering a man in cold blood, then so be it.

Reithan spent the intervening time examining the room in detail. He glanced at the books scattered on Dirk's desk and spent an inordinate amount of time studying the chess game in progress on the small table near the unlit fire, seemingly uninterested in conversation. There was no point trying to escape. Dirk had taken the precaution of posting guards outside. He claimed it was for the sake of appearances, but Tia didn't believe him.

At the sound of the door opening, Tia spun around to find Dirk stepping into the room, but his expression gave nothing away.

'Where have you been?' she demanded.

Dirk did not answer. He walked to the couch and squatted down beside Eryk, shaking the boy awake gently.

'Lord Dirk?'

'Are you all right, Eryk?'

'I'm a bit sleepy.'

Dirk smiled at the boy. 'Well, you'd better wake up. I need you to pack some things for us.'

'Are we going thomewhere, Lord Dirk?'

'Yes. But just pack a small bag. We can only take what we can carry.'

Eryk nodded and slid off the couch, rubbing his eyes as he walked towards the other room.

'Going on a trip?' Reithan asked.

'With you.'

Tia laughed derisively. 'Do you really think we'd have anything to do with you after what you did?'

'I want you to take me with you,' he told Reithan, quite deliberately ignoring her. 'To Mil.'

'Are you insane?' she cried. 'We're not taking you anywhere near the Baenlands!'

'Then stay here and face Antonov's wrath,' he said with a shrug. 'I'll find it on my own.'

She stared at him in disgust. 'You're unbelievable! First you kill Johan and then you expect us to betray our friends and family by taking you back to Mil with us!'

'I don't think that's what Dirk is after, Tia,' Reithan suggested thoughtfully.

Tia turned on him angrily. 'Then what is he after, Reithan?'

Reithan didn't answer her immediately. He studied Dirk for a long moment.

'Sanctuary, is my guess.'

Dirk met Reithan's gaze without flinching.

'Something like that,' he agreed.

Reithan nodded. 'It's not going to be easy. Just getting out of the palace in one piece may be more than we can manage.'

'You let me worry about that. Will you take me to Mil?'

'Are you sure about this? Once you join us, there's no going back. An empty belly and a few nights in the open, and Antonov's court may not seem such a bad place to be.'

A fleeting smile flickered over Dirk's lips. 'Trust me, I'll not change my mind.'

Reithan nodded. 'Then, assuming we can get out of the palace in one piece, we need to get to Paislee.'

'Reithan!' Tia cried angrily. 'Have you completely lost your mind?'

'Not completely.' Reithan turned to Dirk. 'When do we leave?'

'Now,' Dirk replied.

Their escape from the palace itself was uneventful. With the sudden departure of the Queen of Dhevyn and her retinue, the palace was in chaos, and they were able to slip through the confusion with ease. Dirk made no attempt at stealth. He didn't need to. He was well known in the palace and already the rumours about what had happened on the balcony outside Antonov's study were beginning to surface. Some of the servants stared at him openly as they walked past, others scurried out of his way. He even ordered the guards to escort them, and then dismissed the men once they reached the stables.

Dirk ordered his mount saddled, and demanded two others for Tia and Reithan to ride. The grooms didn't question his reasons; they simply hurried to obey.

'You can ride, can't you?' Dirk asked Tia, as the groom led the saddled mounts towards them. One was a truly beautiful chestnut with a white star on its forehead; another was a mottled grey. The third was a smaller, much less impressive dun that Tia suspected was as docile as Dirk's horse seemed spirited.

'A little,' she replied, eyeing the animals warily.

He looked at her. 'Define "a little".'

She glared at him defiantly. 'Why didn't you ask Reithan if he could ride?'

'So the answer is no.'

'I can manage.'

'With no experience and a wounded hand?' he asked sceptically.

'You just get me on the beast and let me worry about whether I can ride or not.'

Dirk shook his head but made no further comment. She

allowed the groom to help her into the saddle and picked up the reins with her good hand.

Reithan rode up beside her with a frown. 'Maybe I should lead the horse, Tia.'

'Maybe you should just concentrate on keeping an eye on your new best friend,' she suggested frostily.

Rolling his eyes with frustration, he clucked at his horse to get it moving and rode up beside Dirk where Eryk sat behind him, his arms wrapped tightly about his master's waist. Tia repeated Reithan's gesture, but the beast wouldn't budge. Finally, she kicked it in the ribs and the dun moved off, following the others at a walk. *Why did we have to ride?* she thought in annoyance. *I can walk faster than this.*

Almost as if he heard her thought, Dirk halted his mount and waited for her to catch up with him.

'If we act like we're supposed to be riding out of the palace, nobody should question us,' he explained. 'Just keep your head up and don't look anybody in the eye. If someone stops us, let me do the talking.'

'That's your plan?' she asked scathingly. 'If we look like we know what we're doing, nobody will question us? I thought you were supposed to be the smart one?'

Without bothering to answer, he leaned over and grabbed her horse by the bridle and urged it forward. Tia held her throbbing hand to her chest, and amused herself by imagining any number of painful things she would like to do to Dirk Provin, starting with cutting the tongue out of that smart mouth of his with a blunt and rusty dagger.

They rode through the palace gates without incident. The soldiers on duty waved to Dirk, but didn't challenge his right to leave or ask who his companions were. Tia glanced back at them as they rode down the wide, tree-lined boulevard that led to the palace from the city, wondering what the men were thinking. Did they wonder who she was? Were they thinking that Dirk was riding into town with some bit of fluff he'd been amusing himself with last night?

'I think we've got a problem,' Reithan said, glancing over his shoulder.

Dirk and Tia both turned and looked back towards the palace. The guards who had been so relaxed in their duties a few moments ago were suddenly rushing about, drawing the large wrought-iron gates closed. A mounted figure appeared behind the gates, riding a magnificent white gelding, accompanied by a full squad of Antonov's personal guard. The rider stopped long enough to speak to the guard commander, and then waved the gates open again before they were fully closed.

'That's Prince Kirshov,' Eryk said, sounding a little puzzled.

'What's he doing?' Reithan asked.

Dirk didn't answer for a moment. By the time he did, the gates were open far enough for Prince Kirshov and his guard to canter through the gap.

'Move it!' Dirk cried, startling Tia with his shout. He kicked his horse into a gallop, dragging hers along with him. Reithan galloped along on the other side as Tia clutched at the pommel, forgetting her damaged hand for a moment. She cried out in pain, but neither Dirk nor Reithan looked to see why. When she looked down, the cobbles rushed past her in a dizzying blur, and the sound of their pursuers drew closer. Clinging to the horse with her thighs, Tia closed her eyes, but discovered that was infinitely worse. She opened them again and risked a glance over her shoulder.

They were far enough away that Prince Kirshov might not recognise them, but Dirk was leaving nothing to chance. As soon as the curve of the road took them out of sight of the palace, he turned the horses sharply into a littered laneway between two shops and hauled both mounts to a halt. He jumped from the saddle and ran to the end of the lane, flattening himself against the wall as the young prince and his men rode past at a gallop.

Tia jumped to the ground to discover she was shaking like a sapling in an earthquake, her hand throbbing in time with her racing heartbeat.

Dirk sagged against the wall and turned to look at them. 'Is everyone all right?'

'You think he's after us, don't you?'

'And they say I'm the clever one,' he muttered, pushing off the wall.

'But how did he know . . . ?'

Dirk shrugged. 'I suppose any one of the several hundred people who know that Rainan left on the *Calliope* this morning could have let it slip.'

'There's no need to be sarcastic.'

'Come on,' he said wearily, as he walked back to his horse.

'Where do you suppose Kirshov is headed?' Reithan asked.

'The docks.'

'You think he's heading for the *Calliope*?' Tia asked.

'Are you really descended from the smartest man that ever lived?'

'Don't you take that tone with me, Dirk Provin. We don't need you or your help. You can just leave us here. We'll find our own way home.'

'Tia, let it go,' Reithan sighed wearily.

Dirk walked past her without further comment. When he reached Eryk, he bent down until he was eye to eye with the boy who was pale and trembling with fear. 'Are you all right, Eryk?'

'Are we in trouble, Lord Dirk?'

'Something like that.'

'What are we going to do?'

Dirk glanced over his shoulder at Tia before he answered.

'We're going to Mil.'

'The hell you are!' Tia called, fed up with his insistence on that insane idea.

'Keep your voice down!' Reithan hissed. 'Do you want to wake up the whole damn city?'

'This charade has gone on long enough, Reithan!' she cried, albeit with much less volume. 'We're out of the palace now. We don't need him any more. And we're not taking him anywhere near Mil! Tell him!'

'Yes we are,' he replied. 'We're in an enemy city, Tia. You're wounded. We have little money, no food, very few friends and very soon it's going to occur to the Prefect that we've escaped. Just how far do you think we're going to get without help?'

'*Help?* Is that why he wants to go to Mil? To help us? More likely the Lion of Senet set him onto us, hoping we'd lead him to our people. I'll bet the two of them staged that whole scene with Johan!'

Dirk glanced at Reithan before turning his back on her.

'Did you toss a coin with Barin Welacin to decide who got to chop my fingers off?' she called after him.

Eryk looked up at her with tear-filled eyes. 'Why are you mad at Lord Dirk, Tia?'

'You wouldn't understand, Eryk,' she tried to explain.

'But he saved my life ... heaps of times.' The child looked quite distraught.

'Don't waste your breath, Eryk,' Dirk advised, with a look at Tia that spoke volumes.

'And now he's saved your life, too, Tia. So why are you mad at him?'

Tia looked at Eryk for a moment, but couldn't answer him. She turned to Reithan, her arms crossed defensively. 'I don't trust him.'

'That's understandable,' he conceded. 'But right now, he's the best chance we've got, Tia.'

Dirk muttered something that sounded like a curse as he fetched their horses, who had wandered up the lane and were nosing around in the trash for vegetable remains thrown out by the tavern on their right. He gathered up the reins and led the horses back to where they were waiting.

'How did you get here, anyway?' he asked.

'We came by boat,' Reithan told him, far too readily in Tia's opinion. 'We landed in Paislee and travelled the rest of the way overland.'

He thought for a moment and then nodded. 'So if

we can get to Paislee, we can make it back to Mil from there?'

'Yes.'

'Then that's what we'll do.'

Reithan took the bridle of Tia's horse and led it forward. He helped her mount, then swung into the saddle of his own horse. Dirk pulled Eryk up behind him and then, without asking her permission, took the reins of her horse and led them back out into the street.

'Are you a man of your word?' Reithan asked Dirk suddenly.

They had been riding in silence since they left the alley. They were several blocks from the palace, riding through Avacas as it came awake.

Dirk looked startled that anyone had spoken. 'Why?'

'Because I need your word on something.'

He shrugged. 'Very well. You have my word.'

Tia looked at him closely, but she couldn't tell if Dirk was lying. Nor was she sure what Reithan was up to.

'We have to make a detour before we leave Avacas,' Reithan said.

'To where?'

'Chandler Street. There's something there I need to collect.'

All their possessions, all Reithan's gear, was still at Ivon's house on Chandler Street. Tia wondered why Reithan didn't just abandon it until she remembered that the marker proving ownership of the *Wanderer* was hidden among his gear. Without it, they would not be able to claim the boat back from the Brotherhood.

'Are you sure about this, Reithan?'

He glanced at her with a shrug. 'We have to risk it. There's no way to retrieve the *Wanderer* without that damn marker.'

Dirk shrugged. 'If you need to make a detour, then we will.'

'And how do we know we can trust you?' Tia asked.

'You don't,' he told her bluntly.

'The man who owns the house,' Reithan explained, with a frown in Tia's direction. 'He's a corporal in Antonov's Guard.'

'And he was helping you and Tia?'

He nodded.

'No wonder you wanted my vow of silence.'

'Will you keep it?' Tia demanded.

'I said I would,' he replied, then he glanced at Reithan curiously. 'I gather it's no coincidence that you and the captain of Rainan's Guard have the same name?'

'We're cousins,' he admitted. 'My father was the Duke of Grannon Rock before the War of Shadows. He fought with Johan and was killed in the final battle.'

'Then why aren't you the Duke of Grannon Rock?'

'Rainan was forced to disinherit my father after she took the throne. The duchy went to my uncle. Alexin is the current duke's second son.'

'That happened a lot, didn't it?'

He nodded. 'Antonov made the queen disinherit all the noble families who sided with Johan.'

'And when Alexin approached me at the ball with his cryptic comments about people needing my help, he was referring to you and your people in the Baenlands?'

'I suppose.'

Dirk looked at Tia for a moment, then turned back to Reithan. 'Considering it was you and your cousin who asked me for help, you'd think some people would be a little more grateful for it, wouldn't you?'

Tia opened her mouth to object, but she caught the warning look in Reithan's eye and thought better of it. Nobody said another word after that until they reached the cat-filled house in Chandler Street.

73

The *Calliope* was gone by the time Kirsh reached the docks. He watched the ship's sails billowing out as the wind caught her near the harbour entrance, watched Dirk slip through his fingers with a feeling of helpless fury. He should have listened to Marqel. She had warned him Dirk might outsmart him.

'Where the hell is the harbourmaster?' he demanded of nobody in particular.

'I sent someone to find him,' the guard captain informed him.

'He'd better have a damn good excuse for letting that ship sail.'

'Your highness?'

Kirsh looked down to find the harbourmaster hurrying towards him, wringing his hands anxiously, a guard with his hand resting threateningly on the hilt of his sword behind him. A small crowd had gathered to watch the commotion, but they dispersed quickly when the captain glared at them. It was never a good idea to invite the attention of the Palace Guard. Or an irate member of the royal family.

'Who authorised the *Calliope*'s departure?'

'Lord Provin, your highness,' the harbourmaster assured him. 'The queen had all the correct documentation. I mean . . . truly, there was nothing amiss . . .'

Kirsh glared at the man, not realising how much he looked like his father, or the effect the resemblance had on people. 'Nothing amiss? Since when do you let the Lion of Senet's ship sail on the orders of the son of a Dhevynian duke who has no formal rank or position in my father's court?'

'But Lord Provin is . . . well, I mean, everyone knows—'

'Just what does everyone know, exactly?' Kirsh asked.

When the harbourmaster couldn't answer him, Kirsh turned to the guard captain. 'What is he talking about, Sergey?'

'I think, your highness, he's referring to Dirk Provin's rather colourful reputation,' the captain replied.

The answer surprised Kirsh. 'You mean people actually take that Butcher of Elcast nonsense seriously?'

'Seriously enough that the Avacas harbourmaster would rather let the *Calliope* sail than defy him, so it would seem.'

'That's not only insane, it's bordering on treasonous,' Kirsh declared. 'Goddess, when I get my hands on that treacherous little bastard . . .' He sighed, realising how childish his threat sounded. 'Is there any point in pursuing them?'

'Not much,' Sergey replied. 'The *Calliope* can outsail anything else in the harbour.'

'I'm not letting that Dhevynian brute get away with what he's done.'

The harbourmaster looked confused. 'Your highness, if you mean Lord Provin, then he didn't sail with the Queen of Dhevyn.'

'He's not on the ship?'

'No, your highness. He wasn't with the queen's party at all.'

'Then where the hell is he?' Kirsh asked. Nobody was able to provide an answer. He turned to Sergey. 'Captain.'

'Your highness?'

'Seal the city.'

Sergey frowned. 'That's not going to be easy, Kirsh.'

Kirshov stared at him coldly. 'I didn't ask for your opinion, Captain. I gave you an order.'

The guard captain debated the issue for a moment, then bowed apologetically when he realised that not only had Kirsh pulled rank on him, he was deadly serious.

'I'm sorry, your highness, I didn't mean to question your orders. I simply meant that Avacas is not a walled city. We can block the roads, but there are any number of other ways to escape.'

'One of which Dirk Provin is undoubtedly taking advantage of while you sit here arguing about it, Captain.'

'Of course, your highness,' Sergey said, bowing again respectfully, before turning to issue the required orders to his men.

Kirsh returned his attention to the harbourmaster. 'As for you, sir, you may consider yourself under arrest.'

'But, your highness!' the man objected, as the guard standing behind him moved to restrain him. 'Everything was in order! The documents were marked with your father's seal!'

'He used the Lion of Senet's *seal*?'

'I would never have let the *Calliope* leave the harbour without it, your highness. Captain Clegg would never have sailed without the correct orders, either!'

Kirsh realised the man was right. If Dirk was smart enough to forge the *Calliope*'s sailing orders, then it was hardly the harbourmaster's fault. And if the orders had been authenticated with the Lion of Senet's own seal, then technically they weren't even forgeries. But to back down now and admit that he was wrong would make him look indecisive. His father had often told him that the secret to being thought of as a leader was to act as if you knew you were right, even if it turned out later that you were wrong.

'Take him to the Prefect,' Kirsh ordered the guard holding the harbourmaster back. 'If he can convince Barin Welacin that he's blameless, then he might keep most of his fingers.'

With the harbourmaster's protestations of innocence ringing in his ears, Kirsh wheeled his horse around and headed back to the palace.

Antonov was in his study, standing by the window staring thoughtfully out over the gardens when Kirsh returned to the palace. The Lion of Senet was unshaved and bleary eyed. He looked like he'd been up all night.

'The Queen of Dhevyn stole the *Calliope*,' Kirsh announced, slamming the study door behind him.

His father glanced over his shoulder at him. 'So Barin informs me.'

'We should go after them!'

'I think not.' Antonov shrugged, turning away from the window. 'Besides, it's not as if we don't know where they're going. And I don't think Rainan has actually stolen my ship. I'm sure we'll get it back in a few days, none the worse for the wear.'

Kirsh stared at his father suspiciously. 'You're taking this awfully well.'

'The temporary loss of my ship is the least of my concerns right now, son. Have you seen Dirk?'

'No. Why?'

'I was expecting him to be here.' His father hesitated, suddenly concerned. 'He didn't sail with Rainan, did he?'

'Not according to the harbourmaster.'

Antonov smiled, looking very relieved. 'Then he's still in Avacas.'

'I ordered Sergey to seal the city. He won't get far.'

Antonov smiled. 'That won't be necessary.'

'Sir?'

'Dirk isn't going anywhere, Kirsh,' Antonov assured him. 'I have plans for him.'

'You can't be serious! He raped a Shadowdancer! He killed Johan Thorn and he rode out of the palace this morning with those two Baenlander spies Barin arrested at the ball. Do you honestly think he's just gone off for a few days of sightseeing? He's running as far and as fast as he can.'

'Dirk knows that his future lies with me.'

His father's words cut Kirsh to the core. Marqel was right. Antonov wanted Dirk. He was the son neither Kirsh, nor his crippled brother, Misha, were cut out to be.

'And if he *doesn't* decide that you're his future?' Kirsh asked bitterly.

'Then I will eradicate him,' his father replied calmly.

'You have to find him first.'

'It's been a traumatic few days for him. He just needs time to adjust. I'm confident he'll come to me in his own good time.'

Kirsh couldn't believe what he was hearing. 'So that's it? You're going to do nothing?'

'Not at all. I've got plenty to do, the first of which is to arrange your marriage to Alenor.'

'I hardly think we need worry about that yet, Father. Alenor doesn't even come of age for another four years.'

'Four years?' Antonov asked. 'I've no intention of waiting that long, Kirsh. You'll marry Alenor as soon as I can arrange it, and rule Dhevyn as regent when Rainan abdicates.'

Kirsh was speechless. With those few words his whole life had been reordered to suit his father's whim. And he hadn't even been consulted.

'What's the matter? I thought you were quite fond of Alenor?'

'I am, sir, but that doesn't mean I want to . . . marry her . . . not right away, at least. I thought I'd have years yet.'

'Well, you don't,' his father informed him. 'You have a couple of weeks at best, so if you're planning to sow any wild oats, you'd better get it done soon.'

Kirsh still couldn't believe it. 'Did Rainan really agree to abdicate in favour of Alenor?'

Antonov pointed at the parchment laid out on his desk bearing the queen's signature. 'Signed and sealed and as binding as I can legally make it.'

'Does Alenor know about this?'

'I imagine she does by now.'

Kirsh wanted to shout, *You can't do this to me!* but he knew how futile it was to rage against his father's will.

'What about the Queen's Guard?' he asked, doing his best to sound composed and accepting of the situation. 'They're waiting for me.'

'The Dhevynian Queen's Guard will just have to muddle by without you, Kirsh. I have far more important things for you to do in Dhevyn than play toy soldiers for Rove Elan.'

'But I want to join the guard,' he objected, unable to contain his disappointment any longer. 'I don't want to rule Dhevyn.'

Kirsh regretted the words as soon as he uttered them. That was the problem, he realised now. He didn't have his father's burning ambition. Perhaps that was what Antonov saw in Dirk. Perhaps that was why he was prepared to, quite literally, let him get away with murder.

'I'm sorry you feel that way, Kirsh, but I'm afraid the matter is not open for discussion.'

Kirsh felt cheated. Everything he had been dreaming of – all his plans, all his aspirations – had just been smothered by the blanket of his father's territorial ambition.

He nodded slowly, conceding defeat. 'May I ask a favour then, sire?'

'Of course.'

'Let me find Dirk. Let me bring him back here to pay for what he's done.'

'Why? Because he got to your pet Shadowdancer before you did?' The Lion of Senet seemed more amused than concerned about what Dirk had done to Marqel.

Kirsh forced himself not to rise to the taunt. It was important that he sound reasonable, important that he give the impression he had thought this through.

'No, sir. He needs to be found because he's Johan Thorn's bastard, and if I'm going to rule Dhevyn, I don't want Dirk Provin running loose and free to stir up trouble. The Goddess knows what he'll get up to.'

Antonov seemed surprised, and more than a little pleased, at Kirsh's reasoning. 'Do you really think Dirk wants the Eagle Throne? I offered it to him. He turned me down.'

The news wounded Kirsh even more deeply as he realised he was his father's second choice for Dhevyn's ruler.

'Dirk wouldn't accept the Eagle Throne from your hand,' Kirsh pointed out. 'He's Dhevynian. But that doesn't mean he won't try to take it on his own. I'll rule Dhevyn as regent if I must, sir, but I'd rather not have to fight a damn uprising while I'm doing it.'

Antonov thought about it for a moment and then nodded. 'I think you're wrong, Kirsh. I spoke to him earlier this morning—'

'And now he's missing.'

His father thought on that for a moment and then nodded, somewhat reluctantly. 'Find him, then. And if he *has* fled, do whatever you must to stop him leaving the city. Just don't kill him.'

'Thank you, sir.'

Kirsh turned to leave, but hesitated when he reached the door. 'When I do find him, shall I hand him over to the High Priestess to deal with?'

'The penalty for raping a Shadowdancer is death, Kirsh. It doesn't suit my plans for Dirk Provin to die just yet.'

'Then you'll let him get away with rape as well as murder?'

'I'm still not convinced he raped anyone, despite what your Shadowdancer claims.'

'I believe her.'

'I'm sure you do, son,' his father agreed, 'but that doesn't make Dirk a liar, or Marqel a victim.' Kirsh opened his mouth to object, but his father held up his hand to forestall his protests. 'I know you like her, son, and Goddess knows she's pretty enough, but that doesn't mean she's not bending the truth a little to suit her own purposes.'

'What do you mean?'

'She's Dhevynian, and I never met one of them who didn't secretly despise us. Never forget that.' He smiled then, sensing some of Kirsh's anger. 'Have your fun, Kirsh. Keep her as a mistress if you want . . . hell . . . take a dozen of them for all I care! Just remember that you are marrying the nominal ruler of Dhevyn and I don't want you jeopardising the annexation of her kingdom because you can't separate duty from lust.'

'You've been sleeping with Belagren for as long as I can remember,' Kirsh retorted, annoyed that his father could so easily trivialise what he felt for Marqel with a few well-chosen words. 'I didn't notice you worry about doing your duty.'

'Your ex-thief isn't in the same league as the High Priestess, Kirsh. Belagren speaks directly with the Goddess.'

'Then maybe she can ask the Goddess why you're so determined to protect Dirk Provin, yet you're willing to let Marqel suffer.'

'Don't let your desire for that girl get in the way of reason. She is a thief the High Priestess took in out of pity. She will never amount to anything. Dirk Provin is far more important to me than some nameless Landfall bastard you happen to be lusting after. He has the potential to hand us Dhevyn on a plate.'

'When did Dirk become so important?'

'The day he was born, Kirsh. He is the bastard son of the only man who has ever dared defy Senet, and I've been waiting for this moment since the end of the Age of Shadows. I let that treacherous bitch Morna Provin live, I suffered Rainan and her passive resistance, I raised Alenor under my own roof . . . all of it, waiting for the day that I could claim Dhevyn and return it to its rightful place as the jewel in Senet's empire. With him willingly by my side, the whole kingdom will be mine for the taking.'

'Then why do you need me?'

'Because I might be wrong, Kirsh, and if I am, then Dirk Provin will die and we'll just have to annexe Dhevyn the hard way.'

74

Tia and Reithan disappeared into one of the rooms of the house on Chandler Street, leaving Dirk and Eryk alone in a small cluttered kitchen filled with cats. A large grey tabby rubbed up against his leg as he waited. Eryk bent down to pat the creature, which purred appreciatively as he scratched it under the chin.

'What are we doing here?' Eryk asked, stifling a yawn. He'd been up all night, and weariness was beginning to take its toll. The tabby looked up at the boy with golden eyes and moved its head around so that Eryk could scratch it in a more pleasing spot.

What am I doing here? Dirk asked himself silently. He knew the answer. *I promised Johan Thorn I would try to save Tia and Reithan . . . just before I killed him.*

The memory was still too raw for him to be able to dwell on it for long. Dirk pushed the last part of that thought away and consoled himself with the knowledge that he had done all he could.

He wondered what had prompted Kirsh to action. Had Antonov sent him? Or maybe Barin Welacin had decided that he was safer taking orders from Prince Kirshov, rather than from Johan Thorn's bastard? There was no way of telling, but Dirk had seen the look on Kirshov's face as he rode past. It was not the laughing, cheerful expression that he usually wore. In that fleeting moment, Dirk had seen genuine anger in Kirshov's eyes. Whatever had been said to Kirsh had sparked a reaction in him that few were able to evoke. For a moment, Dirk felt a pang of loss for his friendship with the Senetian prince.

Dirk didn't fool himself into believing that he could go back to the palace, didn't try to pretend that he wanted to. Living under Antonov's roof had taught him more than the finer points of court etiquette. Antonov's ultimate revenge on Johan Thorn would be the total corruption of his son. He knew, as surely as he knew the first sun would rise tonight, that to accept the Lion of Senet's patronage would be to embrace the persona of the Butcher of Elcast. He couldn't do that and retain his sanity.

Dirk was still uncertain that throwing in his lot with the rebels hiding in the Baenlands was the wisest course of action. Perhaps he should find a berth on a ship sailing south to the faraway islands of Galina, or maybe find an overland caravan heading into the bleak northern wastes of Sidoria? He could find a way to visit the ruins in the northern mountains of Omaxin, perhaps, where it was rumoured that past civilisations had risen and fallen long before Senet or Dhevyn were populated. He could even visit Damita and meet his maternal grandfather . . .

But no, like an idiot, I'm trusting my life to a bunch of angry rebels who might string me up as a murderer the first chance they get.

But somehow, it felt like the right thing. He smiled faintly, wondering if he was driven by the idea that *finally* he would be doing something Johan might approve of. Dirk closed his eyes for a moment and, for the first time, he allowed himself to relive that awful moment on the terrace. He let the scene play out in his mind and discovered that the most lasting memory he held of his father was the look in his eyes as Dirk plunged the dagger into his throat.

It wasn't fear, it wasn't pain and it wasn't forgiveness.

It was gratitude.

He realised that now. It was not feigned to comfort Dirk, but was the final, unguarded emotion of a man who knew he was about to die.

'Tia! Reithan! Are you here?'

Eryk looked up sharply at the sound of the unexpected voice as the front door banged shut and heavy footsteps sounded in the hall. For a fleeting moment, Dirk thought that Kirsh had somehow managed to track him down, then he realised that this was not one of the Lion of Senet's famed fighting force. This was the corporal who'd been aiding Tia and Reithan.

'Johan is dead! You have to flee Avacas! Aagghh! My Lord Provin!'

Eryk jumped to his feet to find a rotund little soldier standing before them. The cat shot out of the room, startled by Eryk's sudden movement.

'You must be Ivon.'

The man nodded, backing away in fear. It took Dirk a

moment or two to realise that the corporal was terrified of him.

'I . . . I wasn't expecting you to visit . . . my humble home . . . my lord . . .'

'If you're looking for Tia and Reithan, they're in there somewhere, packing.'

'Packing, my lord?'

'As you so wisely advised, Corporal, they're leaving Avacas.'

'And . . . you, my lord?' Ivon inquired carefully. 'I had heard that you—'

'You've nothing to fear from me. I'm just here to see them safely out of the city. Once that onerous task is taken care of, you'll never hear of the Butcher of Elcast again.'

'An onerous task? You're a great one to talk about that.'

Dirk looked up to find Tia emerging from the other room dressed in leather trousers, boots and a worn linen shirt. Before he could respond, she dumped her knapsack on the table and disappeared into the pantry, emerging a few moments later with half a wheel of cheese and a loaf of dark bread, which she shoved in the bag before attempting to tie it off, a task she found next to impossible with one bandaged hand. Ivon stood as if nailed to the floorboards, his terror solid enough to touch. Dirk watched Tia struggle with the knapsack for a minute or two, then offered to help. She slapped away his proffered assistance in annoyance before finally admitting defeat and standing back to let him finish the job.

'I could have done it myself. Eventually.'

'We don't have time for you to stand on your pride, Tia,' Reithan said, as he walked back into the kitchen carrying a knapsack almost identical to Tia's. 'Do you have everything?'

She glanced around the kitchen and nodded.

'Let's get going then. I don't know how long it's going to be before it occurs to someone to seal the city.'

'Can that be done in a city this big?' Dirk asked.

'I'd rather not risk finding out.' Reithan turned to Tia. 'How's the hand?'

'It's not bothering me at all.'

Dirk knew she was lying. He could tell she was in agony, just from the sweat that beaded her brow and the way she grimaced every time she brushed her hand against anything. Still, if Tia wanted to pretend that an amputated finger didn't bother her, that was not his problem.

'Let's get out of here, then,' Dirk said.

His new allies picked up their gear and they headed outside to the horses. Dirk glanced up at the second sun, wondering how long he had before the Lion of Senet realised that his protégé had turned his back on the glittering future he had planned for him and simply run away.

75

Marqel paced Kirsh's room anxiously, waiting for him to return. Her body ached where Belagren had beaten her, but that was the least of her concerns. Marqel had been beaten plenty of times before by Kalleen, and the High Priestess's blows had been delivered for maximum visual impact, rather than any true desire to cause her pain or injury. The bruises would fade eventually.

But her mind was in turmoil. Had she said enough to Kirsh? Had she said the right things? She felt as if she were balanced on a knife's edge, one part of her trying to stay in the High Priestess's favour, the other wanting nothing more than to be with the man she loved.

The acrobat smiled to herself suddenly, knowing that it wasn't that simple. It wasn't just Kirsh she wanted; it was everything that came with him; the wealth, the prestige, the power . . . If only there were a way she could stay here in the palace. Belagren had been Antonov's lover for years, and look at what she had achieved. How hard would it be to secure that same power for herself? Antonov wouldn't rule for ever, and she knew for a fact that Belagren would never let Misha inherit the throne of Senet . . .

She stopped her pacing and walked to the armchair by the fireplace. With regal poise, she sat down and looked around the room as if the chair were a throne and she the queen of all she surveyed. Closing her eyes, Marqel peopled the room with her subjects. In her imagination, Kalleen was there, on her knees before the throne, begging her forgiveness. Lanatyne was there, too. Marqel waved her arm and smiled as her personal guard dragged Lana kicking and screaming from the room. That disgusting little butcher from Elcast was there, offering her money, his life . . . anything for the chance to be with her one more time . . .

And Dirk Provin was there. In chains, she decided, looking very forlorn and sorry for himself. What would she do to him? What punishment could she devise for the Butcher of Elcast?

'Cut his balls off,' she declared aloud. 'And then make him eat them!'

'I *beg* your pardon?'

Marqel's eyes flew open and she jumped guiltily to her feet to find Ella Geon standing in the doorway.

'My lady!'

'I cannot even begin to imagine what you're doing, Marqel.'

'I was . . . I wasn't really—' Marqel shrugged helplessly, realising there was no way she could explain. 'I was waiting for Prince Kirshov, my lady.'

'I see,' Ella replied, although it was patently obvious that she didn't. 'Did you do as the High Priestess asked?'

'Yes, my lady. Kirsh will find Dirk Provin for us.'

Ella nodded. 'In that case, your work here is done for the time being. You may return to the Hall of Shadows.' She stood at the door expectantly, waiting for Marqel to follow her.

'But—'

'Yes?'

'Kirsh . . . Prince Kirshov asked me to wait for him, my lady.'

Ella debated the issue for a moment and then nodded. 'Then I suppose you'd better be here when he gets back. Come and see me before you leave.'

The Shadowdancer turned to leave. Marqel took a step towards her, realising this might be her best, her *only* chance, to stay in the palace. 'My lady? I was just thinking . . .'

'That's always a dangerous trait in an acolyte,' Ella remarked sourly as she turned back.

'Well, if the High Priestess wants me to . . . assist her . . . with Kirsh, wouldn't it be better if I stayed here in the palace?'

'You mean permanently?'

'Perhaps I could be placed in your care, my lady?' she suggested warily, not sure what reaction she would receive. 'That way I could stay close to Kirsh and learn from you at the same time.'

Ella seemed surprised by the idea, but she didn't scoff at the suggestion. She stared at Marqel for a moment, then nodded. 'That may not be a bad arrangement, actually. But I will have to discuss it with the High Priestess.'

'Of course, my lady,' Marqel said with a small curtsey. She lowered her eyes so Ella couldn't read the triumph in them.

Ella studied her suspiciously, and then she shrugged. 'In the meantime, you may . . . carry on . . . with whatever it was you were doing . . .' she said as she closed the door behind her.

Kirsh returned about an hour later. He slammed the door shut behind him and leaned against it, shaking with anger.

'What's wrong?' she asked, hurrying to him. 'Did you find Dirk?'

'Not yet. I've arranged to seal the city. He won't get away.'

'And doesn't that please you?'

'I'm getting married.'

'I know, but—'

'Now.'

'What do you mean, *now*?'

'I mean my father has decided that he doesn't want to wait for Alenor to come of age. He's arranged for us to get married straight away. I'm to rule Dhevyn as regent.'

'But that's wonderful!' she cried, thinking Kirsh should be happy to gain such a position of power so young. Then she saw the look on his face and added tentatively, 'Isn't it?'

'No, it's not wonderful,' he snapped. 'It's a disaster!'

'But—'

'Don't you see what this means? I won't be permitted to join the guard. I'll be married to Alenor and stuck sorting out border disputes and fishing rights and . . . bloody grain quotas for the rest of my life!'

She reached out and touched his face with a smile. 'You'll be a king.'

Her touch seemed to drain some of the anger from him. He slumped against the door with a sigh. 'I don't want to be a king, Marqel, and even if I did, a regent isn't a king. I'll be baby-sitting Alenor in a court that will hate me and distrust me, just because I'm Senetian.'

'How could anyone hate you, my love?' she asked with a smile.

'Don't you?' he replied bitterly. 'You're Dhevynian. My father says he's never met a Dhevynian who didn't secretly despise us.'

She kissed him. 'Does that feel like I hate you, Kirsh?'

'I don't know.' He smiled hesitantly. 'Perhaps you should kiss me again so I can decide.'

Marqel did as he asked. He pulled her close as she closed her eyes and pressed her body against his. She moved her hand down between his thighs and felt his startled response.

With a start, Kirsh pushed her away, holding her at arm's length. His breathing was ragged, his eyes wide. 'It's not even lunchtime,' he said, a little scandalised by her eagerness.

'So?'

He suddenly laughed.

'What's so funny?'

'I just had this vision in my head. Of Alenor. I was trying to imagine her saying the same thing.'

Marqel smiled and quite deliberately placed her hand between Kirsh's legs. 'Why don't you forget about that frigid little virgin for a while?'

'I'll be married to her . . . in a couple of . . . weeks,' he pointed out, visibly trying to resist the effects of Marqel's expert touch.

'Then we'd best make the most of the time we have,' she purred, as she began to unbuckle his sword belt.

'But I have to find Dirk—'

'You've sealed the city,' she reminded him as the belt and his sword clattered to the floor and she went to work on the laces of his shirt. 'Let the guard find him.'

'But what about you? After what happened . . .'

Marqel suddenly realised her mistake. She was supposed to have been raped yesterday, and here she was feeling Kirsh up like a tavern whore. Snatching her hands away from him, she let her eyes fill with unshed tears and turned her back to him.

'I'm sorry . . . I suppose you don't want anything to do with me now that I've been spoiled by another man . . .' She sniffed back her tears and turned, reaching out to put her hand on the doorknob, as if she were planning to flee. 'It's all right. I understand. I'll just go—'

'No!' he cried in alarm. 'That's not what I meant!'

'You don't have to explain, Kirsh.'

He took her face in his hands and kissed her tenderly. 'I just don't want to hurt you, Marqel. You've been through a terrible experience. I thought maybe the memory was too fresh . . . too raw.'

'I was hoping you'd give me a better memory to replace it,' she sighed.

Kirsh hesitated for a moment and Marqel wondered if her tears had been enough to cover her error.

'I truly don't want to hurt you.'

'You could never do that,' she assured him aloud, thinking: *For the Goddess's sake, Kirsh! Stop talking about saving my feelings! Just get on with it!*

Finally convinced, Kirsh took her hands and drew her close to him again, gently and carefully. He kissed her fingertips, then her palms, her lips, her throat, then her ear, sending shivers down her spine. Marqel deliberately did not respond.

Let Kirsh think he's seducing me.

If she was ever going to own this prince, in body and soul, then it was important that Kirsh believe he was coaxing her back from that awful place in her mind where Dirk Provin lurked.

And at least, she thought irreverently, as her shift dropped to the floor, *I won't ever have to call him Daddy.*

76

They reached the outskirts of the city just after midday. The Paislee Road was jammed with traffic, which was further hampered by a roadblock manned by soldiers wearing the gold-and-white livery of Antonov's personal guard. Dirk reined in several streets from the barricade and turned to Reithan questioningly.

'Now what?'

'Any chance we can bluff our way through?' he asked.

Dirk shook his head. 'There's a good chance someone there knows me. And Tia's bandage is a dead giveaway if they're looking for her.'

'Is it worth trying to make a run for it?' Tia asked.

'The way you ride?' Reithan asked. 'They'd catch us before we got half a mile up the road.'

'Well, what do you suggest, then?' she asked in irritation. 'We can't stay here.'

Dirk glanced around at the cluttered street. The guard had just let a convoy of fully laden hay wagons through the barricade, and there was a line of near-empty wagons waiting for them to pass before they attempted to get back on the road so they could leave the city. The drivers of the incoming wagons were cursing the traffic jam loudly as they tried to push their vehicles through the crowded street.

'Maybe . . . if we create a diversion,' he suggested thoughtfully.

'What sort of diversion?'

'The sort nobody in a crowded city can ignore,' Dirk said, pointing to the hay wagons.

She stared at him blankly. Reithan understood immediately, though.

'Fire, Tia,' he explained.

She turned her gaze to the hay wagons inching their way towards them. 'What are you going to do?'

Dirk dismounted and handed Eryk the reins of his mount as the boy slid forward into the saddle. 'Try to get closer to the roadblock, but not so close that they get a good look at you. And when I find you, be ready to ride like hell. We won't have long.'

Dirk didn't bother to explain anything further or look back to see if they were doing as he asked. He ducked between two of the empty wagons and into a small shop he'd spied across the street. The store was dingy, the smell of herbs and imported spices sharp, almost overwhelming. The shelves were cluttered with jars of all shapes and sizes, and bunches of dried herbs hung from the ceiling. The apothecary looked up as he entered, straightening his vest as he took in Dirk's finely cut clothes, marking him as a man of means.

'How can I help you, my lord?'

'Do you have any lamp oil?' Although the hay would burn well once it got started, Dirk wanted to make sure the fire could not be extinguished before they got a chance to get past the roadblock.

'Don't get much call for lamp oil these days, sire,' the

storekeeper told him, scratching his stubbled chin. 'What do you need it for?'

'I thought I might set fire to those hay wagons out in the street,' Dirk told him.

The storekeeper stared at him for a moment and then roared with laughter. 'Oh! That's a good one, sire! Very good!'

'So? Do you have any lamp oil or not?' Dirk asked again with a smile.

Still chuckling to himself, the man nodded and disappeared through a curtain behind the counter. He came back a few moments later with a small jar full of viscous yellow liquid.

'It's rare these days, lamp oil is,' the man told him as he placed the jar on the scrubbed wooden counter.

'How rare?' Dirk inquired, silently groaning as he recognised the opening gambit of the merchant's haggling routine.

'I couldn't part with it for less than twenty silver dorns, milord.'

'Twenty dorns for that?' Dirk scoffed. 'That's extortion!'

'A man has to eat, sire.'

'For that much, you could feed half of Avacas! I'll give you five coppers and not a single dorn more.'

'Fifteen is as low as I can go, my lord, without selling one of my children into slavery,' the man lamented.

'Eight. And you can throw in a flint and tinderbox.'

'Twelve, and my babies will still starve at that price.'

'Ten.'

'Done!' the merchant cried happily.

Dirk handed over the ten copper dorns and took the jar and tinderbox with him. He stopped just outside and surreptitiously worked the stopper loose from the jar. Glancing up the street he couldn't see Reithan, Tia or Eryk nearby, so he squeezed back between the wagons and began to walk towards the hay carts.

The jostling crowd pushed him up against the lead wagon. He tipped the jar over the edge as he walked alongside, emptying the contents into the dry hay as he went.

When he reached the end of the wagon bed, he dropped the empty jar into the hay and pulled the tinderbox from his pocket. He glanced around to see if anyone was paying attention to him, but in the dense crowd nobody cared what he was doing. The lamp oil caught on the third strike. He blew on the flame gently for a moment to make sure it was well alight, then walked away as casually as he could manage.

He spied Reithan, Tia and Eryk ahead of him. Tia was looking around nervously, just as the first cries of alarm went up. Once it caught properly, the hay roared like a furnace behind him. He could feel the heat searing the back of his neck. With an anxious look at the roadblock, Eryk handed him the reins to his horse.

Reithan smiled as he looked back towards the roaring fire that was causing a general panic a little further up the street. 'When you create a diversion, you really create a diversion, don't you?'

An errant clutch of flaming straw landed on the wagon behind the first one and it too, began to burn. By now the soldiers manning the roadblock had noticed the fire and were calling out for someone to put it down. They didn't abandon their posts immediately, but Dirk knew it wouldn't be long. The houses here were close together, and many of them were constructed of wood. A fire might destroy a quarter of the city if it raged out of control for long enough. Eryk fidgeted behind him, his head swivelling back and forth from the fire to the roadblock.

'If you try a bit harder, Eryk, I'm sure you could act even more suspiciously,' he remarked.

'I'm thorry, Lord Dirk.'

The officer manning the roadblock ordered his men forward to help put out the fire. The soldiers hurried past them without so much as a glance in their direction.

'Now!' Dirk hissed, grabbing Tia's mount by the bridle. He didn't trust her to get the dun moving on her own. He pushed his horse forward, careless of the people in his path, ignoring the curses they hurled at him as he forced his way forward.

They reached the roadblock, and the one man left on guard, but he was too engrossed in the excitement going on further down the street to notice them. A few more shoves and curses and they were on the open road. Dirk kicked his horse forward and gave the chestnut its head, still towing Tia's mount behind him.

77

The *Calliope*'s sails snapped in the crisp breeze as Senet dwindled to a blur on the horizon. Although she had never stopped calling Kalarada home, Alenor had been away from the Dhevynian capital since she was eight years old, and she found the thought of returning oddly discomforting. People she remembered as being young would have grown older; others she might not recognise at all. Alenor realised with some dismay that the friends she had left behind would have moved on to other things. Their lives had continued without her.

She was returning home a stranger.

The last day had passed in a blur of misery and unhappiness for Alenor. The welcome news that she was finally allowed to return home had been overshadowed by recent events, and most of them were directly related to Dirk Provin. She could not understand why Dirk had slept with that damn Shadowdancer. But she didn't believe Dirk had raped her, any more than Prince Antonov did. And she was hurt beyond words that Kirsh was so upset about Marqel he was willing to fight Dirk over her. She could not imagine what had driven Dirk to murdering Johan Thorn, or come to terms with the fact that he was Johan's bastard son.

Perhaps worse than that, she could not understand why her mother had so willingly agreed to abdicate the throne of Dhevyn in favour of her daughter.

'Alenor.'

She turned to find her mother climbing the companion ladder to the foredeck. Rainan smiled as she approached.

'You must be pleased to be heading home,' she remarked as she stopped beside her.

'Very pleased,' Alenor told her mother. Her tone belied her words.

The queen looked at her with concern, then smiled suddenly and spoke up for the benefit of the sailors around them. That was the worst of it. They were on Antonov's ship with his crew, his people, watching their every move, listening to their every word. There was no chance to let down her guard. No chance to talk to her mother. Here in the bow, where the wind whipped away their words as soon as they were uttered, was the closest thing they had to privacy.

'Look, there's Alexin! Captain, come here! We'd like to thank you personally for the sterling job you did protecting us in Senet.'

Alexin Seranov was on the main deck, talking to one of his men. At the queen's summons, he dismissed the guardsman and headed forward. A few moments later Alexin climbed the companion ladder and approached the queen and her daughter with a low bow. He was a tall man, with warm brown eyes and a ready smile, and looked very smart in his blue-and-silver uniform. Alenor had grown to like him a great deal in the short time of their acquaintance. Her mother seemed to trust him, too, which was a little odd. There was still a fair amount of residual resentment in Dhevyn over Alexin's father so readily denouncing his brother in order to inherit his duchy. There weren't many people left in Dhevyn who were willing to trust a Seranov.

'Your majesty. Princess Alenor.'

'Captain.'

'Mother seems to think your efforts in Avacas require special commendation, Captain,' Alenor remarked, thinking the praise a little undeserved. If Alexin had done his job properly, he should have stopped Dirk from killing Johan Thorn.

For a moment, the young man's eyes clouded and Alenor wondered if he was thinking the same thing.

'I'm not sure I'm worthy of any praise, your highness.'

Rainan glanced around to ensure none of the Senetian sailors could overhear them.

'You did everything you could, Alexin,' the queen assured him quietly. There was more to her words than a simple expression of gratitude.

'But not as much as I would have liked, your majesty,' Alexin replied.

'I think we all find ourselves in that position, Captain,' the queen agreed.

'Mother—' Alenor began, a little irritated to think that with everything about to befall them, all her mother could do was think of stroking the ego of a guardsman who had barely even done his job.

'And have you worked out a way to get me out of it?' Rainan said, ignoring Alenor's interruption.

Alenor looked at her mother in surprise. She had thought the queen quite accepting of the whole idea of abdicating in favour of her daughter.

'I suspect the Lion of Senet is too clever to leave a legal loophole for you to wriggle through.'

Rainan nodded in agreement, turning to study the smudge on the horizon that was the coast of Senet. 'Then what do we do, Alexin? I'm damned if I'm going to hand over my kingdom to a Latanya to rule as regent.'

'Maybe we can stall for a time?' he suggested.

'How?' the queen asked.

'Kirshov,' Alenor said with quiet conviction.

'Kirshov Latanya is at the root of the problem, Alenor,' her mother remarked. 'The Lion of Senet wishes to appoint him Regent of Dhevyn.'

'Dirk said Kirsh didn't know anything about this.'

'I'm not particularly interested in Dirk Provin's opinion, Alenor,' Rainan said frostily.

'This is nothing to do with Dirk, Mother. My point is that Kirsh has his heart set on joining the Queen's Guard.

He's obsessed with the idea. He doesn't want to rule Dhevyn. He wants to be in the guard.'

'His father has his heart set on Kirsh becoming regent,' Alexin reminded her.

'What if we *could* stall it, though? Isn't there some way we can convince Antonov that Kirsh needs to serve some time in the guard first?'

'That's not a bad idea,' Alexin conceded. 'And once he's there, it wouldn't be difficult to arrange some sort of accident . . .'

'No!' Alenor cried in horror. 'That's not what I meant!'

Rainan smiled faintly. 'Appealing as it might be, Captain, I don't think we should tempt fate quite so blatantly as that. For the time being, Kirshov Latanya must remain alive and healthy, I fear. But you may have hit on a solution, Alenor. If I can convince Antonov that Kirsh won't be accepted as regent until he's spent some time in the guard, we might be able to delay the abdication by a few months at least.'

'And how does that help us?' Alenor asked. 'In a few months, we'll still be right where we are now.'

'A lot can happen in a day, Alenor,' Rainan sighed wearily. 'The whole world could be a different place in a few months.'

Alexin nodded thoughtfully. 'You speak of the Provin boy?'

Rainan leaned against the railing. 'Who would have guessed that Johan and Morna had a son?'

'Is he likely to claim the throne?'

'Dirk would never . . .' Alenor began, but her voice trailed off. She never thought Dirk could kill a man, either.

Rainan shrugged. 'I have no idea about the workings of that young man's mind. Or what his relationship to Antonov is. They seemed very cosy right up until he murdered my brother.'

'I think he did the only thing he could, your majesty,' Alexin suggested.

'Really? If Dirk Provin wanted to help Dhevyn, he could have plunged that dagger into Antonov's throat, not Johan's.'

Alexin shook his head. 'He'd never have come within spitting distance of Antonov armed with a naked blade, your majesty, before someone brought him down. As it was, he saved the life of my cousin, prevented Neris Veran's daughter from falling into Belagren's hands, stopped Johan from revealing if Neris still lives and his location, and he got us out of Avacas before Antonov could force the wedding between Alenor and Kirshov to take place. That's a pretty tidy day's work, in my book.'

'Then you don't think Dirk betrayed us?' Alenor gasped. The relief she felt was palpable.

'I think it was the single most courageous act I've ever seen, your highness.'

The queen did not appear convinced. 'Even so, Belagren's interest in the boy concerns me almost as much as Antonov's obvious fondness for him. She wants him to join the Shadowdancers. She didn't even care that he was Morna's son. I think the High Priestess wants Dirk Provin very, very badly.'

'For what?' Alexin asked.

'The next Neris Veran . . .' Alenor said. 'Antonov called Dirk that once. The next Neris Veran.'

'And what did Neris Veran ever do,' Rainan scoffed, 'other than start a war, then throw himself off a cliff to avoid facing the consequences?'

'If he's as smart as Neris Veran, why does Antonov want him?' Alexin asked. 'You'd think it would only be Belagren who needed his talents.'

'Antonov wants him because of *who* he is,' Alenor said. 'Belagren wants him because of *what* he is.'

'That's the problem, isn't it?' Rainan sighed. 'It's a two-headed monster we're fighting. On one hand, we face Antonov and his desire to conquer Dhevyn, and on the other, we face Belagren and her cult of Shadowdancers. The two of them feed off each other. I don't see how we can fight one without bringing down the other. And if Dirk Provin has thrown his lot in with either Antonov or Belagren . . .'

'Mother, why don't you just tell them both to get out of Dhevyn?' Alenor snapped impatiently.

'I wish I could, Alenor,' the queen sighed, taking the suggestion quite seriously. 'But I would be on my own. There's not an island in Dhevyn strong enough to defy the Lion of Senet, and with my luck, the Age of Shadows would return the very next day, and I'd have Belagren and the whole damn kingdom ready to string me up.'

'You don't believe that Belagren really brought back the Age of Light by making Antonov kill his son, do you?'

'I suppose not,' the queen admitted. 'But I'll not make the same mistake that Johan did. Until and unless we can prove otherwise, the vast majority of people will continue to believe in the Goddess, and there is nothing any of us can do to change their minds.'

78

They made it to Paislee in nine days. Dirk and Reithan pushed the horses hard, and they frequently rode through the bright ruddy nights, past small campsites set up by the numerous travellers on the road. Tia wished they'd let up the pace a little. There had been no sign of pursuit, and the long hours in the saddle had chafed her inner thighs raw. However, other than checking her hand occasionally, neither Reithan nor Dirk apparently had any thought for her pain or discomfort.

Eryk chatted away constantly, but the others didn't talk much as they rode. Dirk appeared to have things on his mind, and Reithan seemed content with his own company. Tia hoped Dirk might be tormenting himself over the terrible thing he'd done, but she wasn't quite ready to press him on the subject.

The problem of what to do about Dirk Provin plagued

Tia constantly. Her personal vow to destroy him for killing Johan had, by necessity, been postponed for the time being. She was honest enough to admit (at least to herself) they might never have escaped Avacas without his help.

But she had another reason to delay her desire for vengeance. Dirk's accusation in the palace haunted her. *You and Reithan came here to kill Johan!* he'd said. *And now, because I saved you the trouble of doing it yourself, you think you can condemn me with a clear conscience.* The words rattled around in her head like a neverending echo. He was right. She and Reithan had come to Avacas for *exactly* that reason. Had Dirk not intervened, she might be facing the same dilemma as Dirk.

Or maybe I wouldn't, she decided, *because when it came to the crunch, I don't think I could have gone through with it*.

Lexie had warned her about that.

'There's a stream up ahead,' Reithan said, interrupting her train of thought. 'We should rest the horses. The second sun will set soon. We could use the rest.'

Tia nodded in agreement and followed Reithan, Dirk and Eryk off the shoulder to a small stream some distance from the road. She dismounted stiffly and led her horse to the water to allow her to drink.

'I've been thinking,' she began, finally deciding to broach the subject that had been gnawing at her all day. She wasn't expecting a positive response, but she still felt that she had to ask.

'That must be a new and novel experience for you,' Dirk muttered as he helped Eryk down and led his chestnut to the stream beside her. He was always like that, bitter and sarcastic – even when she was trying to be civil. 'Eryk, go and see if you can find some firewood.'

'How much, Lord Dirk?'

'As much as you can carry.'

The boy scuttled off into the undergrowth in search of kindling, leaving the others to tend the horses.

'I was wondering what you're going to do once we get to Mil?' Tia asked.

Dirk continued to ignore her in favour of his horse.

'Are you going to tell everyone who you are?' she persisted. 'What you did?'

He glanced at her with genuine amusement. 'Are you serious?'

'Then what *are* you going to do?'

'I haven't decided.' He turned his back on her again and continued to unsaddle his horse.

'Tia, we can settle this some other time,' Reithan suggested, as he pulled the saddle from his own mount.

'No, Reithan, we can't,' she declared. 'This needs to be settled before we get anywhere near the Baenlands. I want to know what he's planning to do.'

'I'm not actually "planning to do" anything,' Dirk told her.

'You said you wanted to join us.'

'Actually, I asked you to take me to Mil. I don't recall volunteering for anything.'

'So you expect our help and offer nothing in return?'

'I just can't win with you, can I?' Dirk said. 'First you're violently opposed to me going anywhere near Mil. Now I'm in trouble because you don't think I'm dedicated enough to your cause.'

Reithan began to rub down his horse with a sheaf of leaves, a little impatiently. 'Tia, leave him alone.'

'Why do you always side with him?'

'I don't. I side with reason. And you're being unreasonable.'

'*I'm* being unreasonable? What about him? He murdered his own father!'

Dirk jerked the saddle from the chestnut's back and dumped it on the ground. 'Don't you understand, Tia? Until Johan Thorn washed up on that beach on Elcast, Wallin Provin was my father! I hardly knew Johan.'

'You must have felt something for him.'

'Why must I feel something? And where do you get off lecturing me about what I should feel for my father? What about what you feel for *your* mother?'

His question startled her. 'That's different!'

'Is it?' he asked, pushing past her to unsaddle the dun. He jerked the buckles on her girth strap free, and pulled the saddle off, dropping it on the ground next to his. 'You're a hypocrite, Tia. Given half a chance, you'd kill your own mother and never lose a moment's sleep over it.'

'He's got a point, Tia,' Reithan agreed.

'Ella Geon turned my father into a drug addict!' she cried.

'Johan Thorn turned my mother into an outcast,' Dirk replied quietly before turning away.

'I don't *believe* you! Either of you! Ella Geon is evil! Johan Thorn was a good man. The best! There is no way you can equate her actions with his.'

'Nobody's trying to,' Reithan said, trying to placate her. 'But now is not the time to discuss this.'

'When is the right time, Reithan? Would you prefer to wait until he's betrayed us to Antonov?'

'Would it help if I gave you my word that I *won't* betray you?' Dirk asked, clearly not expecting her to believe him.

Tia glared at him, trying to read what was going on in that unfathomable mind. In the end she shrugged. There was no way to tell.

'I suppose if we have to take the word of the Butcher of Elcast, then we have no choice.' Dirk stopped and turned to stare at her. She'd finally said something to crack that icy facade. 'How many people does one actually have to kill to be called a butcher, I wonder?' she asked, deliberately goading him.

Dirk stared at her for a moment and then he shrugged.

'Not nearly as many as I'd have to kill to be called a conqueror,' he said.

Later that evening, after they ate the last of the bread and cheese from Ivon's house in Avacas, Dirk announced that he was going to check the road, to make sure they were still free of pursuit. Eryk hurried after him, as if he were afraid to let Dirk out of his sight. Tia was immediately suspicious.

'Tia . . .' Reithan warned. The night was warm, and the small fire had burned down to glowing coals. Reithan stretched his booted feet out and folded his arms behind his head.

'What?'

'Leave them alone.'

'I wasn't—' she began, then sat down again with a guilty sigh. 'All right, so I was going to follow them. How do we know he's not leaving a message for someone, so they can follow us?'

'We don't. But I'm willing to bet he isn't.'

'Just remember it's my life you're gambling with, too.'

'Stop being so paranoid, Tia. We're safe for the moment.'

'You're joking, aren't you? We'd be safer still trapped in Avacas. Actually, I think we'd be safer standing on the lip of a volcano that was about to erupt.'

'Dirk has nowhere else to go,' Reithan pointed out.

'He's got a whole damn world to get lost in. Why, in the name of the Goddess, does he want to go to the Baenlands? What does he really want from us, Reithan? Do *you* know? He doesn't seem interested in joining us.'

'I'm not sure he knows, exactly.'

'And yet you expect me to trust him? How do you know he isn't just doing this to find out all he can about Mil? How do you know he isn't planning to run straight back to his friends in Avacas as soon as he's learned everything about us?'

'I don't. But I *am* certain that *you'll* drive him back to Avacas if you don't stop goading him.'

'I'm supposed to just forget that he murdered Johan?'

'I think you're jealous, actually.'

'*What?*'

'Dirk Provin is everything you want to be—'

'That's absurd!' she cut in angrily.

'Is it?' Reithan asked. 'I think you're jealous that he had the courage to do what Johan asked, and you resent the fact that he's Johan's son. And while you're thinking on that little paradox, you might like to wonder what your hatred is going to do to Mellie when we get back to Mil. Do you realise he's her brother?'

'Don't you dare bring poor Mellie into this! You're insane and you're wrong! I don't envy anything about him. He's a cold, heartless, spoiled Senetian lackey, and I think you're an idiot for trusting him! He doesn't care about us or what we're fighting for.'

'This may come as a shock to you, Tia,' Dirk said from behind her, making her jump, 'but the vast majority of Dhevynians live perfectly happy lives without ever feeling the need to fight for your noble and ultimately futile cause.'

Tia turned on him angrily. 'The ones who aren't burned at Landfall Festival, maybe,' she retorted. 'But then, I guess that wouldn't bother the Butcher of Elcast, would it?' It was the quickest way she knew to rile him, to call him that. 'And for your information, Dirk Provin, our cause isn't futile.'

'Isn't it? Johan thought it was. Otherwise, wouldn't he have done something to reclaim his throne? You don't have the resources to take on Antonov, and you haven't a chance of breaking Belagren's grip on the hearts and minds of Dhevyn's people.'

His statement echoed Johan's sentiments so closely it frightened her. How many times had she and Reithan asked Johan why he wouldn't do something to free Dhevyn? And how many times had Johan replied with almost the exact words that Dirk had used? She found herself falling back on the same argument she had used with Johan. 'We *could* reclaim Dhevyn if we knew when the next Age of Shadows was due.'

'Ask your father,' he told her, disinterestedly. 'Isn't he the one who's supposed to know it all?' He turned to Reithan, as if the subject was closed. 'Eryk's taking the first watch. I'll relieve him in an hour or so. That's about the limit of his concentration span.'

Tia was annoyed at his dismissal. And suspicious of it. He was faking this disinterest, she was certain, but he simply sat down and lay back, resting his head on his saddle and stared up at the red sky.

'Aren't you even curious to know the truth?'

'I know the truth. Johan told me.'

'And you're prepared to do nothing? If you're as clever as everyone claims, then you might be the only person alive who could work out when the next Age of Shadows is due. But you won't, will you? You're just going to sit there and let the world roll on around you, pretending that it's not your fault?'

'I don't have to pretend it's not my fault, Tia, because it never was. Stop trying to make me feel guilty about something I had no part in.'

'So you're just going to walk away?'

'Actually, I thought *running* away would be smarter. Look, even if I was this genius everyone claims I am – which, incidentally, I'm *not* – I was training to be a physician. I don't know anything about the suns or the skies.'

'Neris didn't work it out for himself either, Dirk,' Reithan told him. 'The information came from somewhere else. He just figured out how to decipher it.'

'What? Don't tell me he had a vision.'

Reithan shook his head. 'He found the secrets in the ruins in Omaxin.'

'Reithan!' Tia cried in alarm. *There was no need to tell him that.*

Dirk ignored her outburst. 'So why don't you just go to the ruins in Omaxin and find out for yourself?'

'After Neris realised what he'd unleashed by telling Belagren about when the Age of Light would return, he decided to destroy the information. He hid it behind a Labyrinth that nobody has ever been able to penetrate. Belagren has lost a score of Shadowdancers trying to find out.'

'What did he do? Fill the Labyrinth with man-eating monsters?'

'You could kill those,' Reithan said with a small smile. 'Anyway, Neris is far too subtle to do anything so crude. The

Labyrinth is a series of puzzles. If you can't solve them – in the right sequence – they'll kill you.'

Dirk stared at them. 'And you think I could solve these puzzles? Or are you hoping I might die trying?'

'Actually, now that I think about it, either one would do,' Tia snapped.

Dirk was not amused. 'Yesterday you were ready to kill me for what I'd done. Now that you've had a chance to think it over, you've decided I might have a use after all. What's next, Tia? Are you going to suggest that I could be the next King of Dhevyn?'

'Would you want a throne you'd killed your own father to gain?'

'I didn't kill Johan to gain his throne, Tia. And if I *was* going to kill anyone for their throne, I'd have killed Rainan, not Johan.'

'They used to call him the Eagle of Dhevyn.'

'What?' he asked, confused by her abrupt change of subject.

'Johan Thorn. They used to call him the Eagle of Dhevyn.'

Tia shifted around on the hard ground, looking for a comfortable position and settled down with her saddle as a pillow.

'What's that got to do with anything?'

'It just occurred to me,' she said, turning her back to him, 'that the next person likely to wear that title is your good friend Kirshov Latanya.'

79

The *Wanderer* was right where Reithan had left it, anchored in the sheltered waters of Paislee Harbour. It took most of the day to track down Blarenov, the man from the

Brotherhood who was minding the boat. Reithan was finally able to arrange a meeting with him later that evening, in a warehouse near the docks. The message insisted that Reithan come alone, so Tia, Dirk and Eryk found a waterfront tavern filled with sailors, and agreed to wait there for Reithan's return. The second sun had set and the docks were bathed in red light, but it was still early enough that the streets were crowded. Several wandering performers were doing their best to add to the general noise and confusion, blocking the sidewalks with the crowds that had gathered to watch them.

Dirk ordered ale for the three of them in the Anchor's Arms. The noise from the bawdy songs and drunken sailors filling the place provided them with privacy better than if they'd been in a locked room out the back. They found a table tucked away in the corner of the tavern and said nothing to each other as they drank. Tia didn't want to speak to Dirk anyway.

'Lord Dirk?'

'Yes, Eryk?'

'Can I go watch the mummers?'

There was a puppet show going on in the street outside, and a small clutch of laughing children had gathered to watch. Dirk glanced over his shoulder at them and nodded. 'All right. But don't wander off. And when the show is over, you come straight back here,' he said, giving him a few dorns to pay the players.

'I will,' he promised. Eryk clambered over his stool and hurried outside.

Tia watched him leave with a smile. She liked Eryk almost as much as she disliked Dirk.

'You're very good with him,' she remarked, somewhat begrudgingly.

Dirk shrugged. 'Somebody has to look out for him.'

'That's what I can't understand about you. You watch over Eryk like a mother hen, yet you killed your own father in cold blood.'

Dirk said nothing for a long moment, then slammed his

tankard down in a splash of foaming ale and left the table without another word.

Tia watched him leave, gloating over the fact that she could rile him so easily. Then guilt replaced victory as another thought occurred to her. She could hear Reithan's voice: *You might like to wonder what your hatred is going to do to Mellie when we get back to Mil. He's her brother, too, remember . . .*

What were they going to tell her? *Hey there, Mel, this is Dirk Provin, the man who killed your father. Oh, and by the way, he's your brother . . .*

How do you explain any of this to a twelve-year-old girl?

Tia was still trying to answer that question when Dirk's seat was taken by a man Tia did not recognise. He smiled at her, looking her up and down for a moment, then nodded with satisfaction.

'How much?'

'What?' she asked in confusion.

'How much?' the man repeated. He was unshaven and dressed in a loose, sleeveless shirt and trousers made of tough material, a common garb for sailors the world over. The man glanced over his shoulder in the direction Dirk had gone and chuckled. 'Guess the boy couldn't afford it, eh?'

'The boy?' Tia said, still puzzling over the man's question. Then it dawned on her what he was suggesting and she stiffened in alarm. 'No! I mean, that's not what he wanted . . . I'm not—'

'Come on, darlin',' the sailor laughed. 'There's no need to play hard to get.'

'I'm waiting here for a friend,' she told him firmly.

'I'll be your friend for the next hour,' he offered. 'Three months at sea . . . I've just been paid . . .'

Tia swallowed the rest of her ale and stood up. 'I'm not for sale.'

Without waiting for his reaction, she walked away from the table and pushed her way through the tavern and out into the street, cursing all men, and Dirk Provin in particular, for leaving her alone in the first place. That she'd driven him away with her anger and her taunts was something she wasn't quite willing to admit to anyone, least of all herself.

Tia glanced up and down the street. The puppet show had finished, and she could see no sign of either Dirk or Eryk. She looked up at the sun, wondering how much longer Reithan would be. She hated Paislee and could not wait to be out of the grubby Senetian port and back in Mil. Across the street, a troop of Senetian guardsmen had stopped to watch a contortionist crossing his feet behind his ears while balanced on his fingertips.

'Hey! Don't you just walk away from me like that!'

Tia glanced over her shoulder to find that the sailor had followed her outside.

'Leave me alone,' she told him. 'I'm not a whore.'

'Listen, sweetie,' the man replied, grabbing her by the arm. 'There's only one type of woman who drinks alone in the Anchor's Arms. Now, are you gonna do your job, or am I gonna have to get rough?' He clutched at her elbow so hard it was painful.

'Get your hands off me!' she warned coldly. For a moment, she debated screaming, but that would bring them to the attention of the guards, and selling her body to this persistent, foul-smelling sailor was actually preferable to falling back into the hands of Barin Welacin's thugs. She looked around, but there was not a familiar face in sight. One of the guards glanced her way and she hurriedly looked down, hoping that if her description had been circulated, it wasn't an accurate one.

'All right,' she said, shaking free of the sailor's grasp and surreptitiously placing her bandaged hand behind her back, out of sight. 'But not here. In the alley.'

The man smiled and let her go. 'That's better! How much?'

'Fifty copper dorns,' she told him. 'In advance.'

The man fished around in his pocket and produced the required coins. He dropped them into her hand, and she made a show of counting them carefully, before turning into the alley beside the tavern. She led him as far from the guards as she could get, but the alley wasn't particularly long, and even a moderately loud cry would easily attract their attention.

At the end of the litter-strewn lane, Tia turned to face the sailor, wondering if she could disable him silently. She had a bad feeling that when she drove her knee into this obnoxious fool's groin (which was the only part of her body he would *ever* get to feel), his shout might alert the nearby guards. It was a risk she would have to take. There was no chance this sordid little interlude was going to end any other way.

The sailor was already pulling at the drawstring on his trousers as she faced him. He glanced at her and frowned impatiently.

'Come on, then,' he urged. 'Get your clothes off.'

Tia assumed he would want to embrace her, giving her a chance to get close enough to knee him in the balls. He was more than an arm's length away from her, and not nearly close enough for her to do any damage.

She smiled seductively. 'Don't you want to kiss me first?'

'I want to fuck you, you silly bitch, not court you.'

This was not even remotely going according to plan. He reached for her, and she instinctively flinched away from him.

'I just thought . . .' she began, realising with dismay that she sounded just like the amateur she was.

Annoyed, the sailor grabbed her by the front of her shirt, tearing it open as he pulled her closer. Tia wanted to scream, but she couldn't. One cry and the guards across the street would come running. His breath stank of ale, and his stubbled chin scratched her face as he tried to force his mouth over hers . . .

'I'd think twice about that one, if I were you.'

The sailor released his grip, and turned to face whoever had interrupted his sport. Tia stumbled backwards, and nearly cried with relief when she realised it was Dirk. Her feelings of relief were followed almost immediately by the desire to howl with shame for the fact that he had found her like this. She would never be able to explain it. And she hated the idea that she might, yet again, find herself indebted to him for her life.

'Piss off, boy. I've already paid for her. You'll have to wait your turn.'

Then again, I might not have to worry about owing him anything, she thought. The sailor was twice Dirk's size. If it came to a fight, Dirk would be annihilated.

'I don't want a turn with her.' Dirk shrugged. 'She's got the pox.'

Tia bit down on her lip to stop herself crying out with outrage. The sailor took a step away from her with a frown.

'How d'you know?'

'My brother had her a few weeks ago,' Dirk informed the sailor. He put his hands in his pockets and leaned against the alley wall, talking in a disarming tone.

Some hero to the rescue you turned out to be, Dirk Provin.

'He's already in the second stage of the disease. That comes a few weeks after the sores on your dick appear. I think the skin rashes are the worst bit, though . . . or maybe it's the weeping lesions in your mouth and throat. My brother says he has them on his arse too, but I didn't really care for a close look.'

The sailor looked quite horrified.

'Of course, he's been pretty poorly since his glands began swelling and the fevers started,' Dirk continued gleefully. 'Aches . . . pains . . . headaches that nearly kill him. But now that his hair is falling out—'

The sailor was gone from the alley before Dirk could finish the sentence. He watched him leave with a smile and then turned to look at Tia, and his momentary good humour faded. 'Are you all right?'

'I'm fine, thank you,' she replied, hastily covering her breasts with her torn shirt. She was having some trouble trying to retain the few shreds of dignity she had left. 'It wasn't necessary for you to intervene, you know. I was handling things quite well on my own.'

'So I noticed.' He shrugged out of his jacket and held it out to her. 'Here. Reithan and Eryk are waiting for us at the jetty. That shirt is ruined. You can wear this until we get to the boat.'

Her first instinct was to refuse his offer, but she couldn't walk the streets of Paislee unclothed. She snatched the jacket from his outstretched hand, and turned her back to him as she put it on. Although travel stained and a little worse for wear, the jacket was made of brocaded silk, and it was quite the most beautiful thing she had ever worn. She almost felt guilty for the sigh of pleasure that escaped her lips as she felt the whisper of silk against her skin.

'It wasn't what you think,' she announced, squaring her shoulders as she turned back to face him. 'I mean . . . it wasn't what it looked like. I wasn't—'

Dirk said nothing. He just let her prattle on like an idiot while he walked to the end of the alley and glanced up and down the street. The guards still had their backs to them as they watched the contortionist across the way.

'It's all your fault, anyway,' she snapped, interpreting his silence as censure. A smattering of applause came from the crowd gathered around the contortionist as he finished his routine. Dirk watched the dispersing crowd for a moment, then hurried back to her as the guards began to turn around. 'If you hadn't left me alone in the tavern, that sailor would never have propositioned me, and I'd never—'

Tia never got to finish the sentence. Dirk quickly grabbed her by the shoulders, pushed her against the tavern wall and put his mouth over hers. Too stunned to object, she let him kiss her as if they were lovers suddenly reunited after months apart.

'Hey! You two! Get a room, for the Goddess's sake!' a male voice yelled from the alley's entrance. The shout was followed by several other men laughing, then it faded as the guards resumed their patrol.

Tia felt Dirk's relief, felt him relax as he realised they were safe. Then she panicked, as she realised that she was kissing him back. She pushed him away, appalled to discover her breath coming in ragged gasps. Dirk stared at her, obviously as dumbstruck by the realisation as she was.

'Of all the stupid things to do . . .' she began, certain she was blushing a deep shade of crimson. 'Goddess! I thought you were supposed to be smarter than everyone else!'

'It worked,' he said, taking a step backwards.

'Only because not even a Senetian guardsman would believe that anybody would try such a lame stunt to hide from them,' she snapped.

His eyes narrowed, the only outward sign of his irritation. 'I could call them back, if you like. Maybe I could think up something better next time? Something that might meet your exacting standards?'

'Don't bother,' she said, pushing past him. 'There won't be a next time. Not ever.'

80

They found Reithan and Eryk talking to the man from the Brotherhood near a small jetty on the western side of the harbour, where the bulk of the fishing fleet was moored for the evening. The boats bobbed gently in the bay, a forest of bare masts and stinking nets lying out to dry. Blarenov was a tall, thin man with a carefully groomed goatee beard and pale green eyes. The man looked at Dirk and Tia curiously as they approached the jetty.

'What happened to you two?' Reithan inquired, glancing at Tia's torn shirt and the jacket she was wearing.

'It's a long story,' she replied shortly, her tone as much as her scowl discouraging any further questions. 'Can we go now?'

'Aye, you'll want to get away as soon as possible,' Blarenov warned, pocketing the coins Reithan handed over from the last of the stash retrieved from Chandler Street. They had sold the horses earlier in the day for a fraction of their value. They were marked with the Lion of Senet's personal brand, so they had not been in a position to haggle about the price.

'Has there been trouble?' Reithan asked.

'Someone burned near the whole western quarter of Avacas to the ground. And Johan Thorn is dead.'

'That's not our problem.' Reithan shrugged. 'The Brotherhood has nothing to fear.'

'We always fear when important people die,' Blarenov replied. Then he looked at Tia and smiled. 'You've moved up in the world, lass. There's a price on your head now.'

'How much?' she asked, looking a little pleased with herself. Dirk wondered if Tia had ever been considered significant enough to warrant a reward before.

'It's only a hundred silver dorns. But there's a thousand *gold* dorns on offer for someone named Dirk Provin,' he added, looking straight at Dirk.

'We'll keep our eye out for him, then,' Reithan replied blandly.

The Brotherhood man smiled knowingly. 'Look, I don't know what happened in Avacas, and I don't want to know. But you people know far too much about the Brotherhood for my people to be comfortable with any of you being caught.'

'I've had a price on my head for years, Blarenov,' Reithan reminded him.

'There's a world of difference between being wanted and being actively hunted by Barin Welacin's men.'

'We'll be careful.'

'You'd better be. There's a school of thought here in Paislee that we might be able to trade this Provin fellow for significant concessions.' He turned his gaze on Dirk again and added, 'If we knew where he was.'

'What are you suggesting, Blarenov?' Tia asked suspiciously.

'Just this, lass: it'll take less than a day for word to get around Paislee that you've come to collect the *Wanderer*. About an eye-blink after that news gets out, people are going to start wondering about your friend here.' He glanced around the jetty and lowered his voice. 'I owe Reithan a favour or two, Tia, and for that I can turn a blind eye for an hour. But no longer. A thousand gold dorns is an awful lot of money.'

'You're telling us we've got an hour to get out of Paislee?'

'Less than that.' Blarenov shrugged. 'We've already been talking for a quarter of that time.'

'Then consider us gone,' Reithan declared, turning towards the small dinghy tied to the jetty.

Dirk started to follow him, then he stopped and turned to the thief. 'Who posted the reward on Dirk Provin? The Lion of Senet or the High Priestess?'

'Neither of them,' Blarenov told him. 'I believe it was Prince Kirshov.'

'We'd better get moving,' Reithan suggested, before Dirk could question the Brotherhood man further. The pirate and the thief shook hands like old friends and wished each other well, as Tia began to negotiate her way down the rope ladder to the boat with one hand. Eryk followed her, making the small craft rock wildly as he jumped down from the bottom rung. Dirk followed Eryk, and held the rope ladder steady for Reithan as he climbed down. As soon as they were all aboard, Blarenov pulled the ladder up and unhitched it, tucking it under his arm.

'Do you want a hand?' Dirk asked Reithan, as the pirate settled himself down between the oars. There were several sacks and a couple of small barrels tucked into the bow. Reithan had obviously arranged for supplies for the trip.

Reithan smiled. 'Save your strength. We're going to have to haul this beast aboard once we get to the *Wanderer*.'

'Wouldn't it be easier to simply tow it?'

'Easier, yes. But the drag will slow us down too much. I want to get away from this town as fast as I can.'

'Do you think we're being pursued?' Tia asked.

'I don't know, Tia,' Reithan said, as he began to pull on the oars. 'Perhaps if I knew why your shirt's been torn half off and you're wearing Dirk's jacket, I might be able to decide what sort of threat we're facing.'

'Nothing happened,' Tia said, pulling the jacket tightly closed.

'Nothing?' Reithan asked sceptically.

'It was just some sailor . . . but don't panic. Your little friend Dirk here came to my rescue in the nick of time.'

Her voice was laden with scorn. Dirk studied her unrelenting profile, trying to reconcile the girl who spoke with such venom to the girl who had kissed him in the alley.

'Why would Prince Kirsh post a reward on you, Lord Dirk?' Eryk asked, providing a welcome distraction from the disturbing direction his thoughts were heading. Dirk glanced over his shoulder at the slowly retreating dock. Blarenov stood watching them as they rowed towards the *Wanderer*.

'I don't know, Eryk,' he lied.

Eryk's expression was puzzled, even a little hurt. 'But he's your friend.'

'Out of the mouths of babes . . .' Tia muttered.

Once the *Wanderer* was safely clear of Paislee, Dirk searched around in the lockers below decks until he found some more antiseptic and a clean bandage to dress Tia's hand. She forced herself to watch as he changed the dressing and removed the stitches from the stump of her little finger. It was clean and healing well, but the sight of it obviously made her queasy.

'It's not infected,' he remarked, noticing the look on her face.

'You did a good job,' she conceded.

'I am good at other things besides getting people killed, you know.'

She studied him for a moment, then sighed, as if she had come to a decision about him. 'When we get to Mil—'

'What about it?' he asked, tying off the bandage.

'We don't have to tell them what happened. Nobody need know it was you who killed Johan. We could just tell them that Reithan and I found a way to carry out his orders.'

He sat back on his heels and stared at her, immediately suspicious. 'Why would you do that for me?'

She held up her bandaged hand. 'You didn't have to do this. But mostly I'm doing it for Mellie.'

'Mellie?'

'Johan was married, Dirk. Actually, now I come to think of it, that makes Reithan your stepbrother.'

'He's my *what*?'

'Your stepbrother. His mother is ... was married to Johan Thorn. You also have a half-sister. Her name is Mellie.'

Dirk was stunned. It never occurred to him that Johan might have moved on with his life once he and Morna parted. It was strange to think of Johan having a wife and child. Even stranger to think he had a sister he knew nothing of.

'She's only twelve, Dirk, and she'll be thrilled to learn she has another brother. I don't want to spoil it for her by introducing you as the man who murdered her father. Neris lives in Mil, too,' she admitted. Dirk stared at her. 'But I guess you've already worked that out for yourself. Goddess, have you any idea how much we're risking by trusting you?'

'Tia—' he began, not sure what he could say that would make her understand he was no threat to her or her people. How could he explain that he simply wanted to get away from Avacas? From Antonov and his seductive power? From Belagren and her insidious religion? He needed time. Time to work out who he was. Time to reconcile in his own mind, the dreadful thing he had done. Time to convince himself that there had been nothing else he could do.

And he needed time to quiet the voice in his head that kept asking him, *But what if you'd done this? Or that? ...*

Unaware of his inner turmoil, Tia took a deep breath, as though bracing herself for what she wanted to say next. 'I just want you to understand something, Dirk. I'm not a blind fanatic – and I'm not stupid. I know Reithan and I – and maybe even Eryk – could have been killed that night in Avacas. I know that when you stabbed Johan you did what I couldn't do. I know you probably saved my hand. Believe it or not, I even appreciate you rescuing me from that damn sailor in Paislee. But Johan and Lexie were like a father and mother to me, and Mellie is like my little sister. If you hurt her, if you *ever* do anything to harm her, I will hunt you down and kill you.'

Dirk was quite dumbfounded by her admission – and didn't doubt for a moment that she meant to kill him if he hurt Mellie. 'I never set out to hurt anyone, Tia.'

'Neris didn't intend to hurt anyone either, Dirk, and he started a war. That's the problem with people like you and my father. You never mean to do any harm, but you're so damn clever . . . all you end up doing is causing trouble.' She checked the bandage and stood up, stooping slightly in the *Wanderer's* small cabin. 'You've got Reithan's trust and, for all I know, you have the best intentions in the world. But that doesn't make you any less dangerous. I'll do whatever I must to protect my people.'

'I've got no interest in betraying you, Tia.'

She met his eye for a moment, but if she believed him, Dirk couldn't tell. He waited for her to say something, but when she didn't reply, he began to gather up the dirty bandages. The puzzle that was Tia Veran was too complex to fathom.

81

Vasili Torrez, the Senetian Ambassador to Dhevyn, returned with the *Calliope* bearing a long missive from Queen Rainan regarding the upcoming wedding of Alenor to Kirsh. Antonov began to read the letter, then threw it down on the desk impatiently and glared at Vasili.

'Goddess! Who wrote this nonsense?'

'I believe the queen had her people working on it for days, your highness,' the ambassador informed him. Vasili was a small man, dapper and as sharp as a new sword and a close friend of Kirsh's father, which was the reason he held the post of ambassador to Queen Rainan's court. It was rumoured that he kept a stable of mistresses on Kalarada, and only visited his wife in Senet once a year. Kirsh didn't blame him. He had met Vasili's wife. She was a vapid, plain-looking woman with little to recommend her other than the vast tracts of land she inherited on the death of her equally vapid and plain-looking mother.

'Rainan's got balls if she thinks she can dictate to me.'

'What does it say?' Kirsh asked. He had been called to this meeting as soon as Vasili had arrived at the palace, as had the High Priestess. Belagren sat by the desk, her hands folded demurely in her lap, as if she was simply there as an observer.

'Basically, it says that she's trying to renege on our deal,' his father declared.

'Actually, much as it pains me to admit it, your highness, she has a point.'

'*What* point?' Kirsh demanded, annoyed that he had no idea of the contents of a letter that affected him so severely.

'Rainan is suggesting that you should marry on Alenor's eighteenth birthday.'

'Why?'

'She says Alenor is too young. She says that her people would view the idea of the princess marrying at fourteen quite . . . disturbing. Rainan is suggesting that we delay the wedding until Alenor comes of age, and that you serve the intervening time in the Queen's Guard. She seems to think it would consolidate your position in Kalarada and make it easier for you to rule as regent.'

Kirsh couldn't hide his delight. 'But that's a wonderful idea!'

Antonov smiled. 'Funny, I had a feeling you'd say that.'

'So did Rainan, probably,' Belagren suggested.

'But how could she know?' Antonov began, then dropped the letter on the desk as he answered his own question. '*Alenor.*'

'Rainan made a valid observation about having Alenor

under your roof for all these years. She certainly knows Kirshov well. And this—' she added, pointing at the document from Dhevyn '– is living proof of it.'

'Do you think she's up to something, or merely trying to save face?'

'A little bit of both, I suspect.'

'But why?' Kirsh asked. 'Even if I serve in the guard for a year or two, I'm still going to marry Alenor. I'll still be regent. I mean, nothing will be any different.'

'Oh? I don't know, Kirsh,' Vasili said. 'You might suffer a fatal accident in training. That would alter things quite dramatically.'

'Rainan wouldn't *dare*,' Kirshov gasped.

'No, *she* wouldn't,' Vasili agreed. 'But the Queen's Guard is the worst hive of Dhevynian nationalism in the whole damn kingdom. It would only take one young hothead to decide he wants to save Alenor from a fate worse than death, and the next thing you know, we'll be tossing petals on your funeral pyre, Kirsh.'

'That's ridiculous! Alenor wants to marry me!'

'*You* know that, but as far as the average Dhevynian is concerned, her marriage to you is just another union arranged for political expedience.'

'Then we will have to convince them otherwise,' Antonov said. 'We need to make it patently clear that Alenor wants this wedding as much as we do.'

'Then why don't we wait until she's eighteen and her people believe it really is her decision?' he asked. 'I don't mind.'

'If Alenor is of age when she marries, Kirshov,' Vasili pointed out, 'there is no need for a regent.'

'Ah . . . I didn't think of that.' He looked at his father hopefully. 'But that doesn't make delaying the wedding while I serve with the guard a bad idea, does it? I've heard you say any number of times that if the Queen's Guard ever decided to defy the throne, we'd lose Dhevyn overnight. That's why you suggested I join the guard in the first place. It's the reason you wanted me to be Lord Marshal of Dhevyn one day.'

Antonov glanced at Belagren before he answered. The High Priestess nodded.

'Like Vasili, it grieves me to admit it, but Kirsh is right. A short stint in the Queen's Guard would go a long way to making Dhevyn easier to rule.' She smiled coldly, adding, 'You just need to make it clear to Rainan what will happen should any accidents befall your son while he's in her service.'

'I can look out for myself, you know, my lady,' Kirsh informed the High Priestess, a little offended.

'I'm quite sure you can, Kirshov,' she agreed with a soothing smile.

'I'm not inclined to give in so easily, Belagren,' Antonov said. 'It cost me a great deal to get Rainan's signature on that damn abdication.'

'Then set your own conditions, Anton. Agree to Kirsh spending time in the guard, but put a limit on it. Set the wedding for Alenor's sixteenth birthday. That should satisfy the cynics, and Alenor will still have two years before she comes of age to get used to the idea of referring everything she does to Kirshov, and through him, to you. That habit will be hard to break – even after she has assumed the throne in her own right. And make sure that our own people are in place in Rainan's court, so that when Kirsh does assume the mantle of regent, he has a well-oiled machine ready and waiting to aid him. Do that, and this stalling tactic of Rainan's will actually play into your hands.'

Antonov glanced at the ambassador. 'Vasili?'

'I agree with the High Priestess, your highness.'

Kirsh waited for his father to ask his opinion, but the Lion of Senet seemed to think it unnecessary to ask the views of the one person these decisions affected most.

'Very well, I'll have my reply drafted and ready for you to return to Kalarada on the next tide,' he told Vasili. Then he glanced across the room at Kirsh. 'On second thought, you can deliver my message personally, Kirsh.'

'You want *me* to sail on the next tide with Vasili?'

'I don't want to give Rainan any more time to come up with another reason why she shouldn't abdicate. Besides, with you there, Alenor may be a little less enthusiastic about finding ways to avoid marrying you.'

Belagren rose gracefully to her feet and curtsied. 'Then I beg your leave also, your highness. I will need to make arrangements to ensure that Kirshov has the right people to attend to his needs in Kalarada.'

'Of course,' Anton agreed with a dismissive wave of his hand.

The High Priestess rose to her feet and walked to the door.

'But not the thief,' Antonov declared suddenly.

Belagren turned to him. 'Pardon?'

'Father?' Kirsh asked, equally surprised.

'You're not to send Marqel to Kalarada, my lady. The Dhevynians need to be convinced that Alenor and Kirsh are in love. That might be a bit difficult if Kirsh is amusing himself with one of your Shadowdancers on the side.'

'But, Father!' Kirsh objected.

'You can have all the mistresses you want once you're married, Kirsh. But until you are, you will do nothing to incur Alenor's wrath. I had enough trouble smoothing things over the night of your birthday party, when she caught you and that thief in the woods. You should be grateful Dirk found you before it got completely out of hand.'

The High Priestess nodded. 'You are wise, as always, your highness. I'll send someone else.' Then she added, almost as an afterthought, 'By the way, have you any news of the Provin boy yet?'

Antonov shook his head. 'He seems to have disappeared off the face of Ranadon.'

'And that doesn't concern you?'

'He'll be back,' Antonov assured her.

Belagren studied the Lion of Senet thoughtfully for a moment. Then she opened the door and glided gracefully from the room.

Kirsh looked at his father angrily. He wasn't sure if it was Antonov's continued insistence that Dirk would return, or that Marqel had just been taken away from him again, that made him so furious. 'You keep saying he'll be back, but there's still no sign of him.'

Antonov shrugged. 'I want him to come to me of his own volition.'

'And if he won't?'

'Then we will *drive* him to it.' His father looked at him and smiled. 'I won't make the same mistake I made with his father.'

Kirsh didn't like the sound of that. 'What do you mean?'

'I mean, Kirsh, I will drown Dhevyn in blood, if I have to, but one way or another, he *will* come to me.'

'You'll do the same thing you tried with Johan?' Vasili asked with a frown. 'What makes you think killing innocents would be any more effective with the Provin boy?'

'Because I'm not going to kill innocents this time, Vasili. If Dirk Provin doesn't return of his own accord by the time Kirshov becomes Regent of Dhevyn, I will start killing the people he loves.'

'He killed his own father,' Kirsh pointed out. 'How are you going to top that?'

'He still has a mother,' Antonov said.

82

Ten days after they left Paislee, Reithan guided the *Wanderer* through the tricky sandbars guarding the delta and Mil finally came into view. Tia's hand had healed sufficiently that she could grip the tiller, but she still couldn't tie a knot or reef a sail. Eryk sat beside her, his hand also resting on the tiller, convinced he was helping. Dirk stood on the foredeck, waiting for Reithan's command to tack for the last time. He was tanned and lean, the voyage stripping off the last vestiges of the life of excess he'd been enjoying in Senet. Tia watched him the whole time, filled with doubt about the wisdom of inviting him into her home.

Their approach had been spotted by a lookout high on the cliffs overlooking the delta, and there was a small crowd gathered on the beach as Dirk helped Reithan pull the mainsail down. There was another ship anchored in the bay: a shallow-draughted trader with a demonic figurehead.

'Porl Isingrin's here,' Tia called from the stern, pointing at the ship.

'Is that a good thing?' Dirk asked Reithan as they hauled on the sail.

'At the very least, it means we won't have to break the news about Johan,' Reithan replied. 'They'll already know about it.'

'Tia! Tia! Reithan!' an excited voice floated out over the water.

Dirk glanced at Tia, surprised to find her smiling and waving. He'd seen very little of Tia smiling, and was astonished at the difference it made in her. Reithan saw the direction of his look and smiled. 'She's not always so obnoxious.'

'Really?' Dirk said, as he tied off the sail. 'I thought that was her natural state. I take it that's Mellie?' he asked, jerking his head in the direction of the dark-haired girl standing on the beach in front of the small crowd, jumping up and down with excitement.

'My sister,' Reithan agreed. '*Our* sister, actually.'

Dirk was suddenly overwhelmed. 'Could we just . . . not tell everyone who I am?' he suggested.

'We could,' Reithan agreed. 'But sometimes, except for your eyes, you look so much like Johan, it's scary. So there wouldn't be much point, would there?'

Dirk nodded reluctantly. Until this moment, he had not realised how difficult it would be to face these people. 'This was a bad idea . . .'

Overhearing his doubts, Tia left Eryk manning the tiller and clambered forward. She laughed sceptically. 'See, I was right, Reithan. One trip through the delta and he wants to go running home to Avacas already.'

'It's a pity Barin Welacin only cut your finger off, Tia,' Dirk snapped, fed up with her unrelenting anger. 'He should have started with your tongue.'

Tia's fist came out of nowhere. She belted him squarely on the jaw, and sent him flying backwards into the jib. Then, without another word, she returned to the stern, snatched the tiller from Eryk's hand and steered them home.

Their arrival was greeted by almost everyone in the settlement. As soon as they had secured the *Wanderer*, Mellie splashed through the shallows and flew into Reithan's arms, laughing one minute, because her beloved brother was home, sobbing the next, when she told him the news about Johan. She then repeated the same exercise with Tia, who hugged the child closely, her own eyes welling with tears.

Reithan introduced Dirk by his first name only.

Mellie eyed him curiously. 'Do I know you?' she asked.

She was a Thorn, through and through, Dirk thought. She had the same warm brown eyes as Alenor, and the same rich brown hair; however, unlike her perfectly groomed cousin, Mellie's hair was a tangled mess of curls.

'I don't think we've met before, Mellie,' he replied as evenly as he could manage. 'This is Eryk.'

Eryk smiled at the little girl shyly. 'My lady.'

Mellie laughed. 'I'm not a lady, silly!'

'Mellie, why don't you take Eryk down to the longhouse and find him something to eat?' Reithan suggested. 'I'll bet he's sick to death of salt beef and stale bread.'

Eryk seemed quite delighted by the idea. 'Can I, Lord Dirk?'

'Sure. Just mind your manners.'

Mellie looked at him suspiciously. 'Why does he call you "Lord Dirk"?'

'It's a private joke,' Tia volunteered, before Dirk could think up an acceptable excuse. 'Trust me, Mellie, there's nothing noble about this fellow.'

Mellie took Eryk's hand and led him away down the

beach to a long, thatched building that dominated the centre of the small village. Dirk watched them leave, and then turned to find another man pushing through the small crowd. His face was scarred, his right eye simply a slit in his badly burned face.

'We were afraid you might not make it out of Avacas,' the newcomer said.

'We had help,' Reithan explained.

'Is that who I think it is?' the pirate asked, staring at Dirk.

Reithan nodded. 'Dirk, this is Porl Isingrin, the captain of the *Makuan*.'

'Captain,' Dirk said, offering the man his hand.

Porl did not accept the proffered hand. 'You'd better go straight up to the house,' he said to Reithan and Tia. 'Lexie wants to know what happened.'

Johan's house was cut into a steep slope. Built on stilts, it looked out over the entire delta. The house was much larger and more substantial than Dirk expected. Constructed of wood, it was surrounded on three sides by wide verandas. Each room in the house opened onto the balcony with wide doorways that let the air flow freely through the house to keep it cool.

Dirk climbed the stairs behind Tia, Reithan and Porl to the main level, where an old, bent woman muttered a greeting to them in an incomprehensible language that the others appeared to understand.

'Finidice, this is Dirk,' Tia announced. Then she turned to Dirk and explained, 'Finidice had her tongue cut out by the High Priestess for heresy.'

With an involuntary shudder, Dirk looked away from Finidice, trying not to imagine how much suffering the old lady had lived through. As he turned away, the old woman quite deliberately opened her mouth to expose the raw stump that was all that was left of her tongue. His stomach churning with disgust, Dirk hurried after Reithan and Porl.

He understood now why Tia had hit him.

Reithan led the way through the house to a book-lined room, where a small, curvaceous woman, her auburn hair streaked with grey, waited for them, standing by the open doors leading onto the veranda. She was not what Dirk expected. For some inexplicable reason, he imagined Johan's wife would look like Morna. Lexie Thorn greeted Reithan and Tia with relief, then turned her attention to Dirk. Her shock was palpable.

'Is this . . .?' she began, unable to complete the question.

'This is Dirk Provin, Lexie,' Tia confirmed. 'Morna's son.'

'You look like your father,' she said eventually, breaking the uncomfortable silence.

'I'm sorry if my presence distresses you, my lady.'

Lexie shrugged. 'I always had my suspicions about your parentage, Dirk. I remember thinking, when I heard Morna had delivered another son to Wallin, that your birth seemed awfully . . . soon. You are welcome here, of course. This was your father's home, and it would be remiss of me to turn away any child of his.'

Dirk was a little surprised by the offer, until he remembered that Lexie was more than just the widow of a dead pirate. She was a noblewoman. Her first husband had been a duke, her second husband a king – albeit a deposed one. If it killed her, she would maintain the poise and good manners expected of her class. His mother was the same.

'Thank you, my lady. I appreciate your generosity.'

Her painful duty done, Lexie turned her attention to the others. 'Words cannot begin to describe the relief I feel at seeing you two whole and unharmed.'

'You've heard about Johan, obviously,' Reithan said.

She nodded. 'The Brotherhood learned of it first. Porl brought the news as soon as he heard.' She searched the faces of her son and her foster daughter. 'Were you able to smuggle something into him? Or did you have to—'

Dirk closed his eyes, waiting for Tia or Reithan to tell their story. He suspected Lexie's generosity of spirit would quickly evaporate once she heard the details.

'It was quick, Lexie,' Tia told her. 'You don't want to know anything more than that.'

Dirk looked at her in surprise. After that comment about cutting her tongue out, he wouldn't have blamed her if she'd told Lexie the whole sordid story. But she kept the promise she had made on the *Wanderer*.

'Then it was neither of you who . . . ?' Lexie asked hesitantly.

'No, Mother,' Reithan assured her. 'Neither Tia nor I wielded the blade that ended Johan's life.'

Lexie sagged visibly with relief. 'That is good. A child should never have to bear the responsibility for ending the life of a parent. Or someone they considered a parent.'

'I'm sure some people cope with it just fine,' Tia remarked.

'I beg your pardon?' Lexie said, looking at her in confusion.

'Nothing.' Tia shrugged. 'Just a stray thought. How did Mellie take the news?'

'She copes. Children are resilient. More than we, I believe. And she's used to Johan being away for long periods. I don't think it's fully dawned on her yet that he's never coming back.' Lexie turned to Dirk with a smile. 'I believe the welcome discovery that she has a new brother will go some way to easing the loss of her father.'

Dirk found he couldn't meet Lexie's eye, but when he turned away, he found himself confronted by Tia's warning glare.

'I'll do what I can, my lady,' he promised.

'If you are Johan's son, Dirk Provin, then I would expect nothing less of you,' she replied confidently, then turned to Porl. 'Now that Reithan is back, we must call a meeting and decide what must be done. Life goes on, I'm afraid, and we cannot risk the lives of everyone in the Baenlands while we mourn Johan.'

'I'll see to it, my lady,' the pirate replied. He turned for the door, then stopped and looked at Dirk. 'One thing bothers me about you, lad.'

'Captain?'

'Why is there a reward out on you? There's no mention of you being involved with us. No mention of any crime, for that matter, yet they've posted a reward as large as the one they had on Johan.'

'I know the reason,' Tia said, coming to his rescue once again. 'The High Priestess Belagren wants him because she thinks he's the next Neris Veran.'

Several days later, Dirk was sitting on the balcony of Johan's house, taking advantage of the cooling breeze that blew across the delta. He had been living a surreal existence since he arrived, in which he was treated like a guest that everyone wanted to gawk at, but nobody really trusted. In some ways, it was exactly like being in Antonov's court in Senet.

Dirk looked up at the sound of footsteps. 'Tia.'

It was the first time he'd seen her in days. She was dressed in her usual garb of trousers and loose shirt, and she held a plate covered with a square of cheesecloth. Tia Veran appeared much more composed, much less angry at the world, now that she was home again.

'Lexie said I'd find you out here.'

'You were looking for me?'

'I thought you might like to meet Neris.'

Dirk made no attempt to hide his surprise at the suggestion. 'Yes, I would.'

'Come on, then. Here, you can carry this.' She thrust the plate into his hands and turned for the stairs.

'What is it?'

'Blincakes. Made to Neris's exacting recipe. Where's your shadow?'

'My what?' Dirk asked as he hurried after her.

'Eryk.'

'Oh . . . I think he and Mellie have gone up to help with the goats.'

He'd hardly seen Eryk since they arrived. He'd been welcomed into Mil as if he was born there and, for the first

time in his life, Eryk was enjoying his childhood. The boy
spent his days looking for mischief with Mellie and her
friends, playing pokeball on the beach – or under the
watchful eye of the schoolmistress, Alasun. Dirk did not
begrudge the child his freedom, or his newfound happiness.
However, it was taking some time to adjust to the idea that
here, in Mil, Dirk did not have to keep a constant watch on
the boy.

Tia led the way down the beach. Dirk helped her push
the boat into the water and clambered aboard as she picked
up the oars and began pulling away from the shore. Her
hand had healed nicely and, except for some stiffness in the
joint of her fourth finger, she was hardly even bothered by
it now. Petra, the old herb woman in Mil, had been quite
impressed with the job Dirk had done.

The air was cooler out on the water. The ringing of the
smithy bounced across the delta, a constant echo that repeated
itself over and over again as it ricocheted off the cliffs. Tia
rowed in silence and, mindful of the extraordinary effort it
must have cost her to finally introduce him to her father,
Dirk said nothing that might upset her.

It took about half an hour to row across the bay to a
narrow strip of shale just wide enough to beach the dinghy.
After helping Tia pull the boat above the waterline, Dirk
followed her up a barely perceptible goat trail that wound
through the scrubby foothills.

Dirk was sweating heavily by the time they reached a
small plateau high above the bay. He turned back to study
the view, stunned at how far they had climbed. The settlement below appeared as small as a child's play set.

'Neris!' Tia looked around in concern. The plateau was
only about thirty yards at its widest point. On the far side
was the dark hollow of a large cave, but there was no sign
of life within. 'Neris!'

'Perhaps he's not here,' Dirk suggested when the only
response was the soughing wind across the wide ledge.

'He's here,' she replied, with a slight frown. 'Come on,
Neris! Stop playing games. People are worried about you!'

'I am the Deathbringer!'

Dirk looked up at the sound of the cry to find the madman sitting on an outcropping of rock about twenty feet above them. He was as thin as a reed, his long hair matted and tangled and so filthy it was impossible to tell what colour it might have once been. He had a straggling beard that covered hollow, sunburned cheeks, and his sunken eyes seemed to reflect pain rather than intelligence.

Tia looked up. 'What are you doing up there?'

'I can see death up here.'

Tia sighed and glanced at Dirk with a shake of her head. 'I was afraid of that.'

'Afraid of what?'

'Once he starts talking about death, nothing will divert him.' She smiled up at her father, attempting to sound reasonable. 'Come down here, Neris. I've brought someone to meet you. And we have blincakes. Your special ones.'

'I am the Deathbringer,' he announced solemnly. 'I am the Bringer of Death.'

'Whose death?' Dirk asked curiously.

'I am the Death of Reason. The Death of Enlightenment. Who are you?'

'My name is Dirk Provin.'

'Dirk? *Dirk?* A dirk is an insignificant blade: too small to be a weapon, too large to be a decent table knife. Just an annoying little poker with grandiose ambitions.'

The madman's words belied his appearance, Dirk thought. Beneath the filth and grime of insanity lurked an educated man.

'Is that what you are, boy? An annoying little poker with grandiose ambitions?'

Beside him, Tia laughed softly. She apparently thought that was rather funny.

'What I am, is hot,' Dirk replied. 'I want to get out of the sun. Come down here, so we can finish this discussion in the shade.'

The Deathbringer studied Dirk through disconcertingly intelligent eyes. 'You seek the shade, do you?' Suddenly, he leapt to his feet and howled like a dog caught in a trap. The sound was primal and unnatural. It sent a shiver down Dirk's spine, and made the hairs on the back of his neck stand up. 'Step into the shade, boy, and taste the Age of Shadows with me!'

Tia gasped, as the madman teetered on the edge of the precipice with nothing below him but the stony ledge where they stood.

'I am the Deathbringer!' he howled. 'Come to me, all ye who lust for destruction, for I am the instrument you seek!'

'Neris! Stop that!' Tia cried.

'You brought him here to find out my secrets, didn't you?' Neris accused, pointing his finger at Dirk. 'Ella promised me that if I told her my secret, things would be better.' Neris's shoulders slumped, his mood changing so quickly that it was impossible to keep up with him. 'That's why I told them. There'd been so much trouble, you see . . . so much suffering. I thought I'd be a hero!' Tears of remorse welled up in Neris's dark eyes. 'I didn't mean for it to turn out like this, Tia. I didn't know what she'd do . . .'

'Neris, why don't you come down?' Tia suggested gently. 'Dirk wants to meet you.'

Neris was instantly suspicious. 'Why? Why does he want to meet me?'

Tia smiled. 'Because Dirk is really very clever, Neris. Even smarter than you.'

'*Is he?*' Neris studied Dirk with a great deal more interest. 'If you're so smart, then, what's a lion?'

'*What?*' Dirk looked at Tia for help, but she just smiled at him.

'What's a lion?'

'A lion? A big cat.'

'How do you know it's a big cat?'

'There are lions all over Senet. It's Antonov's family crest.'

'Yes, but have you ever *seen* a lion? A real one?'

'No.'

'Why not?'

'I don't know,' he shrugged. 'I suppose it's because they're not real. They're creatures of myth, like dragons and fairies and wolves.'

'Ha!' Neris declared. 'He's not so smart.' Then he looked down at Tia with a frown. 'I know what you're up to. It won't work. I won't tell you anything. Not now. Not after what happened.'

'It wasn't your fault, Neris,' Tia said with the weary resignation of someone who had repeated the same assurance over and over. Her words did little to console the madman.

'I am the Deathbringer,' Neris muttered.

She sighed and turned to Dirk. 'He'll start to go into withdrawal soon, if we can't talk him down.'

'Can I do anything to help?'

'Actually, you can.' She faced him squarely, almost defiantly. 'You can repay the trust we've placed in you by offering you shelter here in Mil.'

'What do you mean?'

'Did you see what happened when I said you were as smart as Neris? He got all defensive and started asking bizarre questions, just to prove you're not.'

'I don't understand where you're going with this, Tia.'

'Neris is like a child and, like a child, he has to prove himself – constantly.' When it was obvious that Dirk didn't follow her reasoning, Tia looked a little annoyed. 'It's all part of the game, Dirk. He does it all the time. He drops hints, quite deliberately at times, and nobody understands them. It proves his secret is still safe.'

'Hints about what, exactly?'

'Neris was right. You really are thick, aren't you?' She pointed up at the second sun. 'To learn how long the Age of Shadows would last, Neris had to calculate an orbit, Dirk. That's a big round thing, in case you didn't know. How could he possibly do that, without discovering both when the sun would arrive and when it would leave again?'

Dirk digested that silently.

'I know you think our cause is futile, Dirk. The tragic thing is you're probably right. I know we can't really do much to hurt Antonov or Belagren. But neither can we stand by and allow them to do . . . that,' she declared, jerking her head towards Neris, 'to anybody else.'

Dirk thought about his answer for a long time. Tia wasn't asking just for his help with her ludicrous plan. She was asking him to throw his lot in with the exiles and pirates of Mil and take part in their struggle.

She was asking him to choose whose side he was on.

'So you want me to outwit a madman, who's not only the smartest person alive, but who's been hiding the secret you want me to uncover for longer than I've been alive? Are you sure it's your *father* who's the crazy one?'

She frowned, looking more like the Tia he remembered. 'Will you help us, or not?'

Dirk looked at her for a moment, then glanced up at Neris. 'Do you seriously think he'll blurt out the secret about the next Age of Shadows just to prove he's smarter than me? That's insane.'

'Yes, actually it is insane,' she agreed. 'But then, so is Neris.'

Dirk hesitated, aware that if he agreed to this, there would be no going back. Then he realised he didn't care.

He didn't want to go back.

'I can try. But I don't think this is going to work, Tia.'

'I am the Deathbringer!' Neris howled from his perch above them.

Tia looked up at her father for a moment, then turned to Dirk and shrugged.

'You've got until the next Age of Shadows,' she said.

CHARACTER LIST

ALENOR D'ORLON – Princess of Dhevyn. Heir to the throne. Rainan's daughter.

ALEXIN SERANOV – Second son of the current Duke of Grannon Rock. Reithan's cousin.

ANALEE LATANYA – Deceased. Princess of Damita. Wife of Antonov. Mother of Misha, Kirshov and Gunta.

ANTONOV LATANYA – The Lion of Senet. Father of Misha, Kirshov and Gunta. Husband of Analee of Damita.

BALONAN – Seneschal of Elcast castle.

BARIN WELACIN – Prefect of Avacas.

BELAGREN – High Priestess of the Shadowdancers.

BLARENOV – Member of the Brotherhood based in Paislee.

BRAHM HALYN – Sundancer living on Elcast. Brother of Paige Halyn, the Lord of the Suns.

CALLA – Mil's blacksmith.

CASPONA TAKARNOV – Shadowdancer in training with Marqel.

CLEGG – Captain of the *Calliope*.

DAL FALSTOV – Captain of the *Orlando*.

DARGIN OTMAR – Master at Arms in the Queen's Guard.

DERWN HAURITZ – Butcher's apprentice. Son of Hauritz the Butcher.

DIRK PROVIN – Second son of Duke Wallin of Elcast and Princess Morna of Damita.

DROGAN SERANOV – Deceased. Duke of Grannon Rock

until the War of Shadows. Killed fighting with Johan against Senet. Father of Reithan. Husband of Lexie.

ELESKA ARROWSMITH – Baenlander. Daughter of Novin Arrowsmith. Mellie Thorn's best friend.

ELLA GEON – Shadowdancer and physician. Expert in herbs and drugs. Tia's mother.

ERYK – Orphan from Elcast. Dirk's servant.

FARALAN – Daughter of the Duke of Ionan. Betrothed to Rees Provin of Elcast.

FREDRAK D'ORLON – Deceased. Duke of Bryton. Killed in a hunting accident not long after his wife, Rainan Thorn, assumed the throne of Dhevyn. Alenor's father.

FRENA – Servant in Elcast Castle. The baker Welma's daughter.

GAVEN GREYBROOK – Pirate on Johan's ship. Killed in the tidal wave that hit Elcast.

GUNTA LATANYA – Deceased. Youngest son of Antonov Latanya and Analee of Damita. Sacrificed as a baby to ensure the return of the second sun.

HARI – Pirate captured in Paislee. Sacrificed on Elcast during the Landfall Festival.

HAURITZ – Butcher living in Elcast Town.

HELGIN – Physician and tutor at Elcast.

JOHAN THORN – Pirate. Exiled King of Dhevyn.

KALLEEN – Leader of Kalleen's acrobat troupe.

KIRSHOV LATANYA – Second son of the Prince of Senet.

LANATYNE – Member of Kalleen's acrobats.

LANON RILL – Second son of Tovin Rill, Governor of Elcast.

LEXIE SERANOV THORN – Wife of Johan Thorn. First husband was the Duke of Grannon Rock. Mother of Reithan Seranov and Mellie Thorn.

LILA BAYSTOKE – Herb woman from Elcast.

LILE DROGANOV – Pirate based in Mil.

LINEL – Pirate captured in Paislee. Sacrificed on Elcast during the Landfall Festival.

MADALAN TIROV – Shadowdancer and aide to the High Priestess Belagren.

MARQEL – Also known as Marqel the Magnificent. Landfall bastard. Performs as an acrobat in Kalleen's troupe until she is taken into the Shadowdancers.

MASTER KEDRON – Elcast Master at Arms.

MELLIE THORN – Daughter of Johan Thorn and Lexie Seranov.

MISHA LATANYA – Eldest son of Antonov, the Lion of Senet. Also known as the Crippled Prince.

MORNA PROVIN – Duchess of Elcast. Princess of Damita. Daughter of Prince Oscon. Sister of Analee. Married to Wallin Provin. Mother of Rees and Dirk.

MURRY – Member of Mistress Kalleen's acrobats.

NERIS VERAN – Sundancer and mathematical genius. Believed to be dead.

NOVIN ARROWSMITH – Pirate living in Mil.

OLENA BORNE – Shadowdancer attached to Prince Antonov's court.

OSCON – Exiled ruler of Damita. Father of Analee and Morna.

PAIGE HALYN – Lord of the Suns.

PARON SHOEBROOK – Cobbler's son on Elcast.

PELLA – Baker in Mil.

PORL ISINGRIN – Pirate. Captain of the *Makuan*. Based in Mil.

RAINAN D'ORLON – Née Thorn. Queen of Dhevyn. Mother of Alenor. Johan Thorn's younger sister.

REES PROVIN – Eldest son of the Duke of Elcast. Dirk's brother.

REZO – Sailor on the *Calliope*.

ROVE ELAN – Lord Marshal of Dhevyn.

REITHAN SERANOV – Son of the late Duke of Grannon Rock and Lexie Seranov. Johan's stepson.

SABAN SERANOV – Duke of Grannon Rock. Father of Alexin and Raban.

SERGEY – Captain of the Avacas Palace Guard in Senet.

SOOTER – Member of Mistress Kalleen's acrobats.

TABOR ISINGRIN – Son of Porl Isingrin.

TIA VERAN – Daughter of Neris Veran and Ella Geon.

TOVIN RILL – Governor of Elcast.
VARIAN – Nurse to the sons of Elcast.
VIDEON LUKANOV – Head of the Brotherhood in Dhevyn.
VONRIL – Juggler. Son of Kalleen.
WALLIN PROVIN – Duke of Elcast.
WELMA – The master baker at Elcast Castle.
WILIM – Officer in the Queen's Guard.
YORNE – Apprentice baker. Welma's son.
YURI DARANSKI – Physician in the palace at Avacas.